In the
Country *of* Shadows

Also by Cindy Brandner

Exit Unicorns Series

Exit Unicorns
Mermaid in a Bowl of Tears
Flights of Angels

Short Stories

Spindrift

In the
Country *of* Shadows

Cindy Brandner

Starry Night Press

Published in Canada by
Starry Night Press

First Edition

Rev. 01/29/2016

For my grandmother,
Violet Brandner,
who first introduced me to the magic of Ireland.

Acknowledgments

The author's thanks to:

My editors – Tracy Bhoola, Denise Ferrari, Carla Murphy and Mary Foley Hurst. I cannot even begin to express my gratitude for all your hard work. The book is so much better for it.

Karen Barth who ended up being my first reader as well as the last set of eyes to look at the manuscript – thank you for both the encouragement and the proofing.

All my beta-readers and proof readers – Connie Lawrence, Marie Sheehy Grip, Marcia Peterson, Lindsey Walsh Smith, Stephanie Williams McCartha, Laura Molina, Jackie Helus, Amy Quarry, Nancy Albano Burley and Marlonne McGuire. Thank you for all the careful reading and picking up of a variety of errata. Any mistakes left are entirely my own responsibility.

Thank you to Yuliya Miakisheva for checking over my little bits of Russian and making sure they were correct and to Isabelle Mulligan for correcting my French – Jamie appreciates it. ☺

Michael O Neil and Arlene Gillen, tour guides extraordinaire, thank you for the best and funniest tour of Northern Ireland imaginable. Mick, you always reignite my passion for Irish history.

Lisa Egan Wanket – both for the use of her name as well as showing me her beautiful city by the bay. Carol Cross for giving me a wonderful tour around the Haight and the Castro while relaying the history of the area.

Stevie Blaue for yet another beautiful cover.

Thank you to the readers who have shared their stories with me over the years, both those of their Irish ancestry as well as tales more personal. You all inspire me.

And last but never least, gratitude to my Patrick for always being my biggest fan and supporter. I couldn't do it without you, babe.

Table of Contents

Prologue

1

Part One – Home

3

Part Two – Count the Stars in the Sky

127

Part Three – Me, Without You

255

Part Four – The Lotus Eater

367

Part Five – A Glimpse of the World Before

405

Part Six – The Far Side of Barsoom

439

Part Seven – The Dark Man

529

Part Eight – The Undefended Heart

575

Part Nine – Cosan na Marbh

681

Prologue

You can live *inside a shadow, for shadows are not as people think. Shadows have a life and substance of their own.*

Watch them roll down the street as a cloud crosses the sun, watch them swallow pavement and light, feel the cold as it touches your spine, feel the fingers of the shadows as they skim through your hair. Feel the chill wind of a mountain against your skin, the snuffing of light as though it were tucked quick in a box when you enter the forest's edge.

Sometimes we think we walk without our shadows, but I tell you this is not true. For when the sun is at its highest, blinding us with the gold of happiness and fortune, the shadow is still there, living within us, dense and whole, weighting our lives with premonition. It is only when the sun begins to sink and the shadow re-emerges, sliding sideways, breathing thick, moist vapors, that we realize it never left.

For in the umbral depths of a shadow reside many things; the dark architecture of need, the cold-breathing well of want, the drifting ship of love lost and hearts betrayed.

Shadows walk with us all our living years; they follow us out of bed each morning, keep to our sides during the day, amble along country lanes hand in hand, and flitter down moonlit pathways before us. We build many things from shadows: dark dreams, regret, vengeance, magic, borders, wars and loss.

We walk from sunlight into shadow, from year to year, all our lifetimes.

For this I tell you true, you can build a country entire out of shadows.

Part One – Home

Ireland
December 1975-April 1976

Chapter One

Home

HE WAS HOME. His lordship, James Stuart Kirkpatrick, having spent two years in a Russian gulag through what had been little fault of his own, (though some might argue that point) had arrived home at long last. His house, locally known by the illustrious name of Kirkpatrick's Folly, basked in the chill light of a December afternoon, its amber stones aglow in the last of the pale winter sunlight.

The house looked much as it had when he had left it three years before, but he had changed markedly during that same time. He brought with him a son, aged one year, a Georgian dwarf and a very pretty young man with inconvenient senses.

The door stood wide, for he was expected. He hesitated for a moment, his son in his arms, the child's blue eyes wide with curiosity, a stuffed cat clutched in his fingers. He took a deep breath, kissed the warm reassurance of Kolya's red-gold head, and walked back into the world he no longer knew.

An hour later he felt that while you could, contrary to what Thomas Wolfe had to say on the matter, go home again, you might find it wasn't the same place that you left behind. Everything felt unfamiliar, even something as simple as the pathway to his bed. He was seeing everything through a scrim of exhaustion, he knew, and a good night's sleep would make him more right with his own world. At least he hoped it would.

They were gathered, at the end of that whirlwind first hour, in the kitchen, the Aga humming warmly in the background, food upon the table, tea at the ready. Shura had already, in his inimitable way, endeared himself to Maggie by complimenting her cooking and the orderliness of her kitchen. He had run an infirmary in a gulag for several years, and appreciated order and mastery when he found it. His command of English was impressive, though the heavy Georgian accent that accompanied it rendered it somewhat less than entirely comprehensible.

Vanya was quiet, taking in the house and its grounds, its inhabitants: Maggie, cook and housekeeper, Robert, secretary to Jamie, and Montmorency, the somewhat unprepossessing dog that he and Pamela had rescued many summers ago. Vanya's amethyst eyes met his own now and again, and smiled as if to acknowledge how very far they were from that frozen gulag which had been the entirety of their universe such a short time ago. Vanya did not look like the refugee that he was but rather—with those eyes and Tatar cheekbones—he seemed a Slavic faun, an emperor in exile from the Babylon of the Snows.

Robert, in his reserved Scots way, was taking in each of them, clearly uncertain what to make of their bizarre troika, plus one. Kolya had crawled across the floor, and pulled himself up with drool-festooned hands, using the impeccable grey wool of Robert's trousers. It was to the man's credit that he merely lifted the baby up and set him on his knee, then gave him his flawless handkerchief to chew.

Maggie, Jamie noted with a pang of sorrow, looked older, her shoulders slightly stooped, but her welcome and love no less vibrant. She took the baby from Robert when it was time to eat and snugged him firmly to her hip.

"He's a beautiful laddie," she said. Kolya merely goggled back at her with his vibrant blue eyes. "But then with yerself for a daddy, I would expect him to be."

"He is Andrei's son biologically speaking, but mine in all the other ways," he said, feeling that Maggie deserved the truth. "I was...I am... married to his mother."

"Married?" Maggie said, looking around suddenly as if she expected a bride to materialize here in the warmth of the old kitchen.

"Yes, for a year in September," he said. "But she is in Russia." More than this he would not say, he did not speak of Violet to anyone, he did not think of her if he could at all manage it.

Maggie, being Maggie, did not ask any further questions. For this, he was inordinately grateful.

Her eyes met his—eyes that had seen him grow from a small lad to the man he was now and he knew she catalogued all the changes, for better or for worse, and kept her counsel about them.

"Ye're too bloody thin," she said, fiercely blinking back tears. "We'll work on fixin' that in the next while. Now, I'd best pour the tea for yez, before it's fit to take the paint from the walls."

With visions of endless potatoes and roasts in his near future, Jamie hugged her tightly, so that she might have no doubt there was still strength in him. He did look, he had to admit, a wee bit like a scarecrow left out in the field too long. He had managed a haircut and shave in Paris in an attempt not to look like a barbarian returned from foreign wars. Apparently, it was not enough to civilize him.

Later, when Kolya had been put down in the bed prepared for him, and Vanya had drifted off to the library, Shura to a bath and sleep, Jamie asked Robert to join him in the study.

The fire was lit and there was tea, steaming gently, on the desk. He had dreamed of good, hot Irish tea during his entire time in Russia. He had dreamed of many things during his time there.

The small Scotsman came in. "Sir?"

"Please, Robert, sit down."

Robert looked tired. Jamie knew the preceding two and a half weeks must have gone hard on him as well. He was very fond of Pamela and her children after all.

"Robert, I will be to the point. Tell me what happened with Casey."

Robert sighed, his small, wise-owl face drawn down in lines of sorrow. "I wish there were something to tell, sir, but there isn't. As far as Pamela can discern, he went out one morning to check the property— something I understand he did on a monthly basis —and he never returned home. He was meant to go to work later in the day and never showed up there. She and Patrick searched the entirety of the property and every other location they could think of, and then called the police."

Jamie raised an eyebrow. The police, all things considered, might feel the disappearance of a man who had been no small figure on the republican scene, a sort of gift. Both Pamela and Patrick knew this all too well and would have exhausted all other avenues first.

Robert noted the lifted brow and translated it accurately.

"And what are the police doing to assist?"

"About as much as you might expect, sir."

"And Pamela?"

Robert rubbed his eyes, as though they pained him. "Again, about what you would expect, sir. She's in denial. Whether that is for the sake of her sanity or something that will go on indefinitely, I do not know. And perhaps she is right to hope at this point."

A heavy silence fell between them, because this was Belfast and the most likely scenario that would have snatched Casey away from his family was one that ended in blood and pain in a wee hillside hut, until the merciful bullet to the back of the head came. Pamela would know this as well as anyone. Those scenarios played out in a week at most and nearly three weeks had passed since Casey's disappearance.

"She was here earlier today. She wanted to be certain all was prepared for your arrival. I think she finds it easier at times to be here, rather than at home. There's a passel of women there just now, and I suspect she's more than a bit overwhelmed."

Jamie nodded. When in the midst of a tragedy she would seek solitude.

The man sighed, his entire frame pensive inside its expensive grey wool suit.

"What is it you're not telling me, Robert?" Jamie asked, setting his teacup down on the desk.

The Scot moved his glasses back up his nose. "Why do you think that, sir?"

"Because it's roughly the size and shape of an elephant, and standing right here on the rug."

"That will be my cue, then," said a sharpish voice from the entry.

Jamie stiffened. "Grandmother," he said, and the tone could not be construed as one of great joy.

"Grandson," she replied and nodded to Robert, who stood and, like the wise man he was, exited the study posthaste.

Small and neat, his grandmother crossed the room to him and proceeded to startle him with a rather fierce hug. It only served to add to his feeling of having arrived in a world unfamiliar in its lineaments.

She held him out at arm's length. "Well, ye're a bit worse for the wear, but that's not anything which can't be mended."

Jamie thought he'd had enough of being assessed. "Would you like a drink?"

She quirked a brow at him in a fashion that he recognized.

"Yes, I will take a drink."

He poured one out for her, but not for himself. He needed to keep a clear head for a few more hours.

She sat, drink in hand, on a hassock by the fire, her bearing almost military in its composure.

"Is the news really so bad that you have to deliver it?" Jamie asked, sarcastically, though inside he wondered what could be so dreadful that hadn't already been imparted.

"Not so bad, mayhap, but personal-like. Pamela would have told ye, but as she cannot at present, it's down to me."

She handed him a picture. He took it and raised one golden eyebrow at her in puzzlement.

"That would be yer son."

"My son?" Jamie said, and laughed. "Is this some sort of bad joke? My son is upstairs, asleep in his crib."

"Aye, well, ye've more than the one. Look at the picture an' tell me ye don't see it clear."

He looked. He blinked and looked again. He was aware of sitting down, the starch gone from his knees entirely.

He was a young man, not a child. At least nineteen years of age, Jamie would guess. And if that was his age, only one woman could be his mother. He took a breath, and looked up at his grandmother. The sharp green eyes missed nothing, and so he schooled his face as quickly as he might.

"You've met him?"

"Aye, he's caused no small grief for all of us, Pamela and yon Scotsman mostly. He tried to take the companies out from under them. He didn't succeed, but it was a fight to the finish. Pamela will tell ye the details of that when she can. His name is Julian."

He looked back down at the picture.

He had his mother's coloring—that dark hair, a rich brown that was like a pond seen through the barest skim of ice, gleaming with golden tints in its depths. His eyes were an intense sapphire blue, an intensity that made his gaze seem alive even in the static of a photograph.

Beyond the coloring... Jamie sighed. Beyond the coloring, there was nothing in him that was not a direct result of Kirkpatrick genes. The irony of it was almost too great. That his one living son should be one he had never seen and had no hand in raising.

"I could have been gentler with the news, but there hardly seems time for it now."

"It's not news that can be given gently," Jamie said.

"So you truly did not know?"

"You think I would have allowed him to go in complete ignorance of me?"

"Aye, it might be wise to have done so. It's neither here nor there now that he knows. He's not an easy lad, but there's maybe something in him worth the saving. That will be up to you."

Jamie realized he hadn't taken a proper breath since he had entered the study. He could not quite absorb the idea of a grown son, one that looked disconcertingly like him. His mind was elsewhere and could not yet light upon this new fact of his life.

He could feel his grandmother's eyes once again assessing him.

"She will be awake," she said. "I don't think she sleeps these days. And she will be wonderin' how ye are, since ye've arrived home. Go see her."

Finola left shortly thereafter, discombobulating him further with a sound kiss to his forehead, something she had not done since he was fifteen. He checked Kolya, left instructions with Vanya about where he would be should anything arise in his absence, and went out to the garage. The car was gleaming with a recent cleaning and turned over without hesitation. No detail had been overlooked around his arrival it seemed.

Twilight touched the face of the land as he moved through it, the car a low hum against the coming of night. He saw it in miniature as he drove—the narrow, winding road set like a scatter of crushed jewels in the larger setting of countryside. His mind traced the path, past the edge of the rubble-strewn city, into the squared-off farmland, banded by high dark hedges, past the tiny smoke-furled cottages and the sheep-dotted fields, the tumbling stone walls, near to the border of the murder triangle. To the sloping hill with the weary ash guarding its head, down the drive to the wee farmhouse, whitewashed and braced with brambles and bare rose cane. A house that had been built with love and hope.

"Where are you, you bloody bastard?" he said out loud.

There were a few cars in the drive, and he was glad that she was not alone. It did not bear thinking about—what these last weeks had been like for her. He took a breath of the frosty air and walked toward the emerald green door. It opened before he could raise a hand to knock.

The woman who stood before him was short, hair a vigorous and perfumed red, her eyes the clear blue of aquamarines, set bold in a small round face.

"Who might you be?" she asked, voice sharp, the blue eyes looking him over the way a crow might look over a corpse for soft spots.

"James Kirkpatrick," he said, smiling and putting out a hand. "I'm a friend of Pamela's."

She wiped her hands on a tea towel and took his own. "Come in then, and be quick about it, it's colder than a witch's teat out there tonight, and I've got bread rising on the counter."

He followed the woman inside, the scent of ham and yeast tickling at his nose. The kitchen was a hive of activity, with several women bustling about, cooking, setting the table, making tea and one, in the corner by the hearth, rocking a small baby who was crying loudly and angrily. The woman looked up at his arrival, dark eyes sharp. He met the gaze openly, for he knew at once who she must be. Her sons favored their father, still there was no mistaking the woman who had borne them. He was looking at Casey and Patrick Riordan's mother. And so the baby crying in her arms must be Pamela's. Of the woman he had come here to see, there was no sign.

He walked toward the woman in the rocking chair.

"May I try?" he asked and held out his arms.

The woman's glance needled over his face, but she stood and held the baby out. "She's been inconsolable all afternoon, might be that a strange set of arms will help."

He took the baby carefully, feeling the strain in the tiny body. He held her against his chest, snugged in the curve of his left arm.

"Her name is Isabelle," the woman said.

"Hello, Isabelle," Jamie said to the small, red face that was crumpled up like an angry cabbage. Perhaps it was only that his voice was that of a man, but she stopped abruptly, dark eyes opening wide, though her lip still quivered like a wee jelly. Her gaze was fierce for one so small and there was no doubting just who her father was, for she had the look of Casey about her eyes. A fluff of dark curls whorled out around her head. She was a beautiful baby, but he would expect no less with her parentage.

"There now, darling girl, you're all right." He walked across the floor with her, joggling her slightly, and cooing nonsensical things. He could feel her tension ease, the pearled spine bending as she relaxed into his arms. She missed her daddy, poor wee girl. He spoke to her softly in Irish, knowing the language would have been natural for her father to speak in the small hours to his daughter. She snuffled, tiny catching breaths, that said she was still on the verge of crying, but willing to consider the possibility of stopping. The dark eyes were fixed to his face, the flush in her skin gone from red to the color of a pink tea rose dipped in cream. She was younger than Kolya by some months.

He held her gaze, understanding instinctively that she sought reassurance, and that to look away would be to start her crying once again. He continued to speak, low and soft, and she gave a small coo, her eyelids beginning to droop. Moments later her lashes lay against her cheeks, still dewy with tears, but her rosebud mouth was open in utter relaxation. She was fast asleep.

The woman raised an eyebrow at him. "Well, ye've the magic touch, haven't ye?"

He merely smiled at her. There was no point in explaining this affinity for animals and babies he'd always had.

"Pamela's in the byre," the woman said simply, taking the baby back from him. "'Tis a bit mad in here, an' she slipped off for the quiet." She smiled wearily. "From what my son Patrick has told me of ye, I don't think she'll mind if ye join her though."

"How is she?" he asked, quietly, so the other women would not hear him.

"Not good, but it can hardly be hoped that she would be otherwise. Ye'll see soon enough how it is with her."

Aye, he would see soon enough.

The dark was settling in earnest as he crossed the yard, the frost thick under his shoes. He could smell the baby's scent on his coat, a sweet note amongst the sharper smells of the chill evening. A small light glowed in the byre, and he could hear the soft whicker of a horse—Phouka, the pewter demon he had rather disastrously gifted to Pamela a few Christmases ago. He was glad she had brought the beast down here to her own byre, for she had always been one to find comfort in horses. He had given her Phouka for that very reason, to curb the pain of another loss, long ago. This time there would be nothing to curb the pain, or the fear.

He put his hand to the door of the byre, hesitated, then took a deep breath and opened it.

The lantern was low making her silhouette ghostly in the dark of the byre. She was as he had held her in his memory, and yet utterly changed at the same time. Time, babies and grief had altered her lines subtly, so that he knew he was seeing the interior changes more than the physical ones.

He said her name, quietly, not wanting to startle her. "Pamela."

She turned slowly, the movement causing her hair to spill over one shoulder like ink diffusing through a gelid winter pool.

"Jamie." She was pale, her eyes burning in her face, even here in the flickering lantern light. And then again, as if she didn't quite trust his appearance, "Jamie."

He crossed the byre floor to her. The hay was fresh and released the scent of clover and summer sun.

"Pamela, I—"

She shook her head, her eyes pleading with him not to say the words. And then she put her arms around him and he held her tightly for a moment. He could feel the terrible strain in her, as though she were trembling glass, delicate and blown to its limits. And then she pulled back, sensing, he thought, that he could read her too well. She could not afford the vulnerability of that just now.

"I'm so glad you're home," she said, and the words were sincere, though her face remained that set, terrible white. He could hardly have hoped otherwise.

They stood mute for a moment, for there were things to be said, but each understood there weren't words for them just now. They had been so many things to one another, and now all the parameters had shifted, leaving them strangers, without a map by which to guide themselves in this new and raw territory.

"I understand you have a son," she said finally, sitting down on a bale of hay and looking up at him.

"Two of them it would seem," he said, but his voice faltered on it, for there had not been time yet to come to grips with the idea of Julian. "I'm sorry, I understand he caused you no small worry with the company."

She shook her head. "It's all right, it's done now and we managed to keep most things safe. How old is your boy?"

"He turned one this month. And you have both a son and a daughter."

"Yes, we do." The emphasis on the word 'we' was soft, but unmistakable.

He could feel him suddenly—the big, dark Irishman who would never have left this woman bar the finality of death. His presence was here; strong, stubborn and with an emphasis that left his imprint behind long after he had left any room or building.

"Who told you about Julian?" she asked.

"My grandmother broke it to me in her own inimitable fashion."

"I'm sorry for that; I had intended to tell you myself."

"It's all right, Pamela. I don't think there was a good way to tell me."

"You need to be careful, Jamie. Julian is a puzzle, and I don't know what his motives may be concerning you."

"And we are so certain that he is actually my son?"

"Jamie, if you had seen him in the flesh, you would have no doubts. He even moves like you. Genetics is a funny thing."

"Pamela, we don't need to talk about this right now."

"No, it's a relief to talk about something other than the fact that everyone seems to believe my husband is dead."

He did not reply to her words for she would not want platitudes and empty phrases of comfort right now; they could not reach her in the far country in which she now dwelt. She, perhaps more than anyone, would know what an absence this long likely meant. She would either understand it or reject it. It was not for him to push her in either direction.

She took a deep breath, as if she was turning away within herself, from knowledge it was too soon to face. "Come sit. I could use the company. Tell me how you managed to get out of Russia and I will tell you what I can about Julian."

He sat on a bale of hay opposite her.

"Tea?" she asked.

He raised an eyebrow.

"I have a thermos of it. I can't seem to get warm since...since..."

"I'd love some tea," he said softly, forestalling her, so she would not have to speak the words. It was hot and strong, and it did taste as good as he had remembered it. Pamela had always made a good cup of tea.

And so there, within the precincts of the lantern light with the smell of horse and hay surrounding them, he told her in outline of his time in Russia; the things that had led, he believed, to his imprisonment and how he had escaped in the end. It was stark in the telling, just outlines, no brushstrokes to fill it in, for there were no words for that yet.

As he spoke, another part of his mind took in the woman before him, how she had changed and how she had not in the time that separated them. The strain was evident in her, her eyes dark and refracted as they were when she was deeply upset. He had seen her so before. She was still unsettlingly beautiful, though he had not expected that to change. Motherhood had only brought that beauty to its full fruition, for there was something softer about her, even now in her grief.

And when he was done, she told him about Julian. It wasn't, he thought, the most flattering description he had ever heard of a boy, but he thought even at that, she was holding something back. There was time enough to discover what that was.

They discussed the distillery, and the plans she had put in place to have it rebuilt. The death of his Uncle, and whom she believed was behind that death and why. And then they spoke of things more personal—children, friends, the loss of their mutual friend David, who had been a British agent. Very suddenly, they came to that place where there were no words left that did not contain Casey and his lack, for it drenched the very air around them.

He took her hand, giving what small comfort the warmth of human touch could give her right now. The tension sang through her bones, her flesh chill to the touch and wires of fear strung tightly along every inch of skin. Her composure, as fragile as the sheathe of frost that crept up to the byre door, was very dearly bought, and it was in danger of melting away completely right now. He took his hand away.

The horse laid his silver muzzle against Pamela's head, as if he knew her sorrow, and would comfort her if he could. Her hair coiled dark against the long pewter nose, glimmering soft in the dimly lit byre. She put her hand up and stroked Phouka's long nose absently.

When she looked up her gaze was naked, and like a knife, cut sharp and short across his chest. Her honesty had always disarmed him.

"I feel like I can't breathe, Jamie. How am I ever supposed to breathe again if I don't know where he is or what has happened to him?"

He would not lie to her; he was too good a friend for such things.

"I don't know, Pamela. I will tell you this though—I promise to do whatever I can to find him."

They both knew the words that were left unsaid, for they hung between them like a weight of sand.

Alive or dead.

Chapter Two

Here, Nevertheless

BY NOON OF THE NEXT day it seemed every soul in Belfast, from the mean-est crook on the streets to the Secretary of State, knew that His Lordship, James Stuart Kirkpatrick, was home and apparently, he thought with some irritation, open for business. He had forgotten the busy nature of his old life and the endless questions he was expected to answer. Just now, though, there were no answers and he was merely playing catch-up on two years worth of news.

The state of his country was much the same. He had lived here too long to expect great change or to think that peace would be anything other than painfully slow in coming. Still, it was disheartening to realize that little had changed, that the cycle of violence and fear was, if anything, worsened from when he had left.

Just after lunch, which had been copious in both content and serving, a guest was shown into his study whom Jamie was very happy to see.

"Patrick," he said, rising from his desk and coming around it, feeling a rush of emotion. This man was a very dear friend to him and he had missed his steady presence over the last few years. He was also Pamela's brother-in-law.

"Jamie."

The younger of the Riordan brothers had changed a bit in Jamie's absence. He was more man, less boy now, something in him had hardened to a fine finish. There was a deep pain in his eyes, occasioned by his brother's mysterious disappearance, and Jamie thought, likely by other things as well. Jamie could only imagine what these last three weeks had been like for Pat.

The dark eyes quickly assessed his own changes, which he knew were far more visible to the naked eye. There was no judgement however, only concern and then he was engulfed in the big man's embrace.

"We're all so bloody pleased that ye're home safe an' sound." He still smelled the same, like a field after a hard rain.

"It's good to see you too, Patrick. Please come and sit down."

Pat sat on the sofa, his tensile strength resounding in the air. His presence was quieter than that of his brother, but still very definite; he was a man that one could not ignore. Right now there was a great exhaustion emanating off him, which was to be expected.

"Ye've seen Pamela, then?"

Patrick had never been one for small talk, and now it would have been ludicrous to even attempt it. It was one of the things that Jamie had always appreciated about the man.

"Yes, last night. She held it together well, but it was clear how distraught she was."

"Aye," Pat said grimly, "distraught is one way to put it. I don't know what to do for her or how to make it better. There aren't words with which to reassure, because the truth is, I'm as fearful as she is."

"I'm sorry, Patrick."

Pat nodded, face suddenly tight with repressed emotion.

"Jamie, if you could have seen her that first night—just running through the woods calling his name, getting more desperate by the second, calling until her voice left her and she was scratched and bruised and bleeding from running headlong through every gully and patch of shrubs that she came across. I thought she might go mad in those first few days. I thought *I* might, come to that. There was no trace, and it doesn't matter who she has appealed to for help, nor what questions she and I have asked—it's truly as if Casey did disappear into thin air. But ye know as well as I do that's none so rare in this country as it might be in others."

Unfortunately, this was all too true. In Northern Ireland, with clandestine illegal armies and their countless splinters operating at all times, people disappeared on a regular basis. Someone with Casey's history— well, it wasn't a stretch to think that he was just another casualty in this never-ending little war. Yet, Jamie had a niggling feeling that whatever had happened to Casey wasn't so simple as that, and that finding the answers was going to be very difficult, particularly in a culture where talking often meant an unpleasant death.

"Pamela says you've been in law school. I'm glad for you. It suits you. I can see a man like yourself doing great good as a solicitor in this country."

"I need to make a difference in some way. The gun is not a natural fit, so I thought I could bash some civility into my fellow man through the uses of the law."

"I wish you luck with that. I've had more than one briefing on the state of things here in our wee country this morning, and I can't say it filled me with optimism."

"Aye, it's worse, though ye'll know that by now. The violence has escalated, lots of tit-for-tat killings, an' of course no results that anyone could agree on from the convention. It seems attitudes an' positions have hardened just that bit more, an', as is usual, total intransigence rules the day. It seemed for about two minutes that somethin' might come of the convention, but in the end 'twas the usual that won out—no emergency coalition, no compromise—the usual Ulster slogan 'Not an Inch'. We seem to have stagnated into an endless cycle of violence. The Brits are hardened into their role of the caretaker an' peacekeeper between the warrin' factions of the insane Irish. I guess it allows them to sleep at night, even if the tale they tell themselves bears little resemblance to the truth."

"I suppose we all need our illusions about who we are, even on a national level, but it's costing us a bit too dear here in Northern Ireland for the British to keep their tale of imperial glory."

"There's more too, somethin' that maybe ye've not heard yet."

Jamie arched a brow in inquiry, a small thread of unease spooling at the base of his spine. Patrick had a look on his face that said the man was about to tell him something awful, and Pat Riordan wasn't a man who frightened easily.

"There's been some killings that are different. These aren't the normal level of violence. These seem something else altogether, an' it worries me."

"Go on."

"There've been two incidents so far. The first was in a spirits shop. They killed the two sisters that ran the shop, an' a teenaged boy that filled the orders for them an' such. While that, sadly, isn't out of the normal line of things, the way they were tortured before death is."

It was like something cold had crept in under the study door with Pat's words. Jamie remained silent, listening.

"They pulled a few teeth—molars—a few fingernails, an' the head was almost severed from the boy's body. The next instance, it was a Catholic man in his twenties, grabbed off the street while he was makin' his way home after the pub closed for the night. He was a bit worse for the wear when he left, the publican said, but not so much that he couldn't find his way home. Only he never did. The body was in a terrible state. My source says some of the police—hardened veterans—threw up at the scene."

Jamie felt as if his blood had pooled in his feet.

"Are you afraid Casey might have been a victim of this gang?"

"Aye, I am, though 'tisn't so much their style to hide a body an' that's the one thing that gives me hope that he's still alive, or that he met a much swifter an' more merciful end."

"Do you think he's dead, Pat?"

He would not have dared to ask the question of Pamela, but Patrick had been born to this hard little city in this hard little country, and had long been toughened to its harsher realities.

"I don't know, Jamie. I hope he's alive. I pray for it every moment that I am awake an' I come up from sleep with that same prayer on my lips an' a flame of hope in my heart. But if he were alive, what's keepin' him away? Because you an' I both know there's not a thing on earth that would keep him from Pamela an' the babbies. An' that's where the prayer turns to ashes in my mouth an' that small flame in my heart sputters."

They sat in silence for a moment, because there weren't words to fill the void that hung in the air or the years that had lapsed since they had seen each other and all that had taken place in that time. They were friends enough not to try. There was, however, still one thing left to be said.

"Pamela will have told ye about David, then?" Pat asked, voice no more substantial than the smoke that filtered up from the peat in the hearth.

"Yes, she did." He chose his next words carefully. "If you ever want to speak of it, Patrick, then you know I will listen. I was so sorry to hear of his death. I will miss him."

David Kendall and Patrick Riordan ought to have been natural enemies. One a British agent and the other a Nationalist boy from the hard end of Belfast and yet through strange circumstances they had become best friends. Jamie knew David's death and the circumstances surrounding it would weigh hardest on Pat.

Pat shook his head. "Thank ye, Jamie. If the time arrives that I feel I must talk of it, then likely I will come to you. I know ye cared for him. Just now, I feel as if I don't have words in my heart for it."

He knew that only too well. He had a list of names in his own heart right now, for which there were no words to speak.

"Robert tells me that Joe Doherty was killed a year back. I understand someone worse has taken his place."

"Ye know how it is, it only takes a few to cause disproportionate trouble in this town. The faces change, the numbers don't."

He understood what Pat was saying. A dirty war was like that, attrition came in a number of ways: violent death, aging out of the cause, the lure of money found on the edges of any illegal organization, the exercise of personal power where men became kings of their own cause, modified along more violent lines and with far more dubious aims. Some left for higher motives, like Casey who had left in the end because he loved his family more than he loved the conflict. Which begged the question of why someone had chosen now to see him as a threat.

"Thus far, I haven't found out anything new, Patrick. I will continue to make inquiries. I'll do everything I can to help."

Pat acknowledged this statement with a weary smile that did not reach his eyes.

"Ye'll have yer own worries, Jamie. An' I'm told ye've brought a son back with ye."

"I have indeed, in fact I think I hear his roar right now. Come meet him."

They followed the outraged howls to the kitchen where Kolya had worked himself into a fine temper over Vanya's removal of a teacup from his hand.

Jamie picked him up and swung him over his head and Kolya's fury changed instantly to shrieks of joy.

"There now, *mishka moy,* you are all fine now."

"He's a hale little mannie," Pat said. Kolya went quiet and looked with wide blue eyes at the big, dark man in front of him. He took him in in parts and Pat smiled when the blue eyes reached his face. Kolya put his arms around his father's neck and peeked out shyly at Pat.

Jamie put him down on the floor. Kolya wobbled for a second and then got his bearings. If it were possible to look like a Russian emperor at age one and one month, Kolya most assuredly did. He walked directly to Pat, as though there had been no fit of shyness, holding his arms up when he reached the support of Pat's legs. Pat swung him up easily, resting Kolya's bottom on his forearm.

Pat stayed awhile longer, dandling Kolya on his knee, while they shared a pot of tea and some of Maggie's biscuits. He chatted with both Shura and Vanya, taking the presence of these two men in Jamie's home in stride, as if everyone brought home Russian dissidents from their time in the gulag.

"I ought to head home, I suppose," Pat said as the twilight began to creep in at the windowsills and slip over them, gathering in soft pools where the walls met the stone-flagged floor.

"Stay to supper. Maggie's trying to fatten me up, apparently within a week judging from the amount of food she has cooked since our arrival."

"It's kind of ye to offer, but well," his face flushed, "supper will be waitin' for me at home."

Jamie raised one gull-winged eyebrow in surprise.

"Aye, there's a woman," Pat said answering the eyebrow with a tentative look. Jamie understood, for he had been very fond of Patrick's young wife, Sylvie, who had worked for him for a short time. She had died the day after they had married, killed by a car bomb that had been meant to kill Patrick.

"I'm glad to hear it. I hope she makes you happy."

"She does, but there is the one thing, an' I'd as soon ye heard it from me. She's Noah Murray's sister."

Jamie coughed, giving himself a minute to cover his surprise.

Pat gave him a sardonic look. "Aye, I know what ye're thinkin' but it happened before I even realized it. I never meant to care for someone so, didn't think I could really, not after Sylvie. Kate was just there though. She's the most maddenin', stubborn, infuriatin' woman imaginable, an' I adore her, an' she loves me despite her own good sense."

Noah Murray. Possibly the one name in the six counties most likely to make a man's blood run cold in his veins. And Patrick was in love with his sister. Mind you if the man hadn't killed Pat yet, he might spare him a bit longer.

Noah Murray ran one of those infamous splinter groups that Pat had mentioned during their conversation. In truth, it wasn't so much a splinter group as an army and a fiefdom unto itself. Noah Murray was the king of South Armagh and he ruled the Provisional IRA in that area, and a more ruthless lot was not to be found in all the various groupings of the Irish Republican Army's history. Not many men frightened Jamie Kirkpatrick, but given thought, Noah Murray might.

"An' on that note," Pat said, "I'd best get myself home before I'm late for my supper."

Pamela arrived some time after Jamie's own supper, when he had removed himself to the study to take a phone call which went on in length and content until he realized he was making noises of agreement but not listening to what was said any longer. He knew it was her because Montmorency, curled up on the rug before the fire for most of the day, had shot out of the study door like a much younger dog. He found his visitors in the kitchen, Pamela talking to Maggie while a small boy played at her feet with a set of wooden cars. Wee Isabelle was held over her shoulder, and the dark eyes stared wide-eyed at him, the tiny face surrounded in its halo of wild curls. He smiled at her and she smiled back, a resplendent expression of healthy pink gums and tongue. Pamela turned and he saw something relax a tiny bit in her expression, at the sight of him.

His own child was dragging himself up on Pamela's leg by clutching her jeans, one jammy hand over the other. She looked down at his son, Isabelle bouncing in her arms and then glanced back at Jamie, her eyes bright with tears. "Oh, Jamie, he's beautiful. I'm so happy for you."

"And I for you," he said softly, looking at her two healthy whole children, and thinking how far they had both come in a short time, and yet such a long time in a myriad of other ways.

"I thought I had half dreamed your return, but seeing you here in your own house makes it real. You really are home." She said it with a sort of relief, as if his presence eased her burdens a little. *If only*, he thought, *that could be so.*

"It could hardly seem otherwise with all this chaos," he said, for Kolya was making his usual imperious noises that meant he needed a cup of milk immediately. Conor was emitting steady car noises and Isabelle, not to be outdone by some impertinent Russian upstart, was escalating from coos to indignant teakettle noises between vigorous chews on her mother's sweater, the shoulder of which was wet with drool. He found the sound of it all quite lovely.

"Did ye bring a bottle with ye?" Maggie asked, walking over and taking Isabelle from Pamela's arms. "I'll sit an' feed her if ye did."

"I did." She bent and took a bottle from the baby's bag at her feet. "It ought to be about right; I heated it before we left home as I knew she'd want feeding soon."

Kolya, handed a warm cup of goat's milk, released Pamela's pant leg and sat on the floor at her feet, big blue eyes intent on her face as he drank with the intense focus of the young with their food.

Pamela's son looked up then, his big dark eyes meeting Jamie's with the calm assurance of one far older. Jamie's breath caught in his chest. Small as he was, Conor so resembled his father already that it caused a small jolt of shock to go through him.

"I know," Pamela said quietly, taking in his reaction. "He's the spit of him, as Casey always says. We joke that Casey brands his children, they both look so much like him."

He smiled at the boy, and knelt down so that he might show him his car collection, which Conor did in such an easy manner that it was as if he had known Jamie since the day of his birth. Each of the small trucks he played with had been carved from blocks of wood, beautifully grained and exquisitely detailed; they were clearly a product of Casey's love and skilled hands.

"My da's away. He be home soon." The little voice was grave, as he continued to run his small wooden trucks across the freshly washed floor.

Jamie did not answer the boy's words, for the self-possession that came off the small, solid body was such that he knew for the boy it was just a statement of fact, and he required no reassurance from an adult.

He caught the expression on Pamela's face as he stood up, and it felt like someone had hit him, for the pain in her face as she looked at her son's bent curly head, absorbing his words and the pragmatic faith that his daddy would come home simply because that's what daddies did, was profound. He reached out and touched her arm lightly.

"Come into the study, there's a fresh pot of tea and a roaring fire."

She looked at him, face almost blank now, and he realized she was ready to collapse in exhaustion. He wondered if she had managed to sleep at all last night, or any of the endless nights that had preceded it.

She glanced back at Maggie who was still holding Isabelle and crooning to her in a soft tone.

"Go on," Maggie nodded at her, "ye know they're fine with me. I'll come get ye should she need ye."

Pamela bent and kissed the top of Conor's head, murmuring a few words to him. He nodded, still preoccupied with his toys, and Pamela took a deep breath and turned to join Jamie.

The study was a harbor of warmth and quiet. The peat hissed gently under the sound of the clinking of china and the liquid purl of hot tea pouring into cups. He carried a cup to her and she clutched it gratefully. She was shivering. He handed her a sweater that was over the back of one of the chairs by the fire.

"Pamela, forgive me for stepping over the line immediately, but you look like you're going to collapse. Have you slept at all these last few weeks?"

She answered the question indirectly, which told him all he needed to know. "The doctor gave me sedatives to sleep," she said.

"Do you think perhaps it would be a wise idea to take them?"

She shook her head. "No, I know I need to sleep, Jamie. To sleep though means to forget for a little bit and then to have to remember when I wake in the morning. Right now I don't think I could bear that—to think he's there for a minute and then have to remember that he isn't."

"You can't keep going this way, Pamela. You'll wind up in hospital."

"I'm managing," she said. "I realize I have to sleep for the children's sake, if for no other reason."

"Would you like a drink?" he asked.

"Maybe just a little of something; I'm still nursing Isabelle."

He poured her a couple of fingers of Hunter's Vodka, knowing it would be best to warm her blood. Vanya had found some in the two brief days they had been in Paris and bought several bottles claiming it heated the body like nothing else. Jamie knew it to be true. He hoped it might take the edge off her nerves which were as taut as a thrumming wire.

He watched her as she sat, legs curled under her, wrapped in the sweater, but still shivering. He realized that she had become, in his absence, an integral part of this household; it was she who had made the decisions, kept a hand on the tiller and become the most important cog in the wheel of the estate. It was what he had intended, thinking he might not survive to return, and now he wondered if he had been wise. He wondered if the burden he had put upon her had cost her the father of her children, had cost her the love of her life.

"Jamie, I have no wish to put my troubles on you. You need time to readjust to your world, and judging from the stream of people who have been to see you already, you won't be allowed much freedom to do that."

She had always been able to read him when others could not; apparently this had not altered in his absence.

"Pamela, whatever changed while I was in Russia, this one thing has not—that I am your friend, not just in name, but in action as well."

"Thank you," she said softly, and even in those two words, he could hear the strain in her voice, the undercurrent of fear so strong that she could not, must not give in to it in any way. Everything about her spoke of an attention that was fixed to a narrow point, in a far distant country. The country where her husband now dwelt, and whether he was alive or dead made no difference to his residency there, for he belonged to the country of the disappeared.

"I think, Jamie, that he was into something that he couldn't share with me, and that's what took him."

"Do you have any idea of what it might be?"

"No, I was so busy with everything here, and I only had Isabelle in July. If he was in trouble, I know he wouldn't want to worry me, despite the fact that we had agreed not to have any secrets with one another. And to be honest, I was so wrapped up in what had happened with the attempted takeover that I wasn't paying attention as I should have."

He could say the empty phrases that came to a man at such times, but here there seemed neither room nor use for them. She was going to feel this was in some part her fault and there was nothing he could say to change that. He would not insult her by trying.

"I hope you don't mind that I came here tonight. I feel safe here and that makes me feel guilty, I suppose. Plus my house is overrun with well-meaning aunties. Deirdre put them on notice this morning. I think she knows I can't manage it much longer."

"Pamela, this house is as much yours as mine, especially after these last few years. I hope you always know that."

She smiled, though it was more of a grimace, as if it hurt to smile. It did hurt for her right now, he supposed. The smallest gestures would hold a terrible cost.

He spoke now to the questions she had not asked, but that hummed in the air. He was gentle because it was not the news she wanted, and it might never be.

"It will take time, Pamela. My connections with the various organizations are tenuous if, indeed, they exist at all anymore. I won't be trusted, not that I ever really was. From what I've been able to gather thus far, no one has found a trace anywhere. I realize someone must know something. It's just a matter of finding that person. Whatever happened to Casey, there's no more sign of it than a wisp of smoke upon the air. I've spoken to the policeman assigned to the case and to a man I know with connections deep inside the Provos."

She nodded and tried to mask her disappointment. Had she been less exhausted she might have succeeded. She swallowed and changed the subject. She had never lacked for courage, and it hurt him to see her exercise it in this way.

"Will you see Julian soon, do you think?"

He sighed, rolling his glass between his palms, the scent of ginger and lemon peel floating up out of the vodka and tickling his nose.

"I suppose I will have to."

"He's not so terrible, Jamie, just very young and, I think, easily led by the wrong people."

He raised an eyebrow at her. "Wrong people—is that what we're calling the Reverend?"

"I think he could be taken from the Reverend's influence. It's possible their bond was shaken when Julian failed to take over your companies and home. Besides, you are his father and I think that matters to him terribly. You have the greatest chance to turn him around, Jamie—when you're ready and feel able."

He felt neither ready nor able; he knew that she understood that all too well. She had grown into something more in his absence, a woman who had taken on the bad guys and won, and then lost more profoundly than anyone could have foreseen.

"You must miss them," she said, voice pitched barely above the soft hiss of the peat and the distant sounds of the household going about its nightly business. There was no need to ask whom she meant; he understood. The rapport between them had always been this way, unnecessary words not needing to be spoken. It was a shock to find it still there between them, this invisible thread which had existed from the time they met, all those years ago on the Vineyard, when he had been a young husband who had lost two sons, and she an abandoned child who needed a friend.

"I do. Were I still there though, I would be dead by now. Things were not straightforward with my marriage, to say the least. She was—or at least it appears that she was—an agent for the KGB." He took a drink, his throat suddenly dry. "If she was KGB it's possible she made a deal and if so, I hate to think what it might have been. We weren't followed out of Russia, and that in itself was odd. We had to be careful and we walked through untrammeled wilderness for the most part, but still the border is not exactly porous. It troubled me at the time, but I was just grateful to get out with my life and Kolya."

"I'm grateful too," she said, voice starting to blur slightly. He held his breath for a moment and then continued to chat to her, keeping his voice low, speaking whatever nonsense occurred to him, the pleasant bits of Russia, embroidered and shed of their cruel trappings so that he might give her something kind, something slightly fairy tale in nature to drift away upon.

He walked across the room to place the blanket, kept always on the back of the sofa, over her. She looked like a delicate flower that had been caught out in a hard frost and now was bent on its stem, petals translucent with shock.

She appeared to be heavily asleep. He added a few bricks of peat to the fire. If she was warm then she might sleep for a bit. He stood at the study door, hesitant, worried that if he left she would wake, but that his presence here might disturb her too.

The kitchen was a haven of warmth and mellow light. The dishes had been tidied away and Shura had left something steeping in a bowl on the counter and was now preparing tea for himself and Maggie. Maggie watched him with a gimlet eye. Jamie was shocked, however, that she was willing to allow Shura free rein in her kitchen. He had never known her to let anyone breach her territory before.

"Where's Vanya?" he asked, for he had only seen his exotic houseguest at meals today, though that meant little, as he had been holed up in his study, with only small forays out between visitors.

"That one," Shura said with one of his eloquent shrugs, "he has been in your library all day."

Vanya was an insatiable reader, in both Russian and English and a library such as this house possessed would seem little short of King Solomon's mines to him. Where he had come by his ability to read English was a bit of a mystery.

"Yasha, you will take more tea for you and your guest?" Shura asked.

"I still have half a pot left in the study, and my guest is asleep." The latter information was in response to Maggie's inquiring look. Isabelle was profoundly asleep in Maggie's arms, an empty bottle at Maggie's elbow.

Conor played quietly near Maggie's knee, and Kolya sat beside him, gnawing on the corner of one of his trucks.

"Poor wee thing," she said and he knew she meant Pamela, not the baby she held. "She's been looking like a ghost gone the far side of the grave this while. It's good that she sleeps as long as can be managed. Best she does it here, rather than wakin' in the bed that's empty of her man."

"Can we manage the children, maybe call her mother-in-law to let her know, in case she sleeps through the night?"

"Aye, we can manage fine. Ye just let her sleep as long as she needs. I can put these wee ones to bed."

He put Kolya to bed himself, for he wasn't ready to allow another the privilege of it. He had been bathed and he smelled sweetly of talc and clean rompers. Jamie held him tightly, allowing the warmth of his small body and the silk of his hair against his cheek to relax his own body. Kolya had been, Maggie informed him, utterly fascinated with wee Isabelle Riordan. Kolya had never seen a child smaller than himself, which likely accounted for much of the fascination.

He put the boy into the crib in which he had slept as a baby, and stood for a moment merely watching him breathe. He thought of how quickly this year of Kolya's life had passed, how much had changed, how far he was from the events that had put this child into his governance. He did not think of Kolya's mother, he had become quite adept at not thinking about her.

Russia had put a strange stillness at the core of him, so that even when events were spinning wildly about him, there was this place inside where he could retreat and view things through a lens of quiet. It was clear he was going to have to call upon that still core in the days and months to come.

He returned to the study once Kolya was deeply asleep, and sat at his desk, working quietly through the mountain of paperwork which had accrued in his absence. There was no fear he might run out before the dawn.

Occasionally he would look up, surprised to find himself in his study, which was both wonderfully familiar and joltingly strange to him after three years away, two of them spent in the gulag. It had always been his favorite room in the house. It had been his grandfather's as well. Sometimes he thought he could still smell the ghost of the man's aftershave and the cigars he'd occasionally smoked. There had been nights, when he had sought refuge here, when he thought he felt his grandfather standing by his shoulder, giving him what comfort he could. Pamela, asleep on the sofa, was comfortingly familiar too, she had done so more than once, claiming that the study had a spell on her, which halted time and gave her sanctuary. It was why he had brought her here tonight, in the hope that the room would give her some small dose of those healing properties, or even just respite for a moment.

He looked around the room, at the worn Bokhara rugs, the gilt-edged bindings on the books, the glass walls, supported by a structure of wrought iron, making it resemble nothing so much as a Victorian bird-cage. The study was an addition to the house, and was built in the shelter of a ring of oaks and clambering rose cane. He realized, after a moment, he was seeing none of it. His senses were turned inward to a face that was blazoned upon his inner eye.

He took the picture out from the drawer where he had put it yesterday. Even with repeated viewings, it was a jolt to realize how much the young man looked like him. He had barely had time to think about this newest ripple in his life today, but the image of this boy had been at the back of his mind through every interaction, through every hour. This young man whom he had not been allowed to see, whom he knew not the slightest part of, other than he held within him a destructive amount of anger. Pamela's words had been soft and designed to soothe, the look on her face, however, had told him far more about his son's nature. He was going to have to take the proverbial bull by the horns and arrange to meet. Julian had returned to Oxford, that much he knew.

Pamela muttered something in her sleep and took a sharp breath, as if she were on the edge of a cry. He held his breath, letting it out only when he saw that she had settled back to her rest.

He laid the picture of Julian to the side and returned to his work, pausing from time to time, looking over to where she slept, huddled tight beneath the blanket, as if it could shield her from the hurts of this city, the loss of her man and the unbearable pain in which each dragging moment of her day was steeped. She was right, when she woke it would be to forgetfulness for a moment and then to remember afresh. For grief, in her arts, was a cruel mistress.

He would be here when she woke, not the man she wanted or needed, but here, nevertheless.

Chapter Three

The Disappeared
January 1976

It was the usual sort of station, the usual sort for Northern Ireland that is, meaning there was a Plexiglas cage between herself and the constable on the counter. There were security buzzers and gates to go through and the constable facing her was wearing a bulletproof vest. This particular police building had been bombed once before. The bomb had done a fair bit of damage despite the fact that the place was built to the specifications of a concrete bunker. She hated coming here, but it was necessary to check in, to ask questions and to prod them to do their job. She wasn't naïve though about how earnest they would be in searching for yet another disappeared person in the six counties. In this case, it was worse, because Casey had been ex-PIRA and would be considered the enemy.

Her neighbor and the children's honorary grandmother, Gert, was at her house with the children, as she knew it was likely she would have to wait before someone could see her, and trying to do that with a rambunctious toddler and a tiny baby was unthinkable. She had become a familiar, if not terribly welcome, face in the last few weeks to the officers here.

She sat to wait, her hands clasped in her lap to still their trembling, or at least to make it less visible. With each day that passed her anxiety went up another notch, so that now it seemed the dark bird in her chest never ceased to flap its wings. She found herself having to stop to catch at a decent breath of air. She couldn't seem to get warm, even now, though the waiting area was overly heated, she still felt a cold that went straight through to her marrow. Just sitting here, as tired as she was, felt like a poor use of time, when she felt she ought to be out searching, scouring every dead-end lane and hollow in the land.

On the day that Casey disappeared she had been gone from early morning until just before supper, away at Jamie's house, tidying up loose ends, signing paperwork and making decisions. She hadn't thought much of it when she arrived home to an empty house, for Casey was often home late, depending on the stage of the building on which he was working. But then the hours had ticked past, and he had not come through the door. She had fed the children, bathed them with a rising tide of panic in her chest, put them to bed with stories, kisses and lullabies, even though her throat felt as though she were choking on needles.

She had come back down the stairs praying he would be sitting in the boot room, apologizing for his tardiness and looking for his dinner, which she had kept warming in the Aga. She had given it another hour, the longest hour, or so she had felt at that point, that she had experienced in quite some time. Then she called Pat, who had done what he could to disguise his own alarm. He had shown up at the door an hour later. Casey had not been at the construction site, and no one had seen him all day.

That was when she truly started to panic. That feeling, that terrible dark blooming in her chest had not stopped since, not even when she slept, which admittedly wasn't often or of any depth. It was a constant feeling that she had no control over anything, that the entire universe had become a whirl of chaos and terror, of thoughts she could not stop and fear that gnawed at every last nerve ending in her body. Gert had come to watch the children while she and Pat searched everywhere they could think that Casey might have traveled that day.

By morning, she knew she had to go to the police. While she had worked with some of the police in the various Belfast RUC stations, she wasn't familiar with any of the men that worked in her own area. She was very much afraid that they would not be terribly sympathetic to a woman who was looking for her notoriously republican husband. She was justified in her fear, as it turned out, because they were not sympathetic in the least. She had left the station and thrown up right outside the doors. They refused to take a missing persons report on Casey until he had been gone a week. She knew the rule was generally 48 hours, not a week, and understood their cruelty was deliberate; that she was going to have to steel herself for more of the same, and also to look for unorthodox avenues of finding out what had happened to him.

Things had not improved much since. She had been assigned an officer—Constable Severn, who did his best to be kind, even if he did not instill much confidence that the police would be in any way effective in helping her to find out what had happened to her husband. He was a bit of a plod, but he meant well, she knew, even if she sensed he had no power at that station.

Today, however, it was not the kindly if ineffective constable who came out to the waiting room. A shadow fell over her, and she startled, for she hadn't heard the man approach. He was standing too close, as if he were one of those people who didn't understand that other people had spatial boundaries, invisible, but very real. She had to crane her neck to see his face, for he was very tall, as tall as Casey was perhaps, though he had a much slighter frame.

He was young and had one of those rawboned faces with an overly prominent chin and a hint of acne peeking out from his collar. His eyes were grey, the sort that held neither water nor light, rather they were pale and predatory, made more so by the sparse lashes that surrounded them.

"I'm usually referred to Constable Severn," she said, hoping the man was here.

"Well, he's not here today, he'd family business to attend to, so I'm to answer yer questions. I'm Constable Blackwood." He didn't shake her hand, or do anything else that might be construed as a social nicety, he only gestured abruptly that she should follow him.

He took her into a dingy room, with a table and two chairs and little else to recommend it. She could only assume it was an interrogation room, and she began to get a distinctly bad feeling. He held a file that looked terribly thin; it couldn't possibly contain more than two pages.

He sat and opened the file and shuffled the two papers around in an attempt, she thought, to look officious. He hadn't offered her tea or a glass of water, something that Constable Severn always did. She never drank it but it was a small comfort to have the offer, as if just the smallest civility somehow kept the reality of her situation at bay.

"I'm here about my husband, Casey Riordan, he went missing a month—"

He held up a hand and cut her off. "I know why ye're here, I looked at the file."

"Is there anything new?"

"No," he said bluntly, and if she wasn't mistaken, with a little scoop of satisfaction that it should be so. There was nothing to hang her hope on, and yet nothing to take it away either. A woman could find comfort in that, if of a small and precarious sort.

"Have ye considered that it might be an own goal by those pricks in the 'Ra?"

"No," she said flatly, wanting to tell him that her eyes were in her head and not her chest, as that's where he kept training his gaze. She couldn't afford to antagonize him because she needed any bit of help she could find.

He shrugged. "There isn't any news. Some police feel the need to mollycoddle families, but I think honesty is kinder in the long run. So ye need to start reconcilin' yerself to the idea that yer husband is dead, an' likely has been from the day he disappeared, unless he was tortured somewhere for a bit first."

She jerked back feeling like the man had slapped her. He might as well have for the shock was the same. He was being deliberately cruel. It wasn't that she didn't understand that an absence this long didn't portend well, but to have it so bluntly stated, with such malice that it fairly dripped from him like cream from the whiskers of an overfed cat, was like taking a punch to the stomach when she wasn't prepared for it in the least.

She stood to go, her entire body tingling with both hurt and humiliation. She intended to be out of the station and safely in her car before she had any sort of reaction. She would not give this man the satisfaction of her pain.

He followed her out into the lobby area. She wished he would just stop, and let her go on alone. She could smell his body odor and it was making her nauseous. Sweat and something else—an undernote like curdled milk.

Her hand was on the door when he spoke again.

"Woman that looks like you won't have no problem findin' herself another husband. I wouldn't fret too much over the one ye lost."

She did not turn, she did not trust herself to look at him and keep her ability to remain calm. If she looked at him, she might well fly at him like a banshee and scratch his eyes out. Instead, she walked out of the station flushed with humiliation and shaking with fury. If he had wanted to make it clear that she could expect no help from the police, then the message was received. She got in the car, aware she was still watched for she could feel his eyes fixed upon her.

She looked in the rearview mirror as she backed out, and wished she hadn't. Constable Blackwood was standing watching her, his arms crossed over his chest and his cold grey eyes trained on her. She thought she might be sick, and was furious with herself when tears started to gather in her eyes. She pushed on the gas pedal hard enough that the car lurched forward before it caught and sprayed gravel, and then it shot out of the parking lot.

She drove. The dark bird in her chest was beating its wings so hard she thought she might pass out. She had been afraid that this might happen, that the police would take against her and her questions because Casey had once been a member of the PIRA.

She drove past the turn-off that would take her home, but only realized it a few moments later. She needed to turn around somewhere; Isabelle would need feeding soon and there was no spare bottle for her in the fridge. Her milk had been unreliable since Casey's disappearance because it had been so difficult to stick to Isabelle's feeding schedule and the stress and anxiety weren't helping to keep up her supply. She stopped at the first lay-by she came to on a narrow country road that was little more than a paved cow trail. The lay-by was merely a small indent in the thick hedgerow which lined both sides of the track. The leaves rustled in the breeze, speaking of the rain to come, or given the cold maybe even a fall of snow.

She was shaking so hard she had great difficulty turning off the ignition. The tears were gone now, though she felt it might have been a relief to cry. It wasn't going to happen, even if it felt most days that there was an ocean of them trapped inside her. Rage and fear she could feel, but not grief, because grief would be an acknowledgement of something she could not admit.

She sat there watching as the drops of sleet came and slid down the windows of her car. She thought she must be in shock sometimes, because despite the pain and panic that were her constant companions there was still a sense of falsity to this, as if she would wake up tomorrow morning and hear Casey whistling downstairs as he made the morning tea or turn over in the bed and find the sheets still warm from his body, the scent of him, dark and musky, there in the sheets. She had not been able to sleep in the bed since he'd disappeared.

She sat until the windows were fogged with her breath and she had regained some small bit of composure, or what now passed for composure. It was a small and miserable shield that did little to protect her from the slings and arrows of living in this country.

She turned over the ignition and squared her shoulders, waiting for the bird in her chest to give a few more flaps. Then she pulled the car back out onto the narrow road. If the police wouldn't help her, she thought she knew someone who would.

Chapter Four

Noah

PAMELA WAITED BY THE STONE wall that set the boundary for the southern end of their property. She stood where the wall ended in a clump of elm, slick-dark and laden with sleet this evening. It had not been an easy task to set up this meeting. It had taken screwing her courage to the sticking point and asking Kate to talk to her brother on her behalf. For two weeks she had waited before his answer came. Pamela was, like most people who lived in the fragile state of the murder triangle, somewhat terrified of the man. The PIRA was a different entity altogether in South Armagh, at times they made the Belfast wing of the Provos look like old world gentlemen. Noah Murray was the godfather of the hard men in Armagh, and he was feared far and wide for good reason.

She shivered, it was a cold evening, and while she was well bundled against the weather, she was never warm anymore. She glanced around, this was her own land, but everything looked ominous to her. Vision became skewed in the wake of a disappearance, roads and paths that seemed merely just that before became sinister in their various turns and twists; the crooked trunk of a tree at a bend in the road, the way water pooled in a familiar depression suddenly seeming a black and ominous divining mirror. Every turning of a path, every fork in every road, now represented something different to her than it had before, because what if that was the place where Casey had vanished, what if that was the exact ripple in the air where he had turned his head and looked back at home one last time?

She understood suddenly that she was afraid she would always be standing here, stuck in time, looping forever around that one instance, the events of a single moment, events of which she did not know the slightest detail and thought, perhaps, she was too much a coward to know the entire story. To find the one person that *did* know, *that* she would give her life for. For someone to tell her, even without mercy or regret—this, this is what happened to your husband, to the man you loved, this is where he was taken, this is where he was left. And yet, when she was awake in the pits of another three o'clock in the morning, did she really want to know, would knowing change anything? Would it ease the pain in her heart and the cold place in the world where, when she reached out her arms, he no longer existed? It was a real danger, the possibility of getting stuck there in that place forever, waiting for someone who was not ever coming home, while the world around you moved on, lived, laughed, loved and breathed without feeling like they had broken glass in their chest.

They were the questions she had to ask herself. Questions about every word, every nuance, every look and every small detail that might be nothing, but might be everything in finding the trail that led to Casey. Why that day? Had he done something that she was unaware of or met with someone unexpected?

If there was one man who might tell her the things she needed to know without mercy or regret, it was the man she had arranged to meet here tonight. For Noah Murray had his finger on the pulse of every heartbeat in the Armagh region, though her knees got rather more shaky when she thought about how many heartbeats he was rumored to have put a full stop to.

Kate had been a bit hesitant when she first approached her with her request.

"Did ye not tell me my brother had threatened to kill ye once?"

"He did, but it was a long time ago, and I haven't poked my nose into any of his business since. Please Kate, will you think about it? He might be the only person who can help me."

Kate nodded, the sympathy on her face stark. "Aye, Pamela, ye know I would do anything to help."

And she had, setting up this meeting despite her own reservations about the wisdom of it. Pamela was having her own doubts just this moment, though it did not matter, for she would do much worse to find so much as a whisper about what had happened to Casey.

Just when she thought Noah wasn't going to show, he walked out of the trees, silent as a wolf, hands in his pockets and his face hidden beneath the brim of a poor boy cap.

He came and stood beside her, taking his cap off. He was a good deal handsomer than she had imagined him. She had half expected the man to look like the monster he was reputed to be. He looked a great deal like his sister, for he was fine-featured with the dark chestnut hair and the distinctive gentian eyes which Kate also had. He was slender and stood about six inches above her, which put him just over six feet. She knew he was four years older than Kate, which made him only three years senior to her. He was just thirty in terms of actual time, but a lifetime older in terms of experience. That quality made itself felt quite clearly.

"What is it that ye want then?" he asked, clearly not one for either intrigue or small talk.

She took a breath for courage and plunged in at the deep end, suspecting there was no other way to approach things with this particular man.

"I want to know if you know anything about my husband's disappearance?"

He didn't seem surprised by her question. She thought it likely Kate had apprised him of just why she wanted to meet with him.

"Are ye askin' if I murdered yer man?"

"I suppose, in part, I am," she said aware that her knees were roughly the consistency of badly-set jelly, but relieved that her voice didn't shake in the least.

"No, I didn't. I had no troubles with him."

"Do you know of anyone who did?"

His eyes narrowed and she felt like a goose had walked firmly across her grave.

"An' why do ye imagine I'd tell ye if I did?"

The man had a point there, why would he tell her? He owed her nothing. She would have to go with the truth once again, because she had no other chips with which to barter.

"Because I'm slowly losing my mind," she said softly, "and though everyone else thinks you're the most cold-hearted bastard on the planet, I think you're maybe not entirely without compassion. The truth is if anyone can find out, it's you. That's why I asked."

He laughed. "I *am* the most cold-hearted bastard on the planet, truth be told. It's rare for someone to have the courage to say it to my face."

She shrugged. "You don't seem terribly sensitive to me, so I doubt it will bother you overmuch."

He laughed again, a soft laugh for such a hard man.

"Ye're not one to butter a man up with soft words, are ye?"

"No, I'm not."

"I only agreed to meet with ye because of Kate."

"I know." She held his gaze; she couldn't afford to falter with this man.

The gentian eyes were cold as the snow that lay thick in the fields.

"If I do this for ye, then I expect a return on my troubles. I'm not like the other men ye've known—the ones who would do anything ye ask, because of the way ye look. I'm not weak for that sort of thing."

"I suspect you're not weak for any sort of thing," Pamela said tartly. She knew she ought to be afraid of him, he was feared county-wide for good reason, but she found his company oddly comforting. She had the sense that he would not lie to her nor would he make promises he couldn't hope to keep. "What sort of return are you talking about?" She was blunt, because there was no other way to be with this man, and because she wanted it clear from the start that she would not go to his bed, if that was what he had in mind.

"I'll not expect ye to sleep with me—I can see that ye scruple at that idea. Occasionally, I may ask ye to put up a man on the run, someone who needs a room to hide in for a day or two. It will be made clear to them that ye're a respectable widow with wee ones to care for, an' they are to behave themselves or answer to me. Trust me when I say Mrs. Riordan, that none of them want to answer to me if they can avoid it."

"I'm not a widow," she said indignantly.

He shrugged. "Maybe ye are or maybe ye aren't, it remains to be seen. Thinkin' that ye're a widow will give ye a respectability in the lads' eyes, an' they are less likely to get ideas in their heads."

"What makes you think they will give me any trouble?" she asked. She could hardly imagine any man's desire overcoming his fear of the man in front of her.

"Just because I'm not weak for it," he said, "doesn't mean that I'm not well aware that other men are. I know ye understand who I am an' know what I've done, but I've made a deal with ye, an' I'll not allow ye to be hurt for keepin' yer end of it."

"How will this work?" she asked, swallowing over the dryness in her throat. It wasn't fear exactly that she felt, only the sense that if she put one foot on this road there would be consequences, and there would never be any turning back.

"I'll let ye know if an' when I need yer help, an' I'll arrange to meet here with ye, should I have anything to tell ye. What I find out about yer husband, whatever that might be, I'll be sure to tell ye right away."

"Okay," she said and for a fleeting second heard her husband's voice clear as day in her head.

"*Have ye completely lost yer fockin' mind, woman?*"

"Yes, yes I have," she replied to him.

"What?" Noah was looking at her curiously, and she realized she had spoken her answer out loud.

She shook her head. "Sorry, it was nothing, just mumbling to myself."

He nodded. "I've got to go, I've other appointments to keep this night. Are ye all right to walk back on yer own?"

"Of course I am," she said stiffly. He merely put his cap back on his head, gave her a curt nod and melted away into the night. She stood for a long time after he left, looking at the spot where he'd stood, but not seeing anything. The wind had changed direction while she'd talked to him, and the sleet had turned to snow. Tiny stars fell, landing on the stone wall, glimmering there for a second before melting into oblivion. She touched one, and felt the small chill on her fingertip, there and then gone. Like her husband, there one moment and gone the next.

She took a breath, feeling the terrible weight in her chest, as if a stone sat there. She closed her eyes and tilted her face up to the night sky, letting the snow fall on her eyes, and nose and lips. And she said the prayer she never stopped saying inside her mind, in her heart.

"*Come home to me, man, come home to me please, please, please...*"

Sometimes she thought if she just kept her eyes closed long enough, she would finally wake from this nightmare, that she could conjure back life as it had been, and Casey would be there in front of her, warm and big and secure. Her man, her husband, her love.

But when she opened her eyes, there was only the night sky above, the trees around her and the heavy silence of falling snow.

Chapter Five

The King of the County

UPON SLIEVE GULLION, on a fine day, you could see eight counties clear as glass, laid below at your feet. It could make a king of the most ordinary man to see such a sight and know it to be his own, even if only for a fleeting moment. For Noah Murray the sight was just that wee bit different for much of what he saw lying below him, glimmering under a light covering of snow, was indeed within the hand of his considerable power. South Armagh was his own private fiefdom. Even the British Army acknowledged that he was the ruler in this tiny kingdom. They had learned long ago to step lightly upon this land, and when they hadn't he had brought it sharply to their attention.

    South Armagh had long been a land apart. Even in a country of rebels and outlaws, South Armagh was considered a wild zone, a no man's land where the Provisional Irish Republican Army had their own set of rules and an autonomy which even the Belfast Brigade dared not gainsay. Geographically it was set up to be a bandit's paradise with the Gap of the North being the only entry into or out of the kingdom of Ulster into the Leinster of old. In other times people refused to come to South Armagh to either trade or buy solely because the chance of being set upon by thieves was almost certain. That hadn't changed much and many people would go out of their way to avoid the county altogether, or lock their doors and make a run for it through the beautiful rolling countryside banded with blackthorn hedges and low stone walls.

The Defenders, an organization that many saw as the seedling of what eventually would become the Irish Republican Army, had its genesis in this land. Enmity was handed down through the generations, old tragedies neither forgiven nor forgotten. Outlaws like Redmond O'Hanlon still lived in memory as if they had only faced the hangman yesterday and the legends of Cuchulain and the Hag of Beara were as much a part of the landscape as the stones of the mountain upon which Noah now stood. It was still a land of legend, of outlawry and savage violence when tribal lines were crossed. And in this land, one man was king.

Noah Murray was considered the single biggest threat to domestic security within the United Kingdom. It was no small thing to be such. His farm was under near constant watch by army surveillance teams dug in close to the border crossing point. In the last five years several million pounds had been spent on building watchtowers just to the north of his farm. But there were ways to elude the army and their intelligence gatherers. They had not caught him yet, though he had endured many a search of his land and house and been beaten more than once at the hand of interrogators. It was a matter of course, and he bore it when he had to and struck back when the bastards least expected it.

The one vulnerable spot in his life was Kate for he loved his sister and was extremely protective of her. He had been alarmed when she took up with Patrick Riordan, and even more so when it became clear that she loved the man in no small fashion. He had reconciled himself with it, however. Pat Riordan was on his way to becoming a lawyer and hadn't taken up the republican sword in any fashion that would bring harm to Kate. He had made it clear to Patrick he would kill him slowly and painfully should anything happen to his sister. Pat hadn't so much as blinked and had said he'd shoot himself, thank you kindly, if any harm came to Kate on his watch. Noah believed him, and appreciated the fact that the man didn't seem to fear him in the least.

Noah took this little war in his country seriously, and he trained his men accordingly. They were crack troops that he would put up against any military in the world—if the numbers were near even, or even if they weren't. He had trained in Libya and had become an expert in arms and explosives. He believed in this war but he didn't feel a great loyalty to the Belfast command. They were moving in a direction with their speeches and philosophies that he didn't think would do much more than throw an aura of glamor over the organization.

There were many in the Belfast wing of the army, he knew, who would not be sorry to see him dead. He understood that. Noah was a threat and he didn't vote along popular lines unless he absolutely believed in the resolutions put forward. He was not part of any inner circle or conclave and had no wish to be so. Noah knew this worried the regular command, but he did not care. He was a man who had always known his own mind. He also knew how to put and keep the fear of God into most men who crossed his path.

That was where he found Pamela Riordan such a surprise too, a wee bit of a woman who didn't shake in terror of him. Noah considered what the woman had asked of him. He had told her he would help and he would, for he believed in certain human decencies, and helping a woman who looked like a breath would crack her fragile composure was a basic decency in his opinion. He had been somewhat surprised when she had requested a meeting with him; it took a rare courage and a rare desperation to approach him in such a manner, with little to offer in return. He wouldn't have seen her had Kate not vouched for her. Women were used by both sides quite often in this war he was involved in. A woman who looked as Pamela Riordan did could make a man take risks he couldn't afford, could make a man lose his wits and flap his tongue. He would have to be certain that any of the men she put up knew the penalty should they feel the need to unburden themselves to that fair face. It would be as dangerous for her as it was for them.

He had met her husband a time or two, first at a meeting long ago with the Belfast brigade. He had respected him, for he had a natural air of command and a clear vision of the future, one that wasn't terribly rosy, but had the smack of realism about it. Once he had run into him at the Emerald Pub, and they had exchanged curt nods and nothing else. The man had been wary of him, and wisely so. Casey Riordan, despite having left the IRA behind—as much as a man ever could—was a threat to a man who had no intention of sharing his power with anyone. At first, Noah couldn't believe the tale he was told—that the man had left the Army because he valued his marriage more than his own history. There was a word for that, and it wasn't polite. Then one day he had seen the Riordans in the village, doing their shopping with their wee boy in a pram. The man's arm had been around his wife and they had been laughing together at some shared joke. It had been clear to him, unromantic as he was, that they had something rare.

Since her request, he had done some digging and put out a few feelers into the dark corners of the paramilitary world. He had twisted a few arms and put pressure where he felt it was best used. He did have some information for her, not as to what had actually happened to her husband but a hint as to why it might have happened.

Noah turned from the mountain view and made his way back to his truck. He had chosen to go to the top of this mountain today for some much-needed time to think, and for the perspective it always gave him. His real destination though lay further down the mountainside, hidden away where there were no tracks, no pathways, and little traffic other than that of badger and fox. He drove part of the way, down the rough road that was barely passable even after weeks of hard frost. He parked the truck about a half-mile from his destination. The rest of the journey would have to be made on foot. The truck was hidden from any stray soul who might chance by, though it wasn't likely anyone would be about on this side of the mountain. The terrain was rough, to say the least, and there were no public footpaths.

It was a tough slog in to reach his objective but that was by design. The cave was well hidden in a small glade of ivy-wrapped trees and low, thick shrubbery. He took a pathway known only to him, stopping where the land abruptly changed to put on a pair of wellies. He had to wade through marsh grass and bog to reach the cave. There was a lacy skim of ice on the boggy ground, though the day was fine for January. He counted out his steps; the cave was so well hidden that it almost seemed to exist in another dimension, as if the entrance to it shifted from one visit to the next. When he was near the mouth of the cave, a cloud scudded across the face of the sun, lending the tiny glade a supernatural chill for a moment. Noah frowned and continued on to the screen of willow that hid the entrance.

Noah stood still for a moment after he had crawled in over the stony lip, pulling out his torch and turning it on. He checked the floor for any traces of trespass. His purpose for being here lay ahead of him, for there were eighteen crates of guns hidden in the depths of the cave, far back where there was neither light nor damp. He walked carefully, torch in hand, always aware that an animal might take refuge here. He had no desire to run into a disgruntled badger in the dark.

The cave stayed dry even during the wettest weather, which made it ideal for the storage of guns. In this country, weapons were both a form of wealth and a hard currency.

This cave was a personal sanctuary and he considered the finding of it a turning point in his life, much as a monk might consider an ecstatic vision, or a prophet a term of forty nights on a wild and isolated mountaintop. For it had been exactly that to him. Long ago, a boy of fifteen had run from his home, in fear and grief, and hidden here. A month later the man had emerged, still fifteen, but no longer vulnerable and no longer afraid. This cave held his memories, his fears and his eventual emergence from the boy he had been into the man he had forged from the ruins of that sensitive adolescent who had loved the beautiful things of the world. He had spent much of the nights inside the cave, and his days roaming the mountain like a wild thing—eating berries and trapping hares and stealing from farms in the gloaming when he got desperate for a bit more food than what the mountain could provide. For the first time in his life, he'd been free and happy. He thought it was the only time he had ever been so.

He had returned home someone changed entirely and the look of it was in his eyes, for his father never raised a hand to him again.

His father had died shortly after that. His time in the cave had created something tough in Noah that allowed him to do what he needed to in order to keep him and Kate alive and keep the farm running. It hadn't been easy; he had to face down men twice his age and find a way to pay the mortgage on the farm each month. Which had been substantial for his father hadn't been the best manager, nor the best farmer come to that.

During Noah's own time, he had managed to pay out the mortgage and improve the function and form of the farm in great measure. The smuggling had come about because of his association with Mickey Devine. In fact the location of the farm—straddling the border between the North and the Republic—had been what had caused Mickey to approach him in the first place. Noah had understood at once that it could be either an opportunity or a road to disaster. He chose to make it into an opportunity, standing firm about what he would allow on his farm and what he would not. He was smart enough to know, even then, that he wanted something kept sacrosanct in the place where he lived. No bombs made in his byre, no weapons stored upon his land, he had stood firm on that until Mickey had laughed and said, "All right, lad, I know when I've met my match." At the time, Mickey Devine had been the acknowledged head of the South Armagh brigade, a position Noah would one day inherit from him.

He had known even at the tender age of sixteen that smuggling had the potential to make him enough money to have lifelong security provided he was smart and careful about it. Mickey had given him his start there and Noah had built it up piece by piece until he was running what amounted to an illegal empire. He had enough money never to have to farm another day in his life. The money was simply a means to an end and it funded his true passion, which was the autonomy of his county, if not his country. No small part of that were the weapons in this cave. This was his space, an enchanted portal that none but him could find. It was why he had hidden the crates here, and a long night of hauling each crate from the back of a truck to the cave it had been. It was his personal storehouse and the weapons were good ones, not hand-me-downs the Libyans had found rattling around in one of their cupboards, which was the source of much of the PIRA's weaponry. He had a pipeline out of Irish America, and most of the weapons were American-made, and had been smuggled over at no little cost and no little trouble. They were worth a small fortune—M16s, AR-18s, AR-15 Armalites, M60s, Smith and Wesson revolvers, Browning pistols and a consignment of Mauser rifles from Germany, all funneled through his American connections.

An odd prickling ran up his body as he went deeper into the dark, and he had a sudden sense that someone else had been here. It was a chill shimmer in his spine, putting up the hair on his nape. He would swear the cave was empty now, but someone had definitely trod upon his territory; intruders left an unmistakable energy behind. He played his torch slowly over the crates, tucked neatly under their oiled canvas sheets. Though it wasn't apparent to a casual glance, he could see one of the crates had, indeed, been disturbed. He pulled back the canvas that covered it and saw that, while the lid had been put back and even fastened properly, it was clear someone had been in it, for the nails were not as neat in their beds as he had left them. He pulled a small crowbar from his bag and prised off the lid. It was immediately apparent to his eye that there were guns missing. Two of them. He shone the torch on the rest of the crates. They appeared undisturbed, the canvas still arranged over them just as he had left it. He would check each and every one before he left just to be certain. Not that it mattered, not now that someone had violated his sanctuary.

Who the hell had been in his cave and then had the temerity to steal two guns? And why only two? Unless the person or people planned to come back with a truck and take them all. He was going to have to move them, even if he wasn't certain to where exactly. His farm was off limits. The only weapons he kept there were those he needed for personal use.

He thought as he checked the rest of the crates, going over the mental inventory he kept in his head, clearing his mind of the anger, knowing he needed to move the guns as soon as possible. He pondered several possibilities and rejected them each in turn as unsuitable for a variety of reasons: too much traffic near the location, too damp, too far away from his farm and base of operations, too close to a British Army base, making movement in and out too risky.

There was an abandoned workhouse he knew of, long buried in the woods roughly halfway between his farm and Pamela Riordan's land. None had passed that way for years, and local legends that remembered the place claimed it was haunted by the ghosts of the many who had died there. It had a decent cellar, dry and cool, and would do for the guns until he could come up with a more permanent plan. He played the torch over the walls of the cave one more time. He couldn't rid himself of the strange cool shimmer in his spine, the feeling that somehow the thief who had been here still lingered in some strange way, as though there was an imprint on the air that could touch him if he stayed in the cave much longer.

Noah shivered, and walked back toward the entrance, wanting the warmth of the sun and the light of day to banish this strange feeling. By the time he crawled out through the screen of willows to find a light snow drifting down from the sky, he had found his anger again. He put it to the side where it would simmer over a cold flame until he needed it. But when he found him, God help the man who had violated this sanctuary, because

Noah Murray had learned long ago that a man always paid retribution in full.

If he had one code of conduct, one family motto that had long ago been scored into his soul it was this—*Nulla misericordia*. It was the only bit of Latin his father had known, but he had taught it to his son in full measure—no mercy.

Chapter Six

New Friends

THE LATE AFTERNOON SUN was gilding the big kitchen a deep and dusty gold when Pamela arrived at Jamie's house, children in tow and files in hand. The files were, she hoped, the last of the paperwork she needed to wrap up before giving things back into his entirely capable hands.

There was only one person in the kitchen, and that was Shura whom she had met briefly the night after Jamie's return. She smiled and said hello, and received a broad grin in return that crinkled his black eyes up at the corners and lit his homely face into something irresistible.

"Yasha is out with the horses," he said. He was grinding herbs in a mortar. The scent was thick and green and soothing.

"Feverfew, lemon balm and peppermint?" she said, sniffing the air.

"So, not just a beautiful face," Shura said, eyeing her with interest. She watched as he placed handfuls of herbs into a large jar and then poured a very good make of vodka over top of them, until they were completely immersed.

"Are you making a tincture for migraines?" she asked.

"*Da,*" he said and then repeated, "Yes, I am. You have the knowledge of plants?"

"A bit," she replied, leaning over the big stone bowl and breathing in the residue of the ground herbs. "Jamie's grandmother has been teaching me over these last months."

"*Da*—yes, Yasha has mentioned her."

From the lift of Shura's thick and expressive eyebrows, Pamela thought Jamie's description of Finola might have been less than flattering. She didn't quite know what the relationship between Jamie and his grandmother was, but she had no doubt that the woman loved him, and that alone would have made her quite fond of Finola. That she had also helped Pamela, in no small measure, save Jamie's home and company for him had endeared the woman to her quite a bit more.

Shura capped the bottle, and then set it to the side. Pamela knew the concoction needed to steep somewhere cool and dark for a few weeks. She thought the cask room below the house would probably serve quite well for the purpose. However, there were other things in the warren of rooms beneath the house that Jamie might not want his guests to know about, so she kept the information to herself.

He rinsed his hands in the big stone sink, dried them on a towel he had draped over his shoulder and then stepped down from the stool he had been using. He walked to Isabelle's basket and leaned down, and looked at the baby who was sleeping the righteous and deep sleep of a tired five and a half month old. There was a fleeting sadness that touched his face, gone as swiftly as it had appeared.

"Do you have children?" she asked.

"*Da*— yes, and no too," he said, and now there was no mistaking the sorrow in his face. She thought his answer, considering that he had recently escaped from a gulag inside the Soviet Union, made perfect and tragic sense.

Conor was peeking out from behind her leg, and Shura smiled at him and coaxed him to come out by use of a small carved toy he pulled from his pocket. Conor, always curious, stepped forward, though he still kept a good grip on her pant leg. It was a yo-yo, painted bright red and spinning down from the man's broad hand.

With another child she might worry that Shura would pose a puzzle because of his size, and that something would be said which could make things awkward. With Conor, she didn't fret for he had his father's easy acceptance of differences in people. Shura's height would not seem odd to him, he would simply see him as an adult of less intimidating proportions. Conor stepped closer to Shura, letting go of her leg, his face rapt with interest.

Shura wrapped the string around the small wooden circle and handed it to Conor, rolling the loop gently over his finger. He then put his hand lightly over Conor's and showed him how to flick the yo-yo so that it rolled straight out and furled back with a distinct snap. Conor laughed with delight, and it made her heart a little lighter to hear the sound.

She realized suddenly that Shura was looking at her, not Conor, and brought her head up from watching the scarlet flash of the yo-yo, to meet his gaze. The dark eyes looked at her steadily, but it had the feeling of a shaman's assessment of his client's needs, rather than a man looking at a woman. He narrowed his eyes and took a deep breath, and she could almost see the diagnosis being formulated in his head.

"I make you tea, something just for you, something for the," he made a fluttering motion with his hands, "in your chest."

She stepped back, startled that he had somehow felt her anxiety. He merely got back up on the stool and started pulling jars from the shelf, muttering to himself. She recognized a medical man when she saw one, and left him to his herbs. She was still astounded that he had won Maggie around enough already to have such free use of her kitchen. She began to gather up Isabelle's basket, only to have him pause in his muttering and turn toward her.

"What you seek is seeking you," he said.

"What?" she asked, confused by the mysterious pronouncement.

"I am reading the poems of Rumi," he said, the 'r' rumbling like a thundercloud in his deep voice. "That line comes to me when I look at you. I am not knowing what it means completely. It is just in here." He tapped one blunt finger to his broad forehead.

She nodded, a swimming sensation in her limbs. The smallest thing, the simplest statement became a life preserver to cling to, to find hope within. She tried to take a breath and found she couldn't. She needed to go sit down and gather herself together. The man would think she was crazy if he knew the torrent of hope, despair and anger that his simple words had set off inside her. He didn't have a crystal ball, nor a psychic premonition. It did not mean that Casey was somewhere seeking her, as she sought him. She smiled at Shura, though she knew it was an extremely tremulous expression; then excused herself.

She took the children to the library to wait for Jamie. She thought she might pick out a book to take home, even if she knew full well she would not be able to read more than a few lines. Books had long been her refuge and comfort when the world became too much, but since Casey had disappeared, she hadn't been able to still her mind or body long enough to read. Still, she thought perhaps just the presence of the books might provide a calming influence.

She put Isabelle's basket on the floor. The baby was still sound asleep, her darkly lashed eyes shut tight and tiny mouth pursed. There was something so like Casey in her face that Pamela had to bite her tongue so she wouldn't cry out. She got Conor settled with his toys, near enough to the fire so that he'd stay warm. There was a big green wingback chair that she often used when nursing her children since the library was always quiet, and none would disturb her here. She turned from the fire to find that wasn't the case this afternoon.

Curled up in one of the big squashy chairs that was turned toward the window, nose stuck into a worn copy of *Bleak House,* was the most exotic creature she had ever seen. He looked up at her and smiled. The smile was like that of a cat, slow and practiced, but no less genuine for that. He had eyes like amethysts seen through a skim of frost and deep red hair framing a face with the cheekbones of a faun. He rose from the chair with a boneless elegance that made her feel suddenly awkward. His skin was the color of snow—snow shaded and made enigmatic by the touch of twilight.

"I am Vanya," he said in a tone that sounded much like 'I am the Emperor of Shangri-La and you are clearly a lesser being, but I will acknowledge you nevertheless.'

"I'm Pamela," she said, taking his extended hand and smelling a scent like spiced tea coming from his skin.

He tilted his head, the beautiful eyes grazing like ice over glass along the sharp cheekbones. "Ah, of course you are."

His English was quite flawless. It was also thick and dark with the steppes and deep forests of his native land. He was dressed in loose jeans and a blue sweater against which the silky red hair flared like a flame.

"Our Yasha has told us of you."

"Has he?" she asked, smiling, despite feeling thrown by this beautiful creature's self-possession. The adrenaline from Shura's simple words was still flooding through her in waves, making her dizzy.

"Of course, you are family to him, I believe."

"As he is to me," she said, realizing it was true. Jamie had long been her dearest friend and in the way that had little to do with blood and names, he was also family.

"We will be friends, too," he said, in a very certain manner. "This I know, Russians always recognize their friends at first sight. We will be very good friends, I am thinking."

She smiled. She felt drawn to him by his candor and certainty. "I think you're right."

He bent over the basket where Isabelle slumbered on. He laughed as one tiny hand shot out in sleep, the fingers curling slowly under, like the rose-pink fronds of a sea anemone.

"May I?" he asked.

"Of course," she said. Isabelle would not wake despite a stranger holding her. Like her brother before her, once she was asleep there was little that would wake her short of an explosion. He picked her up gently, tucking her into the curve of his elbow and smiling down at her recumbent form.

"I love the babies," he said. "They are not complicated, just love and eat and sleep. It is lovely and easy."

"It is," she agreed. She liked this exotic looking young man already. He was right; they were going to be friends.

Jamie came in then, clad in dusty jeans and an old sweater, his son in his arms and the scent of the stables—fresh hay, horses, oats and well-oiled leather—coming in with him. She breathed it in, and felt the knot in her chest loosen the tiniest bit. Isabelle stirred in her wrappings as if she sensed his presence. Deirdre had told her Jamie had worked magic on Isabelle that first night when he had come to visit.

His eyes swept over her and he smiled, one of his beautiful, heart-stopping smiles that always made her feel the world could be righted, as long as his hand was at the helm. She was terribly grateful that he was home. It might not make a difference to finding Casey, but it made her feel like the universe was slightly less out of kilter.

He let Kolya down and the tiny boy promptly went over to Conor, determined to get near this human who was of a size more interesting than the adults. He plopped down beside Conor, and promptly grabbed one of his blocks and attempted to shove it in his mouth. Always unflappable, her son didn't so much as give him the side-eye. Conor was a great deal like his Uncle Pat, and didn't let much ruffle his feathers, which was no small miracle considering the present circumstances under which they found themselves. He hadn't asked much about where his father was. His silence worried her, for he ought to be asking more, of that much she was certain.

The next hour passed in chatter, and Pamela found herself relaxing a little. Jamie got the fire roaring in the hearth and the heat of it reached her where she sat. Shura had brought in a tray with tea on it and she noted that hers was in a separate pot. It tasted of catmint and something else that she couldn't identify, the flavor was pleasant enough though. Isabelle stayed sleeping in Vanya's arms, as he crooned to her in Russian. It sounded incredibly comforting, the warm rumble of it carrying notes of steaming samovars and ephemeral dachas in its threads. Between the sound of Vanya's voice, the fire and the tea she was having a hard time keeping her eyes open. She wondered why she could not sleep at home, yet could barely stay awake here.

Jamie got down on the floor with Conor and Kolya to build a complicated tower out of blocks, and Pamela was happy to see that Conor was utterly engrossed in the construction. There was a sense of normalcy here in Jamie's house that did not exist just now in their home. Isabelle woke just then, letting out a lusty cry that said her belly was well and truly empty. Pamela rose, still feeling half asleep and retrieved the baby from

Vanya's arms. She took one glance back at the children, but Conor was happily building, and Vanya had slid down to join the group on the carpet. She took Isabelle to the study to nurse.

The fire had been lit in the study as well, and tongues of warmth reached out through the room. She changed Isabelle's diaper swiftly, for the baby never liked air hitting her skin when she was hungry.

Isabelle set to nursing with that slightly desperate air babies sometimes had when starting a feed. She drained one breast and then Pamela switched her over to the other. She looked around the study as the baby nursed, the stress in Isabelle's tiny body easing perceptibly.

This room was her favorite, and she had done most of her work here over the last few years, behind the big oak desk which graced the northern wall of the room. The room had changed a little already, as if it clearly recognized the presence of its true resident and had resumed its long ago air of security and privacy. There was a decidedly more masculine feel to the entire house already.

Isabelle finished nursing and Pamela looked down at her daughter, to find dark eyes looking up at her with the lovely intensity baby gazes had. She felt a rush of love so profound that it made her tremble, coupled as it was with a terrible fear that this tiny girl would have to grow up without her daddy. Isabelle had been daddy's girl from the first day of her existence. Casey had called her 'the tiny tyrant' and it had been utterly apt, as she had demanded his attention the minute he arrived home each night. If Casey didn't come home—no, she rubbed her forehead hard, as if she could rub the thought out, and by so doing prevent it from ever becoming truth.

She righted her clothing and stood, putting Isabelle to her shoulder and patting her back. Jamie walked in just then, Montmorency at his heels.

"I'm sorry," he said, "I wasn't thinking, I needed a pen and I knew I had some in the desk."

"Don't be ridiculous, Jamie. It's your house. I daresay it will take a little while, but eventually I will stop treating it as my own. We've gotten very comfortable here these last few years. Conor is used to being at the house every day, so you're going to have to forgive our manners for a bit until we adjust."

"Pamela, this has been your home since that first night you arrived, dancing your way into our lives. That will never change and it goes without saying that extends to your children as well."

Isabelle reached her arms out to Jamie as if she recognized him, and Jamie took her as though it was entirely natural to do so.

"Stay for dinner," he said, patting Isabelle's back, "and don't bother lining up all the reasons you shouldn't," he added, as she began to protest, "just stay and break bread with us. There are too many men in this house; we could use a feminine influence for a few hours."

"I can't—," she began and then halted feeling like someone had hit her, the rush of anxiety back full force. She had almost said that she needed to go and start supper before Casey arrived home.

Jamie took in the expression on her face and said, softly, "Just stay."

"All right," she said, relieved that she could put off facing her empty house for a few more hours.

They joined the others then, making their way to the kitchen. Conor was holding Kolya's hand, the two of them fast friends already. Shura tucked a little bottle into her hand as she sat and then took his seat to the left of her.

To her surprise she found she was a bit hungry as they sat down to dinner. Maggie had made a roast with all the trimmings, and there were biscuits as well, something she normally loved. After about five bites, she felt as though the food, as lovely as it tasted, had congealed into a lump that sat heavily in her stomach.

She put her fork down and watched and listened, and was happy to see that Jamie had not been alone in Russia. He had formed a family of sorts with these two men—the exotic faun and the apothecary dwarf. That they cared for Jamie was clear, and she could imagine how such an experience—their time in the gulag—could have bound them, forging a family from disparate and foreign pieces.

After dinner, they stacked plates and silver ware, washed glasses and cups amidst a hum of noise. The boys were playing with Conor's beloved wooden cars, Isabelle cooed and babbled in her basket and Shura sang in a deep and rumbling voice that sounded like the warm and dark winds that blew across his ancestral home, deep in the Caucasus Mountains.

When the kitchen was clean, even to Maggie's strict standards, Jamie turned to her and said, "Come to the study with me for a few minutes."

She looked around. Shura was showing Conor a very complicated cat's cradle, Kolya had fallen asleep curled around one of Conor's cars and Isabelle had drifted off to sleep as well. Vanya kneeled on the floor watching Shura, and, even here in the bright light of the kitchen, he looked like something from a Russian fairy tale. "Go, I watch the babies," he said.

She followed Jamie to the study with nervous trepidation. If he wanted the privacy of that particular room, it was because he had something important he wanted to say to her.

Someone had lit the lamps and the study glowed in the low light, burnished and comfortable as a favorite blanket. She sat down on the sofa, knowing Jamie preferred the squashy old wingback chair, covered in a rather lurid green velvet, that had once belonged to his grandfather.

"Would you like a drink?" he asked. "I'm going to drive you and the children home, so you can have one if you'd like."

"You don't need to drive me home," she protested.

"I'm going to whether you feel it's necessary or not, you look all done in, Pamela. So you can either stay here in your old room with the children, or I can drive you home. Those are your two options."

"I see Russia did little to temper your high-handed ways," she said, feeling slightly testy.

"Do you want a drink or not?" he asked and she gave in, knowing that when Jamie laid down an ultimatum he became an immovable force that one resisted at one's own risk. She was tired, and the thought of someone else driving them home did appeal. She did too much thinking in the car.

"Yes, maybe just a little of that vodka you gave me the other night."

He poured her a rather generous amount and then poured himself somewhat less.

Jamie handed her the glass, the vodka a rich and shimmering amber inside. He looked more rested and at ease than he had even a week ago. He sat down on the couch beside her and his scent reached her, lime and sandalwood and comfort, interspersed with the cloves and birch fire of the vodka.

"You didn't eat much," he said, quietly, looking down into his tumbler. She noted he wasn't drinking it, and had merely poured it out of courtesy to her so she would have the illusion of not drinking alone.

"I haven't had much appetite of late," she said, "it's certainly no fault of Maggie's cooking. What I did eat was delicious."

He looked up then and met her eyes, his own candid and she knew what he was going to say. She took a sip of the spicy vodka, hiding her face in the thick crystal for a moment. And then, because he was Jamie, he just said it.

"I'm worried about you, Pamela."

She nodded. "I know. I'm coping. I have to for the sake of my children. Turnabout is fair play. After all, I've spent the last three years worried about you."

It was a weak joke, but he smiled and the tension in the room went down a notch.

"Jamie," she began and then stopped. Sometimes she didn't want to put words to the questions that slammed around inside her head constantly. He anticipated what she had been about to ask, and saved her the effort.

"Do you want to know? There isn't much to tell, Pamela. If there was news you know I would have told you the minute I saw you."

"Would you, if the news was bad?"

"Yes, even if the news was bad. You have more right to know it than anyone."

"I think I want something concrete, something real, an answer to anything. Then I think if I get it, and it's not what I want, and I do know how likely that is, then that will be worse. I feel like a bat that has touched an electrical wire—I'm flying in all directions and my radar is completely messed up."

He reached over and touched her forearm and she took a breath, his touch was light and reassuring. It eased something in her the tiniest bit, so that the horrible buzzing in her skin began to fade.

"Pat said you'd had a bad experience at the police station."

"Yes," she said, "but that's not terribly uncommon here, is it?"

"He also said you'd asked for a meeting with Noah Murray."

"Perhaps," she said coolly, "it would be easier if you told me what Pat *didn't* tell you." There was an edge of defiance in her voice, because she knew she wasn't imagining the disapproval in Jamie's tone.

"Pamela, you know what he is, you're playing with fire."

"I know, that's exactly why I approached him," she said. "Nothing happens in that corner of the countryside that he doesn't know about, or can't get information on somehow."

"Because people are afraid of him, and for good reason. I'm wondering why you *aren't?*"

She shrugged. "I am a little. It doesn't matter though, as long as he can help me find out where Casey is."

"I would ask you to stay away from him, but I know you're as likely to listen to me as you are to the wind."

"Jamie, I would walk through the gates of hell and make a deal with the devil if it meant someone could tell me what has happened to Casey."

"I know you would; that's what worries me."

She took another drink of the vodka, and felt the warmth of it as it went to her belly, the taste of fennel and horse radish lingering hot on her tongue.

"How are the children?" he asked, holding her gaze.

"Isabelle is too small to understand, of course, though she fusses during the night, which is when Casey would spend time walking her up and down the hall, or just comforting her so I could sleep a bit. Conor isn't asking many questions and I don't know how to answer even the few he has asked. He's so little, I don't know how much is right to tell him. The fact is *I* don't know anything. I don't know the truth, so how can I possibly give it to him?"

"Just answer his questions as they come, anything more will confuse him. It will be some time, Pamela, before he asks the really tough questions for which there are no real answers. With luck, that day may not come."

It was a relief to talk to him, and to admit how frightened she was. It was just a relief to have him home. She had not been joking when she'd spoken of her worry for him these last few years. She had never dreamed that when he finally returned, she would have lost her husband.

"You know what is ridiculous—I can't cry. I feel like it would be such a relief if I could and yet I can't. I feel everything else—loss, anger, terror—but I can't seem to shed a tear."

"There are some things, to paraphrase Wordsworth, that run too deep for tears. We both know that all too well."

Poetry had long been their shared language, and was often the way they understood the world, made sense of both its pains and its pleasures. It was a common root for the two of them, going back to the summer when they had first met.

"I'm going to England for a few days," he said, and she was relieved at the turn in the conversation.

"Will you go see Julian?"

"Most likely, yes. I can't say it's an interview about which I'm excited."

"Well, if anyone can manage him, it's you."

"Thank you for the vote of confidence, but I have to say I don't quite feel equal to this task. I had no idea of his existence. He isn't likely to believe that though, is he?"

She shook her head, rueful. "No, probably not. He's somewhat disposed to take against you, for lack of a better way of putting it. I wish I could be more encouraging, I just don't want to see you get hurt or caught in the crossfire between him and his mother. My sense is, she has twisted him with ideas about you that bear no resemblance to reality."

Jamie looked down at the glass in his hand. His hair and eyes and cheekbones were underlit by the fire and the lamp that glowed on the small table next to the couch, so that he appeared softly gilded. But his fingers were tight around the glass, knuckles sharp against the skin. He saw her glance and unclenched his hand, setting the glass gently aside. "Her reality has clearly been very different than mine. I wish she had told me about him at some point. I think I understand why she didn't, but damn it, I wish she had."

She saw for the first time since her arrival home how badly the news about Julian had upset him. With his history, she could only imagine what it had done to him to discover he had a son who was nineteen years old and completely unknown to him until days ago. She leaned over and put her hand on his.

"Jamie, he's old enough that she can't control everything he thinks and feels. He's not a child anymore."

He looked up, the green eyes dark, his expression bleak.

"That's my worry, Pamela. What if it is too late?"

She did not speak for she knew there was no answer she could give, nor did he expect one.

Chapter Seven

Black Taxi

THE STREETS WERE his hunting ground. In this city people disappeared all the time, mostly for the grave sin of wandering off into the wrong bit of geography, down the wrong street, into the wrong pub, or merely associating with someone who was a known criminal of the political sort. Either way it was to a hunter's advantage. Prey went missing, people assumed it was political in origin and that The Troubles had taken yet another victim into its ravenous maw, all in the name of cause or creed.

A city was a living organism, its streets the arteries through which humans moved in predictable patterns. In this city there were cross-points, places through which people must move into a strange no man's land, but one could always tell whence they had come. He had the patience of the natural born hunter—he watched, he waited, he saw.

An unofficial, messy little war served many purposes, it covered over many sins, hid things that would otherwise find the light of day, allowed atrocities to masquerade as tribal warfare and as the collateral damage of conflict. This war was perfect for him for it gave relief to the hunger that ruled his life. He could not remember a day in his life in which the hunger hadn't ruled, though he knew there must have been a time when it had not. For so long now it had controlled him with an iron hand, and he had long been its willing slave.

He drew hard on his cigarette, considering his options. The smoke floated and curled out on the damp air, blue tendrils sliding amongst the molecules of oxygen, infiltrating and dissipating, just as he himself did through people and streets. He was, he thought, as good as invisible, for he killed any witness to his actions.

It was time to move on, better hunting perhaps tomorrow. He touched the keys, and turned over the ignition when something flickered in the corner of his eye, a bit of blue cloth, not much to the average person's senses, but to his own a prickle of fire along his skin, and that strangely pleasant shudder that told him the prey had come out into the open field where he might play with it at his leisure, until he no longer wished to continue the game.

It was a young man, alone, and just a bit worse for drink. Precisely how he liked them. He eased in the clutch, let the car roll forward, and turned on the light on the top of his car.

"Will ye want a ride, lad? 'Tisn't the best neighborhood to be caught out in, ye know."

Gerard's voice on the telephone had been grim. "Be sure to bring a strong stomach with ye, I think it's only fair to warn ye that it's one of the worst I've ever seen."

Pamela could not begin to imagine how bad it was for Gerard to say such a thing. They had worked together after the bombs of Bloody Friday had left body parts scattered in the streets. She still had nightmares occasionally to do with what they had witnessed that day.

She knew she ought to have said no, ought to have told him her husband was missing and that he needed to find someone else. She never considered saying any of it though, because she had to know, she had to see the body, to see if it was Casey. She hadn't done this sort of work in a while, not since before Isabelle was born. Running Jamie's companies had taken up a great deal of her time, and so she had only worked sporadically when the police couldn't find another photographer on short notice. Having children had changed something inside her and she found the scenes much harder to deal with in the aftermath.

When she arrived there were policemen milling everywhere. Some nodded at her, some did not and she was used to it. Gerard had been right, she couldn't have begun to imagine how bad it was. The body had been dropped over a railing and lay in a filthy stairwell, a bloody heap that was barely recognizable as having once been a human being. She could see the hair color and it was not black, it was a fair, dirty blond. It was not Casey, and there was some small part of her that felt the relief of that confirmation, even while recoiling in horror at the state of the body. Still, a thrum of panic, never far from her these days, began to beat in her blood, sending out its cold tendrils of fear and nausea.

The camera was her only defense in such situations, to do what she had been brought here to do and do it well, to give the dead person their due from the living. So that is what she did—laying out the instruments of her trade, the shaking in her hands slowly subsiding as the camera fitted itself to her fingers. She could quell the panic long enough to get this done, she had to, so she bit down on her lip and pulled in her focus. All she needed to do was get through the next half hour. She got out the ruler, the grey card, the lens and filters she thought most suited to the scene. There was a weak sun flickering through the clouds and a whiff of rain in the air. As long as the rain held off for a bit it was perfect weather for this job. Nighttime shooting required much more fussing with lighting and lenses so that depth perception was as accurate as a daytime shoot and a bright, sunny day would have presented difficulties of its own. She took her preliminary notes quickly, knowing Gerard's would be more in depth, but needing her own record to submit with the pictures. Then came the overview photos, the basic sketch of the scene, and the photographic record of each item of evidence.

It was how she had to view these scenes—as evidence, as something that was owed to the victim and to those who had loved him or her. Even a scene outside had to be approached as though it were a building, like she stepped into a room with four walls and a door—a room of blood and death, but a room nevertheless with exact boundaries. All angles and approaches had to be covered, the way the body was lying, its alignment to the buildings and cobblestones beneath it. Any other items within the vicinity of the scene had to be photographed twice—once with the measuring device and once without. The pictures were meant to be a precise record, scientific in their exactness, without emotion coloring any part of them. She catalogued each aspect as it came into her camera's view, and hoped that it did not come back to haunt her later.

The boy's throat had been cut, a jagged open wound that made it clear that the neck had been slashed with such force and brutality that it was sheared down to the backbone. He had been, for all intents and purposes, decapitated. There were thick shards of glass in the victim's forehead. It appeared that a beer glass had been forcefully shoved into his face at some point. There were bruises and abrasions on every inch of skin she could see. There were two depressions in his skull, obvious to her eye, even though parts of the hair were matted black with blood and other matter that she knew, from previous scenes, was brain. His arms had been flung up above his head when he was thrown here, for it was clear this was not the primary scene, and she could see deep abrasions on his wrists that indicated he had been bound with something sharp—wire maybe. Each wound had to be photographed separately and close up; this part never felt as difficult as the overview shots, perhaps because she could parse the victim up into his or her various injuries, rather than seeing the whole human being.

Time took on an odd feel at crime scenes, sometimes it was short and tight, confined to each *whirr* of the camera's shutter and other times it was drawn out fine until it felt like a wire in the blood, thrumming with primal fear, with the full knowledge of the human body's ultimate fragility—how a living, breathing, laughing creature could be reduced to this—this bloody pulp—in a mere matter of moments. In real time the photography took two full hours, because it was a complicated scene in some ways. It wasn't the original location for one thing and the narrowness of the street, the overhanging buildings and the depth of the stairwell made both light and positioning difficult.

She stood when she was done and walked over to Gerard who was still making notes, face impassive, his tape recorder tucked into his shirt pocket. The rain had started to spatter in fitful drops, the crime scene would soon be compromised; she had finished just in time.

"I'm done," she said, feeling as if she had run for miles without air or water, without sustenance or reprieve. She felt faint, her vision was slightly fuzzy, the grey telescoping warning her that the anxiety which was her constant companion was about to become something far worse. He nodded, still scribbling in his notebook and so she busied herself with organizing her equipment. A shadow fell across her and she glanced up briefly, black spots dancing across her vision. It was only Gerard though, his sharp eyes damnably observant.

"Are ye all right?" he asked, as she repacked her camera, putting the lens in its coddling velvet lined bed.

"No, I don't think I've ever…" she stopped, pressing a hand to her middle. She tried to take a breath and then tried again only to feel it catch hard on the shoals of panic, like a dam bursting and pouring its flotsam, jagged and sharp through the spillway of her nervous system. She could not, must not have a panic attack here. If she did, she would fall apart, would not be able to get in the car, would not ever get another job photographing dead, battered, bloody bodies.

"Pamela?" Gerard hunkered down beside her, concern written large over his weathered face. He patted her back, and slowly her breathing resumed something near its normal pace.

"I…my husband is missing. He's been missing for over two months," she said flatly, her hands clenched so hard that the bones sang with pain.

"Missing?"

"Missing, disappeared without a trace, gone into the wind, and everyone except me and his brother thinks he's dead."

Gerard didn't comment, merely rubbed her back for a moment longer and then said, "Pamela, ye ought to have told me about yer husband. Ye shouldn't be here, an' ye know it."

She took a deep breath in, trying to ignore the heavy scent of blood that lined her nasal passages. "I'm all right, I just need to get past the initial shock." It occurred to her that life in this city was always about getting past the initial shocks. And then one day, what if she wasn't shocked anymore? She dreaded such a day ever arriving.

She snapped her camera case shut and got to her feet. She couldn't feel her legs properly. She thought if she could just get in the car and sit down that she might be able to stop the precipitous slide into the abyss of panic. Gerard picked the case up and walked to where her car sat, battered, but still reliable.

He put her camera case in the boot and then stood back and looked at her.

"I can't have ye here if emotion is cloudin' yer ability to do the job, ye know that well enough."

"It won't happen again," she said, her body so tired that it felt like it was aching in every joint and cell.

"Pamela, I hope ye won't mind me askin', but why the hell are ye still doin' this?"

"I need the money," she said bluntly, because soon enough it would be true. She had put aside some of what she had been paid while running Jamie's companies but she had also sunk most of it into their mortgage. Casey had been against it, feeling that the use of Jamie's money to purchase their home wasn't right. But she had finally talked him around to it because she wanted the security of the land, she wanted to know the house was theirs forever, even should some terrible event befall them. He had looked at her long and hard and finally said, "All right then, I can't argue with ye over that." He had understood that for her, it was a necessity, because it was her first real home, it was the home in which they were raising their family. Nothing less would have convinced him, she knew, for he had not liked her coin coming from Jamie's coffers. Right now, the construction company was barely breaking even, and she knew without Casey it was going to be a hard sell to keep contracts, even small ones, coming in. It was important to her to keep her relationship with Gerard intact, and to keep her work as professional as it had always been so that she didn't lose a source of income.

"Fair enough," he said. "Just tell me next time if it takes ye sideways, we can't afford to have anything off with the photos."

She understood that Gerard meant the two of them specifically, as they were both Catholic with affiliations inside the Nationalist community. This meant their work needed to be beyond reproach in every single aspect. She respected that and held herself to that higher standard—always—because she knew too well just what was at stake for herself, for her children and for the Catholic/Nationalist community as a whole. Sometimes it was the only defense a person had, rising to a higher standard, sticking to it through the bloodshed and violence and hatred that had once been unimaginable in her life. Their work was used in court, what she did provided a permanent record for the police and the legal system to refer back to on the pathway to providing some sort of justice for the victims.

"It won't happen again, you don't need to worry over me," she said, striving to keep the nerves from her voice. He nodded at her, though there was still a look of doubt in his face as he waited for her to get in her car and then shut the door for her. He leaned in the window of the Citroën, brow furrowed.

"Pamela, I'm sorry for what's happened."

She nodded, because she could not yet say meaningless, polite words like 'thank you' for something this profound. Gerard would understand.

"Are the police—are they helpin' ye?"

"As much as they would help any wife of a known rebel," she said bitterly.

"If ye need anything, if there's anything I can do, don't hesitate to ask."

She nodded tersely, just wanting to be away from the stink of blood and fear and pain, just wanting to be gone from the sympathy in Gerard's face. She drove carefully, because it would be all too easy these days, with her exhaustion and the constant anxiety eating at her nerves, to have an accident. The rain was coming down in earnest now, keeping the wiper blades going at full throttle.

She was a good distance out of the city, nearer to home than to Belfast when she stopped the car, got out on the roadside and threw up the little she had eaten that day, and then just stayed there on her knees in the cold, wet grass, rain beading through her hair and sliding down the back of her neck. The road was thankfully deserted. She was quite certain she did not have the strength to get up. The last of her reserves had been depleted by the death scene. She had not slept again, not properly, since the night in Jamie's study. She knew she was in danger of making herself seriously ill if she didn't find a different way to cope with the situation, with the lack of Casey in every second, in every breath. For the sake of Conor and Isabelle, if nothing else, she had to find a way to sleep, to eat and to breathe her way through the days to come and not have every second wracked with the thought of what might have happened to her husband.

There was a pain in her chest, like some black and terrible substance held in a vessel blown fine and thin as a wish; which sat waiting, smoking and acid, to break the vessel and flood her entire being. This was fear she knew—fear of the grief that would swamp her and take her over if she allowed it. If the vessel broke, she feared she might die; she feared that she would no longer be able to keep thoughts of what may have happened to Casey at bay and that wasn't something she could manage; that was a nightmare from which there would be no waking.

Get up off yer knees, Jewel. Get up and go home.

She startled, Casey's voice so vivid and stern in her head that she was certain she had heard it right there in the air behind her. She turned quickly, wrenching her neck with the strain. The shock of it stunned her. It was like being punched hard without warning—the sound of his voice and the empty road behind her.

"I'll listen to you, you bastard," she said angrily, "if you will listen to me and just fucking come home."

She hit the ground, her fist sinking into the wet verge, coming away muddy and cut from a stone she had grazed. She stared at her hand and then drove it into the ground again, blood pounding in her head and face, blurring her vision. It felt good as much as it hurt, it felt like the only real display of emotion she'd had since Casey had gone off to walk their property and not come home. Disappeared like a fairy tale figure, as if he had never been real, so absolute was his vanishing. She hit the ground again and again, mud spraying up into her face and over her clothes. She kept hitting and hitting until her hand was running with blood and her hair was dripping with rain, rivulets of it running down the channel of her back and soaking her clothes.

"Come home, come home, *just fucking come home!*"

"Are ye all right there, lass?" She came around to the fact that there was an old man standing beside her, a look of concern on his wrinkled face, his ancient lorry chugging away behind her car. She had no idea how long he had been there. She hadn't even heard the truck stop behind her. She wiped her face with one muddy, bruised hand. She must appear a lunatic to him, kneeling here, beating on the ground, rain running down her face, as she shouted at the air.

"I...yes, I'm fine," she said, seeing the dubious look on his face and not blaming him in the least. She knew she looked a right virago—bloody, wet, filthy and furious.

"Well, if ye're certain," he said. She nodded and stood, brushed herself down as best she could and walked back to her car, got in and waved at the old man who still stood watching her through the rain that was falling in great silver sheets now.

Sitting in the car, she took a breath, turned the key in the ignition and pulled out into the roadway. And then she went home to where her children waited.

Chapter Eight

His Father's Son

JULIAN HAD BEEN BORN WANTING. It was a condition that many were born into, some in poor countries, some with poor hearts; Julian was of the latter, ever wanting only those things which nature had not fitted him to have. Yet at first glance it seemed that this should not be so, for he was fitted, as the world saw to such things, to have everything upon which his glance might alight with desire.

Julian had always loved beautiful things, had seen them as a birthright. After seeing James Kirkpatrick's home, he decided that it was something he had inherited from his father.

After he returned, in some small disgrace, from his attempted coup of his father's home and empire, he had decided to finish out his degree at Oxford, as his father had done before him. His rooms at Oxford had been an attempt to recreate, in microcosm, some facet of Jamie's gilded universe. His own magpie tendencies had overwhelmed the original décor. He liked the jumble as it made him feel oddly secure. He had added the books and globe after spending time in the comfort and warmth of Jamie's study. He supposed the man had actually read the books in his study; he supposed he might actually read his own collection one day.

He found, however, that one could not recreate that patina, the steeped golden light that seemed to exist only within that strange study: the worn Bokhara rugs, the rump-sprung chairs, the jewel tones of floor and shelves, the frayed bindings of gilt-edged books, the worn edges of the big oak desk that had passed through countless generations, the sunlight that touched the edges of things and seemed to have woven itself into the very fabric of the iron and glass room. His facsimile of it was just that, a facsimile—one with slightly dark edges, as if some far more sinister thing crept and wove through his own rugs and chairs, books and shelves. It made him very angry.

He entered his room, thinking of the Kirkpatrick house and its sweeping grounds and of the ghost-like specter that hung over all of it—the man he had never met, his biological father, Lord James Stuart Kirkpatrick—only to find the man himself in the flesh there in his room. Julian stopped as though he had walked full tilt into a mirror, but a strange one that added years and changed coloring.

It had been one thing to see pictures of the man, to regard him theoretically as one's father, as the precursor of the blood, at least in part, that one had running through one's veins. To see him sitting in your humble parlor was another thing altogether. He had not been prepared, despite being duly warned, for the man's physical presence.

James Kirkpatrick sat with one long leg canted over the other. He wasn't a man who needed to stand in order to intimidate others. He knew what he was, he didn't need cheap tricks to prove it. Dressed impeccably in a dark grey wool suit, tailored no doubt to fit him exactingly, with a black wool coat hung loosely over one arm and black shoes polished to a fine sheen, he was the epitome of a wealthy man who was entirely comfortable in his skin. His hair was gold, but not gold—it held every shade within it from caramel to honey to wheat, to a near white and a shade like that of newly minted guineas. His eyes were a cutting verdigris with little warmth in them at present. Julian felt his own sapphire eyes narrow in response. The man smiled, his lips finely-cut, but of the sort that women would like. Julian knew because he had the same lips.

"Lord Kirkpatrick, I presume," he said voice as formal and chilly as he could contrive when his pulse was thumping madly. The man appeared utterly relaxed, as if he were here on a cordial call and hadn't just broken into Julian's room.

"So formal, Julian? Aren't you going to call me daddy? I understand you haven't been shy about shouting it from the rooftops in my absence."

Fair enough, Julian thought. He had been warned that the man could be a cold bastard. But so could he, and he felt secure in the knowledge that he did not carry the same deficits as this man. He knew those deficits to a fault, for he had studied each of them tirelessly, as if he was expecting to get a degree in all the finer points of James Kirkpatrick's weaknesses.

"What, no paternal warmth?" he said, matching his voice to Jamie's and knowing it didn't quite come off the way he had hoped it would.

"Do you feel you deserve any after the stunts you've pulled with my companies and home? Undermining my friends and trying to take over lock, stock and, as they say, smoking barrel? Not to mention your unholy alliance with the Reverend Broughton. That being said, I don't expect any filial loyalty or warmth from you either. We will both of us have to earn that, if we choose to."

Julian felt a little smacked off-center. Was the man offering to have a relationship with him? His opening salvo had not indicated such. He would have to proceed carefully, and yet the arrogance of the man assuming he wanted a relationship with him, when it was far too late for such things, irked him.

"We're both adults and I will treat you as one. It's too late for us to have a father to child relationship, so we will have to make of this what fits our circumstances. What you want from this will be for you alone to determine. Trust is something that will have to be earned on both sides."

Julian had the discomfiting sense the man was reading his mind.

"Why should I have to earn your trust?" he asked haughtily, while inwardly steaming that the man should be so presumptuous as to instruct him in what was needed in order to earn his favor.

"Why? Because you went after a woman, who had more than enough to concern her, to whom I had entrusted the care of my business and home. That you also did it in cooperation with a man who hates me and would do anything to destroy those I love and that which I hold dear—all this I take as an overt act of hostility if not that of outright war on your part."

"You're very defensive of her," Julian said, for he well understood that Pamela was a chink in this man's armor; he had been assured of it. He had dealt with her himself and knew not to underestimate her influence over his father.

"Pamela requires no defending from me."

"Doesn't she?" he asked, and then sat for he felt oddly at a disadvantage, standing while the man sat, still looking as relaxed as a lion on a stretch of sunny veldt. It did not improve his humor to have to remove a hat, two books and dirty clothes from the chair before he could sit.

"Tell me, Julian, what is it that you want?"

"What makes you think I want anything from you?" he said, and knew even as the words left his tongue that he sounded like a sullen child.

"Don't you? I am home now, and you are more than welcome to visit the estate, on the understanding that you are a guest and will be treated as such."

To Julian's own surprise, he found himself replying, "Is the invitation an open one?"

The man gave him a long look, the green eyes less cold, and more calculated. "Yes, it's open. I think if we're to get to know one another, that's the best place to do it. You're familiar enough with the house and grounds to feel comfortable there, I think."

"I am," Julian said, fighting not to rise to the man's words. Clearly he knew just how familiar Julian had made himself with the house and grounds that he had believed would be his own.

"With that, I will take my leave." Jamie stood and Julian fought the urge to leap up and back away. He had a presence that Julian had not reckoned with, for it wasn't quite as his mother had told him. She had described a man with a brittle glamor to him, but this was nothing like that. This was like a force of nature, barely leashed and disguised within the perfect suit, the impeccably cut hair, the indefinable accent. His mother had warned him that the man had a cunning which must never be underestimated, that there was always a secondary agenda when dealing with James Kirkpatrick.

'He's a master of figurative sleight of hand,' she had said, 'he distracts you with one hand while the other is picking your pocket.'

He wondered just what the man was distracting him with by this offer of a visit.

"What do you want from me?" he blurted out, his tone not the cool one he had hoped to convey.

The man paused in the doorway, the morning sun twining its gilding strands in his hair.

"Simply this; I am offering you a relationship. I am offering to find out if we can get along well enough to be friends."

"Friends?" Julian said, increasingly off-kilter due to the man's unruffled surface.

"Yes, friends. It's not an offer I make to many people, but I am making it to you."

"You think we can be *friends*?" The snarl was evident in his tone. He couldn't seem to keep his temper in check.

"That," said His Lordship, James Stuart Kirkpatrick the Fourth, "remains to be seen, Julian."

"Yes it does, Your Lordship," Julian said to the closing door, the whisper no louder than the hiss of a grass snake, and yet he was left with the discomfiting notion that somehow James Kirkpatrick had heard him.

Jamie walked swiftly through the grounds of the university. Memory spoke from every cobblestone and stone façade and from the bridges and curving streets. Some echo of his young self still resonated in the air here and he half expected to turn a corner and see himself and Andrei plotting their next bit of madness, most likely illegal and most certainly great fun.

He had not thought too much about Andrei since his return home. It wasn't an easy task, given that he saw the outlines of his imperious face each time he looked at Kolya. There was too much going on at home, things that were both immediate and raw. Settling Kolya into a world where his mother was absent and quite possibly would always be, was just the beginning. Trying to help Pamela find her feet without Casey, was another. She was not the girl he'd taken in all those years ago, she had grown in his absence into something fine and resilient. She was also infinitely fragile just now and while he knew he could not mend that for her, he would still take care of her in whatever manner possible. Or, he thought, more accurately, in whatever manner the woman would allow. He had forgotten just how stubborn she could be. The fact that she had gone to Noah Murray for help infuriated him, but he knew to handle her gently. He understood, after all, the desperation behind the act. Still, he didn't like it at all. She had never been one to shy away from danger, in fact she had actively courted it at times, but Noah was a beast of a totally different stripe. He only hoped she understood what sort of darkness lay within the man. And now by no means the least of that list of worries—a son, *his* son, a man grown, physically at least. That he was intelligent, Jamie had no doubt, but he thought much of the boy's intelligence was of the low and cunning sort. He suspected this had been cultivated in him and that there might be something more beneath the surface anger and resentment that could be brought forth, with time and infinite amounts of patience.

He hadn't been certain what he would feel when confronted with Julian, but he had not expected to feel angry, he had not expected to feel a faint, underlying revulsion that he was certain the boy had sensed on some level. And it had thrown him to see himself so exactly in counterpoint, like he was looking in a mirror that took away years, changed colors and gave him back himself in a way he did not like. The reflection was not less true for that dislike though.

Despite his harrowed-up feelings, he hoped that Julian would accept his invitation to visit. He wanted to get to know him, as much as was possible, in an environment where they could both relax, in theory at least. He also wanted the advantage of home territory and to be surrounded by those he loved, so that Julian might see what the Kirkpatrick house was in reality—a home. One that he might embrace if he could learn to stop conniving and hating.

Jamie looked down at his watch, aware that he was being followed. He assumed this fellow would follow him onto the train platform and then contact his colleague in London and then someone would be waiting for him when the train arrived in London. He smiled, he could use a bit of rough play, his skills needed sharpening. He couldn't allow it to slow him down too much, though, for he had a meeting with an old friend which he could not miss.

Chapter Nine

The Lion and the Fox

HE LEANED AGAINST THE RAIL in the arrivals area, watching for the trains coming in from Oxford and sipping at a plastic mug of tea.

He had been assigned to follow the man while he was in London. Keep his distance, report back on where he went, with whom he met, what he did, and if possible get close enough to overhear his conversations.

He felt a touch smug when he spotted the man getting off the train. The target was dressed impeccably in a dark suit, dressed beautifully really, though it was his hair that was going to make it so Agent 274, also known as Gareth Jones in his daily life, would have an easy day of it. The hair shone like a bright golden coin, standing out in stark contrast to all the duns and blonds and blacks around it. The man carried a briefcase, and while he seemed sharply aware of his environment, Gareth thought if he hung back far enough the man would have no idea he was there. Gareth could blend into walls and curbstones if need be. He had been trained by the best and had improved on his teacher's methods in the intervening years.

By noon he was no longer feeling smug, even if he was still grimly confident that he could keep up with the man through sheer dogged determination if nothing else. He had been on three buses and two trains and had to run through the muck of a riverbank, ruining his new shoes and twisting his ankle, still he had managed to keep on the man's tail. He was sweating, his heart was pounding, he was a touch angry, having lost his spy cool some miles back, mainly because of a sneaking suspicion that the man was leading him around London like a calf with a ring through its nose. Whether he was doing it for his own amusement or had a more nefarious agenda, Gareth did not know, but he was getting frazzled, something which was heretofore unknown in his experience.

The man was heading down into the bowels of Charing Cross. Gareth heaved a breath of relief, he would at least get to rest on the train for a bit. He eased back a little, he would be able to see the man now in the limited space of the station, regardless of how many people were milling about. He didn't want to tip his hand too far just yet. But when he got to the bottom of the stairs, despite the relatively low density of people, he could not see the man anywhere. Gareth swore and struck his fist into his other hand. It wasn't possible. He turned in a circle, a thrum of panic starting below his breastbone. He was going to be in trouble if he lost him. He stood on the stairs, ignoring all the annoyed people having to walk around him, muttering impolite things, some just saying them outright.

"F'in wanker, move yer arse out of me way."

He did move eventually, because he couldn't see the man and needed to walk the platform. There was a thud of excitement when he saw a flash of that singular hair up ahead of him. It must be inconvenient, he thought, looking as the man did. It would make him recognizable anywhere. He walked swiftly toward the far end of the station, the color dancing on the air ahead of him like a tantalizing mirage.

Gareth smelled the drunk before he saw him; the cloud of stench traveled ahead of him. Gareth caught sight of the man in his peripheral vision and turned his head. He had a dreadful limp, one leg must be a few inches shorter than the other to give him such a gait. He had matted grey hair, stuck to his head with what looked like several months worth of grime and grease. This was topped with a dreadful floppy hat, which would have looked more appropriate on a commune dweller's head.

The man sidled up to him, giving him an obsequious smile. He wanted money, of course. Gareth blew out a breath of exasperation. He could not afford to be distracted for a second.

The man was tugging at his sleeve. "Please sor, can ye spare a wee bit of coin for a man. I's hungry an' have no place to put me head tonight."

"You'll only drink it," Gareth said distractedly, pulling his sleeve out of the man's bent claw. "Leave off, I haven't got anything for you."

"Jest a few coins, sor, I can sing for it if ye'd like." Much to Gareth's horror the man began slurring his way through the opening bars of *Silver Dagger*. Gareth dug frantically in his pocket for loose change and flung the bit he found at the man.

"Ten pee, s'bit sheep," the drunk hiccoughed, a wave of cheap alcohol fumes wafting forth as he launched into the next bit of the song.

*'All men are false, says my mother
They'll tell you wicked, winnin' lies…'*

Christ, the man was a dreadful singer, off-key, voice cracking before it even climbed halfway up a note.

"Here," he dug in his pants pocket for another coin, "now go away, would you?"

"Five pee—fuck am I 'sposed to do wif fifteen pee? Sheep bastard."

"Sheep?"

"Aye, sheep," the man said, and began to sing again.

*'My daddy is a handsome devil
He's got a chain five miles long
And on every link a heart does dangle
Of another maid he's loved and wronged.'*

It belatedly occurred to an indignant Gareth that the man was calling him cheap, rather than comparing him and his thick and curly hair, to the woolly farm animal.

"Go the fuck away!" he hissed at the drunk. The old man stepped back and ceased his singing. He looked, Gareth was amazed to see, really quite offended.

"Lor' you gots a filfy mouf on ye, son."

Gareth considered that this was a tad rich, considering the man's own mouth.

"Please just get away from me!" His voice was rising in anger, and people were beginning to turn their heads to view the spectacle the two of them presented.

The drunk held up his hands in surrender. "Oiright son, no need to telt me twice, I'm be off an' away then."

Gareth gave a short pent-up bark of relief and turned, his eyes clocking every head in the place. He couldn't see the man anywhere, heaven help him if he had given him the slip.

The drunk was tugging on his sleeve again. Dear Lord, what did the miserable sod want now?

"That feller ye're lookin' fer—I think he just got on that train." The drunk pointed a filthy finger to the trains moving in the opposite direction, toward Waterloo.

"What makes you think I'm looking for someone?"

"Well, ya keep lookin' about like ye're a puppet on a string, figured ya was lookin' for someone. Thought it might be the feller with the yaller hair."

"Yaller hair?" Gareth echoed.

"Yis sir, him was lookin' about like he thought he were bein' followed, an' you were lookin' about as if you'd lost someone, so I figured as you might be lookin' for him. He's only jist gettin' on now—see there he is!"

Gareth looked about wildly, panic fluttering at the edges of his composure. Sure enough he caught the blazoning flag of gold that had kept his quarry in sight all day. He threw a pound note at the old man and ran toward the train, just barely making it through the doors before they closed on him. He looked about wildly, wondering where his quarry had disappeared to. There wasn't a single head in the car with that distinctive golden hair. Duns and dirty blonds, black hair and grey, and even a redhead but not one with that shimmering gold hair. He looked out the window, wondering if the man had run in one door and out the other. The train was moving now and it was too late.

The old drunk was still on the platform, standing straight and tall, no slouch to him anymore. He saluted Gareth in a most jaunty fashion and then swept a low bow and took off his hat. With it went the filthy and matted grey hair, to reveal a head as gold as a guinea coin.

Gareth hit the dirty glass between him and the man. "Fuck, fuck, fuck!!"

"The filthy mouth on you, you ought to be ashamed!" The sharp tip of an umbrella stabbed him in the arm, the old woman on the other end of it looking at him censoriously.

He was ashamed, but not for the reasons the old woman thought he ought to be. He got off the train at Waterloo and dragged himself up the stairs, his fury turning to a grudging respect for the man.

In fairness, he thought, limping down the street, he had been warned.

Sergei the Fox was late. In Jamie's experience the one reliable thing about Sergei was that he was never on time for anything. He was a little late himself, for it had taken longer than expected to give the slip to the young fool MI6 had following him. The boy had been fairly proficient, but Jamie had been followed by the best in the business and he ran on Moscow rules, which kept it simple and was entirely effective. One always assumed one was under surveillance and acted accordingly.

He approached the hotel from the back. It was, to put it kindly, a down-at-the-heels establishment, renting rooms by the week or month to people down on their luck. Most of the clientele were alcoholics or drug addicts. If anyone saw him or Sergei, they weren't likely to remember their faces later.

The lobby, which still had its furnishings from Victorian times, was a bit gloomy and very quiet on this sunny afternoon. He retrieved a room key from under a potted palm. The receptionist was asleep, gently snoring with a copy of The Telegraph on his chest, open to the racing results, the pages fluttering a little with each rise and fall of his breath.

He took the stairs to the second floor swiftly. There was seemingly no one about. He let himself into the agreed upon room and closed the door gratefully. The room was dingy, the wallpaper a design of William Morris' which had likely been put on the walls when the man himself was still alive. The carpet was a faded blue with a scrollwork of overblown pink roses undulating around its grimy edge. He sat in the threadbare armchair by a window which looked out over the narrow alley that ran behind the hotel. There was a distinct whiff of urine wafting up from the alley and the sound of a bottle breaking in the distance. He took a breath, bringing his mind into the here and now and out of that book-lined room at Oxford.

The door opened with a quiet snick. Jamie turned.

Sergei the Fox fit his nickname well. He was a small man with a sharp-pointed chin, fading ginger hair and narrow blue eyes. He was the sort of man who looked like a minor hustler or petty thief, and as such he blended into any city landscape in any country. Appearances, of course, were often deceptive and his looks worked to his advantage in a world where a man wanted others to forget his face five minutes after they had seen it.

Jamie pulled out three packs of Marlboro cigarettes and put them on the table in front of Sergei. All the rest of their trade would be in the nebulous form of information.

"Cigarettes," Sergei clapped his hands together. "How well you know my weakness, James. Sit down, man. You will take a drink with me, no?" Sergei pulled a paper bag with a bottle in it out from under his arm with a theatrical flourish.

Jamie nodded. The sound of Russian words was oddly comforting, in the way that icy vodka was comforting—it might burn like hell, but it gave a warm afterglow. He accepted the small, smudgy glass of vodka that Sergei poured for him. A man didn't refuse to drink with a Russian, especially not one he was priming for information.

Sergei pulled a cigarette out of his cuff. He would save the Marlboros for later, or use them in one of his own trades. He lit up the home-rolled cigarette and took a long deep drag on it, then breathed out in great wreathes of blue smoke, lending him a rather Mephistophelean air. Jamie took a drink of the vodka, and the taste was memory itself, of snow and fire and blood and the bone weariness of the camp. It brought to mind other things, too, but he shut the door on those things as swiftly as the vodka opened it.

"You heard about Tony?" Tony had been Sergei's handler for more than a decade.

"No, I am out of the loop, having just returned from the gulag, where information was somewhat thin on the ground," Jamie said, acidly.

"He got caught in compromising circumstances in a French brothel. There was him and a *chef de cabinet* and a boy strapped naked to a table. I will leave it to you to fill in the blanks."

Jamie rather thought that Sergei hadn't left any blanks to fill. It was an ignominious end for a man who had been considered one of the most talented agents in MI6. He had met Tony more than once, at parties in London, and his friend Jonathan had known him as well. He had been a kind man, and good at his job. His homosexual escapades aside, Tony had been a damn good spy. The situation sounded like a set-up.

There was a certain pattern to their exchanges and Sergei was given to abrupt shifts in subject, in part because he didn't see the point of small talk, nor in the fine stitching of politeness to pull together the different cloths of their conversation. Sergei often replied to questions Jamie hadn't asked, but he didn't mind, it was an effective way to get information without appearing overeager for it.

"And so, Russia." Sergei shrugged and lit another cigarette. "Russia—is anything ever clear cut? Well, Stalin was clear cut, I will give you that," he said as if Jamie had made a slur on the man. "They are moving chess pieces about on the board, courting Syria and wooing Arafat. It is, as ever, say one thing, mean another. It is the game, and the game never changes, only the players."

"Except in this game the players die when they lose," Jamie said.

Sergei smiled, a slightly frightening exercise as he was missing a few teeth and had four of the remaining ones capped in gold.

"Ah, that is what makes the game interesting, no? The risk."

Sergei had a point there, it was why many of them got into the game. The love of risk. It was why many of them were no longer amongst the living as well.

Sergei paused to delicately pick a piece of tobacco off his tongue, and having retrieved it, flicked it to floor. No one could accuse the man of an overabundance of etiquette. He took another drag on his cigarette, and spoke on the expelled cloud of smoke.

"So, not finding what they want in the quagmire of Middle East politics and players, they have turned their faces to other pastures."

"Africa and Central America," Jamie said.

"Astute and to the point as ever, my friend."

It made sense to him, as much as Russian policy and paranoia could make sense. They lived in strange times, and the spy world was as surreal as an acid trip at times. A bad one. The signal intelligence base in Cuba, less than one hundred miles from the US coast, was rumored to be the largest of its kind in the world with acres and acres of antennae fields and intelligence monitors, not to mention more than two thousand Soviet technicians. The Red Menace was real and far too close for comfort. The Soviet Republic was always looking to plant its flag in another country, to find another foothold, to protect its own borders while encroaching upon others.

"What I have to tell you is to do with another area entirely. The most valued bit of real estate in the world," Sergei said, blowing another succession of smoke rings into the already foggy room.

"Svalbard." Jamie said it automatically. Svalbard meant one thing—the oil interests of both West and East, and Soviet paranoia that any oil rigs operating there could be equipped to monitor the surface ships and submarines of the Soviet Northern Fleet. Soviet paranoia was overblown, but not necessarily wrong. With Russia's immense naval facilities to one side of the Kola Peninsula, it was a foregone conclusion that in any kind of battle of the Atlantic, the Soviet military would seize Norway first and take questions later. Svalbard was too close to Russia *and* the West, and it had the potential for far too many riches for either side to shy away from it. Why Sergei had brought it up was another matter, however. A matter which became clear with his next sentence.

"Our man in Norway has just been appointed as undersecretary to the Law of the Sea negotiations." The Law of the Sea negotiations were to determine who had rights where concerning the world's oceans. The Soviets had long had a man on the inside of Norway, who had now been appointed to the negotiations—it would give them a huge advantage on knowing what was coming and when.

"That's putting the fox in with the chickens."

"I'm giving you the shotgun for the fox," Sergei said.

"I'm not in the game anymore," Jamie said.

Sergei shrugged. "Use it or don't, it might be the last useful bit I have for you. I've been summoned home to Moscow."

Jamie knew what such a summons usually meant. It wasn't going to be a friendly téte-a-téte with his master. The look on Sergei's face said he was fully aware of this.

"I will likely not make my appointment and that means I am going to have to make myself scarce for a time. We will resort to our original channels for the passing of information. It will be like the old times, my friend."

'For a time' was a euphemism for 'the rest of my life' in spy speak.

"And now, James, what do you have for me?" Sergei butted out his cigarette and leaned back, wiry arms crossed over a narrow chest.

What he had wasn't high grade information, at least not that he was willing to share with Sergei. They had their own version of détente, and Jamie had never been fool enough to trust the man. He assumed and hoped that Sergei exercised the same caution with him. What he told him was enough to satisfy him, and it was enough so that he could trade it wherever it might be of most use. It wasn't information that was going to harm anyone, but it might buy Sergei time or favors when he needed either commodity. He was likely to need both in the near future.

"And so to the real reason we are meeting here today," Sergei said, putting another few inches of vodka in his glass.

Jamie took another swallow of his own drink. He would have liked to drain the glass, but then Sergei would refill it, and things would spiral down from there. He had no wish to compromise his faculties right now, as tempting as the idea might be.

Sergei fished a grubby pot of tobacco out of his equally grubby pocket. He took roll paper from his other pocket and set to making himself another cigarette. Jamie thought he was going to be a candidate for emphysema by the time he got away from the man. He waited, outwardly patient while Sergei tamped and rolled and licked and lit.

"I asked the questions you wanted me to ask. I do not think the answers will give you satisfaction."

Jamie merely raised an eyebrow. Sergei knew well enough that he didn't expect happily-ever-after answers to come out of the situation he had left in Russia.

"Do you want to know, Jamie? Think before you answer."

Did he want to know? Sergei had a valid point there, and Russians understood the price of information better than almost any other people. Information exchanged or overheard, could cost a man his life, or a woman as it were.

"Yes, I want to know," he said, and realized that he did, for he wanted to close off the trailing bloody ends of his Russian chapter before proceeding with the rest of his story.

"It could be that I am telling you what you already know, James. Yes, she is an agent. Once the KGB has their hooks into you you can never get them out, but you know that too, no?"

Jamie didn't answer, he wasn't going to give Sergei anything, not even acknowledgement of the rumors that flew like cotton tree fluff around the spy world. His time in Lubyanka and the resulting consequences of it were not something he discussed with anyone, ever.

"Whether or not she was a willing servant, I do not know. Whether or not she is still alive," Sergei shrugged, "I do not know. I can continue to ask questions, if you like. It may take a long time. I have to be careful."

Jamie eyed the small man in front of him. Sergei was as cunning as the fox for which he was named. It wasn't impossible he was stringing him along for his own purposes, which were myriad and often nefarious. Such was the spy world. He would have to take his chances because there was information he wanted and needed and there were very few channels more effective than Sergei.

"As to the others. Your friend is dead. That is the word in places both high and low. The other one—the *vor*, of him I can find neither rumor nor whisper."

Jamie nodded. Gregor had merely been a *zek*, a prisoner like the rest of them, and of little account, whereas Andrei had been an astrophysicist and a chess master. He had mattered as much as one human being could in the scope of the great and terrible machine of the USSR.

"And now we will speak of your own handler?"

Jamie knew Sergei wasn't talking about his current handler, but the one who had started him out in the circus. Diane Landel. Who also happened to be Julian's mother.

"She hasn't been my handler in many years," Jamie said quietly.

"I know. She's the one who brought you in though and she's the one you need intelligence on."

"I just want to know if she's still in the game?"

"Yes and no. Do any of us really ever get out?" Sergei said gloomily, making Jamie think of Eeyore. He was starting to relate much of life to the children's books he read to Kolya. It was one of the strange quirks of parenthood. Just the other day Pamela had asked him how he was feeling and while he had understood she was wondering how he was finding the transition from life in the USSR to life in a house filled with children, friends, dogs and on one memorable day last week, a sheep, he had found himself replying, "Oh, you know how it is, Pamela. From there to here, from here to there, funny things are everywhere!" She had laughed, because she knew the quote all too well, having been made to read the book five times that day alone. He had taken a deep delight in making her laugh, yet he noted how her expression turned stricken in the wake of her laughter.

"Jamie?" Sergei's voice was harsh, and he snapped his focus back into place.

"My apologies, my mind wandered for a moment," he said, hoping his face hadn't revealed anything.

"She's not running agents anymore, but she's still important to the company. She's not the ring master, still she's awfully close with him."

"Felix Plum?" It was a rhetorical question, as everyone knew who the grand master was of their claustrophobic little world.

"Yes, and he wants you to stay in, at least that's the butt-scuttle."

Jamie politely refrained from laughing at Sergei's turnabout of words, something he thought the man did purposefully to make himself seem less proficient in English than he actually was.

"Well, he's going to have to live with disappointment, because I am done."

"Be careful with her, Jamie, you weren't once and you got yourself badly burnt. Don't allow her to do it again."

"I won't," Jamie said. "I just need to see her."

"I understand that, but you loved her once, no? Even the memory of love can make a man weak." Sergei splashed more vodka into his glass and leaned back, still with that same strangely sad look on his face.

Jamie left. There was no more to say, no more information to exchange. They would leave separately, spaced by time so that there was no possibility of them being seen together.

He thought about what Sergei had said, as he walked the river embankment. The day was fine, though there were racing clouds coming in from the east. It would rain by the time his plane was leaving to go back home.

His life in Russia already seemed strangely distant in many ways, as if the people he had known and loved and left behind were figures in a play, one for which he did not know the ending and knew he might never find out. It was like he was peering through a frosted glass to watch each of them in their turn—Gregor with his fierce brutality, his friendship and the sacrifice of his life on the altar of their friendship. Nikolai who had felt like a father in ways he could not give words to and Violet, his wife. His traitorous, lying wife. Or so it appeared. In Russia, it did not serve to ever take things at face value, because all of life was a Potemkin village, a façade that served many purposes.

Vanya had asked him one night, as they sat quietly by the fire in the library, if he wanted to talk about Russia, about the people they had left behind. Vanya who, he thought, understood him better than most. He had quietly said, "No."

Chapter Ten

The Devil You Have

THE WEATHER HAD BEEN filthy all week. Tonight the dark had come down early, the fog shuttling in thick as cotton, muffling the world and restricting sight to just a few feet in front of one's nose. The drive home from work, with a stop to pick up the children and then a few groceries, had been a long one. Pamela had to drive at a crawl due to the limited visibility and Isabelle, hungry and teething, had been crying in the backseat from the minute they had left Gert's until they pulled down the drive to the house. She'd had a long frustrating day at the building site, which had left her feeling completely helpless, a state which always made her angry.

She paused for a moment, putting her head to the steering wheel. She was exhausted. Sometimes it swamped her this way, the knowledge that she was so damn tired. It seemed to her that every cell of her body held grief, the weight of which was more than cold iron. She thought she might never be warm again, that she would never sleep a full night, that she would never be rid of this terrible pain in her chest and this ache over her whole body. She wanted to turn the car around, screaming baby and all, and drive into Belfast, turn up the mountainside and flee into the safety and warmth of Jamie's home. She knew she couldn't keep doing that, she had to learn to be on her own with the children, how to function, how to breathe without the distraction of Jamie's house and presence. Better yet, she wanted to walk into her own home, and find her husband there, big and warm, his arms open, waiting for her like he had never left, never been taken from her. She wanted to fall asleep with his hands on her, wanted to hear his voice ribbon through bedtime tales for their children, wanted him to soothe the cries of their daughter and reassure their son.

Barring all that, she wanted to get out of this car, fall on the ground and beat her fists into the dirt until they were bloody. She wanted to tear her own skin away and get out of herself, walk away from the pain that seemed to be all that she was anymore. The only other thing that existed inside her was her love for their children.

Isabelle's cries were escalating. Pamela gritted her teeth and opened the car door. Got out, got Conor out and took Isabelle from her seat in the back, her small face red with fury. She needed to freeze a clean cloth for her to chew and rub her gums down with whiskey. She grabbed the groceries, one-handed, awkwardly, not wanting to come back out to the car once she managed to get the children inside.

"Who dat, mama?" Conor asked. The hair on the back of her neck went up immediately, as she realized they were not alone in their yard. There was a man standing, legs apart, casual and yet with the sense that came with certain men that said violence was merely a matter of course for them.

"I don't know, sweetie, you just stay behind mama."

"Can I help you with something?" she asked, trying to sound brave and feeling anything but with two small children in tow and a stranger blocking her way to the door of her home.

"I'm here to collect on yer husband's debt," he said. He wore gloves and a dark coat, hobnailed boots and a knit cap pulled down to his eyebrows. He looked like a thug, likely because that's exactly what he was. She could feel her groceries slipping from her hand and thought, rather ludicrously, that she would have to return to the store for milk, because the bottle was going to break. She let the bags go, hearing the crack of the milk bottle, and put her hand behind her to touch Conor's head in reassurance.

"My husband isn't here at the moment," she said, striving to keep every trace of fear out of her voice.

"Yer husband isn't ever goin' to be here again, lady. I know that, so ye need not bother with yer lies. He owed us money, one last deposit so to speak, an' I've come to collect it," he hissed this last, advancing until he was almost close enough to touch her. Conor was hanging onto her leg and she could feel him staring at the man.

She judged the distance between herself and the house. Even had she been alone, key to hand, odds were she couldn't outrun him. With the children and having to fumble through her pockets for the key, it would merely be reckless and likely to get one or all of them hurt.

"I don't know what you're talking about," she said again, joggling Isabelle, who had passed beyond angry and was well on her way to inconsolable. It was the truth, she *didn't* know, unless it was a continuance of the graft Casey had told her about after a terrible beating he had taken for his refusal to give any more money to a sordid pair of men who worked on the fringes of the PIRA.

She backed up, stumbling a little. Isabelle was howling now, both startled and feeling her mother's fear. It wasn't beyond some of these men to hurt a child, or to hurt a woman and leave her children to fend for themselves. Behind her sat the wood pile, if she could just grab a good-sized chunk of wood and throw it at him, maybe she could make a dash for the door.

"I suggest ye leave the lady alone." The voice was quiet and emerged from the side of the house. Noah Murray walked out into the open, seemingly unarmed but with an authority, she knew, that one ignored at one's peril.

The man swallowed and backed away a little. "Now, I never meant the lady any harm."

Noah merely looked at him. Clearly the man knew just who he was facing, for the tension that came off him hummed in the air. Noah stood in a relaxed fashion, as if he had merely stumbled across them during a countryside ramble.

"Get off her property now, or I'll take ye off myself. An' tell yer boss that he's to consider his bill paid in full. If he doesn't like that, he can come to me for an accounting." He made a clicking noise with his tongue, a dismissive sound, a sound one might level at a stray dog that posed no threat. "Threatenin' women an' babbies, is this what the Belfast chapter has come to?"

From the fish-belly hue of the man's face, Pamela thought an accounting with Noah Murray had little to do with money, and a great deal to do with blood and pain. He added something then in Gaelic that made the man pale even further and then the man simply turned and ran. Her Gaelic had never been good, and Casey had only taught her the words of love, both the gentle ones and the blue ones, but neither served her now. She had caught the word pig and something she thought might be slit and she could understand all she needed to from those two words.

Noah turned to her. "Take yer children in the house, Mrs. Riordan, it's best if ye're not outside for the next few minutes."

She nodded, leaving the groceries where they had fallen. Isabelle was taking long stuttering breaths now. Pamela's hand was still clutched around Conor's and he followed her inside without a sound.

She set Conor at the table with bread and jam and a glass of milk. His big dark eyes followed her as she sat on the sofa to nurse Isabelle. She couldn't see anything other than the side yard from her position, though she was aware of Noah moving around outside. It felt strange to have a man in the yard, walking about, checking things. She didn't want to think of what else might be taking place outside. She took a breath and looked at her son.

"It's all right, sweetheart," she said to him, forcing herself to sound brave. "The bad man is gone, and he won't be coming back."

He nodded, but she didn't think he was convinced. He was such a steady little soul that she worried at times about what he kept inside, how he was dealing with this world of his which had been turned upside down with the disappearance of his daddy. She tried to present him with her brave face as much as she could, but she knew, small as he was, he wasn't fooled by it often. She took a shaky breath, wondering just how gone the bad man was.

There was a light knock at the door just as she finished nursing Isabelle. She laid her down carefully, tucking pillows in beside the baby's recumbent form, and called out. "Come in." She swiftly checked her clothing to make certain everything was righted and that she was decent.

Noah stepped in, stood on the mat and took his hat off. He held her bag of groceries in one hand. The bag looked dry and tidy; he had clearly gotten rid of the milk and broken glass.

"There was a loose board on yer shed, I nailed that down, an' fed the horse an' the sheep. Ye'll not have to venture out again tonight, though he won't trouble ye anymore. There's no one else about, an' no sign of anythin' amiss. He'll take his message back to his boss, an' there will be no more bother to ye. Just to be certain, I'll have a word with the Belfast command. They don't want to fall foul of me, so they tend to listen when I have a word with them."

She was aware of Conor listening to the man, his crayon stilled in his small hand. She had to be careful of what she said. She didn't want to make her wee boy any warier than he was already.

"How did you know?"

He merely looked at her, the gentian eyes clear and completely unreadable.

"How did you know to come along just then?"

"We made a deal, you an' I, this is me holdin' up my end. How I manage that is not for you to worry over."

"I never asked you to protect me," she said, worried that the parameters of their deal had shifted without her agreeing to the new terms.

"Not as such, but I did say that I would see that no harm came to ye."

"Well, thank you," she said, aware her tone was a bit stiff.

"Ye're welcome," he said, matching her tone. She had a feeling he was amused, and it made her somewhat prickly to know it.

"I'm making tea, you're welcome to stay and have a cup."

"Thank ye, but no, I've cows that need milkin'."

With that he left, and she locked the door behind him, sighing with relief that he had not taken her up on her offer of tea. She could not quite imagine herself making small talk over a cuppa with the man. '*So did you have to kill anyone this week? No? That must make a pleasant change for you.*'

She sat down, her knees were as wobbly as jelly, and it took a few minutes to find her equilibrium. Conor had moved on to playing with his cars, running them over and around the very patient Finbar, whose expression was that of canine martyr. Isabelle slept, cheeks flushed shell pink, mouth a tiny oval of blissful unconsciousness.

Everything seemed extraordinarily ordinary, in that strange way life often did after a surge of adrenaline.

"For supper, mama?"

"Warmed-up stew," she said.

Conor nodded, his curly head already bent back toward the dog and his cars. He took so much in his stride, so much he shouldn't have to.

She watched him play, her mind going to what Casey would think of this situation. She knew exactly how the man would respond to the idea of soliciting Noah Murray's help and she indulged in the small fantasy of him giving her what for in her head.

"*Damn fool woman, always getting' yerself out of one scrape only to leap headfirst into the next. Ye'll be the death of me with yer antics.*"

She allowed the fantasy to fill out, to see him in her mind's eye, the frustration in his face, the way his eyes went a bit smoky when he was truly angry with her, how he would take her shoulders with those big hands and look into her eyes to reinforce whatever point he was trying to make with her. She could feel her heart speed up and her skin prickle with need, so vivid was her imagining. She could smell him, and breathed it in, the complicated notes that were only Casey—wood and musk and a deep, dark note that had always sent her pulse to racing.

It hurt too much to keep the image close, hurt too much not to have those hands on her, not to have those arms to go to when the world was a harsh, cold place. She opened her eyes to his absence, feeling the pain of it as if someone had cut off her oxygen and taken away her ability to breathe. She had to stop doing this to herself.

He had one last thing to say, before the fragile bubble of his presence floated away on the winds of reality.

"*If ye make a deal with the devil, prepare to burn a wee bit yerself.*"

She sighed, and got up to warm the supper. The words were true enough, but when the devil was all you had, you made your bargains and just hoped to get out alive.

Chapter Eleven

'In Falls of Sky-Color'
April 1976

"CHRIST HAVE MERCY, it's another young one," Gerard said. Pamela nodded in agreement, for the victim *was* young. She was young and had died in a ditch filled with bluebells—falls, in the words of another Gerard, of sky-color filling the narrow ditch from side to side.

The present Gerard looked at her and said, "I don't like the young ones. We'd best get to it, it's fine now but it's goin' to rain soon."

She nodded and took the cap off the lens of her camera. A half hour of quiet work ensued, with Gerard writing his meticulous notes and her slowly circling the body, recording the scene with each whirr of the shutter.

They were out in the countryside, on a narrow lane that petered out in a farmer's field. She could smell the scents of freshly dug earth and steer manure and the light honey scent of the bluebells that proliferated all through the fields and ditches and even in the cracks of the roadway. The farmer's collie had found the body early that morning.

Gerard was right, she was very young and there was something strangely lovely about her, even here in death. The breeze ruffled her hair, hair the color of a fawn, that light, silky brown which turned gold when the sun played across it. Her face, terribly still and blank, was delicate in its structure, and Pamela could tell she had been a pretty girl. She'd possessed the shy sort of beauty that isn't first noticed, but which lasts longer with the observer than the more obvious sort. This one was going to stick with her, as she knew the sight of that face—so young that there was still a hint of baby softness around her jawline—would haunt her for a long while. The girl was lying on her side, knees curled up toward her body, fully clothed in a white blouse and thin white pants. She knew once the girl was turned over, the peace and stillness would be gone. She had been shot in the head at point blank range. The coroner's van was sitting on the side of the verge, waiting to take the body when all the attendants of violent death had done their jobs.

"Pamela?" Gerard's gruff voice startled her. "What's amiss?"

"It's just that this feels wrong."

"Aye, well murder rarely feels right," Gerard said, drily.

"I mean it's not like the other scenes we've attended recently—neither kind."

"No, it's not."

She knew he understood what she meant. Generally speaking there were two sorts of scenes they worked; the ones where the hate and violence were clear, and the other where the scene was almost clinical, despite the violent manner of death. There was just a feeling, an energy left behind on the air, the executions felt flat, as though the air were missing its whirl of electrons. The ones motivated by hate felt dark, and the energy was still there swirling, pricking along her skin, warning, and often leaving her with a heavy feeling for days afterward.

"There's not the same fury here. Gerard, you've seen exactly what I've seen. Can you tell me this one doesn't look and feel different to you?"

He bent down next to the body again, his hands, still gloved, held casually over his knees. "All right, tell me what ye're thinkin' here."

She hesitated for a moment, she often went on instinct, though in the matter of photographing bodies she operated from a place of logic and a methodical precision. Her private thoughts often went in a different direction. Once home, after attending and photographing such a scene, she couldn't help but mull the details over in her head. She always knew which deaths were going to linger with her, like an oily smoke that coated her mind until something in the daily round of life banished it. What she thought of as the typical scene—executions, bar brawls gone too far—no longer stuck fast in her mind. They were all too common and she had seen too many of those scenes. It was work and she had learned to put it in its own drawer so that the stain of it did not leak into her home. Granted this had become a harder task since Casey disappeared, still she attempted to do it because she didn't want the taint of those scenes to show in her face or to touch her children in any way.

"This seems personal," she said trying to inject some certainty into her voice, because she couldn't have said why it felt so, only that it did. "Like whomever did this loved her, or did at one time."

Gerard squinted up at her. The day was fine, and the sunlight bright making it hard to see detail. "Loved her so much he shot her in the head?"

She gave him a pointed look. "Gerard, we've been in this profession long enough to know there are three reasons for murder—lust, lucre, and love and love's opposite, which I suppose technically makes it four. Well, here you have to add in politics, too, but those first four reasons still stand good for much of what we see. It wouldn't be the first time love thwarted turned out this way."

"All right. I suspect ye have more reason than that to say this one is different. Even in the executions hate is always involved, which is, as ye pointed out, only the darker side of love's coin."

"It's only that her body didn't fall that way. You know most of the scenes when someone is dumped in a spot, it means just that—dumped—like their body was refuse. But she's been placed carefully, like she's sleeping."

"Aye, an' so?" He was always one to get to the point, was Gerard.

"Who would do that, who would place a body just so? Only someone filled with remorse, so that someone cared for her a great deal. My guess is a lover."

"She's naught but a baby!" Gerard said indignantly.

Pamela shook her head. "You say that because you're a decent man who looks at her and sees a child, but there are men who don't view a young girl that way."

Gerard gave her a shrewd glance. "Aye, I know that well enough, an' I suppose ye attracted a few men like that yourself at the same age."

"More than a few," she said. "A young girl can easily be dazzled by the attentions of an older man. Then again it could be a boy who did this, but somehow it doesn't quite feel that way."

Gerard gave her on odd look. "Ye're gettin' all that from how she's lyin'?"

"Yes, aren't you?"

He looked back at the girl and tilted his head, taking in the scene with narrowed eyes.

"Aye, I see what ye're sayin'. Hopefully we actually find out one day if ye're right."

She sighed, understanding exactly what he meant. In their line of work they rarely knew the end of the cases they worked on, in the main because the police didn't know either and the cases didn't end up at a trial or they ended without any sort of closure or knowledge of events at all.

She looked around. Everyone was busy at their appointed tasks. Even here, though everyone was polite and professional for the most part, there was a divide. She and Gerard were often the only two Catholics working these scenes. There was a formal restraint even now, after a few years of working with these men. She knew they were good people for the most part, trying to do a difficult job in a more than difficult country. But there were also the ones like Constable Blackwood who took out his hatred on the closest Catholic standing. Now and again, she would catch one of them looking at her and then looking just as swiftly away. Rarely did they smile though, as if even so small a thing could be seen as a betrayal. Which, she knew, it could in either community.

She packed up her equipment and stood, her shoulders tight from holding the camera so carefully for the last half hour. She sighed and closed her eyes for a moment. Oddly, there was no smell of decomposition. It couldn't have been very long since the body was placed here in its bower of bluebells.

Gerard was right, it was the young ones that were the hardest. It was the thought of a light so new, eclipsed before it could even begin to truly shine. It was all the lost promise and blighted hopes of the parents, and the ripples of pain and loss that spread out from there, moving out to the edges of the lives of those left behind.

She looked back. There were rain clouds rolling in, the color of old silver, and the breeze had sharpened just the slightest bit, carrying the scent of water with it. The fields spread green and verdant out around her, bounded by blackthorn hedges and the sweet scent of newly sprouted hay. And in a ditch lay a young girl, surrounded by falls of sky-color.

Chapter Twelve

Tomas Egan, Esquire

TOMAS EGAN, ESQ. had not been terribly keen to take on a young untried solicitor so that he might complete his training under supervision. Tomas Egan, Esq. in point of fact, had told Patrick Riordan sans Esquire to 'Feck off yerself an' the horse ye rode in on, boy.' Patrick Riordan, a man of no small stubbornness himself, merely waited out the old buzzard, which was how he thought of this fearsome man of law. This man who had once had three separate test cases against the British Government pending in front of the European Commission on Human Rights. This man who, it was said, told the British Prime Minister that he could go shag himself seven ways from Sunday when he proposed sending yet more troops into Tomas' embattled hometown. He was possessed of a roaring intellect, a gift of oratory and a fierce sense of justice. He might have been, some said, anything he had chosen to be—council to kings and prime ministers, a judge for the Privy Council, or even the leader of the country entire. He had one love beyond that of justice, though, and that was whiskey. Ultimately whiskey won, and the once fiery young lawyer found himself in a seedy office with flies on the windowsills, taking on cases that no one else would touch.

There had been other firms to choose from, but Patrick had decided himself weeks before, it was Tomas Egan or bust. And so he merely stood his ground (partly because there was no chair on which to sit) in the run-down office, where piles of papers covered every conceivable surface, and dust lay thick as velvet over most of them. And there he stayed, all six foot two of him, stubborn to his final inch. He was a Riordan, and Riordans stood their ground, particularly with crusty old solicitors, even if said old buzzard had once been lauded as a judicial genius.

"Ye need the help, I'd say," Pat said, in response to a needling query on what the feck he thought he was doing barging into a man's office, unannounced. Pat knew that this was not a man who needed flattery or finessing, he would recognize it for what it was. Blunt honesty seemed his only course. "Ye don't even have a secretary."

"Don't need one," the man said, "not enough for her to do here, not many calls to field an' no dictation to take. An' I've certainly no need for some wet-nosed pup who imagines himself a lawyer."

"Well, that's the point, I'm not a lawyer yet. I need yer help with that."

"And why is it you think I should be interested in helping you?"

"Because I asked ye to. I've not got anything else in my favor, only that I need to do my training under someone an' ye're my first choice."

The man leaned across his desk, blue eyes suddenly sharp. "How desperate are you, son, that an old shambling alcoholic is yer first choice?"

"Ye're the best at what ye do, an' I would learn from the best. It's that simple. I could have gone elsewhere, but I came here first. I've passed my rights of audience an' I'm bringin' a case with me that I think ye might find interestin'."

There was a spark of curiosity in the old man's face, though it was swiftly veiled.

"Ye've got a case? Well, why the feck would ye need me then?"

Pat took a breath, appealed to his own particular saint and answered the man politely.

"Because clearly I can't try it, but you can."

The old man laughed, and laughed, until Pat, clearing a space on a stool he'd spotted under a pile of files three feet deep, sat down to wait him out. Patrick, unlike most of the men in his ancestry, had the patience of a saint, or as his father used to say, the stubborn will of an obdurate bulldog.

"Let me guess, it's one of those do-gooder, entirely suicidal cases that suck a man down into a tribal quagmire from which he's not likely to ever emerge."

Pat merely maintained a dignified silence, having nothing with which to refute the man's last statement. It was, in many ways, just as Tomas had described it. It was also one of the worst miscarriages of justice he had ever seen.

"Ah, I see I'm right. Such a case will get ye killed, an' bein' that ye're young an' hale I don't see why ye're intent on stickin' yer neck into that particular noose."

"Because it's the right thing to do, someone has to defend those who cannot defend themselves."

"I know who ye are, boy, or leastwise I know who yer family is. I don't meddle in republican affairs."

"Ye used to," Pat said mildly.

"I used to wear short pants too an' eat more candy than was good for me, but as ye grow older ye leave the bad habits behind."

"Really?" Pat looked pointedly at the whiskey bottle that was none too well hidden behind the toppling stack of papers at the man's left elbow.

Tomas Egan merely leaned back at this provocation and eyed Pat more shrewdly than he had before.

"So why me then, boy? Of all the solicitor's offices ye might have strayed into, why this one? Tell me the truth, no buttering me up the right side an' down the left, just the cold hard truth."

Pat took a deep breath and then told the truth, which he sensed was the only tactic to take with this man.

"Because I think ye might be the only lawyer mad enough to take this case on. Also, I was tellin' ye the truth when I said ye're my first choice."

Tomas Egan, Esquire, gave him a ruminative look, narrowing his eyes until they were mere rheumy blue slits.

"Flattery will get ye a cup of tea, boy an' maybe five minutes of my time. That's how long ye have to convince me that I shouldn't just kick ye out the door."

Pat smiled, feeling an uprush of hope. If he had the measure of this man, he was certain he wouldn't even need the full five minutes.

Tomas poured them each a whiskey rather than the aforementioned tea. Pat, normally not one to imbibe before evening, was grateful for the fortification.

"Outline the case for me, an' then tell me yer own particulars."

The case wasn't a simple one, but Tomas Egan had never specialized in simple. A young woman had been raped, beaten and strangled to death in a cemetery. It was a cemetery she cut through on her way to work each day, and she was known to spend her lunch hours there from time to time. The young man who tended the grounds of the cemetery was charged and convicted in the case, having been found with blood all over his shirt, cowering in a tool shed. He had a mental age of roughly twelve, and the reading comprehension of a child of eight.

After ten hours of non-stop questions, during which it was alleged the police had pulled his hair, slapped his face and shouted at him for many of those hours, he had signed a confession which he could not comprehend, merely to make the interrogation stop. The confession had been written in pencil, allowing, it was also alleged, changes to be made afterward.

A blood expert had testified saying the only way the young man could have gotten the blood on his shirt in the pattern it was in was if he had committed the crime. There were at least three other very viable suspects though. A cuckolded husband, a married lover, and a strange man who had been known to follow women into the cemetery and expose himself to them. None of these men had ever been so much as questioned. All this Pat outlined in broad strokes, giving just the facts and not coloring it with emotion.

"An' why is it that ye think they didn't bother to look at the other men?" Tomas asked, though Pat suspected he already knew the answer.

"Because Oggie's—that's the convicted lad—last name is Carrigan, an' so I suspect they charged an' convicted him to get their own back on his older brother."

Tomas would be more than familiar with Oggie's older brother, a social justice campaigner and it was rumored a former IRA member who had been involved in the killing of two RUC officers many years back.

Tomas sat forward, tenting his hands under his chin and narrowing his eyes at Pat. "All right, I'm imaginin' the family wants to appeal the conviction, though they've been turned down already."

"Aye."

"An' they approached you?"

"They didn't know I wasn't a fully trained lawyer yet. They know they can't look to the police to open an inquiry, so they are trying to force their hand with an appeal."

Tomas nodded. "All right, tell me about yerself."

Pat refrained from grinning, but he felt a rush of jubilation at the question. He had a foot in the door, even if only just.

Two weeks later, his joy over convincing the old man to take him on was somewhat tamped, though he in no way regretted it. It was going to be a hard twelve months, but he would know what he was about when it was over. Tomas wasn't going to spare him in the least, that was clear. It was, he believed, what was referred to as learning on an extremely steep curve.

It became clear to him almost immediately that if he wanted to actually get the full worth of his pupillage, he was going to have to convince Tomas to take on a secretary. They desperately needed one so that Bob, Tomas' clerk, could get on with the job of clerking properly. The man was good at his job, he was just spread far too thin. He brought to mind Bob Cratchit, Scrooge's much put-upon clerk in *A Christmas Carol*. He was a small, thin man with a smattering of red-gold hair in a fringe round his face, and a flyaway cap of it on the dome of his head. In the little bit of time he'd had to get to know him, Pat had decided he quite liked the man.

When he suggested the notion of a secretary to Tomas, he got a grumble of what he decided to take for agreement, despite the fact that the man was knee-deep in papers and couldn't find his wig for court at the time. Pat decided he would act in haste and repent, no doubt somewhat copiously, at leisure. He told Tomas three days later when the taste of a victory in court was still sweetening the man's mood.

"I've hired a secretary," he said, quailing a little on the inside but holding fast on the outside, which it seemed to him was what much of working in the law required. Regardless of what hard-nosed judge he came up against in the future, he didn't think he was likely to find any of them as intimidating as his own boss…unless it was the aforementioned secretary he had just hired. The simple truth was they needed someone to organize them and see to clients. It would take away a good bit of the burden Bob Gibney was currently staggering under, and allow the man to do what he was meant to do, which was to bring in clients, sort out court times and perform the Herculean task of trying to keep their budget out of the red.

Miss Dervla Mundy (he had made the mistake of calling her Ms. Mundy thinking an independent woman such as she appeared to be might prefer the title—he would not make that mistake ever again) was a woman of comfortable proportions, steely grey eyes and a fearsome bun of dark hair that looked as if it had not grown as normal hair grew, but rather had been placed there upon her head at birth, like a crown bestowed for sensibility and valor in the face of a feckless world. Had Miss Mundy been presented to the Queen, she would have dealt with the meeting, Pat had no doubt, in the same manner in which she took him in hand during the interview. She would have disabused the Queen of any notion she might have of her place in society and the larger world as having any importance greater than that of a hobo begging his meals in a ditch. She was, thank God, highly qualified, but even had she not been, Pat didn't think he would have had the wherewithal to tell her she didn't have the job. And so Miss Dervla Mundy joined the company of Tomas Egan, Esquire, his law clerk, Bob Gibney and his pupil of law, Pat Riordan.

Tomas gave him a dressing down about it, calling him a Fenian bastard who was going to need to learn his place if he wanted to stay in his law firm, by God. Pat said nothing until Tomas was done raging. He merely took the dressing down, as it was fully expected and then said, "Can ye deny that we need the help here?"

Tomas fired him a look out of bloodshot blue eyes that would have shriveled a lesser man. Pat merely looked back at him; after two weeks with the man he was well used to his rages.

"She can have a trial period of one month. I reserve the right to fire her at the end of that time."

Bob was hovering in the corridor, a small stack of briefs in his hand, when Pat came out of Tomas' office. He gave Pat a nod of encouragement.

"He'll rage at ye, but he will allow her to stay. I think even he has the good sense to be afraid of her. Meself, I'm terrified, but I'll not deny she's efficient. I've had loads more time to actually get clerking done this week. It's brilliant, really." He beamed at him, and Pat thought that alone made it worth suffering Tomas' wrath for a few more days.

"I know I'm lucky he didn't show me the door, I didn't see how we were goin' to get properly organized around here, though, without some help. I don't know how ye've managed as long as ye have, Bob."

Bob shrugged. "He still brings in money, not as much as he once did, mind ye. He's never missed my wages, even if he's usually late with them. I worry about him though, he squanders too much money on the dogs an' the drink."

"Ye've been with him a long time," Pat observed, thinking with Bob's talents he might have worked in any number of solicitor's offices.

"I sense there's a question in that simple statement," Bob smiled. "I stay because he's the best there is, when he remembers it leastwise. I'm fond of the old man, truth be told. Who'd look after him if I weren't here? Well, other than the formidable Miss Mundy." He cast a wary glance down the hall, as if they were both truant and about to be caught out by the headmistress. Which pretty much summed up how Pat felt. The woman was a wonder, though, even if the office was so clean now that they couldn't find their tea mugs in the morning.

Bob handed the briefs to him. "Study up, he'll expect ye to present the cases to him so that he can take the ball an' run with it. How are ye findin' it here?"

Pat grinned. "I love it."

Bob grinned back, his untidy hair lit red as a Roman candle in the afternoon light. "Aye, I thought ye might."

"Are you two school girls goin' to work today, or merely hang about gossipin' in the corridor?" Tomas bellowed.

Pat tucked the briefs under his arm and realized the truth of what he had said to Bob. He did love it here. He surveyed the office around him, all surfaces of which had been divested of their burden of dust within twenty-four hours of Miss Mundy's employment. The sun had been a rare presence this week. It was shining now though, through the well-polished windows, highlighting just how shabby the furniture and carpeting was but also giving the place a glow. There was a hum to the activity that was lovely to hear.

He was, he realized, happy. Or as happy as a man might be who had a beloved brother missing. In moments like this when he landed on some island of contentment, it reminded him how life moved on. Like water, passing around a rock in a river, life was inexorable and would simply keep going. Joy would be felt and sorrow, too. Just now though, any sort of happiness felt like a blasphemy. The guilt hit him like a brick in his chest and for a second he couldn't breathe. He could hear his brother's voice in his head suddenly, as clearly as if the man was standing next to him.

"Sometimes the world we believe we live in is just an illusion. Things change, people we love die, an' suddenly ye have to bid farewell to the world you thought ye lived in."

Not yet, my brother, not yet, he said inside his own head. He was not ready to say goodbye to that world in which his brother might still be alive.

And then he took a breath, and got down to work.

Chapter Thirteen

The High Cost of Truth

IT WASN'T YET LIGHT when she set out for Noah's farm. The distance from her home to Noah's wasn't great in terms of real miles, but it was vast in terms of atmosphere. When she crossed from County Down into County Armagh, heading down the Silverbridge Road toward Crossmaglen, her tension notched up a little and she could feel her shoulders start to inch up toward her ears. This wee bit of land, this small green mountainous beauty, was a world unto itself. South Armagh was beautiful, but it put a shiver of cold silver in her blood every time she visited it.

Pamela left the car at the mouth of a walking path that was very near to Noah's land, and then cut away through the woods bordering the path. She was going in on foot, so as not to alert any of the various security forces that were watching Noah's farm at any given time. He knew to expect her, so hopefully none of his guards would take her walking onto his land as trespass. She was familiar with the farm, as she had been there a few times to visit Kate, admittedly only when Noah was absent.

She had left the children snug in their beds, as Deirdre was visiting for a few days. She didn't think she could have stood anyone else for company just now, but she found a comfort in Deirdre's presence. Despite the fact that Casey and his mother had been estranged for a very long time, she still felt that outside of Pat, only Deirdre felt the loss of Casey as sharply as she did. Deirdre didn't expect her to talk or pretend to a strength that she did not feel.

It was a chilly morning. The sun was pinking up the horizon already though, and it looked like a fair day might lie ahead. It was a relief to be away from the house, away from the ever ringing telephone. She felt like there was an invisible chain that bound her to the thing. Every time it rang her heart went mad in her chest, and she would start to pray as she dashed to answer it. She didn't know what to pray for because some information had a cost that was far too high. There was always the fear that a voice might one day tell her that her husband was gone and no more returning. She had more than one hundred entries in the notebook she kept by the telephone, each one a meticulous record of the phone calls—sometimes just people who were praying for her, praying for her husband, a few phone calls from Constable Severn, kindly and well meant, but utterly useless. Others far more sinister, promising that they had information, knew where Casey was, or what had happened to him, could take her to his body all for a tidy sum of money. Constable Severn had told her that this was all too common, "They're like lice that scuttle in at the scent of vulnerability."

Deirdre had chased one away the evening before. It wasn't the first time the woman had shown up at the house. She was a middle-aged grand-motherly looking sort who had, at first, seemed rather harmless. Pamela had been willing to hear anything she had to say, grasp at any thread the woman offered her and the woman seemed to have credible things to re-late, as she somehow knew small details of their life. But somewhere deep inside, Pamela knew she was using the tidbits of information to stay in denial about what a charlatan the woman was.

She skirted the wood that edged Noah's fields, thinking about David Kendall, the British agent who had been her friend, and whose life Noah had spared for reasons still unknown after a firefight of epic proportions had taken place on his land. David had died at the hands of an evil man just a short month later, and considering the manner of his death, or what she knew of it, it might have been better if Noah had killed him on that fateful bloody day. She crossed herself reflexively, the way she always did when she thought of David, praying that he was at peace and that he knew how much he was missed.

She stepped from the wood, and walked across the fields. She knew which one the bull lived in and avoided it with great care. The ground was gilded with a light layer of dew, every cobweb in the grass strung with diamond drops glimmering in the first light of day. She stepped with confidence and tried not to look around too much, she needed to appear like she belonged here. It was a beautiful piece of land, nicely situated, but knowing some of what had gone on here over the years gave it a dark aspect in her eyes, and she always had a feeling of foreboding when she was here.

She caught a glint in the corner of her eyes, a small dance of light from the hedgerow that grew thick along the drive into the farm. It was odd that there should be light reflecting out of such thick shrubbery, and yet being that it was Noah's farm, not really odd at all. She would have thought the British security forces or Special Branch, whichever unit was watching Noah at present, would have learned a bit more subtlety over the years. Personally, she wondered that they were foolhardy enough to come onto his land in this way.

Proximity to the border, a lack of a Protestant population and the hilly landscape as well as a deeply rooted sense of rebellion had made it the *de facto* independent Republic of South Armagh. British soldiers feared the posting to Forkhill or Crossmaglen more than any other posting in the world. Their living quarters had been compared to submarines they were so heavily mortar-proofed. The soldiers weren't allowed to sit outside, ever, and they always had to be on high alert, forever aware that in this territory they were the ones whose freedom was severely circumscribed. One Captain of the Parachute regiment had compared it to being a target on a conveyer belt, going round and round, just waiting to get knocked down. In South Armagh it was never a matter of if, only when.

Noah opened the door as she stepped into the yard. He seemed to have the radar of a bat in the night sky. He tilted his head, indicating she should follow him into the house. She walked behind him through to the kitchen, where it was blessedly warm, the old room glowing as the sun flooded in, more gold than pink now, over the deep windowsills.

He turned to look at her. "Might I ask what the reason is for ye creepin' through the shrubbery just past dawn?"

"I know this whole area is under heavy surveillance," she said. "So I thought I should come in on foot as circumspectly as possible."

"Usually we meet on yer land," he said, leaning back against the counter, arms crossed over his chest. She swallowed, wondering if he suspected her of spying on him in some way.

"My mother-in-law is staying with me for a few days and I thought it best if she didn't know about us."

He nodded and turned away from her. "D'ye want somethin' hot to drink? It's cold an' ye look half blue."

"That would be nice," she said, clutching her sweater more tightly around her.

"Ye can sit," he said gruffly, "I'll not lash ye to the chair an' pull yer fingernails out if that's what ye're worried about."

"I'm not worried about that," she said with some asperity.

"Good, because I'd not do that to a woman, I'd take yer toenails instead."

She laughed, caught off guard by his black humor. At least she hoped it was humor. She sat down at the scrubbed wooden table. It held a jug of milk, a small pot with sugar and a bottle of tick medicine for sheep.

Noah handed her a thick blue mug filled with the delicious scent of strong coffee. She warmed her hands on the mug gratefully as she was still chilled through from her tramp through the woods. She put in a little cream and a half teaspoon of sugar.

"I think you have company in your hedges today," she said quietly, voice half muffled by the coffee cup. The coffee was surprisingly good. It wasn't a staple in most Irish households and so it was a rare treat for her to have it.

"Aye, I know," he said, apparently unconcerned with spies roaming his land at will. "They like to take cover in the blackthorn hedges. They set up with their camouflage an' nettin' an' are near to invisible as such, except to the dogs an' cows, an'," he smiled, "the long sticks we use to beat down the bushes."

"I don't imagine they take kindly to that," Pamela said, taking another swallow of the hot coffee.

"I don't give a damn what they take kindly to, as ye well know. I'm not a fool. I know given the chance, they will kill me without provocation. I'll have to be that wee bit more careful about my business and movements. I'm pretty certain I'm under a new set of surveillance."

"New?"

"The latest intelligence splinter, I suspect," he said, "there have been rumors that the SAS might be movin' in soon."

"The SAS?" she echoed. The Special Air Services was serious business.

"Aye, they've been here in dribs an' drabs before, attached to other units an' the like, but never sent in full force. If they are, it's because they mean to step up the battle with the IRA." She wondered if she only imagined the slight relish in his tone at such an idea.

"Does it worry you?" she asked, curious, for the countryside was fairly bristling with army personnel these days and there was a heightened tension that prickled along a person's skin even when out for a simple walk.

Noah shrugged. "Those bastards are used to shootin' first and askin' questions later, so we'll all have to be on our toes around here if they truly are sendin' in a squadron. Somethin' tells me they might be waitin' for just the right provocation to put them in."

Seeing him here in his own kitchen, which was surprisingly cozy and clean given that he was a bachelor for all intents and purposes, threw her off a little. He wore a neatly-pressed blue shirt that matched his eyes and a pair of navy colored dress pants. His hair was freshly trimmed and his face clean-shaven. He looked preternaturally alert considering the some-what unholy hour. Mind you, he was a farmer and well used to rising with the dawn.

"I have news for ye," he said.

She was suddenly nervous, the queasiness she had managed to quell all morning flooding through her stomach. She wished she hadn't drunk the coffee now.

He sat down across from her and she felt the force of the man's au-thority. He had long been used to command and wore it as a second skin. She wondered if anyone had ever penetrated past that layer with him, be-yond his sister and long-lost parents.

She realized he was watching the expressions that crossed her face, as if he could see her every thought. She flushed under the scrutiny of those gentian eyes. He looked considerably less frightening today, but it would never do to lose sight of who and what this man was.

He smelled clean, of soap and hay and something else, something amber in tone. Being that he had roughly a couple hundred pigs, a flock of sheep and a great number of cows, it was no small feat, she thought, for him to appear so clean and well-dressed. He had hired laborers, some of whom lived on the property, still she knew he did a fair amount of the work which was necessary to keep a farm this size not just ticking over, but running like a well-oiled machine. Not to mention his smuggling net-work and his position as the godfather of the South Armagh PIRA.

"Look, I want ye to understand up front what I am about to tell ye is merely hearsay. I would ask ye this as well—are ye certain ye want to know? Because we all believe we know the people we love, but do we really? There are some nasty surprises to be found along the pathway of another man's life. So, if it's information that changes the way ye knew yer husband, the way ye remember him, do ye really want it?"

She wanted to blurt out 'yes', wanted him to just say whatever it was he had to say, and not ask her permission to do so. She felt irrationally angry at him. She knew it was shoot the messenger syndrome, but that did little to lessen her anger.

"Yes, I have to know. I think knowing has to be better than this never-ending wondering." She wasn't certain at all, actually, but she had to hear whatever it was he had to say.

Noah eyed her shrewdly, as if he knew she was lying in part. She wished the damn man would just get on with it.

"I think he killed someone."

She wasn't sure what she had been expecting, it wasn't this though. There was a small echo of dismay deep inside that told her she had half suspected it could be something of this nature.

"Who?" she asked. Her stomach was cramping and she put her hand to it, not wanting to break down in front of this man.

"The men who attacked ye in yer home—at least one of them was killed. Word is your husband did it. If that's so, it's only what the bastards deserved, so ye need not feel any sorrow on their part."

"Oh, I don't, believe me, I just—I didn't know and if he disappeared because of something he did to protect us…" she trailed off. Her body hurt and she felt disconnected from it at the same time. It wasn't shock, but rather another set of stones to be put into place in the wall of stubborn denial behind which she lived, scant as their shelter was proving.

"Maybe I'm wrong, Pamela. I didn't know yer man well, it seems to me, though, that he would not think it a waste of his life, did he die protecting those he loved."

Unfortunately this was true, but what the bastard hadn't thought about was how she would survive without him; how she would raise their children alone, how she would sleep in a cold bed for the rest of her life, how she would feel as if she could never draw another breath without pain, and if the day came when she could manage any of those things, it would hurt even more. The salient point of what Noah had said suddenly sunk in.

"You said one of them, but there were two."

"Aye, there were. It's the one that's left that says yer husband killed his friend. I'll be honest, Pamela, I'm not just that sure I believe him. Mind, he was adequately persuaded to tell the truth, but it may be that he doesn't know the truth in its details."

Her mouth went dry. She was quite certain she didn't want to know what Noah meant by 'adequately persuaded', however she had lived here long enough, and had measure enough of this man to understand it would not have been pleasant and that he would not have stopped until he had the information he wanted.

"Thank you for telling me," she said. Every word was an effort, like it had to be pushed through a dam of ice to make it to the surface of her lips.

Noah shook his head, blue eyes dark. "Do not thank me for bad news, it's ill luck to the both of us to do so. Just take it for what it is, information that might be true or might not be."

She nodded, unable to say anything further. She needed to go, needed to get away where no one could see her. He offered to drive her back to her car, but she said no and managed to get out of his house without a further word spoken between them.

Outside, she walked off toward the tree line, beyond the north field. She didn't even care if the entire British Army was taking pictures of her from the shrubbery. Let them, let them watch her through the sights on their goddamn machine guns.

She managed not to get sick until she was well within the tree line. Then she threw up bile, hot and acidic, because there was nothing in her stomach other than a few swallows of coffee. She sank down to her knees, the frost and damp ground soaking her jeans immediately. She didn't care, nothing mattered right now other than the fact that Casey might have killed someone and if that was so, and she knew it might well be, then it was also likely he had been killed in retaliation. What the hell had he been thinking? And yet, she knew; she understood. She had been there after all, the afternoon those two men had invaded their home. She remembered all too well the terror, the fear they would rape her, hurt her child, both the one in his bed up the stairs and the one in her belly, for she had been five months pregnant with Isabelle at the time. She knew their neighbor Lewis, who'd once killed for a living, had told Casey he should have shot both men then and there that day. In a country where blood was common currency, it made sense to her in a terrible way.

She took one shaky breath and then another, her head still pressed into the tree trunk. She felt like most days she kept her head just slightly above the waters of a silent, heavy sea, one that was intent on dragging her down into its depths, and that she had to fight every minute to keep breathing. And in the midst of that strange, silent sea in which she knew she might well drown, there was now a wire of anger, bright and crimson, to which she could grasp. She touched it in her mind and felt it steel her spine.

She got up, brushed off her knees and kept walking.

Chapter Fourteen

'Should Time Dissolve This Prison'

THERE WAS AN EMERALD shimmer to the woods as she entered them, spring had sprung in all her forty shades of green and the woods were wet and flush with the sound of birds about their business. It wasn't the most obvious spot for a clandestine meeting, she thought bending to disengage her pant leg from a low thorn bush.

The approach was made through Father Jim, much as that must have galled the man who made said approach. She returned his phone call at the appointed time from a payphone in Belfast. She had raised an eyebrow at his suggested venue, but agreed nevertheless. He was a scary man to be certain, but she knew he had no reason to hurt her. To give him credit he was straying pretty close to the borders of South Armagh in order to meet up with her. This was a gesture of faith on his part, so she tried not to curse too loudly at the undergrowth through which she had to wade.

She was very damp and somewhat piqued and flushed by the time she reached their appointed meeting spot. The woods had originally been the parkland of an earl's estate. Both earl and estate had long faded into the annals of time, but a few things remained that gave echoes into the present day of what the site had once been. Such as the garden bench, well mossed, that William Bright sat upon, looking about as if he expected evil gnomes to come to life and attack him at any second. A country boy he clearly was not.

Pamela had not thought to see this man ever again in her life. She had not particularly wanted to either. He was the most feared man in the hardline Loyalist world, and that was saying something in a world where blood and hatred were a given. In some ways he was a walking cliché. Short, barrel-chested, covered in tattoos and looking every inch the hard man that would kill you without giving it a second's pause.

"Mr. Bright," she said and sat down beside him on the bench.

"Mrs. Riordan," he replied, with the slight mockery in tone that she remembered from her only previous encounter with the man. "By the by, I want to start off by sayin' I'm sorry about yer husband."

"Thank you." She knew she sounded stiff, but she could not discuss her missing husband with this man. "All right, what is it that you want?" she asked.

"I do like a woman who knows how to get straight to brass tacks, an' none of yer small talk to it."

"Why me?" she said, striving for a cool tone, despite a dry throat and a tongue that felt as thick as a wool sock.

"Because I know ye're friends with dat journalist, da Catolick one that's got the death wish."

He meant Muck, she knew, there were only so many journalists that fit the 'death wish' descriptor. As a teenager, Muck had been a member of the Official IRA, drawn to them because of their socialist-republican politics. He had been interned as a result in 1971 and spent a year in the Kesh in the Official IRA compound.

Muck occasionally wrote under an assumed name. Sometimes he disguised the names of the people about whom he wrote, giving them nicknames, but describing them in such vivid detail that they were entirely recognizable within the narrow tribal world of Belfast. It was a safe bet that he didn't have any Loyalist fans, which begged the question of why this man wanted to use Muck's particular talents.

"I have a story to tell ye. Let me just tell it through so I don't miss any of the details an' then ye can ask me any question ye like. Will that suit ye?"

"Yes," she said, intrigued despite herself. It had to be something very serious for him to have taken the risk of meeting with her.

"First, I believe ye took death scene photos not so long ago of a young girl, fifteen years old, light brown hair?"

"I did," she said, unsurprised by his knowledge. This wasn't a country for secrets, at least not in some respects.

"Ye've been on the Mullabrack Road, so ye'll remember what a lonely, isolated stretch it is?"

"Yes," she said, remembering too clearly the morning she had been on that particular bit of roadway. She had been waiting for a car to come and pick her up to take her to meet with the man beside her now. She well remembered the isolation of it.

"Well, imagine that same road at midnight, an' imagine ye're a fifteen year old girl wanderin' along it, maybe a touch worse for the drink. Imagine that ye've just had a bit of a disagreement with a friend an' ye're goin' to go tell yer married lover that ye're pregnant with his child."

"Pregnant?" she asked, thinking of the forlorn little corpse in her bower of bluebells.

"Aye, pregnant," he said heavily.

"What was she doing out on that road in the middle of the night?"

"Meetin' her man, apparently he wanted to be circumspect about their relationship."

She raised an eyebrow and he laughed a short barking sound that resembled a hostile seal.

"Aye, too little, too late."

He took a breath and then coughed, a long wracking sound that was disturbing. It sounded as though the fabric of the man's lungs was rending in two. It took a few minutes, and he had to get up and hit his chest several times, before he could get his air back. He pulled a handkerchief from his pocket and muffled his face in it for a moment. She sat waiting, wondering if he was ill. He took the handkerchief away from his face, and in the second before he hastily stuffed it in his pocket she saw a bright scarlet stain in its snowy folds.

He sat down again and resumed telling his tale, as if he hadn't just coughed up blood. He was plain in the telling, but she could see it clear, the young girl, frightened by the news she had to impart, standing on that dark lonely road in the middle of the night, easy prey for anyone who might happen along. She must have been terrified. Pamela tried to push the delicate face out of her mind—the delicate face with the soft line of childhood still there in the chin and the round of the cheek.

"So this man does pick her up, though he claims he's not the one with whom she was havin' relations. An' he drives her back toward Portadown. He stops to run an errand he says an' while he's out of the car—for two minutes—she shoots herself in the head."

"And so they think she committed suicide?"

"Aye, well they would, despite a whole lot of evidence to the contrary."

"Why is that?"

"That's the question, isn't it? An' this is where it gets interestin'. It was one of their own in that car. The man that picked her up was an off-duty RUC officer."

The need for secrecy suddenly became clear. She felt ice-water gather in a pool in her stomach. The man was mad if he thought Muck could break this story, even with credible witnesses to back him up, of whom she suspected there would be none.

"And he's saying she grabbed his gun, and killed herself for no apparent reason?"

"Aye, that's about the size of it," he agreed. "Though she's left-handed an' apparently shot herself in the right side of the head, at a bugger of an angle."

"Oh, that poor girl," Pamela said. "Is it possible he's telling the truth and he wasn't the man she was having an affair with?"

"No, it's not possible. He did know her, mind ye there's little to prove it other than her wee girlfriend sayin' it were him Janie were havin' relations with. She says Janie was pregnant, an' that the baby belonged to the policeman. I think she asked him to meet up with her, so she could tell him she was expectin'. He's got a wife an' a family already, he's panickin', she maybe threatens to tell his wife an' in his panic, he kills her. Dumps her body in a ditch an' away he goes, thinkin' he's scot-free."

"How do you know she died in the car?" Pamela asked. "We found her in a farmer's field, after all."

"That's not where she died though, right?"

"No, she had been placed there." She recalled the strong sense she'd had that the girl had been put there by someone who loved her.

"Her girlfriend said she'd gone to meet this man that night, an' she told Jane's family. Jane's daddy went there straight off, found the man cleanin' his car. He said he could still smell the blood in it. The man called the police, said Barry—that'd be Jane's daddy—were harrassin' him. They carted Barry away, an' stuck him in a cell until he cooled off. So they bring in their colleague for questionin' an' he admits the girl was in his car, but that she killed herself. An' that's that apparently, case closed. The evidence is bein' made to fit the events, essentially."

"Why aren't you dealing with this inside the Loyalist community?" she asked, though she feared she knew the answer.

"It can't go that way, Loyalists are loyal to the RUC. Nobody is goin' to talk, an' if they did their life would be bound to get difficult real quick-like. Their neighbors would turn against them an' the police would harass the ever-livin' bejesus out of them."

"Whereas they would just put out a hit on us pesky Catholics," she said drily.

"Yer journalist friend has more death threats against him than raindrops fallin' from the sky on any given Belfast day. Do ye really think it will give him pause? As to yerself, there's no reason why yer name has to be connected with any of it. I came to you because I know the journo is a friend of yers. An' because frankly, I need to keep this outside my own community."

"Why are you talking at all then?" she asked.

"Because there's a wee girl that's been killed an' her mammy an' daddy need answers. They've stained her memory by sayin' it's a suicide, when it's not. The police don't like me anyway, I've little to worry about." He rubbed a hand over his bald head, and gave her a questioning look.

She sighed. "I'll take it to Muck, and I'll let you know what he says. I'll send word back to you through Father Jim. I'm assuming," she said somewhat tartly, "the communication line runs both ways."

He smiled. "I believe it does."

She gathered up her purse and stood, but William Bright had one last thing to say.

"I hear ye're keepin' interestin' company these days." He wasn't looking at her as he said it, but rather gazing out over the broken walls, the sun gleaming on his bald pate like a ring of fire turning him into a wide boy version of Lucifer.

"Do you?"

"Aye, I do. Some say ye're Noah Murray's woman now."

"People can say as they like," she retorted sharply, "it doesn't make it so."

"I told ye once lass, that ye were right to be afraid of me, an' I will also tell ye this for free—I haven't been afraid of any man in my life but two—my father an' that bastard Murray, an' if he's got ye in his grip, he isn't likely to let ye go."

"I'm not here to talk about Mr. Murray," she said.

William Bright shrugged and turned back to look at the flowers. "Fair enough. Just remember my words."

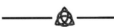

Pamela made a stop before heading home. She needed time to clear her head and sort her emotions before she could deal with the children and set about all the homely tasks of the evening. She had long been familiar with this old estate, and there was a spot that was particularly dear to her.

Casey, knowing her as he did, knowing how she loved history-haunted places, had brought her here more than once, to this estate, abandoned so long ago that it wasn't even on the map anymore and very few people knew of its existence. It was part of why she loved it here, because usually she could ramble without interference, and feel like she was caught in another time altogether. They had come with Conor now and again too, to traipse through the old gardens, and sit by the pond, where crumbling statues glimpsed their ghostly reflections. It was to the pond that she now headed.

There still remained parts of the ancient house, lines of stone beneath the velvet of grass and lichen, partial walls rearing up out of nowhere, statues that lay over abandoned, long buried in a shroud of vines and bramble. A chimney still stood, stones the size of a trunk partially mortared together and sporting reams of plant life. It was an incredibly romantic spot as well as a sad one. There had been rumors of late that the National Trust might be eyeing the property. She didn't see how strewn rocks and broken statues would be worthy of that august institution though.

The earth was mucky near the pond, but the water reflected the sun, edging the pale gold in pewter, taking the orb of light in and rinsing it soft so that it became something else—the moon of a drowned land. She walked near the edge of the water, listening to the soft *quork* of the frogs and the household chatter of the ducks, all of which had scuttled to one corner of the pond upon her arrival.

The last time she had been here she had been pregnant with Isabelle and Conor had been just a tot. The acknowledgement of how much time had passed since that day gave her a hollow sensation. She always knew the date, and measured it from the day Casey had disappeared.

She took a few deep breaths, not really taking in the scenery in front of her, realizing suddenly that she was angry. While she had been upset by William Bright's story, able to understand the poor girl's plight, and horrified that her short life had ended in such a terrible fashion, her primary emotion right now was anger. For the truth was, his final words to her had upset her more than she cared to admit. There had been a time when Casey's presence and love had kept her as safe as a woman might expect to be in such a hard land. It was clear that was no longer true, for now she was a woman alone with two small and very vulnerable children, which in turn made her that much more vulnerable as well. She had put herself under the protection of Noah Murray and she had taken the steps that led people to believe he was now a man in her life, if not indeed *the* man. Gossip was as rife in a small Irish village, after all, as it was anywhere else.

Part of her anger was directed toward Casey himself, she knew. Because he had not come home and had disappeared leaving her with what might become a lifetime of unanswered questions.

She closed her eyes against the peaceful scene in front of her, wishing that she could bring that peace inside herself, could feel a bit of it, even if only for a few minutes of respite. And yet, would she? After all, to feel peace would seem like a betrayal of Casey. It was moot anyway, as she knew she wasn't capable of any sort of tranquility right now, as much as she might long for it.

If she didn't open her eyes, maybe she could transport herself back to the last time they had been here together and could find one of those rifts that she imagined existed on this old estate. They had been sitting by the big boulder down near the pond's north end, Casey wet and laughing from playing in the reeds with Conor, her keeping a tight eye on their son as he mucked about in the mud, rocks clutched happily in his hands, and more disreputable objects shoved in his pockets. Conor was one of nature's natural magpies, and had been since he was old enough to grasp things between thumb and finger.

The day was a beautiful one, the light that pale, soft green that spoke of all things new and growing, things beginning, both root and soil moving, opening up, burgeoning with life—rather like her own self, six months pregnant and feeling like a waddling duck.

The rosebuds were just opening, giving a filmy glimpse of the wash of pearl pink that would cascade down the broken walls and through the wild hedges in another week. Finbar was picking his way through what she feared was a patch of stick burrs. Half of her mind was rebuilding the estate, planting it with Elizabethan herbs and Irish wild flowers, and peopling it with the lords and ladies of that time, while the other half wondered what to make for dinner, watched her son, and tried to remember how long since the baby had last moved. Such were the vagaries of a pregnant woman's mind. She was lying on a patch of dry grass, her head in her husband's lap, one hand held lightly over the contents of her belly.

"Do you think he was part of the Flight of the Earls?" she asked, for her husband was well versed in all his Irish history, not just the parts rife with rebels. He would know the history of the man who had once lived and ruled here.

"No, he wasn't. He'd led an attack on an English fort near Dublin, set fire to the colony an' was considered a traitor for his deeds. He got what traitors got from the British—no mercy an' the headsman's axe. They put his head on a pike as a warnin' to any other rebel Irish who might get ideas. But ye know, we Irish, a head on a pike just encourages us. My da used to refer to them as the 'Twilight Lords', bein' that it was the twilight of the Celtic world."

"It's a twilight place—an edge place, so it's fit that a twilight lord should have lived here." She reached up and brushed a stray lock of hair out of his eyes. "Maybe if we came here at twilight we'd slip back in time and the house would be whole again, and the lords not yet fled the country."

"Aye," Casey said encouraging her flight of fancy. "An' would ye like that, to be there in the Celtic twilight, before the English razed what was left of us to the ground?"

"I would, though maybe not forever. I'm rather fond of hot baths and kitchen appliances, after all. Likely I would have been the scullery maid anyway."

"You?" Casey said softly. "No, I think not, Jewel. Ye were born to be a lady, there's no mistakin' such a thing. Ye're my lady, after all. Which makes me what—the highwayman or the boot black boy?"

"Outlaw suits you best—stirring up rebellion around the countryside."

"After havin' made off with the earl's daughter."

"And knocking her up, not once but several times, bad man."

She could conjure it up in her mind's eye: the house, the grounds, the clothes, the music drifting out on the wind, played by an old blind harper. The twilight lord, the last of the great Celtic chieftain-warriors, knowing his world was dissolving around him as certainly as time had crumbled the walls of his house. The English had put paid to what was left of the Celtic world, thinking them barbaric and savage, belonging to a world of myth and legend and not having a place in the modern universe.

"What happened to his wife?"

"She died givin' birth not long after he was executed. Their children were orphaned and turned out of the house. Heaven only knows what happened to them."

She shivered a little, despite the warmth of the day. Had she been a woman of that time, she knew it was highly likely, with the number of pregnancies she'd had, that she might not be alive at this time in her life. Conor's birth had been straightforward, but she remembered the fear that had accompanied it all the same.

"Ye're driftin' off to dark thoughts," Casey said, "I can tell because ye've a wee crease above yer nose. Ye always get that when ye're troublin' over somethin'."

"I suppose I was only thinking about how many women died in childbirth in those times," she said.

"An' ye're thinkin' about yer own impendin' labor, I suppose."

She shot him a very green look.

"Darlin', it's only natural that ye should feel that way. Women did die in childbirth a great deal in the past, so it could be that it's a sort of ancestral memory, passed down through the blood."

There was something to what he said for she could feel those women in her blood, the ones who had died during the most natural process on earth.

"You can feel the ghosts here, can't you?"

"I'd think ye have enough Irish blood in ye, Jewel, to know that ghosts are real an' don't require our belief. They come to us in any manner of ways. Sometimes it might only be through memory, but the haunting is real enough."

"I'd come back if I could, I'd haunt you," she said and plucked the clover he was chewing from the corner of his mouth.

"Would ye?" He quirked a brow at her, all lechery. "It would be quite the experience, I'd imagine, makin' love to a ghost. Ye'd not have the limits of flesh, so just imagine the sort of things ye could get up to. I'd be utterly at yer mercy."

"Are you saying you aren't now?" It was her turn to quirk a brow.

He laughed, and leaned over to kiss her. "Aye, ye've a point there, woman."

He looked oddly serious all at once, the playful banter gone. "I would haunt ye, too. I'd like to think I could come to comfort ye when ye needed it. When ye wanted me."

"Then you'd have to be with me all the time because I would always want you."

He took a hand and smoothed her hair away from her face, and then held her chin while he looked into her eyes.

"Aye, it seems so now, an' I feel the sense of what ye say, but it'd not be right to live wantin' a phantom by yer side all the time. Life is for the livin', after all. An' I would not want ye to be alone all yer life, ye do know that?"

"Casey—" she began, wanting to cut him off, wanting to stem the words she knew he meant to say.

"Jewel," he said firmly, "just listen for a moment, would ye? My da always said live life to the fullest, hope for the best, plan for the future, an' sort all yer business as if today is yer last. I want ye to know what's what an' where, in case anything at all should happen."

"Nothing is going to happen to you," she said, glaring at him. Conor's small head popped up from where he was digging a good-sized hole that was already filling with water. His big dark eyes were wide with concern. He always responded to any upset in her tone. She smiled reassuringly at him and he went back to his digging.

"Aye, well," Casey said with some exasperation, "I'm not plannin' on it or anything, but it's irresponsible to act as if we're in a fairy tale where naught can touch us."

"Just don't, just please..." she pleaded. She understood the sense of what he was saying, but didn't want to hear it. She felt as if it were courting the dark fates to speak such things aloud, especially when she was pregnant.

He took in the look on her face and sighed. "Darlin', come here." He coaxed her into his arms so that her head was against his chest. She held herself stiffly, still upset at his words. "Lord woman, ye're stubborn as a goose an' a mule combined. I'm not seekin' trouble, only tryin' to make it less should it come, regardless of our intentions."

"I'm just feeling fragile; I did when I was pregnant with Conor too." She capitulated to his touch and settled into his arms, breathing in the calming scent of him.

"Aye, I know, I maybe picked a poor time to bring up this topic, only I think it's not wise to put off until tomorrow what can be dealt with today."

"I love you, man. I love you so much that I can't breathe or think straight at the idea that you might not be here with me, every day of our lives."

"It's the same for me, Pamela, surely ye know that? But everyone makes wills an' talks about matters that need to be known should somethin' happen. Only should, not when."

"Can we just wait until after the baby comes, Casey? I just can't talk about these things right now. Just until after the baby comes."

"Aye," he held her tighter, putting his face in the curve of her neck and kissing her softly there. "It can wait for now."

She wanted to stand here forever and hang onto him, cling to the echo of his voice, the feel of his hands on her, the comfort of his body and presence. She wanted him to tell her what to do, how to proceed and wanted him to tell her to keep waiting, to keep faith because if she did, if she tossed every bit of salt over her shoulder, avoided every black cat and ladder, carved their initials into the bark of an oak under a midnight moon, then he would come back to her. He would arrive just as the fairy tales promised the man would if you obeyed all the rituals and signs and portents. But for the sake of their children she could not do that.

'Should time dissolve this prison, or prison dissolve such time...'

The Jack Stuart line ran through her head, and she thought for the first time she truly felt the import of the words, and wondered at what crossroads of grief and time Jamie had been poised when he wrote them.

She took a long breath and allowed the sounds of the world to return, the frogs and the ducks, the distant bleat of lambs and the chug of a car passing on the road above. She turned and walked into the woods, on the path to her car, back to a life in which she well knew she might never hear her husband's voice again. But at the edge of the parkland she turned and looked back to where the stone sat, ancient and imperturbable.

"I should have let you tell me, man. I'm sorry for that, I'm sorry I didn't let you say what you needed to say."

Chapter Fifteen

No Small Thing

IT WAS ON A WARM DAY in late April that Patrick took Pamela and the children to meet his new boss. Kate was spending the day with Noah and he was seizing the opportunity to introduce two people whom he thought had much in common, even if it wasn't obvious on the surface. He sensed that the old codger would be good for Pamela, and vice versa. He hoped to heaven he wasn't wrong, because Tomas could be very off-putting when in a sour mood.

He cast a glance over his shoulder into the back seat of the car, where his nephew and niece sat. Conor was utterly absorbed in a picture book about birds that Jamie had given him, and Isabelle was gabbling like a tiny magpie in a lovely swooping baby voice. He felt a wave of emotion sweep through his chest. He loved these children of his brother's as much as if they were his own, which he supposed they were in part, now that Casey was gone. He glanced sideways then at his sister-in-law, and felt that strange hollowness he often did when he was with her. It was her grief, he knew, and he better than anyone understood her loss, because in many ways it was his own too.

They chatted about many things on the trip to Tomas' house, everything from the state of the construction company to the eruption of Isabelle's latest tooth. He had kept careful watch of Pamela since his brother's disappearance, and shared the same fears Jamie held for her—fearing that she might actually grieve herself into a serious illness. He wasn't fool enough to believe she would ever get past the loss of his brother, if it should turn out that the loss was permanent, but he thought she might make her way back to life eventually, given time and love.

"Kate said ye've stopped visitin' the police." What he really wanted to talk about was just whom she had turned to after that.

She shrugged, looking out the window. "They aren't inclined to help me, to put it politely. I check in every two weeks still, fruitless as that endeavor feels. We're on our own with this, Pat."

"That's not entirely true, is it? Kate told me about yer deal with Noah."

"You sound like you disapprove, Patrick," she said.

He didn't answer at once, because the truth was he didn't approve, in fact the whole mess reminded him of something Casey had once said about Pamela.

'She's pure bloody reckless, an' ye might as well try to stop a train with yer bare hands as stop the woman when she's taken a notion into that head of hers.'

He couldn't fault her. He understood why she had struck a deal with Noah, only he was very much afraid she wasn't going to get what she wanted from it and that the price might end up being far higher than she anticipated. Then again, perhaps there was no price too high in her mind. It was that notion that worried him more than anything.

"Ye know what he is, Pamela, an' yes that gives me no little worry."

"Yes, I know what he is; I know exactly what sort of man it is I've asked for help." Her voice was cool, and there was an edge of steel in it. She would not be dissuaded and he knew it was best to let it lie for now.

He turned down the crooked drive to Tomas' house then, and Pamela's attention was caught by the avenue of overgrown, shambling beeches that provided a long and enchanted entry to Tomas' property.

"Oh my goodness," Pamela said, head craned so that she could see up ahead. The trees formed an overarching tunnel of ancient smooth-barked branches. Today the pale spring sunshine wove its way through the new leaves, and the long tunnel looked like the portal to a fairy world. And then they came around the corner and the house rose into view.

"Oh, Patrick," Pamela said softly, her hands going to her chest. "It's beautiful."

He wasn't sure about beautiful, but he had known Pamela would love it, as she always loved broken things. And there was a beauty to it, if a somewhat moth-eaten one. It was something straight out of a fairy tale, but a fairy tale with dark things at its core: impenetrable woods, sly crones, moldering huts, and wise old men who didn't always have the best of intentions. There was, literally, a tree growing up through one part of the roof, a huge old spreading oak, which in this season was newly leafed with a shimmer of pale lemony green. The roof around it was built tight though some of the shingles were curled up on the edges, where the spread of the oak had ousted them from their positions. The shrubbery around the gates and the front of the house was overgrown and the house seemed to glower out its windows, peering over the brambles and branches, the cascades of ivy and clambering rose cane. The paint was faded from what had once been white to a soft grey. The great double doors that fronted the house were arched, and had once clearly been beautiful, but were battered by time and weather now to a nondescript pattern and color. It was hard to know where to look, for there were miniature turrets and a tower on one corner complete with stained glass windows that had been shattered inward at some point and never repaired, and a walled off garden at the other end, with briar rose cane throwing an impenetrable guard over and around the crumbling stone walls.

He pulled the car to a halt and they sat quietly, Pamela taking in the details and Pat watching her.

"It's disappointed," she said and Pat started from his reverie.

"What's disappointed?"

"The house," she replied. "It expected to be filled with children and warmth and light, but it never was and it's disappointed."

Pat raised a brow at her.

She colored up and shook her head. "Don't listen to me; I'm just having one of my flights of fancy."

"No, it's not that, it's that ye sound like Casey. He always felt houses held emotion too, that they were the sum of all the energy of those that had once lived in them. Yer own home, for instance, he always said he knew the people that had once lived there had loved each other well and known joy, as well as sorrow, because he could feel it from the first time he walked through it."

"I know he did," she said softly.

"Of course ye do," he replied, feeling ridiculous. Pamela knew Casey in ways he never had. His brother had told him once that Pamela held his soul between her two hands, only he didn't intend to make that too clear to her being that she was well aware of her power over him as it was.

"Well, let's beard the old lion in his den," he said grimly, causing Pamela to arch a dainty brow at him in question. They stepped from the car, Conor scrambling out on his own, with Pat steadying him so that he didn't fall in one of the several mud puddles that pocked the drive. Pamela picked Isabelle up, snugging her to her hip and then together they walked up to the large double doors that fronted the house.

Tomas answered the door immediately, something Pat had never known him to do. In fact, he'd had to scale the ivy to the second floor and crawl through a window he knew was never locked to gain entry the last time he had been here—into the room, no less, where a badger lived—and search the house for Tomas, only to find him passed out, drunk as the proverbial lord of the manor, in the vast library fireplace.

"Tomas Egan, this is my sister-in-law, Pamela Riordan, an' my nephew, Conor, an' niece, Isabelle. Pamela, this is Tomas, the most feared man of the law in all the kingdom."

Tomas took one look at Pamela, as she stood from taking off Isabelle's wee coat, her face flushed from the warmth of the day and the green eyes deep as emeralds against the rose and ivory of her skin. She looked well today, Pat thought, and the smile she gave the old reprobate was a lovely thing to behold. He had been right to bring her here, and he felt relief sweep over him.

"Christ have mercy on a man's heart," Tomas said, sweeping an elaborate bow over her hand. "This is yer sister-in-law?" he turned to Pat, grizzled eyebrows raised. "Where have ye been hidin' her?"

Pat merely smiled, feeling rather smug. He had never seen Tomas flustered, but he believed he was witnessing it now.

Tomas fussed about, taking Pamela's coat and the children's, offering tea and whiskey and juice and even sandwiches. Pamela accepted the tea, wisely passing on the sandwiches, much to Patrick's relief. The state of the man's cupboards did not bear thinking about.

"I feel I should apologize for gawkin' at ye like some gormless boy, but I suspect ye're well used to men starin' at ye, so I won't. I will tell ye this—were I a few decades younger, ye'd never be able to beat me from yer doorstep."

Pamela raised an eyebrow at him, and laughed. "Patrick didn't tell me you were a charmer."

"Didn't he, then?" Tomas winked one red spackled blue eye at her. "Could be the lad doesn't bring out the charmer in me."

Tomas offered Pamela his arm, and she took it, Isabelle snugged to her shoulder, small rose petal fist stuck firmly in her mouth, which was glistening with drool. She smiled at Pat, one of those four tooth grins that simply melted him. He grinned back causing her to laugh and put her face down to her mother's shoulder in delight.

"So I imagine wee Patrick has brought ye here to seduce me into taking his latest mad case, hasn't he?"

"I don't know," she said. "Have you, Patrick—brought me here to seduce Mr. Egan for your own nefarious ends?"

He opened his mouth to protest his innocence, but Tomas waved a wrinkled hand at him. "Never ye mind, boyo. I know well enough what it is ye're up to. I mean it's not as though we're still wadin' through the muck of the first one ye brought to me."

Tomas turned back to Pamela, not waiting for Pat to protest. "Ye may commence the seduction in a few minutes," his eyes twinkled under the grizzled brows, "but may I show ye about the house before ye start?"

"Oh, yes please," Pamela said eagerly.

Tomas took them around the bottom floor to begin, saving the jewel for last, for it was the upper story, Pat knew, that held the greatest enchantment.

The kitchen was large and shabby, but it held a cozy homeliness in its scuffed floor and beamed roof. There was an enormous old ceramic sink, filled near to overflowing with dishes, though Pat knew Tomas had an ancient housekeeper who came out from the village once a week to haunt the halls, and apparently did little else. There was an Aga in one corner, puffing out heat like an old man with a pipe, and a long butcher block table that looked as if someone had hacked it here and there with a sword at some point.

"When was the house built?" Pamela asked, as Pat swung Conor up so he might have a better look out the windows. Conor was a child of the outdoors and was far more intrigued by the weedy pond he could just glimpse through the open back door than he was by ancient architectural details.

"Durin' the 16th century," Tomas said. "It's a bit of a bastard's house, bein' that changes have been made in every era since. But it's got the original bones an' some things that were native to that time. There's a buttery, an' a beer cellar an' a salt house an' dry larder. They lived large did the Elizabethans. If ye can rightly ever call an Irishman such. There are two hundred an' forty-three oak beams in this house. Ye can see if ye look just there that there was a fire here long ago. The English tried to burn the family out durin' the Nine Years' War." They had moved out into the hallway, where oak panels lined both sides of the long expanse and scorch marks were wraith-like stains upon the walls and ceiling above.

"The man who built it must have been one of the great lords, to own such a house," Pamela said, lightly touching one of the panels.

"I think the one who lived here was well in favor with the Queen, but then he fell out as so many did, durin' the Tudor conquest of Ireland. Now come on up the stairs, there's somethin' there to see that I think ye'll fancy."

The stairs were a long smooth flight, above which ran an open gallery that had once been for minstrels to sit and play. Pat knew which room it was that Tomas wanted to show Pamela, and he knew why. He only hoped the tenant was out for the day.

Tomas opened a door near the very end of the gallery and then stood back so that Pamela and the children could take in the view.

"Oh my," she said, breath held in wonder. Tomas smiled, just looking at her. Pamela had that effect on men, Pat thought. They took happiness in making her happy, even when they were complete strangers who weren't likely to encounter the woman ever again.

The oak grew up through the center of the room, its large trunk twisted and curved, boughs stretching out to the corners, two resting on the floor, like ancient arms that had tired of their burdens and had lain down for a rest. The light in the room was like that of sunlight under water, restless and green, flimmering and flickering in the corners. In a fairy tale house, this was the core. Conor's eyes were wide, and Pat wondered how long it would take before he asked his mother if they could grow a tree in their own home.

She walked into the room, the pale green light washing over her skin, lending her an otherworldly aspect as if she moved over the floor of the sea.

"A mermaid," Tomas said, with some satisfaction. "That's what she puts me in mind of, a mermaid cast out from the sea with her babies."

As a metaphor it was apt, Pat thought, because she was like a mermaid cast out from the sea, only the sea had been his brother; which was a rather ironic metaphor considering Casey's views on the ocean.

Just then something moved, a flutter of white in one of the dark corners of the room. It drifted out, a phantasm of floating alabaster. Pamela jumped back, startled, automatically clutching Isabelle to her chest, and cradling the back of her head. Pat automatically stood in front of them, Conor peering out from around his uncle's long legs, more curious than afraid.

It was a white bird, more particularly an owl, flapping its wings in a panic and then rising up through the branches of the tree, like a ghost in the mottled green light. The owl settled up near the ceiling, peering down at them with great eyes that were a deep gold tourmaline in the strange light.

"Sorry about that," Tomas said, "she usually sleeps up high in the branches, not down near the floor."

"They say owls are messengers to the underworld," Pamela said, voice quiet. "They would guide souls through the transition from this world to the next." There was a look of longing on her face that Pat had to turn away from.

"They are also the carriers of wisdom and have the ability to see in the dark. I would imagine that means spiritual darkness as well," Tomas added, his tone gentle.

Pamela smiled. "Forgive me; I tend to look for portents even in my morning cup of tea these days."

"There's naught wrong with that," Tomas said and Pat wondered if he had walked through to another dimension, what with Tomas' gentlemanly behavior and the scent of cleaning fluid all about the house.

"She did just about cause a fainting fit, I have to admit. I didn't expect an owl in an upstairs bedroom."

"Aye, she's just the bit spooky, but 'tis her room, well her tree to be more accurate. She likes the quiet of it, I think. She's the only one brave enough to share the room with the badger."

"The badger?" Pamela echoed, turning to Pat with a look of bemusement.

"Aye, Basil, he's my most constant lodger, we rub along together rather well."

"It's because the beast is likely yer spirit animal," Pat observed drily.

Tomas snorted, which was the man's version of a laugh. Considering that he was usually about as socially malleable as a badger that had been poked with a stick one time too often, he might well laugh. Pamela had clearly worked no small magic with her presence.

"Shall we go downstairs where it's warm, an' ye can tell me what it is ye've come here to discuss?"

"That would be grand," Pamela said and smiled again. Pat felt a profound gratitude to the deities that he had thought to bring her here. Though in truth, it was a bit more of an earthly deity as Muck, now running with the story of wee Jane had put the thought in his head.

The old buzzard was actually possessed of a great deal of charm, Pat thought, following Pamela down the stairs with Conor in his arms. Apparently all he needed to display it was the company of a beautiful woman.

There was a roaring fire in the study, which was slightly less shambolic than was its norm. Apparently Tomas had made some effort at tidying up. The room actually looked welcoming rather than appearing like Miss Havisham's study, which Pat had taken to calling it privately.

Isabelle was deposited onto the floor on a clean quilt, several small, brightly colored toys arrayed around her. Pamela had come prepared to make an afternoon of it clearly. Good thing too, because it might take that long to convince the old man to even consider the madness they were about to propose. Conor had his own set of toys, mostly things Casey had made for him. Today he had brought a small train with him, as well as his bag of treasures from which he was never too far. Pat was always just a little trepidatious when Conor offered him a peek inside the bag—there had been a live frog in it once, which had almost given him a heart attack when it leaped out of the bag, narrowly missing his nose.

Tomas presented each of the adults with slightly smudgy tumblers of whiskey and Pat saw Pamela sigh a little. The woman did not have the palate for whiskey, despite her long association with one of the best whiskey makers in the world. She made a slight face as the smell hit her nose, but gamely sipped it when Tomas turned around and looked at her.

He noted how she was dressed. He had gotten so used to seeing her in jeans and his brother's old shirts that the transformation was startling. She wore a pale pink blouse paired with a light grey skirt. It was businesslike but also decidedly feminine and designed, he thought, to display her charms to best advantage. She had disarmed Tomas from the minute he had opened the door, but she had come here planning, he thought, to do just that. She sat back, crossing one long leg over the other, and took a swallow of the whiskey, green eyes leveled over the top of the tumbler at the old man, who was eyeing her back with undisguised admiration.

"So, Mr. Egan, shall we get down to business?"

"Aye, hit me with it, girl. Clearly the lad has brought you here to see if he can't stun me into agreeing to whatever madness he's got in mind."

"How does taking the police force to court strike you?" she asked sweetly and took another sip of her whiskey.

Tomas laughed and sat back in his big chair, shaking his head. "Oh Lord, I might have known it was goin' to be this. On what charge exactly?"

"Murder," she said.

Pat leaned back into his chair, and smiled to himself. He might not even need to talk; he could just watch the show. He had not seen this side of Pamela before, though his brother had told him of it.

"All right ye've got my attention young lady, but ye'd better have a damn good story to tell me."

"Patrick did bring me here to tell you about it. I know the details best, after all."

"Aye, an' the boy well knows that a man is not as likely to say no to a lovely face like yours, as he is to an ugly mug like his own."

She smiled and it was such a thing of lovely innocence that Pat almost believed she had no knowledge of exactly what she was up to.

Pamela took a second, smoothing the line of her skirt down and taking another sip of her whiskey. "First, I think it's important that you know that it was William Bright who brought this story to me."

"An' why is the likes of William Bright talkin' to you?"

She eyed the old man steadily over the rim of her tumbler, the whiskey glowing gold in its belly and casting a pale flickering light over her face. "Because he knows me from a prior meeting. And I know Patrick and Patrick knows Muck. It's that simple."

She sketched in the story of Jane, and the suspicious circumstances surrounding the girl's alleged suicide. It was bald in the telling, and Patrick marveled that the woman knew to keep emotion from the tale, and only give the old lawyer what was necessary. But then he remembered the tales his brother had told him of her handling of politicians in Boston, and thought it was a natural gift for her, this—knowing how to gauge what each situation required. There were a number of reasons that Jamie had chosen her to run his companies in his absence, and her deft handling of people wasn't the least of them.

When she finished, Tomas sat silent for a moment, a gleam in the blue eyes and one finger tapping his upper lip thoughtfully. Tomas had the face of a great poker player—entirely unreadable. Pat felt his pulse pick up a little as the silence stretched out. Pamela, on the other hand, still looked cool and completely unruffled.

"So, Pamela, are ye like yer madman over here thinkin' we should go after the RUC for this?"

"Just the guilty party," she said, not so much as blinking under the beetling gaze of the old solicitor.

Tomas laughed, long and loudly. "Just the guilty party is it? Well, that's no problem then, is it? As a point of interest, does madness run in the family, did ye catch it from his brother?"

"Shouldn't the supposed law keepers be subject to the law?"

"In another country, Miss Pamela, I'd agree, but in this one that doesn't work. The kill rate for justice reformers in this country bein' rather high last time I checked."

"So we all stop expecting or hoping for justice? That seems an odd attitude for a lawyer, if I may say so."

Tomas smiled. "Miss Pamela, I expect that ye don't ask anyone for permission to speak yer mind. But I'll tell ye this for free—lawyers are some of the most cynical bastards about. Young Patrick hasn't had the idealism beaten from him yet, but a few years of this work will do the job to him."

Pamela arched one sooty brow at him. "I don't think so. Riordans are some of the most stubborn people you're likely to come across and my husband always said his brother was the most stubborn of the lot."

"Aye, well," Tomas cast a look in Pat's direction, "clearly yer husband was a shrewd judge of character."

"He knew his brother well, I daresay."

"An' how exactly do ye think we're to go about doin' this?"

"Wrongful death," she said, cool as a lemon ice. "If it's a civil case directed at one man, the police are less likely to see it as a direct attack on them. Not to mention it will be easier to win."

They had discussed this before, after Pat had taken the time to mull the whole situation over in his mind, as well as having a rather spirited talk with Muck about it. Approaching the situation in this manner wouldn't eradicate the risk but it would lessen it substantially.

"I need to change the baby," Pamela said, bending down to pick up Isabelle who had begun to fuss. "I'll leave you gentlemen to confer upon the matter."

Tomas watched her leave the room with a bemused expression. He was anything but bemused when he turned his regard back to Pat though.

"That was a bit of a dirty play on yer part, man."

"How so?" Pat replied with the innocence of a lamb.

Tomas snorted. "Has anyone ever said no to that woman in her life? If so, I'd like to meet the man with the fortitude for it."

"There's a cardinal in Boston who would likely agree with ye," Pat said. "Ye'll do it then, ye'll take the case?"

Tomas gave him a hard look. "No, son, *we'll* take the case. Ye're not sidesteppin' this. Ye brought it to me, ye're goin' to help me see if it's got merit. I tell ye it will be a trial by fire, no less. The feckin' RUC are goin' to see this as a direct attack on them. But if Miss Pamela there can keep such as William Bright sweet, we'll maybe have a whisper of a prayer."

They spent a few moments then talking over what would need to be done simply to get the unwieldy gears of the law in motion.

Pamela returned with a freshly-changed and fed Isabelle, who gave one of her completely infectious grins to Tomas. He grinned back, scaring the baby who put her head to her mother's shoulder, peeking out now and again at the white-haired man. Conor walked over to Tomas, completely unafraid of him despite his rather gruff manner and handed him one of his little cars.

Tomas looked up from where Conor was now making tracks in the dust on his desk. "Stay to dinner, Miss Pamela. I think ye owe me the pleasure of yer company considerin' what ye've just talked me into."

"All right," she said gamely. Pat thought that she was either brave or mad; being that the thought of any food Tomas might conjure up in that cavernous old kitchen was likely to be, at best, inedible and at worst poisonous.

"Ye needn't fear, Patrick," Tomas said, "I'm goin' to run to the local chipper to get dinner. I wouldn't inflict what passes for cookin' in this house on this lovely woman an' her children."

It was a very pleasant evening in the end, and Patrick was glad for more than one reason that he had brought Pamela here to present their case. She smiled and even laughed at one point, and he thought for perhaps a moment or two she managed to put thoughts of his brother to the side.

Tomas saw them out when they took their leave. He bent over Pamela's hand with a flourish and kissed it. "It has been a pleasure, be sure to come back as often as ye please an' bring yer wee ones with ye, it's lovely to hear the noise of children in this old house."

"We will come again," Pamela said, and Pat saw that she meant it. She had thoroughly enjoyed the company of the old curmudgeon.

Tomas stood watching them until he was a tiny figure in the rear view mirror. As soon as they cleared the drive, Pamela collapsed against the seat and let out a long breath. Pat looked over at her and smiled.

"Well done, you. Though I'm not sure I should be thankin' ye all things considered."

"Probably not," she laughed, but it was a hollow sound.

"Are ye all right?"

"I'm fine, just tired. It's been a long day and Isabelle was up at five this morning."

"Are ye sleepin' any better at night?"

She shrugged. "A bit here and there. I sleep with Conor in his bed, or I sleep on the couch downstairs. I manage in bits and pieces. That applies to sleep and life," she said, voice as insubstantial as an abandoned moth's wing. "I'm trying to live a normal life, however much that is possible in this country. For their sake," she nodded toward the back seat, where both children were already fast asleep.

"Ye have to do it for yer own sake too, Pamela."

"I know, Pat. Right now that seems like a very tall order, but some day I'm sure I'll feel like it matters again."

She neatly changed the subject then, as she often did when the topic of moving on with her life came up.

"Are you certain about this, Pat? What you're embarking on if charges are brought against this man?"

It was a question he had asked himself more than once since Pamela had told the story to him. He had spent several restless nights thinking it over. Kate, being Kate, had said he must follow what his heart felt was right.

His heart said that a man had to believe in something larger than himself and in this case whatever small comfort justice could bring to the girl and her family. His head said he was a mad man for even considering tangling with the forces of law and order, such as they were, in the Six Counties. But then what was a life lived without conviction, without passion for a cause greater than oneself?

"Aye, Pamela, I have thought it through. It's a rock an' a hard place, isn't it? I need somethin' bigger than my own well-bein' in order to really be alive. Do ye understand?"

She turned toward him, her expression unreadable in the dim of the car. "I understand, but I am afraid too, Pat. I don't want to lose you because of some nebulous idea of a larger purpose, which may not amount to anything in the courts, and could get you killed."

"Aye, I know that, Pamela. I promise to take as many precautions as I can. Life is a chancy thing under the best of circumstances, but I'll try to keep away from the razor's edge as best as I'm able. Bringin' it as a civil suit makes it less risky."

She nodded, the sparkling and witty woman of an hour ago now gone. At times like this, when her defenses were low, her grief was palpable. He had known she loved his brother a very great deal. He thought perhaps he had not really understood just how much until these last few months.

Pat helped her take the children in and settle them in their beds and then checked that all the doors and windows were battened down tight for the night. For a few minutes he stood in the kitchen with her. It struck him how tired and thin she was looking, concerns that Jamie had voiced the week before. His worry must have shown in his expression because she looked at him and said, "I'm fine, Pat. Kate will be worried, it's getting very late."

He gave her a quick hug, shocked by how insubstantial she felt in his arms. At least she had eaten her dinner tonight. He left then, feeling helpless and inadequate to the task of caring for his brother's family.

He halted in the yard, the night cold around him. He worried for her, in more ways than just the obvious. For one there was her association with Noah. He knew why she had gone to the man, but he wished the woman had the sense to be afraid. Damned if he knew what to do about any of it. He knew had the shoe been on the other foot, Casey would have felt the same. He wished someone were here to give him advice and guide him in what was best for Pamela and the children.

He spoke then to his brother, here in the yard of his home, spoke with frustration and fear, and with the worry that he might always be speaking to a ghost. "Ye promised me, man, ye promised me ye'd always have my back, don't ye remember that?"

He looked up at the sky, Orion setting in the west, with all its frosted glitter. It recalled the night they had picked out their stars—him, his father and Casey. His daddy had told them each to pick a star.

"Pick one, pick a star from the sky an' it will be yours, all yer life."

"Ye can't keep a star for yerself," Casey said, sounding rather dubious about the idea.

"An' who is to say ye can't, boyo?"

"I don't know, but I think the priests might have somethin' to say about it."

"Well, we just won't tell them, 'twill be a secret between the three of us. Now pick a star."

They all lay silent, putting thought into their choices. It was cold and each of their breaths was a slipstream of sparkling frost upon the air. They were well bundled up and his daddy had brought a thermos of cocoa for them which he poured out now as they mused over which star in the sky would be theirs.

"Betelgeuse," Casey said a moment later, his voice certain.

"Why that one?"

"I like the color of it, an' it's a warrior's shoulder that gives strength to his arm."

The choice suited his big brother, even at his age, for he had much of the natural warrior about him.

"It's a warrior's heart that gives him most of his strength," Pat said quietly.

"Aye, ye're right, wee man," Brian said and stroked the soft curls on his son's head. "Ye know warriors must take care for those around them, those that are not given to the constant fightin'." This said with a bit of playful teasing, being that Casey had been in trouble twice in the last month for fighting.

"I'll keep watch over my brother," Casey said, with an unaccustomed serious tone to his voice, "if that's what ye're hintin' at, Daddy."

"Well, no son, I wasn't hintin' at that, but it's good to know ye'll protect him should he need it. An' what star would ye choose, Patrick?"

"The blue one," he said.

"That's Rigel, Orion's foot," he said. "Why that one?"

"Because it carries the warrior into his adventures," Pat said.

They were quiet for a time after that, the three of them sipping their cocoa and staring up into the night. The sky was clear as an angel's breath, each star a pinwheeling fire within that ether. Lying there with the earth soft beneath their bodies, it was easy to feel the movement of the planet; it was as natural as the blood moving through their veins.

It had been one of those rare perfect nights, held carefully in his memory, tucked away in a box in a room he didn't visit often because it was too painful. He thought of a quote his father had shared with them that night, a night which now seemed a lifetime ago.

'*And I sense when I look at the stars*
That we are children of life.
Death is small.'

Brian had taken his hand and held it as he spoke the words, and Pat had snuggled up to him, feeling happy and safe, because his father and his brother were there with him, and thus his world was complete.

He took a breath of the raw spring night and looked back at the house. He could see Pamela moving about the kitchen, putting things to rights before she went to her sleepless bed.

"No, death is *not* small," he said, and knew not if he spoke merely to his own anger and grief, or to his departed family. "It's not small at all."

Part Two

Count the Stars in the Sky
May 1976-July 1976

Chapter Sixteen

You Take a Breath,
and Then You Take Another

PAMELA WAS LOST, and not, she thought, in her usual fashion. She had dropped off a set of blueprints down near a wee town called Keady, and had made a wrong turning somewhere, only to find herself in unfamiliar territory. She was tired and her mind was filled with architectural drawings and specs, which she only half understood, as well as orders for wood and stone and concrete, and just where a woman might find a traditional thatcher at short notice.

She was learning the business slowly, but it was a hard curve and with two small children at home for whom she was the only parent, she didn't feel she had the wits left by day's end to get further up on her construction know-how. She had hired a new supervisor, though she could ill afford him, who did know what the hell he was doing, and thankfully didn't seem to mind that he worked for a woman. This was only in the most nominal sense, as he went ahead and did what needed doing without making a fuss. She had her suspicions about where he had come from and just why he was willing to work for so little.

The road she was on was like many in this part of the countryside, narrow and dark with high hedges, relieved only by the occasional ditch and lay-by cut into the hedges. She pushed down an incipient wave of panic. She slowed down and looked around; there was no one behind her so she could take a moment to get her bearings. She thought she might be somewhere near Noah's farm, and if she could find that, she could make her way home easily from there.

Ahead the road widened, and she spotted a flash of color. It looked like there might be a roadblock. She took a deep breath and felt the panic rise in her chest again. Roadblocks made her very nervous. The soldiers posted to South Armagh were on edge more than their colleagues in Belfast and other locations in Northern Ireland. She didn't blame them, but it was always a very tense few moments while one waited to go through.

She slowed even further, readying herself for the questions and the suspicion. That was when she heard the distinct *rat-a-tat-tat* of an automatic weapon laying down fire and knew this was no ordinary roadblock and the men up ahead were not British soldiers. She realized her mistake too late, for the clothing was indeed khaki green, but balaclavas covered the face of the three men she could see. British Army didn't do that—that left Loyalist paramilitaries or the South Armagh wing of the PIRA and if the latter, then these would be men acting under the law of Noah Murray. Either way the odds were better than even that she was going to be dead in about two minutes if she didn't get the hell out of here.

There was a bus halted in the road, its doors open. Beside the bus there were men standing at the roadside, maybe a dozen of them, and the men in the balaclavas were shooting them. Six men standing, and then five, then four, three, two and then one. The world slowed its spin as she saw the gun at the last man's back, saw each tiny jerk as the bullets entered him, watched him crumple like old cloth, stained and torn, to finish on the ground. The man holding the gun turned then, and looked directly at her.

She yanked the car into reverse, trying not to panic, for the car was old and didn't respond well to bullying of any sort. She heard it slip into gear and put her foot to the gas, knowing that it was going to be hell trying to back up this lane, twisty and narrow as it was. There was little hope that she could outrun these men, even with wheels in her favor. And then the car stalled. She looked up to find the masked gunman walking toward her, gun cocked over his elbow, his steps firm, his mind set on the one task he had to tidy up before getting clear of this massacre.

The entire world telescoped to the barrel of the gun. She said a wordless prayer, too panicked to form coherent thought, a prayer for her babies, that they would be safe, that they would not have to grow up orphans entirely. That if she had to be shot, she would somehow survive it.

She was frozen, cursing the car under her breath, cursing herself for throwing it into a stall. She couldn't take her eyes off the gun, but she didn't fool herself into thinking that making eye contact with her potential killer would help her in any way. The man was close enough, that had he not been so camouflaged behind his balaclava she would have been able to see the color of his eyes and she took a breath, a small ribbon of calm forcing its way through the panic, the strange calm of finality and knowing that she no longer had any control over her own fate.

He could see her face now and she looked back at him, with defiance. She would take that much dignity with her, small as it was. He halted and walked back a step or two. A chill chased hard down her body. Despite the fact that she couldn't see his face, she knew under the balaclava was a man she would recognize. For it was clear that he recognized her. He backed up further and a tiny hope began to grow in her that he wasn't going to kill her here in this deserted laneway. Then the gun came up and she heard the fire even as she felt the impact of it. There was no pain, just a horrid rush of adrenaline, no life rushing past her eyes, just a white void of utter panic. She sat with her hands over her head, until the realization that she was still alive penetrated through her. She raised her head, ever so slowly, not even daring to draw breath, though her chest felt like it was on fire.

The man had returned to the van and was jumping up into the back of it even as she looked. He cast her one last glance over his shoulder, from behind the utter anonymity of his hood and then slammed the van door shut as it roared off up the road and out of her sight. She waited a heart-beat and then another, before getting out of the car, still terrified that they would come back.

The roadway was littered with lunch pails, thermoses and sand-wiches; she nearly tripped over an apple that had come to rest on the lip of the ditch. She counted swiftly, ten men all lying very still, some in such unnatural positions that she knew without checking that they were dead. Just ordinary working class men slaughtered at the side of a lonely road, for the sin of what—being the wrong religion in the wrong place? She suspected it might be retaliatory in nature, for two brothers from a Catholic family had been killed three nights previous for no apparent reason other than bloody sectarian hatred.

She went to each man in his turn, her heart hammering and her breath loud in her ears. It was immediately clear that most could not possibly have survived, for they had been shot at point-blank range. She crossed herself reflexively, then thought that had been a foolhardy thing to do, for if someone was still watching they would know she was Catholic, and she didn't know if these dead men were Catholic or Protestant, though her money would be on Protestant today.

Just then she heard a moan, so quiet that she thought she had imagined it. Then it came again and she knew it was not her imagination; one of the men must be alive. She looked about frantically, for it seemed as if there were bodies everywhere, blood everywhere. Then a hand moved, just the slightest bit, but she was so jumpy it seemed as if he had waved at her. He was half in the ditch and half in the road way.

She crawled over to where he was, too frightened to stand upright and make herself a clear target. His chest was a mess of blood and there was a pool of it gathering beneath him, leaking through into the cracks of the road, shimmering like rubies in the green of the grass. A drift of white blackthorn petals had caught in the man's hair and tumbled through the blood onto the road. The soft, musky scent of them mixed with the acridity of cordite and the copper of blood.

His eyes were a clear blue, his face rough-hewn and he looked like he was in his forties. There was likely a family at home depending on this man. She felt a sweep of rage and despair push down the terror inside her.

"Is there anything I can do for you?" She schooled her face so that he would not know there wasn't a damn thing she could do for him, for it was clear to her it was far too late.

"Could ye hold my hand, lass? I don't want to go all alone."

"Of course," she said softly and took the big, work-roughened hand in hers. She saw that he understood he was not going to live and she felt sorry for him, that the knowledge should come in the wake of such terrible hatred, on a lonely country road with only a strange woman to keep him company in these final moments.

She heard a car pull up, and a door open and was afraid to look for fear one of the men had come back to finish her off. There were steps behind her, and then a voice she knew.

"Jesus—what the hell happened here?"

Pamela took a half breath of relief. It was Noah. She looked up, knowing he didn't need an explanation, the carnage was self-explanatory.

"He's the only one left alive," she said. There was no need to say more, Noah could hear his breathing and see the lake of blood that was still spreading out from under him.

"There's a farm up the lane, I'm goin' to go back an' get them to call for the police an' ambulance. Will ye be all right here, until I get back?"

She nodded and he took a second to look her over, assessing her for injury, before running back to his car. The sound of the car fading down the lane was one of the loneliest sounds she had ever heard. The sun was warm and the sky a tender shade of blue as it was sometimes in April— this cruelest of months. She could smell the bitter leaves of meadowsweet, like some strange, silent melody woven around the echo of gunfire and the screams of men who knew they had seconds left to live.

She turned her attention back to the man whose hand she held. His breath whistled in ever shorter gasps, the blood that pooled beneath him congealing at the edges, so that it was a thick black now under the sheen of sunshine.

"Could you pray?" he asked. Blood bubbled at the corners of his mouth—dark blood. He had been shot through at least one of his lungs. He was drowning in his own blood.

She prayed out loud, voice pitched to encompass the two of them, stumbling and terrified as it was. She prayed for him, and she prayed, she knew, for Casey, prayed that he had not come to an end like this one without someone to hold his hand or to pray for him. She prayed for the man's wife and children, and for her own children and all the children that weren't going to get out of this filthy little war alive. She prayed while blood soaked into her skirt and stockings, coating her skin with its slick lividity.

The man's hand was growing cold. A cloud crossed the face of the sun, and a damp shadow passed over her, tiny drops of rain hitting her face. She knew she needed to move, the police would be here soon and now that the man was dead, it was probably best if she was gone. There weren't any questions she could answer for them, and even if she could it would be suicidally dangerous to do so.

A hand touched her shoulder, and a voice spoke, echoing her own thoughts. She startled, she hadn't heard Noah come back.

"We need to get ye out of here, the police will be here any minute an' as all these dead men are Prods, it's not wise to get caught here."

She let him pull her up; her knees were wobbly still and the road slippery with blood. She had seen many things during her years of living in this country, but somehow none of it had hurt like what she had seen today. She felt like she no longer had any protective covering, as though her nerves were exposed to every cold wind of chance and misfortune that passed.

"Ye'll take my car an' head to my house, I'll bring yers along. Here's the key, now go."

"I don't know that my car will run, one of the men shot it in the engine. Or at least I think that's what he did." She passed a hand over her face, her skin was numb and her lips buzzing with delayed shock.

"Pamela," he said gently, "it is still runnin' but bein' that it has steam comin' from under the hood, I'd as soon drive it myself. The house is only two miles from here, be careful on the way, ye'll not be yerself just now."

She obeyed, feeling like her mind was on autopilot and that some piece of it was going to be back there on that road for some time. The drive to Noah's was a matter of reflex, rather than conscious thought on her part. She was surprised to find herself suddenly shifting the car into park in the front of the tidy farmhouse. She simply sat there, uncertain what to do, though she ought to be safe enough in Noah's car. A strange vehicle in this drive would, she knew, bring men with rifles to the car window.

The events of the last hour began to sink in. She was shaking hard enough that she clutched at the steering wheel in an effort to stabilize herself. She was terribly cold, the blood that soaked her clothing clammy against her skin. The scent of it was thick on the air and she swallowed back a wave of nausea. She wanted Casey so badly that she felt it in the marrow of her bones. He had always been her anchor for every storm, every catastrophe and now there were no arms to run to, there was no security left in her world.

The door opened and she startled, putting her hand to her chest. She looked in the rearview mirror to see her car gently smoking in Noah's drive.

"Come inside," Noah said. She followed him into the house. The kitchen looked surreal in its normality, its warmth and brightness.

"I...I need to get this blood off me," she said, the shaking so hard now that her teeth felt like they were rattling in her head.

He nodded. "Bathroom's right there, I've got hot an' cold runnin' an' all. I'll make tea while you're in there. Could ye take a bite, do ye think?"

She shook her head. "Tea will do, I'm not sure I can keep even that down."

He nodded. "I'll get ye somethin' to wear, ye can't stay in those." He nodded at her gore-stained clothing.

"I'm sorry, I shouldn't have come in like this, I wasn't thinking."

"Well, it was either that or strip down in the yard, an' while I think the boys who work for me would appreciate that, I'm thinkin' you wouldn't. An' a bit of blood isn't likely to bother me."

It was on the tip of her tongue to say, "No, I don't suppose it would." But she quickly thought better of it and kept silent.

He handed her a pile of clothes. "Shirt's mine but it'll do to get ye home, an' the trousers are an old pair of Kate's, they ought to fit ye well enough."

"Thank you," she said and went into the bathroom. It was, like the rest of the house, immaculate and spartan, tiles gleaming and fixtures old but kept in good condition. There was a stack of clean towels to the right of the sink. She washed up as best as she could, grateful to get the blood off her skin. She put her clothes into a neat pile, the bloody parts folded in so she didn't have to see them.

Noah's shirt was too big, but it was clean and soft with many washings. The pants fit well enough. She took a quick glance in the mirror before she went back into the kitchen. She still looked shocked, eyes wide and dark with it, skin pasty white. At least the blood was gone, even if the scent of hot copper still lingered in her nose. She thought about the car and wanted to cry. Casey had picked it up at an auction a few years back and if it couldn't be fixed, it would be another link to him gone. It seemed to her that was what her world consisted of, losing one more link to him, each and every day, even if it was just the turning of the page on the calendar, or finally putting his old jersey away, the one that he'd thrown over the back of the rocking chair in their bedroom the night before he disappeared. She put her hands on the edge of the sink, the chill porcelain steadying her. She took a breath, and then another because that's what you did in this land, you took a breath and hoped to God you were allotted another.

Noah, his sleeves rolled up and slippers on his feet, was just putting tea on the table when she emerged from the bathroom. He appeared entirely unruffled, and was in good clothes. He had been to town from the looks of him. He couldn't have been one of the men in the roadway in balaclava and camouflage, there was no way he could have run off and come back looking like butter wouldn't melt in his mouth a few minutes later. That didn't mean he hadn't ordered the massacre. She couldn't ask, though he knew well enough that she was likely to think it.

She realized, to her consternation, he was looking back and taking in her scrutiny of him. He knew exactly what she was thinking, she could see it in his face, though his expression never changed.

"Drink yer tea," he said.

She sat and took a sip of the tea, it was good and hot, but not scalding and it was sweet with sugar. Did every bloody Irishman know to treat shock with tea and sugar? Noah, she suspected, was more used to dealing out the blows that caused shock than trying to repair the after-effects.

He sat down across from her and drank his own tea, quiet, watching her steadily. It only felt like casual observation though, not as if he was searching her for signs of imminent hysteria.

"I see horrible things all the time. I don't know why this got to me so badly."

"I would imagine," Noah said quietly, "it's because ye're seein' yer husband every time ye go to a scene now. An' while I know ye've seen some dreadful things with yer work, I don't imagine ye've had men shot right in front of yer face before."

"I had a realization when I was out there," she said, looking up to find his eyes on her with a calm curiousness in them. "I want to live, even though most days I feel like I will never draw a deep breath again and I still dread waking up each morning."

"It's how life is," he said, "life asserts itself even when we think it can't possibly want to, it does. Life is ruthless that way, an' it doesn't take our feelings of how things should be into consideration."

"You would tell me, wouldn't you—you would tell me if you ever found out he was dead?"

He regarded her for a long moment. "It's why ye came to me in the first place, no? Because ye know I'm not goin' to be tender about yer feelins'. So yer answer is yes, if I knew, ye would know too."

"It's comforting somehow, that you would tell me, that you wouldn't spare my feelings."

"Ye're a strange one, Pamela."

"I'd rather know, even if it kills me. It would be better than this. I feel like I'm in purgatory much of the time."

He didn't say anything to that, just accepted the words as she said them.

He made a rough dinner for the two of them, and she was shocked to find that she was famished. He fried up potatoes and a rasher of bacon, did up eggs in the bacon fat and put a well heaped plate in front of her when it was cooked. She ate it all and even accepted a slice of bread and two more cups of tea. She pushed her plate away, feeling guilty, but comfortingly full at the same time.

"How can I be hungry after seeing all those men dead and dying? How can I want to eat?"

Noah considered her over his last forkful of potatoes. "It's not uncommon for death, even a violent one, to give a person an appetite. It's like the body needs to reassert that it's alive, an' so ye might find ye're hungry, or thirsty or needin' to bed someone. It's just how it is."

"Is it?" she asked, slightly shocked at how candid he was.

"Aye, it is. Ye've seen more than yer fair share of the horror this country can inflict, did ye never go home an' take yer man straight to bed right after takin' pictures of one of yer dead bodies?"

She felt herself flushing, a flare of heat starting at her neckline and washing up over her face and ears. She considered what he said, about life asserting its appetites to reassure itself.

"Yes, I suppose I did do that more than the once. Is that what you do?" she asked and immediately regretted the question.

He laughed. "Ye're not shy, are ye? Aye, I've a woman for such times an' others. I know they call me the Monk, but it's not for the obvious reason."

"I see," she said, aware that she sounded rather prim.

"Do ye?" he asked, the amusement clear in his voice. Yet there was no sense he was mocking her.

"Yes, I do."

"Aye, I thought ye might."

She felt slightly surreal having this conversation with him, and yet she felt strangely comfortable in his presence. As if things were simple, were black and white and she didn't have to worry about finding herself in a grey area with him.

"You're maybe not so terrible, Mr. Murray."

He paused part way through putting his mug down on the table. He looked at her, expression utterly serious. "No, I am. I'm every bit as awful an' monstrous as yer friend on the hill will have warned ye. Ye'd be advised to remember it, Pamela. I tell ye this as a kindness, don't ever underestimate how ruthless I am. Don't ever cross me because I'd rather not prove my words to ye."

There seemed little point in answering to that, so she merely finished her tea and then stood.

"Thank you for everything, but I need to go get my children now. Do you think my car will make it home?"

"No. Ye can take one of mine."

"I can't do that."

He stood up, took their dishes to the sink and turned. "I don't see that ye have a choice."

They walked out to the byre closest to the house. That it didn't contain animals was at once apparent, for though it was freshly painted and kept in good repair there was no animal smell wafting out of it.

Noah pulled back the doors, and the scent of hay filled the air around her.

The truck was covered in a canvas tarp. He pulled it back, wisps of hay floating out on the air. It was a deep blue and maybe a year or two younger than she was. She gave him a dubious look.

He laughed, interpreting the look correctly. "I don't want ye drivin' in something that's recognizable as mine. This truck is old, but she runs well an' no one is goin' to associate it with me, which is the most important factor."

"I can't take your truck," she said.

"Ye bloody have to, or ye'll not have any way to get to work in the mornin', nor pick yer wee ones up tonight. Don't be silly, I don't drive it anymore an' it's good for the engine to run every now and again. I'll have one of the boys look yer car over an' see if it can be fixed. Ye can't take it into a garage, or there will be questions about the bullet holes."

She got into the truck and put the key in the ignition. It turned over without hesitation and had the rough volume of a cannon.

"I'll get it back to you as soon as I can," she said, wanting to be clear that she wasn't taking favors from him that she could not hope to repay. She suspected she had passed that point already.

He shrugged. "Keep it as long as ye need, it will just go back in the byre when it returns."

She eased the truck out of the building, the scent of hay sweet in her nose. The inside of the truck was immaculate, and she wondered how much work he had put into this vehicle. Heaven help her if she scraped it or banged it up against something. It felt a tiny bit like driving a tank. She stopped outside, the light of the day starting to fade a bit at its edges. She was suddenly impatient to pick up Conor and Isabelle and just hold them, feed them dinner, give them their baths, read them a chapter from *Winnie the Pooh* and lie down beside them to watch them fall to sleep. It sounded like the most blissfully normal thing imaginable.

Noah walked out with the truck and stopped by the open driver's window.

"It wasn't me who ordered that hit," he said quietly. He looked her in the eyes. "I know ye were wonderin', but those were not my men out there today. I'm not messy like that, an' I don't do things for sectarian reasons. I have never killed a man because of his religion."

"Okay," she said. He didn't owe her explanations, and she knew he was not a man normally to give them. She wondered why he had made an exception today. Then thought, perhaps, that was another question she didn't truly want answered.

"That's all," he said and waved her off.

He was a puzzle, was Noah Murray. She looked in the rearview mirror and was slightly perturbed to find him still standing in the lane watching her drive away.

Chapter Seventeen

Count the Stars in the Sky, Noah

THE WORLD THAT NOAH MURRAY lived in was a shadow land, and of this dark place he was the master. This world had its own hierarchy, its own rules and someone had broken those rules and broken them badly. Someone had forgotten that to commit crime in Noah Murray's territory without his advance knowledge and permission, was to speak a death wish to the wind that wove through the lanes and over the walls and high dark hedges of South Armagh.

Noah had never been afraid of wet work; he had started out as an enforcer for Mickey Devine, many years ago now. He had become rather infamous for his ability to make men talk before they died. He rarely did this anymore, rarely held another man's pain in his own two hands, pushing the man to the fine edge of madness, knowing when to stop and when to begin again because breaking a man was an art. A messy art, but an art nonetheless.

Some transgressions required direct contact; the shooting of ten Protestant men two miles from his home was one. Today he had received word that his men had taken one of the shooters. He had forewarned them that he alone would deal with the punishment. They knew where to take the man.

Thus he stood outside an old stone byre, long abandoned, deep in a forgotten corner of his realm, deep enough in the hills and hedges and byways that no one could hear a man scream, no one could save a man from his fate. He looked up. The sky was clear tonight; it had been a fine day with only sporadic showers, clearing to a world of tender blue near evening.

"*Count the stars in the sky, Noah.*" His mother used to say that to him to calm him, to get him out of the house, to get him away from his father. It was an old habit this, counting the stars in the sky, actually attempting to do so in earnest when he was a wee boy, before he understood that such a thing was impossible even for astronomers. Later, it had become a way to quell the terrible anger that rode him like a scorpion on a frog's back. Some nights it had been the only thing that had kept him from killing his own father. Counting those tiny pinpricks of cold fire, one by one by one. And then counting them again, lying on the hill beyond the house, half-frozen and counting the fucking stars so that he would not slit his father's throat, gut the bastard like the pig he was. No matter the blood, the pain, the rage, no matter the agony, no matter the loss of a boy's soul, no matter the lack of poetry and love and music and tenderness and art. No matter the bruises and the blood and the words that rained like stones upon his head. There were still and always stars in the sky. Still and always his mother's voice, pleading with him to forgive, to understand, to survive into another day. It was what she said to turn him from the realization that life wasn't going to change, things were not going to get better and he wasn't going to suddenly awaken in a household that understood him. The stars were a place to put his mind, while nasty things happened on the ground below. It was a place to hide and to believe that there was, despite all evidence to the contrary, beauty and goodness in the world.

Count the stars in the sky, Noah.

He took a breath, the evening was chilly, and when he exhaled clouds of silver streamed out around him.

The man would be hard-primed now, blood pumping furiously, panic lighting up his nerve endings like match sticks. It thinned the skin, fear did, it heightened the pain, lent it a ragged red edge that broke a man down far faster than a sudden violent attack. Noah would give it another five minutes, which would feel like both five seconds and five days to the man awaiting him. Fear did that, it both compressed time and stretched it out to unbearable limits. It was his friend in these situations, it was the enemy of the man at the end of his hands.

He knew what it was to be on the receiving end of pain, to be utterly certain that death was coming for you, and to believe it was not going to arrive gently, but in a crimson wave of pain and terror. He thought that only someone who had been subjected to pain could ever really apply it properly. What he had learned as a boy, he had done as a man, and so it went. He had never hurt a child, a woman or an animal—it was a code of sorts, something that set parameters around this shadow world. Parameters kept a man sane.

Count the stars in the sky, Noah.

He had planned to go by and visit Pamela Riordan this evening, check to see if she had recovered from her experience the other day, and to make certain the truck was running well. It would have to wait, for he wouldn't go near her, not with another man's blood on his hands, not with another man's fear thick as oil upon his flesh, which it always was after such a night as that which lay before him. Some women had the ability to scent violence on a man, to know what he had done if not in its particulars then in its general darkness. He felt instinctively that she was such a woman. He would need to avoid her for a day or two, until it was washed from his eyes and his skin. Noah wondered at himself that he wanted to see her, that he felt drawn to her, that he worried about her safety, despite the warnings he had put out. She was not for him, and he didn't entertain such a notion, for he didn't have relationships with women, other than his sister. He did not have love for any other than Kate; he was not capable of it. Once, perhaps, but no longer.

Count the stars in the sky, Noah.

"Ye ready?" a voice asked, quiet, respectful, just a wee bit afraid, for even Noah Murray's own men held a bit of fear for him, a bit of a clenching in their bellies. A filament of scent reached him. The man had already pissed himself, even though Noah had yet to enter the byre. He knew Noah was coming and Noah's reputation walked ahead of him into every meeting room, every dark hedgerow, every lonely hut on an abandoned hillside in this country. Because he had made damn certain a long time ago that his reputation was backed up by his actions.

He pulled his gloves on, and walked into the old byre, the scent of another's man's fear thick in his nose.

Count the stars in the sky, Noah.

Chapter Eighteen

Qui Audet Adipiscitur

TRUE TO NOAH's prediction the SAS was deployed into South Armagh. It was done in a blaze of dubious publicity by the British Prime Minister in the wake of the bus massacre of the ten Protestant workers. He had told the House of Commons that SAS units were being sent in to stamp out cross border banditry and murder. The plan for the SAS to initially operate only in South Armagh was an indication of just how serious the situation there was considered to be.

Captain Edwin Forest had been a SAS commander for five years. He had seen action in Malaya and Aden but he had never seen anything quite like the ground in South Armagh. They had been briefed on the situation, though that briefing, as black in tone as it had been, could only partially prepare a man for the reality of life as a soldier in this land. The leash was far shorter in Northern Ireland than it was in any other location in which the British Army was stationed, because nominally this place was part of the United Kingdom. Captain Forest thought most of the natives hadn't gotten the memo on that particular detail. They had been told they were here to protect the civilians, but the civilians weren't appreciative in the least. In fact, he had never come up against a more actively hostile population.

He was awaiting a briefing more narrow in scope at present, though certainly it was connected to the larger scheme of things as well. The young man in front of him had a fresh look to him, but he had survived his time in South Armagh which meant he was tough and smart.

He set a folder down on the desk and flipped it open to a picture of a charming and well-kept farmhouse in a dell of woods and fern; it was the sort of home that might be featured as a slice of old Ireland on a travel poster. He looked up, waiting for the young man to begin.

"There's been a bit of activity around this farmhouse, always at night, they come and go through the woods on the property. It's not constant, but Noah Murray has been seen there on more than one occasion."

"Noah Murray?" There was no name in the county, no enemy he had ever encountered, that made his blood boil more.

"Yes, sir, Noah Murray. We're not entirely certain what is going on. There's a widow who lives there with her two small children."

"A widow?"

"Yes and no sir, one Pamela Riordan. She was married to Casey Riordan, who was a longstanding member of the PIRA. Or she still is, I suppose. He's classified as missing."

"And is he missing?"

"As far as we know, yes."

"You think this woman is running a safe house of some sort, or that Noah Murray actually has something other than ice water in his veins and is courting a woman?"

"Well, sir, if you had seen the woman in question, you'd understand why it might be visits of the romantic sort."

Captain Forest raised a brow. "Do you have a picture? I'd like to see the woman who could turn Noah Murray's head."

The soldier smiled. "I thought you might ask, sir. Just flip through the photos."

"How long have we been keeping a file on this woman?"

"Well, she was married to a known IRA leader; he was pegged to run the Belfast wing of the PIRA before they packed up and moved to Boston. They came back here a couple of years later. He still had ties within the Provos when he disappeared. And, sir, it is likely worth noting that she also lived with James Kirkpatrick for some time."

The captain sputtered over his tea a little. "Lord James Kirkpatrick?"

"Yes, sir. It's my understanding they were not romantically involved, but merely friends."

The captain turned over the picture of the house. There was more than one photo of the woman. He flicked through them quickly; each had been taken from a distance, for the subject was clearly unaware of the camera's eye upon her. The pictures were innocuous enough, showing her in simple day-to-day tasks or actions—riding a horse, pushing a pram, presumably with a baby inside, though in Belfast it didn't pay to presume anything. She was lovely, there was no denying that, and something more, something that made itself apparent even here in the static medium of a photo. He couldn't quite put his finger on what it was, but to have such a draw even in a picture, he knew it must be very powerful in the actual presence of the woman. And if Lord James Kirkpatrick was involved with her in some fashion, it took her importance in the scheme of things to a whole different level.

James Kirkpatrick was surrounded by a blackout of information that resembled a big granite wall, and that told the captain a great deal about just what His Lordship's extra-curricular activities were. If he was more highly-placed than the SAS, it meant he was intelligence and someone was very concerned with keeping his history secret. James Kirkpatrick was someone he did not particularly wish to tangle with, and it was possible, the snarled threads of Ulster being what they were, that keeping an eye on this woman could attract the man's attention. You pulled one thread here and the entire picture unraveled before your eyes, revealing something underneath that was far more trouble and far uglier than what you'd bargained for.

"And what is her connection to Noah Murray? This is not a man who socializes with the neighbors after all."

"His sister is involved with the younger of the Riordan brothers. It's possible they met through her."

"If it's not romance, then what? And if it is romance, you will be able to knock me off this chair with a feather."

"We're not certain, sir. He comes and goes at odd hours, not so much like a lover, but rather like a man who is trying to keep something secret."

"What, is the question? And why this woman? Is her land convenient to something, or is she connected to something larger that he wants a piece of? You know this man doesn't do anything without an eye to his own advantage."

"Well, sir, it could be her connection to James Kirkpatrick that he's interested in."

The captain contemplated that nugget for a moment. The situation had all the hallmarks of something that could turn into, to use a term the Americans had for situations like this, a clusterfuck of phenomenal proportions. No man messed with British Intelligence without being fully aware he was stepping into a viper pit. But the potential here for finding a way into the incredibly tight network Noah Murray maintained in South Armagh was too great a temptation.

The captain tapped his finger on a picture of the woman.

"I want you to look into everything—her connections, her financial situation, if there's anyone she's afraid of, et cetera. I want to know if we can turn her into an asset for our side. I want a full report before anyone makes a move, understood?"

The young soldier nodded. "Consider it done, sir."

Chapter Nineteen

The Visit

EACH TUESDAY, PAMELA spent the afternoon at Jamie's house, going over a variety of business, mostly the leftover bits and pieces from her time managing the companies. He said he enjoyed having someone else understand the whole wooly ball of the business, rather than each person he dealt with having acquaintance with only one or two aspects. She brought her children with her, so that they could visit with Maggie, Vanya and Shura—all of whom were very fond of Isabelle and Conor. More often than not they stayed to dinner at Jamie's insistence, and the latter half of Tuesday had become a bright spot in her week.

Today, however, there was a strange car in the drive in front of the house and a sense of tense expectancy about the house itself when she let herself in through the kitchen entrance.

Conor rushed to Maggie, who leaned down to engulf him in a capacious hug. Pamela put Isabelle on the floor and removed her pale pink sweater. Maggie kept a box of toys in the kitchen for the children, and Pamela fished out a ragdoll that wouldn't be harmed if Isabelle drooled on it and handed it to her daughter, who clutched it up and stuck an arm directly in her mouth.

Maggie looked at her then, and Pamela knew she hadn't imagined the strange tension outside.

Maggie, as was usual, was to the point. "Julian is here. He arrived an hour ago."

"Did Jamie know he was coming?"

"Aye, he only gave a day's warnin', barely enough time to change the sheets an' put together a decent dinner. I tell ye," Maggie harrumphed, "the boy flusters a person, he looks too much like Jamie for anyone's comfort."

"I know," she said, dreading the encounter. "Perhaps I should just go home."

Maggie laughed, a somewhat grim sound. "Oh no, ye won't get away that easy, Jamie said to send ye on through when ye arrived. There's no runnin' for it now, he'll have heard that truck ye're drivin'."

She sighed. There were few things she wanted to do less than see Julian once again, but Maggie was right, Jamie would know she had arrived.

"Let me take the tea in then, Maggie, it will give me something to do with my hands." Maggie had been assembling the tray when she walked in, and now she poured water into the teapot and added a delicate lavender teacup that was Pamela's favorite to the tray.

Maggie nodded. "All right, saves me goin' in there. The tray is a bit heavy, so mind how ye go."

A bit heavy was an understatement. Looking down at the array of sponge cake, lemon drop cookies and sugar-dusted scones, Pamela wondered if Maggie was trying to lull everyone into some sort of sugar and starch détente. She traversed the long corridor without incident, and was relieved to see that the door was ajar. She tapped it lightly with the edge of the tray, so that she wouldn't come upon the two men unawares.

They rose as one when she entered the room. Each man was a study in that same cat-like grace; it was like being in some strange hall of mirrors. Seeing the two of them together in the same room gave her a slight case of vertigo. The china rattled in an alarming fashion, and Jamie quickly took it from her, setting it down on the low table between the chairs. She sat down and was dismayed to find that her knees were knocking a little. She had first met Julian when he had arrived unannounced with Jamie's Uncle Philip, at a Christmas party she was hosting in Jamie's absence. She had very nearly been sick from shock that night. In subsequent encounters with Julian, she had come to see how different he was in nature from Jamie, and it caused a neat divide between the two men. But now, seeing them only feet apart, Jamie with the elongated look to his eyes that he only got when truly furious and Julian mirroring that expression in sapphire across from him—well it was entirely disconcerting. If she'd had a fan handy she would have used it, and smelling salts wouldn't have come amiss either.

She wasn't sure what they were talking about, though Jamie drew her into the conversation with his usual skill and Julian greeted her like she was an old acquaintance of whom he was fond. Which, she thought turning her gaze to him, could not be further from the truth. Today he wore a shirt that highlighted the dense sapphire of his eyes and a pair of charcoal grey dress pants. Both were custom-made and she had a funny feeling that the clothing had been made by Jamie's own tailor, as the cut was the same. Jamie was far more casual in a cream sweater and jeans that had seen better days. He looked like he'd been caught working in the stables when Julian arrived. It didn't appear to bother him, for he seemed relaxed, annoyingly so. Her own nerves did not feel quite so sanguine.

She was, truth be told, surprised that Julian dared to show his face here after all the trouble he had made in Jamie's absence. She had no great fondness for him, but he was, regardless of her own issues with him, Jamie's son. Jamie would want to get to know him, as was his right.

She poured the tea and handed a cup to each man, though Julian had a tumbler of whiskey in front of him. Jamie watched as she did this, observing Julian's reactions to her and hers to him, which might be best described as icily polite on her end and restrained on Julian's. And then it was her turn to observe as she sat back in the chair and sipped at her tea. Jamie's face, of course, gave nothing away. Since Russia, he was even harder to read, as if his time there had forged an opacity to his daily interactions.

She of all people understood what this meant to Jamie—Jamie who had buried three infant sons because of a genetic heart disease, Jamie who had never thought to have a living son of his own body. She only prayed he would not allow it to make him vulnerable to this beautiful boy across from him, for Julian was as treacherous as the rocks that lay just below the surface of a calm sea. She had been likewise susceptible to him, due to his remarkable resemblance to his father, but fortunately she had also distrusted him in equal proportion, understanding that looking like Jamie did not make Julian his equal in character. He had proved in short order that he was not anywhere near the man his father was by trying to steal not only his companies but also the house in which they now sat. She felt distinctly twitchy, like there were ants crawling in a mound at her feet ready to swarm up her legs.

"We have been discussing," Jamie said, "Irish history."

Discussing Irish history with Jamie, Pamela well knew, was akin to stepping out into a minefield whilst hopping on one leg. Hopping while carrying lit dynamite she amended, as she realized the subject at hand was the recent withdrawal, by the British government, of special category status for Irish republican prisoners. Because England's occupation of Ireland had no real legal underpinning, Irish republicans had long been treated as political prisoners. Now suddenly it had been withdrawn by an English politician who ought to have known better.

"You're part of the United Kingdom, and therefore subject to its laws," Julian was saying, in defense of the reversal.

"British law?" Jamie laughed. "Britain has always had one set of laws for herself and her wealthy, and another set for those she sets out to conquer and considers savages. Britain has, as I'm sure you know, been the biggest transgressor of her own laws."

"No," Julian said with a rather superb haughtiness, "I don't know that. You can hardly expect a whole separate set of rules for your little corner of the United Kingdom. It doesn't work that way."

"Perhaps perfidious Albion is so black and white, but I can assure you Northern Ireland is not." Jamie took a bite of a scone, as if they were discussing the weather, or cricket. Pamela arched a brow at him, wondering if he was deliberately baiting the boy. Jamie merely smiled at her, in the maddening fashion which told her exactly nothing.

"Perhaps it would benefit all of you if you realized that the law and the world sees you as British."

"We prefer to define our own nationality here, rather than have it handed to us at the end of a gun."

"I think you all have a greater fondness for the gun than do your neighbors across the sea. After all, we don't kill our own with such appetite. Murder is murder, regardless of whether it is wrapped in the flag of nationalism."

"Oh, the civilized Englishman, rarer than the Dodo bird, and far more elusive," Jamie said softly, but there was no mistaking the icy edge to his words. "Would you like me to list the atrocities that have been committed in this country at the hands of your oh-so-civilized countrymen?"

"Englishmen are your countrymen, lest you forget," Julian replied, no small edge in his own voice.

"Ah, that's what *your* countrymen tend to forget—this is not England and never will be."

"And yet still it is British law that rules this land," Julian said, tipping the crystal tumbler he held, so that the light swam like a delicate water sprite through the gold of the whiskey.

"If that is true," Jamie said, wiping crumbs from his sweater with a brisk hand, "then British law would have to truly apply. It doesn't here. You can't say, as the politicians have been saying—a crime is a crime, murder is murder and then apply different consequences to it. You can't have the SAS hunting these so-called ordinary murderers down, nor can you have special prisons manned by special guards, nor Diplock courts where a trial, and I use that term loosely, takes twenty minutes and has no jury. You can't keep prisoners on remand indefinitely, postponing their trials again and again, just to keep them locked up for as long as possible. There is no internal logic to such a system that says these crimes are equal and ordinary, regardless of the root cause, and then apply special punishments to said crimes."

Pamela felt as if she were a spectator at a rather brutal game of ping pong, watching the ball being hit back and forth with ever more vigor and anger. Jamie was right, and Julian could not possibly understand just what a complicated snarl the mix of history and politics was here in Belfast. Murder was never just murder here, nothing was straightforward, most acts of violence had roots that twisted their way back to a very deep place, where many factors played a part: family history, the street you lived upon, the grammar school you had attended, the way you prayed before you closed your eyes at night and which sports teams you supported. Here the political was personal, always.

"Is there logic to it? Eight hundred years of rebellion and madness and brother killing brother—can there be logic to such a thing?"

"It's not something insiders understand, never mind outsiders," Jamie said quietly. "This country has been riven down the center, often by outside forces whose interests have never served the Irish well. There is a saying that if you're not confused, you don't understand the situation. That tends to be rather too accurate in Northern Ireland."

"Well, one thing isn't confusing," Julian said, putting his tumbler down with a small thump, "and that is the English are clearly the villains of this piece, and all the internecine killing can be laid at our feet, rather than taking a long look in your own mirror."

Pamela cleared her throat, harboring a wild hope that she could think of a new subject that was less fraught with potential bombs. It was a howl of outrage from Kolya that put paid to the conversation. Jamie excused himself and left the room.

The tension went down a notch, but no more than that, for she found herself eye-to-eye with Julian. The sapphire eyes were discomfiting, for he had Jamie's trick of making it seem as if he looked right through you, only with Jamie it was because her friendship with him often made her motives and feelings transparent to him. She was vulnerable to Jamie, but she did not mind because he would never abuse that fact. With Julian it felt like exploitation, as though he would pick over a person's soul and look for any weakness to use later to his own advantage.

"I was sorry," he said, "to hear about your husband."

"Were you?" she said, very cool, though the teacup in her hand was near to shattering from the pressure of her fingers. "Somehow I don't think so." She would not discuss Casey with this man, nor would she suffer any false sympathy from him, and false she was certain it was.

"You do not like me, I know this," Julian said, his eyes holding a small umber flame within. It was only the reflection from the fire, but it gave him a slightly demonic glow.

"You gave me little reason to," she said frostily.

"Perhaps we can start fresh," he said, "for my father's sake, if nothing else."

"Perhaps," she said guardedly, remembering how overly familiar Julian had been with her and how he had offered to take her on as his mistress, once he took over Jamie's house and life. He had assumed that she had been such to Jamie and as he had rather succinctly asked, 'Do I inherit you along with the house?' No one could accuse him of a lack of hubris at least.

"You spend a deal of time here?" he asked, like he was merely making conversation, but it was never so simple with him.

"I do, not that it's any business of yours."

"No," he drawled in imitation of Jamie's most irritating tone, "I suppose it isn't, though you should bear in mind that he does not keep his mistresses long. Just ask my mother how long she lasted."

"Then I needn't worry, need I? Because his friends, he keeps forever."

Suddenly she realized that Jamie was standing in the doorway, the air around him still as if he stood in a place apart. She tensed a little, as this was always an indication that he was well and truly angry. Clearly, he had overheard the last of their exchange.

"You," he said looking at Julian, "are a guest in my home and as such I will give you what that courtesy demands. I would ask that you give the same in return. If you feel you cannot, then you may leave." His tone was mild, but Pamela shivered a little on Julian's behalf.

Julian colored, a tide of red rising from his collar to stain his cheeks. Like Jamie, he had fine skin and the flush turned his eyes a deeper blue, almost black in its density. Jamie's eyes turned dark like that when he was in the grip of high emotion too.

"I have plans for this evening," he said, somewhat stiffly, "so I won't be here for dinner. Friends are here in the city and I've promised to see them tonight. I will be back later if that's still all right by you."

"Of course it is," Jamie said easily, "you'll find Irish hospitality is without stint. I don't take disagreements personally. I do, however, take insults toward my friends as such. You owe the lady an apology."

She shook her head at Jamie, but he merely gave her a sardonic lift of one eyebrow in reply.

"No, he's right, I do owe you an apology. I'm sorry if I offended you, Pamela," Julian said, and she feared for a moment that he might actually take her hand or touch her just to emphasize his words. She would hit him if he did, or throw the tea left in her cup in his face.

After Julian's exit, it felt like there wasn't enough oxygen in the air to pull in a proper breath.

"I apologize, Pamela, you shouldn't have had to witness that little tête-à-tête."

She shook her head. "Don't apologize, Jamie. You're going to be prickly with one another, that can't be helped. It will take time to get to a place where either of you is comfortable enough to have a normal conversation."

Jamie went to the windows that looked out toward the drive. "Do we know who his friends are in Belfast?"

"Well, we know one," she said.

"You think he's enough of a fool to go visit the Reverend?"

She shrugged, not wanting to malign Julian without proof. "I've learned the hard way and so have you, not to underestimate just what Reverend Broughton is capable of. If he wants to use Julian to pull you back into his game, he will."

The Reverend Broughton was an old and implacable enemy of Jamie's who had long sought to make his life difficult. For some reason he believed that he and Jamie shared a father though there was no proof of such a thing.

"Yes, I know that, I don't quite see how to stop him, though, short of killing him, and the law tends to frown upon that, unfortunately. You would think," he sighed, "that the game would be getting just a bit dull to him by now."

"You'd think so, but you'd be wrong," she said. "Jamie?"

"Yes?"

"Are you all right?"

He shook his head and took a long breath in through his nose. "Yes, I'm fine, or I will be once I've calmed my temper. Would you care to go riding? I think that might restore me to a more civil frame of mind."

"I—"

"Maggie will be more than happy to keep watch over the children," he said, anticipating her protest. "We can check on them before we go."

"Yes, let's go," she said, the thought of a ride immensely appealing.

They saddled the horses in a companionable silence. The stables and paddock lay in a pool of afternoon light and the smell of horses and feed and leather was soothing to the senses. Jamie was riding an Arabian stallion named Naseem Albahr, which he had bought the month before. The horse shimmered coal black from nose to tail and stood sixteen hands high. He was impossible for anyone other than Jamie to ride, or handle in any way. Even with Jamie he showed his impatience regularly. She was riding a lovely bay named Danu, with an even temperament and an energetic gait to her. The filly also possessed the invaluable attribute of being the only horse in the stable that would tolerate Naseem Albahr's high-hoofed behavior.

They set off at a brisk canter, down the main trail away from the stables. This land led down the mountainside and into a small, lovely valley filled with hazel and oak and ferns that grew to almost prehistoric size. She hadn't ridden Phouka since Casey had disappeared, a cause of great guilt for her. Jamie had offered to have him back in his stables, so that he would get regular exercise. She thought she might have to take him up on his offer, because there was never any time, nor could she leave the children alone on the off chance she might have a spare five minutes at some point.

She loved this side of the mountain, loved the strange magic that seemed to linger here and the sense that the wee bloody city below and all its tragedies did not exist. A soft breeze floated in from the west, and the scent of fir needles and wet earth rode in upon it. A green mist lay over the woods and bracken, lighting the hollows with celadon fire.

A fox darted across the path just then and narrowly missed being trampled by Jamie's demon of a horse. Naseem reared back, hooves slashing at the air and Jamie cursed, tightening his grip on the reins. She hurriedly took Danu off to the side, where the filly let out a long whicker, and then set to munching the new grass at the trail's side, as if to make clear she had little concern for tetchy stallions or stray foxes.

Pamela stood and watched, reins clutched fast in her hands. There was nothing she could do to help Jamie, odds were she would get herself trampled if she tried. Besides, Jamie had the best hand with horses of anyone she had ever known. If he couldn't calm the stallion, no one could.

With some horses Jamie used soft words and soft touch, but with such a spirited stallion he used an entirely different approach. She knew some of the Gaelic curses, but Jamie knew them all, and used them to great effect.

"You bloody bastard!" he said, and clamped his thighs hard on the stallion's rib cage, pulling the reins to turn his head. She gasped as she saw the stallion's neck make contact with Jamie's face. She covered her eyes after that, certain that the horse was going to kill Jamie or break its own legs in the attempt. After that it was all sound, thrashing, cursing, and a severe impugnment of the stallion's dam and the snap of tree branches breaking off.

There was a lull suddenly in the proceedings, and a dry voice said, "You can uncover your eyes now."

She glanced up to find Jamie giving her an amused look from the vantage point of Naseem's back. The horse was still snorting, coat gleaming and Jamie had moss and bark in his hair, as well as a black eye that was going to be truly impressive.

"Bastard had the last word," Jamie said, and slid down off the stallion's back, taking care to stay clear of the bobbing head and snorting nostrils, before putting a hand gingerly to his rapidly swelling eye.

They were near to his grandmother's cottage.

"Jamie, I think we should stop and see Finola. She can have a look at your eye."

Jamie opened his mouth, no doubt to protest, when Pamela caught a flicker of movement in her peripheral vision and turned to see the woman in question moving toward them through the dim of the woods. Finola was a small woman, but one with a fierce presence. She had her herb gathering basket over one arm and the other hand clutched a variety of wet and muddy plants.

The green light of the wood made Finola appear as if she had just crossed the border from that other world, the one that seemed to shimmer right along the boundaries of Jamie's land, a place apart, enchanting but also frightening. Pamela had spent a fair bit of time with her only a few months back, and it had convinced her that the woman was part witch, at least where plants and their uses were concerned.

"Come into the house," she said without preamble, her eyes narrowed against the sunlight, "an' I'll have a look at that eye of yers." She put her basket down, tucking the muddy roots in with the other plants she'd foraged, and then looked up at Jamie, touching one hand lightly to his eye.

"We should probably get back to the house," he said, politely, but with an edge to it.

"Ye can spare a minute to let me tend to yer eye an' to drink a cup of tea," Finola said crisply, "not to mention a little civilizing wouldn't hurt ye just now, I'm thinkin'. I've a pot of comfrey already brewed an' cool, ye won't have to hang about long, if that's what's worryin' ye."

Jamie cast a glance at Pamela and she nodded. She liked Finola, and wasn't averse to stopping for tea. Mostly, she wanted Jamie's eye attended to, for like most men he was too stubborn to have a doctor look at him when he was hurt.

She followed Finola into the cottage. It was just as she remembered, though she suspected it had remained much the same for decades. She could feel Jamie behind her, the electricity fairly crackling off him. She had been here one strange and dark night with Casey, a night where time and space had seemingly been suspended in this small cottage and she had reached out to find the man who now stood beside her.

Pamela sat, her skin thrumming with the electric charge in the room. Jamie and two of his relatives in one day might be more than her nerves could manage. Finola had a will of steel as well as a mind as sharp as her grandson's. Pamela thought perhaps this was why they seemed at odds with one another—they were just too much alike. There was something more, though, something that simmered just beneath the surface and could be felt now, roiling about the room. Finola had never said what caused them to fall out, nor had Jamie. She didn't suppose either one was about to enlighten her now.

Finola, never one to waste time or words, set about making a compress for Jamie's eye. She soaked a pad of cheesecloth in the tincture, which Pamela knew would be triple the strength of ordinary comfrey tea, and then wrung it out a little and put it on Jamie's eye. He put a hand up to hold it, and used the other eye to glare at his grandmother, who returned the look with interest. While Jamie did not look much like Finola, his eyes were the mirror shade of hers, a dark green jade, bright with anger at present.

Once the tea for drinking was made, she handed them each a mug and then sat down opposite them on a three-legged stool by the fire. With her usual tact, she got straight to the point.

"I suppose the reason for yer fine temper today is because yer son is visitin' ye."

"And how do you know that?"

"Just because you rarely grace me with conversation doesn't mean others on the estate don't talk to me."

He shot Pamela a sideways glance with his good eye, and she started guiltily, despite the fact that she hadn't known about Julian being there until she had walked into his house today.

"It wasn't Pamela, she only just arrived, so ye can scarce blame her."

"Do you have some sort of underground psychic network going?"

"No, simply civilized chat over the gate. Have ye forgotten what that's like?"

"Might be that I have," Jamie said and laughed, "living in a gulag, while good for the character, plays havoc with a man's manners."

"I suppose ye've let him get under yer skin?" Finola said, narrowing her eyes at her grandson.

"I suppose," Jamie said shortly, "I have. He's a maddening boy—you *have* met him, haven't you?"

"Aye, an' he reminds me in no small way of yerself when ye were just the wee bit younger than him."

"He is nothing like me," Jamie said hotly, and Pamela wondered if either of the two would notice if she quietly slipped out the door.

"Oh, he is, it's only that yer ego won't let ye see it." Finola had her hands on her hips, green eyes sparking through the dim cottage light. Jamie's visible eye was narrowed in the cat-like way that said he was positively furious. All that was missing was the hissing and spitting. Pamela bit her lip to stop herself from laughing. There was a decided resemblance between the two in front of her right now, though she was quite certain neither would appreciate her pointing it out.

"My ego, is it? Well, thank you for the compliment."

"Oh, laddie, 'twasn't meant as a compliment an' well ye know it."

"I'll take it as I like."

"Ye don't get to be childish, man, but I think ye can forgive him if he is childish for a bit. He's likely to feel such when he's visitin' ye for the first time in his life. I think ye forget just how intimidatin' ye are to people meetin' ye for the first time."

"Me, intimidating? I've been hospitality itself since he arrived."

Pamela stifled a laugh, which caused her to cough in what could only be described as a dubious manner.

The narrowed green eye was on her now. "I'm not intimidating him, am I?" With the dripping cloth still clasped firmly to his eye, Jamie looked less than the picture of righteous indignation.

"I would prefer not to venture an opinion just now," she said and buried her face in the solidity of the mug, the steam from the tea heating her face.

Jamie laughed, and the tension went down a notch.

"It's up to you, James," his grandmother said, in a slightly more conciliatory tone. "It's yer responsibility, not his. He doesn't owe you anything, but you do owe him a chance an' ye need to lend him yer understandin' as well."

"Just as it was lent to me at a similar age?" he asked, and there was no mistaking the iron in his tone.

"Ye were a high-strung laddie, an' ye had the deficits of such a temperament, but ye also had good advisers an' guides who loved ye."

"Meddling Jesuits and meddling women is what I had," he said with no little frustration in his tone.

Which rather accurately described his current set of advisors too, Pamela thought. It seemed to her that the conversation had officially entered territory that did not bear witnesses. She stood and went to put her mug by the big stone sink, then having done so, sidled toward the door. Two or three steps and she would be out of the cottage and could wait in the garden for Jamie, where there was no danger of getting caught in the familial crossfire.

"Pamela," he said quietly and she froze in her tracks. Damn the man anyway, he never missed anything even when he was in the grip of a dreadful temper. "I'll leave with you, so don't try to sneak off."

"I'll wait outside," she said meekly and shot out the door before he could say anything to stop her.

Outside, she took a long breath of the warm air. Finola's extensive herb garden was softly hazed with new growth. The herbs in this garden were arranged according to their various uses: the herbs for blood-related illnesses at the top of the round—hyssop and motherwort, sage and angelica; followed by herbs for the heart—yarrow and rosemary, with the hawthorn—both leaf and berry; herbs to draw out bruising—comfrey and arnica; herbs for the head and the soul—clary sage, geranium, St. John's wort, borage, valerian and chamomile. The final arm in the spiral were women's herbs, for fertility and for preventing fertility, for bringing on the bleeding and for promoting labor in a woman gone past her time—raspberry leaf, blue vervain, the root and leaf of the dandelion, mug wort and tansy. Then there were the herbs for love charms, for spells to bind either man or woman to you and charms to thwart an enemy, herbs to turn aside evil and bring luck, and one low herb that crept along the ground, said to bring the dead back to walk amongst the living. The poisonous herbs were separate, with the deadly nightshade plants outside the wheel and in a pattern of their own that followed the path of the moon from dark to full and back again.

A whiff of new fennel, warm and sweet, ribboned past on the breeze. There was an old stone dyke at the bottom of the garden, and she walked down to it. It was thick with moss and small starry flowers, blush pink against the worn grey stone. Long ago, someone had planted a small copse of fir here and they exuded their dark magic; the scent, thick and golden, of resin like a perfume brought into being by the warmth of the late afternoon sun. She closed her eyes and breathed it in, letting it relieve the tension that had built up in the cottage. When she opened them, she caught a flicker of movement in the long grass at the base of the firs. It was a fox, golden eyes fixed to hers, a shimmer of roan amongst the sun-dappled green.

She realized suddenly that Jamie was standing beside her, his presence hadn't disturbed the fox in the least.

"Are you all right?" she asked, softly.

"I suppose if I hadn't had steam coming out of my ears when we arrived, her words might have been a less bitter pill to swallow," he said.

"I think she only meant he's like you in terms of general stubbornness," she said.

"Well," he laughed, a sound of chagrin, "what infuriates me most with her is that she's usually right. I suppose she is this time as well."

"She does have your best interests at heart, Jamie."

"She usually gets her way," he said drily, "you needn't worry on her behalf, Pamela."

She laughed. "Oh, I'm not worried about her in the least. You, on the other hand, I am worried about."

"Why?"

"I'm afraid Julian will hurt you. Regardless of what you say, I know you're vulnerable to him."

"Do you think he's like me?" His tone was considerably softer in asking for her opinion than it had been with his grandmother.

She looked at him in the light, the firs dark behind his head and the sun touching his hair gold and yellow, platinum and wheat. Even now, when she kept company with him on a daily basis, his beauty could take her unawares and she felt that catch in her throat that sometimes occurred in his presence.

"In the obvious ways, he is very like you; in the more subtle ways I think he could not be more different. There is something fine in you that Julian lacks and will never have. Whether it was present at birth and his mother managed to flail it out of him, I don't know. But it's not there. He can hardly be blamed for that, because what you are is rare. You're magic, Jamie, surely you know that by now."

"Magic?" his voice was off a shade and there was something both mocking and vulnerable in his tone.

"Don't do that, not with me. Surely you understand what you are?"

"Magic—what is it really? Smoke and mirrors, distraction without substance."

"You're starting to annoy me." She gave him a pointed look and he laughed.

"Come on, Pamela, let's go back up to the house and see if dinner is ready. Being in a temper always gives me an appetite."

Naseem was nuzzling Danu's neck and blew a raspberry in their direction as they approached the two horses. "Now *he*, on the other hand," Pamela said, nodding toward the stallion and trying not to laugh, "most assuredly *is* like you."

Chapter Twenty

Man of God

ELSPETH DOWDELL HAD A SECRET. She was in love. In love with a man of God, the purest, holiest, kindest man imaginable. She had been in love with him for five years. From the moment she had met him she had felt a certainty in her life that had not existed before.

Elspeth was the sort of woman upon whom churches are built, and ministers rely on to carry out the brunt of church work. She was scrupulous in her attendance to both the Temperance League and Sunday services. She never missed an opportunity to help the Reverend in whatever capacity he might need of her. She cleaned the church on Tuesdays and his home on Fridays. This gave her the sort of access to his life and his thinking that other women, and there were more than a few in the congregation, could only dream about. The Reverend was a busy and important man—there was no more important man in the Protestant community—and she was there to facilitate his great work. Which was, of course, to cleanse their society of the Roman Catholic scum that infested it. She knew all about them, about their strange rituals and unholy worship. She knew the horrible little warrens they lived in, without proper bathing facilities, and how none of them wanted to work, but rather to live off the state and drink and fornicate so as to produce their endless offspring.

Today was Friday, which meant Elspeth was in her favorite place in the world—the Reverend Lucien Broughton's home. She always started her cleaning in the kitchen and then moved to the parlor and then the bathroom. The Reverend's house was immaculate, but she still cleaned it with a fervor that was a religion in itself. She saved the best part of the house for last.

She always quivered with delight when she entered his bedroom. No other woman was allowed into this sanctum, just she, mousy little Elspeth Dowdell. She'd heard one of the young mothers refer to her that way, and laugh a little after. A cruel little laugh. Well, the girl could laugh as she liked, she was married to a great lump who already had a red nose from the drink, and him not even thirty yet.

The bedroom was on the second floor and had two large windows that looked out to the east. It was filled with light in the mornings, during which time she knew the Reverend prayed, sometimes for two whole hours. He was beautifully pious.

She checked his hairbrush for stray hairs, and found to her delight that there were five today. She gathered them and tucked them in the small envelope she kept on her person for just this purpose. She had almost enough to finish the doll she was making of him. It was her hobby, a small passion that she had, making dolls to resemble people she knew. There wasn't anyone that she knew, not even old Mrs. Cruikshank, who could stitch as finely as she could. She had a trunk at home, her father's old army barrack box, which was filled with scraps of cloth and bright beads, threads in jeweled colors, tiny buttons and bows, and bits of leather to fashion shoes. When she could she liked to use real hair for the dolls, though it was difficult to procure. In making the Reverend's likeness she wanted it to be as authentic as possible and so she had collected his hair when the opportunity presented. She knew some people thought her hobby was creepy, but the Reverend didn't. She had shown him the doll she had made of the Queen, and he had exclaimed over the bright yellow wool suit and the marcelled brown curls in delight, saying he'd never seen such a likeness. It was then she'd had the idea to make one of him, for him.

The bed was made, just as it always was, with military perfection, corners tight and the sheet folded down over the blanket to an exactness that pleased her soul. Elspeth loved order, exactness, cleanliness, holiness. The sheets were white, none of your brash colors for the Reverend. She pictured him lying here at night sometimes when she was in her own narrow spinster's bed, and her breath would get short and her skin would feel swollen all over. Sometimes she would get up and pray for the impure thoughts to go away. Sometimes she would just allow it to happen.

Today was the day she washed the linens, a task she loved. There was something almost religious about it, washing the linens, hanging them to dry, ironing them with long strokes and then putting them, still warm, on the bed. Then smoothing the sheets over the mattress with her hands and sometimes kneeling there for a moment at his bedside, smelling the clean scent of the bedding and knowing he would lie upon that which her hands had made ready for him that very night.

She took the coverlet off, and folded it carefully, laying it on the stool the Reverend kept by one of the windows, where he knelt for morning and evening prayers. The sheets were always pristine, the Reverend didn't have any of the nasty habits that most men were afflicted with. One would almost think no one slept in this bed, only she knew he did, because she could smell his scent on the sheets when she lifted them to her face and breathed in deeply. He smelled pure and yet somehow very masculine at the same time, it was almost an absence of scent. The smell made her think of swans on a river, or fields of cotton under a silver grey sky.

She stripped off the top sheet and then frowned. The sheets were *not* pristine today, for there was a hair on the snowy white linen. A long black hair. She picked it up, a sick feeling rushing up from her stomach, for this was a woman's hair. She walked to the window, to better look at it. It shone iridescent in the filtered sunlight, glittering with tints of violet, green and blue. Released from the sheet, it spiraled down in loops. Why was there a woman's hair in the Reverend's bed? It made no sort of sense. She had never seen him so much as glance at a woman, nor had there ever been one in this house since he had taken up residence. She had never even seen a woman who had such—such *temptress* hair. Had he tracked it up perhaps, on his socks, on the sleeve of one of his immaculate sweaters? She clutched one arm across her middle, she felt sick at the thought of the Reverend giving in to a man's baser nature.

She looked at her reflection in the mirror over the bureau. Her face was mottled with anger, eyes wide with shock. It wasn't flattering. She whirled away from the mirror, her well-ordered world shaken by this simple discovery of a woman's hair in the Reverend's bed. Her sleeve caught on the corner of the bureau, and the top drawer, situated on well-oiled runners, flew out and landed with a crash, depositing all of its contents onto the floor. She felt a moment of horror—what if the Reverend should come upon her and think she was snooping through his things? It was just sweaters, as the Reverend kept separate drawers for particular articles of clothing—underwear in second drawer down, socks in the next, vestments and collars in the bottom. In the jumble of pale woolens now spread across the wood floor, she saw a flicker of brown—an envelope, sealed and thick. She leaned down and picked it up. There was nothing written on it, but it was substantial. She ran her fingers over it, wishing the flap was unstuck. She took a shaky breath. It would be the work of a minute to unstick it and then she could easily smear a dab of glue on the flap and stick it back together. The Reverend was across the way in the church, going over the arrangements and details for a marriage he was conducting this weekend. She would have plenty of time. She gathered up the sheets to take down to the laundry tub, she wanted to wash the filth of the woman's hair away as soon as possible. She put the kettle on to boil while she put the sheets in the washer. She added a little bleach along with the laundry powder, just to make certain the sheets would be entirely sanitized.

The kettle was letting out puffs of steam when she returned to the kitchen. It took two minutes to unstick the flap. She turned off the stove and headed back up the stairs, the damp envelope clutched to her chest.

Inside the bedroom she knelt down on the wood floor and shook the contents out of the envelope. There were papers in a bundle, a small leather-bound book, a long narrow envelope, and several pictures. She started with the papers, which appeared to be legal documents, property details and bank accounts. There were also dossiers on a few policemen, one a name that she recognized. She committed the names to memory and moved on to the notebook. Its pages were filled with tiny crabbed writing, line after line of it, so small she could hardly make it out. She could read snatches here and there, but knew it would be foolhardy to linger too long over deciphering it. There was a name repeated in it a few times, a name that she was familiar with because she had often seen it in the pages of the newspaper.

The pictures were of a variety of people, some women, some men and some families merely getting into their cars or walking together in a park. Half-way through the photographs, she came to the woman with the dark hair. There were several pictures of her. Some with a tall dark-haired man, and some just with children, clearly the offspring of the man. She peered closely at the pictures and determined that this was indeed the woman from whose head the incriminating hair originated. What to make of it? Why did the Reverend have pictures of the woman? She was clearly married, and Elspeth couldn't fathom that the Reverend would take up with a married woman.

Her mother had taught her that men had no control over the appendage between their legs and therefore it was the woman who must always be the guard over her own virtue. If the Reverend had this woman in his bed, it was because he was, like all men, weak in this area. She was pretty, very pretty, and Elspeth understood how much that was valued by men and how daft it could make them. She would not have thought the Reverend particularly vulnerable in this area, and found it rather disappointing that he was. She sighed; men could not be held accountable for their own actions when such a woman practiced her wiles upon them. She felt a wave of hatred for the woman so profound that her skin turned hot with it, small droplets of sweat breaking out on her face. She picked up the long narrow envelope last, and was happy to see that it wasn't sealed, but rather that the flap was just tucked inside. She opened it. There was something wrapped in tissue inside, something dark and silky. She unwrapped the tissue carefully, and then gasped in horror. It was the same hair, only there was a bunch of it here, carefully ordered, shimmering in the rare sunlight that was pouring in through the windows. The hair was neatly tied with a white ribbon. A man would have to be madly in love to do such a thing, to have a woman's hair in his bureau, bound in ribbon like it was a precious object, treasured as a love lock. She thought of her own mousy thin hair. There would not be enough to bind together, even if she were to shave her head bald and present the Reverend with the harvest.

"Elspeth, what are you doing?" The voice was calm, but she startled in horror. There was no way to fix this now, his sweaters were still in disarray on the floor and the pictures, the glossy wee squares, gleaming evilly, were everywhere. She was still clutching the silky hair in her hands, and the ribbon had come undone, the hair spreading and falling from her hands, winking like jeweled threads. His eyes were so cold as they looked at her. Surely he would fire her and maybe even banish her from the church. Everyone would know her shame; just walking down the streets to get milk from the corner shop would be an exercise in humiliation.

He knelt down beside her and took the hair from her hands. He was not smiling, but then he rarely did. He did not seem angry either. And then he said the words she had wanted to hear from the day she had met him, the most desirable words in the world.

"Elspeth, I need your help."

Chapter Twenty-one

Life, Death and Lemon Loaf

To HAVE A LOVED one missing was to exist in some strange alternate universe in which that person was neither dead nor alive, but rather in a dreadful limbo which had all sorts of legal ramifications, and yet no real help forthcoming from the actual law. Life itself took on a ridiculous aspect, simple things that used to have meaning no longer did. Choosing what to wear in the morning seemed silly at times, because what could a shirt or a pair of shoes matter anymore? Pamela was surprised if she managed to wear two shoes from the same pair, if she remembered to comb her hair more than once a day, if she remembered to eat, to sleep, to breathe. These alone still felt like monumental tasks each day.

No one warned you about the macabre visions that went along with all the uncertainty. The things that haunted you and belonged to the necropolis through which your mind wandered during the wee hours while the living world slept. The worry that he was cold, that he had suffered pain, that his body was now in some anonymous hole where it would never be found, and there would never be an answer for her, for Patrick, for Conor and Isabelle, for Deirdre. Or worse yet that he'd been left to the elements, to wind and rain and animals to scavenge and scatter. It was incomprehensible to her that his big body, so strong and capable and loving, could be gone, could be hurt and harmed and made to stop, like a great light snuffed out, leaving a dark hole in the midst of her own universe.

Then there was the search for answers. On that front she was banging her head into the same patch of brick wall over and over, regardless of the figurative blood and bruising she kept sustaining. There was always the hope, admittedly getting smaller by the week, that at some point she would ask the right question, or discover the one tiny detail that would lead to finding out what had happened to Casey. And on the underside of that there was the fear that she would never find the right question, never stumble across the truth, and that if she ever did, she wouldn't be able to bear it.

The truth was she had no patience left and she was exhausted by the ridiculous and ultimately meaningless dance she had to do each time she wanted any sort of update on whether the police had found something—anything—to indicate what had happened to her husband. Today had been especially unpleasant as it had been Constable Blackwood and not Constable Severn who came out to talk with her. It was her third time meeting with this constable, and he wasn't getting any more pleasant with familiarity. There was something about the man that made her feel like she needed a hot shower after even a few minutes spent in his presence. Patrick had gone with her the last time, and had no better luck than she in determining if the police were doing anything at all to follow up. She was driving home from her latest encounter with the constable, hoping that the soft late spring day would take some of the taint of the meeting away before she picked up Conor and Isabelle from Gert's.

Another season, come and nearly gone. It was hard to watch the pages on the calendar go past, flicking faster and faster and causing time to blur. Because, as it turned out, even when your heart was broken the seasons still changed, and life, as inexorable as a river in full spate, kept moving. Leaves broke free of buds, rivers rose and fell, lambs and calves were born and grew, and so did children.

Up ahead was a roadblock. A soldier was in the roadway motioning her to slow down. She sighed, this roadblock was a new one. It must have been erected after the shooting of a soldier last week. It consisted of a barricade of sandbags across half the extremely narrow road, a gate that had to be opened manually and a hastily constructed tin hut. She slowed to a stop and rolled her window down. Roadblocks were simply part of her daily life, but she was still uneasy any time she was stopped. In a country filled with flashpoints roadblocks were just one of many, it was a place where tensions naturally rose and things could quickly go awry. At least this soldier didn't aim his rifle at her face—that had happened more than once, and while usually it was just the soldier using the telescope to get a better look to determine who was driving, it was still terribly unnerving.

She rolled her window down, as one of the soldiers approached. She put on what she thought of as her 'neutral face', though Casey had always told her she didn't possess any such thing.

"Good afternoon, Ma'am."

Whether it was a good afternoon was highly debatable, but Pamela felt it was unwise to argue with the man carrying the machine gun. She knew the drill, and already had her license out to hand to him.

"Where are you coming from today, Ma'am?"

"Newry," she said.

"And where are you going?"

"Home—just outside of Coomnablath."

He nodded and stepped back and she got out of the truck and opened the bonnet for him. He gave it a cursory once over and nodded. "I'll be back in a minute," he said and retreated to the tin shed from which came the insistent crackle of a radio. She got back in the truck confident he would come back out and wave her through in a few seconds. He was several minutes, though, and when he emerged from the tiny hut he had an uneasy look on his face.

"I apologize. I'm going to have to ask you to pull aside, Ma'am. There's a P-check alert on your vehicle."

"A what?" she asked blankly, distracted by the thought that she would now be late.

"It means you're on the list of vehicles that have to have their license run, and *that* means we have to get authorized permission each time for the release of your vehicle through the stops."

"I…since when?" She wanted to bang her head on the steering wheel in frustration, this was going to add at least another half hour to her trip, and not just today but every blessed time she had to pass through one of the numerous roadblocks that pocked the countryside. She had been driving Noah's truck unimpeded through roadblocks for weeks now, so this was a new development.

The soldier shook his head. "I don't know, Ma'am. I'm only following instructions. I'll need you to pull over to the side."

She sighed. There was nothing for it except to do as he told her to. It wasn't his fault and there was little use taking her frustrations out on him. She pulled over and turned the truck off. It scared the hell out of her that the vehicle had been registered as one to be watched by the security forces. It was likely this was down to her association with Noah. She knew the Army kept an eye on Noah constantly, and so it stood to reason that they might want to keep an eye on anyone associated with him, regardless of the reason.

The soldier came over to her window. She rolled it all the way down and looked at him.

"I've radioed through, but sometimes it takes them a bit to run the plate and get back to me. So I'll have to ask you to be patient."

"This is ridiculous," she snapped, her self-restraint worn thin, "I'm going to be late to pick up my children."

"Well, most things here are ridiculous or hadn't you noticed?" the soldier said, and smiled, taking the sting from his words. "I'm sorry, ma'am. I'm only following orders."

"Yes and how many sins have been glossed over using those words?" she said sharply.

The soldier gave her a mild look. "Probably a great many, but none here today. Unless you count the lustful looks Jock," he nodded toward the stocky soldier who was the only other being at the roadblock, "was throwing at the sheep that ambled through a half hour ago."

She laughed in spite of herself, and he smiled. "I know it's a pain in the arse, but being that neither of us has any choice about it, we'll try to make it as painless as possible."

She left the window down, for the day was fine and there seemed little point in shutting herself inside the car where it would soon be too warm to sit comfortably. Most of the soldiers posted to Northern Ireland were painfully young. Eighteen-year-olds who often would not see nineteen, and were woefully unaware of the politics that had brought them here. One should have the privilege of naiveté at eighteen she supposed, though it was a costly vice when one was a soldier.

"How old are your children?" the soldier asked.

She hesitated before answering. Every bit of information could be used against a person in this country, and she found it was merely habit now to pause and consider before responding to even the simplest of questions. She didn't see how her children's ages could be used against her because she had no doubt that information was already on file.

"My son is three years old and my daughter is ten months."

"I have a baby girl; she was born right after I was sent over here." There was a distinctive longing in his voice. "She's just the one month old."

Damn him anyway, he had gone and made himself a human being when she had been hoping to just keep him as a uniform.

"It must be hard being away from her," she said.

He nodded. "It is. I'd love to go home. As much as you would like us out of the country here, we'd like to go."

"I'm sure you would. I fear we're stuck with each other for the time being."

"That we are." He smiled, a careful smile. He had clearly been here long enough to understand it wasn't wise to trust the natives. Of which she supposed she was one, though she didn't often feel it. She smiled back, finding that she liked the young soldier instinctively. He had lovely deep grey eyes, fringed in sooty lashes and dark hair cut very short in the military fashion. He was tall and thin, but was one of those men who conveyed an impression of quiet strength. In short, he wasn't someone to mess with.

The other soldier came up then, short and solidly built and with an electric air about him, as if he were just waiting for something to happen—Mutt to his colleague's Jeff.

"Everything all right here, corporal?"

"It's fine, private, I'm just passing the time of day with the lady here. There's a P-check on her vehicle she wasn't aware of. I'm waiting on the radio call to release her."

The young private looked at her goggle-eyed. She smiled, slightly nervous under his unblinking gaze. The corporal cleared his throat. "Jock, I think you're making the lady uncomfortable."

The short soldier turned brick red as he realized that he was staring. "I'm sorry, ma'am, I didn't mean to stare."

"Women are all he thinks about." The corporal laughed. "I can't say I blame him, mind you. It's boring as hell here when the locals aren't using us for target practice."

She raised a brow at him, trying not to laugh.

"Did I just insult you? You don't sound like a local."

"Well, I'm American by birth, but Irish by marriage," she said.

The two soldiers were Gordon Highlanders, from the northeast corner of Scotland. The corporal was from Dundee, the private from a tiny fishing village on the coast, the name of which was so long and filled with Scottish consonants and growls that Pamela couldn't remember it a minute after the private sounded it out for her.

"We were about to have a bit of tea, would you like some?" The private asked when it became clear it wasn't going to be a short wait. Between the remote location, boredom and the hostility of most of the people they encountered, it was likely a very welcome anomaly to find someone willing to be civil.

"Oh, no, but thank you for offering," she said.

"Are you certain? My mum sent over one of her famous lemon loaves. It's very good, are you certain you won't have a slice?"

With impeccable timing her stomach growled, reminding her no food had been sent its way since the early hours of the morning, and that only a cup of tea and a hastily toasted piece of bread. It was ludicrous that even a slice of lemon loaf should become such a political quandary. A person could write a book on all the various ways to get yourself killed in this country—*Life, Death and Lemon Loaf: A Practical Guide to Survival in the Six Counties.* She bit her lip to keep from laughing. It wasn't funny, though it was at times ridiculous, in the way things were ridiculous on the steps up to the gallows. It frightened her, because some days she felt she couldn't recognize or acknowledge basic human decency anymore. A small curl of rebellion unfurled in her blood. These were just young men trying to be decent and make a tense situation somewhat less so. They hadn't asked to be here, and were as much at the mercy of fate and authority as she was.

"Yes, I think I will—have a bit of the cake that is."

The private smiled, and it was one of those smiles that lit the space around like a brace of fireworks.

"That's better, and you'd best have some tea to wash it down too." He went to their tiny shelter at the side of the road, and came back with a tin mug of tea and the lemon loaf.

She accepted the tea gratefully, and spent the next half hour engaged in chat with the two young men. They kept an eye on the road in both directions but managed to have an amiable conversation as well. At the end of the thirty minutes she knew both their names, their family histories and their romantic status. The corporal—Callum—was married and the private—Jock—was currently unattached and eager to change that condition, to the extent that he actually asked her if she knew of any eligible young ladies who might be willing to date a soldier.

"Alas," she said, laughing at his hopeful expression, "I do not." The private was a nice young man, and she wished that they both lived in a world where she could introduce him to an equally nice young woman, with whom he could fall in love and build a life. She didn't actually know any eligible ladies, but she wouldn't have introduced a soldier to any of them if she had. It was too risky for both sides.

The radio crackled to life with the permission for her to proceed through the roadblock, just as she as she swallowed the last of her tea. Real life flooded back then and she brushed the crumbs from her skirt and gave the corporal the tin mug with regret. She saw the realization in the deep grey eyes—what was normal here was not in other places, and so it stood to reason that what was normal elsewhere could not ever be so here.

"It's all right," he said, quietly. "It was only tea, and no one saw."

She had become so wary of soldiers these last few years, that these two young men had taken her off guard. She hoped to God the corporal was right and that they hadn't been spotted by anyone.

She realized she was trembling as she drove through the road block and ignored the private's cheery wave. The lemon cake had turned into a cold lump in her stomach. Because while it might have only been tea and pleasant conversation for most, it was punishable by death in the world in which she lived.

Chapter Twenty-two

The Weight of Blood

THE KNOCK UPON THE DOOR came right at the witching hour, just as Pamela was readying herself for bed. She had put Conor and Isabelle to bed hours before and then had spent the intervening time setting the house to rights, getting wood in for the night, checking on Phouka and Paudeen—her lone sheep—in the byre and then returning to the house to make a cup of lavender tea in the vain hope it might send her off to sleep. She'd added three rows to the little pink sweater she was knitting for Isabelle while the tea steeped and then given it up to prowl restlessly around the house. There was something in the wind that pricked her nerves so that her skin felt like an open coursework with icy needles of water trickling through it. A visitor at this hour of the night turned that trickle into a churning flood.

"Who is it?" she called from her side of the door, Finbar growling at her heels, and a stout length of blackthorn in her hand that Casey had long ago carved into a shillelagh to hang upon the wall. She wished she had retrieved the pistol from the tea tin.

"It's Noah," came the answer, quiet but terse.

She took a breath of relief and undid the bolt and opened the door. Noah stood on the step, face grim and rain plastering his dark hair to his head. "I've got a man in bad shape here, I need yer help," he said, turning back toward the night even as he spoke. "Meet me by the byre," he added and strode off into the dark streaming night. She stood for a moment, certain that whatever lay out there was not something she was eager to face. Then she took a breath, grabbed her coat and headed out to the byre.

She smelled blood, even through the rain, and knew the man's injuries must be very bad. She caught up with Noah halfway across the yard where he was trying to hold up a boy who kept sinking to his knees. For it was a boy, not a man, bleeding in the glare of the one outside light. She came up on the other side of him. He was slim and looked to be no more than seventeen or eighteen. She propped the boy's other shoulder up with her own and helped Noah get him across the yard. She could feel a spreading warmth on her side and knew it was blood. She let him go as they neared the byre and Noah took his full weight so that she could go ahead and open the door.

Inside she lit the lantern. Phouka was chuntering in his stall, wondering why his mistress was out in his domain at this time of night. She touched his muzzle, trying to reassure him. He was a high strung horse at the best of times. Paudeen merely stuck his woolly face through the slats of his pen in curiosity.

"He's been shot, has at least five bullets in him as far as I can figure," Noah said, coming in on her heels. The boy sank to the floor, as if his bones had dissolved, his clothes sticky and red. Phouka whinnied a little, stepping sideways in his stall. Like most horses he did not like the scent of blood. Noah shot a look sideways at the horse and then, stripping off his coat, knelt down by the young man, ripping his shirt down the front.

"I wish to God I didn't need to move him, but we couldn't stay where we were."

She didn't ask him just where that had been, she would know by tomorrow when the news of it spread like wildfire along the community branches—it was never more than whispers and hints; enough whispers and hints though, and any story could be pieced together to make something that was near to whole in the telling.

Pamela knelt down on the other side of the boy, thinking rather frantically that she felt somewhat like Phouka about blood—panicked and certain it held ill portents. She placed a medical kit beside Noah having stowed it in the byre after the last wounded man had passed through. Then she watched as he brutally and efficiently set about assessing the wounds. There was so much blood that she didn't see how he could possibly know where most of it was coming from.

"Here," Noah tossed her a couple of packages from inside the kit. "Put these over the worst of the bleeding. There and there." He indicated just below the man's ribs on one side and a wound in his groin. The packages contained thick wads of gauze. She stripped the covering off and took the pads out and then put them over the wounds Noah had pointed out.

"Put yer hand here and press down," he said and placed her hand over the major artery in the groin. It would reduce the flow of blood from his thigh, there was little they could do about the chest wound, it was difficult to apply pressure with the rib cage in the way. Even now she could hear the whistle of his wound as the air moved in and out, less regular than it had been even a minute before. One finger was blocking a hole just below his abdomen, her elbow on that same arm desperately trying to keep pressure on the gauze pad. She felt like she was playing a very serious and rather gory version of Twister.

The boy's pulse was stuttering, like a record that skipped so a song was only half heard, until it stopped entirely and there was only silence left. She saw the knowledge of it in Noah's face as he started chest compressions, a grim concentration laying over his face, like he could will the boy to stay alive and force his survival, even though the slick floor of the byre told her that the blood loss was too great.

Time stretched out as if she could hear every tick of it on a clock, and she could feel the corresponding inertia in the body on the floor. Phouka was still grumbling, and she looked up at him when she could, making eye contact so that he wouldn't panic and take the back wall out of the byre in his fear. She would never forgive herself if he was hurt because of this.

Her senses were heightened, the wash of panic having made her hearing and sight that much sharper. Out in the night somewhere, she heard a barn owl call on the wind, warning prey of its approach. Inside she was aware of the pool of light they were bounded by and the heavy breath of the horse outside it, the rustle of hay, the play of light on Noah's hands as he raced against time to save this boy's life.

The gauze was slick and heavy with blood, and it had breached the pads and was sliding along her fingers now and dripping from her wrist, turning cold as it moved. The flesh beneath her hands was not as warm any more either; it was flaccid and inert. Despite the chill of the night, she was sweating, her heart pounding in her chest so that she felt the slam of it in her throat with every beat. Her arms were tingling and the bones in her hands ached. Beads of perspiration had popped out on her forehead and around her hairline. A line of it trickled down her backbone, cold as ice.

"I feel like the little Dutch boy, trying to plug a dam with his fingers," she said, wiping her forehead against her shoulder so that the sweat wouldn't drip into her eyes and blind her.

"There aren't enough fingers between the two of us to plug all the holes he's got in him," Noah said and she could hear the frustration in his words. He kept on for a few more minutes and then, "Ye can stop," he said, and blew out a breath that he had clearly been holding on to for the last several minutes. He looked exhausted, red-eyed and disheveled. "He's been gone twenty minutes by my count, even if I could bring him back he'd be brain damaged."

Her hands came away with a sucking pop, sticky with drying blood and still slick where the last of the boy's life had poured over them. Her knees were stuck to the byre floor and Noah looked like he had been butchering pigs for the last hour.

She staggered to her feet, and made her way outside to the rain barrel. The night air was raw and rain sluiced over her as soon as she stepped outside. The water in the rain barrel was cold but she plunged her hands in. It was a relief to wash away some of the blood. Phouka was still whickering, but he hadn't panicked and for that she was grateful. Noah covered the body with a blanket and for the horse it was out of sight and at least partially out of mind.

Noah came out behind her, taking a deep breath of the night air.

"I'll get the body moved before dawn," he said, his tone somber and weary. She nodded; feeling like her very marrow was weighted with lead.

"Come in for some tea," she said, "I'm sure you could use the warmth."

"All right," he said and followed her to the house, shedding his boots in the small porch, his clothing wet with rain.

Inside, she went directly to the sink, turned the water as hot as she could bear it and scrubbed her hands. There was still blood under her nails, embedded in the lines of her hands and traces of crimson on the edges of her cuffs. Noah stepped outside briefly and she suspected it was to radio for his men to come and help him remove the body.

Noah washed while she checked on the children. Both were still deeply asleep. Isabelle had kicked off all her covers, so Pamela gently replaced them, putting her hand to the baby's soft halo of curls. Isabelle snorted slightly in her sleep, something that Casey had sometimes done. She bit her lip and drew in her breath. Conor looked like his father, but his mannerisms were more like his uncle and Pat said, his grandfather as well. Isabelle, in nature, was entirely her father's daughter.

Downstairs she found Noah sitting at the table, having put the kettle on already. She made the tea in silence, for small talk seemed entirely beyond her scope at present. She had left the shirt he had loaned her out on the table and he'd changed into it so that he was clean and free of blood on his top half.

When the tea was done steeping she put the pot on the table, steaming, and then took day old scones out of the bread box, put them on a plate and placed them on the table along with butter and jam. Scones were one of the few things she had mastered the baking of and so wasn't afraid to serve them to the man.

He took two scones and then poured out the tea for her and himself. It felt odd to be sharing a cuppa in the wee hours with any man who wasn't Casey, but it wasn't uncomfortable or awkward.

"Ye have a beautiful wee home here," he said, looking about the room. "Yer man did the work himself, no?"

"He did. He's a natural craftsman."

"Ye always talk about him in the present tense."

It was a blunt statement, but somehow she didn't mind bluntness from Noah.

"I know I do. Likely I seem crazy to you. You know what a disappearance like my husband's means in this country, and so do I. Only I just don't feel that he's gone. I know how that sounds, but it's just the reality of the situation for me."

Noah nodded and addressed himself to the tea and scones. What he said next surprised her.

"Ye were brave tonight. Not many women have the sort of steel in them that ye showed out there. Wherever he is, yer man must miss ye, ye seem a rare woman to me."

"Thank you," she said, though she wasn't sure how complimentary it was to be called a rare woman by the likes of Noah Murray. "Where did you learn your medical skills?" she asked.

"Well, ye'll hardly countenance this, but I learned from a British Army medic."

"What?"

He laughed. "Have I finally managed to surprise ye, Pamela?"

"Yes, you have. It's not the most obvious of answers, you have to admit."

"No, I suppose not. He was someone I knew when I was a boy. He was kind to me, an' he taught me how to stitch up a wound, an' how to restart a man's heart, and how to triage someone bleeding out."

"I guess what surprises me is that you even knew a British soldier, much less were friends with one. How did you meet him?"

He looked at her steadily and she felt like he was trying to answer something for himself, before he replied. "My father was beating the hell out of me in the fields one day, the soldier happened along an' had got his directions muddled up, or so he said, when he came across us. He made my father stop. I was twelve, an' he would check in with me from time to time after that day. He tried to be my friend, but I was as wary as a crossed badger an' not the easiest child to become acquainted with—still, he taught me things, an' even then I could appreciate that."

They were quiet for a bit then, as the aftermath of the night settled in. She felt numb and exhausted and everything had a slight haze around it: the kettle on the Aga, the mugs hanging over the counter, the whiskey bottle glowing amber from its place on the sideboard. She thought about having a drink, just to take away the immediacy of all that had happened. In the window over the sink she could see the two of them reflected, side-by-side, Noah's eyes meeting hers there in the glass. Even in the night-dark window his eyes were a deep and brilliant blue.

"What will happen to him now? Does he have family that will be missing him?" she asked, looking away from the shared reflection down to the table, uncertain why she was asking. She was digging a thorn under her own skin with the question and they both knew it.

"Aye, he did. I'll go tell them. He'll be given a burial with full army honors."

"And will that comfort his mother?" she said, angry suddenly at the waste of a young man's life.

"No," Noah replied mildly, "I don't imagine it will. If it matters I did try to discourage him from joinin'. I thought he wasn't right for the life."

"What qualities make a man right for the life?"

He looked at her for a long moment before answering. "I think ye know the answer to that question well enough."

Pamela stood and took the dishes from the table. They rattled together as she carried them to the sink, for she was shaking, whether it was with delayed shock or rage, she couldn't be certain.

She filled the sink and put the dishes in. Her hands still felt like they were sheathed in blood and she thought the warm water might be a relief, that something as routine as wiping up the dishes might return her to some semblance of normality. Noah came and stood beside her, took the tea towel from her shoulder and began to dry the dishes. She thought she might break into hysterical laughter. There was a body in the byre still to be dealt with, and here was the most feared man in the UK drying her dishes as if he hadn't a care in the world.

She swayed a little, vision going grey at the edges. She clutched the edge of the counter, and Noah put a hand to her back to steady her.

"Are ye all right? It's the blood an' the death, it takes some people badly. Blood has a weight to it, an' it weighs heavier on some than others."

"Does it, then?" she said with no small sarcasm. "You couldn't tell by watching you, you're cool as a cucumber."

"Ye're angry with me," he said, and continued to dry the dishes and place them on the counter, neatly stacking each piece. She could feel the spot on her back where his hand had been.

"Yes and no. It's not that," she said, the lightheadedness growing. "It's... it's Casey, I..." her voice faltered, she could not say the words, for that terrible black heaviness in her chest was threatening to break apart. She couldn't allow it; if she did, it would drown her, right here in her own kitchen. She tried to take a breath and found she couldn't. Then Noah stepped toward her, and she could smell him, his own particular scent—something inexplicable, like fresh hay and also the chill smell of rain clouds just before they released a downpour. He touched her face, smoothing her hair back and then, without warning, pulled her to him and held her. She was too startled to do anything but allow it. And then to her surprise she found it was a relief to be held, to feel another body against her own, another's flesh and warmth. It did not even seem terribly odd that it should be Noah Murray. Not after the night they had gone through together. She had half expected him to smell of blood, not unpleasantly, just that she had thought he would carry the copper heat of it on him, always. Especially tonight.

She knew she did not have to explain herself to him, he wouldn't ask, and she did not need to fill the silence with the whys and wherefores, because there weren't any really, there was just the fear that what had happened to that young man out there—the panic, the blood, the inglorious end on a byre floor with strangers—was in some way the same as what may have happened to her husband. Noah knew it as well as she did.

It was easy to be held by him, perhaps because the man did not need anything of her, did not want her as a man wants a woman, did not have expectations of anything between them. And then memory surged, and she thought of the last time Casey had held her in this kitchen, and how they had danced with their tiny daughter between them, and she stepped back from the embrace. She felt her face flush, even as she looked up to find him watching her, his expression unreadable.

She didn't quite understand what it was that drew her to this man, to his company. Perhaps it was that the lonely child in her recognized the lonely child in him.

"I'm sorry, that was maybe a bit forward of me," he said, his voice quiet.

"No," she replied, "it's all right. It just hit me that the last person to hold me here in the kitchen was my husband, that's all. We were dancing together late at night, with Isabelle."

"It sounds nice," he said.

"It was." She flushed again, feeling as though she had given him a glimpse into an intimate corner of her life, something that had belonged only to her and Casey before. She busied herself with wiping the counters down, waiting for the heat in her face to subside. She could feel him watching her and turned once she felt her expression was sufficiently neutral. He had a curious look on his face, his head tilted to one side, tea towel still held lightly in his hands.

"What is it?" she asked.

"It's only that I was wonderin' why is it that ye're not afraid of me?"

"I don't know," she said, "maybe it's just that I'm not afraid of much these days, unless it's something happening to my children."

"Fear is not always a bad thing, Pamela. It teaches us that there are boundaries in the world that it's best not to cross over. Sometimes consequences, as ye know, are far too permanent. It's true everywhere, an' perhaps more so in our wee corner of the world."

"I know, only I think I am tired of fear. I've lived with it too long and it hasn't stopped me from losing people I love."

"Aye, I can understand that."

She put the dishes away in silence. The quiet with Noah was not uncomfortable. It was clear that he neither expected nor indulged in small talk merely for the sake of filling the silence.

He looked toward the door suddenly. There had been no sound, and no indication of movement in the yard. She turned toward him, a brow cocked in query.

"My men are here to take the body away, I'd best go see to them," he said, folding the towel neatly and hanging it over the rack by the Aga so it would dry. He was a man of details, even in the midst of trauma.

She locked the door behind him. She didn't want to see the body being removed; she'd had enough blood for one night. Noah was right, blood had a weight, and right now it felt like stones upon her back. She started up the stairs, hoping that she might be able to doze for a bit, before facing a full day with energetic children who, thankfully, had no notion of the previous night's events. She paused on the narrow landing, where the stairs turned at a right angle before they continued up to the top floor. Casey had installed a small octagon window here, saying eight was a fortunate number and therefore all views out this window would be happy ones.

The yard below was already empty, the byre door closed tight and no trace of the last frantic hours left upon the land. Everything looked entirely normal, each building snug against the night's rain, each animal tucked up where it was meant to be.

The haze was still there around her vision, so that the dawn was a rolled pearl coming in across the horizon, touching soft as down upon the weather vane on the byre's peak, the red door of the shed, the overturned soil in the garden. The view from this window was no longer happy, so much as empty, because she could not expect to see Casey stride across the yard, spade in hand, or axe, or any of the other implements with which he had kept their small homestead running smoothly.

It struck her sometimes, when she was tired and could not push the thoughts away, nor firmly tamp them into place with the nails of sheer will power, how much her life had changed in such a short time. There were times when she hardly knew herself, or what she was willing to do to find any scrap of information that might lead to an answer.

She put her forehead to the glass. Her eyes were burning behind the dome of her lids and bright blossoms of crimson, the same shade as the blood on the byre floor, bloomed across the dark landscape inside her head. Closing her eyes provided no relief, for the night of which she had spoken to Noah rose up in front of her, soft as the dawn clouds, and as painful to her as needles drawn fine through her heart.

It had been the night before he disappeared. Pamela had awakened in the wee hours, breasts tight, slightly panicked that Isabelle had overslept her feeding time. Isabelle was not one to miss her meals. When she turned over and sat up she realized Casey was out of the bed and had been for a bit, for the sheets were cool to the touch.

She had found father and daughter in the kitchen.

The light in the kitchen was low, just the small one over the Aga was on. Casey was singing softly, an old Irish lullaby called **Seoithin, Seo Ho.** *It was, Casey had explained to her the first time she had heard him singing it, a warning to babies to sleep before the fairies could come to lure them away. She peeked around the corner and saw that he was dancing, a slow shuffle, with his daughter over his shoulder. Isabelle was quiet, her daddy's voice being the most magic of soothers to her. He was barefoot, clad only in jeans that he must have pulled on when he heard Isabelle crying. The contrast between the delicate tiny baby that was her daughter and the big man that was her husband put a knot in Pamela's throat.*

At the end of their dance, he held Isabelle out, one hand on the small diapered bottom, the other hand cupping the back of the fragile skull. Isabelle's dark eyes were big and round, gazing intently into her father's face, as he spoke to her in the soft voice he used with her. He always spoke lovely nonsense to the children, tales he'd thought up during his work day, or bits of sage advice that they didn't understand but took in like they were imprinting each word on their souls. Tonight the vein of his conversation seemed more serious as if something weighed on him which he could only express to someone he loved who could not understand the full import of his words.

"My daddy always said ye could tell a wee one yer heart an' soul, because they never would judge ye for the contents of either. These days my heart an' soul seem to be filled with yerself, yer brother an' yer mammy. I worry about things I never did think to find myself worryin' about. The three of ye have made the world seem a different place all together, more beautiful, an' far more terrifyin' at the same time. All the trouble that I've become accustomed to over my life seems so much darker now, an' I'm terrified of it touchin' yerself or yer brother in any shape at all. An' I hate that it has touched yer mammy too many times already."

Isabelle stretched her chin up toward Casey, her dark eyes fixed to her father's face and cooed softly as though acknowledging everything he had said. Standing in the shadow of the stairs, Pamela felt tears prickle at the back of her throat. How she loved this man, and the children they had made together from a love which had weathered so much, and come out stronger in the end. More than the house that he had built to shelter them all, this man was her home and the place in this world where she went for sanctuary. She took a moment to admire him, the depth of his chest, the long lines of him, the dark hair that whorled across his chest and down his belly. The brute strength that kept her safe, but was gentle in her service and that of their children.

He was still talking to the baby, who was patting his face with her tiny ivory and rose fingers.

"I want to make the world a clean, beautiful place for ye—aye, ye can purse up yer wee mouth, but it's true. I wish I could fix it all, control everything that comes yer way. I know that I can't, an' that's maybe the hardest thing about bein' yer daddy. Let me tell ye wee lady, ye'll not marry a man like yer da. I'll chase him off with a shotgun if such a one comes sniffin' round ye. I tell ye, I don't know what yer mammy was thinkin' when she married myself, but we'll not question that too much then, or she might come to her senses an' head for the hills, no?"

Isabelle burbled with laughter, as if she thought her daddy was the funniest man who had ever walked the planet. He bent his face down to Isabelle's and kissed her forehead, nose and chin. "I adore ye, wee girl an' don't ye ever forget it. There will always be a man in the world that loves ye, come what may, even if he is yer old da'."

Pamela crossed the kitchen floor, the wood cool and smooth beneath her bare feet. Casey turned and smiled, as though he had known she was there for a while.

"It was the smartest thing her mammy ever did, marrying that boy," she said softly, reaching up to kiss him.

"Well, I'm not entirely certain 'twas smart, girl, but I'm glad ye did lose yer senses for a bit at least." He pulled her to him with his free arm. She reached her arms up around his neck. He began slow dance steps, humming softly in her ear. It was an old song that she had always loved.

'See the market place in old Algiers…
Send me photographs and souvenirs
Just remember when a dream appears
You belong to me…'

She swayed with him, her body melding to his own, following his steps with ease, and it occurred to her that he was as much a part of her flesh now as her very fingers or the slope of her shoulders. He was essential to her, the scent of him, the feel of him, his heat that always warmed her.

"There is nothing I wouldn't do for you woman or for our children."

The words startled her out of the half sleepy state she was in and she looked up at him in alarm. "Why are you saying that?" she asked, with the unsettling feeling that there were words he wasn't saying, words that he ought to speak but was afraid to.

"Because it's true," he said, dark eyes unfathomable in the low light. "I would do anything for the three of ye."

"I know that, Casey," she said.

"Aye, but it deserves sayin' now an' again."

"It goes both ways, man."

He kissed her very gently. "I know, ye've proven it often enough in the past. Ye're a wee bit scary when someone crosses yer family too."

She kissed the top of Isabelle's downy head, tears pricking at the back of her eyes again. She always felt terribly fragile for months after giving birth, as if the world were suddenly a porous place where the ground might crack beneath her feet, taking someone she loved without warning.

"I wish I could keep you safe too, man. So while you're busy protecting all of us, take care for yourself."

He had kissed her then, silencing her fears and they had gone upstairs together, the baby drowsing on Casey's shoulder. And then, after she fed Isabelle and they returned her to her crib, they had retreated to their own bed, and he had given her the security of his body, the reassurance of it in that wordless way that spoke so deeply of what lay between them.

'I'll be so alone without you...'

She spoke the words, without a tune, the tone of them broken and fragmented, hearing in her head the song as he had sung it, the soft whisper of his voice in her ear and the final sentence he had spoken that night.

"I'll keep ye safe, darlin', that's my job an' I take it seriously."

And now, standing alone at their eight-sided window where the view would never be the same, she wondered if he had taken it so seriously that it had killed him.

Chapter Twenty-three

Dealings With Badgers

"Tea, whiskey, salmon, soda bread and a pie," Jamie said, handing a box filled with the listed items into Pamela's arms. "Maggie believes none of us are capable of feeding ourselves, so she's sent along rations to keep everyone going."

"They are gratefully received," Pamela said, taking the box from him so that he could remove his coat and shoes. "Tomas has a moldy block of cheese, milk that went off last week, and a clutch of withered carrots. Kate brought food though and is in there now cooking up a storm, so I suspect we're going to be spoiled for dinner."

Jamie straightened from removing his shoes and smiled, taking the box back from her. "Lead me to the kitchen."

Jamie had done a bit of covert snooping on Patrick's behalf, and was here to present his findings today. It was a working bee for the lot of them, as Patrick and Tomas prepared to make a run at convincing the courts that Oggie Carrigan deserved an appeal.

Truth be told, she was a bit nervous for Jamie to meet Tomas. Both men meant a great deal to her, albeit in very different ways. She wanted them to like one another, though she could hardly fathom anyone disliking Jamie. Tomas, on the other hand…she sighed. She trusted implicitly in Jamie's ability to hold his own however, even with someone of Tomas' unpredictable temperament. She had spent a few evenings here with the children, as well as a Saturday, during which she had given the kitchen a rather fierce scrubbing while Tomas played outside with Conor and Isabelle took her afternoon nap. She felt comfortable in the old man's company, he was blunt and prickly, but he was also kind under the gruff exterior.

Tomas was in the kitchen where Kate was cooking on the gleaming stove, which Pamela had taken the time to black and polish during her cleaning spree. Pat sat at the table, a stack of papers three feet high in front of him, and a steaming pot of tea adorning the center of the scrubbed oak. Jamie set the crate of food down, and took out the bottles of Connemara Mist and placed them handily by the tea. Pamela added the smoked salmon and bread to the array of food Kate already had simmering, baking and braising in and on the ancient stove. Isabelle was playing with a stack of rings and Conor was next to her, absorbed in a coloring book.

"Tomas, this is Jamie, Jamie, Tomas." She stood back a little as the men shook hands, Tomas eyeing Jamie up and down in his usual bluntly assessing manner. Jamie was genial but cool, as was his own wont when first meeting someone.

"It's all right, lass, I won't bite him," Tomas said, lingering back with her as Jamie moved forward to hug Kate and Pat, Conor already looking up at him and smiling.

"I'm not certain I believe that," she said, but she heaved a sigh of relief nonetheless.

Twenty minutes later they were all settled with tea in hand, Tomas' fortified with a tot of Connemara Mist. Kate had just put a plate of still-warm ginger snaps on the table and the children were still happily occupied with toys and crayons and books.

There was a palpable tension around the table, everyone eager to hear what it was Jamie had found out.

"Well then, Mr. Kirkpatrick?" Tomas said, voicing the impatience everyone was feeling.

"It's safe to talk?" Jamie asked, and Tomas needed no further explanation. He did seem to bristle a little in his reply. She saw what Patrick meant about the badger being his spirit animal.

"I've had it swept for bugs, just two days ago. Someone has been *in situ* ever since."

"Good," Jamie said, blandly, as if everyone had their house swept for listening devices on a regular basis. She knew he had his own house swept every few months, the way most people would have their chimneys cleaned or their windows washed. It was a hazard, she supposed, of working for a spy agency.

He took a swallow of his tea, and then set his cup down on the table.

"Here it is then. There were at least four policemen involved in the matter. Certainly there are more that knew—one died of a heart attack six months back. The other two have some sort of oath of secrecy, even my source couldn't get a peep out of them. The remaining member of the quartet might be amenable to certain kinds of persuasion. He's drowning himself in drink, due, my source believes, to guilt over Oggie's conviction. My source says the other two men are worried about him because they think he'll talk when he's drunk. He hasn't so far—though I think the biggest fear they have is pillow talk, as he's a bit of a womanizer. He's on his own, an outsider, because he was discharged from the RUC only six months after the trial. His name is Andrew Donaldson, and he is your weak link."

"How is it this man hasn't come to our attention before?" Tomas looked over at Pat, who shook his head.

"He didn't come up in any of the interviews, this is the first I've heard of him. He wasn't involved in the initial investigation that's for certain, because there's no documentation—the little I've been able to access—with that name on it."

Jamie took a bite of a ginger snap and another swallow of tea before answering. "He tried to make complaints, but it's not on the record, anything he said or did has been erased or not taken down in the first place."

"So how does yer source know this then?"

"Because he's placed to know such things," Jamie said. "He can be trusted; his information has never been wrong."

"Because ye pay him?" Tomas asked.

"No," Jamie replied coolly, "I don't pay for information, it taints it and then the informant tries too hard to please and tends to jolly up the information in order to make it as palatable as possible. What I've given you is only slightly useful because without a named source or witness it's inadmissible in court anyway, as you well know."

Tomas tapped his finger to his pursed lips. "Aye, it is, but I think we might be able to pull a few strings usin' the information to encourage others to talk, or even to scare a few of them."

"You'll have to be exceedingly careful," Jamie said, "these people have lied for some time, and they aren't going to take kindly to anyone trying to open up a worm can they thought they had put the lid on long ago."

They got down to work then, with individual breaks to see to the children, or make fresh tea or go outside and get some fresh air to relieve burning eyes and stiff backs. Pamela had, with Tomas' permission, cleared the formal dining table and they set up in the big room which had the advantage of light pouring in from the garden, and no other distractions beyond the sound of the birds and the occasional exclamation over just how corrupt the entire proceedings around Oggie Carrigan had been.

They stopped near to six for dinner, Maggie's salmon, bread and cheese and Jamie's whiskey having made a neat tea earlier in the day. They had accomplished a fair bit, sorting through endless paper and placing each piece in its appropriate stack as to its importance and relevance. Over the ambrosial dinner Kate had made, the chat was general and light, flowing along with the food and drink.

After dinner, they moved to Tomas' library, where the fire was built high and hot in the huge hearth. Between the food and drink and heat there was a soporific lull to the atmosphere.

"How did the two of yez meet?" Tomas asked, leaning back and folding his hands over his belly and looking pointedly at Pamela and Jamie. Pamela was settling Isabelle who had fallen asleep on her shoulder at dinner and so she let Jamie answer for the two of them.

He looked over at her and smiled. "On a midnight shore, far distant from here, a very long time ago. I mistook her for a selkie dancing in the waves."

"Sounds like a fairy tale," Tomas said.

"It felt like one at the time," Jamie said. "I thought I had maybe imagined her at first, until she had an accident involving a horse and I came across her just as it happened."

"He rescued me and in thanks I threw up on his shoes. At which point he knew I wasn't a mystical creature of any sort."

Jamie laughed. "I wasn't going to mention that."

"Jamie is my oldest friend in the world," she said, turning back toward Tomas. It was true, he was the oldest and dearest, as well as the person to whom she had turned during some of the hardest times in her life. Just as she had these last months. He had never once let her down. Jamie smiled at her, and she noticed Tomas watching the two of them with a shrewd light in his eyes.

She looked about her, Kate's cooking and the small glass of brandy she'd had after dinner relaxing her so that the bird in her chest was, for a small space, quiet. The firelight gilded the shabby edges of the room, rendering the entire scene into a sort of Renaissance painting, brushed fine with gold leaf round its edges. The scarred desk, heaped high with papers, the scored floor, where she was certain badger droppings still lurked, despite her best efforts. The bookshelves chock-a-block with legal tomes, history books, and papers tied with fading ribbons, for Tomas kept to the old system of tying documents with the affiliated colors—black for wills and probates, green for land matters, pink for defense briefs and white for prosecution briefs.

And the people inside the painting, the living heart of it. Patrick all dark shadows, whiskers tinted blue in the light; Kate straight-backed beside him on the lumpy sofa, but with a hand laid lightly within his; Tomas lord of the wild manor, his veined nose and reddened eyes softened by the fire-light; Isabelle, asleep on a mattress that had been dragged down from the attic. On the hygiene of this article Pamela chose not to dwell, and at least the blankets were clean. Jamie was sitting opposite Tomas, now engaged in the sort of debate the old lawyer loved, on the topic of just where Irish history had slid off the rails, and what exact events had led to their current quagmire in Northern Ireland. Conor was falling asleep, curly head propped up against Jamie's knee, with Jamie's hand on his head, steadying him so that he didn't fall over.

She waved off Jamie's offer of a chair and curled up on the rug at his feet beside Conor. She sat quiet and let the words flow back and forth over top of her, from Tomas to Patrick, to Jamie and back again, the conversational ball never dropping, but lofting from one man to the next, sometimes with great fervor and at others with a gentle sally.

Around her Elizabethan Ireland came to life through its lords and peasants, its wars and famines as they discussed the history of the house in which they all sat.

"Yer own ancestor was one of the twilight lords, as Patrick calls them, was he not? Silken James Kirkpatrick, first of the name."

"He was, indeed," Jamie said with a smile.

"He was rather legendary," Tomas said, "for more than one reason, if the history books are to be believed."

Jamie laughed. "Yes, he was fairly illustrious, to use a polite term. He was once in great favor with Queen Elizabeth, but fell from grace rather spectacularly by the end of his life. He fought in the Desmond Wars. That is the fate of so many of we Irish, to fight in losing battles, sometimes all our lives."

Tomas' eyes lit up and he rose without explanation and went to his shelves, where he began to rummage, muttering to himself all the while. He came out with a sheaf of papers between two blackened and bowed boards, the whole thing held together with dusty and moth-eaten ribbon. He walked across the room and handed the whole parcel to Jamie.

"Yer ancestor stayed here for a bit, did ye know that?"

"No, I did not," Jamie replied, taking the bundle of paper into his own hands.

"Those are a few letters, an' a sort of journal. I'm certain they're his. Ye're welcome to have a look. Take it home if ye like, ye can return it through Miss Pamela here, next time she chooses to grace me with her presence."

"Thank you," Jamie said. He laid the papers to the side, though she saw his eyes linger on them for a moment with a curious longing.

"Does his blood run in you?" Tomas asked, and there was no mistaking the challenge in his tone.

"If by that you are asking if I'm willing to throw myself on the blazing pyre of republican martyrdom, the answer is a resounding no."

"Most men would be proud to have such an ancestor."

"Most men, yes, but not me. He was, after all, like every rebel before him and every one since. He died worn down and humiliated, just as did the Great O'Neill and Tyrone, and Wolf Tone and Parnell. This country will take every last drop of blood a man has, and every last drop of pride until finally it takes his last breath, and then the wheel simply grinds on without him. Was it Spencer who said that change is like the wind on the sea? Water moves, but it never alters. The history of this country is as water, it moves but it never truly alters. And so we continue to fight and shed blood and revolve in our unending cycle of patriot martyrs."

"O-ho, a poet *and* a cynic. Well, laddie I know better than to fight with such a creature. A man might as well try to fight with the wind. It does not bother ye then, to have British soldiers in the streets of yer own city, to see young men on their knees with machine guns held to their heads?"

"It bothers me more than I could express to you had we a month of conversation ahead of us, but I do not see how more blood is going to finish it and give the next generation hope for a better life, one without soldiers in the streets and killers in our country lanes."

Pat, ever the diplomat, changed the tack of the conversation.

"Perhaps we should get back to the business at hand?"

Jamie smiled gratefully. "Yes, Pat you're right."

"So what can we do with the information we have? Is there a way to turn it to our advantage? There's only one man who we know of that is rotting with guilt, and he's where—I think we can all agree—we will have to make our attempt. Is the alcohol a big enough weakness? We need somewhere," Pat said, "to poke in the knife."

"Well," Tomas said, "beyond the drink, his weakness, as ye mentioned, is women." His eyes lit on Pamela, and he opened his mouth to say something only to have both Pat and Jamie abruptly cut him off.

"Absolutely not," Pat said, glaring at Tomas.

Jamie, the wiser and more experienced man in this situation, directed his glare and comment at Pamela.

"No damn way, don't even think about it, Pamela."

"Think about what?" she asked, her indignation fueled more by the fact that he had guessed her thoughts so quickly, rather than any innocence of said thoughts on her part.

Jamie merely raised one golden brow at her. "Seducing information out of some sot in a bar. It would be far too easy for you, and far too dangerous."

"Good heavens, Jamie, I wasn't planning to do anything of the sort."

Jamie made a sound that could best be described as dubious. She stood, attempting to look offended at his doubt and began to clear away the glasses and dishes that had collected in the room over the evening. She took them to the kitchen, and ran water in the ancient stone sink, absent-mindedly swooshing her hand through the water to encourage the soap to bubble. Jamie's words had upset her because there was a dark truth to them, and at the heart of that dark truth were the things Casey had believed, the things of his past which he had been trying to leave behind so that their own future might be more secure. It bothered her also because she knew Jamie only partially believed his own words, for many of his actions, however covert he might believe them to be, spoke the opposite of the eloquent speech he had just given in Tomas' study.

It was easy, she knew, to judge and draw conclusions from the outside. It was easy to say what was right and what was wrong when you weren't afraid of dying, when you hadn't been born to a particular world and could draw conclusions from books and two minute montages on television. What she had believed normal even a few years ago, no longer held authority in her world. Normal was something else entirely in gritty Belfast, in green and austere South Armagh, in wee Derry with her winding walls. Normal looked very different even now in her own home than it had just a few months ago.

Tomas came up beside her, and began to dry the dishes.

"I have a woman comes in to do this, ye know. Ye don't have to clean every blessed time ye're here. Ye're meant to be a guest, not a housekeeper."

"I know you have a housekeeper, I'm just not certain whose house it is she's keeping because it's certainly not this one," she said tartly.

"I like him," Tomas said.

"Really? It was a little hard to tell."

"The man is no fragile flower, he held up just fine. He's the sort of man ye can't quite get on an equal footing with—mind, you seem to hold yer own with him well enough."

"Jamie has been my friend for so long that I don't always remember how intimidating he can sometimes be."

"I suppose it helped bein' a child when first ye met the man."

"It did, I didn't know well enough to be intimidated. He was incredibly kind to a lonely child; the poor man hasn't been able to rid himself of me since."

"He doesn't seem to mind," Tomas said. "He's right fond of ye."

She cast a glance over her shoulder to make certain that neither Pat nor Jamie had moved into earshot.

"That matter you were discussing before, about the weak link?"

"Aye?" Tomas said.

"I think I can help."

Chapter Twenty-four

Nothing to Lose

PAMELA LINGERED A LITTLE at the entrance to the hotel. She was, to be frank, still quite stunned that Tomas had agreed to her plan.

"Come on, Pamela, buck up, you've faced worse," she muttered it under her breath, but the man passing by on the sidewalk still gave her a bit of a berth. She tottered a little on her heels as she crossed the marble floor of the hotel lobby. She hadn't worn pumps in a very long time since her life rarely called for dress up of this sort. She pushed down her nerves as best as she could and thought that she was going to allow herself a drink, a large one, to quell the racing of her heart. She had, indeed, faced worse before, and managed to walk away from the situation, if not triumphant, at least still with all her bodily parts intact.

Tomas had had his misgivings right up until he had watched her walk off across the street to enter the hotel. "He likes all women—short, tall, narrow, wide, young, old—but I suspect he's never seen a woman quite like yerself. He'll be round ye like a bee to a honey bowl. It's gettin' him to talk that will be the trick."

"Don't worry, just leave that to me," she'd said. She didn't feel quite so confident now in her ability to make the man open up. In the drink or not, he was likely to be wary if she started quizzing him about particulars. From somewhere Tomas had procured a wire, which felt like a burning brand against her skin. She hoped it would work, the setup hadn't exactly looked like the latest in spy gadgetry.

Forgive me, she said to the man who lived in her heart. She seemed to spend more time in silent communion with Casey these days than she did with God. He would be beside himself with worry if he knew what she was about to do. Or, if she were being honest with herself, he would be so furious he wouldn't have the space for worry. She had a fleeting fantasy of him coming into the bar and putting her over his shoulder and carting her out. She smiled. It was a nice fantasy, but she needed to keep her focus in the here and now. Never mind Casey, Jamie and Patrick would have her head if they knew what she was up to.

The hotel bar was a nice one, as such things went. She knew it was a place for people to relax after a day of business, to unwind before heading up to their hotel room, or a place for assignations. Tomas was waiting outside for her, though they had come in separate cars.

She got up on a stool, trying to maintain a look of nonchalance. The bead of sweat that was currently running down the hollow of her spine and the trembling in her hands, however, wasn't doing much to help maintain her façade. She crossed one leg over the other, the slit in her skirt aligning as it was meant to—enough thigh to make a man sit up and pay attention, but not enough that he thought she was a complete tart. She didn't want things getting out of hand too quickly. Other than playing it cool and sitting here having a much needed drink, Tomas hadn't given her much of a script. He seemed rather more certain than she was that the man would find his way to her.

Tomas had been right, for she hadn't done more than sip at the vodka tonic she'd ordered when a man heaved himself up on the stool beside her. He smelled strongly of dirty copper, the way people who drank too much often smelled.

"Hello," he said, voice overly loud, causing a few heads to turn toward them. She looked at him.

"Hi," she said, swallowing nervously. This suddenly seemed a catastrophically bad idea.

"Not from around here?" he asked, and she thought that chat up lines in bars seemed standard regardless of country.

They had decided her cover story should be as close to the truth as possible. "I'm American, from New York." Which she was, just not recently. She sipped a little more of the vodka tonic, so far it wasn't doing anything to calm her nerves.

"Here for pleasure or business?" he asked. The edge of his voice was broad and melted, the way it often was in people who were always partially inebriated.

"A little of both. I'm hoping to see some of the countryside while I'm here too. My family came from Ireland a couple of generations back."

"Ah, ye can tell, ye've the look of an Irish colleen about ye. What with the lovely skin an' the eyes."

Pamela rather thought most women, regardless of national origin, were possessed of skin and eyes, but forbore to share this observation with the man.

He ordered her another drink, without asking, though she was not even halfway through her current one. The second would be her limit. Tomas had told her this man had the almost bottomless capacity of the chronic alcoholic. There was no way she could keep up with him, or she would have to be taken out of here on a stretcher. Two drinks was her absolute limit, she had a notoriously low threshold with alcohol.

"Ye're very attractive," he said, and smiled.

"Thanks," she said, turning her body ever-so-slightly toward him so that he would think she was receptive. In truth, she felt mildly repulsed, and also sad to see what the drink had done to the man. He bore very little resemblance to the youthful police officer in the pictures Tomas had shown her.

"What about you, what is it that you do?" she asked.

"I'm a policeman," he said, "or I was."

"Really, a police officer?" She leaned forward a little more, and put her fingers an inch or two from his arm on the bar. "That must be fascinating work. My father was a policeman back in New York, part of the 94th."

"Was he? Then you know how it is—how we're the bad guys all the time, even when we try to do something right. Dealing with the scum of the earth most days, an' somehow we're in the wrong, we're the persecutors."

"Oh, I do know," she agreed, heightening her accent a smidge so that it was more Long Island than where she had grown up in Manhattan. "My dad had this case that almost destroyed his life. He took early retirement because of it, well that and they pushed him out because he liked his evening tipple. It was that last case that started him drinking though. He'd stop at the bar on the way home at night, to take the edge off." She hesitated for a moment, because the story was going to have to be just right, neither veering too close to his own, nor too far away. It was a delicate balance she had to achieve.

"It was one of those messy cases, you know, where it's just a shambles from the get go?"

He nodded, bloodshot eyes trained on her face, as if her story might offer him some sort of absolution.

"So this prostitute gets killed, but she'd been a CI for the police for a long time, because she was connected to some really big players in the drug scene. She's found dead one morning, face down in the Hudson River, shot in the head. It's execution style. So it's sending a message, yeah?"

He nodded to show he was following her, and she took a few seconds to push from her mind another prostitute, not an imaginary one, who had been found facedown in another river in a different city.

"They thought it was a hit, or maybe her pimp. He was this real nasty sort, the kind that's in trouble from the time they're old enough to make trouble. You know the sort? Little greasy guy, they called him Carlos the Weasel behind his back. Thing is my dad found out it wasn't him that killed her, but another policeman, someone he'd known and trusted for years. Turned out the guy had been having a fling with her and she was threatening to tell his wife. The pimp gets twenty-five years for the murder, and then he gets killed his first year in prison. He wasn't a good guy, but he died for something he didn't do. My dad thought the cop arranged to have this guy killed in prison, to keep him from talking. He went to the top brass, told his story, gave his proof and they shut him down so fast and cold he didn't know what had hit him. By the time he understood, they'd pensioned him out, blackened his name and ruined his life. That," she said, allowing a quiver into her voice, "is when he started drinking in earnest."

She decided that was enough of her hard luck sell, he would either buy it or he wouldn't. Too much detail sounded like a lie, not enough would never convince. She hoped that she had hit the right balance.

"I'm sorry to hear that. What happened to yer father?"

She looked down into her drink, she didn't have to fake this part because her father was gone and she missed him, especially of late. "He died a couple of years later, cirrhosis of the liver." She shrugged, "It sounds like one of those sordid stories you expect out of New York. I'm sure you don't have that kind of corruption here, it's such a beautiful part of the world." She switched gears back to slightly naïve American.

"Oh, ye'd be wrong thinkin' that, wrong entirely."

"Really?" she said, mixing an equal part of breathiness with a touch of dubiousness. Which was no easy feat while trying to maintain a Long Island accent.

He got a look on his face, which she recognized. It was of a man who was sure he was about to impress her.

Please God, she muttered to herself, please God that he might be about to tell her the right story and she wasn't about to spend an hour listening to a drunken ramble.

It *was* a drunken ramble as it turned out, but it was the right drunken ramble. Fortified by another shot of Bushmills with a pint on the side, he began. With his first words she felt a quiver of excitement go through her.

"There were this case we landed some time back, wee girl gets killed in a cemetery—terrible scene, lots o' blood, throat's cut, clothes are in total disarray, in such a way as to know that she's been raped. Sometimes there's no suspects, or not even one good one but this case had too many. Four of 'em to be exact. One weren't guilty of much other than bein' in the wrong place at the wrong time, an' havin' looked at the girl more often than was smart. She'd told people he give her the creeps, an' so he were an obvious suspect in that light. He weren't in other ways, though. He were a slow lad, but he didn't mean much harm, or that's what I believe, believed it at the time, too. The other three were more interestin' an' more likely in my view; she were havin' an affair with someone's husband, she'd broken things off with her own fiancé just recent like. An' there were a strange character, too, hung about the cemetery, showin' his bits to whatever lady had the misfortune to wander through. All three had motive, means an' opportunity, an' admittedly so did the wee slow lad, but I knew he wasn't guilty, right from the start. Nothin' fit, ye know, how things are just that way sometimes, like a puzzle where the pieces just won't click together, but a toddler shoves the pieces into place, breakin' them in the process to make them fit. That's how the whole case was, start to finish."

She hoped to God that the wire was picking every word up, she could only tilt toward the man so far, without risking him seeing the wire and also making him think she was offering him a night in bed.

She nodded sympathetically and patted his hand in a manner meant to be both encouraging and comforting. He trapped her hand with his own though, so that hers was palm down flat on the bar. He gave her a look that was a frightening mix of lust and anger.

"Why are ye listenin' so close? Most women don't like stories like this one. Most women want sweet words an' promises."

"I told you, my dad was a cop, I grew up with stories like this one."

"Are ye lonely?" he asked, and there was something both cunning and pathetic about the question.

"Sometimes yes, most of the time actually," she said, because it was the truth and the truth was always recognizable, even to a drunk, perhaps even more so to a drunk. The tension in his hand eased, and the anger faded from his face.

"Hard to imagine," he said, words clear, "how a woman like yerself could be lonely. What are the men thinkin'?"

"I lost my husband," she said, "a while ago."

He gave her a long look, one eye squinted almost shut, like he was trying to keep her down to one image. Then he nodded. "I'm sorry."

The simple human decency of it made her want to tell him to stop talking and not tell her anything more. She suddenly hated the thought that Tomas was hearing all of this. The words started again and she realized it was a confession of sorts, from a man who knew there wasn't any redemption for what he had done. He was speaking more to himself than to her, she knew, trying to find some wisp of relief, some small handhold by which to pull himself out of this quagmire of guilt that was slowly but surely killing him.

"It were this man, Mungo Hanna that fitted him up, his partner was killed in a shootout with the boy's older brother a few years before. He wanted blood vengeance every day after. This was as close as he could get. Think it would have done less damage had he just killed the man."

"How long has this boy been in prison for a murder he didn't commit?" she asked, striving to keep her voice free of judgement, and not betray how much this one question mattered. If she could get him to answer it then she was done here for the night.

"Four years, poor lad, four years for somethin' I'm dead certain he couldn't have done."

Sin sin. It was how Casey had always said, "That's that."

The man was still talking, however, and there wasn't any way to graciously extract herself just yet.

"Sometimes I think I'm haunted by the ghost of who I could have been. D'ye know what I mean?"

"I do," she said.

"Aye," he nodded, and she could almost hear the contents of his head sloshing about. "I believe ye do. What's yer ghost, then?"

"My life with my husband, how it was then, and how it is now," she replied, softly.

It was strange how sometimes one had these moments with a total stranger, where one told truths that one didn't often admit to oneself.

She understood that it was guilt that had done this to him, more than the alcohol, because he had started drinking to drown the guilt.

"I knew it weren't him. I told my bosses, I tried to make it right. There weren't no proper proof the lad had done anything."

She felt a wash of guilt go through her. This man had tried to do the right thing, a little too late, but he had at least tried. And he'd been repaid by the loss of his career, his wife, home and family, all of which had clearly meant a great deal to him. And here she was trying to trick him into telling her all the heartbreaking details so they could be used in court to possibly hurt him further. She reminded herself that an innocent young man was currently in prison for the mistakes and cover-ups this man had assisted in making.

She touched his forearm, giving it a small squeeze so that he might know she saw a human being in him, and not the monster he felt himself to be.

"Sometimes I feel like the drink is me cheatin' on the guilt an' the loneliness. It's an easy way out, an' I deserve to feel the pain, but then I can't manage the pain without wanting to blow my own head off."

"Maybe you need to tell someone. Maybe that would help alleviate the guilt a little."

"I just told you, didn't I? Not sure how much better I feel. Only forgetting can do that for me an' I can only think of one way to forget." He put his hand on her thigh, the disturbing mix of anger, fear and lust there in his face again.

In truth it wasn't lust for the body, but lust for oblivion. It did not matter how desirable he found her, if he indeed did, she could not give him that. And that lust for oblivion had one cause, fear that you would never stop feeling this way, not even for a second for the rest of your life. Temporary oblivion was the best that one could hope for. It was past time for her to leave because things were getting to a place where she could no longer easily handle them. She gently removed his hand.

"I need to powder my nose," she said and slipped off the stool. "I'll be right back."

She walked away, aware of his bleary regard following her, a niggling guilt in her chest for lying to the man. At the same time she was relieved to be leaving the building having accomplished what she had set out to achieve, and all without any real trouble. She felt a tiny bit smug as she stepped out the back door into the dark parking lot. This feeling was abruptly squelched when she realized Tomas's car was gone.

She panicked and sped up to a half run, her heels hampering her from moving any faster. She couldn't imagine the man would leave her alone unless something bad had happened, like he'd been spotted and pulled in by the police. And then she saw exactly why he had left, for Jamie was standing in the lot, leaning up against his car, arms folded across his chest, an exceptionally unpleasant look on his face.

She swallowed a very big desire to bolt, and slowed her run to a steady walk, or as steady as she could manage. James Kirkpatrick angry was not a thing she enjoyed in any way, shape or form. How on earth the man had known where she was tonight she couldn't imagine, then again it was Jamie, she might be more surprised if he didn't know what she was up to.

"Good evening, Pamela," he said, and there was no mistaking the even tone for anything other than disapproving anger.

"Where is my truck?" she asked, looking around in bewilderment.

"I had Vanya drive it up to my house. I'm going to drive you there because I'd like a few words with you in private."

She swallowed, her nerves back in full force. "I am not a child, Jamie," she said, aware that she sounded defensive.

"I know you're not, but you're acting a little like one. Get in the car please, I'd rather not have this conversation out here."

She got in the car, because she had no other alternative. If she had a decent pair of shoes she would bloody walk home, even if it took until the dawn. She noted that the receiving end of the wire was in Jamie's car now, and she felt a little queasy knowing he had heard everything that had passed between her and the man.

The car was cold, in marked contrast to the man in the driver's seat, who looked like he could easily produce steam out of his ears right now. He didn't speak, merely pulled the car out into the street and began the journey toward his house. He was driving fast, which wasn't uncommon for him, though she noted how tightly his hands were wrapped around the steering wheel. She clasped her own hands in her lap, feeling ridiculously like a penitent school girl, a Catholic one, caught out with her skirt rolled up and cigarettes in her pocket. Though to be certain, James Kirkpatrick, angry or not, was no one's idea of a dour-faced priest.

The silence became increasingly fraught as they left the lights behind and drove up the mountainside to his property. They were about halfway to the house, when he pulled over in a break between two large oaks, and turned off the car. The silence felt oppressive. She was about to blurt out an apology just to break the tension, when he turned to her.

"Have you lost your mind entirely, Pamela?" The words were said calmly enough; the look on his face was anything but. Even in the dark of the car she could feel his anger, and something more, a strange pulse to the air that she didn't quite understand.

"N...no," she said. Jamie mad was one thing, Jamie furious in a confined space was another thing all together.

She realized the slit in her skirt was on the same side as Jamie and had ridden rather high up her thigh. The leg seemed to be glowing with a phosphorescent light. Jamie noticed her glance and raised an eyebrow at her.

"Did it work?" he asked, and the sarcasm was gone from his voice. Instead there was a peculiar tension there, the strange pulse that she had sensed before.

"In a way. I left him there to his drink; I never had any intention of letting it go further than a harmless flirtation." She sounded defensive she knew, which was not the tactic to take with Jamie.

"There's nothing harmless about it, anything might have happened to you, Pamela. You know that."

She did know it. It struck her how her actions of not just tonight, but these last several months must appear to him. She reached over and took his hand. He was shaking, whether with fury or upset she wasn't certain, she felt incredibly ashamed, regardless of the cause.

"Pamela, I got a phone call tonight from a contact inside the police force. My contact said there's been talk in certain circles. Your name has come up, and not amongst good men. When I found out what you were up to tonight, I could have cheerfully murdered you myself. You can't take chances like this anymore."

"I really did just want to help Tomas and Pat with their case. It was only a conversation."

"Which could have gone horribly wrong. He might have dragged you off, done anything to you. This kind of stuff, as simple as it seems, can get you killed here. You know that better than most."

He was right; the risks here were higher and played out for far greater stakes than they might in another land.

"I really am sorry, Jamie," she said and meant it.

"Oh, I believe you're sorry for making me worry, but I don't believe you're sorry for doing it in the first place."

He gave her a long, level glare, which she quietly took in because she really didn't want to aggravate the man any further tonight. Suddenly he laughed.

"You're never dull, Pamela, I will say that for you. I'm surprised Casey didn't tie you to the bed posts before he left for work in the mornings, just to give himself peace of mind for the day."

"He did mention it a time or two," she said, relieved that the worst of his anger seemed to have passed.

"I'm acquiring a much deeper appreciation of the man's forbearance."

"I'm not quite *that* much of a handful, James Kirkpatrick," she said indignantly.

He merely laughed, and she felt annoyance replace some of her relief.

"Well, did you get any valuable information out of the man?"

"Some," she said, feeling badly for the poor wreck she had left back there on a stool that was far too familiar with his backside. "His mind isn't all it could be, and he rambled a bit, but I think all together, yes, it's useful. None of it can be used in court, directly, but it gives Tomas and Pat some leverage with him. Maybe enough to convince the courts that an appeal is necessary."

He didn't respond to that, and her general impression was that he was less than impressed by the rewards reaped versus the risks taken. His index finger was tapping out a vigorous rhythm on the steering wheel, and she thought she was quite happy she couldn't read his mind. Then again, it's likely he still had a piece or two of said mind to give her, so it was probably best to get it over with.

"Say it, Jamie. To paraphrase Pat, spit it out and save your spleen."

He took a sharp breath in through his nose and she braced herself, lest he was about to let fly with one of his rare lectures. They tended to be pointed and razor-sharp in their assessments, and entirely unpleasant.

"When men have nothing to lose, Pamela, they do desperate things. That man in there tonight, has nothing left to lose, and he might have done something awful and taken you with him. You would have been nothing more than collateral damage in his view."

"I wouldn't have left the bar with him. I'm not that crazy."

He was looking out the windscreen of the car, his jaw still tight with tension, face drawn in troubled thought. He managed a derisive, "Hm-mphmm," which she thought was meant to disagree with her statement as to the degree of her craziness.

"Is that how you felt in Russia, like you had nothing to lose?" she asked. He didn't speak of Russia, not about the serious things, not about the woman who was his wife or the man who had been his friend and died for it.

"Sometimes, yes."

"Do you feel that way now?" She worried about him, his life was so splintered among a variety of personas, both public and private, and because of his bipolar disorder, she knew he often lived near the edge of a very particular sort of disaster.

"No, because I have Kolya to raise, and apparently," he smiled, "you to look after as well."

"I *am* sorry, Jamie," she said for the second time that night.

"I know you are, Pamela, I just don't think that will stop you the next time."

They sat quiet for a few moments. Silence with Jamie, unless he was upset, was always a comfortable thing. As he seemed to have moved past the worst of his anger, she leaned back into the seat and felt some of the tension leak slowly from her body. She was exhausted. She could easily fall asleep here, with the security of Jamie beside her, and the sound of the night breeze roaming through the leaves on the oaks around them.

"Do you ever feel that way, Pamela? Like you have nothing to lose?"

She thought about telling him a half-truth, something to relieve the worry she could still feel emanating from him. But he had asked an honest question, and so she owed him an honest answer.

"Sometimes," she said, "at three o'clock in the morning, when I haven't slept for yet another night and I think there may never be an answer to the one question that burns me from the inside out—then yes."

And because he was Jamie, he did not remonstrate with her or tell her she had children to raise and friends that loved her because he knew she understood all that. He knew that it was possible to have all those things to live for and still feel, in the midst of a white night, like you had nothing to lose. He simply took her hand and said, "I'm here."

Chapter Twenty-five

Carpe Diem

THINGS MOVED RATHER SWIFTLY after Pamela's slightly sordid evening. Tomas and Patrick had listened through the tape several times and then had approached the former policeman at his home, which was a rundown bedsit over a tobacco shop in Atlantic Avenue. He'd been furious at first, but then had admitted he thought something was 'mucky' about a woman like Pamela being so friendly with him. Still, he'd spilled his guts and being that it was on tape, didn't seem to see a reason not to do it again with Pat and Tomas. Pat recounted all this to Pamela across her kitchen table one night, after having dinner with her and the children.

"To be fair, he was half-cut at the time. I think he's sort of given up all together, an' feels he might as well shrive his soul to lawyers as to anyone else before they kill him. That's about how he put it leastwise."

"Will they really kill him?" she asked, even though it sounded naïve to her own ears, and she knew the answer.

Pat nodded. "Aye, if they can find him. He might feel he's nothin' left to lose, but they have plenty. One of his former colleagues is high up in the RUC now, an' not a man to be taken lightly. Tomas has Andy stowed in a safe house now, even I don't know where it is. Tomas says it's best if I don't, so the bastards can't torture it out of me if they take a mind to." Pat laughed, but it was, as was often the case in this city, a bit of a gallows laugh.

"Tomas is tryin' to keep him relatively sober, though that's a bit like puttin' the fox in charge of the hen coop. I suspect that means they drink together more than anythin', an' then Tomas takes the remains of the bottle home. We have to move quickly, because as ye know Andy's just the wee bit unstable, an' I don't know how much longer the man's liver is goin' to hold out, he was the color of a banana last time I saw him. So we've put together his statement an' pieced together a timeline, also we're lookin' at the other three suspects. Once we looked at the girl's history it wasn't hard to figure out just who was who—one man is dead, but the one we think most likely to be guilty is still alive. Mind, we don't need to prove he did it, just prove that there were at least one or two points of law that were fudged over or not attended to properly."

Pat hadn't expected to be in court with Tomas, as thus far much of his work had consisted of conveyancing, succession work and accident compensation, with the very rare divorce thrown in for variety. However, he did have his certificate in advocacy which gave him the right of audience in the higher courts. It was the same path Tomas had taken, which had allowed him to advance to the rank of Queen's Counsel. Tomas had insisted that Pat having brought this 'feckin' quagmire of a case' to him, could suffer through all the legal proceedings that resulted from said quagmire.

The hearing was this morning, and as a result she had a case of butterflies on their behalf that neither tea nor toast had drowned. The house was quiet around her, as she stood wiping up the breakfast dishes. She had dropped off Conor and Isabelle with Gert earlier, to give herself a chance to catch up on her book keeping.

Later, she thought she might run a box of baby clothes up to a young mom in Newry to whom she'd promised them. She'd packed the clothes up the previous evening and had sighed over every wee dress and pair of socks that had gone into the box. It was as if she was closing the door on ever having more children by giving them away. Casey and she had discussed the possibility of more, she feeling three would make a nice number and he more inclined to four. Still, if he did not return, it wasn't likely that she would ever have any more children and the thought of that made her sad. She picked up the box, resolved. She would put it in the car now, so she didn't spend her morning gazing at it and feeling melancholy.

She put on her shoes and opened the door, jumping back in startlement and dropping the box, which spilled tiny sweaters, booties, frilly dresses and tights all over. Pat was standing on the doorstep, his hand raised to knock. Rain was dripping down his face and darkening the shoulders of his suit.

"What on earth are you doing here? I thought you were in court this morning," she said. He hunkered down with her to pick up the clothes.

"I'm meant to be there in two hours," he said grimly, "but Tomas is drunk as the proverbial lord an' I've done everything I can to sober him up. All to no fockin' avail I might add. Pamela, ye've got to help me. He's in the car, passed out."

The man's desperation was clear, Patrick wasn't one to swear.

"I thought he was off the booze this week, or at least until the appeal was over."

"Aye," Pat said, "he was meant to be. I'd confiscated everything I could find at his house, but he must have had some stored away because he appears to have gone on a real bender last night."

She stood from re-packing the last of the baby clothes and brushed down her pant legs. "What is it you think I can do?"

"For some reason, heaven help us, he sees ye as his good luck charm. If ye could just help me sober him up a wee bit an' then give him a talkin' to, I'd owe ye somethin' terrific. Not that I can repay it, but ye'd have my eternal gratitude."

"You can't go to court soaked as a wet rat, let me run upstairs and get you a dry suit. You can change into it when we get Tomas sorted."

"Pamela, I—"

"Patrick, I don't mind you wearing his clothes. You're his brother. Not to mention," she said briskly, "you're the only person who would fit them. Now, go bring Tomas in."

He leaned forward and kissed her on the cheek and said no more. Patrick had always been wise in that way. A moment later, the two of them were bent over Tomas, whom Pat had laid out on the sofa by the hearth. Pamela feared he was unconscious until she had leaned over him and one puffy and excessively red eye looked back up at her. He lifted a hand and patted her face, smiling beatifically, "Ye have the eyes of a mermaid, lass, has anyone ever told ye that? Ye're like somethin' borne in upon a wave, Venus on the half shell." He hiccoughed, and a wave of whiskey scent wafted toward her. Pamela sighed and then grabbed him, rather ungently, by his dirty collar.

"Listen you old sot, if you ruin this for Patrick, I'll drown you in a vat of whiskey and do it happily. He needs your help, he can't present the damn arguments by himself. If you make him go out there alone, it will be a fiasco for him and I will never forgive you. What's far worse is that you will never forgive yourself once you sober the hell up. Patrick, help me get him up and into the bathroom."

Between the two of them they got him into the bathroom, where he slumped on the toilet lid, and began to sing *Tiny Bubbles*. She turned the cold tap on full in the tub. "Stick his head under and show no mercy."

Twenty minutes later, Tomas was presentable and nearing sober. He was still damp from his forced ablutions, but he no longer smelled like the inside of a whiskey barrel and his eyes had gone from red to pink, rather like those of a querulous and somewhat pissed rabbit. He was seated at her kitchen table, while Pat was upstairs changing his clothes.

Pamela handed Tomas a cup of coffee strong enough to take the silver off a spoon. She adjusted his collar, which she had cleaned with a damp cloth and a bit of soda while he was in the bath, and then took a brush to his hair. "Drink that bloody coffee, we don't have much time here."

"Ye might look like a mermaid, but ye act like a bloody fishwife," he grumbled, though he drank the coffee meekly enough. Patrick came down the stairs a few minutes later, in a clean suit, which Casey had last worn to their grandmother's funeral, his hair tidied as best as he could manage and a look of nervous anticipation on his face that set Pamela's butterflies to fluttering in her stomach once again on his behalf.

Ten minutes later they had Tomas in the car, relatively sober and presentable. Pamela had decided her bookkeeping could wait and she could easily deliver the baby clothes another day. There were a couple of things she could do in Belfast while Pat was in court, and for now she could offer him moral support.

"Yer brother must have had his hands full with that one," Tomas grumbled from the back seat, as Patrick took off at a fast clip, looking dark things best not uttered. At Tomas' words though he looked over at Pamela and smiled.

"Aye, he did, an' ye never saw a man happier for it."

When they pulled up to the courts, Pamela felt like all of Patrick's nerves must have transferred over to her stomach. It was one of those rainy dark Belfast days and the Crumlin Jail, situated directly across the street from the courts, didn't look the better for it. It had an imposing façade as it was. The prisoner would be led from there through a tunnel that ran under the road to the court which sat, just as imposing on the opposite side of the street.

"Give us a kiss for luck, dear Pamela," Tomas said, and presented her with his freshly shaved cheek. She kissed him, and was happy to find he no longer reeked of alcohol, instead he smelled pleasantly of the Bay Rum cologne she'd splashed liberally upon his person. It was Casey's cologne and the scent lingered pleasantly in her nose, even if it did make her feel a pang of longing for the man who had once worn it.

Pat had explained to her that it was the details that would make the difference in whether or not this case stood a chance of being retried. Those details had to be gone through at length, but also made compelling enough so that the judge would stay awake throughout and be swayed to see their side of things. Most appeals failed at the first gate, so the odds were stacked against them going in, and unless there were valid points of law that had been ignored or subverted, the case wouldn't stand a chance. Tomas, despite his alcoholism still had a great deal of respect within the legal community, and his summations in the courtroom were legendary. She only hoped he could pull his wits together because, while she suspected that Patrick would one day be capable of greatly moving oratory, she didn't think he was prepared for it today. She knew, however, that he had crossed all his 't's' and dotted every last 'i'.

She left them to their legal battle and went to run her errands, one of which was to drop off a set of proofs to a couple whose wedding she had photographed the week before, and then she needed to stop by the Tennent Street station and pick up a check that was waiting for her.

Once in the station, she waited, skin prickling, for she wasn't comfortable in a police station. She always had the sense that her Catholic baptism, as long ago as it was, ringed her in a green halo here; as if the men in this building, Protestant almost to a man, knew her entire history and geography merely by looking at her. Tribal lines ran so deep and long here that it was likely they did know. Belfast was one sticky web of communication, and if you trod one strand of that web, the vibrations of it rippled out to every other line, so that people knew what you'd done and who you were before you understood those things yourself. Her last name alone was enough to condemn her.

She heard his voice first, clipped and harsh and yet with something sibilant in it, for he drew his consonants out in a manner that she thought he had decided was threatening. She didn't want to turn around; she didn't want him to notice her at all if she could manage it. She wondered briefly what he was doing here in this station, rather than his base in Newry. She chanced a glance up. It was Constable Blackwood, out of uniform and chatting with another officer. She shuddered, the internal shudder of prey that wishes it had a handy hedge to hide in. There was no way to avoid his notice.

Pamela put her head down and pretended to be studying the counter with great interest. The man raised the fine hairs on the back of her neck and she hated even being in his proximity. The policeman from behind the counter returned just then, and handed her the envelope. She muttered a 'thank you' and turned for the door, hoping to make a quick exit. But she felt the constable's antennae prick up just then, like she was a rabbit and he a hound that could smell the fear that bubbled through her blood. She heard him excuse himself to the man he'd been speaking with, and turn toward the door. She bolted out of it, uncaring about who noticed now, just wanting to get away as swiftly as she could. She turned up toward Crumlin Road, walking as fast as she could manage without actually breaking into a full run, her adrenaline shooting off in small geysers, adding a manic little hop to her walk every few feet. He was behind her now, and she looked back, to find him looking right back at her, a nasty grin on his face.

She kept her head up and kept walking, even though she felt like every vertebra in her spine had been suddenly exposed to a cold wind. He kept pace behind her, staying just a few steps back, so that she could smell the sour scent of him. She picked up speed, weaving in and out of the people on the sidewalk with her. He walked faster too. The area had long made her nervous, and she wished now that she hadn't been seized by the notion of walking. It was a very Loyalist area, replete with Loyalist murals and Union Jacks flapping wetly in the wind and drizzle.

There were three cars coming out of Crimea Street, turning onto Crumlin Road and so she had no choice but to stop or be run down by one of them. Her whole body was prickling like it had been brushed with nettles, and she was as aware of the man at her back as she would have been a gun muzzle pressed to her neck. It seemed as if the traffic flow would never change, as if she was going to be standing here for the next hour or day or week, with this man standing behind her, breathing his hot, sour breath. A sudden gust of wind blew her hair into her face so that she was temporarily blinded. It was then that he put a hand to the small of her back and shoved her lightly, jarring her enough so that she stumbled into the street, to the tune of brakes shrieking and the claxon wail of horns. She closed her eyes and tried to step back, and then a hand yanked her hard, and she fell, out of the danger of the road way.

Touch was the most primary of the senses for her. She was highly responsive to it, a trait Casey had been very fond of. His touch had been both security and passion; but mostly it had been home. She had been touched before by rage, both literally and figuratively, and though this was like that feeling, it also wasn't. It was a threat, made without words, still it was entirely effective. She looked down, catching at her breath, trying to calm her shaken nerves and then turned to look behind her. There was a crowd gathering, people clucking with concern, but the constable was gone, melted into the bricks and dirty cement and the low grey clouds of the city, as if she had imagined him.

"Are ye all right there, lass?" The driver of the car which had narrowly missed hitting her, was standing over her, visibly shaken. He put his hand out to help her up. She rose shakily, hoping her knees would bear her up.

"I tripped," she said, "I'm sorry."

"No need for that," he said gruffly, "I'm glad ye're not hurt, that was too near a thing all together."

"I'm fine, just a little shaken up," she said. She looked around, a small crowd had begun to gather to see what had happened, and she felt a fine dew of perspiration break out on the back of her neck. These might be perfectly kind people in their everyday life, but let a small mob gather and realize she was a Catholic woman in their neighborhood and they might not remain kind and concerned.

She walked quickly back toward the courthouse, stopping only to dampen the back of her neck with water from a fountain. The small of her back still had an unpleasant tingle where Constable Blackwood had pushed her and she felt the first flush of fury start in her body. How dare he touch her, how dare he put her in danger because he'd formed some baseless dislike of her due to her religion and her name. She was shaking as she wrung the handkerchief out and then wiped her face with it.

She waited in a teashop for a while since she didn't think she could stomach being patted down by the security at the courthouse right now. She took her time drinking the tea, grateful for the heat and the fortification of caffeine and sugar. After she was done, she walked back toward the courthouse, its grim façade only topped by the razor-wired front of the Crum opposite. She had waited until she thought the time was close for them to come out, as it wasn't safe to loiter anywhere in Belfast and particularly not outside a court of law, situated across from one of the most notorious jails in the land.

By the time Patrick emerged, looking ridiculously formal in his lawyer's garb, she was composed, at least outwardly; inwardly she was still slightly nauseous and entirely furious. Pat grinned at her and gave her a discreet thumbs up, his wig ever-so-slightly askew on his dark curls. She took a deep breath of relief that tingled all the way down to her toes. He walked over to her and she stood, waiting to hear the details of what had taken place.

The relief in him was palpable, and she realized just how exhausted he looked. Between his work and his worry for her and the children, and the fact that she knew he was the one person on earth who was every bit as haunted as she was by Casey's disappearance, it was a wonder the man hadn't collapsed at some point.

"I don't think it could have gone better, frankly," Pat said, answering the question that was on her face. "Tomas was a wonder, sharp as a brass tack an' didn't miss a point anywhere. The judge didn't even hesitate in his decision, just said there were clear grounds for an appeal, an' that he was appalled at how the original case had been handled."

"Congratulations, Patrick. I'm so pleased for you both."

He smiled. "This is when the real fun starts, I guess. I'm not sure I know how I feel about it, truth be told."

She knew too well what Pat meant by that statement. If the RUC hadn't been paying attention before, they most certainly would be now. With the rumors going about that there were off-duty officers involved in the random shooting of Catholics, some in the city, others out in the countryside, an act like this was tantamount to painting a scarlet bullseye on their own backs. It could bleed out to all of them, affect their lives or take their lives. It didn't require much of anything in this country, catching the wrong eye in the wrong moment was enough. She half expected there would be no more work photographing the dead once this was out. In truth, she was surprised they had continued to offer her work for this long as it was.

She thought briefly about telling him of the constable's threat, though there was little enough to tell and she didn't want to ruin Pat's moment of victory. There would be time enough later. For it wasn't just the shove into the road, it was that after the hand had yanked her back she'd heard the words, spoken in that guttural hiss, "Next time, bitch, next time."

"Pamela, don't look like that. I'm just having a moment of doubt, because I thought we'd lose an' I'd go back to conveyancin' and writin' up wills. We'll dig our heels in, do our job properly an' take what precautions we can. Beyond that…" He looked down at her and smiled, trying to impart reassurance to her. She took his hands and smiled in return, though she was still cold all over from the touch of the constable's hand.

"Beyond that," she said, "we pray."

Chapter Twenty-six

Tea Spot

IT WAS, TO SAY THE LEAST, nerve-wracking to play host to IRA men on the run. What struck Pamela at times was how young many of them were, and how likely it was their lives would end either in a hail of bullets or in a very long prison stint. Often both eventualities played out to their inevitable and tragic ending. It was a process sometimes referred to as republican university.

There was a young man asleep in her shed this very morning. Noah had arrived with him in the early hours after a skirmish with an Army patrol the night before outside of Newry. Right now the ground was too hot to move him. She had made him breakfast after she returned from a short visit to her neighbor Lewis. Conor had stayed with Lewis who had promised to bring her son back after lunch. She had packed the food for the young man in a feed bag, so that she could move it from the house to the shed without raising suspicion, lest the British Army had eyes on her and her property. Noah had promised to move him after nightfall.

She opened the door to go out to the shed, only to find herself confronted by a man standing in the small covered porch attached to the side door. She jumped back, cursing inwardly as she felt the tea in the bag slosh.

The man standing before her was clean cut—short brown hair, dark brown eyes, and healthy pink-cheeked skin. He was dressed in a sweater and jeans that were far too new. He looked familiar though it took her a moment to place him. She had bumped into him in a local shop the other day, and he had knocked her groceries out of her hand and been extremely apologetic afterwards, trying to make small talk while he helped her pick up apples and butter and bread. Then she had seen him at Gallagher's Pub, having a casual pint, and telling Owen he was a tourist that was lost. That he should show up here, unannounced, was far too coincidental to be co-incidence. She got straight to the point.

"I've seen you three times now. Even in a country this small, the odds aren't in favor of that. What is it that you want?"

"I was told this was a safe tea spot."

Pamela frowned. "What on earth would make you think that?" A tea spot was essentially a safe house for a British soldier if things got too hot on the ground, which in Belfast and its environs was more often than not. Their house had most certainly never been considered a warm and fuzzy sort of place for a British soldier. Not that she believed for a New York minute that this man was a regular soldier. She knew that it was common for intelligence to try to make casual contact with someone they felt might be a potential informant ahead of time to decide how amenable that person might be to any recruitment overtures.

"I understood one of our officers used to come here on a regular basis."

She knew he meant David Kendall, but considering that the man had worked undercover for the most part, it struck her as odd that this young man would know anything about his movements. David had been a friend, though, even if he had been using Casey for information that last year.

She thought about the young man in her shed, and said a silent, but very fervent prayer in her head that he would not wake up and walk out into the yard. The word awkward would be beggared for belief in the light of such a situation.

"You're not welcome here," she said, giving the man her best hard stare. That was the truth. It could be a death sentence for her if it should be discovered that the British thought they had a welcome of any sort at her house. She would be branded a tout and shot in the back of the head without a care for her children. Rumor was enough to kill a person in this land. Proof was not necessarily required in the court of retribution.

"Either you let me in or I will call my superiors and tell them about the young man in your shed."

If blood could actually freeze in the act of moving through veins, she was quite certain hers would have then and there.

"Am I to believe you won't tell them anyway?"

He put a hand to the door so she couldn't close it. "For now, yes."

She put the feed bag on the bench in the porch, and stood aside.

"You have five minutes," she said, "and no more."

"Five minutes isn't even time for a cup of tea," he said, and there was no false friendliness in his face any more. He was here on business.

"What is it that you want, Mr....?" She let the address hang in the air, as he hadn't given her a name even though she knew it was unlikely she would get a real name, just a cover.

He didn't take off his shoes, which were rather mucky from coming across her yard, and no doubt tramping through her property. He sat at the table without being invited to do so, apparently there wasn't even going to be a pretense at cordiality.

"Davison," he said. "Mr. Davison."

"Please just state your business, Mr. Davison, I don't want to prolong this encounter."

He smiled. It wasn't a friendly expression, but more like a baring of teeth.

"A woman who likes to get straight down to business, I like that. I'll lay it out for you just as baldly. We want an end to the conflict here, and people like Noah Murray are playing a long game. He's pacing the war and that gets in the way of us ending things here. We want certain players removed from the board in order to clear the way for a series of moves."

"Pacing the war?" His chess analogy annoyed her, as if the people of this country were merely pieces to be moved about in some greater game, which sacrificed humans like they were little more than wooden pawns.

"Low intensity, striking now and again, but not so much that it becomes an open conflagration that they can't control. If you keep it going, you have a purpose—keep it going long enough, maybe you finally defeat your enemy, through boredom if nothing else."

"Boredom? Is that what you call state sanctioned terror?"

"We're not the terrorists here; that would be your friend Noah Murray and his ilk."

"Oh, that's right, just the mad Irish fighting with each other, no other hand stirring the pot. No eight hundred years of occupation by a foreign power, and certainly never any abuse of said power."

He waved a broad-fingered hand, as if to dismiss eight hundred years of history. "It's not us keeping it going, we're merely here policing. It's a dirty little war, and someone has to oversee it."

She laughed. "Oh of course, the great peacekeepers because the mad Fenians can't be expected to control themselves all alone. Just why is it that you think the British Army is here?" she asked. "If it's a dirty war, it's because you made it so a long time ago. You people play games in Ireland; you play games and use the locals as pawns and sometimes we die for a game we didn't choose to play."

"You're talking of play in a game you didn't choose, and yet you were married to a PIRA rebel and now that he's gone, you've taken up with a known terrorist."

"Taken up?" she said coldly. "You could phrase it more clearly, Mr. Davison, I'm not squeamish about words."

"Noah Murray. You're close with him." He emphasized the word 'close' so that she could have no doubt what he meant. It wasn't mere innuendo. "You didn't waste much time, did you?"

Pamela crossed her arms over her chest and leaned back into the support of the counter. She didn't want to betray her nerves in any way to this man, though he had to know how terrifying it was to have an intelligence officer in her kitchen.

"Let's cut to the chase," she said. She didn't want Conor to return home to find this man in their kitchen and Isabelle could only be expected to nap for a short while longer. She did not want her children to be seen by him, even if they had been taking pictures of the lot of them all along.

"Money, it seems to us that you might need some. We'd be happy to help you out in that arena."

"I don't want money, and if I did I certainly wouldn't take it from the British government," she said hotly. "You have no business prying into my finances."

"It's neither here nor there as to whose business it is, the fact of the matter is you have what—three mortgage payments left in the bank, and you're losing business right and left. Unless you find a new job, and find it soon, you're going to lose your property."

"I don't want your money, I don't want anything to do with you or anyone you represent, be it queen, country or covert organization. Now, if you don't mind, I have things I need to do and I would like you to leave."

He leaned back in the chair, crossing one booted foot over the other, bits of dirt crumbling and falling onto her freshly washed floor.

"Your husband had no trouble taking money from British coffers. I'm surprised you're so scrupled." His smile was chilly and repugnant.

"He would never have taken money from you or your like," she said, furious. On this much she was certain, Casey would have rather begged in the streets for his meals and lost the house from under them than take traitor's money, which is how he would have viewed such a thing.

"You think not? Well, I suppose if it gives you comfort, it's best to stick tight to your illusions. If you want to know what happened to your husband though, we'll be more help to you than Noah Murray."

"How is that? The police have no idea where to look, why should I believe you do?"

"We have resources the police don't have access to."

It could be true, and then again, it might not be. It wasn't beyond the forces to lie in order to manipulate and get what they wanted. There had been a scandal not long ago in which it had been revealed that one of British Intelligence's top informers had been killed by another informant in order to protect his own identity. There was a hierarchy within the world of touts that made it a lethal pecking order. In the end, she trusted Noah more than she trusted this man and his superiors.

"Please just go." She hoped her voice didn't convey her desperation because if he scented weakness, she would never get rid of him.

He stood, and she stayed where she was, partly because she needed the counter to hold her up and partly because she would not give him the courtesy of walking him to the door. He needed to understand he was not welcome here.

"Before I go I will say this, this man you've gotten into the figurative bed with—he's a smuggler, he's got an empire going with illegal activities of all sorts and he's well known as the godfather of the South Armagh PIRA. In bandit country, he's the king bandit and yet he's never been arrested, never taken in by British forces. You might well ask yourself, Mrs. Riordan, just why that is." He handed her a card. She took it, just wanting an end to this visit. The only thing on the card was a number.

"Please go," she said coldly.

He nodded and left. She closed the door firmly behind him and locked it. She ran upstairs and watched out her bedroom window to be certain he left the yard. He was already gone though, disappeared in the way that spooks did. That he worked for Special Branch or British Intelligence she had no doubt, which wing was up for debate, but she would guess MI5 or any of their covert splinters. Regardless, it was deep water in which she now found herself treading.

She collapsed onto the bed, her knees going out from under her all at once. She put her head into her hands, vainly trying to regain her equilibrium. It made her lightheaded with fear to know that British Intelligence had such knowledge of her circumstances. It had been naïve of her not to realize it, especially after their association with David. She had been so distracted by Casey's disappearance that many things that ought to have been obvious to her had slipped her notice all together.

It wasn't personal, she understood that. In his view he was only doing what he needed to do to get his job done and further the aim of his superiors. He wanted to seed doubt in her regarding Noah, and regarding Casey. It was the first step, fear plus uncertainty amounted to making decisions in a state of panic. Just then, Isabelle let out a howl, putting a halt to her train of thoughts.

She rose, knees still shaking and went down the hall to the children's bedroom. Isabelle was standing in her crib, one small hand clutching the railing and the other tugging at her ear. The latter was always a sign that she was getting ready to cut a new tooth. She reached up her arms as Pamela came near, and Pamela picked her up and held her close. The baby was still sleepy and cuddled tightly to her, putting her head on Pamela's shoulder. She kissed Isabelle's frowsy little head, and stroked her back. She needed changing, and would soon want to be fed. Conor would be home shortly too, and she would have her family around her, which was all the normalcy a woman could hope for in this country. Maybe any country, come to that.

She put Isabelle down on the changing table and removed her tiny onesie and diaper. She wiped her down and powdered her. Isabelle was a tactile baby, and of late she loved to be naked whenever possible. The room was warm, and Isabelle was flushed, her cheeks the same shade as the nodding heads of the pink and white peonies out in the garden.

She breathed in the baby's scent and the warm air of the afternoon. She realized she was still trembling, still afraid and her mind was whirling, avoiding letting the man's words sink into her head and heart. She couldn't allow the seed of doubt to take root, she couldn't afford it. She was tired of fear and doubt, afraid if she stood still, if she allowed herself to be quiet and think, the abyss of loss might open beneath her feet and send her on a fall that she knew would never have an ending.

Isabelle burbled at her, happy to be bare-skinned and have her mother's attention solely for herself for a few minutes. Isabelle kicked her feet up and Pamela caught them in her hands and covered the soft, velvety little soles with kisses. Isabelle shrieked with delight, a beautiful smile spreading wide across her tiny face. Pamela's heart clenched inside her with the realization of how much Isabelle had grown and changed since Casey had disappeared. The first year of a child's life was that way, change was so rapid, and trying to hold any moment in your hands to keep was like trying to grasp stardust—when you opened your palms the moment was already past. So many of those moments had come and gone in Casey's absence.

"Oh, Isabelle, I miss your daddy," she said softly, fixing the pins in the baby's diaper and putting a fresh pink t-shirt on her. She picked her up to carry her downstairs, holding her closely, so that her flesh almost seemed part of her own again. She felt the fear there under the denial and the tales she told herself at three o'clock in the morning during another sleepless night. And so she held their daughter a little tighter, kissing her fiercely, as if she could keep her safe by just loving her hard enough.

No, you couldn't grasp stardust, because in the grasping you lost it, but you could hold it carefully for a time, and see it shimmer in your palms before the winds of fate or fortune blew it on its way. She knew this because for a little while, they had done just that.

Chapter Twenty-seven

The Colors of Men

KATE CAME UPON HER in the garden a few afternoons after the visit from British Intelligence. Pamela heard the motor in the lane above and stood, shading her eyes, the low churn of fear starting immediately in her stomach, until she spied Kate's delicate outlines against the bright afternoon sun. She hated this; the fear that came with normal day-to-day events, including things as simple as a car pulling into one's drive.

Kate walked down the drive, presenting a pretty picture in a dainty sundress the color of cornflowers, a shade that made her eyes even more striking than they normally were. She had a neatly folded quilt over her arm, which she presented to Pamela with her usual no-nonsense air.

"'Tis for you," she said. Her tone was brisk but there were two clear streaks of deep pink in her cheeks that told Pamela this moment had meaning to her.

Pamela took the quilt and unfurled it across the garden gate, careful not to let it crush the delicate tendrils of the sweet peas. It was absolutely beautiful with every shade in it from the softest of shell pinks to a crimson that was almost black. Beautifully constructed rag roses anchored each corner of the quilt. The blocks were made from a variety of materials, from thickly-brushed flannel flocked with tiny rose buds to ruched velvet and bits of satin appliqued onto blocks of blush pink cotton in the form of briar roses which spread out from a thick cane, replete with grass green thorns, pricked with silver thread on their tips. One square held a perfectly rendered vardo, a bright blue flag in the midst of the reds and pinks and greens. She and Casey had conceived Isabelle in such a caravan under a full moon when the tides ran as high as they had for a century, both those of sea and man. There was a silhouette of a mermaid, too, holding a baby to her breast, gazing off to far horizons, pearls scattered through the dark satin scrap that made up her hair. There was a square that held a small, woolly sheep with Paudeen's dark face which made her laugh out loud. A long streamer of pewter grey silk with black button eyes and filaments of ragged silk made up the haughty beauty that was Phouka. There was a pair of mating doves in the center of the quilt, positioned sitting upon a branch of the briar rose. Another square held corduroy stones, and birds feathered in scraps of taffeta and velvet, representing Conor's two passions in life.

It was their life depicted in cloth. It was a work of art, and it never failed to astonish her how Kate created such beauty when she could not see what she was doing.

"Oh, Kate." Her words were slightly choked with emotion and she put her hands to her chest, touched beyond measure by the gift.

Kate shrugged, visibly uncomfortable, the deep pink in her cheeks brightening to red.

"I've never had a good friend like you before. I just wanted to make ye something that would keep ye warm at night. I started it for the both of yez—you an' Casey. It was meant to represent how love is, how there are thorns amongst the roses an' yet that only makes the roses that much sweeter. For a long time I thought it best not to give it to ye, but then I felt today that I ought to because I had made it mostly because of our friendship, an' it was meant to be yers."

"It's absolutely beautiful, Kate, thank you so much. I still can't fathom how you manage to make quilts. I feel very honored that you've made one for me."

"Tisn't as difficult as it might seem. I can see the colors in my head when I'm workin' on the bits an pieces. Pat does for me what Noah used to do an' sorts them in their piles, an' then he tells me what each piece of material looks like as I touch it and then I envision the pattern in my head an' know where I want to place each piece."

"Were you always blind, Kate?" Pamela asked, curious, for Kate seemed to have a fine understanding of color as well as direction and form.

"No, I could see until I was four an' then I got sick with a terrible fever an' I lost my sight by the time all was said an' done. The doctors have never been able to understand just why it happened. I'm legally blind, but ye know I can see the rough outlines of things. I can't see detail well, an' I can't make out color. I remember it though, I remember it fine. It's how I see people, too; I see their colors in my head when I meet them."

"You do? Like an aura, do you mean?"

Kate shook her head. "No, not so much, just that people have their own colors. Patrick was a lovely deep an' clear green the first time we met, despite how irritatin' he found me."

Pamela laughed. "He didn't find you irritating so much as he was completely addled by you."

Kate smiled, her eyes lighting from within. "Aye, well so was I. I came here expectin' to find yerself an' the wee man an' here was this tall, dark man with gentle hands an' a gentle heart. I was a bit angry when I left, truth be told. I had never been so comfortable in a stranger's company before. I trusted him immediately and that threw me right off my axis."

"And now what colors do you see for him?"

"'Tis the same, like a green spring rain or a cool still pond with moss round about its edges. Mind, his greens are just a wee bit more murky with this case he's workin' on. No surprise there, though."

"No," Pamela agreed stroking her hand over the quilt and reveling in both its beauty and the thick weight of it. She worried for Pat and Tomas endlessly, and after the years of worry for Casey, she knew all too well how Kate felt.

"Would ye like to know yer own colors?"

"I have colors?"

"Of course ye do, daftie. Why wouldn't ye?"

"It's only I feel a little transparent lately," she said, "as if I might simply evaporate into the wind one of these days."

"Aye, I can see why ye would feel so, but I still see color about ye, though it's changed since—" Kate paused, the pink flares in her cheeks turning almost scarlet.

"Since Casey disappeared. It's all right, Kate, you can say it. It's the reality of the situation."

Kate looked at her, the gentian eyes depthless and unfathomable. "Aye, doesn't make it easier to say an' certainly not easy for you to hear. Are ye plantin' rosemary?"

Pamela took the abrupt change of subject for what it was meant to be, an escape route from speaking of hard things.

Kate came into the garden then, for like Pamela, she could never resist the opportunity to work with green growing things. Pamela folded the quilt gently, placing it so that neither recalcitrant sheep nor small drool-festooned hands could molest it. She eyed the sky suspiciously. She wanted to finish her herb garden today, and while the sky was currently a blame-less and limpid blue with nary a cloud to be seen, she was well enough acquainted with Irish weather to know that could all change in a moment.

Pamela settled on her knees to resume her planting, Kate beside her sorting through the plants by scent, passing the small pots swiftly beneath her nose, and ordering them thusly.

"Shall I tell ye yer colors now?" she asked, as she gently squeezed a lemon balm from its nursery pot and took it firmly in hand.

"Yes," Pamela said, "I'd like that."

She cast an eye toward the shed where she just knew Conor was digging some sort of hole to China. Phouka had almost broken a leg in one of Conor's 'tunnels' last week and she had warned him that all holes must be filled, to which he had rather smartly replied that if it was filled, it wouldn't be a hole any longer. She had given him what Casey had always referred to as her 'scorched earth' look and he had proceeded to meekly fill it back in.

"Ye're all soft like lavender shot through with bursts of silver an' grey, or ye were when Casey was still with ye," Kate said. "Yer colors are darker now, more indigo at times than lavender, though there's always a hint of the sea in ye—greens an' blues, like water reflectin' the sky."

"And Casey—did you see his color, too?"

"Aye," Kate said and handed her the nicely separated roots of the lemon balm. "He was like a sunrise, so bright it burned. When the two of ye touched, it turned to something else, it became the color of roses, the deep ones that are given for passion. It's why I made the quilt in the shades that I did. Those are the colors that are the two of ye together."

"Oh, Kate," she said and hugged her friend.

Kate squeezed her back and then said, "Away with ye, girl, we've plants to attend to."

Pamela smiled and took up the lavender pots, touched by Kate's summation of her and Casey's aura together. She was curious now about the color of others.

"What colors are the children?"

"Well, they're still just wee, so their colors are a bit more changeable. Conor is like his uncle, lovely greens an' browns. He's a child of the earth like his da, no?"

"He is, or at least," she sighed, as her son hove into view, grass stuck in his hair and his fresh pants liberally besmeared with mud, "he's a child of the muck."

Kate turned at the sound of Conor and smiled. He ran over, throwing his grubby arms around her and giving her a smacking kiss on her cheek that left a small trace of mud on her fair skin. Kate adored Conor and Isabelle and never minded their exuberant affections. Pamela reached over and brushed the dirt off Kate's cheek. She sighed; Conor had managed to get dirt on Kate's lovely cotton frock as well.

Correctly interpreting Pamela's sigh, Kate said, "Not to worry, 'tis only a bit of dirt. I love it." She pushed away a strand of chestnut hair where it had caught in her lashes. "Livin' at home, the way things often were…" She looked down at the lavender plant in her hand, fingers stilled in the task of separating the roots. "It was a sterile existence. After I met Pat I started to see another life, an' then to be taken into yer family without anyone so much as turnin' a hair over it—well, it's absolutely lovely."

"It is, isn't it? I think Casey and Pat got their talent for family life from their daddy, he sounds like he was quite a wonderful man. His boys certainly loved him."

"Aye, it makes me sad that neither of us will ever know him, beyond the memories."

"Yes," Pamela said. She knew the tension in her voice was audible, especially to one as tuned to nuances of tone as Kate. It was so exactly what she feared for her own children, that their father would be little more than a memory to them, a man made of shadows and stories.

Kate, in her usual unflappable manner, merely picked up the main thread of their conversation, knowing there were no words to comfort Pamela's fears.

"Isabelle's got this wee pink puff cloud about her, unless she's mad, then it turns fiery red, rather like her daddy in that aspect."

"Oh, aye, she does have Casey's temper," Pamela said as Isabelle, having heard her name, looked up from her scrubby array of stuffed animals. She was drooling vigorously on a tatty elephant with pink velveteen ears which Casey had brought home when they had found out they were expecting for the second time. Pamela smiled at her and Isabelle returned it with a gap-toothed grin and an excited wave of her hands. She felt a pang in her heart for how much she loved these wee people of hers. But behind that pang was always the hollow echo of Casey's absence and what he wasn't here to witness—Isabelle's six teeth, Conor's skinned knee and the fact that last week he had read part of a sentence to her out of one of his books, sounding out each word with careful gravity. She had been so proud of him, and wanted to share the news immediately with the only person it could possibly matter to just as much as it did to her.

"What about Jamie?" She bent her head to the task of gently breaking the roots a bit before putting the lavender in the small hole she had made for it in the rich black soil.

"Ah," Kate's fine, clear brow wrinkled a little, "Jamie, well he's more complicated. There's a lot o' colors with him, likely ye'll know that already. Some that are very dark, an' some that shine so hard ye can hardly keep yer breath around him. I knew he must be a beautiful man, because when he walks into a room where there's folk that haven't met him before, there's always a bit of a gasp an' then a stunned silence like a swarm of bees that have been heavily smoked." She smiled and bent to sniff the lavender that she was removing from its pot. "It's somethin' more with him, isn't it? It's who he is at his core; his soul is a contradiction to itself. It's beautiful all the same."

"It is indeed," she said. Jamie was the most complex man she knew, and yet at times, he was as easily read as ink on paper. But that was when he let his guard down, which he only did with a select few.

They worked in companionable silence for a while, planting rosemary and parsley, sage and thyme, Pamela humming *Scarborough Fair* under her breath, relishing the spiky scent of the rosemary and the dusty warmth of the sage and thyme. There was one person Kate had not mentioned and Pamela wasn't certain she should ask, but curiosity got the better of her.

"What about Noah, Kate, what are his colors?"

Kate looked up beyond the pines and the clouds that were flying in as fast as geese racing across a late autumn sky, and the blue eyes, so like her brother's, were as those of a seer gazing into distances invisible to most.

"He only has the one. Black."

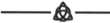

Kate stayed to lunch and she fed Isabelle while Pamela fixed a sandwich for Conor along with a glass of milk. Duly fed, mouth still rimmed with milk, Conor shot back out into the fair early summer day, followed by a muddy-pawed Finbar. The clouds that had threatened before lunch had raced on to the west like an unspooled skein of dark grey. Conor, like his father before him, was never fazed in the least by a bit of rain.

Kate was happily situated on the sofa, Rusty the cat curled up at her elbow and Isabelle ensconced on her shoulder fast asleep. Kate made a picture there in her blue dress, her hair loose and tumbling around her shoulders. She looked lovely, and there was a glow about her that Pamela knew was entirely due to Patrick. She used to glow that way herself, once upon a time. She sighed and returned to the freshly dried basket of laundry she was folding.

She missed it, the anticipation that would set up in her as the day drew down to its close. The knowledge that Casey would arrive home soon, that their household would rearrange its dynamic to include husband and daddy. Even now the thought of it set her fingers to tingling, as if her skin had a memory of its own, separate from the knowledge of her heart. She took a breath, and rubbed her fingers against the small romper she had picked up to fold. She looked out into the side yard; the windows open so that she could hear Conor. She could see him, his cap already abandoned somewhere, and his sweater undone. Like his father, he always ran a bit warm and keeping coats and sweaters on him was a challenge. He was happily playing, building something with a good chunk of the wood pile, and keeping up a running patter with Finbar while he did so.

"Ye know how I said before about things bein' sterile when I was livin' at home. I wouldn't have ye think that was Noah's fault."

"I wouldn't think that of him," she said, still watching her son, her mind only half on the conversation.

"Ye've been spending some time with him of late, no?"

Pamela turned and looked at Kate. There was a sudden and peculiar tension in the woman, even if her expression was easy enough. She had the sense Kate had only been waiting to bring Noah into their chat in order to begin the conversation she really wanted to have.

"I suppose I have," she said, though she wondered how Kate was privy to that knowledge. She didn't think Noah was likely to be discussing their visits and the nature of them even with his sister, regardless of how much he trusted her.

"He's not had an easy time of it, my brother," Kate said quietly.

"No?" Pamela said, folding the last of Isabelle's fresh diapers and adding them to the pile in the laundry basket. This wasn't really news to her; one didn't have to listen terribly hard to hear the rumors that were rife in the countryside about Noah and the things that had gone on at the farm when he was a boy.

Kate hesitated for a moment, smoothing one fine-skinned hand down Isabelle's back.

"Ye know we lost our parents when we were still young?"

"Yes."

"We were close with our mam, but not so much our da. He was a hard man. We had an older brother who was shot by the police when he was just fifteen. They said it was an accident, mistaken identity an' John bein' where he oughtn't to be late at night. We knew better, for it wasn't the first such incident of that sort—well, ye know how 'tis here well enough, Pamela."

Yes, she knew well enough all right. Just the week before a couple and their three sons had been shot in cold blood in their home as they had gathered around for an evening game of cards. Their particular sin, as near as anyone could figure, was that the father was running for the local council and was Catholic.

"Our father never forgave Noah for the fact 'twasn't him who was killed that day. John was his favorite an' his death turned him bitter. We all missed him, but da' an' he had been close. I was close with Noah though, not John. John had a wee bit of a mean streak in him, he was like our da' that way."

She took a breath, the blue eyes turned down to some invisible point of memory.

"Noah wasn't hard an' mean like them. It's true, raise yer eyebrow at me as ye like, he was very different when he was young, our Noah."

Pamela laughed and the sound startled Isabelle so that she lifted her curly head from Kate's shoulder, eyes half open. Both women held their breath, Kate patting the baby's back until she settled again, with a soft sigh.

"Now, how did you know I had a raised eyebrow?"

"Because I know ye well enough now, an' I know what ye're likely to think of my brother an' no fault to ye for it. Ye wouldn't know it now, but he was a sweet boy. He liked to read an' help mam in the gardens, he liked music an' poetry, he liked beautiful things an' said so. Da' called him a nancy-boy an' John would bait him an' do nasty things to him, an' da' would laugh. Noah never said anything, just lived inside himself an' did his talkin' with me an' mam when the other men of the house weren't there to hear. My mam said Noah was like a star left in a basket of rocks, an' John would always be jealous of him for that, an' da' would hate him for it."

"What about you, Kate? Where did you figure in that constellation?"

"Well, I was blind an' a girl, not of much use, an' not likely to do great harm either."

There was a world of explanation in that one small sentence, but Pamela knew it was not what Kate wished to speak of, so she held her silence and let her continue.

"My mam was diagnosed with the cancer the year after John was shot. They gave her two months to live, an' she managed only a week more than that. My da' finished drinkin' his liver to death six months later. Noah became my father an' mother an' big brother all in one go. The farm was mortgaged to the hilt, an' my father had let it run down after John died. Noah was sixteen years old, an' had to build it back up. He worked two jobs outside the farm and somehow managed to make certain I was still bein' schooled an' fed an' properly cared for. I think there were times he didn't sleep more than a couple of hours a night, an' I worried for him that he would break his health, tryin' to keep us together. He never complained, just said 'We're all right then, Kate, aren't we?' It broke my heart sometimes to hear the exhaustion in him, though he tried hard not to let me know. He was right smart, too, but he never got the chance to finish his schoolin'. I think if he has one regret that might be it."

The flow of Kate's story was interrupted by Conor bursting into the house, looking for a snack for himself and Finbar. Conor, in the way of small boys, needed feeding on a regular schedule. She gave him two cookies and an apple, only to look out the window a moment later to see Finbar happily polishing off the last of the cookie Conor had clearly given him.

"He's such a good laddie, isn't he?" Kate said. Isabelle was awake now and squawking for her mother. Pamela took her, changed her diaper and warmed some mashed peas for her.

"He is. I'm lucky he's so easy. Deirdre says he's not quite as daredevil as Casey was at the same age. She said Casey was forever getting into scrapes and getting stuck in out of the way places, like the neighbor's chimney and his grandmother's china cabinet."

"He'd a restless streak in him even as a grown man, no?"

"Yes, he did," she said and felt the pain of the past tense even as it slipped from her tongue. She wanted to correct the word, turn it to the present, but didn't because people, even Kate, were starting to look at her with pity in their faces when she spoke of her husband as if he were still here on the same earth as her. Sometimes she felt a fool for believing that one day he would walk back through that door, put his arms around all of them, and the world would be right again.

"You were saying about your brother?" she asked, wanting Kate to start talking again, so that she didn't have to think about Casey and didn't have to think about speaking in the past tense for the rest of her life. She spooned peas into Isabelle, only to have her purse her wee mouth and spray the spoonful back out in disgust. Isabelle was very clear on her likes and dislikes, and peas it appeared, could be added to the dislike list.

Kate resumed her tale as Pamela wiped the peas from Isabelle's face and went to fix something the baby would deem more palatable.

"Noah'd learned the hard way not to say his truths. As he got older he became more withdrawn, even a wee bit cold sometimes. After we lost our entire family he changed, he became someone who I didn't always recognize, someone who frightened me, though I've never let on as such to him. People forget sometimes that I'm only blind, not deaf too, an' they say things in front of me they wouldn't were I sighted. I know that he's done some terrible things, things I can't reconcile with the boy he once was, an' the man who is still good to me an' has protected me my whole life."

"I know he's good to you, Kate. Perhaps that's all that matters."

Kate shook her head. "Pamela, ye know that's not true. It can't be all that matters, I can't pretend he's still that boy I knew growin' up. I can't look away, pardonin' the pun, from all he's done an' been."

Pamela could feel tension creeping up her spine as Kate continued talking.

"Kate, why are you telling me this?"

"Only this, that boy he used to be, that sensitive boy born to the wrong father—I think Noah set out to kill that boy. I think he did, an' he has paid a terrible price for it."

"Why do you think I need to know that?" she asked, a strange premonition shivering through her, even as she asked the question.

Kate looked up, her eyes resting on Pamela's face. "I don't know, only that I have this feeling it's goin' to be necessary for you to remember it one day soon."

Chapter Twenty-eight

Hope is the Thing With Feathers

THE PUB WAS CROWDED, the stink of wet wool and mucky boots heavy on the air. Pamela got her shandy, for Manny, the owner, had seen her come in and poured it right away. He nodded and winked as she took it, and she smiled gratefully. Men nodded in her direction, some smiling and adding a word or two, asking how the babbies were and would she need hay for the summer? Casey's disappearance had broken the last reserve the community had with her. They had gathered round, showing her their sympathy in various ways—a loaf of bread left on the porch, wood culled and cut for the stove, a load of hay that had mysteriously appeared in her byre. Like good fairies, they came and went, leaving whatever they thought might be needed in their wake. Many of them had lost more than one loved person to the Troubles; some had lost children, grandchildren, wives, husbands and lovers.

Curious eyes followed Vanya, as the two of them made their way to a small table in the corner. Eyes followed Vanya everywhere she thought, for he was one of nature's exotics and would always attract attention wherever he went. He had been as prescient as a seer when he had told her, upon their first meeting, that they would be friends. For they were, and she found a great deal of pleasure in his company. He had come along with her today to help with photographing a family reunion that had been held just outside Newry. They'd stopped on their way home to have a drink and something to eat here at the Emerald.

She left Vanya with the drinks and went to the washroom. There was a tiny cracked mirror, green with age, above the sink. She tidied her hair, tying it back with a length of twine she had in her pocket. She sighed; she was so madly busy with the business, the house and the children that she never seemed to have time to pay attention to her appearance. She couldn't remember the last time her hair had been cut or even had a decent brushing. Truth be told she didn't give a damn how she looked without Casey to appreciate it.

She left the small room, and made her way back down the narrow hall toward the pub. There was a man blocking her way at the end of the hall, standing still in the stygian gloom. His head was down, hands shoved deep in his pockets, like he was trying to hide his identity. She went to sidle past, he was making her nervous and she wanted back out into the bustle of the pub, where there were plenty of people around.

"Missus," he caught her by the sleeve, and she pulled back instinctively.

"What do you want?" she asked, thinking he might just be drunk and snatching at any woman who had the misfortune to walk by.

"Can I have a word?" He didn't sound drunk, though most Irishmen could hold their liquor well enough that it wasn't always obvious at first blush how much they might have imbibed.

"Certainly," she said, though she couldn't quite imagine what he felt the need to discuss with her. She didn't recognize him, the hallway was too dark to make out his features and the hat he wore covered the top half of his face.

"Ye'd be Missus Riordan?"

"Yes," she said, and her heart began to thump in that horrible slow way it did when one both anticipated and dreaded the next words from a person's mouth.

"Someone would like to speak to ye about yer husband's disappearance."

"Someone?" she asked. She felt a chill suddenly, as if the door had opened and a cold wind had blown through narrow hall.

"Aye, an' this someone would like to meet with ye."

"When?" she asked, throwing any caution she might have to the wind.

"Soon. Ye can't say anything to anyone, it has to remain with you alone."

She nodded, her heart pounding so hard she could feel the thumping in her temples. Her tongue was thick in her mouth, causing her to stutter.

"P...please—do you know if he's alive?" The man looked alarmed and she realized she was clutching his arm hard enough to bruise him. He glanced behind her suddenly, attention caught by someone further back along the narrow hallway.

"I have to go, Missus. You just remember what I said—tell no one." He patted her hand and then moved off down the hall, exiting out of the narrow back door.

She leaned against the wall for a moment. What on earth had the man meant? Had he truly been speaking about Casey? Or did she only want that so badly to be true that she was willing to twist any set of words into the constructs of him being alive somewhere, somehow? And if he was alive, what would that mean? What would it take to keep him from her, from Conor and Isabelle? That was where her thoughts always stopped cold, because there were few things on this earth that would keep him from his family, and those things did not bear thinking about. She took a breath and righted herself, touching her cold hands to her cheeks, which contrarily flamed with heat. She saw an old man looking at her curiously, and forced herself to smile weakly and walk out into the teeming pub.

"Pamela, what has happened?" Vanya asked her, amethyst eyes filled with concern as she sat down across from him. From the look on his face, her expression must be truly alarming.

She shook her head. "Nothing, I'm fine really, just tired." She tried to smile but her lips felt frozen. She could see he didn't believe her, but she wasn't about to tell him the man's cryptic message, not here in a public house. She wanted to hug the information, veiled as it had been, to herself for a moment, rather than see the doubt in another's face and have it chip away at this surge of possibility that washed through her. She couldn't even run this information past Noah, the man had made that clear.

Manny brought their sandwiches to the table, ham and melted cheese, and Vanya bit into his immediately. Manny's sandwiches were delicious and a meal unto themselves.

"You're not eating, *moy podrooga*, something is wrong. You are as Yasha says, pale as the ghosts."

"I'm all right, just lightheaded." She forced a smile to her lips and took a bite of the sandwich. She would have to eat a bit in order to assure him she was as she said, just fine.

Burning a hole in her pocket was a tiny piece of paper that the man had palmed into her hand when he patted it. All she wanted in the world right now was to get out of here, and to read what the paper had to say.

Vanya was staying the night, rather than making the trip all the way back to Jamie's house. There was the bedtime routine to go through with the children and Isabelle had napped longer than usual so was up later, needing to be rocked to sleep. Pamela had tea with Vanya after. It was nice to have someone here to talk to as the dark of night settled in around the house.

It was very late when she finally went outside to get a breath of air. She fished the piece of paper from the pocket of her jeans. She sat down on the small garden bench, which was near enough to the house that the light from the kitchen window allowed her to see the note clearly. She hesitated before unfolding it, afraid of what it did contain, and more afraid perhaps of what it did not.

She sat there in the night, the air filled with the scents of thyme and lavender, their oils rising as the air cooled. A breeze rustled through the tops of the trees so that they whispered secrets to each other and the stars above. A world of possibility existed inside the folds of the paper she held in her hand—possibilities that included hope or overwhelming grief. Hope was often the most painful of emotions she had found. It was, indeed, that thing with feathers that Emily Dickinson had described. Only for her the bird was the one trapped inside her chest, the one that fluttered its wings in panic at the idea of what words might be upon this plain little square of paper. As long as the paper remained folded the possibility still existed, the hope, even if it squeezed her heart like a cold fist, could still live.

Unlike Dickinson's wee bird that asked her for not so much as a crumb, Pamela's hope had cost her dearly and did every day, because it had in some ways crippled her, she knew. Perhaps this was how it always was for anyone who had lost a loved one in this way, where there was no end to the story, only the place where they had disappeared from your world, where their path had forked from your own and you turned to realize you had lost them at some indefinable point. And so you stood on that path, waiting and waiting and knowing that you might well stand there forever to no good end.

She knotted her courage together and unfolded the paper. It struck her as surreal that life should come down to this—a tenuous few words on a soiled piece of paper.

It was a date and a location, merely that and nothing more. A wash of both disappointment and relief went through her. It wasn't news of any sort, it wasn't anything concrete, but, if nothing else, it allowed her to hope for a few more days.

Chapter Twenty-nine

Circumstances and Madmen

THE MILL DATED BACK to the late 17th century, and had been in use until the previous decade. It had not taken long for it to become rather derelict in appearance and soundness. Casey had always told her buildings were only as good as the people who inhabited them. Once a building was deserted it always went downhill quickly.

"It's the people who live or work in a buildin' that are its soul, Jewel."

This building looked as if its soul had turned to a ghost which waited for its people to return. But no one had ever come back and the mill had been left to the depredations of nature and time. She felt a strange kinship with it, for she too understood what it was to wait and wait and to feel resignation creeping in like cold, dirty water under a door sill. She went through the door at the back, a narrow opening supported by a rotting oak beam. It was chilly inside and it took a moment for her eyes to adjust to the gloom. She walked carefully, these old structures had been built solidly with the idea that they would last for centuries, but she knew that exposure to the elements could cause damp rot and soft spots in the floor and ceilings.

She had left her car at home, the walk here had taken an hour but it allowed her a certain amount of caution and subterfuge that driving up and parking the car somewhere would not have.

The mill was tall and narrow and built entirely of local stone. It was three flights of stairs to the top, to what had been the old loading area where the grain had been hauled up by pulley and dumped, and then fed down to the storage bins on the floor below. There was heavy dust coating the walls, and dancing in golden motes as the evening sun leveled through the narrow windows. She stifled a sneeze, not wanting to alert anyone to her presence. She'd found the plans for the mill in a book of local history, and had taken the time to study the layout.

He was waiting in the loading bay, just as the note had said. He stood just out of the light falling in from the window, but visible enough that she recognized him at once. She had encountered the young corporal several times since that first meeting at the roadblock. It was the young Gordon Highlander, Corporal Callum Ainsley.

"You?" she said in disbelief. "You sent me the note?"

"Yes," he said. He twisted his cap in his hands. Out of the uniform, he still looked every inch a soldier, wearing civvies wasn't going to fool anyone. "I'm sorry, I know it's risky, still I had to take the chance."

"You had no right to take the chance for me," she said in a low hiss. "I have two small children. If anyone was to see me talking to a British soldier, I could be executed. You ought to know that by now. If you were bleeding to death in the street and I came across you, I'd have to step over your body or I could be killed for showing you any compassion. You have been here long enough to understand that. You don't have the right to risk my life and the lives of my children because you think you have information for me."

"I'm sorry, but I can hardly ring you up on the telephone, now can I?"

"I apologize," she said. "This scares me, it would be bad for you too, you know, if anyone were to see us."

"I do know, I thought it was worth the risk."

"Well," she said briskly, "get on with it."

"Can we sit?" he said.

There were two crates that he had obviously set out for that reason. He had covered them with old flour sacking, and while it made for a damp seat, it was relatively clean and comfortable. She clasped her hands in her lap to keep from twisting them in nervousness.

"After we met you those few times going through the roadblock, it occurred to me that there was never a man in the vehicle with you. I wondered where he was, your children are so young and all. And forgive me, but you seemed sad. So when I heard some of the officers mention a woman whose husband had gone missing—one of those 'IRA bastards' to quote—I had a feeling it might be you. So I listened more closely and managed to catch his name. It matched yours, so I knew it had to be your husband."

"All right," she said warily, "but this is hardly earth-shattering news, I know all this after all."

He smiled. "I know, I wouldn't ask you to meet unless I'd heard something that really got my attention. Something I feel you ought to know."

"For heaven's sake, what is it?" She was aware she sounded angry, but didn't care.

"I was in our captain's office a week back. Sometimes when you're a squaddie like me, you're just a bit of furniture in the room. They forget that you're there. Also, they have no way of knowin' that I know you. So they were discussin' this man who had disappeared, and saying that they knew someone who had put the word out on him, thinking he was an informant. Someone in his organization. They hadn't managed to get to him, though they had set up a date for one of their interrogations and expected him to show for it."

"What?" she asked, feeling sick to her stomach. Often IRA interrogations went on until the person broke and admitted to things they hadn't done, just to make it end. "How...how did they know this?"

"Well, that's the interesting bit, isn't it? If they know it's because whoever told them is an informant who is more highly placed up the ladder. It's not beyond them to sacrifice a lower level informant to protect a higher placed one. It's happened before."

"My husband wasn't a tout," she said. "Yes, we had a friend who was a British soldier. He was sometimes a go-between for elements in the IRA who wanted to explore possible peace with the British government. In return he was given names from the soldier to pass along to the republican elements about hits that were about to take place. They saved several lives between the two of them. That was as far as it went."

That might not be strictly true, as she now knew, but the young corporal didn't need to know that.

"Anyway, it seems to me it can't have been the IRA that disappeared your husband, nor the Army because clearly neither knows why he disappeared before his scheduled interrogation took place."

"That's not an answer to what happened to him. If anything it leaves me with more questions."

"I thought maybe I could poke around a bit, see if there's anything more that the captain knows. *If* there's a file on your husband. It just sounded like there was more to the story, but then the man in there with him seemed to realize I was listening and shtummed up."

"And what would you want in return?" she asked. There were never any free answers, not when it came to the security forces here.

"Well," he said slowly, "I know my bosses would look favorably on any information about Noah Murray that might come their way."

She shook her head. "I can't do that. I would be sticking my head in the noose and begging him to tighten the rope. He's a very smart man, corporal. I have children to look after; I can't risk my own neck in that way. I don't see what is in that deal for you, unless you're looking to head down the intelligence path."

He opened his mouth to speak and was cut off as the air around them cracked, like someone had broken a plastic comb on the edge of a table.

"Gun," he said and pulled her to the floor. "Keep your head down."

She did as she was told, though she put her head up far enough to see what he was doing. He was crab walking toward one of the windows, likely to scout out the area and see if he could spot the shooter. He needn't have bothered, for a voice, clear and succinct, came through the window.

"We've got ye surrounded, so come out slowly an' if ye've hurt the woman, we won't hesitate to kill ye."

She sat up abruptly, a blind panic lighting her nerve endings. "Oh my God," she said, "it's Noah."

"Noah Murray?" Corporal Ainsley looked like he might get sick on the spot. She couldn't blame him one bit.

"Yes." The words struck her suddenly, and just how carefully Noah had phrased it. He was making the others believe she had been taken hostage by this man.

"I'm a dead man," he said, face a perfect blank. It was just a statement of fact, he didn't even sound particularly sorry about it. "I'll never get out of here alive. How the hell did they know we were in here?"

"He must have followed me," she said, lips and extremities numb. She wanted to run, but knew there wasn't a door or window out of this place of which Noah wouldn't be aware.

"Do you think he'll torture me first, or just shoot me in the head?"

"I don't know," she said faintly, pulling herself up to her feet and feeling a stray nail snag her sweater. She needed to think, and to understand why Noah was making it sound as if she had been taken hostage. He was giving her an out; she just needed to somehow use it to save this young man as well as herself.

"How well do you know the woods around here?" she asked.

"What? I don't—"

"Listen we don't have a lot of time—how well do you know the area and how fast can you run?"

"I know it quite well, though I hazard not as well as Noah Murray."

"Then let's hope you run a great deal faster than he does."

"What are you thinking?" he asked.

"He's suggesting you've taken me hostage, *I* suggest we take his advice."

"Isn't that bloody dangerous for you?"

"A bit." It was more than a bit dangerous and he likely knew it as well as she did, it was also the best of her very limited options and far better than having the men out there believing she'd met willingly with a British soldier. A few years ago, a widow and mother of ten had been 'disappeared' by the IRA. Rumor had it that her sin had been helping a British soldier who had been shot in front of her, but other stories said she had been working for the British forces. It had never been confirmed that there was any veracity in either rumor. The truth was Pamela didn't know for certain what Noah might do. His words echoed queasily in her head.

"I'm every bit as awful an' monstrous as yer friend on the hill will have warned ye. Ye'd be advised to remember it, Pamela. I tell ye this as a kindness, don't ever underestimate how ruthless I am. Don't ever cross me because I'd rather not prove my words to ye."

She swallowed down the lump of ice cold fear in her throat. "I wish I had a better solution but I don't."

"He's giving you a way out. That tells me he believes you're innocent."

"It doesn't matter," she said, thinking she might actually throw up from fear. "If he thinks anything is off about this, I'll have to answer for it."

"But surely—" he began and then stopped as she gave him a withering look.

"No, not surely and you ought to know that well enough by now, Corporal Ainsley. This country does not run on the normal rules. It has its own set and they are brutal. So here it is, you're going to take me hostage, just as he has suggested that you do."

"You're taking an awfully big risk," he said, though there was a tiny spark of hope in his voice.

She shrugged. "It's the only option we have at this point. Pull me back toward the line of the forest, when we're inside the edge of it, throw me down and run like hell."

"I don't want to hurt you," he said, grey eyes troubled.

"Just do it, if I get a scraped knee and a couple of banged up elbows out of this it will be a very small price to pay. To make it look real, you're going to need to be mean and a little desperate, okay?"

"Desperate shouldn't be difficult," he said and swallowed, the narrow column of his throat shiny with perspiration. "I'll do my best."

"When we go past the windows, put the gun to my head," she said, swallowing over the fear that rose up like bile in her throat. It tasted like cold and sour metal. She might well get them both killed and she prayed that Jamie wouldn't be too shocked when her will was read and he discovered she wanted him to raise her children.

She took his hand and gave it what she hoped was a reassuring squeeze. "Are you ready?"

"I won't cock it," he said. "Are you certain about this? We could both end up dying in a hail of gunfire."

"I know, yet I have to believe Noah won't allow them to open fire if it looks like I'm being held against my will." She wasn't absolutely certain about that actually, but didn't think it would help the corporal's nerves to be privy to that knowledge. She swallowed and turned her back to him, presenting him with her all too vulnerable neck. "You better put me in a chokehold."

He put his arm around her neck and she smelled the sweat of his fear, or maybe it was her own, it was hard to know at this point.

They went down the long corridor in a half crouch, darting past the windows, lest someone take a shot, uncaring which of them was hit. The stairs leading down to the door nearest the wood were narrow and half-rotted, and so they proceeded with great caution. Her nerves almost failed her on the stairs, and she did, indeed stumble. It was only the corporal's arm around her throat which kept her from plunging to the bottom and breaking her neck.

"Once we're outside, I'm going to drag you, so stumble a bit and put up a real fight if you can, we need to convince them."

She nodded, throat too dry to speak. The damp air of the mill clung to her skin, and the corporal's hands were clammy.

"This is it," he said grimly and pushed the door open. It squeaked horrendously on its ancient hinges, sounding like something out of a low budget Hollywood horror flick. And then they were outside and she felt more vulnerable and exposed than she had since a night, long ago, on a train. She found she couldn't breathe, her chest so tight with anxiety she felt like she was choking and black spots were dancing in front of her eyes. Apparently it *was* possible to faint with fear. Casey had told her once, long ago, how fear delineated one's surroundings so that every detail seemed outlined in a finely inked line, brought into focus so sharply that everything was heightened and yet slightly surreal at the same time. The breeze was welcome even though she was already chilled with a cold sweat. Twilight was thick, pooling softly at the base of the trees, beseeching night to come and spread its sheltering cloak over the land. She could hear every rustle of the leaves her hearing heightened by fear.

It was like that, this country, a simple mistake, taking the wrong pathway home, deviating to the right instead of the left and you suddenly found yourself facing death. If it all ended in a few minutes, would she see Casey again and know at last what had happened to him? Mind you, he'd be angry as hell that she had left their babies alone, if he was on the other side of this edge place where she now stood.

It wasn't hard to put up a real fight, because panic took over in the horrible sudden way that it did. It was like someone had dropped a black, suffocating curtain down over her head and she couldn't see or breathe properly. Black spots danced like rain in front of her eyes and the bird inside her chest flapped its wings furiously. She couldn't breathe and she grabbed at the corporal's arm, trying to pry it away from her throat. She was afraid she would faint for real and then he would be left dragging dead weight. She stumbled backward, with the horrible sense that she was going under murky water and it would close over her head and she would never breathe again. She could feel the round of the gun barrel against her head, hard and cold.

She could, in the few seconds of stumbling toward the trees, see the men only in silhouette, the sinking sun limning them in liquid fire and making them merely black hollows at the center of all that light. She counted four, not that it mattered, one with a weapon would be more than enough to kill them both.

"I'm going to let you go, as soon as we're in the trees," he said tersely, "just stay there, down on the ground in case they start to fire."

It felt like the trees were a thousand miles away, and it took forever to get there, her heart crashing against her ribs. Her feet were clumsy and not obeying the signals from her brain. She could feel the men moving in. Then the trees closed around the two of them, the leaf mold beneath her feet, the scent of the forest floor, filling her lungs with a thick, dark scent. The corporal pulled her with him for several more feet, and she stumbled, choking for air.

Finally he stopped, letting her go. She clutched at her throat, desperate to breathe.

"Are you all right?" he asked, voice broken and thick with panic.

She nodded, flapping a hand at him, indicating that he needed to run like hell. She could hear the men crashing through the underbrush, hot on their heels. She dropped to the ground, just as he had instructed, knocking her head rather sharply on a branch on the way down. She fought for breath, hoping to God none of the men stumbled over her in the twilit gloom of the wood. She couldn't cry out for help, there was no air in her lungs for it.

The wood around her grew quiet and the shouts of the men moved further off and away from her. She was still struggling to breathe but managed to get up onto her hands and knees, hoping to make it to her feet and see if that would restore her breathing in its entirety. There was little more than a thready whistle moving through her lungs, but she thought if she could just calm herself enough, her breathing would resume. She would focus on something, just as Jamie had taught her to do. There was lichen on a tree trunk in front of her, white with the palest of green along its frilled edges. Jamie had told her about a lichen that only grew in the presence of the human voice. She wished this one would speak *to* her, it might be enough of a jolt to give her back her breath. The lichen did not speak, however just then a hand hit her on the back, not hard, but not gently either. It did have the effect of opening up her airway though. She drew in a half breath and pushed herself up off her hands. Noah stood over her, his face drawn into severe lines. She couldn't quite tell if he was furious or sick with worry.

"Can ye stand?" he asked and put a hand out to her. She took it and he drew her up. She was still gulping at air, feeling like her lungs had been starved of oxygen for hours, rather than the few minutes it had been since the panic had seized her.

He rubbed her back firmly and her breathing slowly calmed and took on a regular enough rhythm that she could speak once again.

"I…I…thank you," she managed to stutter out.

Noah merely shook his head. "Let's get ye clear of here, ye look like ye're in a wee bit of shock. Ye need heat an' some sugar in yer blood." He took off his coat and threw it around her shoulders.

She felt numb on the way to the car, wondering where in the night his men had dispersed and if Corporal Ainsley had managed to elude them.

His car was sitting in a mess of churned leaves and deep furrows where the tires had spun across the soft ground that led to the mill. He had come after her in haste. She wondered where he had gotten his intelligence, or if one of his people had followed her.

The mill rose up dark and ominous, like an old mausoleum. She shuddered, thinking how easily she might have died in there, if Noah had not told his men to stand down. She followed Noah's quick strides across the mill yard. He had his rifle in the crook of his elbow, but she had the sense he was still fine-tuned to every movement and noise in the area. When they reached the car he told her tersely, "Get in," while he scanned the area one more time. He put the rifle between the seats of the car, so that he could easily grab it.

"Stay low," he said.

"I will," she stuttered out, feeling the fine tremors of her nerves fibrillating out like narrow wires under her skin. Noah put the heater on full, but kept the lights dowsed while he turned around in the mill yard.

"Did you find him?" She chose her words carefully, worried that Noah was already suspicious of her.

"Not yet."

The 'yet' chilled her blood. She said a small, silent prayer that they would not catch up to him. She hoped that Corporal Ainsley would get himself out of that wood alive and the only place they would meet again would be at a perfectly boring roadblock.

"Did he hurt ye in any way?"

"No, he didn't. He frightened me, nothing more than that."

Noah made some sort of indecipherable noise and pulled the car into the narrow pitted road that led away from the mill. He kept a silence that she found unnerving as they made their way toward the Silverbridge road that would take them home. He was never a big talker, but just now she would have dearly loved to chat about the weather, or a rare sheep disease, or parts for his tractor, anything but this fraught silence which seemed to grow more ominous by the minute as they drove along the road, stone walls and small well-kept houses flashing past. He slowed suddenly and turned down a tiny dirt road, bringing back her nerves in a nauseous rush.

"What are you doing?" she asked, as he brought the car to an abrupt halt in a leafy alcove which ended in a gated pasture.

He turned the car off and the silence of the night was as thick as the blood that swooshed in panic through her veins.

He turned to her, the blue eyes so intense that she quailed a little.

"I need to know what ye were doin' in that buildin', Pamela."

She had known he would ask, she could not blame him for that. Still it made her feel like a cat on a hot brick. She needed to give a version very close to the truth, because those were always the safest lies—the ones that were right on the border of the facts.

"I got a note telling me to meet someone at the old mill, it said they had information about Casey."

"An' did he?"

"No, not really, not anything I haven't heard before." She held his eyes, knowing she must not blink either literally or figuratively right now. "I think he lured me there under false pretenses."

"An' just what would those false pretenses be?"

"I don't know, he hedged around about Casey, he said that the Army had information and would be willing to trade it if I was willing to pass information along to them. Truthfully, I don't think they know anything, they just want someone to spy for them."

"Spy on who?" he asked softly, though there was a steely note that ran through his words which shot a jolt of adrenaline through her.

She had decided on this bit beforehand, knowing it would come up.

"You, of course."

He nodded, face inscrutable.

"An' what did ye say?"

She looked him full in the face. "I said no, Noah. I wouldn't spy on you, I'm not a fool." This bit *was* the absolute truth, she would never pass along information about Noah; it would be tantamount to committing *hara-kiri*.

He seemed to relax a little, his eyes narrowing just a bit, taking in the expression on her face in what she felt was every tiny nuance. She fought to hold that gaze, praying the traitorous blush of pink would not stain her skin, as it often did when she was nervous. It would be apparent even in this dark car, for she swore the man would be able to feel her blood wash up through her skin.

"I can't have anyone thinkin' I'm coverin' for ye, nor cossetin' ye."

She understood that. Noah's reputation was all, he held an entire county in thrall by the mere force of that reputation. It was well backed by action though, and she did not kid herself about just what this man was capable of doing. He had spent years putting that reputation in place and he could not afford to have a woman making it appear he had cracks or vulnerabilities.

"I wouldn't expect you to," she said calmly, even though the tremors in her nerves had turned into tiny spastic jumps, like someone was applying low voltage electrodes to her skin. This, she thought, was the least of what Noah would do to her if he found out the truth. It wouldn't be low voltage either. Hysterical laughter rose in her throat. She didn't dare let it out in front of this man, so she put her head down to her knees and fought for control.

She was chilled to the bone, and yet there was a fine trickle of sweat beading along her backbone. She was sitting in a car in an isolated spot with a man who had tortured and killed men in ways she could not allow herself to think about. Granted it wasn't a hillside hut, deep in the countryside, but it was a lonely enough spot that no one was likely to hear her scream. She felt a sneeze coming on, her entire body and every inch of clothing was coated in dust from the mill. She sneezed three times, prompting Noah to put a clean handkerchief into her hands. She put it to her face, grateful to hide in the starchy folds for a minute while she regained her composure.

She got herself under control and sat up to find Noah watching her. His gaze could be unnerving at the best of times—cool and calculated, as if he could pick over a person's most secret thoughts and desires like a crow would pick seeds from decaying fruit.

"Are ye all right now?" he asked, and his tone was merely one of concern and not the terrible flat tone he had used before.

"Yes, I'm all right."

She took as deep a breath as she dared, not wanting to start another sneezing fit. She looked out into the night beyond the car. They were parked in front of a gate and she jumped a little, realizing they were being watched by some monstrous figure standing in the field.

"'Tis a cow," Noah said, taking in her nerves. It was indeed a cow, the shape of it materializing out of the night at his words. It worried her that he could guess her emotions so easily, because then perhaps he could sense when she was being less than truthful. She wondered where he started with an interrogation—a few direct questions and then on to pulling fingernails, or maybe breaking a toe or two? She felt the bubble of hysteria behind her windpipe once again.

They sat that way for a long moment, the cow looking solemnly over the gate at them, the deep twilight silhouetting her big ears. The field beyond her was awash in the last light of the day before the black of night swallowed everything—deep lavenders and indigos, and the spill of a narrow early moon touching the far hills. The contrast of such peace and utter tranquility with the madness of the last hour made the moment entirely surreal. She could never reconcile the two—the beauty of the land with the conflict that was so deeply rooted in its soil. She could not reconcile many things though, not the least of which was this man here beside her who treated her with kindness and respect, and the things she knew he did to keep his powerful hold on this wee county.

He took her hand in his, and gave it a light squeeze. The strength there was apparent. It was the hand of a man who had worked hard every day of his life since he was capable of work. He turned her hand toward him and used the fingers of his right hand to trace the pathway of her veins, blue against the pale translucence of her skin.

"I should hate for anything to happen to ye, Pamela."

He let go of her hand and put the car into reverse, backing slowly out of the narrow lane.

She did not know if his statement was meant as concern or as a threat, though frankly she wasn't sure which option frightened her more. She understood that he had just made an exception for her, and that she was going to have to pay for it sometime in the future.

Chapter Thirty

Shooting Lessons

GIVEN THE NOTE THEIR last meeting had ended upon, Pamela was a trifle startled to find Noah outside her door two days later, holding a rifle in his arms.

She looked pointedly at the rifle and then up into his eyes.

"It's a gift," he said gruffly.

"Of the South Armagh variety?"

He laughed. "Aye, I suppose ye could say that."

"What would you propose I do with it?" she asked, stepping out into the yard and closing the door behind her. Conor was with Lewis for the afternoon, for the old man had taken a shine to him from the day he was born and he would sometimes come around to take him on a ramble in the woods. Isabelle was with Gert, and Pamela had been planning to go pick her up early as she had a rare afternoon free from work of any sort.

"I'd suggest ye use it to shoot anyone who comes on yer property without permission. Truth is ye seemed worried about the killings in the area and I thought it best if ye had a means of protectin' yerself, if someone were to try to enter yer home."

"You think we could be targets?"

Noah shrugged. "I don't know, but I should like ye to take the rifle all the same. There doesn't seem to be either rhyme or reason to the targets, so I would think bein' Catholic an' breathin' is enough to make a target of ye."

She sighed, there were times she wished the man was just a tiny bit less honest in his summations.

"Ye know how to use it?"

"I do, Casey taught me how to shoot. He was very good, his own father said he could take the eye out of a gnat from fifty yards away."

"Aye, well, just reassure me by hittin' a few targets, would ye?"

He took six targets from the back of his truck and lined them up along the edge of the tree line. While he was thus occupied, she fetched a pair of shoes and put them on, remembering to take the tea towel from her shoulder at the last minute. She went out to where he waited for her, the gun held loosely over his elbow, as natural a part of him, it seemed, as his hands or feet.

"Load it, just so I know ye understand how," he said handing the rifle to her.

She took it from him, feeling the heft and cold weight of it. The grip was smooth as silk, no doubt it was a good rifle and likely very expensive. She wasn't sure how she felt about being gifted such a thing. She wasn't terribly comfortable with guns, and never had been, despite Casey long having kept a pistol in the house.

She cracked the barrel and loaded the shot, snapping it shut with a forceful click. She did not care for guns, but she understood them. She stepped forward, aware of Noah's eyes assessing her stance and hold. She felt slightly prickly under his gaze.

She lined the barrel up, looked down the site and focused her will on the target. She shot each target, knocking it back, before coolly moving on to the next. She managed to hit all six targets dead center. Casey would be proud. She lowered the rifle, the heat of the barrel radiating out against her leg, though she had set it a good four inches clear of herself.

"He taught ye well," Noah said, and she felt absurdly pleased to have impressed the man in such a way.

"He did," she agreed, and he had, drilling her over and over on how to hold the gun so it wouldn't kick back and bruise her face or shoulder, how to sight in on a target, and when it was necessary to use it.

"It's one thing to be able to hit a sedentary target an' quite another to shoot a human bein'." His words were matter-of-fact.

"I do know that, theoretically at least. I haven't actually shot anyone yet." It occurred to her that she had maybe put a wee bit too much emphasis on the personal pronoun and that this man *had* shot people, and brought death with far less savory tactics too.

"Ye can ask if ye want," Noah said, his tone dry. "I know ye're thinkin' it."

"Thinking what?" she said, trying for a genuinely puzzled tone and knowing she fell far short.

"That I know well enough what it is to kill someone."

"I'm not sure," she said, devoutly wishing the heat would die down in her face, "how one begins such a conversation."

"I don't know, Pamela, but it seems to me that ye're not one that's shy about yer thoughts an' feelins', nor do ye seem to stand much on ceremony."

"Is that your polite way of saying I'm tactless?"

"No, it's my way of sayin' I've rarely met a creature so honest."

She laughed. "Yes, it's one of my larger failings, I admit."

"I would say it's a virtue, not a failing."

"Is it? I'm sure there are several people who know me who might disagree with that."

"I like yer honesty. I know if ye say a thing to me, ye mean it. There's not many who tell me the truth so freely."

"And why do you suppose that might be?" she asked tartly, immediately regretting the words.

Noah looked at her narrowly and then laughed. It was a genuine laugh, light in its parts and she couldn't help but to laugh with him, mostly with relief.

"There's another reason I've come to see ye today." It was like a shade had come down over his face, abruptly changing his mood and tone.

"There is?" She felt suddenly nervous, the lighthearted atmosphere abruptly gone. She wondered if this was about the other day and if he had changed his mind about how far he could trust her.

"Aye, there is. There are only two reasons the British would think to butter ye up for an approach an' it's either they've led ye to believe that they can help ye with the search for yer husband, or they've checked yer finances an' think ye might be open to a series of payments for information. Or they're usin' both."

She swallowed, his information was terribly exact. Honesty was the only path through this particular minefield, and so she said, "The last option."

He nodded. "I thought as much. Could we go inside for a moment?"

She wasn't sure she wanted to be in an enclosed space with this man right now, but on the other hand, as fastidious as he was, she didn't think he'd kill her in her kitchen, as the mess would be much worse there than in the woods.

She walked ahead of him, her legs stiff and uncooperative, her skin prickling with tension. Inside, the house looked innocuous, floor boards glowing dully in the mid-afternoon light, the Aga gleaming bright blue from this morning's cleaning and the air scented with the herbs she grew year-round in the windowsills. She turned round to find Noah looking bemused and fishing in his pocket for something. His shirt pocket was not large enough, thankfully, to carry any sort of weapon, unless he planned to kill her with a pen, which she didn't think likely.

"Here, just in case they're watchin' ye, I don't want every interaction between us on photographic record." He was holding out a slim piece of paper to her, well away from the view of any windows.

She took it warily, wondering if he had written down a message on it. '*You will die slowly and terribly*' or something of the sort. What was on the paper was more shocking than that. She took it in and then looked up at him, her hands shaking with unpleasant surprise.

"What is this?" she said, the figures still dancing in front of her eyes. She wasn't sure if shock or outrage was uppermost in her right now.

"It's a loan. I'd be a fool to leave you open to such temptation as they are offerin' ye. Also, ye're a friend, an' ye don't leave a friend without the means to keep their own roof over their head."

"I can't take this," she said, holding the check towards him. The amount on it frightened her, as if she were being bought, her silence or maybe something more.

"Ye'd rather be beholden to the British?" he asked, tone light, but she knew the question was deadly serious.

"No, I turned them down, too, but thank you for thinking so little of me."

He sat down on one of the kitchen chairs and looked up at her. "Pamela, I am not a fool. Ye've been left here alone in a situation no one would envy. I know the buildin' company is not goin' so well for ye, ye've said as much. So if ye're short of money, it's no wonder. What sort of man would I be if I just left ye to it? I am yer friend, though to be candid with ye, that surprises me a fair deal. The money won't put me out, it's not like I'm goin' short on anything. Ye can pay me back if an' when ye're able."

She was still standing, but felt like she might faint. Noah pulled out the chair closest to him and she sat down in it.

"I don't mean to seem ungrateful, Noah, this is very generous of you, but I can't possibly take your money."

He looked at her steadily, the blue eyes dark, as a shadow passed through the kitchen. The clouds must have rolled in over the sun. Not for the first time, she wondered what went on in his head. "Cash it or don't, just keep it until ye know that ye can keep yer head above water."

"Well, thank you." She wasn't certain what else to say, because it was, indeed, a very generous thing for him to do, even if he was buying himself assurance that she wouldn't turn traitor for the British.

"If there comes a day when ye want to sell the buildin' company, let me know, I can probably help ye find a buyer."

She nodded, and walked him to the door, watching as he got in his truck and left. She stood in the doorway for a few minutes; she needed to put the rifle away somewhere safe that the children could not find it, and then tidy herself up and go pick up said children. The quixotic sunshine was out again, the heat of it comforting on her skin. She leaned into the doorway, absently stroking Finbar's head, where he had come to rest it against her leg. She realized she was clutching the check. She looked down; it was rumpled and damp from her hands. The mere presence of it made her uneasy.

She tucked it in an envelope and pulled a chair over to the tall cupboard that was wedged between the hearth and the stairs. The shelves were narrow, but went back a long way and she had to stretch to reach the hidden slot at the back of it. She pressed the lever and heard the snick of the tiny door opening. Casey had installed the cupboard so that they had a place to put things they wanted safely hidden. She would put the check in it, and close the door on it. Her fingers touched something else; the small cubbyhole was filled to its limit. She poked at it with her fingers, it felt heavy and solid, something wrapped in a worn paper bag. She managed to hook her fingers around it and stretching up on her tiptoes, she pulled it out of the cupboard. It was a solid block, rectangular in shape, the paper bag wrinkled and now torn from her pulling on it. She opened it and looked inside, sneezing as dust dispersed in a cloud. Clearly, it had been there for some time.

It was money, a lot of money. Money of the sort she and Casey did not have. She took it out and checked the bag to see if there was anything else in it. There wasn't.

She fanned the money; at a quick glance it looked to be about two thousand pounds. Enough, she realized to keep the wolf from her door for a little bit longer. She didn't know where the money had come from and so thought perhaps she shouldn't use it. She laughed, though it was a laugh with a manic edge to it. She had been worried about paying her next mortgage payment an hour ago and now she had two thousand pounds in hand, and a check for ten thousand more. All of this money, and a strange certainty that she mustn't use any of it. It was then that the words of the intelligence operative echoed in her head.

Your husband had no trouble taking money from British coffers.

No, she could not believe it. Not Casey, he wouldn't have done it. They had not been rich, but they hadn't been struggling or in a bind at the time. Unless he had been more frightened by the graft than he'd let on, though being that it had almost gotten him beaten to death at one point, it was possible it had.

She looked to the chair where Casey had always sat for meals, for talks, for late night tea and the comfort of each other at the end of the day. It seemed there were many things she had not known, though it was possible he had wanted to tell her but she would not listen. It was also possible that his male stubbornness had told him she didn't need to know, that he was protecting her by not telling her. She felt anger bubbling up through her veins, what else hadn't he told her? What other small traps lay in wait for her, things he hadn't found the time, nor courage to tell her? Sometimes it felt like her future was mined, and just when she was settling into an ordinary day, week, or month, something would explode—something small, or maybe looming out there was the thing that would rip her life apart at the seams, though the seams felt pretty ragged and pocked with big gaping holes already.

"You bastard!" She spoke to the empty chair, the words tearing her throat as they emerged, each one ragged and painful. "You bastard—why didn't you tell me?"

She put her forehead to the door of the cupboard, the polished oak cool and solid against her skin. She could hear the ticking of the clock, the hum of the Aga, the twitter of an excited sparrow that had nested in the eaves of the house, and the sound of Finbar's breathing, warm on her ankles as he gazed up at her.

From the chair there was only silence.

Chapter Thirty-one

If Wishes Were Horses...

SUMMER ARRIVED IN a series of fine days, setting the countryside to blooming in the green of both hedgerow and garden, and the wild flowers that grew in the ditches and along the hillsides. The lambs and calves had grown strong and were gamboling through the fields away from their mothers. And still Pamela counted days and weeks, and felt as if the calendar with the days all neatly squared away was a personal affront.

Tonight, despite a fine day, a heavy rain drummed on the roof and slapped at the windows, the wind screeching around the corners of the house like a scorned woman. Pamela was tired; it had been a long day of it. Isabelle had been cranky much of the afternoon, and even the normally unflappable Conor had only eaten half of his supper and then fallen asleep on the couch while she wiped up the dishes. He felt warmer than usual when she carried him up the stairs to his bed and she was worried that both children were coming down with something. She couldn't afford them to be ill, not with the way things were going at the construction site. Murphy's Law was reigning supreme there, with every last bloody little thing that could possibly go wrong having done so in the last two weeks. Even Frank, her imperturbable foreman, who rarely got upset no matter how awry the world was and who never swore, no matter how pressed, had said damn in her presence and then apologized profusely for it.

It was Friday though, and so she could look forward to two entire days without the pressures of the business. She would have to do the books on Sunday night, but until then she intended not to think about wood orders, recalcitrant stone masons, or ugly columns of figures that seemed to bleed red at the slightest touch. Tomorrow, God willing, Isabelle would sleep past six A.M. and then they were invited to Jamie's for the day. He had recently acquired a pony and had asked if Conor would like to come riding. She hadn't seen him in a week, and she missed him. Just being in his presence tended to relieve a lot of the stress she operated under almost constantly.

She had one foot on the stairs, ready to head up to bed and a few hours of oblivion when a knock came on the side door. A knock on the door in any town or country this late at night was disconcerting, but here in the murder triangle it was downright terrifying. She fought the desire to crouch low on the landing and put her head down until whomever was at the door went away. Only two weeks ago there had been another shooting, this time of a newly-married couple who were working on renovations on a cottage they had bought as their first home.

Hiding was a luxury she did not have. She was the only protection her children had. She took a breath, and turning from the stairs, went to the cupboard by the Aga. The second knock came just as she retrieved the pistol she kept hidden high upon the top shelf, in an ancient tea tin. The rifle was too long at close quarters, the pistol would be more accurate should it be needed. A certain cold stillness came over her, even if her hands trembled as she slotted the bullets into their respective chambers. She put her thumb on the hammer, ready to pull it back.

"Who is it?" she asked, trying to steel her voice so that her fear wouldn't be too apparent to the person on the other side.

"Pamela, it's me, 'tis all right, ye can open the door, an' put the gun down too."

A wave of relief went over her and she opened the door. She wasn't putting the gun away until she was certain she wouldn't need to use it. Right now, she thought she might like to brain Noah over the head with it for scaring her.

There was an old man standing in the rain with a hat literally in his hands, the wild wind blowing thick white hair around his face. He looked like the shadow of an oak tree, ancient and strong but twisted and bent hard by time. Noah stood beside him, rain dripping from the brim of his cap. He nodded at her, but allowed the old man to speak for himself.

"Beggin' yer pardon, I've no wish to impose upon ye, lass, but if ye could spare me a fire for a few hours it would be greatly appreciated."

"Please, come in out of the rain," she said, flicking Noah a questioning look over the man's shoulder.

"I apologize," he said. "I didn't dare call ye. Ye'll understand why in a moment."

She tucked the gun away, noting that there was an odd tension between the two men, invisible but as present as a wire strung taut and thrumming between them. Not for the first time she wondered why so many of these men sought out Noah when they needed help. There were men, hard men, even in the Belfast command who walked in fear of him, after all. Then again, needs must when the devil drives, she thought, for she had been terrified of him and yet had sought out his help too.

She pulled an old armchair beside the fire so that the man might dry off properly. Looking at him she saw that he had a very advanced case of rheumatism, his hands were clawed inward so that she could hardly see how he could use them to any effect and he walked carefully, as if his feet hurt him terribly. If he had been on the run for some time, sleeping rough in byres and damp sheds and whatever else passed for a night's shelter had likely exacerbated it badly.

She saw the old man seated comfortably, as Noah pulled a bottle of whiskey out of his coat and unscrewed the lid. She brought him a glass and he poured in a generous amount. The scent of it wafted up to her nose, making her eyes water and causing her to sneeze.

"Not a whiskey drinker, lass?" The old man asked, smiling at her, an action that transformed his face and she found herself smiling back. She could see he had once been a fine-looking man, broad of shoulder and long of limb, with a genial expression hidden amongst the lines that incessant pain had carved into his face and body.

"No, I'm afraid not," she replied, handing him the glass and trying not to breathe in.

Noah took her to the side, his hair slick with rain despite the cap he'd had on. She handed him a towel from the stack she kept in the boot room and he gave his face and hair a perfunctory and rough rub down before handing the towel back to her.

"Here 'tis then—he's been in exile in America for the last thirty years, but his sister is dyin' an' he's on his way through to Derry to say his good-byes. He doesn't dare go to the funeral, for the police will be keepin' a look out for him. They still have him on their files, an' it would be no small coup for them to capture him. He doesn't require more than the warmth of the fire, as he said, an' the bottle is his. He likes a drop for his rheumatism before sleep. I'll be back in the mornin' to move him on."

"Who is he?" she asked, keeping her voice low.

"Dan Connelly," he said. "He's a bit of a legend in the republican world."

Her eyebrows shot up toward her hairline.

"Aye," he said, "*that* Dan Connelly. Mind, where he used to be fire he's now a simmering bed of coals, but trust me when I say his was a name once feared throughout the land. Just let him stay by the fire, an' keep his whiskey glass filled. He'd never touch a woman, so if ye don't mind I would as soon ye didn't banish him to the shed, as I've advised with most of the men I send yer way."

"I wouldn't," she said, thinking of the damp in the shed.

"I'm away then," Noah said, and merely nodded to the old man and then was gone again into the night, into the mad wind and lashing rain, leaving her alone with a total stranger by her fire. And yet, in the strange way that history and an illegal rebel organization formed intimacies and connections, he wasn't a total stranger.

Casey had told her about him, and she knew her Irish history well enough to understand that she was, indeed, in the presence of a legend. Dan Connelly was famous for his rebellious stand against the British occupation of his country. He had an infamous personal history as well, having been married three times and fathered seven children. He had been living in New York for the last thirty years, and moving about the United States when it looked like his history might catch up to him at a few points. His first wife had died, the second up and left him when she realized she couldn't hack the life of a rebel's wife and the third one was still married to him, for all the good it did her. Before he left Ireland he had been in prison more than he had been out. This wasn't uncommon for an Irish rebel, not of that time, and not of this one either. Songs had been composed about him, and were still sung in pubs at closing time. He had given his life to the cause, and lost almost everything to it.

He had witnessed the Easter Rising, though he had only been a young man of fifteen at the time. The massacre of many of the men who had been part of the Rising had left its mark upon him as it had so many of his countrymen at the time. He joined the Irish Republican Brotherhood shortly after that, and stuck with it through all its various incarnations.

The second time he was jailed he went on a hunger strike, in the long held Irish tradition. His jailors had put him in a straightjacket and tried to force-feed him through a tube. It took six men to hold him down, and two more to force the tube down his throat and into his stomach. He had suffered through beatings and humiliations beyond count, and yet his spirit had remained unbowed. The British could not break him, though heaven and its saints knew they kept on trying.

One by one, the men who had brutalized him in the jail disappeared as if the wind had taken them away. But everyone knew it wasn't the wind, and that each man's end had not been a pleasant one. It wasn't that she felt that such men deserved mercy, only that it took a certain sort of ruthlessness to act as this man had done throughout his life.

Yes, she understood just who it was sitting in the chair beside her hearth.

She readied the fire for the night, smooring it expertly so that the flames would burn low yet the peat would throw out a good heat for hours. She then set a blanket to warm near the fire, arranging its folds neatly in an effort to appear calm and collected in front of her company. She knew she ought to make conversation, though where one began to small talk with a famed rebel such as this man, she did not have a clue. He saved her the effort by speaking first.

"Ye're goin' to have to forgive me for I've been a blunt sod all me life an' that's not goin' to change now, an' so I will say this, grateful as I am to ye for the fire an' shelter, I do wonder what sort of business ye have with Noah Murray that ye owe him favors?"

She looked up from the blanket to find the old man's gaze keen and sharp upon her.

"Why do you ask that?"

"I don't know," he said ruminatively, the whiskey in his hand glowing a soft amber in the firelight. "Only I wonder what a woman such as yerself is doin' with the likes of him. Ye remind me of a tale my nan used to tell, of a woman who was part mermaid, part human. It's as if someone as lovely as yerself can't really be fully of the human world."

"I'm not involved with him romantically," she said, and put a jot more whiskey into the old man's glass, then left the bottle near to hand for him so that he might help himself.

"Maybe not, but it's a bit more complicated than merely doin' his biddin' in return for whatever hold it is the man has over ye, isn't it?"

"He has no hold over me," she said, aware that her tone was far more defensive than it ought to be.

"Has he not?" The old man looked at her with some sympathy in his face. "My mistake then, an' ye'll forgive me for it, I hope."

"There's nothing to forgive," she said, and took the blanket from the back of the chair. It was hot to the touch already, and along with the flow of whiskey, it ought to ease the old man's bones.

"Thank ye, dear girl," he said as she tucked it around him. He sighed, as if breathing a bit of his pain out.

She straightened up at the sound of small feet on the stairs. Conor stood on the landing, one hand rubbing his eyes, the other clutched around his tatty yellow bunny that he'd had from the day he was born. He came down the final two stairs and padded directly to her side.

"Mama, who's this?" Conor asked, staring wide-eyed at the old bent man by the fire.

"He's our guest, his name is Mr. Connelly," she said, picking up Conor and settling him in her lap. He would be next to impossible to get to bed now that he knew there was a stranger in the house. There was no harm, she thought, in allowing him to stay awhile. Conor was fascinated by old men for some reason. Perhaps, she thought, because he did not have a grandfather.

Dan Connelly winked at her and then looked at Conor with great seriousness.

"Ye'll not want to stay up too late, boyo, for night is the realm of the Good Folk, an' it won't do to get caught awake by them. Why they'll take ye by the hand, just as ye are, in yer nightwear an' barefoot an' away ye'll go, no more to see yer mammy, nor any bit of this world."

"Do you believe in fairies?" Conor asked.

"Oh, boyo, 'tisn't a matter of believin' or not, fairies don't need our belief to exist, they just do. Shall I tell ye a story of a night when I met with the Queen of the Good Folk herself?"

"Aye," Conor said and leaned forward eagerly, so that Pamela had to hold on to his pajama top to keep him from tumbling from her lap to the floor.

Pamela watched the old man, feeling the shiver of anticipation in her son, and the echo of it in her own body. Such a night lent itself naturally to the telling of tales, for the wind was moaning eerily round about the chimney top, and the rose canes scratching against the windows had the sound of spectral fingers, tap-tap-tapping at the windowpanes.

Like a true seanachie, the old man pulled a wisp of reverie from the night, from the elements of fire and air and then took a swallow of his whiskey in a manner that said he was going to get down to the serious business of storytelling. He leaned forward a little, crabbed hands inscribing the air about him with another time and another place.

"The world was different then, 'twas as if the doors were open between this world an' that one, particularly of a moonless autumn night. People believed an' so they saw, now people are blind because they don't believe. But I've seen the Good Folk, an' no man will ever make me doubt the sight of them.

"'Twas the dark of the moon, an' the night so thick a man could barely see his hand upon his own nose. I'd been down the pub, havin' a pint an' a bit of craic with my friends. I was a young man, not yet married to either woman or cause. It was autumn, an' near to All Hallows' Eve. The night had felt ordinary enough when I went into the pub an' the sun was settin' on as fine a day as a man is like to see. It was harvest time an' I'd had a full day of it, an' maybe just the wee bit too much to drink for I was tired an' wantin' to get home to my bed. So I took a shortcut, past a patch of bog land that I normally would've avoided that time of night. It was the sort of land that seemed haunted even on a fair day—wee twisted trees grew here an' there upon it an' the water was a dull color, like bronze clouded by time an' dirt. It put the hairs up on the back of my neck at the best of times, an' it could only have been the drink cloudin' my judgement that made me decide to go past the beaten old path that ran along its edge.

"I was halfway along its rim when I heard somethin', a strange high sound that I thought was a bird at first, maybe somethin' hurt an' trapped in the bog."

The old man's eyes were lit with memory, and Pamela shivered slightly despite the heat of the fire, for she could feel the night as he described it, and smell the smoke and earth of the bog under an autumn sky.

"I stopped, so that I might hear better an' know which direction the noise came from an' if there was some desperate creature in need of assistance. It took a moment or two to realize it was voices I were hearin', but like no voices I'd ever known before. It was as though the wind could suddenly speak in words, or the waves of the sea rose up an' told ye a secret. Ye'll know," he tilted his head toward Pamela, "what I mean, for I daresay with those eyes, the sea does whisper its secrets to you."

She merely nodded, wanting him to keep on with the flow of his narrative, even as the chill of it crept into the house with them, settling in along her backbone and creeping out along her nerve endings. Conor snuggled more tightly to her, and she ran a hand over his curls in reassurance.

"It wasn't a language I knew, but I understood it though I know that makes no sort of earthly sense. Yet, I could glean the gist of what they were sayin', even if the words themselves meant nothin' to me. There was a feelin' of waitin' upon the air, an' as if there were a great crowd o' folk that had gathered for a specific reason; ye know how that energy is, when everyone is waitin' an' yearnin' upon the same thing. It shifts the very air, that sort of energy.

"I came round about a clump of trees an' there they were, in the middle of the bog, a crowd of little people, each not more than a foot in height. The clump of trees had hidden them from the path, but once I stepped off I could see them clear. I was certain I was hallucinatin' an' yet nothin' in my life had ever seemed more real than that scene before my eyes. I knew it wasn't a good thing to be caught watchin' them, an' so I kept behind the trees. It was as if I was lookin' through a glass that sharpened the edges of everythin', an' into a world beyond my own. A world of silver an' gold, an' trees that bore both flower an' fruit at the same time.

"I didn't dare move, I didn't dare to breathe for fear they would see the fog of it upon the air. 'Twas then I heard the sound of horses' hooves, soft thuds along the ground, echoin' through the earth so that I felt the thrum of it to the marrow of my bones. There was an old oak that had fallen partway into the bog; the bit that was out was a huge gnarled branch, one of the sort that is near to a tree itself in size. It arched into the water like a bridge that led to the depths of the bog. Local legend had it there was no bottom to that bog an' some of the old women did say it opened into hell itself, for more than one creature had disappeared into it, never to be seen again. 'Twas over this oak came a carriage pulled by six tiny horses, black as coal, all I could see was the light of their eyes, glowin' red in the night air. The carriage they pulled was like onyx reflectin' moonlight, though of course there was no moon that night. 'Twas lit up like a star sat within it on fine cushions. I kept tellin' myself I was seein' things, that there'd been somethin' in my pint of bitter that made such madness appear before my eyes.

"One of the wee men rushed to open the carriage door, an' a woman stepped down, light as air, an' I could see clear it was her they had all been waitin' for. 'Twas as if a sliver of moonlight had been carved off the full, an' transformed into this small woman, this creature, and alit there in the bog. 'Twas clear to me she was someone of great importance to them, an' she carried herself as an empress would, for sure an' wasn't that what she was?"

There was a look of longing on the old man's face that made Pamela wonder if this story was not all together the fairy tale it seemed to be.

"She walked as if she were moonlight too, just driftin' across the dark wet ground, her skirts held high in one hand. It was then that the music began. 'Twas the sort of music that defies words, only that it drew the soul from a man's body an' returned it as somethin' less an' somethin' more at the same time. I've been in many a pub an' heard many a pipe an' fiddle since that night, but none that satisfied me nor sounded half as lovely as the music did that night by the bog.

"She danced when the music began, an' what a sight she was. When I turned my head just so, I saw she wore a simple dress, brown an' homespun, lookin' like 'twas woven of beaten rushes an' sere grass. But then if I turned my head to the other side, she wore a gown all of silver to match her eyes an' skin. Her face was always the same—fierce it was, with somethin' unholy in the set of it, an' yet I'd not seen a lovelier woman in all my years, until I set eyes upon yerself this very night. Ye put me in mind of her, ye look delicate an' yet there's somethin' wild about yer beauty that might frighten a lesser man than a Riordan."

She started slightly and Conor stirred. "Mama?"

"It's all right, Conor, Mr. Connelly just surprised me a bit."

The old man continued on, after a glance at Conor's sleepy countenance.

"She danced like she were no more than a bit of thistledown on the wind, an' yet the dance was both deliberate and wild. At one point her little shoe fell off an' I saw her foot—an' it worn't like no human foot you ever see'd, but webbed an' delicate as a frog's foot, outlined in frost, or so it appeared, for it glittered so.

"It seemed only a moment before I felt the shift that comes in the late hours, when suddenly ye know that night is loosin' its hold upon the spinnin' world an' the stars fade to smoke an' the sun trembles behind the hills, waitin' upon its turn. 'Twas then they left, disappearin' into the last of the night, as if they had never been more than a scent on the air, a vision of somethin' that was once, but could be no more.

"I stood there for a long time, 'twas as if I were hypnotized. I could smell the water an' wood on the wind in a way that I never had, an' just a tracery of the fairy smoke, richer than peat an' earthier, too. I felt like I had no flesh an' the air moved direct through my bones an' blood, an' stirred my soul to somethin' dark an' strange. I was terrified at the same time, for I had looked into the wee woman's eyes, an' I knew it was wrong even as I did it. I knew I ought to move, for I was sore tired for my bed by then, but still I stayed because there in that moment 'twas as though I knew all the ages of the world, all that had come an' gone, an' all that was still to come, an' was sad for it, too, with the sadness of the ages. I'd been given a vision of a world that might be, but I knew in my soul that it wouldn't ever come to pass, an' yet the hell of it was that now I would always know the difference.

"I think it's true what the old ones used to say, that if ye chanced to look upon the Gentry an' had them look upon ye in return, ye'd lose yer soul to them. An' though they terrified a man, he'd yearn the span of his life for just one more look at them." He took a sip of his whiskey, setting it aside with the careful movement of a man long used to rheumatism. "Noah is like that in a way. He'll take a piece of yer soul an' not return it to ye. Only it will be because of his own hunger, not because he's enchanted it away from ye, girl."

Coming at the end of the story as it did, the statement took her off guard. She didn't say anything, for she knew the man was not looking for a response, he was merely giving her a warning. His words bothered her. Because, of course, they were true in many ways. She owed Noah and that was never a position she was going to be comfortable with.

Conor was asleep now, his head heavy against her chest, his breathing slow and deep. She needed to put him in his bed; she needed to go to bed herself. Yet it was pleasant here by the fire and her limbs felt heavy with the heat and weariness.

"Yer man is Brendan Riordan's grandson?"

"Yes, he is. Did you know Brendan?"

"Aye, but mostly as legend not as a real man. My da' was holed up in a house with him one night, where they were keepin' safe from the British soldiers that were scourin' the land huntin' for them. He said he was dismayed at first to find himself in the company of Brendan Riordan, bein' that he was the most wanted man in the land at the time an' he knew there was little the soldiers wouldn't do to claim such a prize.

"He told me 'twas as if Brendan was a figure of legend already, an' that the real man was trapped inside that legend, unable to live the life he truly desired because of it. He was a big man, with the presence of some mythical figure, like Finn MacCool or Cuchulain, an' my da' said 'twas impossible not to be awed by him. He said though, after a night spent in his company, he had never met a man more human. He meant it as a compliment, to be certain, but his face was always sad as he said it.

"People used to say of the Riordans that they were the sort of men others thought were either blessed or cursed, an' some would say they were touched by fairies in their cribs, an' that the touch of that fairy curse would cause them to long for freedom all their lives, an' to always have rebellion like a hard tide in their blood. Well, I suppose you would know the truth of that yerself, bein' married to one."

Oh yes, she knew the truth of it, and she knew the price of it. It was curse, not blessing, to want freedom so. Jamie had warned her long ago, but she had walked willingly into the fire with Casey, only now she was alone and the fire tasted like ashes in her mouth.

"I would ask you one thing," she said softly, "was it worth it? Everything you've lost, all the years in prison, all the friends killed along the way and the loss of your wives and your children—was it worth it?"

There was a long silence and she looked up finally to find the old man's gaze upon her, sharp but not without sympathy.

"That's not an easy question to answer—was it worth it? Is my country undivided, is it free from tyranny—no, so in that sense did anythin' I do, did anythin' I lost have meanin'? I cannot say. But if I were to go back in time, knowing what I know now, knowing how terrible the cost would be, I can't say I would do anythin' differently. There was never a way to just stand on the sidelines an' hope that time fixed history's errors for us. The fight matters, even if lost."

She nodded, though she felt as if something cold and sharp was lodged in her throat.

"Noah told me what happened with yer man," he said quietly. "Ye must miss him terrible, no?"

"Like the rain misses the earth," she said. She stood, and crossed the room. She put her son down on the end of the couch and then made the old man a bed upon it; the heat of the fire would still reach him there. She picked Conor back up and his arms came around her neck and he mumbled from the well of dreams. "An' six black horses…"

"Good night, then," she said to the old man, who still sat by the fire, one last swallow of whiskey in his glass. "Thank you for the story."

He nodded to her and she could see he was still far gone into the world he had pulled from the ether of night and air and fire. His voice, soft and filled with an understanding that made her throat tight, reached her just as she stepped on the small landing where the stairs turned abruptly right.

"Perhaps, lass, he's only away with the fairies for a while."

She closed her eyes, not wanting to look out their eight-sided window, where the stars, which ought to have fallen from the sky eight months ago, continued to shine.

"If that were so, he might never come back."

"Well, if anythin' can bring a man back from a strange world, sure an' wouldn't it be love?"

"And if wishes were horses, beggars might ride," she said, and then holding her son tight to her body, she climbed the stairs to her lonely bed.

Part Three

Me, Without You
August 1976-April 1977

Chapter Thirty-two

Pressure

"That fucking man makes me fucking furious!" Captain Edwin Forrest flung his pen across the room, nearly impaling the young soldier standing before him. "Fucking bastard thinks he's fucking untouchable, does he?"

The soldier remained quiet, uncertain of whether he was meant to respond to this statement. He chose the more discretionary route, thinking it was likely the captain was just blowing off steam.

"I asked you a question, corporal."

"Apologies, sir, I thought it was rhetorical. I do believe he thinks he's untouchable, but that's mostly because he is."

The captain glared up at him, face turning an unflattering shade of red. "Why do you say that? If you were to shoot the man, I believe he'd bleed, would he not?"

"Well, sir, we'd all like to think so, but we've not had the chance to test the theory."

The captain gave him a hard look and then opened one of his desk drawers and pulled out, much to Corporal Ainsley's surprise, a bottle of twelve year old Balvenie scotch.

"Do you drink, Ainsley?"

"Only occasionally, sir, and never on duty."

"Sit, man, while I have a drink. My duty is ostensibly over for the day; consider yourself off the clock as well."

The captain poured them each a generous measure of the Balvenie, in glasses that he'd pulled out from the same drawer the bottle had been in. The smell of it—heather and honey, vanilla, autumn leaves and the smoke from a fire on a cold night—brought the corporal home to Scotland. Just the one swallow had given him a warm glow in his midsection. It might be, he thought, the first time he'd been properly warm since arriving in this land. He thought longingly of his wife and wee daughter and how lovely it would be to be home with them.

The scotch relaxed him a little and he took a long breath for courage. He didn't want to speak in error and further enrage the captain. "Forgive me, sir, but what about the smuggler who we turned?"

Captain Forrest leaned back in his chair and sniffed his whisky appreciatively, his rage seemingly under his command once again.

"We found him in a car in Omeath Forest with a suicide note pinned to his shirt, so I don't suppose he'll be of much value as an informant, will he?"

"Oh."

"Yes, bloody 'oh'."

"Did the note say why he killed himself, sir?"

"He didn't bloody kill himself, did he? He was put in that car, and no doubt wrote the note under great duress. That bastard Murray was smart enough not to leave a mark on him. You heed my words, corporal, his fingerprints are all over this mess."

Corporal Ainsley knew that the mess to which the captain referred wasn't just the suicide of the smuggler, but also the bombing that had taken place last week near the border. A backhoe had been stolen from a local farm and taken to a bridge a few miles away where a Renault van was waiting. The van was packed with a 2,200 pound bomb. The JCB was used to knock down a stone wall, between the van and the ultimate goal, the rail line, which happened to run right next to a checkpoint. The van had been fitted with specially constructed wheels designed to run along the rails. The stones from the knocked down wall along with a few pieces of wood were used to build a ramp and then the JCB lifted the van onto the railway line. A firing pack was attached to a command wire that was more than a mile long. In the meantime, members of the PIRA had set up roadblocks to divert traffic out of the area, with some dressed as Gardaí and signs indicating that the detour was due to a Department of the Environment issue. The van was run down the tracks and detonated as it reached the sangar. The soldier inside, who had only just come on duty before the bomb tore apart the sangar, was killed instantly when the impact of the bomb threw him against one of the sharp corners of the small shelter, fracturing his skull and lacerating his brain. It also destroyed the watchtower that hovered over that particular checkpoint.

"We have the strength here and the fire power, albeit with one hand tied behind our collective back, and yet that bastard outguns us every time. He lives on a farm, like some bucolic shepherd and he runs the biggest smuggling operation I have ever seen and we can't touch him. I will give the bastard this much, it was well planned and well executed. If he was on *our* side, we'd be in far better shape. So here we are, Ainsley, back to square one." The man took another drink of his scotch, and then eyed the little remaining as if the peaty depths were an augur that could forecast the future. Corporal Ainsley had a sick feeling he knew just what the man was about to suggest.

"We need to put a little more pressure on the woman then, don't we?"

"How do you suggest we do that, sir? We've offered her money, hinted that we can maybe find out what happened to her husband, and she didn't budge. She looked horrified at the very idea, truth be told and I don't think we can blame her for that, considering what we know of Noah Murray."

"Well, *can* we find out what happened to her husband? Or were we lying about that?"

"Well yes, sir, but we did try. We haven't been able to trace him at all, though. It's like he vanished in a puff of smoke, there's no trace of him anywhere."

The captain's lips narrowed to a thin line. "Well he bloody didn't go up in a puff of smoke, did he? Is this fucking mystical country seeping into everyone's brain here? He wasn't stolen by the fairies, now was he? He can be found, or at least his corpse can. I want to know what happened to the man. Meanwhile, I think it's time to tap our friends in Special Branch, don't you?"

"Special Branch, sir?" Corporal Ainsley did not like the idea of approaching Special Branch. It would make the waters they were wading in that much murkier; it also opened them up to even more possibilities of informants, double cross and death. Special Branch always played dirty. "It's only, if you remember, sir, Special Branch already made an approach to her. She didn't bite."

"Because the fools offered her money—why would a woman who has James Kirkpatrick for a friend need to take up spying for extra cash. The idea was ludicrous. No, that's not how you get to this woman."

"How then, sir?" Corporal Ainsley wasn't happy with the direction this conversation had taken. He felt badly for Pamela Riordan. A widowed (as far as anyone could establish) mother of two children, trying to stay afloat both emotionally and financially, and here was his commander suggesting they use her in a fashion that could well get her killed.

"Corporal Ainsley, please don't play the naïve soldier with me. The woman has a history, let's exploit it." He drank the last of his whisky and put the empty glass on the desk in front of him. "I think while we're at it, Ainsley, we ought to see if our compatriots in MI5 will put a fire to James Kirkpatrick's feet."

"Why would we want to do that, sir?"

The captain smiled, cool as damn.

"Because if we're going to get to Noah Murray through the woman, we need His Lordship distracted."

Chapter Thirty-three

Me, Without You

THE FIRST KILLINGS IN her own area took place only five miles, as the crow flies, from Pamela's house. She was well used to hearing of violent acts; the whisper of them always rode the wind in this area, like a narrow slipstream of blood, scenting the air with copper. This one was different. An entire family had been killed in their home, for no reason that anyone could fathom. They were an ordinary family—a mother, a father, a son and a visiting friend all sitting around after the week's work, anticipating the weekend ahead. None of them was affiliated with any paramilitary group or even any social movement that might have drawn the attention of the less savory elements of their warring society. They had lived on a small farm only ten minutes distance from her. It had jarred her badly. She hadn't felt secure since Casey's disappearance anyway, but this heightened the anxiety that was her closest companion of late.

She had other concerns, however, more immediate at present. She had lost another contract today; that left her with two, one of which would be completed by week's end. There was no other work in the offing, nothing on which to bid, nothing with which to continue to meet her bills and pay the men who worked for her. Or, if she was being brutally honest with herself, worked for the memory of Casey.

The clients liked her and they were kind to her, but on some level they didn't take her seriously and so the contracts were starting to go else-where. She couldn't blame them, she was in over her head and well she knew it and clearly they did too. She thought the work she did still have was in large part due to people feeling guilty about leaving for another contractor when her husband was missing.

It was the end of a particularly trying day in which Murphy's Law had prevailed with a vengeance: one of the men had broken a hand when a load of schist came off the truck sideways, the company truck had broken down part way to the building site, and her best carpenter had regretfully told her he was going to be working elsewhere starting the following Monday. Just now, though, the house was quiet around her, other than the burble of the radio she had left on downstairs and the sound of Finbar moving around the kitchen, looking for a stray crumb left from dinner. The children were asleep, Isabelle exhausted from a day of cutting a tooth, which had blessedly popped through in the late afternoon, leaving her and her mother exhausted. She had gone to sleep easily though, and Conor had followed shortly after, tumbling down into his accustomed heavy slumber halfway through his bedtime story.

Pamela was tired, but needed a bath and to give her hair a thorough wash. She leaned over the tub in the bathroom, and turned the taps on halfway. If she turned them on full, the pipes would rumble and shake the floor, and she wasn't willing to risk waking Isabelle.

She sat down on the edge of the tub, feeling a surge of anger towards her absent husband. She was so tired that every cell ached, both with sheer physical exhaustion and with need of him. She was tired of pushing the thoughts away that came every day, all the darkness that was simply part of her life now, all because Casey had walked through their woods one day and never returned.

Water poured into the tub, the scent of lavender bath salts rising with the steam. She took off her clothes, shucking them to the floor. She turned the water off, the rush of it fading to the mere plinking of drops within seconds. She got into the tub, the heat of the water prickling all along her skin. She sank in up to her neck, and closed her eyes with the sheer bliss of being warm for the first time all day. The anger was still there, a red pulse in her chest, an ache in all her joints. It shocked her a little to realize just how furious she was.

Having a family meant everything to her; it had made her world whole and given her a security she had never known before. She was angry at Casey for taking that away from her, as nonsensical as it might be to blame the man for something over which he'd had no control. But choice—well that was another matter, because if he had actually killed that man, as Noah had suggested, then he had known such an act would pull out the supports, as shaky as such things were in Northern Ireland, from under their lives. And for that, though she understood why he might have done it, she was furious with him.

She sometimes felt like there was no longer ground under her feet and that she was forever walking on a crumbling precipice. She had foolishly thought she was used to the violence, used to living on her nerves, used to worry and strife being a constant. But the truth was a person could never be so accustomed to those things that it didn't affect them each minute of every day. Her incipient panic was proof enough of that. Every act of blood, every death, every time she looked over her shoulder certain that she felt the bead of a rifle sighting along her back—all these things reminded her that she did not live in an ordinary country, she did not live an ordinary life. Particularly not for an American girl who had grown up with money and safety, for she'd had those things until her father died. She had changed a great deal from the naïve girl who had come to Ireland all those years ago in search of Jamie Kirkpatrick. That naïve girl who had, in ways she had never expected, found her home here in this violent land.

Casey had the talent of that—home, family. She thought perhaps it was something both he and Pat carried naturally with them into the world, something their father had provided for them and so they had a simple expectation of it. Her own father, though he had loved her well, had not had that talent and so while their homes had been beautiful she had often been lonely in them despite their aesthetic appeal. With Casey, regardless of the surroundings—the two-up two-down they had shared in the Ardoyne, the top floor of the triple-decker in Boston, the tiny cottage on the coast of Kerry, this house here—it was always home, because his love and strength had surrounded her from morning until night. *He* was home, and now with him gone she wasn't sure how to keep that feeling, how to provide it every day for their children. She wasn't certain about any of the dozens of decisions she had to make each day.

She tried to shut her mind off; she could never make cogent decisions when she was this tired and if she made plans or thought her way through any of the difficulties that presented each day at work, she would forget her solutions, flimsy as they might be, by the time she got a pen and paper to jot them down.

She needed to toughen up and find a way to understand the business better, to run it better, so that clients felt that they could trust her to get the job done properly.

Her thoughts drifted back to Casey, not that they ever truly left him. Thoughts of him were a constant, like a piece of music that played relentlessly in the background, distracting her at all times. She felt porous, as if everything flowed through her, good and bad. Like the Echo of myth, she felt like she might eventually disappear through the sheer strain of longing for something she could no longer have. If she let the longing take over it would swamp her and she wouldn't be able to function, and she could not allow that to happen. She had to take control of what she could, and leave the rest. Conor and Isabelle were her number one priority, and in order to look after them properly she had to establish some sort of steady income. It was more likely to come from keeping the company solvent than her occasional jobs photographing crime scenes.

She sat up in the tub and began the arduous job of washing her hair. It was a big task as it fell in a curly mass to the middle of her back. Casey loved her hair, which was why she hadn't cut it in such a long time. She mostly wore it tied back in a ponytail these days, having neither the time nor the patience to tend to it. She desperately needed a trim, but she didn't see where she was going to find the time for an appointment. She put a large dollop of conditioner in her hair, working it through, the scent of rosemary and honey surrounding her. Once that was done she washed her body quickly; the water was starting to cool and she wanted to keep as much of the warmth in her skin as she could. She rinsed her hair under the tap and then wrung the water from it before getting out of the tub and toweling off. She was already making a list in her head of all the things that needed to be done tomorrow. There was a list two weeks long just for the company alone. The list for the household was daily, weekly and seasonal. Casey had looked after so much of it, and it was a big task taking over all of that, even with Jamie and Patrick's help.

Determined to winnow her list by one item, she padded downstairs in her towel to retrieve her scissors. They were good and sharp and more than adequate to the task. Upstairs again, she cleared one side of the mirror and before she could change her mind made the first cut. Snip by snip her hair fell to the floor, forming a blue-black cloud on the tile. She was taking something away, shedding something. It felt like a powerful act, stripping away this one harbinger of femininity. As though she were an inversion of the biblical Samson, and shearing the hair away would give her strength and make her less vulnerable. Before she really understood what she was doing, she had cut all her hair off, leaving only about two inches on her head. She looked into the mirror, resolute, lifting her chin and giving herself an honest assessment.

Her eyes looked enormous in her too thin and too white face. She felt a moment of regret so pure and sharp that it made her sick to her stomach. What had she been thinking? The back of her neck felt horribly exposed, and the length of it seemed suddenly ludicrous, like she was Alice and had swallowed the contents of the *Drink Me* bottle and grown grotesque in parts. She knew it was only a matter of what she was used to and that given a few days she would adjust to this woman in the mirror with her strange eyes and overly-long neck. She had hoped somehow that the severe hair cut would make her appear no-nonsense, all business and capable. Instead she looked like an alien child, not quite of this world, but uncertain in which world she did belong. It could stand as a metaphor for her life, as she truly didn't know where she belonged since Casey had disappeared.

She trimmed off a few last unruly pieces and then stood back. The hair was so short that she no longer had any curls. She sighed, at least she wouldn't have to fuss with it anymore. It was definitely a wash and go sort of hairdo. She ran a hand over her shorn head, and grimaced at herself in the mirror. The first thing on her list of to-dos and she had made a frightful mess of it.

She looked at her reflection. She didn't look fierce or unafraid. She looked tired, lonely and indefinite, as if even her edges were insecure and wavering and that she might dissipate along with the steam. She had told Casey long ago that when she was a little girl she had believed that if she touched the surface of a mirror her fingertips would one day melt through and she would be able to follow, stepping into another time. She touched the mirror now—if she could go through, would she? Would she seek out that girl and warn her or would she choose to start over again, maybe never meet him and spare herself the heartache that was her every day companion? She felt a shaft of pain at the very thought—no, never that, she would never choose that, despite the terrible void in the universe which was his absence.

She could, with effort, conjure him leaning in the doorway behind her, his arms crossed over his chest, relating his day, or just watching her with that look in his dark eyes that said she was soon to find herself in bed, entirely and happily at his mercy. Big, strong, capable and yet gentle with her and the children, he had been the axis on which her world turned.

"Tell me what to do, Casey," she whispered, as if anything louder would scatter the carefully-constructed apparition in the mirror. "Tell me what I am supposed to do—with the company, with the house, with our babies, with the rest of my life."

She touched the image, knowing it was as illusory as a reflection in a funhouse mirror. The mirror was warm on her hand, quicksilver and mist, letting her believe for just a moment. She wondered what he would think if he could see her now, what he would say to this woman with the haunted face and butchered hair. This uncertain, stumbling woman who jumped at her own shadow some days.

She needed to move, to feed the dog and bank the fire, to lie down in a bed that was not her own and go to sleep. But first she spoke to the mirage in the mirror and to the woman beside him.

"This is me, without you."

Chapter Thirty-four

The Anatomy of Desire
August 1976

It had taken four months of painstaking repairs before her car was in good enough nick to drive again. She was happy to return Noah's truck to him, as it had felt a wee bit like driving a Shorland tank down their tiny country lanes and she was certain everyone in a five mile radius could hear her approach each time she took it out.

It was one of those summer days when the clouds scudded light as thistledown across the face of the sun and the occasional spatter of rain dusted the land and then just as swiftly turned to a bright sun that gilded the fields and dusted the hedgerows with diamonds.

Pamela paused as she got out of the truck, casting an eye over the land around her. The fields were a rich luxuriant green with plants that would soon need harvesting. Casey had loved this time of year and had spent many hours after work each day in the garden, pulling up the vegetables and readying the soil for the following spring. She had always loved when he came in from the garden, smelling of earth and plants, and excited by the fruition of the new things he had chosen to grow that year. It was a love they had in common and they had often spent winter evenings with their heads bent over seed catalogues, dreaming green dreams. She took a breath and pushed the thought away. She had been able to get her panic under control in the last few weeks, but thinking about Casey could bring it on again.

Noah was in from the fields, working in the small kitchen garden he kept at the back of the house. He was digging up potatoes, swiftly, rhythmically, as it seemed he did all things. He looked up at her approach and wiped the back of his hand across his forehead. It was one of the fine parts of the day and the sun, standing near its zenith, was hot.

"I came to return your truck," she said, "thank you for the loan of it, it's been a great help."

He shrugged, uncomfortable, she sensed, with her gratitude. He really looked at her then, his eyebrows rising as he took in her hair, or rather, the lack of it. In typical Noah fashion he went straight to the point.

"Did ye have a reason for scalpin' yerself?"

"I don't know," she said, feeling suddenly self-conscious about her shorn head. "I just wanted to be less visible somehow."

Noah gave her an odd look. "Well, let me be the first to tell ye, if that was yer intention, ye've failed miserably."

She flushed hotly. "I'm well aware I look like a scarecrow, thank you very much."

Noah propped his arm on the top of the spade and looked at her in a very direct manner. "If that's what ye think ye resemble then ye need to take a longer look in the mirror. Ye don't exactly blend in, an' it's not because of yer bald head."

"I'm not bald," she said indignantly.

"Near enough to it," he said and turned back to his digging, the warm scent of soil and sun floating on the air. She bent and started collecting the potatoes he'd dug up, their skins cool with rich, fragrant black soil.

"You aren't one to soft soap a girl, are you?"

"Ye know well enough that I'm not one to flatter, if ye need that ye'll have to go elsewhere. Nor am I blind, Pamela. Ye're very pleasing to the eye, an' somehow takin' off all yer hair has only made it that much more obvious."

"Well, that wasn't my intention."

"No, I don't imagine it was, but there it is."

"I thought somehow," she said, feeling unaccountably irritated, "I'd become less visible, I'd fade into the background."

Noah gave her a look of incredulity. "What—like some farmer's wife with a weather-beaten soul showin' in her face an' limbs? Surely ye must look in a mirror now an' again, Pamela? An' even if ye don't, I would imagine men's faces are mirror enough."

"I don't really look at men," she said, realizing it was true. She barely saw people sometimes, which was dangerous in this country. So much in life seemed like a blur since Casey had disappeared.

"I can see why ye would feel that way now. But ye must realize that men desire ye. I tell every man I ask ye to put up that if they so much as look at ye sideways, I'll have their kneecaps shot out."

"You do?" she asked, slightly shocked and yet aware he rarely said anything he didn't mean, even in jest.

"Aye, I'm no fool. Men will feel what they do and desire is no bad thing, it's not as if they can control the feeling of it, they've just been warned to control their actions. Has one of them made ye uncomfortable?" His tone had changed with the last sentence, and she felt a chill slide through her, despite the warmth of the day.

"No," she said, for though one young man had made his interest clear, she didn't want him to end up in a ditch somewhere merely for making a pass at her. Noah gave her a dubious look, as if he could see straight through what she said.

"Well, if any one of them does, ye be certain to tell me."

"I can look after myself," she said, aware her tone was sharp and that her pique had little to do with the words he was saying.

"Are ye sayin' ye have no need of men's desire?"

"There's only one man's desire that I want, and he is gone," she said, "so I would just as soon not have to contend with the rest."

"It's none so simple as that, men are men an' they will want, particularly if they think they can't have. Ye've been runnin' around lookin' as ye do long enough to know that."

She ignored this statement, though he was right; however, he likely knew that already and didn't need her confirmation of his opinion. She was finding his assertions somewhat annoying. She leaned down and picked a few more potatoes from the soil. It was companionable with the warmth of the sun and the snick of the spade in the earth. His voice, when he spoke, startled her slightly.

"Ye might want to think about it one day."

"Think about what?" she asked putting one hand above her eyes so that she could see him properly.

"Havin' a man in yer life. A man's desire keeps a woman safe. If a woman accepts that desire, a man's want puts a line around her, a boundary if ye will that keeps other males away. Men are predatory by nature, but they are even more territorial."

"I'm doing all right on my own."

"Ye're not truly on yer own. Yer man on the hill would do anything he needed to keep ye safe. Yer husband kept ye safe to a certain extent when he was here with ye, an' now Mr. Kirkpatrick does, no?"

"And you as well," she said, meeting his gaze directly.

"It was part of the deal we made, you an' I."

"No, it wasn't," she said quietly. "The last man who came through said he knew I was your woman and that no man would dare touch a hair on my head, knowing what it would cost them."

He shrugged. "If they believe I desire ye, what does that hurt? It keeps them clear of ye, does it not?"

"It does, though I am aware some men fear little when it comes to women."

He leaned down to collect the seed heads off a few poppies which grew at the edge of the garden, and they worked in silence for a few minutes, the breeze bringing the soft sounds of the farm to them every now and again. There was a tractor trundling along somewhere in one of Noah's fields, and the thin bellow of a calf sounded every now and again.

"Hand me that basket over there, would ye?"

She picked up the basket from the fence post where it was perched. It was filled with neatly-folded waxed paper, each labeled in a firm, squared-off hand that was unmistakably Noah's.

"Seeds," he said. "I gather what I can in the autumn. I've got strains of some things that haven't been in circulation here since the last century. It was one thing my father taught me."

He was a conundrum wrapped in a riddle, this man, she thought, watching as he carefully sorted through the papers until he found the one he was looking for and removed it, and then carefully poured the seeds he'd gathered into the small fold of paper. Thoughtful and careful with his land and his sister and yet she knew what else he did, what else he was—a man of blood and violence. It was hard to reconcile the two things sometimes, especially now as he handed the basket to her and pulled the weft of the conversation back to its original thread.

"I suppose ye will have experience of men who don't like to hear no."

"I think all women have experience of those sorts of men. Only in my own case it's a bit more. I was raped by four men on a train," she said. "I'm not a fool, I know a woman is never truly safe. I know I am kept safe by their own basic decency or else fear of you. Don't think I'm naïve, I'm anything but."

He looked at her for a long moment, gentian eyes thoughtful. "I'm sorry that happened to you, some people are pure animals an' need to be dealt with as such."

"They were, I believe," she said quietly. "They are all dead, as far as I know."

As usual, he understood what was not said, for he had lived in this country all his life and knew what forms justice took here.

"I would have done the same," he said. "Such acts do not deserve understanding, nor compassion. I think ye'll find, occasionally, that two wrongs do indeed make a right. Only blood answers for blood. Such men do not feel remorse." He looked up at the sky and then back at her.

"Come away into the house, it's goin' to rain any minute."

He was right for the clouds had come in swiftly, blotting out the sun and turning the bright green of the fields a dark emerald. The wind had picked up and she felt the chill of it on the bare nape of her neck. She followed him in, carrying the basket of seeds and waiting in the kitchen for him while he stowed his tools in the wee lean-to that was built onto the side of the house for that exact purpose. She filled the kettle and put it on the stove to heat and then wandered to the window that looked out over the fields to the dark hedges that bordered much of Noah's farm.

Noah came in then and she turned from the window, putting a hand to her shorn head. She felt exposed to him in a way she had not before. He pulled out a chair for her at the worn wooden table where he sat to eat his solitary meals. He always seemed to sense her discomfort. She supposed he was well used to reading others and then using it to his advantage.

She sat and watched while he got the tea prepared, his movements swift and certain even in a task as small as this. He took out a tin and put a few biscuits onto a plate and brought it to the table along with the large blue teapot that looked like it had been through the wars, but was serviceable and made a hot and aromatic brew. The cookies were homemade and smelled strongly of ginger and brown sugar.

"Kate comes home once a week or so, an' makes cookies an' bread an' such. She thinks I'll starve to death without her to look after me."

"Are you angry with her—for leaving?"

He took a moment before he answered, sitting down across from her first.

"I was at first—well, not angry so much as worried. She loves him, ye know. I hope he loves her just as well."

"He does, he never would have agreed to her moving in with him if he didn't."

Noah nodded tersely and she understood that was as much conversation as they were going to have about Patrick and Kate. She felt a small frisson of relief on Patrick's behalf. She had thought merely having a relationship with Noah's sister had been an act of suicidal bravery on his part, never mind living in sin with the woman. Not that, Pat had assured her, he'd much to say about the matter. Kate had told him he needed looking after and before he knew it, he said, she was there cooking his meals, and ironing his shirts. He had said it with a fond exasperation in his voice that told Pamela he didn't mind in the least. She had worried for him, after Sylvie's death, that he wouldn't recover enough to love again, but once she had seen him with Kate, she had understood that Patrick had met his match in more than one way.

She turned her attention back to the man at the table. He was pouring cream into a mug, then he filled it the rest of the way with tea and placed the mug on the table in front of her. It startled her to realize he knew how she took her tea.

They chatted away about the farm, about her own wee bit of land and the things that she needed to fix before winter set in and about the cost of hay and feed and what was the best remedy for the split hoof Paudeen had developed over the summer. From there, as was inevitable, they moved to the wider neighborhood and the events that had happened two days before.

There had been another killing—a couple on their way home with their teenage daughter, shot in their car as they turned into the drive leading to their farmhouse. The daughter had managed to escape by exiting the car and running across the field, even though she ended up in hospital with three bullets in her. Noah had his own theory on just why these murders were occurring.

"There's a pattern here that's maybe not readily noticeable in the midst of such tragedy but it's there nonetheless. Everyone who's been killed has been workin' their way up into the middle class. Or had arrived there already. God forbid that a Catholic should aspire to get out of the muck of bein' impoverished and uneducated."

"You really believe that's it?"

"Aye, well it's part of it, it's not everythin' entirely of course. Nothin' in this country is ever that simple."

"I suppose it's fortunate for me that I'm running the construction company into the ground then and will soon bounce myself out of any hope of middle class membership," she said gloomily.

"It's not so bad as all that, surely," he said. He leaned back in his chair, easy and relaxed and awaiting her answer. There was always the sense with this man that he listened carefully to everything that a person said and that he heard even more clearly what was not said, and tucked it all away like a squirrel storing nuts against a harsh winter, to be used for a future day.

"Yes, it is. People don't have faith that I know what I'm doing, and they have a point there. I can't fault them. I have a great foreman and he does know what he's doing and he's teaching me when he's got the time. But it's not easy securing new contracts. I'm pretty sure what I have gotten is Jamie somehow finding a way to send work my way. I still worry about those men coming back looking for more money, too."

"None will touch ye an' yours, ye needn't worry about that."

"How can you be so certain of that?" she asked and then realized the naïveté of the question even as it crossed her lips.

"Because as ruthless an' awful as those men are, Pamela, they understand that I am more ruthless an' awful still. They tested me on it a few times in the past an' I taught them a lesson they are not likely to forget any time soon."

It seemed that every time she forgot who she was dealing with in this man, he had a way of reminding her just whom she had gotten into the figurative bed with all those months ago. Despite all this she felt relaxed here in his home. It wasn't necessary to talk around Noah to fill up empty space. He was comfortable with silence, though she supposed living on his own as he did that silence was a regular part of his life.

The light was fading in the kitchen and a vague chill heralded the approach of evening. It was time for her to go. Noah would have evening chores that needed his attention.

"Can I use your telephone?" she asked. "I need to call Pat to come get me on his way past."

"I'll take ye home," he said easily. "Yer brother-in-law won't be comfortable with ye bein' here, so we'll save him the worry, aye?"

"All right," she said, "thank you."

She stood and took the tea things to the big old stone sink. Noah had disappeared into another room, so she filled the sink with a bit of sudsy water and quickly washed the dishes. The smell of ginger still lingered in the air, along with the earthier scent of discarded tea leaves.

Noah came back into the kitchen, a bundle of papers tied with a piece of twine in hand.

"Here," he said gruffly, "these are for you."

She looked down to see that the papers were the small, waxen envelopes containing carefully collected seeds. Each envelope was labeled with its contents—lavender, hollyhocks, lettuce, beets, kale and so on. There were at least a dozen packets tied up in the twine.

"But," she protested, "these are your saved seeds."

"Aye, an' ye're one of the few people I know who will appreciate them. Grow somethin' lovely for yer windowsills or plant them out in yer garden."

She looked up at him, puzzled as she often was at the two faces of this man.

He laughed. "Pamela, 'tis only seeds, not a sign of my goin' soft. Take them or don't. I just thought ye might like them."

She flushed, feeling foolish. "Thank you, it's very nice of you."

He shrugged and grabbed his jacket from the back of the chair where it hung. She stood, tucking the packets of seeds into the pocket of her sweater. Despite the gruff tone, she knew it wasn't something he would have given to just anyone and she was touched by the simple gesture.

He drove her home in the truck, quiet for the most part, focused on the narrow lanes. She was a little nervous with him behind the wheel, being that she was all too aware that the price on his head was higher than the price on any other head in Northern Ireland. It would be a coup of immense proportions for the security forces or any Loyalist paramilitary to kill Noah Murray. They would have no compunction about killing anyone in his company either.

He drove down the narrow lane to her home. She took a breath, as she always did when arriving home because the hope that one day Casey would be there, returned and safe, never completely left her.

Noah brought the truck to a halt, looking out over the yard, surveying the perimeter, as he always did in any new environment. It was something Casey had always done, too, and she recognized it for what it was. He looked casual; one arm draped lightly over the top of the steering wheel, but there was an energy coming off him that wasn't casual in the least. He turned then and looked at her and she shifted uncomfortably in her seat, hand on the door, wishing she had leaped out as soon as he had pulled to a stop.

The gentian eyes made her prickly with unease; he saw too much, more than she was comfortable having a man see in her right now. Still, she didn't expect the next words that came out of him, his usual forthrightness notwithstanding.

"Ye spoke before of not wantin' a man's desire, of wantin' to be invisible to men," he said quietly. "But I am a man, an' yet ye seem to have no worries about me."

"You've never said anything that made me think you even see me as a woman," she said, feeling a blush rise hot in her face. "Not until today anyway."

He looked long at her, his eyes cool and appraising. "Just because I don't act on it, doesn't mean I don't feel it."

She got out of the truck, and stood, feeling somewhat stunned, watching as he put the truck in reverse and backed it up her narrow drive. He waved in his abbreviated fashion as he pulled away down the lane, heading back toward his farm.

She stood for a moment longer, though she needed to get inside and start dinner before Pat dropped off Conor and Isabelle. They would be hungry and the evening routine would have to be gone through, even if it was started late. Conor was a stickler for those things, and she knew in part it gave his world a security since his father had disappeared and so they adhered to the routine at all costs because it was something she could give him to keep a boundary on his universe.

The sound of Noah's motor died away into the evening light and his words echoed uncomfortably in her head. She wondered now if those words had been meant as an offer, rather than the casual comment they had seemed in the moment.

'A man's desire keeps a woman safe. If a woman accepts that desire, a man's want puts a line around her, a boundary if ye will that keeps other males away.'

Chapter Thirty-five

Baptism of Light

"AND BEHOLD, *a woman comes to meet him, dressed as a harlot and cunning of heart.* Because men by design will and do sin, and so women must be the example of good faith, of purity and morality. Women must help to guide men in the paths of righteousness for you are more innocent by your own design."

The Reverend Lucien Broughton looked over the rim of his gilt-edged bible at the women clustered like a clutch of broody hens in the front pews. Elspeth sat alone, off to one side, keeping herself away and apart. She looked well tonight, she knew, and she didn't want anyone wrinkling her new blue dress by crushing up against her or touching the material with their rough hands. It was silk, and by far the most luxurious garment she had ever owned in her life. She touched it now with a careful fingertip; it felt like a cloud, something light and airy and beautiful. She felt pretty in the dress. She pulled her attention back to what the Reverend was saying. He was, after all, speaking to her, which gave her no small thrill sitting here amongst all these women hanging breathlessly on his every word. And they were breathless, silly bloody cows with their tongues half lolling out, as if he would notice any of them. She realized suddenly that he was wrapping up his sermon and she ought to be listening closely in case there was an extra message for her in his final words of the night.

"*I discipline my body and make it my slave, so that, after I have preached to others, I myself will not be disqualified. And I am afraid, when*

I come again, my God will humble me among you, and that I shall bewail many which have sinned already, and have not repented of the uncleanness and fornication and lasciviousness which they have committed."

The Reverend Lucien Broughton closed his bible with a sorrowful air, his head bowed. Elspeth clasped her hands together until they ached, the bones singing with pain where her nails dug into the palms. Oh how she wished she could soothe his pain, the pain he carried because of the weakness of a man's flesh, the pain caused by that whore with the dark hair.

"Let us pray," he said. The light from the stained glass window above him fell in a bright shower of blue and gold all around him, limning his skin and hair with a delicate translucency. She closed her eyes, but then opened them a little to look around and see which women were watching him and not attending to their prayers properly. There was that little hussy, Sarah Taylor, who went through men like most women went through knickers, gazing at the Reverend—*her* Reverend—as if she was trying to forge a psychic link with him. She would eat him up and pick her teeth with the bones that one would, given half a chance. Well, she wouldn't get the chance. What that strumpet didn't understand was that the sermon tonight was for her. The message was a secret, a secret only she knew, told through bible verse.

After the prayer, he kept his head bowed for some little time as though in deep contemplation of his conversation with God. The women all held their breath, none moving until he brought his head up and gave them a weary smile. It was their cue to get up and move toward him. The usual crowd clustered around him, like flies to meat, Elspeth thought, narrowing her eyes at the lot of them. Half of them were married, too, but you'd not know it watching how they behaved. Like a bunch of gaudy parrots all trying to chatter away at him and get his attention for themselves. Imagine if they knew what he'd been up to and with a Papist whore no less. Yes, she thought with a wave of smugness, just imagine *that*.

"Miss Dowdell, if you could stay behind, I need to have a word," he said, and then turned back to that chit, Sarah. Well, it wasn't Sarah he'd asked to stay back, was it? Sarah shot her a look of hot jealousy, to which Elspeth responded with a cool smile. She could afford to be magnanimous with these harlots now. She had the Reverend's ear, she had his trust. She was his confessor. She didn't like using the Roman Catholic term, but there was a delicious intimacy to the word that appealed to her. She waited patiently, invisible in the shadows, always invisible to these gaudy women who clustered around the Reverend after his sermons.

Eventually, all the women left, most casting her curious glances wondering, she knew, why she of all people had been asked to stay back. The

Reverend waited until the last one had left the church before walking across the well-polished floor to her.

"I need you to come across the way with me," he said.

She followed him without question. His house was quiet and dark, and he did not bother to turn on any of the lights when they went in. He gestured to her with one thin hand that she should follow him up the stairs. She quailed a little when she realized he was leading her into his bedroom.

He went and stood by the window while she hovered uncertain in the doorway. She could hear him sigh. He braced his hands against the windowsill and bowed his head. She wondered if he was praying, beseeching God for comfort or for guidance back to the pathway of the righteous.

The dark had settled in, and a beam of light from a street lamp came in through the window, anointing him. He turned, the sad air still emanating from him. She longed to take the pain from him and bear it herself for she would happily do it if only he would allow her.

"Elspeth, what I want—what I need…" he put his hands over his face and she felt her heart break inside her.

She went to him, drawn by his pain and suffering. "What is it that you need, Reverend? Tell me and I will do it for you."

He looked up, his face a mask of pain. He took her hands in his own and pressed them to his chest. Elspeth was both alarmed and excited. "We need to be washed in the blood of the lamb," he said. "I would baptize you and me—together—here this night so that we might both be washed clean and begin anew to our purpose."

"I…I," she stuttered, wondering what he meant by baptized; it could be a euphemism for any number of things. Not to mention the possibly dubious theology of baptizing oneself.

"With water," he said gently, clearly discerning her difficulty. "It would be best if you took your dress off. I know that you, Elspeth, always wear modest undergarments, so you will still be suitably clothed."

She hesitated only a second, and saw his glance harden. She supposed someone like that whore whose hair had been in his bed would take off her clothes without question. She knew there were more than a few in the congregation who would do it only too willingly as well. She took the dress off and folded it fussily before laying it to the side. She was shocked to realize that he had removed his shirt too, and stood before her bare-chested. His skin was uncommonly fine everywhere. He took her hand and led her to the chilly bathroom, where the tile gleamed from her recent scrubbing. He lit two candles, and she felt a twinge of alarm, this was feeling all a little too papish in nature to her.

He handed her into the ancient tub, and then paused to collect a crystal jug which had been sitting on the floor. They kneeled together in the tub, the cast iron creaking as they took their places, facing each other, close enough so that she could feel his breath on her face and neck.

He lifted the jug and spoke, voice low and filled with a sorrow that she could feel in her very bones. "And thus we are made pure by this blood of the Lamb that we may go forth and do His will and cleanse the earth of sin as we are washed clean by his blood."

Elspeth shivered as the water slid over her body, soaking her slip and raising goosebumps on her fevered skin. She felt as though he poured light into her, *his light,* and she was blessed above all other women, or at least above all others in the congregation. Oh if only that nasty Sarah could see her now, how she would envy her. She looked up and saw the Reverend looking down at her with such tenderness in his face that she could feel tears gather behind her eyes. He trusted her with his weakness, and it was apparent to her that his weakness was great. No one could lead him toward redemption as she could. He had made that clear to her, when he'd confided his sins in her. He had confessed to her and for the first time in her life she understood the Catholic sacraments and why this particular one had such appeal. There was an intimacy to it that bound the one confessing to the confessor. It was an intimacy no other woman had ever or would ever have with him, an intimacy greater than that of sex. Her whole body strained and yearned, and she felt that her ecstasy was that of the Lamb, of becoming one with his vessel here on earth, the man still wet with their baptism across from her. She thrilled to the words as they resounded through her body, *their baptism,* it was like a marriage, only holier and more sacred, for it would not be sullied by fleshly passion. A shudder of pure ecstasy rippled through her body, leaving her flushed and warm and slightly breathless.

"Elspeth, there is something I need you to do for me."

He put his hands on her shoulders and he shone silver in the moonlight that fell through the window. His chest gleamed with water and his hands were hot on her skin.

"It's about the woman, the one with the dark hair, the one you made the doll for."

Elspeth felt a wave of fury—just the thought of that woman was enough to make her see crimson. Why, oh why must he bring her up now in their greatest, most sacred moment together?

"Yes," she said, striving not to let her irritation come through in her voice. "What is it you would have me do?"

After Elspeth left, Lucien washed his hands for a full five minutes, making sure to soap all the way up to his elbows where the woman had grasped him. He could still feel her touch clinging to him, like a smear of dirty oil on an otherwise pure vessel.

It was not an easy dance he had begun with her for he had to balance things well enough so that events didn't spin out of his control and start a conflagration before he was ready to deal with it. He also had to conceal his revulsion at her touch. She had been sexually aroused, but he knew her well enough to understand that she had convinced herself it was something else altogether. Some form of religious ecstasy.

Coming upon her that day with her hands filled with Pamela Riordan's hair he had realized he had two choices—either to kill her, or to bind her to him irrevocably by making her believe he had the same failings as other men. It was unfortunate one of the woman's hairs had ended up in his bed; it must have gotten caught on some piece of his clothing and wound up on his sheets. Of course Elspeth had assumed that he'd had a woman in his bed. Which was all to the good, for now she believed she could save him. And that was all he needed to control her and put her in play as the most destructive piece on the board. He had saved himself from disaster that day, for if she had paid proper attention to the files and the names therein, if she had truly understood the import of what she had seen he would have had to kill her right then and there in his bedroom. Which would have been messy and unfortunate. So he had spun her a tale, a tale of a man who was tormented by the desires of his flesh, and a woman who had cunningly seduced him. That it was all a lie had only made it easier to embroider and embellish. He had been tempted to tell her the truth for a minute—that he had once killed on the woman's behalf, but had restrained the impulse to do so. He had reassembled his pieces so carefully, putting roots down through the chessboard of politics and violence, and nurturing the tendrils in dark soil so that now he had players in all the Loyalist factions, both the faithful church and lodge members, and in the pubs where only the hard men drank. Both those merely political and those political and terrorist. And in the case of a few men—vicious killers.

Elspeth had thought he wanted her in his bed, he had seen that in her face when he had told her to take off her dress. He had felt a certain repugnance at the notion. He was not a man of the flesh. However, if he had been, he would not have taken dowdy little Elspeth to his bed. She had her uses for now, though, and that gave her value—for a time.

When it was done, when the game had been played out to its conclusion it was likely he *would* have to kill her. There was always collateral damage, after all, even in the smallest and most personal war.

Chapter Thirty-six

The Peace People

"THERE'S SOMETHING I'D LIKE to talk about with you." Father Jim knelt beside her in the garden, helping her pull up onion sets and put them in the bucket she had brought out for the purpose. He had come for Sunday tea after church and stayed to help her bring in much of her garden. It was early September and while the weather was pleasant during the day, the nights had become chilly enough that she knew it was time to bring in her harvest, as meager as it might be in comparison to previous years.

She turned, peering out at him from beneath the brim of her battered straw hat. "Yes?"

"Well, it has occurred to me, Pamela, that it might be good for you to take pictures of something positive, rather than all the maimed bodies you've been subjected to of late."

He sat back on his heels, and poked a finger inside his dog collar. The sun was still high enough that it was hot in the garden. "Help yourself to more lemonade, Father."

He poured out a glass for each of them and she took hers gratefully, the cold prickle of lemons with the edge of sweet a relief to her parched throat. The air around them was filled with the fruits of summer: fat bees humming as they addled along on frowsy wings through the green and gold air of September, butterflies, delicate as lace fans, floating in drafts of sunshine and the last of the blackberries hanging thick from the brambles. Paudeen was happily asleep in a patch of clover next to the garden and Conor was mucking about in his own patch of garden, where he had, over the course of the summer, grown six straggly peas, a gaggle of ragged carrots and one enormous turnip. Isabelle was asleep on a blanket in the grass, having played herself out some time ago. If Casey were here, the day would have been one of those slow perfect ones, which were rare and therefore all the more cherished. He would smell of earth and starch, from digging up the last of the potatoes and he would taste of lemons and sugar when she kissed him. Conor would be by his father's side, helping him with the harvest, and learning the ways of the world through Casey's observations. If she closed her eyes, she could conjure the scene to her, could hear Casey's deep voice, humming something old and lovely, the words of the song floating out along the air just as the butterflies did, caught in sunlight and shadow.

"Pamela, are you all right?" Father Jim's voice knocked her back into the here and now, and she gave herself a firm mental shake, flushing hotly under the priest's scrutiny.

"So what event is it that you want pictures for?" she asked briskly, slapping her gloves together to get rid of non-existent dirt. She had visions of church functions dancing in her head, therefore his answer surprised her.

"There's going to be a peace rally this Saturday. I think it's something that ought to go on record, just to prove we're trying to change here in this country, if nothing else. You're familiar with the organizers?"

She rubbed the end of her nose with the edge of her glove, the scent of onions warm and comforting on her skin.

"I am, but only so much as anyone else who reads the papers." She knew the broad strokes of the story—a mother had been walking her children home from school, when a car with two IRA men fleeing a British patrol was shot up, and with the driver dead and passenger too injured to act, had ploughed into the mother and children, killing two of them outright and badly maiming a third—a two-year-old, who tragically died the next day in hospital. An IRA man dead, three Catholic children dead, their mother permanently injured and a small heap of wilted flowers, a string of rosary beads, a snuffed candle at the roadside and prayers that felt futile, left behind. Except that this time, something changed, for the mothers of Belfast turned out a thousand strong the next day, pushing their prams, their children held by the hand, in a protest for peace. The aunt of the three dead children, sister to the woman who was still lying in the hospital, had gone on camera condemning the violence that was costing everyone more than they could afford, even in a lifetime. Another woman, a Catholic housewife, saw the report on the television and began with a simple question to her neighbors—'Do you want peace?' A raggle-taggle petition, signed on scraps of paper, bus tickets and pages from notebooks was born and bloomed into six thousand signatures within forty-eight hours.

"There's going to be a huge march. They are expecting upwards of fifteen thousand or so to march up the Shankill. I think you should come and photograph it."

"You do?" she asked.

"I do. You need to see something positive. Things have been terribly dark for you for a long time, I think you need to go out and see a movement for change in the making. You and Patrick used to be at all the marches."

"It seems a very long time ago now," she said, feeling slightly wistful. There had been a feeling in the air then, a burning hopefulness that real and lasting change was coming. In some ways it had, and in others it had not come at all. She had met Father Jim at one such event, a civil rights march from Belfast to Derry, during which she had been attacked and left with a long scar on her face as a result. It was due to Father Jim's skills as a medic that it was only a narrow line of white down her cheek, and not a large disfigurement.

"Will you do it? I can arrange a sitter for Conor and Isabelle, if you need one?"

"There's no need, I'm sure if I ask Gert, she will be happy to watch them for me."

The look on his face was half hopeful, half worried. He was her one American friend here in Ireland and he had been a quiet comfort to her through this very long last year. "Will you do it, then?" he asked.

"Yes, I'll do it," she said, feeling a small thrum of excitement at the prospect of an afternoon taking pictures of something that didn't require her to rub mentholated grease beneath her nose.

And so it was that she was there when twenty thousand people marched up the Shankill, her Leica in hand, extra film and lenses in her bag and the humming excitement that attended such large gatherings when people were intent upon one goal, even if it was that most elusive of causes—peace. It was a beautiful September day, the air as clear as glass and the sun held in it like early autumn wine.

She took her first shots off the top of a building, a smooth hum to her movements, as she framed each shot, checking the light, the arrangement within the borders of each picture, and that thing, always elusive, which made one photo stand out from the next.

On the ground was where she found the real gems, though—there was a lightness to the air, both in atmosphere and mood that she had not felt since those heady days of the civil rights marches. There were mothers pushing prams, Protestants hugging Catholic nuns, grandfathers in tweeds and grandmothers in hats, teenagers in bell-bottomed jeans and scruffy coats. The road was scattered with flower petals, and young girls held bunches of flowers in their hands. She got a perfect shot of a little girl, gap-toothed with a halo of cotton fluff hair, handing a flower to a man who was trying in vain to give out leaflets on the sidelines, blaming the British for the deaths of the children. They didn't seem to understand that no one cared about pinpointing blame, they just wanted the violence to end, full stop. Another shot was of a mother bending down to pick up a tired toddler, a peace sign held in her other hand, and then a line of nuns, four abreast, expressions of fervid determination on their faces, the sun frisking light over their crosses.

She lost herself entirely to the process, to the people caught by her composition, faces like flowers preserved in amber for all time, here for a fleeting moment brought together in their desire for a society without soldiers and gunmen in the streets, for a world in which their children could walk home from school in relative safety and where gunfire and tanks were not the first lullaby their babies heard in their cradles. When it went well, photography was like ballet, one move flowed into the next, a moment captured like a perfectly-aligned movement, pure emotion in content and muscle.

She was brought forcefully out of her reverie when she was knocked unceremoniously to the ground, falling hard on one knee. Her camera was jarred from her hand by the fall and hit the pavement and bounced in a manner that made her feel sick. She grabbed it up, relieved to see that it appeared relatively unharmed. Casey had given it to her for Christmas a few years back and it was irreplaceable. When she went to right herself, she found a man was offering her a hand up.

"Apologies, Miss, didn't mean to knock ye over like that," he said and leaned down to take her arm. She looked up but the sun was in her eyes, and she was nearly blinded. The man was wearing a hat with a brim that fell over his face, making it impossible to see his features. Despite the warmth of the day, his hand was cold and she could feel the imprint of his fingers through the thin cloth of her blouse.

"I'm fine," she said, standing and just barely refraining from rubbing her arm where he'd touched her. He was already gone, though, slipping away into the crowd and disappearing in seconds. She couldn't even see the odd hat he was wearing weaving its way through the mass of people. She shivered, looking around her, but he was gone. He'd hit her quite hard when he'd bumped into her and she looked down to see that the fabric of her jeans was ripped, and her knee bloody.

She limped off to the side and shot off another couple of pictures, just to make certain her camera was in working order. Her knee would have to wait. To her great relief the camera was unharmed. It would have broken her heart had it been damaged.

The rally wound up with speeches and with a rousing rendition of *When Irish Eyes Are Smiling*. There were certainly plenty of smiling eyes today, Pamela thought, ignoring the pain in her knee to shoot off the rest of her film, catching as much as she could of the day. The sound of twenty thousand voices raised together, in one accord, brought tears to her eyes. She blinked them back, wondering why she could cry for this, and yet not for her husband.

Father Jim came up then, face flushed from the warmth of the day, a middle-aged woman beside him who immediately bent over to have a look at her knee. She had treacle brown hair and a no-nonsense sort of manner to her, as if she were pressed for time.

She took in Pamela's dishevelment as well as the blood still leaking from her knee. "Ye've a nasty cut there, did ye take a tumble?"

"I did, or rather someone helped me to," she said. She had the oddest feeling the man had knocked into her on purpose. She still felt uneasy that she hadn't been able to see his face and she thought that too had been purposeful.

Father Jim bent down and looked at the knee. She was starting to feel rather conspicuous. "It doesn't need stitches," he said, "but it will need to be cleaned out with alcohol and bandaged up. I can take you back to the car and fix it up for you, I keep a kit in there. Apparently, when you're around I ought to be packing it on my person."

"I'm all right, really I am," she said. "I can fix it up when I get home. It's little more than a scratch."

He gave her a somewhat dubious look. "Just be sure that you do, you don't want an infection."

He stood up and gestured to the woman at his side. "Pamela, this is Bettina Edwards, Bettina, this is Pamela Riordan."

She shook the woman's hand. This was the housewife who had started the petition and had gotten much of the momentum going. She looked a tiny bit flustered, and well she would for much of the press here today would want to interview her, and she would need to be both inspirational and on point which was no mean feat.

"It's wonderful what you've done here," Pamela said, gesturing around to the crowd now milling, some departing and some staying to drink in the atmosphere, heady as champagne, in a city that was too used to violence and darkness.

"I had to do somethin', I'm well tired of this shite—the bombs an' the guns an' scrubbin' blood off the pavin' stones. When wee babbies aren't safe to walk home with their mother, it's turned to madness, it has then."

There was a loud noise just then and the three of them jumped in startlement. There was always the fear of a bomb anywhere that people gathered in numbers greater than two or three. It was merely a car backfiring.

"Ye see, we need to stop it. It's like we're livin' in an earthquake zone, waitin' for the next thing that will rip the ground apart beneath us. It's why I had to do somethin'."

"Well, I admire it, pulling all this together. The city needs a movement like this one."

The woman shrugged. "War is a downhill run, peace is rollin' a rock up a hill, but it's worth it if the end result is a better world for the next generation. Ye ought to join us. Father Jim tells us ye were part of the civil rights movement a few years back."

"Did he?" Pamela asked, directing a glare in Father Jim's direction.

"It would be good to have some young blood along for the ride, give it some thought."

"I will," she said, and found it wasn't just a politeness she was uttering, but that it was something that appealed to her. They said their goodbyes then, for there were reporters lined up to talk to the woman and Pamela was happy to escape their scrutiny and slip away to her car, exiting the city ahead of the mass of people.

The drive home was quiet, the roads, once she got out past the limits of Belfast, nearly deserted. Her knee was throbbing, but other than the unpleasant encounter with the strange man, it had been a good and productive day.

Pamela thought about what the woman had said, and wondered why it was that peace was so hard to achieve, and once achieved, so terribly hard to hold. She thought back to those heady days when she had been involved in the civil rights movement. She had been on the periphery and not in the midst of it like Patrick, but it had been very exciting, and they had believed for a brief and shining moment that it was possible, that the future could arrive and be welcomed, even here in the Six Counties. She had liked Pat from the very first moment she had met him, and felt warmed in the glow of his friendship and his revolutionary spirit. And then, of course, she had met Casey, and that had been that, as the saying went. Unlike his brother, Casey had not been a man of peace, he had a warrior's nature and spirit. She should not have been so immediately attracted to him, as he had, in some ways, represented everything she was against. From the first moment they had set eyes upon one another though, it had been the end of rational thinking for the both of them. He had let go of his rebel life; he had changed so many things for her and the children and in the end, it seemed, it had caught him up in its terrible net anyway. The past was like that here, it walked a few paces behind always, and if you so much as paused to look back, it caught up and its shadow fell over you and everyone you loved.

As she turned off the main road to head down the narrow lane that led to their house, she realized that she felt strangely tranquil. Father Jim had been right, it had been good for her to witness an event so positive and filled with the possibility of change. She thought about what the woman had said, and considered that it was something she might do. It would be nice to be a part of something good, something that could change the future for her children, and give them a better life.

She pulled into the drive, slowing down to a crawl. Hope was like a fishhook in her heart sometimes. Hope that he would be there, even if there was no earthly reason to believe he would be. Hope was a strange thing, both a reason to get out of bed in the morning and a prison without doors or windows—some days one thing, some days the other, or at times changing from moment to moment. She wondered if she would always feel it for Casey.

Something fell from her pocket as she got out of the car. She frowned down at it, and then leaned over to get a better look. She reached out to touch it and then gave a small cry as something sharp pricked her hand. She bent down, careful not to get too near the thing. It was a doll, her own face in miniature looked up at her. She stepped back from it, a feeling of revulsion rippling through her body. How on earth had the thing wound up in her pocket?

She bent over and looked more closely at it. The doll was stuck through with blackthorn twigs. That was what had pricked her finger. The thorns had been placed with the sharp end out, just barely so they weren't noticeable until you pricked your flesh upon them. She felt slightly sick just looking at it, for it was clearly meant to resemble her. She shuddered, she would go inside and get gloves and then burn the horrible thing in the fire.

It had to have been the strange man; he must have put it in her pocket when he knocked into her. But why? She left the doll on the ground and half ran to the house, wanting to get inside and lock the door behind her. While she was digging for her keys, she saw something wedged into the door frame. She frowned; she'd had enough surprises this afternoon already.

It was a big envelope, thick and silver-grey. It was the sort in which invitations to posh events usually arrived. Several of the sort landed on Jamie's desk on a regular basis. She took it, wondering at who had dropped this off. Odd that they had left it here on the porch, rather than the front door, which was the door visible when you came into the yard.

She went into the house, which was unnaturally quiet without the children. Finbar walked over to her and sniffed her pant leg, and then growled low in his throat, his nose to the fancy envelope. She put her camera bag on the table, her skin prickling with apprehension. She put the envelope on the table, too, realizing that she'd smeared blood across it from her finger. She went to the sink and washed her hand and then got the bandages down from the cupboard above the Aga. Between the blank envelope and the blackthorn dolly in the yard, she was entirely spooked.

"Horse feathers," she said out loud to relieve the tension of the strange silence that wrapped the house in this uneasy feeling. She opened the envelope and pulled out the thick paper it held. She realized she was holding her breath and let it out, before unfolding the paper. She cried out like the paper had suddenly scorched her hand and let it drop to the floor. Finbar continued to growl at it, his hackles rising high on his back.

He looked up then just as she heard a noise from the upstairs, as if someone with a lame foot was dragging it across the floor. Finbar's growl turned to an agitated bark and she ran up the stairs before she could consider the wisdom of it, Finbar streaking past and ahead of her.

Her bedroom window stood open to the late afternoon, the breeze blowing the curtain in so that it rippled and waved like a ghost caught in brambles. The window had been closed when she left the house—closed and locked. She felt a ripple of pure fear, cold as ice water, go down her spine, the hairs on her arms and the nape of her neck quivering.

She heard the sound of a motor and froze until she recognized it. She looked out the window her heart hammering so hard she could feel her pulse in her ears and temples.

A car was coming down the drive; she recognized the shape and color of it flickering through the leaves. Jamie, it was Jamie, thank God. She ran down the stairs like she had wings instead of feet. Finbar was already at the door, his body a shimmer of wagging tail and clattering paws. He knew the sound of Jamie's car and was, like everyone else with a pulse and blood in their veins, entirely besotted with the man.

She opened the door before Jamie had even brought the car to a halt and Finbar shot out, barking half hysterically. She wasn't aware of crossing the yard, but suddenly she was in Jamie's arms, trembling with relief.

"Hey, hey," he said, holding her close and rubbing her back. "What's happened?"

"I think someone was in my house when I was gone."

"Where are the children?" he asked.

"With Gert, I was at the peace rally this afternoon."

"Good. I'm going to go in and look around, you go check that the telephone is working and if you still have that ancient pistol of yours, make sure it's loaded."

She did as she was told, checking the locked cupboard where she kept the rifle Noah had given her as well. She checked the phone, happy to hear the reassuring hum of the line. The pistol was where she always kept it, tucked far back in the highest cupboard in an ancient tea tin. She checked over every inch of the downstairs, but nothing appeared to be missing, nothing was out of place. She glanced up the stairs, making certain Jamie was still occupied. Then she pulled a chair over and checked the package at the back of the narrow cupboard. The money was still there, as was the check. She shoved it back behind the tiny door, and got down from the chair to find Jamie standing at the bottom of the stairs, looking at her quizzically.

"Jesus!" She put her hand to her chest. "Did you float down the stairs?"

He didn't bother replying to this. "I shut and locked the window and I made certain all the other windows were secured, too. There's no one up there now, though I think you're right that someone was before."

"You do?" she said. She had been hoping that she was wrong. That maybe she hadn't closed the window and the wind had blown it open, despite the fact that it had been an uncommonly still day.

"Is anything missing?"

"No," she shivered, "I wish there was, because I could chalk it up to a simple robbery."

Jamie didn't reply, but stepped over to where the paper she had flung down in her panic earlier had drifted under the table. He picked it up, read it and looked at her.

"Was this in the house when you got home?"

"No, it was in an envelope wedged into the door frame," she said. In the fear of an intruder she had forgotten the envelope and the hideous message it contained.

"Have you gotten anything like this before?"

"No," she said, "that's the first."

"Do you have a bag I can put it in? I'm going to have someone look at it."

She fetched him a bag, glad to have anything to do, rather than look at the paper he held by one corner, an expression on his face like she had not seen in very long time. She was relieved he was taking it away from the house.

He tucked it in the bag, careful to only touch it by one corner, and then locked it in the glove compartment of the Bentley. She waited for him on the doorstep, unwilling to go back in the house without him.

"I have to go get Conor and Isabelle," she said as he neared her. Her teeth were chattering despite the warmth of the evening.

"I'll take you," he said. "You're not going on your own."

He double-checked the lock on the door and looked up at the windows of the upper floor, as if he half expected to see a face peering back down at him. She didn't like it when Jamie was rattled, being that very little got under his skin.

"We'll take my car," he said, "go, get in." He tossed her the keys and then went to her car to retrieve the baby seat. She was just unlocking the door when he said, "What's this?"

She looked over. Jamie was looking down at the ground, his brows drawn together and the vertical crease in his forehead sharp. He bent down and picked up something, holding it up to the light to see it properly. She had forgotten the doll in her momentary panic. Now it seemed even more ominous than it had at first, considering all that had happened in the last half hour.

"A man knocked me down at the march. I think he must have shoved it in my pocket when he banged into me." She hugged herself, the memory of the man's chilly touch still there on her skin.

Jamie turned the doll over, handling it carefully to avoid the thorns.

"Pamela." He was looking at her with the oddest expression on his face.

"What?"

"The hair on this thing, isn't just real hair," he said, "it's *your* hair."

"It doesn't make sense," she said, for what must have been the tenth time in the last hour. She was talking in a low tone, barely more than whispering for Jamie had taken her to pick up the children and they were home now, door securely locked and the entire premises, byre and shed included, thoroughly searched and secured. She shuddered. "It would have to mean that someone was in the house cleaning out my brush before I cut my hair off. But whatever for?"

"I don't know," he said, "but it does seem to be your hair."

He had untangled a few of them, very carefully, from the doll's head and she had watched with ice forming in her veins as each long and quite curly hair came off the doll. It had to be hers, or someone who had incredibly similar hair to hers before she had chopped it off.

"It just seems so strange and..." she trailed off not wanting to put her fears into words.

"And what?" he looked up, his eyes sharp with worry.

"Well, it almost seems like something the Reverend would do—just something strange and creepy, using my hair as a way of letting me know he's been in my house."

"The Reverend?"

She could feel Jamie's tension rise at the mere mention of the man.

"Well, he's been awfully quiet since you arrived home. Which seems a bit odd, don't you think? He has to be festering over his inability to weasel his way into your companies using Julian." She removed a pot of potatoes from the stove and drained them, then set to mashing them with a bit of butter and milk while Jamie broke up leftover salmon and added some garlic and a few spices to it. They were making dinner together while the children played. Gert had tended to her knee, exclaiming over the state of her clothes. Despite Pamela's protests that it was only a scratch, Gert wasn't happy until it was cleaned and bandaged. She had asked them to stay to dinner, but Pamela didn't want to arrive home in the dark, and so had declined.

"Yes, it's odd, though I was just hoping he had given up." He met her look with a rise of his brow. "I know that's naïve, but is it too much to ask for a cessation of intrigue and strange happenings?"

"It would appear so," she said, deftly stepping around him to fold the potatoes in with the salmon. Jamie made the salmon patties while she dealt with the vegetables and tea, stopping now and then to remove various articles from Isabelle's mouth, much to the baby's outrage.

She mashed up some carrots and added a tiny bit of butter and salt to them for flavor and then put the mixture in Isabelle's bowl to feed her. Much of it would likely end up on the floor or in Isabelle's hair but as long as even half of it made its way to her belly it would be a triumph. She put Isabelle in her high chair, always a battle royal as she took about as kindly to being strapped into it as a bear might to being chained in a fighting pit. She sat down with her, putting the cooled carrots within Isabelle's reach, as well as a mound of mashed potatoes. While she usually attempted to spoon feed her, Isabelle preferred to touch her food and then put it in her mouth one not-so-dainty bite at a time. It was messy, but more effective than spooning it in only to have it spit back out.

With Isabelle happily occupied with her food, Pamela ate her own. She was shocked to find she was hungry. All things considered, it wouldn't have surprised her if she hadn't been able to choke down a bite. With Jamie here, though, they were all safe for the moment and she could relax a bit. She always felt like it wasn't possible for any kind of harm to touch her or the children when Jamie was near.

Both Conor and Jamie ate well and even split the last salmon patty. Men, she thought, looking across at the two of them, it took more than home invasion and ill wish dolls to put them off their food.

Isabelle, a mess of carrots and potatoes, needed to go directly from the table to the tub. Jamie nevertheless lifted her out of her seat and didn't so much as flinch when she put her potato encrusted arms around his neck. Pamela ran her a bath, and was tempted to put her in it, clothes and all, she was so mucky. The front of Jamie's shirt was a mess. She bathed

Isabelle while Jamie cleaned the kitchen with Conor keeping up a steady stream of questions which Jamie answered with great patience.

Clean, clad in soft pajamas and given a cup of warm milk, Isabelle fell straight to sleep. Pamela carried her back down the stairs with her, not wanting the children on a separate floor from her tonight.

She had brought downstairs a pair of pajamas for Conor too and ordered him to the bathroom to change into them. She would have to supervise the brushing of his teeth and the washing of his face, for while Conor was fiercely insistent on doing these things himself, he wasn't terribly thorough about it.

She settled Isabelle on the couch on a quilt and covered her lightly with a thin flannel blanket. Like Casey and Conor, Isabelle ran warm all the time. Jamie was seated on the floor, where he had clearly been playing trains with Conor. He looked relaxed, green gaze focused on a series of knots in the string of Conor's yo-yo, which he was patiently unpicking.

"So what's the bit you're not telling me?" he asked casually, flicking her a glance.

"What makes you think there's something I'm not telling you?"

"Well, isn't there?"

She sighed; sometimes Jamie's preternatural percipience was more than a tad annoying.

"The man that knocked me over when I was at the march? It could have been an accident, only somehow it felt deliberate. I think he meant to knock me down. He helped me up and his hand was cold, unnaturally so, because it was so warm today. I felt like I couldn't wipe his touch off me afterward. I couldn't see his face, because the sun was right over his shoulder in my eyes."

She glanced over at Conor, knowing that he often had the acuity of a bat just when she most wanted him not to listen. He, however, was blissfully absorbed in his trains once again, his pajama buttons askew and his face most certainly not washed.

"Remember the night when the house where Casey and I lived burned down, and he thought I was dead for a bit?"

"Yes," Jamie said, "I don't think I'm likely to ever forget that night."

"Well, when the man reached down to help me up I had the same strange sensation I had that night when the Reverend came in and killed Constable McKoughpsie."

"What sensation?"

A faint line of unease crossed her face. "I don't know, it's fear, but it's an absence of feeling too, as if he's a void. When he touched me that night I felt like he was taking something from me, trying to fill something in himself, like he's not complete." She shrugged. "I don't know if I can explain it properly beyond that."

"I think what you've said covers it," Jamie said. "If you don't mind, I think I'll stay here for the night. I'll kip on the sofa and keep an eye out. I don't want you alone tonight, you won't sleep a wink. Kolya has plenty of minders at home," he said, before she could protest.

"Of course I don't mind," she said, "I'm grateful." She was, too, she would still be nervous as a flea on a griddle, but at least she wouldn't be terrified.

Conor was thrilled to have Jamie stay for the night. He went upstairs and returned a few minutes later, laden down with five books, two blankets and two pillows, determined to set up for the night on the rather small sofa with Jamie. Pamela attempted to dissuade him, but Jamie just shook his head.

"I don't mind, it will be cozy down here with the lot of us."

It turned into a lovely evening, despite the fear that was still knocking at the back of her heart like a tympan drum. They made a nest on the floor of blankets and pillows and an old mattress Pamela dragged down from the attic. Instead of reading to him, Jamie told Conor stories from his own imagination, which were lovely and far more entertaining than most books. Conor fell asleep that way, with Jamie's voice still weaving its tale over and around him, securing him into the safe land of story. She felt the spell of it too, and was yawning by the time Jamie's voice came to a halt, the tendrils and airs of that far bright land he had brought into being here in the homely space of her kitchen still wound round about her.

Jamie sat, the firelight gilding him, his face in repose, though there was still a line of tension in him, visible now that the children had fallen asleep.

"Any news regarding Casey?" he asked, and the bright land burst like a bubble on a thorn.

"No, nothing," she said. "I have my regular meetings with the police, during which they tell me nothing of use, or they actively harass me. Here at home, I get ten phone calls a week now, instead of the thirty I was getting at first. I've only been approached by one psychic claiming to know where he is this month—San Francisco, in case you're wondering—and only one person has implied that he likely left me for another woman and another life. All in all," she said bleakly, "things are looking up."

"I'm sorry," he said, "I shouldn't have asked."

"Of course you should, you're one of the few who still does."

She yawned widely enough that her jaw cracked. The events of the day had caught up to her while Jamie had woven his tale. She realized he had done it in part to distract her, so that she might relax enough to sleep tonight.

"I swear Jamie, you have some sort of Sandman effect on me."

He quirked a brow at her. "A man could perceive that as an insult."

She laughed. "James Kirkpatrick, you know better than that. You are the least boring man on the planet."

"Perhaps it's only that you feel secure," he said.

"You do make me feel safe, Jamie. I don't often thank you for it, but you do."

"You don't need to thank me for it," he said quietly, looking down to where Conor was sprawled next to his leg, breathing so deeply that she could hear the outrush of air every time his chest rose and fell.

"I do—need to say thank you. I don't know how I would have managed these last months without you."

"I'm only glad you didn't have to."

"Sometimes I think it's some strange universal juggling act; once you were found, I lost Casey, when I had him here and safe, I spent every minute worrying about you. I can't have you both it seems." She flushed suddenly realizing how her statement sounded. "I'm sorry that came out wrong."

He reached over and took her hand. "It's all right, you can say whatever you need to. Surely you know you don't have to censor your words with me."

"I do know that and I'm grateful for it," she said.

The ticking of the Aga and the soft hiss of the fire, the breathing, even and deep, of the children and the tiny snore of Rusty who was curled up, nose to tail, on the back of the sofa were tiny tympanic notes of ease. Despite all the strange and outright frightening things which had happened today, she felt oddly calm. It was due to the man sitting next to her, she knew, and she felt a flood of gratitude for the forces that had seen fit to bring him home.

"Jamie?"

"Yes?"

"I'm awfully glad you're home."

He gave her hand a gentle squeeze.

"So am I."

It was late, Jamie thought, maybe four o'clock. The darkest hour was always the one just before dawn. He had dozed off and awakened to Pamela asleep, warm and limp against his arm. He could feel the soft crush of her body all along him. He took a breath in and leaned back a little. She tipped over further, into his lap. Her short cropped hair had begun to grow out a little, though her neck was still bare and left her terribly vulnerable look-ing. It wasn't only in looks, she *was* terribly vulnerable. He didn't like her living here with the children; the location, while undoubtedly lovely, was too isolated. Anything could happen, and no one would hear a thing—not gunshots, not a scream, not a cry for help.

He eased out from under her, placing a pillow beneath her head and covering her with the blanket from the back of the couch. Finbar looked up at him from his position by his mistress' side, dark eyes alert. Jamie tucked Isabelle in by her mother. He smiled down at her. Her small arms were thrown above her head in the abandonment of baby sleep, cheeks flushed with warmth. Conor was curled up on the floor in a mess of blan-kets, most of which he had already kicked off. Pamela was deeply asleep too, the low light of the fire casting her in gold and shadow. There was a fine pucker to her brow which told him she had carried her worry along with her down into the land of Morpheus. Asleep, with those fierce burn-ing eyes closed, she looked more fragile than ever. He was afraid for her and angry that he seemed to have so little help or comfort to offer her.

He clicked his tongue at Finbar, and the dog rose quickly, careful not to disturb the humans arrayed around him.

"Come on, boy, let's go do the rounds."

Outside it was still with that strange hush which seized the earth as it waited for dawn, as if everything—every rock, every bird, every creature of the forest floor and pasture—held its breath and waited for that first pale finger of dawn along the horizon to exhale and begin the slow movements of those first hours of the day.

He could see well enough to make his way around the yard without a torch. He checked on Phouka first, who rolled one eye and snorted at him sleepily. Paudeen didn't even bother lifting his small, woolly head, appar-ently of the opinion that if it didn't worry a high-strung horse, it wasn't going to worry his unflappable ungulate self. He checked the shed, and found it locked and dark and without, he thought, any rebel occupants this night. Pamela thought he didn't know about the bolthole program she was running for PIRA boys on the run, but she was wrong on that score. She was a grown woman, though, and she had made her deal with the devil. When she had told him she would walk through the gates of hell to find Casey, he knew she meant it. It was up to him, as her friend, to make certain the burns she sustained weren't permanent.

He walked the perimeter of the tree line, moving in and out, branches brushing against the top of his head, Finbar off ahead, snuffling the ground. It was a warm night and the air felt like milk on his skin.

In his mind, he saw the letter; he could close his eyes and it would be imprinted there like a brand, crimson and smoking. It had been writ-ten in blood, the letters oddly tidy despite that. It meant someone had collected blood enough to fill an ink pot and then used it while it was still fresh to write the words. The letter had been to the point, but you only needed so much space to call a woman a whore and threaten her with gruesome death along with an attendant bible verse about loose women and their downfall. It had unsettled him deeply and he could well imagine how frightened Pamela must be. The letter had a decidedly feminine feel to it, and he was almost certain a woman had written it.

Regardless of who had written it, the letter needed to be taken seriously, and it was down to him to find out who was behind it. The police weren't going to pay it much mind, and a few had made it clear to Pamela already that they weren't inclined to help her. Between Casey's PIRA connections, Patrick's court cases and her own history with the civil rights movement, every odd was stacked against her in regards to police assistance. He was going to have to pull in some favors to get what he needed, but it seemed a small enough price to pay, even if he had promised to never ask his intelligence colleagues for another thing as long as he lived. The question remained—was someone merely trying to frighten her, or did the person intend to follow through on their bloody threats?

Not for the first time he felt angry at her absent husband. Because he had disappeared she would stay here in this house waiting for him on the chance, however slim, that he might one day return from the land of the missing. If he believed in fairies, he would be certain Casey had been whisked away by them. That's how complete the lack of information was, there was nothing to be found, not a whisper, not a hint, not a glimmering trace left in the air.

Finbar sensed it first, the change in the air around them, a disturbance in the dark. Jamie put his hand lightly to the dog's ruff, which was standing up stiff as porcupine quills. He stepped back into the pool of darkness under the heavy branches of an elm. There were men in the woods, not just one, but a few. They were moving stealthily, but not perfectly silent. Finbar was growling low in his throat, a steady hum that threatened to escalate into a full-on fury of barking.

He had a good idea about just who these men were, and thought it was best if he revealed himself before someone took a shot at him. He stepped out into the open, and without warning found himself face down on the ground, his arm twisted up behind his back and a light in his eyes so bright it obliterated the world around him. Someone was kneeling on his back and he was having trouble breathing. He felt a surge of panic. In front of him he saw high walls, dripping with water and darker substances and he felt his own heart high in his chest, surging at the back of his throat. With one part of his mind he knew it wasn't real, he knew he wasn't trapped in that damn horrible room deep in the heart of the USSR, but the other part of his mind saw it, felt it, heard the endless hammering questions and felt the anticipation of pain, applied with skill and leisure. For that part of his mind it was more real than the trees before him, and the whicker of Phouka in the byre and the barking of Finbar which seemed to come from a great distance.

"What the hell are ye doin' roamin' around here at night?"

"I could ask you the same thing," Jamie said. He felt the cold prod of a rifle muzzle at the base of his neck.

"Let him up," said a voice. The man eased off his back and let go of Jamie's arm. He stood, the light still bright in his face, though not aimed into his eyes anymore. A man walked into the light.

James Kirkpatrick was not a man to bow before any other man's authority but he always recognized it when he saw it. He had never met him face-to-face, yet the resemblance to Kate, especially the eyes, was too marked for this to be anyone other than Noah Murray.

"Take the gun off him," Noah said. "He's a friend of Mrs. Riordan."

The gunman moved back from him, and Jamie stepped away toward the house, making it clear he stood between its occupants and this group of thugs. Finbar moved with him, his hackles still up and his growling down to a low hum.

Jamie heard the door open behind him, and Pamela came out, his coat pulled on over her nightgown, but her legs and feet bare. The men all looked at her and he saw her suddenly as they must. The pale light was like lilac smoke against her skin, the long bare legs and the too large coat making her appear little more than a young girl, her eyes wide with worry. She looked like a woodland creature, a dryad escaped from a man's erotic yearnings, made flesh here in this lonely dooryard. He wanted to tell them not to look at her for she was too vulnerable to take the weight of their gazes, and the thoughts that lay behind them. He wanted to hit each and every one of them. Noah Murray, he simply wanted to kill.

"What's going on out here?" she asked, her voice taut with fear. She took in Jamie's state, his dishevelled clothes and hair and the dirt on his face and hands.

"I don't know," Jamie said, "perhaps you could ask your friend Mr. Murray. I was just checking to make sure no one was about and found these men roaming your property."

"If ye're goin' to have overnight company," Noah said, addressing himself to Pamela, "perhaps ye could warn me ahead of time, so I don't accidentally shoot one of them." His tone was polite, if hard, but there was an edge to it that communicated something else entirely. He wasn't happy to find a man here with Pamela.

"Jamie is here because I came home to find someone had been in my house when I was away," Pamela said. "Your men must have missed that." There was a sharpness to her voice that carried to the man at whom she looked. She'd always had a foolhardy amount of courage. She was more than equal to this man, though, of that Jamie was all too aware.

Noah looked around at the men behind him and Jamie felt a twinge of sympathy for them. He didn't think any of them were going to have the ability to make mistakes in the near future. Noah looked back at Pamela and something flickered in his eyes, a pure blue flame, there and then just as quickly doused by force of will.

"I'll talk to you later," she said, drawing herself up and somehow, even with bare feet and clad in a rumpled night gown, managing to look like an empress.

"Ye needn't worry, it won't happen again," Noah said, and nodded to her before walking off into the rising morning with his men.

Inside, it was quiet, the children still asleep, the morning sun sifting slowly in over the windowsills, and the fire died back to ashy coals. Jamie felt suddenly very tired, the adrenaline had petered down to random jolts in his blood, and he realized he had only slept briefly.

"Jamie?"

He looked up. Pamela was staring at his hands, concern writ large over her face. He grasped his hands together, realizing how badly they were shaking. It happened sometimes, usually he could hide them, or leave the room when he felt the tremoring begin. Only Vanya had noticed until now. It had been the memory—rising up unexpectedly and vividly—the memory of blood and pain, and the point, narrow and unknown, where the mind finally broke. He had come far too close to knowing where that line was in his own mind, and sometimes his hands remembered that knowledge.

"When did they start shaking like this?" she asked quietly.

"In Russia." She looked up at him sharply, but forbore to continue her questioning. Russia was for him still a closed door, one he dared not open for fear of what might come through. She seemed to understand this instinctively and so she did not ask that which he could not afford to answer.

She pulled his hands between her own, at first just holding them still and then slowly massaging them until they were as warm as her own, as if her blood had flowed through the chill veins of his body and provided him with respite. The tremoring ceased as quickly as it had come.

"Sit down, Jamie. I'll make you some breakfast."

He sat, the morning sun high enough that he could feel the warmth of it on his back. It was going to be another fine day. He watched Pamela as she moved about the kitchen, cracking eggs and putting a rasher of bacon on to fry, cutting bread to toast, putting oats on to cook and setting the kettle to boil.

The sun was touching her too, outlining her in pale gold, and making, he was disconcerted to see, her nightgown rather transparent. He looked away, feeling like someone had hit him in the solar plexus. Desire prickled along his skin, and he had to focus to take a breath and resume his mask of cordiality. He understood only too well what that flicker of fire had been in Noah's eyes.

She put a bowl of oatmeal on the table in front of him, along with a pitcher of cream and a jar of honey. They ate in companionable silence, Pamela getting up now and again to bring the eggs from the warmer and refill the toast plate.

He watched her drizzle honey, thick and amber, over her porridge. She looked tired still with dark smudges beneath her eyes and her skin so pale that he could see the delicate blue of her veins and the pulse of blood that flowed through them.

She looked up suddenly, her eyes the dark bottle green they were when she was troubled. "What is it, Jamie? I can feel words sitting on your tongue, just go ahead and say them."

"Just this—be careful."

As she so often did, she understood the words he had not said and answered to those rather than the ones he had said.

"He's an acquaintance, Jamie, we have an understanding. It's no more than that."

He opened his mouth to protest but just then Conor awoke and made his way over to them, rubbing his eyes and yawning. "Mama, I'm hungry," he said.

Conor came and sat beside Jamie, while his mother got up to fix him breakfast. He leaned into Jamie's side, still half-asleep, the weight of him warm and comforting. He put his arm around the boy and felt some of his tension subside, though his worry did not abate in the least.

Pamela believed what she needed to believe at this point, and he knew from long experience that she didn't always understand her effect on men. But he did and he knew what he had seen in Noah Murray's face when the man had looked at Pamela out there in the yard, with the morning light touching her like smoke. It was a man who wanted possession of a woman, pure and simple. And he wondered, as he watched her move about the kitchen, warming milk for Isabelle, and fixing oatmeal and toast for Conor, just how far the man was willing to go to secure that possession.

Chapter Thirty-seven

From Dawn 'Til Dark, From Dark 'Til Dawn
November 1976

PAMELA KNEW THAT the first anniversary of Casey's disappearance was going to be very difficult and that no amount of putting her head down and working her way through the day was going to change that. So she had taken the day off, driven the children to Gert's and then gone to the one spot where she thought she might find some relief. She and Casey had stumbled across it one day during a long country ramble, nearly two years ago.

The shrine was an ancient one; it had been there as long as the memory of the land. It lay deep in a small mossy wood and had the feel of a secret well kept. There were three well-worn stone stairs that led down into the dark hollow. The well was at the end of a shallow cave, and the walls of the cave were thick with letters and appeals to Saint Bridget—that she might heal the sick, find the lost and soften the grief of those left alive to survive without their loved one. Pamela had brought a set of beautiful beads today, made from Baltic amber, ones her father had given her long ago, to offer up to the Saint along with her prayers.

She knelt and felt the damp seep into her trousers right away. The cave smelled of candle wax and smoke, incense and living water bubbling from deep beneath the earth. It was the scent of respite from pain.

She placed the beads carefully around the statue of the Saint. It was an old statue, the face barely discernible beneath moss and the wear of time. She breathed out, some of the tension she always carried with her pricking along her skin and then releasing into the quiet. It was peaceful here.

Bridget was one of the three patron saints of Ireland, and the only female. Pamela felt her prayers were better addressed to one who had the heart and mind of a woman. She began with the prayer, knowing the words would give breath to her own thoughts, would coalesce some of the pain in her heart and body and allow her to put it into words, and perhaps in the wake of an official and oft-repeated prayer her own words would not seem so small and naked.

> *Brigid of the Mantle, encompass us,*
> *Lady of the Lambs, protect us,*
> *Keeper of the Hearth, kindle us.*
> *Beneath your mantle, gather us,*
> *And restore us to memory.*
> *Mothers of our mother, Foremothers strong.*
> *Guide our hands in yours,*
> *Remind us how to kindle the hearth.*
> *To keep it bright, to preserve the flame.*
> *Your hands upon ours, Our hands within yours,*
> *To kindle the light, Both day and night.*
> *The Mantle of Brigid about us,*
> *The Memory of Brigid within us,*
> *The Protection of Brigid keeping us*
> *From harm, from ignorance, from heartlessness.*
> *This day and night,*
> *From dawn till dark, From dark till dawn.*

The words, spoken quietly, were a meditation. She felt the anxiety she carried everywhere with her abate a little, enough that she could breathe with ease. She sat silent for a long moment, not waiting for anything other than the time when it would seem right for a more personal prayer, a plea really. The words came simply because they were always in her heart, and the silence and peace of the cave gave them form so that she could speak them.

"I know you can't bring him home, I know people plead with you a thousand times a day for those kind of miracles and it's not always possible. I won't ask for that, I won't ask for you to bring him home safely, I will only ask you this—if you can't bring him home, if you can't let him come back to me, please make it hurt a bit less. Just a little less every week." She leaned her head against the smoke-smudged wall, unheeding of the press of the beads and letters and pleas against her flesh. "I don't want it to ever go away entirely, and I know it won't, but if you could ease it a little, I would be so very thankful. Because I don't think I can survive if it keeps on this way."

She understood now why people often said that someone had died of a broken heart, rather than whatever the medical cause was determined to be, because you could die from a pain this profound, this heavy. If it wasn't for their children, she wasn't sure how she would manage. Conor and Isabelle's dependence on her remaining strong enough to get through the daily routines and to love them, was the one thing that kept her going.

She got up off her knees and took a breath. It was a deep one, full of damp and incense and the scent of a thousand hopes and prayers and fears. It filled her lungs, and when she let it go, she could have sworn some of the pain, just a little, went with it, like one needle leaving a stack.

She turned back on the top stair and felt the sigh of the small cave, as if it breathed out around her. The letters, the pleas and the pain were encompassed in that narrow passing breeze. She was merely one voice amongst an enormous choir in this country, but she felt a shiver of hope in her chest nevertheless. She put her hand to the silver cross around her neck and spoke to the woman in whom so many hopes and prayers resided. Her voice was small, but steady.

"But if you have a spare miracle then please, please let him come home to me."

Chapter Thirty-eight

Silence and Dignity

THE FIRST FROST ARRIVED in late November and by early afternoon of the next day the thatch on the house still glimmered with it. The cobwebs, strung fine and delicate, were embroidered silver and the breath of both humans and animals was visible in small rising clouds. Winter had settled in on its hoary old bones and was breathing out across the land, withering berries, stripping branches and turning the ground to iron.

Pamela was seeing to the last of the winterizing. Patrick had come by a few days before and put the storm windows up and the byre was filled to the rafters with a season's worth of hay. There were always the small things to attend to like taking up the last of the frost-bitten stalks, and covering the flowers that required protection from the cold. She used to love small tasks like these because it allowed her time to think and plan for the next spring, or just let her thoughts drift fancy-ward. Now she dreaded time alone because her thoughts wandered into very dark territory which had nothing of the fanciful about it.

Pamela had been on edge ever since the letter and the incident of the doll. She had a hard time relaxing even in her own home, though she tried not to show that to her children. Conor was far too attuned to her moods as it was and she didn't want him to be frightened. If there was one gift she could bestow upon her children, it was that they should feel secure and that their home should always be a sanctuary for them.

She paused for a moment and looked about. The yard lay peaceful, the sun low and insubstantial as it was this time of year and the scent of peat smoke both sharp and comforting on the air. She drew in a breath of it and stood quietly. It was the thin time of the year, a time she usually loved because it seemed to her that ghosts lingered in the chill and smoky air, making it seem possible to cross the divide between the material world and the one that lay just beyond, out of reach. Dreams came thickly when the nights were long; laying their touch upon the dreamer so that it seemed the divide *was* crossed, even if it was only for a few moments in the depths of a November night.

She had dreamed about Casey last night, so vividly that she had smelled his skin and felt the rough warmth of his hands as he reached out to touch her. She had awakened with tears on her face and her hands still reaching back for him. The fine webbing of the dream had clung to her senses all day, making her feel rather melancholy.

She glanced into the house through the kitchen window, a flash of red having caught her eye. Conor had dashed in to make a sandwich. She had left the cheese and bread cut for him so that he wouldn't need anything more lethal than a butter knife to put together his own snack. He was an independent little soul, and liked to do things on his own as much as was possible at three and one half years of age. The sandwich would not be a thing of beauty, but it would be roughly edible once he was done.

The crunch of car tires turning into the top of her drive distracted her from Conor's depredations in the kitchen and she turned, frowning, a small spurt of adrenaline coursing through her as it always did when a stranger entered her yard. Every now and again it struck her just how alone they were here. There were two men in the car and a woman in the back seat. She froze to the spot, her mind frantically trying to ascertain where the nearest weapon was. There was a spade leaning up against the house, so she grabbed it, the haft slippery against her gloved hands.

As soon as the first man emerged from the car, his chilly grey gaze fixing her like a slap of snow to her face, the small spurt of adrenaline turned into a flood. It was Constable Blackwood.

She stepped forward warily, the spade still clutched in her hand. She didn't want to give them an excuse to shoot her, but if this was a kill squad, she wasn't going without a fight. She didn't think they would arrive in broad daylight in uniform, in truth, though, she had no way of knowing for certain. She would have to fight as long as she could to give her children a chance of survival. She'd had a talk with Conor about it last week, a talk that had been like walking a high wire between trying not to frighten him but also making certain he understood what to do if something should happen to her. She'd had to acknowledge that even though her son was not yet four years old, there were realities to living in this country that required a different kind of knowledge for him. Conor was a quick study fortunately, and had mastered the dialing of the numbers he needed to know some time back. He knew where the bolt for the door was, and he knew who to call—Gert as she was very near and almost always home and then the list moved to Lewis, Uncle Pat and Jamie.

The second man emerged from the car. He had white hair and a red face, neck bulging above his tight, starched collar. He, too, was in uniform and clearly of a higher rank than the constable. Neither man appeared to be armed, but she clutched the spade a little tighter just in case. It was the white-haired man who walked toward her.

"I'll ask ye to put the spade to the side," he said.

"Why are you here?" she asked, wary but polite, she couldn't afford to antagonize them, not with two small children to protect.

"We need ye to come in for questionin'," he said, blue eyes officious but not unkind.

She put the spade aside. She took the gloves off and wiped her hands on the front of her jeans, a cold stillness coming over her.

"Questioning about what?"

"The murder of Philip Kirkpatrick."

She turned cold all over and she thought for one dreadful moment that she might faint as her blood plunged down into the vicinity of her toes.

"Murder?"

"Aye, murder." This last was said by Constable Blackwood with a bit of relish. He had come to stand by the other police officer, a look of smugness on his face.

"Mama?"

Conor was standing in the doorway of the house, his cheese sandwich clutched in one hand, Finbar in front of him, teeth bared.

"Finbar, enough," she said sharply. She didn't want the dog to be shot because he was trying to protect them. The dog gave her a baleful glance, sighed and sat down so that he was still shielding Conor.

"He was shot in the head at point blank range before his body was burned to a crisp along with the distillery."

"Mama?" Conor's voice was rising in panic. He'd walked out to stand behind her and she turned to take him in her arms and give him the comfort of her embrace. He put his arms around her neck, and she felt the cheese sandwich squish against her shoulder.

"It's all right, baby," she said, even though it wasn't.

Constable Blackwood stepped toward her and Conor turned to glare at him, as if daring the man to come any closer to his mother. She turned away so that Conor wasn't looking at the men anymore. She put him down and gave him a gentle push toward the door. "Go in the house, sweetheart. Remember what mama said to you about calling Gert."

Conor backed up in to the house, his hand on Finbar's furry back. He looked from her to the policemen, and the WPC who having exited the car, stood further off, her hands folded in front of her, her face completely blank.

"You can't expect me to leave little children here alone. Please, just let me call someone to come and stay with them."

"They will have the WPC to take care of them until further arrangements can be made."

Those three words 'until further arrangements' stuck a sliver of fear in her heart. She had to hold it together and make it seem like she wasn't frightened and that it was nothing terribly untoward to be questioned about a murder, a murder that she was only too aware certain police would be happy to pin on her.

She glanced back at her son. He was near tears, his small face terribly white. She was incredibly grateful that Isabelle was sleeping through this. She had to do something to reassure him, to shore him up until an adult who loved him was here to look after him.

"Conor, call Gert now. Remember everything that mama told you to do. And please check on your sister."

He nodded, small fists clenched. She gave him a look intended to stiffen his spine. He drew himself up to his tallest and she saw the strange reserve come over him, his wee face losing all expression, the way his father's did when he didn't want anyone to know his thoughts or to suspect his feelings. Conor had already learned the hard lesson of this land, and that was to give no one your vulnerability. She hated that someone so small already knew this, even if it was only subconscious. Or maybe it was only part of his genetics, the Riordans after all, had never been friends with the police.

She thought it was not a coincidence that the police had chosen this time, being that Jamie was away in the States. They had waited for their opportunity and then seized it. It would explain why they had not asked her to come in for questioning, as had been the case in the past.

She said nothing on the ride to the station, merely sat with her hands clenched in her lap, and prayed with a desperate fervor that Gert would be home when Conor called. She could well imagine the Valkyrian fury that the WPC was going to have to deal with when Gert arrived.

She did quail a little when she realized they weren't taking her to her local station, but into Belfast. It was, however, more likely she would know some of the police there, which might help mitigate her terror. Not that any of them could help her, but it would be nice to see a face that wasn't hostile.

They took her to the Tennent Street station, which increased the flood of ice-water in her intestines since it was in the heart of Loyalist territory. Once there, they escorted her into an interrogation room with a shabby tiled floor and four uncomfortable chairs seated around an equally shabby table, which was bolted to the floor. She sat down and clutched her hands together, to still their trembling.

She was dressed in old clothes, her skin smelling strongly of cold earth and clean straw. She could still feel the dirt in the lines of her palms and the sweat that was gathering around the particles despite the chill deep set in her flesh. She was wearing an old sweater of Casey's, for the day was cool, and she had been cold working out in the yard. Wearing his clothes gave her a sense of holding him close, as if something of him—his scent, his aura, his strength—remained there in the weft of the threads. She pretended for a moment that he was here, the strength of his big hand curled around her cold one, telling her she could manage this without breaking down. For a fleeting second she thought she could feel it, the heat of his skin, the calluses that made the palm of his hand hard.

"Ye don't ever give the bastards even a crack to reach ye through. If they want to come after ye, ye make it difficult just by maintainin' yer silence an' yer dignity."

'Easier said than done, you bastard,' she said to the man in her mind. She was only a Riordan by marriage after all, not by blood. She didn't have that remote indifference that they could cloak themselves in, seemingly at will. If anything, every thought and feeling she had bloomed fully on her face like a rose in summer heat.

Despite the bright lights, the room was horribly dingy and smelled of sweat and dirt. It was the smell of fear, the smell that was, she knew, rising off her own body right now. She was shaking hard enough that her teeth were chattering together. She only hoped the men across the table from her couldn't hear it.

They had made her empty out her pockets before coming in to the room, and so were treated to the detritus of a mother's day: the ear of a velveteen elephant, which needed sewing back to said elephant's head, two dusty humbugs which Conor had asked her to hold on to for him, a vet bill for Paudeen, and a shiny hazelnut which she had dug out of Isabelle's protesting mouth this very morning. She had to turn away from the objects when the officer began placing them in an envelope, afraid the sight of the homely bits and pieces would make her cry. Right now, she would have given much to even have the torn velveteen ear to clutch in her hand, as though that tiny touch of home would give her the strength she needed to get through this without breaking.

She swallowed, her throat dry. They hadn't so much as offered her a drop of water. It was clear they wanted her to be uncomfortable. The phantom touch of her husband had stiffened her resolve and she sat up, keeping her expression neutral.

Across from her sat two men. Constable Blackwood, whose chill and wet gaze she studiously avoided, though the hair on her arms stood upright in revulsion at his proximity. The second man had been a surprise for it was Mr. Davison, whom she was now quite certain was Special Branch. That raised her anxiety level a little higher—Special Branch was the level at which things could get very ugly, very quickly. His trying to recruit her to spy on Noah made far more sense now. Noah had told her Special Branch had been trying to turn someone near him for years, though it had never worked, and for good reason.

They took a moment sorting papers, taking sips of water and conferring with each other in half-whispers. It was all designed, she knew, to unnerve her and make her more susceptible to the game they would force her to play.

She cleared her throat, and both men looked up at this. She addressed herself to Mr. Davison, refusing to look at Constable Blackwood. She knew there was no set of circumstances under which the man would be reasonable with her.

"Before you begin, I would like to know where my children are," she said. She would play their game if only they would let her know that Conor and Isabelle were safe.

Constable Blackwood smiled, a cold gesture that caused the trickle of ice water in her stomach to turn to a flood. "They'll be put in care temporarily, better for them no doubt."

"What?"

"Ye heard me, we couldn't just leave them there unattended now could we?"

She had gone cold all over and the floor under the chair seemed to have tilted sharply. The thought of how frightened Conor must be, and Isabelle waking up and not understanding in the least why a stranger was there and not her mother or at the very least a familiar face. She was the one constant in her children's lives and it made her furious that these men had shaken that faith even the tiniest bit. Please God, let Patrick know what to do. If Conor had managed to call Gert before they took him away, then Pat would know and he would move heaven and earth to get the children back.

"You should have called my brother-in-law; he has the legal right to take them when something happens to me."

"Yer brother-in-law? Would that be the same brother-in-law who is the solicitor that's suin' us?"

"Is that what this is about?" she asked.

He smiled, and her blood chilled. "Of course not, we're here to discuss the murder of Philip Kirkpatrick."

"Yes, so you said."

"We understand there was bad blood between the two of ye."

"You already know this; I was questioned at length right after the incident."

"Incident? That's a bit of an odd term for a body burned beyond recognition in a fire which destroyed the distillery you were in charge of at the time."

"I'm not sure how you'd like me to refer to it," she said. "I did not like him, but I wouldn't have wished him such a terrible death."

"Ye were heard to say, an' I quote, 'I'd as soon see him dead as allow him to get his hands on this company or this house.'"

"What? I never said any such thing." Certainly she had thought it, but she had been careful not to say it out loud.

"We have the sworn statement of someone who heard you say it." Mr. Davison finally spoke, his voice calm but firm. She wasn't sure which of the men she was more worried about. There was no point in asking just whose sworn statement that might be. They wouldn't tell her and it might be a bluff on their part any way. She had a very good idea just who it was, however, if it was, indeed, true. She had the sense that this interview was about something other than Philip's death, murder or otherwise.

"Men have died around ye before, no?" One side of the constable's mouth was turned up, as though in a smile.

"I don't know what you're talking about," she said, though she did. How on earth these men could know about that long ago nightmare was another matter altogether. There was one man who knew outside of Pat and Jamie, one man who had ties within the policing community. She wondered how much the Reverend had to do with today's events. There wasn't any proof linking those dead men back to her and the horrible things they had done to her and Patrick on a train. She knew Jamie and Casey between them had made damn certain of that. But having these men know about the rape and beating and having them use that knowledge to threaten her was a violation of another sort.

"Don't ye?" he said, the half-smile still twisting his mouth.

"When was the last time you saw Philip Kirkpatrick?" It was Davison again.

"Two days before his body was found in the distillery," she said.

"And did you argue at the time?"

"No, we disagreed. I wouldn't have called it an argument, it didn't escalate far enough for that."

"What did you disagree about?"

"A shipment of whiskey he had arranged, it wasn't part of our regular shipments and it would have shorted our standing orders had he gone ahead and done it. It was the twelve year whiskey, and since it's made in smaller quantities, it's in high demand. He wanted to use it as a gift to someone with whom he was trying to curry favor. I refused to allow it."

"You refused? That sounds rather strong."

"Does it? Lord Kirkpatrick left his business in my hands, and he trusted me to keep things going, and to meet the commitments of said business. I was merely doing that."

The questioning went on in a similar vein for some time. Her head had begun to ache rather badly, and she realized she hadn't eaten nor had anything to drink since breakfast which seemed like it was weeks ago now, rather than eight or so hours. Davison had taken over from the constable, and she could see that Constable Blackwood did not like having his power usurped at all.

She wasn't certain how much time had passed, as there were no windows in the small room and the pain in her head was causing one question to run into the next. She was lucid enough to realize they had nothing other than their 'witness' statement, which amounted to no more than hearsay. The wonder was that they had felt the need to drag her in here with such flimsy evidence. This only shored up her certainty that they had another agenda entirely. The questions just continued on into what she thought surely must be the evening. It would be full dark now and she prayed Conor and Isabelle were somewhere safe and warm where someone would feed them and take care of them. Please let them be with Gert, or Pat and Kate. Then they would be fine, even if Conor had understood enough of what was going on to be panicked for her.

"I'm not sure what I can say to make you understand," she said finally, weary of answering the same questions, phrased ever so slightly differently for the tenth time. "I did not kill him, but I think perhaps you know who did."

Davison made a face of incomprehension. "I don't know what you mean, Mrs. Riordan. There isn't anyone else we suspect. And there are times circumstantial evidence is more than enough. Do you understand my meaning?"

"Unfortunately, I believe I do," she said, too weary to summon up any tartness to her tone.

"Excuse me for a moment," Davison said, and exited the room, leaving her alone with Constable Blackwood. She longed to stand up and stretch her legs and to have a glass of water. Her head hurt so badly now that she thought she might get sick from it. She couldn't remember ever having a headache come on this suddenly and intensely. She wondered if they would even allow her the dignity of a trip to the washroom.

Constable Blackwood got up and began to pace the small room. It seemed an innocuous enough act, but she knew it was designed to make her nervous. He paced the entire room until he was behind her. She stiffened, afraid that he might actually hit her. She had the sense there was no oversight committee to worry these men about just how they behaved in this interrogation room. He put his hand on her shoulder and squeezed, hard enough that she had to grit her teeth together to keep from crying out.

"I think ye know exactly what it is I was talkin' about. There was a policeman died after spendin' an evenin' in your company. He was my sister's husband."

She swallowed, her throat so dry it felt as if it were stuck fast. This man was Bernard McKoughpsie's brother-in-law. Bernard McKoughpsie had been the ringleader of the four men that had raped her that long ago night on the train. This made the whole situation worse, but it also explained just why the constable had such an intense dislike for her. How he knew what his brother-in-law had done was the question that truly frightened her.

Her collarbone was beginning to creak under the pressure of the man's fingers but she sat as still as she was able, knowing it might well break her collarbone if she were to move too suddenly. The touch of his long and clammy fingers sent shivers of revulsion through her body, as if venom leaked from his skin and into hers. The pain in her collarbone was near to unbearable, and she thought she was going to have to risk pulling away from him just to alleviate the agony.

Davison returned just then, and took in the situation in the second it took the constable to let go of her and step back, as though he had merely been walking about the room. Davison was clearly not fooled and he gave Constable Blackwood a long unpleasant look. He was not the arrogant actor who had visited her kitchen some weeks back. This was, she realized, a man to worry about.

"Are you all right, Mrs. Riordan?" he asked, though the sharp gaze was directed toward the constable.

She nodded and he put a glass of water on the table for her. She wished she had the wherewithal to refuse it, but she needed it desperately. It took everything she had not to gulp it down. Her head hurt so badly that small whirling flashes were hovering in front of her eyes. She thought she might confess to anything at this point just to make them stop. If they threw in a few paracetamol it would be a done deal.

Davison cleared his throat. "Perhaps, Constable Blackwood, I could have a few minutes alone with Mrs. Riordan."

The constable didn't like being ordered about, and his scarred face turned an ugly red. He had to defer to this man, though, Special Branch put Davison far higher in the pecking order than a mere detective constable.

He waited until the door shut behind the constable and then turned the tape recorder off and put his hands on the table. "I would like to suggest to you," he said, the hazel eyes resting calmly on her face, "that there are other ways to deal with this situation. We are willing to see our way to a sort of contingency plan."

If her head hadn't hurt so badly she might have laughed at him. So this whole thing, the terror, the questioning and the fear that she might not see her children any time soon, was all so they could test the waters and see how far they had to push before she agreed to spy on Noah for them. She suspected it was a kill-two-birds-with-one-stone situation as well—get her to spy on Noah and fire a warning shot across the bow for Pat and Tomas.

She stared back at him, refusing to dignify his suggestion with a response.

"If that's the way you choose to play it, Mrs. Riordan, you might well come to regret it," he said quietly. "I'll give you some time on your own to have a think about what I've said."

They put her in a cell after that. She was relieved to be alone. She was exhausted and trembling, starting to see double and her head hurt so badly that she couldn't think clearly at all. She tried not to think about her children, as panic set in the minute she did. It was possible the constable had lied to her, just to frighten her, but it also was possible they were in care. She had heard too many nightmarish stories of children taken into care by the state or by the church that were never seen again by their mothers. She was, for all intents and purposes, a single mother in the eyes of the system, and the system didn't always deal fairly with mothers who were alone.

She was cold, tired and frightened. She curled up on the bed, which was only a very thin mattress with a solitary and very scratchy blanket. She put her hands to her eyes, so that she could rest the burning pain against the coolness of her palms. And she prayed for all of them—her babies, Pat, Tomas, Jamie and herself—that they might survive this country.

Pamela slept for a bit, huddled under the scant comfort of the rough blanket. Her dreams were a muddle of fleeting images and the constant sense of fear. She was caught on a staircase, trying to climb it, hearing a baby crying—Isabelle crying—up somewhere in a room at the top of the stairs. But the stairs went on and on spiraling up into some great darkness which seemed like it must stretch out beyond the stars. Then suddenly she was in a boat, and she could feel water soaking into her skin, cold and salt and slick with kelp. There were no oars and the boat was leaking, and she was frantic wondering how she could ever get to shore. She paddled with her hands, for the baby's cries were escalating and she only knew she must reach her before she disappeared. Suddenly, she was swimming, waves hitting her in the face, her lungs burning with cold fire, her arms the consistency of lead as she tried to find the shore. She rolled over on her back, desperately needing to rest, and found that the sky above was a cascade of stars, the Milky Way a visible spine of light holding up the world. Wearily, she thought that maybe she could orient herself and find her way home by the stars, using them as way posts in the infinite.

The water closed over her head without warning and she knew she was going to drown, the shore was too far away and despite the stars, she knew she would not make it. There was a strange relief in the knowledge, as if she could just let go now and drift down, down, down where there was no pain, only darkness and an all encompassing quiet. But a hand reached down and pulled her up, shaking her and making the red pain in her head rage and boil through her blood.

She pulled away from the hand, angry that it had brought her back up from the cool quiet depths. It took a moment to realize that the face hovering above her was a familiar one. Constable Fred. She had worked with him on more than one crime scene and had come to know him as an innately kind and decent man. He was a Protestant, but one who paid no mind to the religious affiliations of others. He held a cup of tea and a bun in his hands, both of which he handed to her.

"The tea is just the wee bit hot there, love, so mind how fast ye drink it. Look, I'm not meant to be in here, but I sent the WPC off on an errand, so I'll have to be quick. I just wanted to let ye know yer solicitor will be in within the hour. Now, I'd best go, eat yer bread there, ye'll need a bit of starch in ye."

Mercifully, the tea was hot but not too hot to gulp down. She drank it all and handed him the cup, which he promptly tucked inside his coat and then he was gone. She could have melted with gratitude just for the knowledge that her solicitor was on the way. She assumed it would be either Patrick or Tomas.

She nibbled cautiously on the bun, though she was without an appetite and felt decidedly nauseous this morning. She just wanted to pick Isabelle up out of her crib, still warm with sleep and dreams, her curls frowsy and standing out around her head like a halo. She wanted to make Conor his breakfast and have him show her a toad or a snail or any of the other treasures he had found during his early morning forays in the garden.

Twenty minutes later she was back in the grim little interrogation room with Davison. He was freshly washed and shaved and looked like he'd had a good night's rest. He had brought her a cup of tea and placed it on the table in front of her. Constable Blackwood was thankfully absent.

He sat down, and she became aware of how grubby she felt. She'd given her face and hands a cursory wash and slicked a bit of water through her hair, though the short curls were springing free already. It was the best she could do with the limited amenities available to her.

He smiled, and there was a bit of warmth in the expression. She wasn't fooled by it in the least.

"Well, Mrs. Riordan, have you had time to think over my offer?"

"What exactly was on offer, Mr. Davison? You don't charge me with false and baseless accusations of which you have absolutely no proof and in return I betray and spy on a man who has done me no harm?"

"Done no harm?" Davison laughed, shaking his head, the hard light back in his face. "Do you have any idea what that bastard has done in this country?"

"Yes," she said coolly, "and I am just as aware of what the police and Special Branch have done. None of it's pretty, but at least Noah isn't a hypocrite about it."

It was a stupid thing to say, and she knew it as soon as the words left her lips. Davison opened his mouth to retort, but it was just then that Tomas came through the door, saving her from whatever the man had been about to unleash upon her. Tomas' red face and bristling brows seemed to Pamela the most beautiful sight she had seen in a long time.

He came to the point directly. "I'll have twenty minutes alone with her, or ye'll answer to the Chief Constable." This was no idle threat. Even the top man ignored Tomas Egan at his own peril.

He put a piece of paper on the table in front of Davison. "Read that please."

Pamela attempted to scan the letter before Davison picked it up, but she had spots dancing in front of her eyes and couldn't make out anything more than the letterhead. She did, however, note how pale the man went as he scanned the letter's contents.

Tomas sat down beside her and glared at Davison. "Are ye plannin' to charge her? Because if not, ye've held her far past the point of legality. Trust me when I say ye're on shaky ground here, an' ye know it."

"No, I am not going to charge her," Davison said with remarkable calm. She suspected it was not the legality of the situation so much as the contents of the letter in front of him. Or at least the signature which accompanied said contents.

"You are free to go, Mrs. Riordan," he said and stood. He gave Tomas a hard glare which was about as effective as giving it to a brick wall and then left the room. She waited for the door to close, and then blurted out her biggest worry throughout the last twenty-four hours.

"My children, they said they put them in care, Tomas."

"No, they did *not*." He looked affronted at the very notion. "Conor ran back in the house an' bolted the door. Yer wee lad is smart as a whip, an' called Gert and Patrick while the police were draggin' ye out to the car. Gert got to him before the policewoman could get the door unlocked. Pat took the two of them up to Jamie's house, figurin' that was the most secure place for them to be right now."

"Oh, thank God," she breathed out, feeling like she might collapse with relief. If she knew her children were safe, she could manage anything, well almost anything. Knowing the police did not have them, nor had they been shuttled into care where she might never be able to get near them, reduced their leverage over her greatly.

"Patrick wanted to come here the minute he had the children safe, but I forbid him bein' that he was ready to rip someone apart with his bare hands. He won't be able to keep a cool head; I was afraid he'd get himself in a heap of trouble if he came through those doors. He has a fine, black temper on him, the boyo does. Jamie flew back from New York the minute he was told. He's fit to be tied, let me tell ye, ears have been ringin' in Stormont an' Westminster these last twenty-four hours."

She nodded. She was glad Tomas had managed to head Patrick off at the pass, because once his temper was roused, he might, indeed, kill someone. Jamie might, too—he would just be more discreet about it.

"Are ye all right, lass? Ye look terrible peaky."

"I've got a bad headache, that's all," she said. The bright spots had moved out into her peripheral vision and she was starting to feel distinctly woozy.

"I'll have ye out of here within the half hour. I'm only sorry it took this long, the bastards have blocked me at every turn."

Knowing that Tomas had things well in hand shored up her fragile reserve. She merely sat and waited, alone in the interrogation room, sipping at the cold tea Davison had left behind.

True to his word, Tomas had the paperwork done and was escorting her out through the doors twenty minutes later. There was a line of police, loosely gathered, with a deliberate air in the waiting area where they knew she had to pass through. She understood it was meant to be a threat. They didn't like Tomas, and they didn't like that she'd been waltzed out of here without so much as a by your leave. This wouldn't be the end of it, but she had faith that Tomas could at least prevent further episodes like this one.

She was hazy with exhaustion, but she held herself ramrod stiff as she walked out the doors. Tomas' face was nearly purple with suppressed fury.

"Hold yer head up until I get ye to the car an' we're clear of here. Do not give them the satisfaction of what they've done to ye. There's a least a half dozen of them watchin' out the door."

She nodded, not trusting herself to actually speak. At the very least she would break down into tears, or she would indeed get sick in front of all those bastards. Tomas was right, she would not give them the satisfaction, and there was at least one of them whom she knew would get pleasure from her pain as he had these last twenty-four hours.

"Come on, lass, just a couple more minutes an' we'll be away from here. I'm goin' to take ye straight to Jamie's."

Once in the car Tomas barely closed his door before driving off and away from the station. "Here, have a nip of this." He handed her an ancient silver flask and she took it, uncapping it. She took a hearty slug, knowing she needed the fortification if she was to get through the next half hour without melting down into a puddle of hysteria. It was brandy, good brandy, though the quality was wasted on her at present. It could have been rotgut moonshine for all she cared, but it did warm her belly and gave her a sense of regaining control over her limbs. The outside world looked surreal to her, everything outlined as if it was a slide in a View-Master and that the viewer had added an extra dimension, acidic colors and a sepia-toned edging to the trees, cars, buildings and roads. She realized she was swaying in the seat and leaned back into it, in an attempt to further shore her nerves. She just wanted to see her children, reassure herself and them that all was well.

"Tomas, was that letter—was it from the Prime Minister?" she asked, still wondering if she had been hallucinating in her compromised state.

"Oh aye, it was," he said grimly, "apparently he owed yer man James a favor."

She laughed out loud, sounding slightly unhinged even to her own ears. Tomas shot her a sideways glance of concern. "Of course he did," she said, and laughed again. Tomas gave her another look and then he too, laughed.

Jamie was waiting outside for them, Isabelle in his arms, Conor running down the drive the minute he heard the car. She was out of the car before Tomas even brought it to a full stop. She knelt down and swept her son into her arms, so grateful for his small solid warmth that she could have wept but knew she must not, lest she frighten him. She stood, Isabelle already reaching her arms out for her, and took her baby and hugged her tight. She buried her face in Isabelle's shoulder, breathing in all her baby scents—talcum powder and a freshly-laundered romper and the pureed apples someone must have fed her for breakfast.

"Come inside," Jamie said briskly, "let's get you a bath and a decent meal. A large drink wouldn't go amiss either, I'm thinking."

She nodded, still not looking up from Isabelle's shoulder. Jamie put a hand to her back and guided her into the house, and just the touch of his hand made her want to weep. She was safe now.

Two hours later she felt somewhat restored to herself. She'd had a bath and a good meal and had held her children long enough that both had become decidedly wiggly. Now she was tucked up on the old squashy sofa in Jamie's study with a drink in hand. It felt like pure luxury to be clean and wearing freshly laundered clothes, even if they were pyjamas. There was a fire in the hearth and the study was warm.

Jamie was sitting across from her, an untouched drink on the table beside him. He looked almost as exhausted as she felt. "All right, Pamela, if you feel up for it, I think you'd best tell me everything that went on these last couple of days."

She nodded, even though the movement set off a crackle of pain through her head. She recounted all of it, from the police arriving in her yard to Tomas finally springing her from their clutches. Jamie's face remained impassive as she told her story but his left hand was white with tension. With Jamie she had long ago learned to watch his hands and not his face to know what was truly going on with him.

"Jamie, it was awful. My head hurt so badly, I couldn't give coherent answers half the time. Mostly, I was so afraid for Conor and Isabelle," her voice broke a little and she put her drink down, worried for a second that she was about to throw up on the priceless Oriental rug that covered the study floor. She put her head to her knees and Jamie moved to sit beside her. He put a hand to her back and rubbed it up and down the length of her spine. It felt as if the last two days were closing in over top of her, drowning her in fear and anxiety.

"It's all right, they just wanted to put the fear of God in you and see if they could rattle you."

"Well they did that," she said, looking up at Jamie and then promptly putting her head back down as a wave of dizziness swept over her. "Jamie, they think I had something to do with your uncle's death. You know I didn't, but they made it clear they wouldn't mind framing me for it."

"They won't. I truly think they just wanted to scare you and I'm sorry they managed to do even that much. If it came down to it, Pamela, I'd take you and the children and flee the country. No one is going to separate you from your babies again. I promise you that." His voice was grim, and she suddenly realized how terrible these last two days had been for him as well.

"I'm sorry, Jamie, what a mess this is. I hate that it has come to rest on your doorstep."

"Don't apologize to me, not for this, not ever." His tone was fierce, and the look in his eyes frightened her a little. He was furious, not with her but with what had happened. She didn't think even Jamie, with all his resources, could fix this, though.

"I'm glad to be here," she said, "I don't think I could have managed to go home tonight. I hate to admit this, but I just don't feel safe there anymore. It breaks my heart because when Casey was there, it was a sanctuary where I did feel safe and happy at the end of each day. Now I jump at every noise and check the locks three times before I go to bed, as if doing it three times will somehow put a magic spell on the house and everyone in it, so that we're safe until morning."

"I'm sorry for that, Pamela. If anyone deserves to have a home that's safe and sacred, it's you."

"For a moment, I did have it. I know how fortunate that makes me."

She shifted a little and realized something had caught Jamie's attention. He was staring at her shoulder. She turned her head and saw that a deep purple bruise had flowered out along her collarbone.

"Pamela?" he said, and the anger in his voice was palpable. So much so that she shrank back a little.

"One of them grabbed my shoulder, that's all. You know I bruise easily, Jamie, it's not...it's not a big deal," she said shakily.

He stood and walked over to the windows and then after a moment he turned and walked back to where she sat.

"It is a big deal. The thought of someone touching you in anger like that..." His lips were in a narrow straight line and he looked like the only thing that might soothe his feelings at present was if he could kill someone with his bare hands. He took a deep breath, and with a force of effort, smiled. "We're meant to get snow tonight, so I think it's best that you are here anyway. You're safe now, Pamela. No one is going to come near you again, not on my watch. Gert packed up some clothes for you and the children. The animals have all been moved here, and Montmorency has even taken to Finbar. I can't insist, obviously, but I think it would be best if you stayed put until we understand exactly what's at the bottom of this."

"Thank you, Jamie."

"For the love of Christ, Pamela, do not thank me either. It's my fault you're in this mess."

"It is not. How on earth can you think that, Jamie?"

"It is, that dead bastard was my uncle, after all."

She laughed, and Jamie turned in his pacing as though he would reprimand her.

"What may I ask is so funny?"

"Nothing," she said, flapping a hand at him. "I'm a little hysterical, I think." It was true she suddenly felt dizzy and slightly breathless. She hoped she wasn't going to have a complete meltdown now that she felt secure.

"I'm sorry," he said and came over to where she sat and pulled her into his arms. She rested her head on his shoulder. It was a relief to be held, to breathe in his scent, which had long reassured her. The tension began to go from her muscles, the tiny groupings in her neck and shoulders, and then the larger ones along her spine. She was terribly tired, and her head was still aching despite the food and tea.

"I'm afraid, Jamie."

"I know you are, but I'm here and I won't allow anything more to happen to you."

Chapter Thirty-nine

The Transitory Nature of Butterflies

PAMELA AWOKE IN THE MORNING to a world transformed. It had snowed during the night and with the snow had come the strange and ephemeral peace that was often its companion. She'd had a restless night, punctuated with nightmares and the headache, which even Shura's remedies had not been able to alleviate.

Jamie went out of his way to make certain nothing worrisome came her way throughout the day. The children were happy to have her back but were more concerned with getting out into the fresh snow to play. This seemed, to her, a very good sign that this incident hadn't harmed them too much.

Tomas came by in the early afternoon and stayed for tea. Her headache steadily worsened as the afternoon wore on, and she had trouble answering his questions, as she couldn't seem to focus on more than half of what he was saying. He left soon after, casting her a worried look, and saying he would be back in a couple of days, as they had a great deal more to get through.

He left just as the early winter sun was sinking, setting Jamie's study afire with a lavender and gold glow. The detritus of afternoon tea still lay on the low table between couches. Pamela's cup was mostly untouched, even though it was the jasmine tea she loved best. Maggie had made it especially for her, but she hadn't been able to drink more than a swallow or two. She was alone for the moment as Jamie had walked out with Tomas. She knew there were things they wished to discuss further, and did not want to do so in front of her.

She got up from the couch and went to one of the long windows that looked out into the small garden that sheltered the study from the worst of the winter winds and summer sun. The snow was glazed in a palette of watercolor paints, from mauve to lavender to a deep grey that was like the feathers of a goose. She rested her forehead against the window, the chill of it a relief to her aching head. Movement caught her eye along one of the branches of the oak which stood in the center of the garden. She squinted to better see and was surprised to find it was a butterfly. It was a gorgeous celadon, its wings picked out delicately in a nimbus of frost. The poor thing would die out in the snow. It seemed odd to her that it had found its way here on such a cold day.

She opened the window she stood next to. There were clasps on all of them so that a person could easily step out into the garden without going through the house. She had long suspected there were reasons other than a want of solitude for this. The chill air hit her skin like a wave of water and she walked out into the snow to get a closer look at the butterfly. Her vision was oddly acute, as though everything was magnified. The folds on the oak bark seemed like they were layered, crevice upon crevice, and she could almost see the years numbered there, telescoping back through time until the massive tree was merely a newly-hatched sprout breaking open an acorn. A snowflake drifted down in front of her and she put out a hand so that it landed on her palm. Winter now and what was liquid had become something different, transient, striving toward unity with the cold. There were more than a billion molecules in this delicate twelve-sided star in her hand, which was already melting and transmuting into a silver sphere of trembling water. Water, ever moving, falling, cascading, streaming, flowing, always yearning to be somewhere else much like humans.

The butterfly was picking its way daintily along the branch, snow capping its delicate feet, and the colors of the sunset shone through the fragile wings, washing the pale green in drifts of purple and crimson. An old poem, one which she had loved as a child, floated through her mind and so she spoke it aloud to the butterfly.

> "You've come each morn to sip the sweets
> With which you found me dripping
> Yet never knew it was not dew
> But tears that you were sipping."

A memory came to her with the strange bits of lucidity which had punctured the grey fog of the afternoon. She remembered seeing monarchs on the bark of eucalyptus trees in California one year, moving in their great rustling ribbons, clustering for warmth and life. Her father had stopped the car and they'd stepped out, careful to keep their distance so as not to frighten the butterflies. On the ground at her feet was a lost wing, just one, stripped of its scales, translucent and torn. She had picked it up, marveling at its weightlessness and at the beauty it held still, even though broken. Around her the very air had trembled with the flight of the butterflies like living flame born on updrafts of autumn air.

"They live such brief lives," her father said, "they have always seemed to me half sunlight, half shadow, for the shade of their ending is on them even as they emerge from the chrysalis, and their life is a frenzy to eat and mate before they die. Some only have days, others weeks, and a few very rare ones, months."

"And then they fly north in the spring," she said, having learned about the monarch's immense migration in school.

"It will be their great-great-grandchildren that return next fall," he said.

"How do they know their way?" she asked.

"No one knows," he said quietly. "Their understanding of certain things is much greater than ours."

The wind picked up and the fragile wing fluttered in her hand, and then took flight, whorling up through the air and disappearing.

"What is it, *a stor*?" her father had asked.

"It's just sad, how brief their lives are." There was more to it than that, but she couldn't express all of it, only that it made her want to cry and run at the same time.

Her father had put an arm around her then, giving her a reassuring squeeze.

"Even a life numbered in days can be beautiful," he said.

And it was then that she had cried for the transitory nature of butterflies, which were born and yearned and died so swiftly.

"Pamela?" Jamie's voice seemed to come from a vast distance, as if he was speaking through a phone on one of those old transatlantic lines, crackling with interference. "What are you doing?"

"There's a butterfly on that branch," she pointed up at the oak branch thick with snow. "I need to catch it so it doesn't die," she said, wondering why he was looking at her so oddly. The snow felt wonderfully cool on her feet, and she thought perhaps she should lie down out here, and it would douse the fire in her head. If she slept in the snow, it would take away the pain. All of it. She sat down at the foot of the tree, between a gap in the roots, the butterfly momentarily forgotten. She put her back up against the

322 • Cindy Brandner

tree. She could feel the snow soaking through her pajama bottoms, but she didn't mind, it felt rather nice.

Jamie's face hove into view, the green eyes dark with worry.

She touched his face, one cold palm cupping his jaw. "You're very lovely, you know," she said and tried to smile, but found it hurt too much. She grimaced, her peripheral vision a soft cloud of grey on each side. There was something wrong about that though she couldn't quite think what it was. Jamie put a hand to her forehead and she sighed with relief, it was icy cold against her skin and it felt wonderful.

Jamie didn't seem to think it was wonderful, though. "Pamela, how long has your head hurt like this?" His voice was sharp with worry and it made her vaguely uneasy.

"Since a few hours after I arrived at the police station," she said, trying to find a spot to lie down properly. She was horribly tired, and it was getting dark so quickly, even for a November day.

Jamie hauled her unceremoniously to her feet and then picked her up. "Come on, I'm putting you to bed, and then we're going to see what Shura can do for that fever. You're hotter than a branding iron."

"Promise me you'll go back for the butterfly, it will freeze to death out there."

"I promise," he said.

"Good, I know you always keep your promises, Jamie."

By the time Jamie put her in the bed, she could only see a narrow field directly in front of her. She closed her eyes; her eyelids throbbing with blood and heat. Every joint ached, and she thought she could see them, each smooth and shiny round of cartilage and the tension of the muscles, scarlet and pulsating with pain.

She felt like she was drifting, and though she could not see, she sensed that the landscape was changing around her, the room melting away to become something small, like the cutouts in a pop-up book, pretty but merely a Potemkin façade.

Behind her someone said her name, and she turned and saw a field of snow stretched out to the edge of a dark wood. She must have walked outside again, she thought, seeking the cold. She longed to lie down in it and just stop for a while until the crimson wires of pain weren't strung so tightly through her body.

Her name again, and a man's voice, beckoning her to where he stood in the shadows, only his silhouette visible to her eyes. She knew him, she thought, though she didn't quite know how. She walked toward him, the snow cold and crisp beneath her feet and the woods dark and deep and welcoming.

———⟨☘⟩———

"How high is it, Shura?" Jamie asked.

Shura looked up at him from his position by the bed, his dark eyes unreadable.

"High, but we will keep an eye on it. If it gets worse, we maybe should consider hospital."

Jamie nodded.

"I am going downstairs to make something for this fever," Shura said. "I will tell Maggie and Vanya, so that the babies are attended."

"*Spasibo*," Jamie said, his mind on the woman in the bed. He had put her in his room, central to the upper floor and the warmest of the lot. She looked lamentably small and fragile in the midst of his big bed, and terribly pale. His thoughts briefly flickered to the last time she had been in this bed. She had been nineteen and attempting to seduce him. It had very nearly worked, in fact if he hadn't had too much to drink that night, it likely would have. How different everything might have been had he—but no, he shut the thought down as quickly as it came.

He was shocked by how frail she felt when he picked her up. He cursed himself for being so unaware. She tended to hide in her clothes these days but he ought to have noticed how thin and white her face was, the bones lying starkly close to the surface. She was exhausted, ill and grieving and trying to cope with everything that had come at her since Casey's disappearance.

He built a fire in the big hearth that graced the west wall of his bedroom until it was a hearty blaze that dispelled the chill of the early winter night. Maggie brought in gin jars that were hot enough that they smoked slightly when applied to the sheets. Shura was right behind her with a tray of hot tea.

A smell, somewhat akin to what one might imagine the borders of hell to smell like, was wafting in drafts of steam from the large tea pot on the tray. Maggie, her nose wrinkled in revulsion, gave him a look that spoke volumes. Shura shrugged and put the tray down.

"It is smelling bad, but is good, you understand? You have to make her drink now."

He woke Pamela, though he hated to do it. Shura was right, they needed to do whatever they could to get her fever down now. Waking her was like trying to bring a drowned woman back to life, despite the fact that it was clear her sleep was anything but restful.

She drank the tea with reluctance, grimacing her way through the first few swallows. He made her drink all of it, though she glared at him when he insisted. Finally she lay back against the pillows, clearly exhausted.

"I feel a bit ridiculous," she said.

"Don't, you're just sick. We will look after everything; you're not to worry yourself."

"Where are the babies?" she asked.

"Downstairs with Vanya and Maggie. They're fine, sweetheart, please don't worry about them. I'll look after them."

This seemed to give her some small but necessary peace, for she fell into a restless sleep again some minutes later. He got a basin of cold water and a small pile of washcloths to soak and put on her forehead. She muttered something that he thought it best he didn't quite catch when he put the first cold cloth on her forehead. The evening passed in this way, with Pamela tossing and muttering, and by turns throwing off the blankets and then huddling in them shaking with cold.

Vanya stuck his head in at one point, Isabelle's tousled head on his shoulder. She was fast asleep, dressed in a castoff pair of Kolya's sleepers. One down, two to go. Conor was such a fixed star, that he adapted to whatever surroundings in which he found himself. As long as someone pointed him to a bed and read him a story he would be fine. Everyone in this house loved Pamela's children as if they were their own.

Shura came in a little later with a fresh batch of cold water, and a pot of tea for Jamie to drink. He went to the bed, and put one thick-fingered hand to Pamela's head. He wore that inward look that physicians or healers often wore when assessing the condition of their patient.

"She is a bit cooler, and she is sleeping better, *da*? You go, spend a bit of time with the babies and eat. You won't be able to help her if you are sick too. I will call you if she is worse. Maggie tells me the phone line is out, I thought you should know."

Jamie nodded, it wasn't uncommon for the phone to go down, the slightest bit of rough weather and it packed it in. "Thank you, Shura. I won't be long."

Maggie had left a plate for him in the Aga's warmer. He sat down to eat, realizing how tired he was. He hadn't done more than snatch a few minutes of sleep here and there since Tomas had tracked him down in New York and told him Pamela had been taken in for questioning. The several hours after that had been a blur of calling in favors and catching a flight home. The flight across the Atlantic felt like it took twice as long as it normally did. By the time he was on the ground in Dublin, his phone calls had begun to bear fruit.

Vanya came in the kitchen then, Kolya toddling at his side. He made a beeline for Jamie and clambered up into his lap. He then proceeded to help himself to what remained of Jamie's dinner. He had turned two just the week before. Jamie kissed the top of his red-gold head, enjoying the little boy's robust good health and energy. Kolya never stayed put for more than a few minutes and was soon down and away playing with Conor's collection of wooden cars and trucks. Conor had gone down to the byre with Jake directly after his dinner to visit the new pony and possibly, Jake had said, to have a ride around the paddock. Jamie had been grateful to his stable manager, because Conor loved horses the way Pamela did and the pony might be the one thing that would keep the child distracted from worry over his mother.

Vanya sat across from him, sliding into the chair with his boneless elegance, the smell of the fresh snow wafting off of him. He had been outside with the children earlier.

"You are worried, Yasha?" he asked, quietly, the remarkable amethyst eyes viewing him with sympathy.

"Yes," he replied, "I am. She's not as strong as she ought to be."

"It is grief," Vanya said, "you know this, you have seen it kill before. It wears masks—illness, accident, suicide or simply becoming a ghost in the flesh. In the end, it is still just grief."

"Yes, it is grief," he agreed.

"She believes she cannot live without him."

"I know she does, but she's wrong," Jamie said and stood, the anger in his veins like a white-blue light, banishing his weariness. If there was one thing he understood about grief it was this—he would rather fight with a disease any day, but he was damned if he was letting Pamela kill herself through mourning.

He returned to his bedroom to find Pamela sleeping a bit more restfully. He went to the windows and looked out over the yard. The snow was lit with diamonds everywhere that the paddock lights touched. Beyond that small halo of light was a deep hush, the absolute quiet of woods and snow and cold.

He watched out over the yard as Conor came back with Jake and the snow continued to fall, building up in the yard, a few flakes sticking to the window through which he gazed, each one a thing of delicate and unique wonder. How long he stood there he didn't know but at some point he realized he was praying, a silent emanation from himself to the night beyond. It was formless, not so much a petition as a plea, not so much asking as hoping that the power beyond would not take Pamela to itself and remove her from those who needed her.

"Jamie," said a small voice from the doorway of his room. He looked up startled, realizing he had been half asleep, his forehead touching the frosted windowpane.

"Conor?" The boy stood there in his pajamas, bare-footed, a blanket clutched in one hand. There was worry in the child's face, worry that he understood all too well. "Come here, Conor, it's all right, your mama is just restless tonight."

Jamie sat in the big armchair that looked out over the grounds and Conor crawled up into his lap. Jamie wrapped the blanket around the boy's small form and then put his arms around him, knowing Conor needed the reassurance of an adult right now. He smelled of toothpaste and soap, his neatly set ears glowing a soft shell pink in the light of the fire and the small bedside lamp, his turf of curls still slightly damp from his before bed wash. He looked up at Jamie, small face grave.

"Is my mama going to die?"

Jamie gave him the respect of looking him directly in the eyes.

"No, she is not going to die, Conor. She is sick, but she isn't going to die."

He nodded, but Jamie could see he wasn't entirely convinced. After all, people had told him his father was going to come home, hadn't they? He had learned the hard way not to trust the word of adults.

"I won't allow her to die, laddie and that's all there is to it. I'm the boss here and I get to say what happens and what doesn't." It was, of course, an enormous lie, but Conor needed a man who seemed entirely in charge of things right now, not a man who understood that a person could actually die of grief.

"Jamie." The little voice was very serious and he dreaded what question Conor might ask now.

"Yes, Conor, what is it?"

"I love you."

Jamie put his face to the damp curls and kissed the boy's head. "I love you too," he said and Conor sighed, as though in relief, and promptly fell asleep.

They sat so for a long time, Conor's little body like a hot water bottle against the chill of the night. Jamie looked over to his bed, where Pamela tossed and turned and reached out toward invisible things in the air, and he prayed over the slumbering body of her son that he would able to keep the promise he had made to him.

He was awakened in the wee hours by Shura gently shaking his arm.

"Yasha, wake up." He came up out of sleep like a diver returning from the deeps. Conor was still fast asleep on his lap and his arms ached from holding the child tight for hours.

Vanya was there, too, and he took Conor from Jamie and left the room in that silent way he had. He would see Conor safely to bed.

"What is it?" he asked, alert now, the worry there in his brain and body like a drum pounding insistently.

"She keeps talking to something that isn't there." Shura looked over his shoulder as if he wasn't entirely certain there wasn't something that only Pamela could see, hovering there in the room. "She calls for you, she calls for her husband, she seems to be seeking and not finding. It is making her very—how would you say?"

"Agitated?" Jamie was out of the chair and beside the bed without any consciousness of his movements.

She had thrashed the blankets onto the floor and was pushing against some entity only she could see. He touched a hand to her forehead, horrified at how hot she was now. The fever must have climbed at least another two degrees while he had slept. While he had carelessly slept. Panic coursed through him.

Shura was wringing a cloth out in icy cold water. He put it to Pamela's forehead, and she cried out like she had been shot. "Yasha, we need to be action."

"It's time to take her to the hospital, I think," he said, inwardly cursing himself for not taking her the afternoon before.

Shura looked up at him, the dark eyes worried. "Yasha, look out the window please, there will be no taking her to the hospital."

Jamie went and looked, and felt a thrill of horror shoot through him. He had never seen snow like this outside of Russia. The snow had already reached the top of the paddock rail; it would be impossible to get a car down the mountainside, not to mention too dangerous lest they get caught in a snowdrift and weren't found for days. The safest place for her was right where she was, with fire and medicine and water readily available. He only hoped he hadn't made a fatal mistake in not getting her to a hospital the afternoon before.

"Yasha?"

He took a breath and nodded. "Yes, you're right Shura, we have to be action. We're going to have to be merciless. Go fill the tub with lukewarm water," he said grimly. "We have to get her temperature down now. We can't afford to wait for the morning anymore." It wasn't worth mentioning that dawn was unlikely to bring any redemption, for the snow was only going to be deeper come morning.

Shura nodded and went off. Jamie could hear the water start to thrum through the pipes. He was going to have to prepare the house for a loss of power as well, which with snow this heavy was likely an inevitability. He was surprised it hadn't happened already.

He went and looked out the window again, as if the few seconds would have somehow changed the grim view. He remembered tales of such winters. He had lived through one himself, though he had only been eleven at the time, and it had seemed like a grand adventure. Driven by easterly gales the snow had covered the entirety of the island, filling every valley and hollow, capping all the mountains and rising in places to the height of the telegraph wires. Cars, bicycles, busses and lorries were abandoned on the roadsides and many elderly, trapped in their homes without adequate food or fuel, died. Livestock wintering out in fields had suffocated in the drifts. Men out cutting peat were found frozen to death days later, packs of turf stuck with ice to their bodies. At home, safe and warm, and too young to really understand how devastating such weather could be, he remembered it now as a time of sledding for weeks and building a snowman so big that it didn't completely melt away until April of that year. The country had been shut down for six weeks, with hard frosts coming down early each night. If they were stuck up on this hill for more than a day or two with a woman who required urgent medical care…it didn't bear thinking about.

A sharp cry from the bed caused him to whirl around. Pamela was sitting up in the bed, reaching out toward something invisible to his own eyes, but he had no doubt that she was seeing something, or someone, there in the air before her.

"Do you see him?" she asked, "Do you?" she was breathing heavily, as though she had been running for a distance.

"See who?" he asked, fighting to keep the panic from his voice. She was hallucinating, which meant her temperature was dangerously high.

"Casey. He's right there, but he can't seem to hear me. Jamie, the snow is so cold, where are my shoes?"

"The snow?" Christ have mercy, where had her fevered brain travelled to? He remembered the episode in Russia where he could have sworn she had traversed half the world in spirit to pull him back from the grave's edge. The woman was half witch, and frankly that scared the hell out of him right now.

He pulled the covers back, and took her feet in his hands. They were so cold that it was painful to touch them as if—as if she had, indeed, been walking in snow.

She was fixated on a point inside the fire now, as if she saw a figure moving through the flames. And then she spoke, the words a toneless whisper, uttered it seemed in another realm.

> *"But I have promises to keep,*
> *And miles to go before I sleep."*

The words frightened him, uttered as they were to that third party whom she clearly believed was in the room.

"Casey!" Her voice was high and frantic. "Wait for me—slow down—wait, please wait!" She had pushed herself to the edge of the bed and was trying to stand, reaching out for a phantom. Jamie grabbed her and pulled her back, afraid she was going to walk straight into the fire. She tried to pull away, crying out in frustration. She turned and looked right into his eyes, yet hers seemed to be looking far beyond this room, and he knew she was not seeing him at all.

"He won't wait for me, please make him wait for me." She clutched at his hand. "Please!"

A ripple went up his backbone, as if small icy hooves skimmed along every vertebra, fleet as a deer crossing a frozen pond. He could feel another entity in the room, as though the man stood there by the fire, waiting for his wife to come to him. That big dark man, who, if anyone could, might well be able to call this woman to him across time and space, across the line between life and death. He felt a surge of anger, the bastard was not taking her. He could not have her.

"Please, Jamie, hurry, he's getting too far away! Tell him!"

Feeling only a tad foolish, for the night was very odd in its lineaments, he spoke to the spot near the fire.

"Wait for her." Wait a hundred years, you bastard, he thought to himself, because she isn't coming any time soon. I will fight you every fucking step of the way.

"The tub is ready. It's going to be a big shock for her body so ease her in a bit at a time." Shura was standing in the doorway of the bath, the exhaustion of the night showing in his dark eyes. "Do you need my help?"

"No, I can manage."

Shura left the room, closing the door behind him.

Jamie began to turn toward Pamela only to have his gaze halt at the hearth. He felt something strange tug at him, like an invisible thread connected him to that spot by the fire, a thread that pulled at his nerve endings. He was aware suddenly that every hair on his body was standing up, acknowledging that something other was indeed in the room with them. And then the tug stopped and the presence was gone. Jamie squelched the desire to go look up the chimney, to see if that something was on its way out.

He took a deep, shuddering breath and turned back to Pamela to find her looking up at him and though her gaze was still far away, he knew she could now see him. Her eyes beseeched him, the skin beneath them bruised with the fever and her restless roving in and out of that strange dream landscape that was causing her such agitation.

He picked her up and she struggled against him, her head turning back to that spot by the fire. He took her into the bathroom, shutting the door behind him. He stripped her down and then picked her back up. Her skin was like fire against him and he prayed they hadn't waited too long.

"I'm sorry, angel," he said and then took a deep breath and put her in the water.

She screamed when the water touched her skin, trying hard to hang onto him and get away from the cold her nerves could sense. He was much stronger than her though, and pushed her relentlessly down and into the water. He got soaked in the process, as she did not go quietly and there was almost as much water on the floor as in the tub by the time he got her fully submerged.

"Jamie that hurts, please stop it! The water is freezing."

"Too goddamn bad," he said ruthlessly, still shaken by the presence in the other room. He was going to bring her back to the here and now even if he had to shock her into it. He did not like the look in her eyes at all; it was as if she was shuffling off her mortal coil right in front of him. He held her by the shoulders, until she stopped struggling and started to cry, silent tears that ran unceasing from those eyes that stood out stark as bruises in the pale face, heavy with fever and pain. She had calmed enough that he noticed other things too, like the way her ribs were sharp against the ivory skin, her legs gleaming lengths of bone with too little flesh. She was far too thin. She was going to damn well start eating after she recovered, he'd had enough of this wasting away in grief. She was going to embrace life if it bloody killed him.

"I just wanted him to wait for me, even for a second, he was right there, Jamie. I could smell him. I swear to you I could almost touch him."

"That's what I was afraid of," he muttered grimly, still feeling a rage towards the entity that had been pulling her to it, out of this world, and into his.

He made her stay in the water for another ten minutes, until he felt her forehead and was convinced that her temperature had come down a few degrees at least. Then he helped her out, toweled her down and wrapped her up in his robe, tying the belt snug.

Her teeth were clacking together, and he picked her up and took her back into the bedroom, put her in the bed and covered her up.

"You're a high-handed bastard, James Kirkpatrick," she said weakly, falling back into the pillows.

"Yes, I am," he said, "try not to forget it."

Shura came in with the mug of his foul fever brew just then, took one look at the two of them, put the mug down and exited posthaste.

"Now drink this," Jamie said, picking up the piping hot mug and putting it to her lips.

"It smells awful," she said, turning her head away. She looked horribly frail, her neck like the stem of a flower that had been crushed under a careless foot.

"I don't give a damn if it smells like the floor of the stable, you're drinking it."

She looked up at him, and then meekly submitted to having it poured down her throat, sip by sip. She was right, it did smell revolting, but he had been subjected to Shura's cures more than once, and knew that while they smelled poisonous they worked extremely well. He would pour a gallon of it down her if necessary.

"Jamie," she said quietly, when the drink was done, "I know you're angry with me, but do you think you could hold me for a little bit. I feel so weak right now, as if I could slip away if someone doesn't keep me tied to the earth."

He swallowed. It was the illness asking, but he knew she needed human touch, needed it while she rode out the specters of this fever. He got into the bed with her and put his arms around her, holding her fast against the night and its ghosts. She sighed and put her head to his chest. He could feel the exhaustion in her, could feel the loss and grief that was making her ill.

She fell asleep there in his arms, fairly quickly, not yet cool to the touch, but at least not the temperature of a lit coal anymore. He relaxed a little, the feeling of her solid in his arms, reassuring him. He spoke low and fierce, looking toward the dying fire. "Let her go. If you can't come back to her, you have to let her go, or you'll kill her."

The fire flared, a small uprush of flame, and then it died back to a glowing bed of coals. If it was an answer, he did not understand it.

Chapter Forty

Prayers and Penicillin

THE NEXT MORNING the household awoke to a wind that screeched about the corners of the house like a banshee and at least another two feet of snow that had accumulated during the night's storm. The wind was the first thing Jamie heard as he slowly regained consciousness. The second thing was the hoarse breathing of the woman beside him. He did not need to put a hand to her forehead for he could feel the heat of her body through the material of his robe. His arms were still around her, her head on his chest. She was cooler now, but that was of small comfort considering the hoarse sounds coming from her chest.

He became aware of stirrings elsewhere in the room, and opened his eyes to find Shura bustling about. He also became aware that his body was very clear about the fact that a desirable woman, *the* desirable woman, was in his bed. He could feel every inch of her along his skin, every curve fitted to his every hollow. He was in the usual state of the male in the morning, and was trying to find a way to ease away from her and not have Shura notice his discomfort.

Shura merely, in the way of a medical man, updated him on what he'd missed during the time he'd slept and, as it turned out, he had slept for some time. He glanced at the clock by the bed—six hours of unbroken sleep. He was slightly horrified that he had slept so deeply while Pamela burned like a coal in his arms all night.

"It is fine, Yasha," Shura said clearly interpreting the look on his face. "I would have woken you if there was any great change for better or worse."

Despite his words, Jamie saw worry there in the dark, soulful eyes. It frightened him perhaps more than any event since Pamela had hallucinated the butterfly in the snow. He got up from the bed, trying hard not to disturb Pamela, who rolled over and moaned a little, her brow furrowed in pain.

"Could it kill her, Shura? Just tell me."

Shura nodded, just a tiny concession to the possibility that she might succumb, that with the snow too deep to pass through and with the shadows gathered thick and deep upon the land, he might not be able to fight off the most formidable opponent of all.

Shura sighed. "Yasha, I have tried all remedies I can think of. She needs penicillin. I think she has—how do you say—an infection of the brain lining."

"Meningitis—is that what you mean?"

Shura nodded. "*Da*, that is what I am meaning."

Jamie sat down, abruptly. Shura was no mean diagnostician and Jamie had known fully-fledged GPs who were far less capable than this man. If he said Pamela had meningitis, then she probably did. The question, of course, was what to do about it. The biggest worry is that it might be bacterial rather than viral, and therefore serious enough to kill her. He got up again a few moments later. He was not going to allow this damn sickness to kill her, he would fight with the last ounce of stubbornness he had in his body before he allowed it to happen.

He went to the bathroom, splashed cold water on his face, ran his fingers through his hair and then returned to the bedroom. It was a scene of disarray—basins of water, damp towels, mugs half empty, packets of herbs and a bottle of paracetamol without a lid. The blankets were half off the bed and all the linens were crumpled. He thought if he tidied a little it might give an illusion of control. The view out the window was much worse and destroyed any illusions he might have about getting Pamela to the hospital any time soon. The phone line was still out, and there was no way to get a car through the endless drifts which had drowned the paddock and yard and lay in great piles against the house. There was no way for a helicopter to land, unless they could manage to somehow hover long enough to take her up in a basket. It was unlikely anything was moving right now, though, weather this unexpected ground everything to a complete halt. He had considered every way to get her down the mountain and somehow then make it through the streets that would be hopelessly impassible to get her to the medical help that was needed. Except there was no phone to call for help, which was where his useless cycle of thought came back to each time.

The day passed quietly enough, considering there were children to feed and entertain and snow to be shoveled, even while it still fell in great white sheets. Shura stayed with Pamela much of the day as she drifted in and out of sleep, sometimes crying out in pain and confusion, and at others lying so still that Jamie, when he looked in, had the desire to stick a mirror under her nose just to be sure she was breathing.

Between the snowfall and the time of year, night fell early and it was full dark by four in the afternoon. Jamie, having managed a bath, fresh clothes and a meal, returned to his vigil at Pamela's bedside and bid Shura, who looked completely exhausted, to go have his dinner and then get some sleep. He checked her temperature and found no comfort in that task. She was still hot, and her skin was dry and taut, with nary a bead of sweat to portend the breaking of her fever.

His thoughts circled back to how to get her to hospital, or even find a way to get a doctor here, culminating in a rather mad vision of bundling her up and flying down the mountainside with her on a sled.

"Jamie." Her voice startled him, intent as he was on crazy plans. She hadn't spoken all day, and he was relieved at her sudden consciousness.

"Yes?" he turned and walked over to the bed. She looked up at him and smiled weakly and he smiled back in reassurance though she looked terribly small and fragile in the big bed, her skin almost whiter than the sheets upon which she had spent a restless day.

"Am I dying? I heard you and Shura before," she said. Her words were barely audible but he could hear the fear in them only too well. He damned himself for speaking in the room; he ought to have known better.

He sat down on the side of the bed and took her hand. "No, Pamela, you're not dying. You are very sick and I'm afraid we're stuck for the foreseeable future as the snow is several feet deep and still falling. The path to the stables is shoulder high with snow."

"Jamie, don't lie to me, please. If I'm dying I need to know. I have always trusted you to tell me the truth."

"No, you're not dying," he said with grim determination.

She looked up at him, her hand tightening on his. Her eyes were fever-bright and pale green rather than their normal deep-water emerald. The intensity in her gaze worried him. Mind you, everything she did and said was worrying him just now. Still, he wasn't quite prepared for what she did say.

"If I die, Jamie, I would have you look after my children."

"I won't allow it to happen, Pamela. You said it yourself, I'm a high-handed bastard. Death won't be allowed admittance here, not today, not tonight, not this month or year—d'you understand?"

"I understand, Jamie. Only, if something were to happen, would you raise Conor and Isabelle?"

He saw that she meant it and that she needed an answer before she was going to be able to rest. He would have to tell her the truth because even in her fevered state she would know if he was less than honest with her.

"Yes, if that is what you want, Pamela, then I will raise them. You know I love them both dearly."

She nodded and gave his hand a squeeze that was meant, he thought, to be reassuring.

"Would you read to me, Jamie?"

"Of course, I will," he said, feeling somewhat relieved by this want of comfort, because comfort was for the living and the striving, and not for the wraiths that haunted the places in between—the places guarded by the elements: fire and water, air and earth.

"What would you have me read, sweetheart?"

"Keats," she said, her voice drifting Lethe-wards, the one word barely audible.

Keats was one of the poets he had long held fast in the storehouse of his mind, and so he did not need pages in front of him. He settled beside her, his eyes on the fire as it hissed high and bright, an open casement between worlds.

He spoke the lines as they were meant to be spoken, soft and then with force where it was necessary and the words climbed the ether of night and became the ghosts of castles long crumbled, of fairy lands once glimpsed from the corner of a child's eyes, glimmering visions which had disappeared along with childhood. And as he spoke he watched and saw other things, the translucent delicacy of her hand against the midnight blue of the quilt, the shadows of her veins so close to the surface of that luminous skin, like rose petals in its soft febrile flush.

He realized in that moment that part of him had always been waiting, like the specter on the edge of the feast, waiting for her to beckon him in out of the shadows into the light of her warmth. He had waited and then had not, and now it seemed with him neither wishing nor willing it, here he was again—waiting. Waiting for what though? That he loved her he admitted to himself, and for a time, it had been the love of a friend for one who was very dear, but now—now, something had once again shifted. Yes, he loved her. He had, he supposed, never truly stopped. Some things were born in a man's cells and beyond that to the inner place that each man must hold sacred or risk losing his soul forever. Or perhaps that which a man held sacred *was* his soul. This woman was tangled up inextricably in all of it, she his soul beyond the confines of narrow flesh.

When he came to the line: '*To cease upon the midnight with no pain...*' She murmured the words along with him, chilling him to his core, despite the heat of her body, despite the fire, burning high and hot. His voice flowed on, up and down, ribboning through the night like some aerial creature, apart from him, giving her thread-by-thread, a skein by which to hold to life, to beauty, to the people who needed her to stay here and not cross that chasm, across which called the phantoms of grief, of joy and love remembered, now beyond human touch, but not beyond a heart that could not accept nor understand such loss.

He stayed with her until she fell back into the phantom sleep that came with fever, her breath sounding like the rasp of sandpaper against wood. He went to the window after, along the same well-worn path he had walked the night before. He stood watching the snow fall relentlessly into the dark bowl of night and he prayed that he had told her the truth and that he would be able to keep the promise he had made her. The one thing he knew for certain was that he was going to have to find help outside this house, even if he died trying to reach it. He sighed; he knew just whose help he needed.

Long ago, his grandmother would have been a *bean fasa*—a wise woman— meaning—like most Irish terms—more than the literal translation. It was understood that such a personage had truck with the fairies, that they had trained her in the ways of medicine and healing and that they would continue to guide and help her throughout her career. If he could believe it of anyone, it would be Finola, for there had long been something of the witch about her—a green witch, steeped in the lore of herbs and their uses, and using methods that could at best be called unconventional to effect her cures. He might not entirely understand how his grandmother practiced her healing, but he trusted her skills implicitly.

He had dressed as well as he could for the elements, though in truth he knew anything short of a fur coat and mukluks wasn't going to be adequate. He was taking the small measures he could to assure that he would find his way back to the house as well. Though small, he thought looking at the ball of twine in his hand, didn't quite cover the inadequacy of those measures.

He had taken the ball of twine and secured one end to a post that was outside the back door of the kitchen. The other end he would tie as far along the paddock rail as he could manage, so there was at least that much of a trail to guide himself home by. It would require finding the paddock, granted, but it was a small comfort to know there was something there.

When he relayed his plan to Vanya and Maggie, Vanya had expressed the notion that it was possible the Irish were as crazy as they were reputed to be. Maggie, being Maggie, had nodded grimly, given him a hug and promised there would be hot food and drink when he returned.

The snow was ridiculously high, and he hoped to heaven he would actually make it to the cottage without getting hopelessly lost and dying from exposure. He had survived worse, mind you; a night in a deep Russian forest hunted by a madman came to mind. Pamela had somehow reached across time and space to save him that time, and he would do no less for her. He would, as much as it made him uneasy, employ the same help she had in that endeavor.

It was going to be a struggle just to find the cottage much less not end up a frozen lump lost somewhere between here and there. He thought grimly of those peat cutters found buried in snow with turf frozen to their backs. A man could be lost and not found for several weeks in severe weather like this. The thaw, when it came, would have its work cut out for it. If he got lost, it would be a long time—too long—before he was found.

At the back of the house, beyond the paddock and stables, there were riding trails. There was one in particular a small ways into the wood which would take him right alongside his grandmother's cottage. Of course every trail was going to be long buried in snow. It would be slightly less deep in the trees and he thought once he was in the wood he would be better able to find his way. There was a danger in the woods as well for if he struck out in the wrong direction he could well end up in the ravine that skirted one edge of it. It would likely be invisible in the snow and he would break his legs or maybe his back and then slowly freeze to death.

Many years ago an Athabascan friend had gifted him two pairs of snowshoes made by one of the elders in his tribe. He had used them a handful of times over the years, and had only remembered them when it occurred to him he might well drown in the drifts if he couldn't find a way to get and stay on top of them. There were spots where he knew the snow was going to be above his head. Between the cold and the wind a hard crust had formed on top of the snow. With the base of the snowshoes he was able to navigate across the crust and not sink down into the lethal drifts. He started out gingerly, testing the snow with each step and getting the rhythm of the shoes. Made from ash wood and elk hide they were built for long hikes in open fields and thick forest. Which was exactly what he needed tonight. The second pair he had strapped to his back for Finola would need them to make the trip back with him.

He noted the man-made landmarks, orienting himself by the stables and other outbuildings which were still, thankfully, visible. He tied the twine at the far end of the paddock, where it butted up against a tack shed. He looked back at that point to find that the big house was already invisible. He hadn't expected he would be able to see it for long but it still gave him a slightly hollow feeling to lose it as a guidepost so early into his journey.

Within minutes he was almost blind from the wind whipping a stinging mix of snow and ice into his face, his eyebrows and lashes crusted with snow and a rime of ice forming already on the edge of his scarf. From here on he was dependent on familiar shapes in the landscape. He went as briskly as he dared, hoping to stay warm enough to ward off frostbite.

It was a slog to get to the woods, but even in such nasty conditions it loomed up before him, though he wasn't sure if he saw it or merely felt the presence of the trees. He stumbled near the edge of it, sliding down into the trees and landing with a knock against a slim birch. He righted himself and was relieved to see that the canopy sifted some of the intensity from the falling snow. In ordinary circumstances he might be able to guide himself by the characteristics of certain trees which he had used as way-markers since childhood: the hazel that leaned to the right and always had since the big windstorm they'd had one autumn when it was still a sapling; the oak with the huge knot on its trunk that looked like an old man with a toothache; the cluster of ash trees which had always reminded him of a group of gossiping old women, turning their backs on the trail and clustering their heads together. Then there was the enormous yew that was near to the cottage. It was so big and so old that someone, long ago, had put a door in the base of it which when opened led to a small hollow in the tree's trunk. It had been just the right size for a small boy to hole up in with a clutch of apples and some books and a torch.

He had been taught navigation on both land and sea by the various teachers in his life—his grandfather, his father and the Jesuit brothers who'd had the molding of both his mind and spirit in their hands. Yet it would be easy to get lost because there was nothing to be seen. The only landmark he might be able to count on was a large standing stone along the way which ought to be visible even in this amount of snow.

Father Lawrence had the teaching of him, too, and his was a truly Celtic soul and so Jamie had been well-steeped in Celtic myth and legend, and the ways of the world before. This landscape was as familiar as the back of his hand and he could navigate it if he depended on a sense other than sight. He closed his eyes against the strain of the snow and dark, and felt the land with his inner eye. He oriented himself to the night and its challenges, and thought perhaps he did know where he was—roughly on the right path and heading in the right direction; he thought he needed to bear west just a little. The stones and trees and earth were all where they should be, still fixed like stars to guide a man through a wilderness of snow and wind.

He stepped forward and found himself face first in a blackthorn bush. This was both fortuitous and painful, and proved that his Celtic ancestors had a sense of humor, albeit a slightly sadistic one. Fortuitous because he knew exactly where he was now for the patch of blackthorn only grew in one place and that meant he was roughly a quarter of a mile away from Finola's wee cottage. Painful because the thorns were a good three inches long. He would take it as a good omen, though, for blackthorn was considered to guard a man against harm.

Time blurred after that as he put one foot in front of another and kept slogging through the snow, moving from tree to tree, and finding the tall stone where it sat humped in snow in the midst of a small glade. He was very close now and he thought he smelled smoke in the whirl of snow. It would be from Finola's fire, as there was no other habitation or building down this way. He had long wondered what it was that caused her to live alone out here, isolated without a neighbor for miles. He had offered, once, to have her come live in the big house with him but she had said no, she was fine on her own out here amongst the trees, with the foxes and badgers for company.

And then there it was, a humped shape in the night, but big enough to be unmistakable. He could have collapsed with the relief of finding it. He put his hand to the stone wall and then walked using it as a guide to the front door. The pathway was recently cleared for when he dropped down into it there were only a couple of inches that had gathered on the path to the door. There was light spilling out of the windows, the shutters thick with small mounds of snow. He took off the snowshoes with some difficulty, being that his fingers were so stiff with cold he couldn't even feel them. He raised his hand to knock on the door just as it opened. His grandmother had a clutch of herbs in one hand, and a pair of boots on her feet.

"What is it?" she asked, clearly aware that only an emergency would have driven him here in this weather.

"Pamela," he managed to gasp out. "She's sick."

"Come in out of the snow," she said briskly, "ye're going to need a spell by the fire before we head up to the house. I'll get some hot tea down ye as well."

"You'll come then?"

"Of course I will," she said. "Now, shed yer coat an' get the ice out of yer flesh. Nothin' will be lost by waitin' a few minutes. I'll need to put a bag together. What is it that's wrong with her?"

"Shura thinks meningitis," he said, dropping his frozen coat over the back of a chair and hunkering down by the fire. At first he couldn't even feel the heat, and then suddenly it was painful as his hands and legs prick-led back to life.

Finola bustled about pulling down jars and tins, and putting them in a canvas bag. Then she bundled up in a wool coat and hat with a scarf wrapped around her face to protect it from the cold. Jamie's own face was tingling as it slowly warmed. He wasn't keenly anticipating the return to the snow and wind but at the same time, he was desperate to get back as soon as possible. Finola made him take a warm drink first, which he gulped, scorching his tongue. She raised an eyebrow at him, as if to say 'I told ye so, laddie.'

"Do you want the fire out?" he asked, wrapping his scarf around his neck and pulling his coat on. It felt heavy and chilled.

"No, it will be fine, it's smoored an' will burn slow. Ye know I prefer to keep it lit this time of year."

She did, it was true. She never let the fire go out from Samhain to Beltane. It was one of her particular superstitions. When he had queried her about it many years ago, she had said it was to keep light in the dark half of the year.

Later, he never could remember the return journey, only that his grandmother's navigational skills seemed to be finely honed, for they were back at the big house within the hour.

Upon arrival, she was her usual brisk self and shed her snowy gar-ments in the boot room off the kitchen, hoisted her canvas bag and marched up the stairs to her patient. Jamie followed her up and watched as she took stock of the woman on the bed, who was still burning up, tossing and mut-tering in what was not sleep but something far less healing. Shura was by the bedside, attempting to put another cold cloth on her forehead.

Finola addressed Shura, one herb doctor to another. "All right tell me everythin' that's happened since she got ill."

He only half heard Shura's meticulous rundown of Pamela's symp-toms for he felt quite suddenly useless. He had brought help to Pamela and now there was nothing more he could do.

He was tired and his senses were both heightened and dulled at the same time, he needed to sleep but didn't see how he could manage it. He thought about the request Pamela had made of him earlier in the night when she had asked him to look after her children. He had said yes be-cause he meant it, and he had not exaggerated when he said he loved them dearly. He realized that in these last months they had been functioning as a family, not the sort perhaps one would find on television but of a sort which allowed them to manage and to not feel so alone. He could not bear the thought that she might not be here to see her children grow; it was tragedy enough that they had lost their father, they must not lose their mother as well.

Suddenly Finola was in front of him, speaking and he brought his focus to bear so that he could take in what she was saying.

"I think yer friend is right about it bein' meningitis. Of course it's not possible to tell entirely without a spinal tap, but that's my guess. It explains the fever an' the pain an' the hallucinating. Whether it's viral or bacterial I don't know. The viral kind simply requires rest an' lots of liquids in order to mend."

"And the bacterial kind?" He didn't know why he asked, he knew full well the problems that could cascade one over the next with bacterial meningitis until it culminated in death.

"Prayers an' penicillin," she said grimly, "a lot more than we've got probably, but it's better than nothin'. We have to find a way to get her to a hospital and the sooner the better. For now though, let's do what we can."

"You have penicillin?" he said blankly.

"Of course I do, herbs are wonderful when they work but sometimes modern medicine is the best choice. I'm not sayin' it will do the job, mind ye, but it's worth the try."

She moved back across the room, and soon there was a bitter smell wafting from the small mortar she had taken out of her bag and the sound of the pestle grinding mixed with the snap of the fire. There was the plink of liquid and he knew she was dissolving the tablets in distilled water.

She held the needle up to the light, and snapped her fingers efficiently against the glass barrel until she was satisfied that there were no air bubbles left. "Jamie," she said, "come hold her still so I don't hurt her with the needle."

Jamie put one hand on Pamela's shoulder and the other on her thigh, and then looked away as Finola pushed the robe up to her waist in order to give her the shot. He smelled the sharp sting of rubbing alcohol and then felt the small shudder that went through Pamela's body at the prick of the needle.

"How long until we know if it's working?"

"A couple of hours." She bustled about putting things away, discarding the needle and replacing the water in the basin. He sat down on the bed, and watched Pamela, as if he expected some sort of miracle to occur from the simple relief of having someone else take charge. "It depends on a few things. Her body is mournin' its other half; it may depend on whether she has the will to pull it back from despair."

"By other half you mean Casey, I presume."

"Aye, I do. The two of them were bound by many threads, but physical love was one of the strongest. His hold on her body, even now, is very strong. You have a hold on her too; it is just made of different threads. Don't let her slip away from ye."

"I'm not sure there's room for me in this equation."

She frowned at him, her green eyes sharp. "When did ye ever think there were only two people in your relationship with her? There has always been the three of ye. 'Tis just how it is. He knew it, an' had learned to live with it, enough that he came to be her anchor the night she came to ye in Russia. He was strong enough to allow ye to be part of his relationship with her, you can do the same."

"Oh, I have," he said, "for a very long time now."

"Have ye?" she said, sounding rather dubious.

She touched his shoulder, and when she spoke again her voice was uncharacteristically gentle. "Stay with her."

He looked up to find her face filled with sympathy.

"Because if this doesn't work, James, she should not be alone."

Chapter Forty-one

Recovery

THE PENICILLIN SAVED Pamela's life. It was another three days before the roads were cleared well enough that Jamie could get her to a hospital but by then the fever had broken and she was out of danger. When she returned from the hospital, Jamie installed her in her old room, where the fire was built high early each evening and he had added small things from her home, so that she might feel more comfortable. Her knitting bag, with a half-knit sweater still neatly rolled around the needles, a few of her books, and her winter clothes. Jamie told her that Gert had helped him pack the things, and reassured her that all was well at her little homestead. Phouka had taken up residence in the stables again, much to the annoyance of Naseem, who wasn't keen on sharing space with some uppity stallion with peasant roots. Paudeen was sharing space with the estate's lone cow, Finbar had settled in with Montmorency, and Rusty was having a love affair with one of the barn cats.

She had awakened in the hospital with little memory of the days that had preceded her stay there. Suffice it to say, the doctor had told her she was very lucky to be alive and without having incurred any sort of permanent damage. He also said it was clear that she was in possession of very resourceful friends. Jamie said little when she asked what had happened, but the lines around his mouth and the dark circles under his eyes told her it had been a very bad time for all concerned. She gathered that she owed her life to Finola having a rather large stash of penicillin.

Her convalescence lasted much longer than she had hoped. The meningitis had left her weak and feeling as wasted as a consumptive character in a Victorian novel. There was no leaving Jamie's stewardship until she was fully recovered either, that had been made clear in no uncertain terms. It was nice though, she had to admit, to have someone else care for her, to help her put the children to bed at night, to talk with over meals. Dinner was a raucous affair some nights, what with Shura's liberal quoting of Sufi mystic poets, Vanya's descriptions of his day (often interspersed with, but not separated from, episodes of whichever novel he was currently consuming), the children's general buoyancy and Jamie's version of small talk which was never small, but rather took in the scope of the universe, from the smallest seed pod to far-flung galaxies. He had brought the children inside his gilded circle, that place of warmth and light which only he possessed in such measure, to make others feel as if they carried the glow into the world after time spent with him. She still stood on the edges of it, both warm and chilled in equal measure, because she could not quite leave her other self, her other life behind.

She had announced her intention of moving her household back to her wee farmhouse in early February. Jamie had merely looked at her and made no comment.

"Jamie."

"Yes?"

"Just say it."

"Say what?"

"I can tell when you have something to say and aren't sure how it's going to be received," she said drily, and took a sip of the rosehip tea Shura had insisted she drink each day since her illness.

Jamie laughed. "Am I so transparent?"

"Sometimes, though not often enough," she said. Her heart was hammering because she had a good notion of what he meant to say and she understood why, but it didn't mean the hearing of it would be any easier because of that.

"I think, perhaps, Pamela, you need to be away from the home—for now—where you stay up nights waiting for the step on the stair that is not coming."

She flinched at his words, though she knew he did not say them to hurt her, only the truth as he saw it; the truth, if she were honest with herself, as everyone outside her saw it.

"There is ample room here and you know this house has always had more empty rooms than is good for a home. Just stay for a bit, let your friends look after you, not because you need it, but because we do."

He was being gentle with her, she knew, and he was right. At home she felt tethered to the pain of Casey's absence, straining with every cell, even now after all this time, to hear him, to sense him somewhere there, somehow. She had to move forward for the sake of the children, for her own sake, and for the sake of the man who sat looking at her with such worry in his eyes. And so they stayed.

With spring's arrival they moved outdoors into the world once again. They hiked and explored Jamie's mountaintop—the ponds and springs and small hidden valleys rich with plant life and little secret things that delighted the children. For Conor's birthday Jamie gave him a microscope and waders and the two of them became amateur botanists for the season. Slowly, she saw her son give his trust to Jamie, how he would take Jamie's hand when they were wading through tricky spots, how he looked to Jamie now for answers to his particular questions about the world. Questions he would have asked Casey. She wondered if she would ever be free of this—this lack of Casey in her world, in the small details of her day, free of the void that carried within it always his absence—absence of body, mind and spirit. Sometimes she thought she would do almost anything to be free of it, and other times she thought she would rather lose a limb than lose that absence of him. Because if that was lost, he would really be gone from her, forever.

As she roamed the hills and valleys with Jamie and the children, she remembered what it was to be a child herself, where an idea could fill your entire body until you felt so giddy with it that you were like a balloon carried on a summer breeze. How an oyster shell found unexpectedly could fill an entire day, a tree with a bird's nest an entire week, the sea and the stars an entire life. She rediscovered the passion she'd had for botany as a child. She assembled a herbarium with Conor, filled with what plants they could find so early in the spring. Many of the pages were taken up with mosses and lichens. Beside each specimen she had drawn small quick sketches of them, and added the name and classification next to it. Through that endeavor she rediscovered her childhood love of drawing and took to sketching illustrations for the stories Jamie had been telling to the children in the evenings.

The world away from this mountaintop seemed terribly distant. There had been no word of whether the police intended to pursue a case against her for the murder of Jamie's uncle, there had been no word of anything, for Jamie had put a moratorium on bad news of any sort, unless it was absolutely vital that she know it. So far he hadn't considered anything vital enough to be relayed to her. Pat and Kate had been up to visit several times, but they were careful in their conversation with her and told her nothing she didn't already know.

When April arrived she knew it was time for her to move back out into the world, and that included returning home with her children, even if she dreaded it a little for the fear that came with living there alone. She wanted to talk to Jamie about it first, in part because he had taken such good care of them all, and also because she tended to want to discuss all matters in her life with him now. She had begun to feel that a piece of news was not properly digested until she had talked it through with Jamie. And there, she knew, lay very dangerous territory for the both of them. It was partly why she knew she must go home.

Two nights later, she had her chance. She had gone home that day to check over the house, and make sure it was still intact. Lewis and Owen had been looking after things but she wanted to set eyes upon it herself. She'd gone alone for she had other business which required her attention as well.

They were alone in the study, a rare event as there was almost always someone around. Shura had retreated upstairs in the grip of one of his dark Georgian melancholies and Vanya was out, having found work at a rather grotty pub in the Cathedral Quarter. The children were snug in their beds, sleeping deeply after an afternoon spent out-of-doors.

"Chess?" Jamie asked. He had brought the beautiful Alice in Wonderland set up from his grandmother's cottage and they had played several games in the intervening weeks.

"I don't think I quite have the mental fortitude for chess tonight," she said. The trip home and her other errands had exhausted her.

He was standing by the chess set where it sat before one of the long windows. Each piece glowed where the light of the fire touched it. There was a sort of fine-drawn tension to him tonight. It wasn't uncommon, only this felt different to her somehow. It was probably time, she thought, to stop keeping company with Russians steeped in mysticism. The next thing she knew she would be consulting the Ouija board to collaborate on her decisions.

"Would you like a drink?" he asked.

"No, I don't think I should attempt alcohol just yet. You know that even when I'm in the pink of health, an eyedropper full can make me tipsy."

He poured himself a drink from one of the decanters in which a very fine make of his own whiskey was kept. She was surprised because he was normally more abstemious than she was. He came, whiskey in hand, and sat down in the chair across from her. The room around them was warm and cozy, a sense heightened by the wind moaning at the windows, and sleet hissing against the glass. It was lovely to be inside, with a fire and only Jamie for company. It was rare to have him to herself and whether it was selfish or not, she did enjoy having his undivided attention every now and again.

She watched him as he relaxed, and was happy to see that he looked well. He'd regained the muscle and flesh he had lost to Russia, and he had enough energy of late to light up a city if they could have found a way to channel it. He smiled at her, as if he sensed her thoughts. A strange intimacy had grown between them throughout her recovery. It was an intimacy which she realized had always existed between the two of them but had been brought into the light because of their time together here away from the usual concerns that haunted both their lives. She had in these months, rediscovered laughter as well, for with the recovery of her body she had found a small corner of happiness and the ability to laugh without feeling like she had betrayed Casey.

"Everything was well at your house?" he asked, turning the tumbler of whiskey in his hand so that it caught the light, fretting it into small splinters of gold that darted and shimmered in the bowl of the crystal.

"Yes," she said slowly, aware that wasn't the question he really wanted to ask.

"And your meeting with Noah? Did that go well, too?"

"How did you know that?" she asked, sitting up sharply, the sense of cozy amiability abruptly banished.

"You didn't take the children with you," Jamie said drily, "and as Conor has been wanting to go home and check on all his haunts on your land for weeks now, I deduced there had to be a fairly good reason you left him behind."

"Jamie, I don't expect you to understand this, but I needed to see him. I fell off the map in a way and I would rather he didn't worry, nor have his men guarding my land when it's not necessary. He has been very decent to me, it's simple courtesy to see him now that I'm able."

"Don't insult me, Pamela. You and I both know it's not simple courtesy."

"I know how naïve you believe me to be and maybe I am to a certain extent. Maybe you have to be born here to be as suspicious and paranoid as I need to be to never put a foot wrong. But I'm not the girl who came here all those years ago, surely even you must recognize that."

"No, Pamela, I don't think you're naïve and that's the problem, isn't it? Because if you're not naïve, then you're being reckless."

"I'm not reckless, Jamie, it's not as though I joined the PIRA and roam the countryside looking for soldiers to shoot at."

"You don't need to look for soldiers, Pamela, they come to you and knock at your bloody door!" He stood up suddenly, clearly too agitated to sit.

"*That* is not my fault," she said and stood up too, facing him. She was shaking but it was with anger rather than weakness for a change. Things had escalated so swiftly that her heart was pounding against her ribs like a trip hammer and her skin so inadequate a defense that she felt like a cracked eggshell, long emptied of its contents and prey to every rough wind which passed.

"Isn't it? Had you not gotten involved with Mr. Murray, I doubt they would have interested themselves in you. Now you're right in their damn crosshairs."

"Yes, they are interested in me because they believe I'm an avenue for them to get to Noah. I refused them. I'm not crazy."

"You don't know though, Pamela, what *his* agenda is."

"And you do know? What about you, Jamie? All the nights you're not home, all the times you tell half-truths about where you've been. Your life is hardly an open book either."

"*I* don't lie to you, Pamela, I just can't always tell you what I'm doing, and you know why."

"And you," she said angrily, "know why I went to him. I would follow Satan through the gates of hell on a brimstone pony if it meant I could find out what happened to Casey."

"That is what frightens me. The truth is if I can't find out what the hell happened to Casey—and believe me I have pulled in every favor and twisted every arm I possibly could—then there's no way Noah is going to find him either. So what kind of game is he playing stringing you along with half hints and rumors, which I believe he knows full well have no foundation to them."

She sat back down and put her hands to her face, suddenly terribly exhausted.

"Pamela, I didn't mean—"

She shook her head. "Yes, you did. I'm not upset, only you'll have to forgive me if I'm not quite ready to give up hope just yet."

"I wouldn't expect you to, Pamela. It may be that the complete lack of information is a good sign. I put things rather bluntly, and that wasn't my intention."

She looked up, and felt as if every day of the last eighteen months was stamped indelibly on her face.

"You know it's *not* a good sign, Jamie," she said wearily. "I just can't help but keep looking, and if Noah can find any little clue that will tell me where to look and what I might find…" she turned her hands up helplessly.

"And what is it you think he wants from you in payment?" His voice was very soft, but she knew better than to mistake it for his temper having cooled. "Do you really believe he's doing this just so he has a safe house now and again for a man on the run?"

She shrugged. "I don't know, and perhaps it doesn't matter."

"How can it not matter?"

"Because I don't have it to give, Jamie. It isn't like that with him," she said, "and even if it was I don't have to succumb to it. I am a rational being with a brain and autonomy."

"I know, I am rather well acquainted with your autonomy, Pamela."

"I'm not the little girl you met on Martha's Vineyard anymore, you can't save me from myself."

"I know that, too," he said. "I realize it doesn't seem like it at times. I just don't want you getting hurt any more than you already have been."

"I can keep my head about it, Jamie. I do understand what he is."

"I know you believe that you do, and perhaps you are right, Pamela. But men are territorial beasts and I have seen how he looks at you. I don't think this arrangement is anywhere near as simple as you believe it to be."

She looked up at him, at the green eyes blazing with anger, and the peculiar tension which still crackled off him. And suddenly she felt like someone had ripped the blinders from her eyes. It caused a visceral pain in her chest, as if she'd been cut across the heart.

"Jamie, is it only Noah we're talking about here?"

"No," he said at last, his voice so low she had to strain to hear him. "I don't suppose it is."

"Jamie, I—" she began, but he shook his head.

"Please don't. I already know what you're going to say and you don't need to. I'm out of line tonight, and I apologize."

She stood, weary and knowing that there was nothing she could say that would help to alleviate this divide which had, without warning, opened up between them.

"You're tired, you should go up to bed." He had walked over to the windows and she understood that he required distance from her.

"Yes, you're probably right," she said, afraid that she was going to cry if she didn't flee his presence. She would not do that to him. Leaving the room was the least damaging option at present.

"I'm going to pack up the children and go home in the next few days, Jamie. I think I've stayed long enough. I'm strong enough to manage on my own now."

He nodded, but did not turn to face her. The subtle tension had become something raw which she knew he did not want witnessed any longer.

She turned back in the study doorway. "I would have you know this—there isn't anything between Noah and me and there never will be."

"You might, Pamela," he said, his tone cold, "want to make sure he understands that, too."

Chapter Forty-two

Fire Without Smoke

Yevgena arrived for a visit near the end of April. She came with her vardo in tow and only a girl for company, a shy young thing called Esme. This lack of a retinue was unusual in itself for a woman who normally had a cluster of courtiers that travelled with her from one country to another, as she followed the sun and seasons. The vardo was parked on the far side of the mountain, away from the house and the view over Belfast, in a hollow ringed with ash and oak and holly.

On the first Friday of Yevgena's visit, she invited the lot of them to dinner at her encampment. And so it was they made their way down from the house in the late April afternoon, muffled in sweaters and scarves, and wool caps, children in their arms and bottles of wine and whiskey to share. Shura carried his balalaika because music at such a gathering was inevitable.

Pamela, Isabelle in her arms, glanced sideways at Jamie, as he walked companionably at her side, Kolya propped up on his shoulders and Conor by his side, taking three steps for every one Jamie took. It had been two weeks since she had moved back home, but she still felt a reserve with him, and while he was as friendly and informal with her as he always was, she sensed that he had, in some way she couldn't quite define, distanced himself from her. She understood why but that didn't make it any easier to bear.

There was a great fire burning when they arrived, its flames leaping high and hot in tongues of crimson and violet and gold. The scent of roasting meat and abundant spices pervaded the air. Around the fire was a circle of low-slung canvas chairs, fitted with quilts in jeweled colors and cushions of silk adorned with feathers and beads. Pamela had long ago decided that Yevgena was in possession of a magic trunk which had a limitless capacity to store treasures of this sort.

Their hostess awaited them in a crimson wool-lined caftan, embroidered with golden thread, her dark hair bound up in a length of violet silk and her hands beringed with a variety of precious metals and stones. Her dark eyes were impossibly huge, outlined with smudged kohl, and a collar of purple stones ringed her throat. Tonight she was pure Roma, a vagabond spirit as mutable as smoke, and a conduit of fortune and fate.

The ancient cauldron in which Yevgena had cooked innumerable meals over the years hung over the fire and was the source of the savory smells. She came forward to greet each of them, enfolding both Jamie and Pamela in her embrace, along with Kolya and Isabelle. Conor, she knelt down to greet, and got one of his rare but effusive hugs for her pains. Vanya kissed her on each cheek and presented her with a bouquet of scarlet anemones, which he had grown in the vast greenhouse on the estate.

"Why thank you, beautiful boy," Yevgena said and kissed Vanya's flushed cheeks. Shura, in a manner totally at odds with his usual gregarious nature, hung back in the shadows of the April dusk, his balalaika forgotten at his side.

"Are you all right?" Pamela asked, wondering what had silenced the man in such a thorough manner.

"She is like an empress from a fairy tale," Shura said, lifting a hand toward Yevgena, his whole countenance one of wonder.

"She is," Pamela agreed, "now come and meet her. If you make her come to you, you may well regret it." She gave him a tug on his sleeve to pull him forward into the firelight.

"You must be Alexsandr Kobashivili," Yevgena said, using the formality of his name as Russians did to show respect.

Shura swallowed and looked up at Yevgena. He appeared to be rendered speechless, and so he settled for bowing low over the hand Yevgena had given him and kissing it with the effusiveness only a Georgian could get away with. Yevgena spoke to him in Russian, the rumble of Slavic vowels and consonants like smoky cold vodka and chilled black earth, causing Shura to smile and look down, his ears bright red with pleasure.

Dinner was a Hungarian stew, well flavored with paprika, onions, tomatoes and peppers and accompanied by a great floury wheel of country bread. The conversation flowed easily, along with wine and whiskey for the adults and milk for the children. There was laughter and talk of everything from cabbages to kings; music and books and travel and the politics of lands other than their own. Jamie led the talk and the laughter, as he so often did, flinging out the filaments of fancy and filigree, poetry and prose, humor and history and they all followed the bright shining threads and helped him to weave a whole tapestry in which everyone partook equally in the making.

Later, when the talk quieted and a certain soporific contentment stunned the company like a hive of bees well smoked, Yevgena rose and went to her vardo, returning moments later with a battered violin case in her hands.

"I have fed you," she said to Jamie, "and now I want some music in return. I do believe," she turned and smiled at Shura, "I saw a balalaika in your hands earlier."

She placed the violin beside Jamie and then plucked Kolya from his lap so that he had no excuse not to play. He looked somewhat bemused by the instrument even as he took it out of its case.

"You play the violin?" Pamela asked, and her voice held a note of incredulity that caused Jamie to laugh.

"I am a rich man's son," he said wryly, "do you honestly think I could have escaped my childhood without music lessons of every sort? How many instruments do *you* play?"

She laughed. "Touché, Mr. Kirkpatrick. The answer is I play none well, but I play three passably."

Jamie bowed to Yevgena and then gave a quick nod to Shura, who picked up his balalaika and settled it on his lap.

"My technique is rather rusty, so let your ears be forewarned."

Jamie played far more than passably. In fact, she was taken aback at just how well he did play. She had spent many months living in his home over the years, and she had never once known him to pick up an instrument.

The balalaika took the low road, frolicking along the lane, stopping to smell the flowers, heating up slowly as the notes rushed ever faster. The violin took to the air, Jamie keeping pace with Shura, and Shura's face lit with joy at finding this unexpected partner in music. They played half a dozen tunes back-to-back, all gypsy melodies, Shura only needing the opening notes to follow Jamie seamlessly through the songs. Jamie put the violin back in its case at the end of the sixth song.

"My bowing hand has found its limit," he said, and Pamela thought for some reason this was not true, and that he simply did not want to play any more music for reasons he wasn't about to share.

The fire was making her pleasantly drowsy, and the enjoyment of the evening showed in the faces around her. The children were exhibiting signs of sleepiness too, though Isabelle still wriggled on her lap like an electrified eel. Like her father, she was not one to sit still often or for long.

"Yasha, will you tell us a story?" Vanya said now that the last rollicking notes had dissipated into the night. He turned to Pamela, "Yasha told us many stories in Russia by the fire at night. He had us all under his spell."

"I have no doubt of that," she said. Jamie merely raised one gull-winged brow at her.

"Oh yes, Jemmy, please do, I have not had the pleasure of your storytelling in many years," Yevgena said.

He sighed. "I know when I'm outflanked. Well, Conor-lad, what will it be tonight?" he asked, looking down at the small boy who was snuggled in to his side.

"Hedge tales," Conor replied without even pausing to think about it. Once she had been well enough, after her illness, to sit in on Jamie's nightly storytelling, she too, had listened raptly to the 'hedge tales' each night.

She looked over Conor's head at Jamie, even Isabelle settling in as a hush fell over the gathering. The fire lit half of Jamie's face, leaving the other side in shadow. It looked like a mask, one of both comedy and tragedy, a storyteller's face. Conor leaned in toward the fire, his own small face alight with anticipation. He loved Jamie's stories, both because they were always magical and because they had provided him with a foundation through their telling when his mother had been sick.

Jamie began with those most ancient words that storytellers had used since time immemorial. "Once upon a time…" And so the magic began, as his words slipped around them all, binding them in his spell.

"Once upon a time there was a boy who lived near a hedge that was forty feet high. The boy had never been beyond the hedge for it was forbidden. Children had been known to disappear and never return when they had wandered too near the great hedge and there were terrible tales about a troll that lived on the other side of it. Fledge was always careful to give the great shrubs a wide berth when he was driving the cows home of a night, even though in late summer the berries hung on it ripe and red and sweet and ever so tempting. But on this particular night when our tale takes place, Fledge drew near to the high dark hedge, for he could hear for the first time, all sorts of things going on beyond it—the bright, rollicking notes of a squeezebox, the shimmering call of mares to their foals, bare feet dancing, and the smells—oh, the smells—nettles rolling in a boil of lavender water, cotton fresh plucked from sun-steeped bushes and woven into blankets, blackberries newly fallen from their thorny perches and sweet as sugar in the nose."

With Jamie's words, a breeze sprang up, as if it had been conjured expressly for his purposes. They sat rapt for the next half hour, even the children quiet, Isabelle asleep on Pamela's shoulder, Kolya drowsing in Yevgena's lap and Conor gazing up at Jamie's face, as Jamie wove a world for him from glowing threads of adventure and adversity and friends and foes. He placed each of them within the story with small details here and there: a faun with amethyst eyes, a shortish man who had a way with poetry, a Gypsy woman with a secret past and the ability to tell outrageous fortunes and a woman who came from the sea and could not find her way back to it. And in the center of it all, a boy named Fledge, who roamed the world over the hedge and had the sort of adventures in which boys both little and big delighted.

A half hour later, the words began to slow, indicating that Jamie was wrapping it up and slowly releasing them from his tale.

"...as far as Fledge's eye could cast itself were caravans and animals and women in brightly-colored clothes and men in rough leather jerkins and boots with worn down heels from many miles of traveled roads. There were camels and packhorses and stallions screaming as they scented mares in heat. There was music and raucous laughter and women calling for children. The children were everywhere. He had not expected children, for the journey beyond the Edge of the World was a very difficult one."

Jamie smiled down at Conor, who was leaning into him, half asleep. "I believe that's the best place to stop for the night."

Jamie and Conor had formed their own relationship when she had been sick. She knew Jamie had done everything he could to allay Conor's fears about her, and now Conor trusted him completely.

She always felt like the world stopped when Jamie told one of his stories, and time was hesitant to take up its run once again when he finished. For a brief moment she had forgotten herself, and the world around her, as if she had been suspended in that far land beyond the hedge. The same regret she felt was printed on the faces around her, as though they were all emerging back into this world and finding the light too harsh.

Kolya was fast asleep by the time the story was done, limp with exhaustion in Yevgena's arms, tiny thumb stuck solidly in his mouth. Jamie walked over and picked him up, easing Kolya's thumb from his mouth with a soft *pop*.

"I need to put this little man to bed," Jamie said.

"Bring him along to the other vardo," Pamela said, "he can sleep with Conor and Isabelle." Jamie's own caravan had been set up a small distance away, in the shelter of a large oak, expressly for the purpose of tired children.

She stood, holding out one hand to Conor, her other arm wrapped firmly around Isabelle.

"Come back for a little brandy, darlings, when you have the little ones down. We can easily hear them from my vardo," Yevgena said, and gave Pamela's shoulder a quick squeeze.

The blue caravan sat within the shelter of an overhanging oak, which cut the worst of the night's chill wind. Isabelle was limp in Pamela's arms; her tiny mouth open in the deep and dreamless sleep of the very young and Pamela laid her down and tucked the blankets around her snugly. The caravan was cozy, for Esme had lit the fire in the cast iron stove a little while ago, so that it would be warm enough for the children to sleep.

Jamie stepped up behind her, and she looked over her shoulder at him. The night wind had ruffled his hair, and the gold of it shone brightly against the flame of Kolya's head nestled on his shoulder. "Fatherhood suits you, you know," she said, smiling over at him.

"Thank you, but it seems rather selective in the arena it chooses for success," he said, his tone dry, with a note of something else underneath.

"Julian?"

"Who else?" He smiled at her over Kolya's head, but there was a particularly bleak quality to his expression that told her things had not improved since Julian's visit of a few months ago.

"Have you heard from him lately?"

"Yes," Jamie said and the brevity with which he spoke the word, made her hesitant to ask anything further.

She took Kolya from him carefully, though once he was asleep there was little short of the Russian Army marching through in full cadence, which would wake the child. She put him in beside Isabelle, making certain they were well covered. The two tiny heads lay in contrast, like that of night and flame.

It took only a matter of moments to get Conor settled, and then Esme showed up at the door, a small stack of books in her hands that she offered to read to Conor.

"I will sit with him," she said.

Pamela accepted gratefully, pausing to plant a kiss on each of the sleeping children's foreheads and to give Conor a hug and a kiss. He was snug in the quilts with the two babies fast asleep on the other side of him, Finbar curled up on the floor below, Esme with a book already open in her hands, pink cheeks aglow in the warmth of the vardo. Pamela suspected some of the pink in her skin came from the glances she had cast toward

Vanya all night. She sighed, and wondered not for the first time why love always had to be so complicated.

Jamie was waiting for her at the bottom of the vardo's steps.

"Shall we?" he asked, and offered her his arm.

They walked back together, quiet, the wind rushing through the branches above them, whispering softly through the new leaves of spring. It was a time of year that Jamie loved, both for the eternal hope of spring's promise and the temperamental nature of the weather. It had been a strange day, one of those where the atmosphere seemed especially thin, as though ghosts flitted through the air around and eyes peered from behind the young greenery. He had long wondered what it was that was present on such days, but was thankful they were rare for it always unsettled him deeply.

He glanced at the woman who walked beside him. She appeared fully recovered now, if still a little too thin. He had been aware of her observing him tonight and had been careful to school his face for he did not want to make her uncomfortable again. The reserve between them had been noted, he knew, on both sides.

In the vardo, Vanya was still chattering away happily in Russian with Yevgena and the scent of Russian tea filled the small space with its rich smoky smell. Shura had left to go back up to the house, pleading exhaustion and still looking like he had been hit by a bolt of lightning.

Pamela settled in on the ornate built-in bench beside Jamie. She smelled of the night—smoke and food and wine, with the threat of rain threaded through her hair. Jamie put his hands on his knees to steady them.

Yevgena sat across from the two of them, a crimson shawl wrapped around her, highlighting the dark hair and eyes. She was ageless, Jamie thought, and still a beautiful woman. He thought it a pity at times that she did not have a man in her life anymore. She had told him once, that after his grandfather died she had closed the book on romance. There would, she had said, never be another. He often wondered how badly she missed him.

Around them the vardo creaked, protesting the brisk wind that had sprung up. A smatter of rain sounded against the windows. Pamela picked up the cup of brandy Yevgena had set before her and took a long swallow, her eyes watering as she put it down.

"Yevgena," she said, and something in the three simple syllables made Jamie turn to look at her. There was a nervous eagerness in her face and he feared he knew exactly what she was about to say.

"Yes, darlink?"

"Would you—would you read my cards? Please, Yevgena. I asked you once before and you said no, and I understand why. Tonight, though, I would like you to read them for me."

Yevgena looked up at Jamie and he saw the worry in her face at the request. Yevgena could read cards in different ways, and usually it was no more than reading the person and their tells and adding in a few things they wanted to hear. But there was another way, and Jamie knew when it happened she had little control over it. This night, this thin spring night, with the wind moving through the treetops like the lament of a ghost... he shivered, this night could well bring a reading of the other sort. Later, he would wish he had stopped them both right there, had claimed a headache and bustled Pamela on her way. Regret was like that—it saw things so clearly in hindsight.

"Because it is you, darlink, I will do it, but they are just cards and they can only make guesses, they cannot give you the exactness you desire."

Yevgena's dark eyes held Pamela's green ones in the flickering light of the candles.

"I know," Pamela said, "it does not matter."

Yevgena retrieved a carved wooden box from a drawer under the vardo's bed and brought it back to the table. It was filled with small velvet bags and Jamie knew each bag held a different set of the tarot.

A shiver of apprehension went through him as he watched Pamela look over the bags. Jamie knew no answer the cards could provide was going to satisfy her. Nothing short of directions straight to a very much alive Casey was going to satisfy her, and that just wasn't going to happen. Despite what she had said, he knew it did matter, it mattered to her too much to play around with half-answers.

"You have to choose the deck. Close your eyes, your skin will know the right cards," Yevgena said.

Pamela's fingers hovered over the velvet bags, sweeping one way and then the other. She touched a black bag, embroidered with tiny crescent moons. "This one," she said and opened her eyes.

"La Luna," Yevgena said, her voice distant like she spoke from a place far away. "O *Shion*. You have chosen the lunar deck. Take the deck out and shuffle it, Pamela."

Pamela did as she was bid, and slid the deck out. Yevgena looked at it and then flicked a quick look up at Jamie, a look of puzzlement. About what he did not know.

"You keep shuffling, I just need to get one more thing." Yevgena stood and went to the narrow cupboard beside the little stove and returned with an object cradled in both hands. In the center of the table, she set a large and lustrous stone, which held in its core the light of the moon. It was the biggest moonstone Jamie had ever seen.

"During the Middle Ages," Yevgena said, "it was believed that if you gazed long enough into a moonstone, you would fall into a deep sleep and dream of the future. The Romans believed moonstones were a bit of the moon fallen to earth, magic made solid. I believe they help the cards to align properly and therefore the reading is more powerful."

Jamie looked at the cards in Pamela's pale slender fingers as she shuffled them. The backs were dark with no discernible pattern or script. He recognized them now and he understood the look Yevgena had given him. He had never known her to use these cards.

"You will remember these cards, Jemmy. Your grandfather traded a perfectly good watch for them in a souk in Marrakesh. I scolded him over that—giving up a nice watch for a tattered old deck of cards."

A grue rippled up Jamie's spine. Oh yes, he remembered it all too well. Yevgena had not been present so she didn't know the whole story of that day's events. He and his grandfather had been deep in the souk and his senses had been swimming with the scents and sounds of the medina: the smells of turmeric and cardamom, fenugreek and cinnamon, saffron and cumin; the bright and vivid colors of the silks and wools and cottons; the baskets spilling over with figs and dates and salted almonds and lemons; the screech of caged birds and the flicker of dark-eyed girls in silks that flowed like ink and the singsong chant of the vendors hawking their wares.

The seller of potions and ingredients for black magic was in a tiny stall with dark cloth covering its walls. Jamie was only fourteen at the time, and was, of course, fascinated by anything occult. He had left his grandfather haggling with a man who sold silk shawls and entered the little shop alone. At first he had not seen the man behind the counter, for he'd been mesmerized by the oddities surrounding him. There had been a fortune teller's table in the middle of the small space, with the seven symbols of Arabic magic carved into its surface. There were tiny drawers stuffed to brimming in a cabinet—filled with strange things: feathers and fur, small balls that looked like twists of string and let off a foul odor, stretched skin that appeared to have once belonged to a reptile, oils with black things suspended in them and spices that smelled bitter and were as dark as jet. There was one last drawer he peered into and then drew back, for it contained human hair of a variety of colors and lengths of cutting. There was something repulsive about it.

The walls were hung with cages and in the cages were live chameleons, cobras and salamanders, rabbits and mice and in one corner, a caged falcon, his back to the room, huddled over in a miserable ball of dusty feathers. The falcon turned as he passed its cage and the one golden eye met Jamie's, sealing both their fates in that moment. Because in that eye was the final desperate plea of an imprisoned animal, whose life was flight. To cage a raptor was worse than killing it.

The man emerged then, startling him, for he moved as silently as a snake. In his hands he held the contents of the last drawer into which Jamie had peered. A snarled ball of hair, black and red and brown. But not a single thread of gold.

"It is the hair of dead men, very powerful this is." The man looked at Jamie's head, shining like a freshly-minted guinea in the dim shop and narrowed his eyes like someone getting ready to barter. He reached out to touch Jamie's hair and Jamie jumped back not wanting the dirty, long-nailed hand anywhere near him. Instead the man grabbed Jamie by the wrist, his nails like long talons and each one inscribed with a dark crescent moon.

He felt his grandfather come into the shop behind him, and the senior James spoke in Arabic, his voice quiet, but with an edge to it that other men ignored at their own peril.

"This one has magic in him, I could teach him many things," the man said, his fingers digging more deeply into Jamie's wrist. He said something in Arabic then, something that caused his grandfather to step forward and detach the man's hand from Jamie's wrist and then put his arm around his grandson's shoulders.

"He is not for you," his grandfather said and Jamie breathed out a sigh of relief. "We need to go."

"I can't leave just yet," Jamie said, though he longed to run out of the dark hovel and back up into the light and color and the surging crowds of the souk.

"The bird?" His grandfather knew him better than anyone else in the world and he understood without Jamie explaining.

The man smiled, his gold tooth winking obscenely. "The bird is special; he came here all the way from the snow covered Koh-i-baba Mountains of Afghanistan. He came with a great magician, who had crossed the sands between there and here a hundred times in his life. He left me the bird and a special deck of cards, and said they must stay together for these two things were all he had left from a lifetime of magic."

"We don't need the cards," his grandfather said.

"If the boy wants the bird, he has to take the cards, they go together or not at all."

"I'll take the cards, too," he said before his grandfather could say no. All he knew was that he had to save the falcon. He was not leaving the souk without it.

"The cards go to the gypsy," the man spit to the side, "that lives with you. She will recognize them for what they are."

Jamie felt a jolt of shock that this man knew of Yevgena, but then Marrakesh was like that, as if a sinuous vine of information ran beneath its streets and people could tap into it at will.

"We need to go, son," his grandfather said, and he realized at no point had his grandfather said his name in front of the man. He took the cage with the falcon in it and his grandfather took the small lettered bag with the cards after handing over his lovely watch, which was the price the seller insisted upon. They did not speak until they were well into the medina and his grandfather stopped to get them each a sweet mint tea. They drank their tea where they stood, the falcon quiet and watchful in its cage.

Even after the tea Jamie was still shivering and the bones in his wrist ached where the little man had clutched them. "What did he want?"

His grandfather looked at him, his face thoughtful but somehow sad. "There are people, Jamie, who want to cage anything they find beautiful and use it to serve their own purposes. I think that is as much as you need to know just now."

He had named the falcon Sameyel, for the hot desert wind that blew in the spring. He had spent his month in Morocco feeding the bird and caring for it until it could fly on its own power. The cards he had given to Yevgena, who had thanked him but had, he noted, touched them with reluctance. He thought she had tucked them away or perhaps discarded them years ago, and now here they were in Pamela's hands and he felt a dread premonition at the sight of them.

Yevgena's eyes were trained on Pamela as she shuffled the cards, though Jamie knew she had heard his own thoughts as clearly as if he had spoken them aloud. There was a terrible concentration on Pamela's face, lashes shuttering her eyes; he knew they were dark and strained, as they had often been these many long months.

Pamela stopped and looked up.

"Lay the top ten cards out in a circle around the stone," Yevgena said. Jamie didn't like the sound in her voice, there was something under the usual Gypsy glamor, something that didn't sound like her at all.

Pamela laid them out one by one, face up, as the tarot required.

"This is the present day," Yevgena said, pointing to the first card that had come up, which was the Queen of Swords. The picture was of a weeping woman alone in a forest, blood dripping from the end of the two swords she held. In the upper left-hand corner was an Arabic symbol. He remembered the symbol from the carved table in the souk that day. Black magic. The sort that was not meant to be trifled with by someone like Yevgena, who had always been a dweller of the in-between places.

"The Queen in this position represents many things—loneliness, anxiety, sadness. She is lost and alone in the forest, but this position also represents change and the hope of direction out of the forest."

Yevgena flashed a look up at Jamie, and he knew she was leaving out part of the card's meaning. The Queen in this position was a widow, which also carried a variety of meanings but Pamela was likely to only see one.

"The Lovers," Yevgena said and Jamie's head snapped up in alarm, for her voice didn't sound like it was her own anymore, but rather being channelled from some other place, beyond that door in the thin spring night. He had seen this happen once before with her and it wasn't something he enjoyed, nor come to that did she.

Pamela leaned forward, and he could see that she was trembling, as if she shook with a great chill. He felt a bit of it himself. There was something else in this caravan with them, something that was standing near, a presence that was undeniable. The same presence he had felt that night in his own bedroom, when Pamela had reached out for a man who was not there. Pamela's eyes had turned a deep and heavy green with agitation, every hair standing up on her arms.

"There is a longing, a yearning that will cross continents and seas, a longing that does not understand its own mind, but that is of little account in matters of love and passion—there is such passion, one that would burn all to ashes that come near it."

The candles flickered suddenly, as if something had passed through the vardo and attempted to extinguish them.

Vanya stood and left the vardo then, a gust of chilly night wind heavy with the scent of hawthorn filling the small space before he shut the door behind him. Jamie did not blame him one bit, he did not like the feeling that had seized the air around them.

"Are you certain you wish to continue, Pamela?" Yevgena asked, and there was something distant in the question that made Jamie fear the worst, that what was coming in the rest of the cards was not going to be anything Pamela wished to hear.

"Yes, I do, please go on," she said. Her hands were fisted in her lap, the skin on her face drawn tight against the elegant bones. Every inch of her spoke of both tension and longing, a longing that would indeed, cross continents and seas, if only it could.

"The Knight of Cups. It is the knight that holds hope; it is his gift after a long search the world over. He has traveled over and under a boundless sea. There is great darkness as well, a darkness that could snuff the moon. And pain, and a very long journey both of spirit and body."

He could not bear to watch the woman at his side anymore, and so he stood and opened the door of the vardo, stepping down onto the stairs. Vanya was nowhere to be seen. There was no moon, and beyond the small glow of the fire, the darkness was absolute. In Russia he had learned the art of hearing but not listening, of shutting the gates to the senses, and allowing nothing through which he did not want to deal with. He had discovered recently that when it came to certain people, certain moments, certain stresses, he was no longer a master of this art. He had seen the cards, all ten—the card of judgment, the djinn, the warrior, the star, the tower and the devil, as well as one strange card in the tenth spot with which he was not familiar. He knew much of what Yevgena would say had she the choosing of her words this night, and knew just as certainly that it was not her in command of the words, but something darker, something that brought with it the knowledge of that world between. Something that had always been with these particular cards.

The bird and the cards go together or not at all.

The seller's words had come true, for although he had set the falcon free, it had returned to the doorstep of the house they rented in Marrakesh, where he found it one morning, its neck snapped and its wings torn. He had learned long ago that he could not alter the destiny of another. He could not make Julian his son in anything but biology, he could not bring Andrei back to life, nor save the lives of his three sons, and nor could he save this woman from her pain and the journey she must make through this darkest of forests, alone.

He stepped back into the vardo a few moments later, hoping the reading might be done, just in time to hear Yevgena say, "And now for the last card."

The words snagged on his ears, and the gates to his senses, jarred, opened again.

"This is the Lazarus card, foretelling of those who die but are reborn. This can mean many things, of course. A fresh start in life, the turning of a corner in a road long traveled, a change of heart. A dying to a life that is done in order to begin again in a new life."

Pamela swallowed, her face deathly white. "That card is upside down, Yevgena. What is the meaning when it's upside down?"

"It means nothing, darlink, please do not worry." She pushed the card to the side, but Jamie saw how her hand trembled and knew the card troubled her greatly.

"Pamela, it's late, I think perhaps—"

"No, Jamie. Yevgena, please, what does that card mean when it's upside down?"

Yevgena shook her head. "I am telling you the truth, Pamela, I do not know what that card means. It should not be in the deck."

"Just—tell—me," she said through gritted teeth.

Yevgena merely shook her head again, the light from the candles casting a gruesome shadow over her face, so that she looked both ancient and forbidding, like some Greek soothsayer of old.

"It is darkness," she said finally and Jamie wanted to stop her, even though it was far too late for such things. "The sort of darkness that is between heaven and hell, what you might call purgatory, but what I would call Gehenna."

"Oh," she said, and it was a small sound, like the pop of a bubble or the last of a woman's hope. "Purgatory or simply death without any life to follow."

"Pamela—please, do not set too much store in what I say. I am only an old woman, I get muddled sometimes and they are, after all, only cards," Yevgena said, her face pained by the effect her words had wrought.

"I think we both know that's not true, Yevgena," Pamela said and stood, slender form rigid with dashed hope. "It's all right, you only did what I asked you to do, it's not your fault if I can't bear the answers. Now, please excuse me, I'm tired. I'll say good night now."

Jamie watched her until she disappeared beyond the edge of the fire's glow and he heard the door of the blue vardo open and close. He looked back at Yevgena, who was huddled in her shawl, looking suddenly exhausted, as if she had held a glamor about her all evening which had suddenly broken and crumbled to dust.

"What the hell was that about?" he asked, for she had upset Pamela badly and he was angry.

Yevgena clasped her hands together, her face pale and drawn. There was not much in this world that could upset Yevgena, and he felt his anger die back a little.

"I am sorry for that, you know I love Pamela, Jemmy, and I thought perhaps I could bring her some small comfort. But I have never seen a spread of cards like that. It's like he is neither dead nor alive, but in limbo or purgatory. And those cards—I have never used those cards, they are cursed! I don't know how they got into the box with the others. I never had the courage to burn them, but I always keep them separate from the rest."

In all the years he had known her, Jamie had never seen Yevgena so agitated.

"They are, after all, only cards," he said, echoing her own words in an effort to soothe her fears a little.

She shook her head. "No, Jemmy, not tonight. Sometimes they are just cards and I am just reading the person, rather than the spread. But a few times in my life, something else has come over me, entered into me and then I know whatever the cards say is true."

"Well, they can't be this time," he said with some exasperation, "because the man can't be both alive and dead at the same time." Her words had unnerved him for he had seen it—seen the shadow that passed over and through her, and had felt Pamela start toward it, a terrible yearning in her face.

"Yes, he could," Yevgena said, clutching her shawl around her tightly, face strained in the low light of the candles.

"How?" he asked, curious but also with a strange feeling stealing over him, as if Casey stood out there in the dark night, just beyond the reach of the firelight.

"Long ago," she said, "I met a man who did not know himself. He wandered into our camp from somewhere in the mountains, he'd been lost for weeks, maybe even months. By the time he came across us, he was half-starved, injured, and more *mulo* than man."

The strange tingle passed over Jamie's skin again. *Mulo* was Romany for ghost. He sat down across from her and took her hands in his own, to steady her while she told her tale.

"You know how Gypsies are, Jemmy, we did not want this outsider amongst us. He frightened many in our camp, for how can a man not know his own person? He was angry, too, so angry—*that* frightened me, though I understand it better now—how could a man not be angry when he couldn't remember his own story, for what are we if we have not our stories to tell?

"He came to me one night, a night not unlike this one, with the wind wild in the treetops and the moon gone away to its dark side so that the very air was like black velvet, so thick you could taste it on your tongue and feel it with your fingers. He asked me to use the crystal ball or the cards and tell him what he could not remember. But of course that is not the way such things work. I tried to do it for him. I was curious, and I felt sad for him, too. He did not frighten me as he did the others, for I was different—of the tribe and yet not, with a history and entire life from before, from that other land, before I met Mihai and married him. And so he spoke to me. He said inside his head it was like a very bad snowstorm, where he was condemned to walk, and that now and again he would see figures in that snowstorm, just outlines but when he reached for them, they would disappear."

She paused for a moment to take a swallow of brandy-laced tea.

"Dreams are strange things, Jemmy, and belong to another realm, one that most of us cannot cross over to without sleep to aid us. All those dreams we have, all the love and hate we feel, all the joy and all the pain, all those things do not leave this world. I think perhaps at night when we dream, those things mingle with the dreams of others—with their hate and their joy and their pain. So there it is, all those things rising into the night, over our humble little vardos, like smoke drifting toward and through the smoke from another person. That night I dreamed his dreams, and felt that he had once been loved and known, that he had once had an affinity for the land, had known passion and gotten a woman with child. But also he had done bad things, had bad intentions in his heart and seen them through to actions. It was both dream and nightmare and when I woke I was sweating and my heart was pounding. I stayed awake for a long time, Mihai and my children breathing peacefully around me. Near dawn I fell back to sleep, and dreamed no more. When morning came, like smoke, all of it had vanished. And so had he. The men looked for him, but they could find no trace of him, it was like he had gone up into the air and extinguished, like the spark from a fire. Later I wondered if he truly had been *mulo* and had somehow crossed into our world, to haunt us for a little time and then vanish again when he found the door back to his own world."

The grue was firmly back in his spine now, though his pragmatic side told him it was a combination of the lateness of the hour and Yevgena's ability to convey the chill of an event that had taken place fifty years before. The cold feathers trailing up his back said otherwise.

"You and I both know that the obvious answer is that Casey is dead and that he has been dead from the day he disappeared. I met the man while you were in Russia, and there is nothing that would stop him from coming back to his family and to Pamela. Their love was a living force; I could feel it all around them."

"I know. I can't see how the man could be alive and not find his way back to her and their children. I know how he felt about her. It just isn't possible that he's out there somewhere. I haven't been able to find a trace of him, Yevgena, not a single clue or sign."

Yevgena shook her head slowly, the wings of dark hair threaded through with a silver like that of fresh forged metal.

"Then tell me, Jemmy, how can a man be both dead and alive all at once?"

Part Four

The Lotus Eater
San Francisco, Spring 1976

Chapter Forty-three

The Lotus Eater

THE BIG MAN HAD come into the shelter on a bitterly cold night two months ago. At first Father Jan had been a little afraid, for the man was rather formidable looking, dark and large and with an aura about him that said he wasn't a man to be regarded lightly. But he had been polite and quiet, merely wanting somewhere to shelter from the weather, which was cold enough to kill a man that particular night. There was something about him for he seemed as if he was dislocated in time and space. That was common enough with the people who sought shelter in his church, mind you. It was more than that though, for he seemed like the sort of man who ought to have a more solid existence, rather than the ghostly one homeless people often led of drifting with neither the anchor of home nor the love of family and friends.

He hadn't spoken beyond please and thank you and had eaten lightly of the supper that was offered. He'd helped with the cleanup and then lain down on the cot allotted to him for the night, turned his back on the room and gone to sleep. By dawn's light the man was gone. He had not expected to see him again, yet on the next cold night, there he was. Father Jan wondered where he went on the other nights, for he always appeared to be clean and well enough groomed. Scary as hell, with those dark, forbidding eyes and powerful body, but clean and always civil, even if there was an air about him that made the other people in the shelter steer clear of him.

He had very few belongings, but that wasn't unusual for a man without a home—a canvas bag which he wore slung across his chest, with a change of clothes and a battered copy of *The Odyssey* in it, which Father Jan had seen him reading at night if there was a light handy by which he could see the words. He wondered if the man identified with Odysseus and his long journey home in some way. He was curious what his story was, for he didn't seem to carry any of the usual crosses of the homeless—chronic addiction, abuse, mental illness—or at least not in any way Father Jan could discern, and he had gotten rather good at guessing people's stories over many years of priesthood and running the shelter. He didn't ask the man though, for he had learned long ago that people either wanted to tell their story or they didn't, and he suspected the man fell into the latter category.

He didn't see him for a few weeks after that, when he heard from others in the shelter that the man had a job fighting. He wasn't sure what that meant until he heard just where the fights were held. He understood then why many of the shelter people gave the man a wide berth.

The next time the man showed up was the night the boiler broke down. The boiler was old and on its last legs and it gave out with a wheezing clang that shook the walls of the building. The night was bitterly cold and the shelter was crowded. Father Jan couldn't find a repairman willing to come before morning for the weather was unprecedented and his wasn't the only boiler needing emergency attention. He sighed, while he was a handy man when it came to the various ailments of the human soul, he was hopeless with machinery of any sort.

The big man came up beside him just as he was rolling up his sleeves in the hope it would make him feel more capable of tackling the boiler.

"If ye have a toolset, I can maybe fix it for ye. I won't guarantee it, but I'll have a look an' see what I can do."

"Do I look that dubious about my ability to fix it?" Father Jan asked, smiling.

"Aye, ye look a wee bit like a bushman confrontin' civilization for the first time."

Father Jan did have an antiquated toolset and he handed it over happily, following the big man down to the boiler room where the boiler was so ominously silent that he was certain nothing short of divine intervention would ever get it working again. Apparently the man was an angelic emissary, for within an hour he had the boiler rumbling and throwing out heat like a forge.

"You have some experience of machinery?"

The man shrugged. "I didn't know if I could fix it to tell you the truth. I just had a sense that I should try and see if I was able."

"Come up, I'll make tea," Father Jan said. The man nodded, which surprised him, and followed him up the stairs and into the small kitchen off the supply closet.

Father Jan made tea in the Polish manner, which required two pots and an enormous amount of tea leaves. He brewed the tea in a small pot and then poured it into a larger pot and diluted the incredibly strong brew with more boiling water and milk. He brought the large pot to the table along with two chipped mugs and a bowl of sugar in case the man preferred his tea sweet. Father Jan watched the man out of the corner of his eye as he did all this, and noted how restless he was. Some part of him seemed to always be in motion, hands drumming on the table or his one foot tapping the floor. And yet, there was a stillness at the core of him that seemed to watch and wait.

"Wow," the man said after his first swallow, "that's got a real kick to it."

Father Jan took a few swallows of his tea, relishing the heat of it on this chilly night. He leaned back in his chair, his cowboy boots tilted up as he relaxed.

"You will forgive my curiosity but I should like to ask where you stay on the nights you don't come here?"

The big man regarded him, the dark eyes looking him over and assessing his trustworthiness. When he spoke his voice had an edge to it, as if the information didn't come easily to his tongue.

"I sleep out, there are places even in the city where a man can sleep relatively safely. Safer than most shelters, an' I don't like to ask for a bed if I don't need it. I shower at the Y an' wash my clothes often enough so that I don't feel like I'm a cave man entirely."

"Forgive me, but you don't seem like a man I'd expect to find on the streets."

The man shrugged and Father Jan felt the suppressed power in so simple a gesture.

"If I had a story, I'd tell it to ye," he said, wryly.

Father Jan raised a bushy eyebrow at him. "Everyone has a story; it's only whether you are comfortable in the telling of it."

The big man shook his head. "No, not everyone. Well, here it is as such, Father, I don't know who I am. What little I do know is because it was told to me by doctors. I was brought off a ship into a hospital in New York five months ago. They didn't know if I'd live. I'd been unconscious apparently for some time. I was in and out of consciousness in the hospital for a few weeks. I'd been beaten an' shot as far as they could tell, the ship's surgeon had attended to me as best he could an' then a couple of sailors dropped me off at the hospital. The doctors at the hospital said it was blows to my head that caused the trauma an' apparently knocked loose my memory."

Father Jan felt a look of incredulity spread over his face. The man noted it; it appeared he didn't miss much.

"Aye, I know what ye're thinkin'. It's more common than ye'd imagine, though."

"What do the doctors say about your memory?"

"Well," he laughed, but there was no humor in the sound, "they have a name for it, just not a cure. They say I ought to be dead, an' it's only that my skull is so thick that it prevented the bullet and the beatin' from killin' me. It's called dissociative fugue, for all the good it does me to know the name, when I can't even recall my own life. My mind might return one day, an' it might not. They can't tell me anythin' definitive on that score. Some things are there—like fixin' the boiler for instance, I just had the sense I could do it."

"Do you have a name?" The priest asked.

"Aye, not one that's mine really, it's Mick—Mick Flaherty. It's what one of the nurses called me—Mick because I'm Irish. I know that I'm Irish at least. I can't get identification, not without a social insurance number, an' I can't get one of those without a history. Fortunately, I can still get work because a lot of the construction projects around the city don't require ID; they're happy enough to pay off the books."

"Did you pick Flaherty? Or did the nurses pick that for you too?"

"No, I picked it. It was the first Irish name that came into my head."

"Maybe it has meaning for you then," the priest said.

"Maybe, it doesn't feel quite right, the shape of it in my head. But I like how it feels on my tongue, an' I had to pick a name of some sort."

"So do you not have the money for more permanent shelter?"

The man named Mick shook his head, placing his big hands on the table and stretching them, fingers digging into the scarred surface. "I'm not entirely skint, but I like to be outdoors as much as I can. I work construction partly for the reason I told ye—because they don't care if ye've a social insurance number an' partly because it's outside. I can't take the lights an' noise of confined spaces for very long. It's why I don't come in here unless it's too cold to stay out-of-doors."

"Some of the people here tell me that you fight at Molly Malone's."

The big man looked wary and Father Jan thought he might have pushed things a comment too far.

"Aye, I do. D'ye have an issue with that?"

"No, only I wonder, particularly when you've had such serious trauma to your head, why would you invite more?"

The man named Mick took a deep breath and then leveled a dark look at Father Jan that made the priest wish he hadn't asked the question. "I get this terrible black anger sometimes. It comes over me an' takes possession like a demon would. The doctors say it's not entirely uncommon in someone with my condition. Mood swings, rage, depression an' so on. For me mostly it seems to be anger. Maybe anger that I can't remember my past. The fightin' is a way of dealin' with the rage. No one gets hurt who didn't sign up for it. The doctors told me if I was a hot head in my life before then the injury makes it worse. They said anger has a quick 'on' button with head injury, it just flashes up an' takes over. The front part of my brain, the bit that says 'no, don't do that, it's a bad idea' doesn't work as well as it ought to. The neurologist I saw told me the front part of the brain is like a thermostat on a furnace, controllin' the heat that the furnace can reach, so basically my thermostat is pretty faulty."

"Do you have any sense of your life before this happened?"

"Sometimes," the big man said, "I have dreams that haunt me durin' the day, they're so vivid an' they hang in the air for a few seconds after I wake, but I can't grasp on to them quick enough to remember them. When I try they seem to disintegrate in the air, it's like tryin' to grab onto a bubble and feel its shape in yer palm. It bursts at the slightest touch."

"Do you think you lived in Ireland before this? Have you thought about contacting the police there maybe, see if someone might know who you are?"

"I don't know, an' truth be told I'd hesitate anyway because someone clearly wanted me dead, didn't they? Until I know why an' what happened to me, I don't know that it's safe to try an' find out who I was. I don't know where to begin to tell ye the truth. My memory only goes back as far as the hospital in New York. I made my way here on a bus a few months ago. I figured if I was goin' to live outside as much as I seem to need to, I'd better find a nicer climate."

Father Jan wasn't surprised. San Francisco had long worked like a magnet and those who were lost or sad, or wanted to leave behind who they had once been, were like so many iron filings that could not resist the lure of this city by the sea.

"There are a lot of people here in this shelter tonight who would like to forget their past, forget who they are and what they've done. It's why some of them drink or do drugs. It takes away the pain for a bit of whatever it is they want to forget. Maybe you forgot because you needed to."

The man shook his head. "Sometimes I feel like Odysseus, an' I've come ashore in the land of the Lotus Eaters an' eaten of the flowers. Trust me, Father, if I knew how to come back to myself, I wouldn't hesitate."

Chapter Forty-four

Molly Malone's House of Blood and Pain

MOLLY MALONE'S IRISH PUB was in the Tenderloin district, where long ago many of the Irish had settled when they had come in their droves to this city by the bay. Molly Malone herself was a more recent arrival having come over from Cork when she was just a slip of a thing. Now she was on the wrong side of fifty, with hennaed hair and a look that could cut a man dead in under a minute. Rumor had it she had once been a rich man's mistress and before they'd parted ways he had set her up with this pub. She still worked behind the bar most nights and it was her and her alone who decided who was allowed down the back stairs behind the bar. If Molly didn't like the look of a man, he was denied entrance pure and simple. Eddy's face was one she knew and liked, so she gave him the nod and opened the counter flap without so much as removing the cigarette that dangled from her lip.

Eddy had come to watch the big Irishman fight. He'd seen him a time or two around the construction site and then heard about the fighting from the men he worked with. As he went down the narrow stairs the smells of sawdust and spilled beer, sweat and slick sticky blood rose up to greet him. He felt the kick of adrenaline that a fighting pit always gave him.

Here the pit was just a big room which ran under the entire pub and a little beyond. The floor had a thin layer of sawdust, mostly to soak up the beer and the blood. There was always something—a ring, a platform, a field with boundaries, a battlefield bounded by stone walls—but all were merely a stage, for fighting was nine parts spectacle and showmanship and one part brutal, bloody savagery.

He knew the things that kept you upright in the ring, the strangeness of it, the urge to half kill a man with whom you had no real beef. Sometimes men did die in the ring and yet even with that knowledge there wasn't fear; there was adrenaline and sometimes rage and the strange stillness that came over a man before a fight. He knew that many people believed fighting was uncivilized and not a natural thing. But he thought for most men it came as naturally as breathing, that it was simply part of the human animal, an ancient part that everyone held in their blood marrow.

The Irishman had just come out into the light, his opponent one of those brute looking men with a shelf for a brow and small mean eyes. The opponent had tattoos down both arms and a big tiger across his back. He was taut and curled, bouncing on the balls of his feet. The Irishman on the other hand was loose, assessing his fellow combatant with eyes that were almost blank in their lack of expression. The referee, a little guy named The Cowboy for reasons Eddy had never been able to fathom, was talking to them now, the three heads together. Then they broke away from each other and the fighting began.

He knew boxing; he had boxed for years and had in his turn taught it to young boys on the reservation where he'd grown up. When you were on the bottom rung, you needed to know how to fight your way up, actually knowing how to physically fight was never a bad skill for a man to have in an often hostile world. Bare knuckle fighting was a beast of another nature though. It was fast and dirty and bloody. Some fights only lasted a couple of minutes; most might go about twenty if the opponents were evenly matched. Which was not the case here at all. The bald man with his tattoos was in way over his head. The big Irishman was doing little more than playing with him, tapping his face or stomach now and again, but the bald guy was already bleeding from his nose and one of his eyes was swelling up.

He looked the Irishman over. Fighters usually weren't so tall, most men fought better with a lower center of gravity. Clearly, his height was not a problem for this man. He had an air around him of barely leashed brutality. He had a reach on him as well that kept the other fighter at bay much of the time. The only way to really hit him hard enough to make a difference, Eddy thought, would be to get in under those arms, otherwise it was hopeless. The man had an incredibly powerful hit on him.

He didn't think he'd seen raw, pure anger like this more than a couple of times. It was the eye of the tiger that the best fighters had, that strange calm fury that existed at the center of the hurricane just before it unleashed its rage and destruction. The Irishman was keeping it chained right now, but Eddy could feel it coming off of him the way he could feel steam coming off a pipe that contained boiling water. He wondered what it was that had given the man this sort of anger. The bald man had managed to get in under the big man's arms, and was trying to maul him which didn't seem to faze the Irishman much. The ref merely pulled them apart and told them to start again.

Gleaming with blood and sweat, the two men faced off again. Eddy didn't think any of the blood belonged to the big Irishman though. Someone, somewhere had taught this man how to box, because he knew how to throw and hold a punch and how to reserve his energy for when it was truly needed. He also was using a flurry of lightning-fast combinations that only someone trained to box would use. Most bare knuckle fights were more like barroom brawls contained in a small arena.

It was here in the middle of a bout that a fighter could lose his heart, lose his drive and go down for no real reason other than the middle minutes could take a man down and make him believe he couldn't last the distance. In boxing the middle rounds were the no man's land of fighting, a place a fighter could get lost and lose his shot at winning. The bald man was tiring badly already and the Irishman seemed to be drawing the fight out so that his opponent wouldn't collapse on him, but it was no more than a cat toying with a mouse that it would eventually kill at its leisure. He could have knocked the other fighter down any time he wished, but it was clear he wanted to just keep fighting for as long as he could keep the other man up on his feet. The fight was at the forty-five minute mark by Eddy's reckoning and that was about twenty minutes longer than it should have gone.

And then he quickly finished it, as if he felt some mercy for his opponent, with an uppercut to the man's jaw. The man went over like a tree that had been axed for a good hour and then felled with one last stroke. The hit was hard; it must have felt like a mule kick to the man's jaw. The big Irishman looked around, his eyes like black fire, hot and consuming, and his stare was a challenge, like he was seeking another man to beat. His eyes met Eddy's a few seconds later. Eddy held the look but didn't respond to the challenge of it. The man glared and then suddenly smiled.

He thought he recognized a kindred spirit in him, if such a term could be used for a man to whom you were drawn because he was lost and angry. He walked over to where he stood.

"Can I buy you a drink, man?"

The big Irishman looked him over, suspicion in his face but curiosity as well. Eddy knew he wasn't the usual rough-faced white man that habituated this place. He merely stood and took the man's scrutiny. At five ten he was a good six inches shorter than this man, and he was on the lean side because he didn't remember to eat more than once in any given day. He had a neatly-bound braid that fell half way down his back. He wasn't a big man, but like this man in front of him, men tended to give Eddy a wide berth.

The Irishman nodded finally. "Sure, why not?"

Eddy waited upstairs for the man, and had a pint of Guinness on the table waiting for him when he came to sit down. The man had showered and had on fresh clothes. Eddy wondered if he lived here. He knew Molly rented out a couple of rooms upstairs, they were no more than single rooms with a shared bath, though.

"You want anything else—a whiskey maybe?"

"No thanks, I don't touch the hard stuff."

Eddy nodded. He didn't touch the hard stuff either, mostly because there was a time he had touched it far too often.

Molly came over and put a plate with steak and fries on it in front of the man.

"Ye all right then, Mick?" she said, handing the man silverware wrapped in a cloth napkin.

"Aye, I'll do, Molly. Thanks for the food."

"Ye're welcome, laddie." She put a hand under his chin and turned his face up to look at her. "Ye've not a mark on ye," she said, sounding pleased. Eddy was struck speechless. Generally speaking, Molly was about as sweet as a grizzly bear with a hangover. She walked off back to the bar sashaying a little, and Eddy couldn't suppress a look of astonishment.

The Irishman noted it. "She likes to mother me," he said, "I think it's because I'm Irish."

Eddy, who had seen the look on Molly's face didn't think mothering was exactly what she had on her mind.

"I didn't know there was a kitchen in this place," he said.

"There isn't as such," Mick replied, "Molly insists on feedin' me after a fight, she knows I don't eat ahead of time as my stomach is too wambly for it. Help yerself to some chips if ye like."

Eddy took a couple and was surprised at how tasty they were. He wouldn't have pegged Molly for a good cook.

The Irishman stuck out one big hand. "Sorry, I don't know where my manners are, I'm just always famished after a fight. My name's Mick Flaherty, an' yers?"

It was a challenge—*Who are you and what the hell do you want with me?*

"Edward Two Feet Walking," he said.

"That's an interesting name," Mick said and took a drink of his beer.

"It's because I was always wandering off even as a baby, my mother was forever tracking me down. I always wanted to see what was over the next horizon, and then when I found that horizon I wanted to see over the next, so I just kept walking. And that is how I got my name. I even signed up to go to Vietnam because it was another horizon. Which just goes to show you how stupid a wandering man can be."

He had been purposeful in mentioning 'Nam. He wanted the man to know he understood fighting because he was pretty damn sure this man knew violence outside of the ring too, and had for a very long time.

"I've seen ye on the buildin' site?" It was a question and it wasn't. Eddy already had the sense that this man didn't miss much. "An' at the mission?" Eddy revised his opinion, the man didn't miss anything.

"Yes, you have."

"So has the good father told ye my story then?"

"Yes, he did. He was pretty brief in the telling."

"That's because the story is just that short." Mick's voice was abrupt. "So is that why ye asked me to have a drink—because ye think I'm a lost soul?"

"And if it is?"

"I don't need yer pity, man."

"Did I say I pitied you?"

"Fair enough."

Eddy might not pity the man in front of him, but he did feel a certain sorrow for him. He was very familiar with the territory of the lost. He had been lost himself for a very long time and the path back to life had been thorny and steep and painful.

"What do the doctors say—on the odds of your memory returning to you?"

"They don't know really, it's a crapshoot. I might get everythin' back tomorrow or I might get some memories back but not others an' then I might not ever get anythin' back at all."

"You're Irish, clearly. So maybe that's where you start. Figure out if that's where you were living when this happened. Eventually, even if your memory doesn't return you'll find out who you were. There are all kinds of ways to be lost, man, but there's just as many ways to be found."

"Ye sound like ye're speakin' from experience."

"You could say that, I suppose. I did three tours of Vietnam because once apparently wasn't enough for my insanity. I came back and found out I didn't have a home anymore. I didn't fit in the white man's world, and I didn't fit in the Indian world anymore either. I had to go on a long trip, physically and spiritually, before I felt like I belonged again, because I realized a man has to belong to himself before he can be a part of anything larger."

"Are ye from here?"

Eddy shook his head. "Is anyone from San Francisco? It's one of those places, you know, it's the edge of something and not just the continent, it's a beginning and an ending. San Francisco was a point of disembarkation for soldiers coming back from 'Nam, some got here and just stayed. When you're already half a ghost you know there ain't nothing for you back home because it's not real anymore. Who you were doesn't exist and the new person you've become has no place, except in streets like these and other places where nobody cares who you are or where you've been."

"So where did ye come from originally?"

"South Dakota—a reservation there to be exact. I'm a full-blood Sioux."

"Do ye miss it—yer home?"

Eddy nodded. "Sometimes, but it's like I said, I didn't belong there anymore. Tomas Wolfe had a point with that whole, *You can't go home again* line."

"Well, I hope the bastard was wrong about that," Mick said and took another bite of steak.

Just then a breeze entered the pub. It smelled of jasmine oil and hash. Every man in the place looked up as if they sensed the disturbance about to enter their midst. Molly Malone's wasn't the sort of establishment that attracted too many women. Other than fight junkies, or rather Eddy thought, watching the woman's eyes light upon the big Irishman, fighter groupies.

The flotsam and jetsam of the 60s had caught up hard when the decade changed and the world suddenly seemed a colder place. But in San Francisco the 60s lingered, even if it was a more tired and tarnished version. The woman who was now standing looking around the dim murk of the pub was one of the bits of flotsam which had caught up on the reef of disillusionment and found her way to the city by the bay. Eddy knew her because he recognized so many of the lost. He didn't particularly like her, though.

"You know her?" he asked the man. The topic could hardly be avoided as all conversation had ceased when the woman had come in the door.

"Aye, she's been in most nights after the fights. I've talked to her a bit."

"She's trouble and not," Eddy said, "the good kind."

"How so?" Mick's tone was merely curious. He hadn't looked at the woman more than once, though her eyes had not left him even as she ordered a drink up at the bar.

"She used to follow the Grateful Dead, and I heard she traveled with the Rainbow Family for a bit, too. I think she found them a little too tame though. I've heard rumors that she lives in some rambling old Victorian house out in Marin County that her grandmother left her."

"So why is she trouble?"

Eddy opened his mouth to answer and then promptly shut it for the woman had drifted over to their table, the jasmine and hash smell of her overwhelming. Bridget Lee was the sort of woman who could render a man mute. She was one of those fiery redheads with milky skin and eyes like sapphires—sapphires fractured with splinters of gold. Tonight, she wore a green dress that set off the flames of her hair and turned her skin to a fine porcelain in the low light of the pub. All around her shimmered a mantle of restlessness, true restlessness, the sort he understood all too well; it was a trait that could ruin a life, forcing a person to move on before ties were forged or roots were allowed to grow and mingle in the soil of family and country.

"Hey, Irish," she said to the big man. She had one of those voices that was like a breeze from some exotic place, low and throaty and making promises even when she was saying something prosaic.

"Hey yerself," he said. He was friendly but it was guarded and Eddy noted he didn't ask the woman to sit down.

Sexual lust, blood-lust, sometimes it was the same thing, especially when you had the women hanging around who were fight junkies, willing to do anything for the bruised and bloodied warriors of the ring at the end of the night. He wouldn't have thought that was Bridget Lee's scene. It *was* lust, though; there was no mistaking the look on her face for anything else. She touched the man lightly on his arm, and even so small a gesture held a wealth of invitation.

"I'll be up at the bar," she said, "if you find you want some comfort."

"What makes ye think I'm in need of comfort?"

She smiled, the cigarette smoke that always wreathed the bar, coiling around her red hair. "Aren't you?"

"Thank ye, I'm flattered, but no, not tonight."

It was polite, it was also dismissal. Bridget colored a little, but then Eddy saw the look that passed through those gold-splintered eyes and knew that dismissal to her was merely a challenge. She walked back to the bar and sat down. She probably thought the man would reconsider before the night was done. She might be right, too, for Mick's eyes followed her as she walked away. Eddy knew fighting often sharpened the other appetites, particularly the primal ones. It was what a warrior wanted after battle—a woman's touch to wash away the blood, a woman's body to take away the pain. When the man looked back his eyes were hollow. There was a deep longing there, but not for the woman who had just boldly offered herself for the night.

"Not many men would turn a woman down who offers to warm their bed, especially not a woman who looks like her."

The Irishman looked down at his plate and shook his head. Eddy noticed that there was a ring on his left hand now. He wouldn't have worn it during the fight, of course.

"You married?"

"Aye, I think I must be. The ring is one of the few things I carried from my life before into this one. I feel married, if that makes sense."

"It does. I think our cells and bones have memories, too. Those aren't so easily banished."

Mick looked up again, and the longing was gone from his eyes as though he had banished it through force of will.

"So is this city where ye found yerself again?" he asked.

"Yes. The story is a little more complicated than that, mind you. I found myself by looking after the lost. Ironic, but true. There are a lot of veterans here and just a lot of lost souls who need help. They need someone to aid them in figuring out the system, or maybe with luck figure out how to get back on their feet. I'm not naïve, I know I ain't no ministering angel or anything and most of the people I help are going to end up back on the streets, shooting smack into their arms again or whatever their poison of choice might be. But that's okay, if I help them find a hot meal once a day or maybe get one off the streets for good then it's worth it."

"Is that what ye do, collect lost souls?" The question was asked lightly, but the look in the man's eyes was hard enough to light a match on.

Eddy shook his head. "No, I just do what I can. I feel for them because there's always a reason they got lost in the first place. Some people stop looking for the lost ones, or they look for a few years and then give up in despair, then they try again for a few more years. It's a heartbreaking cycle, and there's always the tug of war in a person's life too—do they really want that lost one back? Because maybe they make trouble every time they're home. Maybe they break hearts worse when they are present than when they're lost. So I look out for them, and if someone comes looking I can help there too."

"Ye must stay awfully busy between that and the construction."

"Well, you know collecting lost souls doesn't pay real well. So I work construction Monday to Friday and I work the streets on evenings and weekends."

"So why the interest in me?"

"I think it's because you remind me of myself."

Mick raised his eyebrows at that statement and swallowed the last of his beer.

Eddy shrugged. "I know anger when I see it, it's like snakes in your head, man. I told you I was in Vietnam, so maybe you'll understand when I tell you I know blood and rage. I just thought maybe you could use a friend, someone who understands anger that eats you."

Mick startled a little and then he smiled, cautiously. "Aye, I suppose I could," he said.

"All right, then."

Eddy thought if the man knew the real reason he had approached him he would have thought he was plumb loco. You could hardly tell a man that your brother, dead now for some time, had come to you in a dream and told you to befriend him. No, you couldn't tell a man such a thing, you could only do as your brother, even if he was dead, told you to do.

Chapter Forty-five

The Dream

HE HAD THE DREAM the night he met the Indian man, as though the rage had ebbed low enough to allow something else in while he slept. He'd had it before, it was always the same. He was in a boat, a black boat with red-brown sails—a mainsail and two smaller foresails. The boat had a clean entry to it and cut the waves like a hot knife through butter. There was earth in the boat with him, solid clean rectangles of it, and the scent of it was soothing, dark with an edge of smoke to it. The boat went easy and so he could watch as the land came into view in front of him. Cliffs soared high against a silver-cloud horizon, gulls flying like small dipping arches in front of the great limestone face, dark and thick with acid green moss. Time came heavy with such a place, for there was wear on the rock, long ages of it, it was a land that knew itself intimately in joy and sorrow. Even in the dream he could feel his heart pounding with fear and excitement. He longed to reach the shore, but was afraid of it too. Why he should fear it, he did not know.

At some point in the dream, he realized there were oars in the boat and he picked them up, though they felt incredibly heavy and awkward in his hands. Still he managed to wrestle them into the sea and then he began to row. Sometimes in the dream he would make progress and at other times, he would not, he would just spin in frustrating circles. Regardless of whether he managed to get the boat to move, he never reached the shore, for just as he could smell the land, thick and sweet as honey in his nose, the weather came racing over the cliffs, the clouds dark and boiling with rain and wind. The storm came then, and pushed him back out to sea, so far that he could not see the shore and there was only water all around him, waves as high as buildings arching over him and crashing down, soaking him, the water in his eyes and lungs, so he had to fight for breath. Eventually the boat began to founder and break apart and he slid into the water, scrabbling at the pieces of wood, trying to grasp anything that would keep him afloat. But the wood dissolved into the raging grey waters, and there was nothing left for him to hold.

It was then he would awaken, just as he began to drown.

Chapter Forty-six

The Fighter

POST FIGHT EXHAUSTION, adrenaline down, muscle and bone starting to feel the beating they had just taken. He sat on the little bench in the tiny locker room, if so small and grotty a hole could be dignified with such a name. He had won, though he never found the fleet nature of victory to hold the same satisfaction as the bloody journey which got a man there. There was a part of him, small but growing, that wished he didn't need the fighting. Tonight he felt tired, both in body and spirit and his knee felt like it was on fire. It had taken every ounce of willpower he had out there to keep from limping.

Men often wanted to fight him. He suspected this had likely always been true for him. His size and something about him made them want to use him as a proving ground for their own masculinity. Finding the fights had been no problem. He'd asked around, but was careful about it, and one night when he'd gone into Molly Malone's just looking for a pint and something to eat he knew he'd found that which he had been seeking.

The redheaded woman had been there watching him tonight, watching him like he was the answer to a question she had been asking herself for years. He wondered how she'd bribed her way in; it wasn't really a female-friendly atmosphere after all. He understood the appeal though, it did something to some women. It was, he thought, the primal nature of it. It was blood and sweat and sex and testosterone and a sort of dark thrumming magic that came alive in the pit, as if life in the cave were only a few feet back and the memory of it no more than yesterday's.

Eddy had been there too. The two of them had become friends after that first drink. He had to admit to himself it was nice to have a friend. Even if said friend made a man roam the streets on weekends handing out blankets and food and listening to people's problems. The truth was he didn't mind, in fact he had found a real satisfaction in the work. He knew what it was to be homeless; he understood when a man was down that far it was hard to rise up. For the women it was even worse, as the risk of rape was ever-present. Some men assumed every homeless woman was a prostitute, albeit one they didn't feel the need to pay. Some of the lost lingered with a man—their stories, their pain, their humor in spite of the direness of their situations. There was one woman who had been wandering barefoot through Golden Gate Park last weekend despite the fog and cold that had permeated the day. He'd stopped to watch her, shivering, cold even inside a decent jacket. She was older, maybe early forties, sometimes it was hard to tell. There was a prostitute they regularly checked in on, who he had thought was nearing fifty, but Eddy told him no, she was just twenty-eight years old.

"The streets will do that to a woman—drugs, sex with strangers—it all tells on their faces. Mostly it's the heroin."

Mick had watched the barefoot woman, as she wove in and out of the oak trees as though performing some sacred rite, her long black hair wearing a net of mist pearls. She was tall, her face weathered but still graceful like she had once been the queen or empress of an ancient land told about in an old tale. She was terribly thin, as if she only ate enough to just keep herself alive. He had asked Eddy about her, knowing he would know her story. Eddy knew everyone down in the Haight and the Mission and they all knew Eddy and trusted him, too.

"They call her the Banshee down here. She cries when anyone dies, it's this horrible keening. It's totally unearthly at night, it puts a cold arrow through a man's heart."

"What's her story?" he'd asked, watching the woman as she swayed back and forth beneath a fall of hanging moss, like she heard beautiful music in her head.

"I don't know, nobody does. She has, literally, never spoken to anyone down here that I know of. If you talk to her she will just give you a thousand-yard stare, look right through you and out the other side. There was a preacher used to come down here and talk to people, he made the mistake of touching her when she wouldn't respond to anything he said. She stabbed him. Cut him pretty bad actually. She'll take food and water from me sometimes, but not always. I think something really terrible happened to her in the past and she's haunted by it. If you're going to offer her a blanket or some socks, just keep a safe distance from her."

He'd nodded, and dug through the bag he'd loaded up at the mission that morning, until he found a thick pair of wool socks that had been knit by a group of nuns who ran a soup kitchen down on Polk Street. He found a pair of boots he thought might fit her, too.

He had approached with the boots and socks held up, so she would know his intent and hopefully not panic. "If ye sit on the wee bench over there," he'd said, "I'll put them on for ye." He didn't think she would be able to manage with her chilblained hands. He'd made a note to find gloves for her; they'd just given out the last pair to a man in a wheel-chair who was panhandling on Larkin Street. He'd knelt down on the wet ground, the cold seeping up into his knee immediately. She had come and sat down, elegant despite her bare feet and dirty skirt. She'd looked at him curiously and then put one foot up as daintily as the empress in a fairy tale he had imagined her to be. He'd rubbed her foot first to get the circulation going. Surprisingly her foot was not as cold as he'd expected it to be. He'd rolled the socks on making sure to align them just right, so that the boots would sit comfortably over them. She'd continued to sit quietly while he put the boots on and tied them neatly, so that they were snug but not tight. He had the sense that she wouldn't like anything constrictive which lim-ited her movement. He understood that all too well.

"There, that ought to feel a wee bit better when ye're walkin' yer miles each day."

She'd surprised him then, by leaning forward and gently brushing her hand across his forehead, like she was trying to wipe away the cobwebs that obscured his mind. And then she had smiled and truly looked at him, and he saw clearly the woman she had once been long ago, locked away inside the woman she was now.

She hadn't spoken, though he had not expected her to. He'd stood and her eyes turned away from him toward the trees and wet raw earth of the chilly spring day. He'd returned to Eddy who was standing with a stunned look on his face.

"Holy shit, if I hadn't just witnessed that with my own eyes, I wouldn't have believed it." Eddy shook his head. "You got some kind of magic mojo goin' on there, man."

Mick had shrugged, the touch of the woman's fingers still cool on his face. Strangely, his head had felt clear. Not that memory had rushed back suddenly to fill his dented skull, only that it felt as if there was room for it should it wish to return one day.

He liked it, working with the homeless. It somehow made him feel less alone and lightened his own burdens. Because if there was one thing that was true, it was that there was always someone with a story sadder than your own, and a wound in their heart that wanted to swallow the world with its darkness.

A man walked into the little changing room, snapping his attention back to the here and now. He didn't like anyone catching him unawares, it always gave him a sick jolt of adrenaline and caused him to wonder what had made him this way, wary and afraid of anyone catching him off guard. This man wasn't unfamiliar. Mick had seen him at fights before, a few where Mick had merely been a spectator and four in which he'd participated.

The man looked like money. Flashy money, but money, nevertheless. His clothes were tailored and cut from expensive cloth. The coat alone would probably pay for six months on a room in the Tenderloin. He wasn't tall yet he managed to make himself seem big enough. He had brown hair slicked back and blue eyes that were just a little too pale for his skin tone. All four of his fights that the man had watched, Mick had won.

"Can I have a word with you?"

"Aye," he said, looking steadily at the man, "ye can."

The man stuck out one hand. "Hale is my name, Elijah Hale."

Mick took the man's hand and shook it. "Mick Flaherty." The man squeezed his hand a little too hard, as if he were making some show of strength. Mick sighed. He met far too many of this kind in the fight world. They were never the fighters but rather those who watched and believed they too could find glory in the ring or the pit, that they too could hurt another man until he was so exhausted that he begged by his very silence for mercy. They were wrong, but it never did any good to tell a man so.

"Ah, you're Irish, well that explains it."

"Explains what?" he asked, voice muffled by the tape he was pulling off his hands with his teeth.

"Why you're such a no-holds-barred fighter in the ring. So many of the great fighters were Irish—Dempsey, Sullivan, McGuigan, Conn—just to name a few."

"An' what do ye think bein' Irish has to do with it?"

"Everything. It's why so many of the great fighters are black in this country—or come from the lower classes—blue collar working stiffs."

"Oh?"

"It's because your fucking necks have been under someone's boot for so long, all you have left is rage. It's the one emotion left when everything else has gone for shit. It's that lush, beautiful rage. You have to know what it is to be down so far you can't fucking see up anymore, all you can do is fight your way back and hope to hell the light is still there."

"Is there a reason for this stirrin' oratory?" he asked. He was tired, his post-fight adrenaline long gone now.

Hale laughed, an unpleasant sound that did not invite one to join in his jollity.

"I see, you're a no-nonsense, get-to-the-fucking point kind of a man. I like that. I can work with that."

Mick was wishing this man was a no-nonsense, get-to-fucking-point kind of man, because he was starting to weary him with his talk.

"I want you to fight for me," Hale said, as if he was conferring some great honor.

"For you?" Mick asked, uneasy. There was only one reason a man would want him to fight and that was money. A deal like that was never to a fighter's advantage, not at this level leastwise and it more often than not included taking the occasional dive.

"Yes, it's a side venture of sorts."

He reminded Mick of the old time hucksters, just a bit smoother and infinitely oilier.

Fighting in and of itself wasn't illegal—what was illegal was the gambling that inevitably went along with it. Molly gave him a cut of the night's profits when he fought in the pit below her bar, but what this man was talking about was something else entirely. It sounded like a bad idea, absolutely rife with the possibility for legal problems. There were things to consider though. He had medical bills from his weeks in hospital that would make a banker weep for their size. He wanted somewhere to live come the winter this year too. Somewhere he could sleep out on the porch if he needed to, but *somewhere* nevertheless. And one day if he found out who he was, he wanted to possess the means to go home.

"What kind of money are we talkin' about here?" he asked.

"Depends on the fight and the odds. Two thousand, five thousand, maybe more if you keep winning."

Mick just barely refrained from letting his jaw hit the floor.

"Per fight?"

"Yes."

Temptation wore a thousand faces and this one was looking directly into his soul.

"Aye," he said, feeling unutterably weary. "I'm interested."

Chapter Forty-seven

The Ghosts That We Are
May 1976

THEY WERE SITTING HIGH in the hills above the bay, looking across to the lights of the city, the scent of the dark pines below them mixing with the salt and cold of the sea. It was a rare clear evening after several nights of being socked in with fog, thick as pea soup and the leading cause of traffic accidents in the county. The fog could kill here.

"You feeling ready for the fight?" Eddy asked, his back up against a large boulder, his black hair like a blot of ink in the night. Mick heard the hissing pop of a beer can tab being flicked open.

"Aye, ready as I can be."

Hale, true to his word had arranged a fight for the following week. It had been three weeks since the man had come into the locker room with his proposal. Mick had used the time wisely. Other than work and helping Eddy down in the Haight and the Tenderloin with his lost souls, he had been training hard—running miles into the hills around the city and out into the winding green lanes of Marin County. Eddy was working as his trainer in the evenings. He was like a drill sergeant, showing no mercy, demanding endless sit-ups and push-ups, making him work the heavy bag and the speed bag until he was sweating and trembling and ready to drop on his knees and beg for mercy. He was in terrific shape though, the best since he'd awakened in that grim hospital bed in New York. He was a little more nervous about this next fight. His opponent was a black guy out of Oakland and he was reputed to be tough as hell and quick as fury.

Eddy took a long swig off the beer he was holding. "It looks like a fucking fairyland over there, doesn't it? I guess it was at one time. I was here in the late '60s a few times and there was something special then; it was a fairyland fueled on acid and psychedelics but you could feel the hope of an entire generation like it had distilled down to something pure— something so pure that if you mainlined it, it would kill you. But what a high, man, it was incredible. I saw Jefferson Airplane in the park one time, Janis Joplin too—man that lady could sing, she made you feel her pain right down to your roots, way deep in your marrow. The fairies that dwelt here were the singers and the bards and the shamans and the mystics and the windy-footed children who came from all over this country, fleeing what was broken in their homes, praying to find something whole in this city. Maybe that's why you wound up here, instead of staying in New York, maybe every lost soul comes here hoping to find something to make them whole."

"Ye think it's not a fairyland anymore?"

"You can ask that, man, after the day we just had?"

"Point taken."

It had, in point of fact, been a tough day. They had gone to visit some veterans who were living in a dilapidated flophouse in the Haight. Mick thought they were probably squatting there because it sure as hell didn't look like a place where a landlord ever came by. A skeleton had greeted them in the upper hallway, a man with so little flesh that he appeared like skin stretched tight over unforgiving bone, as though the dim light in the place should shine right through him. He had been in a panic, grabbing at Eddy's arm and dragging him down the hall to a sty of a room. It was, Mick thought upon entering, one of Hell's inner circles. Around them were bodies, men barely alive, strung to the fulcrum of the world by the dark thread of heroin. It was like walking through a cemetery where the grave digger had neglected to do his job for several weeks. The room was littered with needles, white powder, filthy sleeping bags, empty beer cans and rat droppings. The man who the wraith from the hall wanted them to see was a young soldier—or he had been once, for he still wore the shreds of a uniform. Now he was a bundle of bones and fever and abscesses and dark veins running with infection. He lay in a pool of fetid sweat, curled around his pain and screaming, eyes sunk so deep in his head that he appeared more skull than face. Mick had carried him out, and it was like carrying bones and air, the only weight that of pain and dirty blood. They had taken him to a doctor who would look at him, help him and not fuss. It was one of the leftover free clinics from the '60s and the doctor who worked there was one that Eddy knew and trusted. The soldier had died later in the afternoon.

"Not my first casualty," Eddy had said flatly. "Probably not the last either. People die down here and go to their graves nameless, nobody knowing who they are, who they were. It's fucking depressing. Or sometimes we do know who they are but no one in their family cares anymore and so they get cremated and buried where ain't nobody ever gonna visit their graves."

Sitting here now, Mick could still smell the man's blood and sweat on his clothes. He had held him in the back seat of Eddy's beat up old Pontiac while they raced to the clinic which was only a few blocks away. It had been too far.

They had driven to the hills because they both knew it was either that or go get shit-faced in a bar, which wasn't a wise move for either of them. So here they were, with a cold wind washing their skins and a six-pack of beer within reach.

"Some days it's too much, another day I could brush it off. You can't be sensitive and work on these streets; now and again though someone gets under your skin—maybe it's because he's a soldier or was at some point. I understand how he ended up in that shithole of a room, shooting smack into his body until it killed him. I almost was him."

"Vietnam?" Mick knew Eddy would either speak of it or he would not. His only responsibility was to listen if the man wanted to talk.

"Yes. Vietnam, fucking Vietnam. That bitch is always gonna be the most important woman in my life. She is always gonna be the one that changed everything and affects everything I do, every decision I make for the rest of my life and sweet Jesus, how I hate her for it."

Eddy looked out over the black water to the lights of the city, his gaze distant and, Mick thought, seeing another country entirely, one thick with green and with air that was even wetter than a foggy night here in San Francisco.

"I was in a Marine Corps Force Recon unit, part of a four man team that they'd insert into enemy territory to scout things out. They'd take us in by helicopter, drop us and leave. We'd be out there for two weeks at a time. There was no medic and no backup if things went squirrely. We didn't even eat our C-rations for fear our scent would give us away to Charlie. Sometimes we'd be only yards from the enemy, watching him, certain he was going to find us, see us, kill us in some god-awful way and no one would ever find our bones or know our fate. We lived in our spines; everything was instinct, right on the edge of our nerves. You live that way enough, staring into that sort of abyss, you don't really ever stop peering over that edge, seeing the darkness in everything. I came home and everything was just grey, didn't know my place, didn't know who I was anymore. I thought I was doing okay, you know, getting by, working here and there on buildings, walking that highwire on the struts, only sometimes I realized that it was just another way of staring into the abyss and thinking about plunging head first into it. Or sometimes I'd walk off a job, not really even knowing what I was doing, and then I'd wake up in another city two days later without any memory of how I got there. Hell man, I wasn't even drinking or taking drugs then, and when you black out without any sort of chemical assistance, well that shit is scary."

He shrugged, uncomfortable. "I think it's because you see shit and you got nowhere to put it, you know? We were moving from one village to another one day and this lady comes along crying and she's holding this little boy, he's maybe eighteen months old, and at first I think he's wearing torn up clothes, and then I realize it's his goddamn skin hanging off him that way. Just in shreds, cuz he's been burned by napalm that we fucking dropped that morning. And I stop, I just stop right there in the middle of a fucking bombed-out crater that used to be a road, and I'm pouring water over her baby, even though I know he's doomed, water ain't gonna help at that point. But I can't stop, I pour all my rations and then I grab another guy's like I'm trying to baptize him, or maybe drown him to end his agony. And that was one day, one dying child and one wailing mother—just one when there were thousands. I took uppers to get through the day, downers to get through the nights. It was like living inside a poison flower, caught inside petals that are slowly strangling you to death. The drugs allowed me to breathe and occasionally to sleep without ghosts yelling at me. Every day I'd wonder, 'Is this the day Charlie gets me, is this the day I drown in my own fear and blood? Is this the day I become a permanent resident of this crematorium they call war? And then it happened. I died there in 'Nam, poison flower caught me up hard."

Mick waited, he knew Eddy well enough now to understand that if the man said he'd died then he had, though dying could take a thousand forms, particularly in a war zone.

"We got caught out by Charlie one morning; he was up on us before we knew what happened. We got shot, they just machine-gunned us down. It was surreal as it happened, hearing the noise, feeling the adrenaline almost geysering out the top of our heads and knowing there was nowhere to run, cuz they had us surrounded. They killed all of us and then piled us up like we were dead animals in the yard of an abattoir. I was on the bottom of the pile. They stripped us of our helmets and gear and went away laughing. I thought I was dead and found it funny that I could hear them.

"I don't remember much after that, just that I woke up about twenty hours later, toe tagged in the morgue. They were getting ready to bag me and ship me home. You can imagine my confusion when I came around, tagged and nearly bagged. They'd pulled us out a couple of hours after we'd all been killed and the doctors said they couldn't find a pulse in me. They were shocked to find me alive, called me Lazarus for the duration of my stay in the hospital."

"Do you remember anything from that time—when ye were dead?"

Eddy looked at him, the brown eyes shrewd. "No, just a lot of blackness for the most part. It was real quiet, you know, the kind of quiet that makes a man itchy. But there was a bit in there—maybe it was just a dream—I was walking with my brother back home, on the reservation. Up in the hills where the stones stick up like a ridge of spine and the pine smells like the coldest, cleanest thing in the world. It felt real, it was part of why I was so certain I was dead."

"How did ye end up here?"

Eddy shrugged, a gesture of great eloquence with him. "How do any of us end up out here? It's the city of lost souls, San Francisco, people searching for meaning, people looking to disappear, people who ain't got nowhere else to go and know it's warm enough to live on the streets most of the year. It was the place to be for a while there, now everybody is just lost and drifting. It's a city for ghosts. Don't you wonder sometimes, Mick—I mean maybe we really are ghosts, you can't remember anything and I can't forget. Don't you feel like you're walking around without any skin some days, like the light and the dark just go through you and nothing stays, nothing remains? Like maybe I never came back from 'Nam and you never left Ireland? Like maybe this here is purgatory."

"Aye, some days I wonder, other days I know."

"You know?"

Mick struggled a little to say what he felt. It wasn't easy to explain how sometimes he caught a glimpse of the world before and it made him feel even more transparent in the here and now, as if he were part of the air, could melt into the fog and drift away over the sea and no one would know the difference.

"It's just that there was a time that I think I was seen and known, an' I think I knew my place in the world. I had roots, now I feel like I'm always at sea in a really small boat."

Eddy tipped his beer can at him in salute. "Well, here's to ghosts, the one that is me—because what the fuck else would you call a man who was toe tagged and dead for twenty-four hours—and the one that is you."

Mick laughed, though it was a hollow sound. "Because what else would ye call a man who has neither past nor name to call his own?"

This time neither of them laughed.

Chapter Forty-eight

The Maid From the Sea

HE HAD BLOOD in his eye and fury in his heart. It was the combination that worked best he'd found, except this time the blood was literally in his eye, which wasn't such a comfortable thing. Around him was the buzz of men high on fight adrenaline, even though it was just that of spectator. It had been the same through time, from the gladiator ring to the carnival fights of early America and then to the professional world of boxing. Men lived vicariously, their own blood rushing and the beast that lived inside each man waking up and roaring as they watched, going to the entrance of the cave and sniffing the wind for the enemy. Every wrong, every slight, every downtrodden moment of a man's life could be soothed for a few minutes by watching two other men beat the hell out of one another. It was basic and it was male. It was an acknowledgement of their own dark side without becoming part of it. Controlled violence was an opiate—a blood-mad, vein-rushing opiate.

The fight was in a big drafty old barn out beyond Altamont. It was also worth two thousand dollars to him. This would be no twenty-minute knockdown of some guy who thought he was tough. This was going to go the distance. He was going to have to reserve some of his energy, keep some of his bigger punches back, and not use everything up in the first fifteen minutes. He felt that out-of-body sensation he always got before a fight, and he took a few deep breaths, trying to bring himself back down to a place where he could feel his bones and muscles and the thunder of adrenalized blood pumping in his ears.

The man was big, not as big as he was, but heavier through the chest and shoulders and thicker through the legs. His head was shaved and his skin was so dark that it shone with a dull blue gleam in the flickering propane torches that lit the barn. He was silent too, moving light and quick on his feet, dancing in and out while he took Mick's measure. And then just when Mick thought he couldn't bear the pre-fight tension anymore, it began.

Mick started out with basic combinations—jab, jab, hook, right cross, jab, hook to the body, cross to the shoulder. Jab, uppercut to the jaw, left hook to the other side. Jab again to make space so he could back away, catch his breath before he pressed forward again. His blood calmed, and he could feel his bones again, he was back with his body and it was working for him like a well-oiled machine. They broke at the ten-minute mark, took a rest and rinsed out their mouths with water. Back in the fight, closing in, smelling the other man's sweat and blood. He still felt light on his feet; the pain hadn't found him and weighted his blood yet. The thrum in his head was there—left, right, left, left, right and then right, right, left—up and down, head, body, body, head—always changing up his combinations, trying to anticipate the other fighter's combinations before they came. This man was good, the best he'd fought so far, and he wasn't entirely certain he could beat him. He liked that, liked the uncertainty of it. Most of the men he'd fought so far had been little more than barroom brawlers. This man understood the art of it. Mick took a few hard punches, a right cross to his ribs that took his breath for a few seconds, and an uppercut that snapped his head a little. He jabbed and went to move in with a left hook when suddenly his peripheral vision went out, like someone had shut off a light. There was a flash in his head like a camera light going off, bright and brilliant and he saw a boy's face, just a wee boy, there and gone just as fast. The blow to the side of his head hit like a mallet and stars exploded in his view—big scarlet ones blossoming like poppies on a black sheet. He shook his head and danced back, giving himself a second before the man pressed his advantage.

He felt a moment's regret; the doctor had been clear about not aggravating the injury to his head in any way. The doctor didn't understand, that a man with no past and plenty of anger didn't always care if he lived or died. The truth was this, right now, locked in sweat and blood and fury with another man was the only time he did feel fully alive—roaring, blood and adrenaline pumping, shot up into the ether alive. The man locked in this space with him felt the same and the two of them fed off each other. The bastard knew how to box, he really knew, he moved and punched and jabbed and threw across the body blows that telegraphed power and pain even before his fist made contact. The exhaustion was going to set in soon, it did after a certain point, there was no help for that. He needed to find an opportunity before then, before he found that place of exhaustion because his knee was starting to pain him and if he got too tired it might seize up all together and then he would be nothing more than a punching bag for the man.

He saw his opening a couple of minutes and three bruising hits to his shoulder later. He took it with a jab and then a feint to the right so the man would think he was going to bring in a hard right cross. Instead he hit him with a left uppercut that snapped the man's head back and dropped him like a hundredweight of flour to the floor. He took a breath and backed away, letting the referee start the count. Here now with the stink of sweat and blood all around, and the numbers slowly building—one, two, three, four, five, six—he was content, he was alive, he was whole.

The win was still thrumming through his blood when he entered Molly's. He wanted the quiet of the place. He wanted to wet his throat and settle his blood before the pain set in. Win or lose, there was always pain, a man couldn't give nor receive those sorts of hits without pain paying him a visit later.

Molly Malone's smelled as pubs always did—spilled beer, smoke, and the fug of male bodies not necessarily well-washed. Molly always lit a peat fire on cold nights and he liked the smell of it, it calmed him and made him feel a fractured yearning at the same time. No yearning was ever whole for him, because he had no understanding of what it was he yearned for.

He reviewed the fight in his mind. What he might have done better, what the other man had done better, his combinations, his surprises, and the angle of his hits. There was always something to learn and store away, something to focus the next weeks of training upon. He wasn't a fool, he knew violence had a cost and he knew it was an animal a man fed at his own peril. He felt a narrow blade of pain down the right side of his head, where the worst of his injury had been. It happened sometimes and was on the opposite side of where the punch had landed. It was just pain. Except this time it wasn't.

"Violence is like a chained beast, boyo, an' if ye feed it too much it will just want more. An' then one day when it gets strong enough on all ye've fed it, it will break that chain an' there will be no controllin' it after that. D'ye understand?"

It was a strange echo, a voice inside his head that came from the very bottom of that deep well where his former life seemed to have drowned.

A voice he had known once, a man, one he had trusted implicitly. How it was he could understand that but not actually recall the man to whom the voice belonged, he didn't know. One of the doctors had told him it was likely he had lived largely by instinct, and had known he could rely on his instincts to guide him well in life, he said it was why he functioned as well as he did in his present world. The gist of it seemed to be that if he allowed instinct to guide him now, it might well lead him back to himself. Tiny echoes in a well that went on forever, and sometimes those echoes made him feel that it was more hopeless than if the silence had just stayed in his head the way it had been, like a snowstorm, ever falling but making no sound. Like the little boy who had flashed across his vision during the fight. Gone now, no matter how he tried to grab at the thin echo of the memory.

"Hey, Irish," said a voice off to his left. He turned. It was Bridget, form slender against the hazy light in which she stood.

He smiled. "Hello."

"Can I sit?" she asked.

"Aye, suit yerself," he said, the words rough but the tone amiable enough.

She sat beside him, so close that her arm was touching his, the scent of her in his nose immediately. Her perfume was spicy, and not entirely to his taste, but she smelled like a woman nevertheless and that was no bad thing after a night in the ring with a sweating, bleeding man.

She put a finger to the hand he had on the table, and traced the bruises and scrapes on his knuckles. Her hand looked delicate and impossibly white in contrast to his, big and brutal looking as it seemed to him suddenly. A hand that was capable of violence. He felt a sudden wash of shame go through him, that he had been flush with satisfaction over that violence only a moment ago. He curled his fingers under, not wanting to be touched.

"I saw you fight tonight. I've never seen anyone fight like that. You scared your opponent and I don't think that man scares easily. You got a lot of anger in you, man. I guess what I wonder is why? What drives you?"

"I don't know," he said, voice rough and the cold copper taste of blood in his throat suddenly. "I guess it's because I don't care like the other men do."

"Don't care?" she queried, her own voice soft.

"If I live or die."

She nodded, and the mere movement flushed a wave of scent off her. He felt slightly sick with it.

"You want to come back to my place tonight?" she asked. She moved her hand from the table to his leg. He swallowed, and almost choked on his beer as her hand slid over his thigh leaving no room for doubt, or anything else for that matter, about just what she meant with her offer. He turned to look at her, and those blue, blue eyes cut through him, her gaze cauterizing as it traveled. "No strings," she said, "just sex."

He shook his head. "I can't."

He couldn't have said why he turned her down; it made little sense to him. The woman was beautiful and desirable and his body was, even now, stirring to her touch. He longed for oblivion at times, the sort found with another body, another's flesh and touch and desire. Something in him recoiled, he just didn't understand what, or maybe he did—a woman he didn't know from a life he couldn't remember. It was ridiculous really. His body seemed to feel it was more than ridiculous and bordering on cruelty.

Bridget got up and went to the bar, and he took a deep breath that didn't contain her scent. She would order her usual, gin and tonic, heavy on the gin. She tossed a look over her shoulder at him, eyes slightly narrowed, reminding him of a Siamese cat with her pointed chin and blue eyes. Most men would count themselves lucky to be propositioned by such a woman.

Several moments later she was back, not quite ready to give up it appeared. She put a shot of whiskey and a pint of Guinness on the table in front of him.

"I don't drink whiskey," he said, "but thank ye for the beer."

He took a sip to be polite, and let it sit on his tongue before sending it down his throat. He allowed himself one pint of the black stuff, and he'd already had that, anything more and he was playing with fire.

He felt a flash of resentment toward her. He wanted to be quiet with his thoughts, even though Eddy was meant to meet him here shortly. The resentment was followed by guilt. It wasn't her fault, after all, that all he really wanted was to steady himself and see if he couldn't summon that wee boy's face into his mind again. What she wanted he knew she could get anywhere and with someone far more willing than he was.

He had expressed some frustration around this particular issue when Molly had asked him why he never had a woman with him. Her reply had been to the point. "It's because you burn, sweetie, that's all. The women can smell it, it's a slow burn, but ye're all the more attractive for it. Besides have you seen yourself?" She quirked a darkly-penciled eyebrow at him and grinned. Mick grinned back; Molly had never made a secret of the fact that she would have been more than happy to keep him in bed for a week or two. She had gone on to express the idea that if he did decide to 'get busy', which she said with more primness than he might have imagined coming from Molly, with some lucky girl, let it not be little Miss Bridget.

"Because she's trouble, I'm sure Eddy has told ye that already."

"Aye, he has. She's not a worry, Moll," he'd said, but Molly had merely given him a rise of her well-painted brow as if to say she was very dubious about any man's ability to sniff out female trouble. She might, he thought a moment later, have had a valid point there.

"Hey Irish, why don't you tell us a story," Bridget said, loudly enough that several heads turned toward them. There was a mocking light in her blue eyes. She was angry that he had turned her down, and determined to make him pay in whatever fashion she could. "I figured you'd know how to tell a tale, the *Oy-rish* are supposed to be grand at that, no?" She was mocking him he knew, but he felt the tingle of it in his blood as if this was natural to him, the telling of a tale beside a fire, with a drink in hand.

"I can give it a try," he said coolly, calling her bluff, though heaven knew just what material he could draw upon to fabricate a story. He relaxed in his chair, threw back the whiskey even though he knew it was a bad idea and then rolled his shoulders to loosen them a little. He was silent for a long moment, looking for a silver glimmer somewhere in his mind with which to begin a tale. He sensed this might have once been familiar territory for him and that a tale could be made to tell itself once it had a start, but the teller must at least find the beginning in order to give the story its first breath. He cleared his throat and began, voice soft and low so that anyone who cared to listen would have to gather in close.

"There was a man, once, who lived by the shore of a distant land, a land of mist an' green soft fields that unfolded like velvet thrown out upon an expanse of rock. Now this man was lonely, though he didn't so much notice it for he was busy all the day through workin' his fields and tendin' to his cattle. Durin' the nights though, when the wind blew from the west an' the stars were thick as salt poured into the sky, he would feel the lack of another, of a woman's warmth an' tender voice.

"One day, after his work was done an' he was feelin' that strange ache which is known to the lonely, he was wanderin' on the shore, for the sea was only a few miles from his farm an' he liked the light of the water at the close of day. He saw somethin' move down near the tidemark, an' he thought it might be a stranded seal, too far up the sand and caught there without water to return it home.

"An' then the seal stood upon two legs, an' he saw that it was no seal at all but a maid so fair she brought the sting of tears to his eyes. She wore only a silver green cloak which she untied an' let drop to the ground.

"She had the eyes of the sea children, green an' deep as a night without a moon. Her hair fell in a tumble of luxuriatin' smoke to the small of her back, black as a crow's wing with the light of emeralds and sapphires within it. An' the skin on her—ah, 'twas like white roses borne in on the waves, come from a far land.

"He had heard legends of such women, an' it was said they made the very best wives. They were said to be under the rule of Lir, Lord of the Sea, an' came from the land beneath the waves.

"He crept as close as he could, watchin' the maid as she bathed in the new moon's light, naked as a newborn upon the cold strand, seaweed fronds ribbonin' through the smoke-black hair. He recalled what he had heard of such cloaks, that they aided the wearer so that they might roam from one realm to the next, from sea to land.

"Finally her cloak was within his reach an' he grasped the hem of it. It was cold and sodden with wet, an' it felt like no earthly cloth he had ever touched, but rather like kelp that had been woven upon a saltwater loom into a strange silk. He clutched the cloak an' then stood, startlin' the maid, who turned as pale as the shells on the shore when she realized he had her clothing.

"He held the cloak out to her to lure her but when she snatched at it, he walked backward. She followed him thusly all the way back to his farm, although the rocks of the fields cut the webbin' between her toes an' caused her feet to bruise and bleed.

"An' so the sea maid, havin' no choice in the matter, stayed with the farmer. In time she bore him a son, a fine boy, firm of flesh an' with none of yer merfolk about him, despite his mother's blood. He was, like his father, a child of the field an' the earth, bound to the land and its ways.

"The farmer could not complain for the sea maid was a good wife, a good friend, a receptive lover, doin' and givin' all that was expected of her. But her heart was never in the day's given tasks, an' so the bread did not rise as it should, the yard was never swept clean, the chickens molted their feathers, the sheets on the bed were always damp, an' the fish her husband caught she would promptly return to the sea. She breathed her damp salt breath upon them an' their gills would flutter an' then they would gasp as she threw them back to their watery home.

"The women of the village never accepted her, for everywhere she went men's eyes followed with the longin' of a sailor for the limitless horizon. She carried the scent of the sea inside, the smell of wrack an' salt, and of the deep places of the ocean where no man had ever been, nor would dare to venture. It was there in her movement, in the way she walked across a field or stood hip deep in a lake—she carried the singin' salt of water in her veins, in the joints of her hips an' shoulders, in the way she danced on the shore of a night, always lookin' away to the west where the breakers rolled ceaselessly, croonin' a mother's lullaby to her.

"But a selkie cannot return to the sea without her skin, for she will drown as surely as any other mortal woman, lungs burnin', limbs heavy and thick with the time of walkin' on earth. For earth inveigles itself into one's bones an' flesh, weights it down, anchors it to keep to the land.

"The man had done his best to be a good husband, an' while he loved her, he knew the sea maid did not love him in return. An' yet he never betrayed by the slightest hint just where her cloak was hidden. Sometimes she thought she felt it, late at night, the sleek, wet chill of it, the salt an' sand slippin' over her limbs, so that she might return home, to her family, to the man who waited for her deep beneath the roilin' dark waves. She walked the land at night, an' would stand by the shore, feelin' the ocean purl about her ankles, the tiny crabs nibbling soft at her toes. She swore some nights when the wind set from the west, just so, she could hear her people an' the soft swish of their language an' then she would weep for she could no longer understand the words.

"Aye, the man was kind to her, but he was neither kith nor kin to her salty soul. His love for her was a burnin' thing that dried her skin, so that she could feel the scales beneath. He wanted all of her, every last inch of her within his possession. He moved her far from the sea, away from where the breath of it, the voice of it could blow over her, could speak to her each day. She couldn't sleep at night for there were no waves to soothe her; only the night sounds of the land, which agitated her an' would give her no peace.

"And so another year passed an' another yet, an' there was a daughter born to them, a daughter who was a sea maid herself. The farmer could see that at once, for the babe was a delicate blue, an' not from any lack of air. She was a tiny mermaid, with hair the color of the sea at twilight, an' eyes deep as any eel's pool. The sea maid loved her daughter, as she had loved her son, but with somethin' more, for the child longed for the water as she herself did.

"Her husband, land bound as he was, did not like this small watery child, he complained that she felt damp to his hands, that she cried when he touched her, that he went cold when she was in the room. The baby did not like him either, an' seemed to sense that he was a stranger to her in all but simple biology, for his hands left burn marks on her fair blue skin, an' scorched the ends of her soft twilight hair. An' so the sea maid kept the child from him, fearing he would hurt her, that he would sense all the water that lived beneath the child's skin, would feel one night the scale an' sleek skin of a creature whose rightful home is water.

"So time passed, as time will, an' the children grew, an' the woman was still the best wife she could manage to be, an' the husband tilled his fields and the tide came in to the shore an' left it once again. Then one spring a powerful storm swept across the land, such a storm as hadn't been seen in a century. It uprooted trees an' knocked down fences, cows blew out to sea an' birds flew upside down. It tore the thatch off the roof of the farmer's cottage an' scattered it into the next county. The farmer spent several days fixin' it, for he knew the old ways an' how to make a roof in the way it had been done for hundreds of years in that county.

"One morning coming back from a far hill, from the top of which the woman could view the sea, she found her son proppin' a ladder up against the cottage wall.

'Whatever are you doing, child?' she asked.

'Why, I only want to look at the beautiful cloth my father hid in the reeds of the roof.'

"The sea maid began to tremble an' gently put her son aside, tellin' him she would look an' bring the cloth down for him to see. She climbed up, an' parted the reeds an' there was her cloak. She clutched it to her breast, an' then made an effort to appear calm. She did not want to panic the boy an' have him run to his father.

"'Tis only an old bit of oilcloth,' she told her son, kissin' the top of his head, while her blood thrilled to the scent of the sea in the cloak. The wind was pickin' up and she could taste salt on her tongue.

"The farmer noticed that night that his wife seemed nervous, she had a flush to her face like the innards of a seashell an' she dropped a plate an' scorched her finger on the kettle. He thought perhaps she was expectin' another child, an' wasn't certain how to tell him. She fed him a big dinner, an' refilled his tea cup an' even put out a glass of whiskey for him. He felt terribly sleepy after dinner an' went to his bed, tellin' his son he would have to milk the cows that evening.

"His son woke him some time later just as the sun was fallin' beneath the land, shoutin' that his mother and sister were gone, an' that his mother had taken the beautiful cloth he had hidden amongst the reeds of the roof.

"The man flew outside, panic beatin' in his chest, an' certain enough the roof was in disarray an' his wife's workaday clothes were left in a pile on the ground.

"He ran for the shore, his son cryin' out for him to wait, but he paid the boy no heed. He was too far behind already. He hadn't stopped to pull on his boots an' so his feet were bruised an' bleedin' by the time he came over the rise an' could see the shore below him. His wife stood with her feet in the water, wearin' only her cloak. She was still every bit as beautiful as the day he had seen her rise out of the sea. Neither time nor hard living had touched her.

"He shouted at her to stop, but she paid him no mind. She held their wee daughter on her hip, the skin of her legs turning to scales, blue an' shimmerin' as the dawn right before his eyes. He could see the water in them both now, as though saltwater ran like the waves to the shore within their veins rather than the blood of a mortal human.

"She turned back at the last just before she slipped beneath the waves, an' he saw the ocean there in her eyes, an' the foam like a bridal crown upon her sleek black hair before she disappeared from his view forever. And the farmer took his son, who was of the earth like he was, an' went home to his farm an' his tilled fields an' his dry sheets an' bread that rose high as snowy mountains, but for all the rest of his days, he would smell the sea every time the wind came in from the west, an' he would weep for the woman who had never loved him."

The sound of the sea faded from his ears, and the crackle of the fire replaced it along with the noise of his listeners stirring, for with the cessation of words, the spell was broken and he came back to his surroundings, though he could still feel the woman he had conjured on the palms of his hands—the small of her back, the nape of her neck, the scent of her like the wind off the sea on a fine day, fading already into the smells of beer and damp clothes, and the smoke from the peat fire.

He stood when he was done, nodded to his small circle of listeners and went outside. His head hurt, as though a hive of bees had been set loose beneath the bones of his skull.

The night was thick with fog, and his breath turned to water droplets at once. He was completely unsettled, not uncommon for him, but this was different, it was like the story had set something adrift inside him that had been firmly tied before.

Eddy was sitting outside on a concrete block, a cigarette cupped in his hand.

"Thought maybe you'd go home with the redheaded woman," he said.

Mick shook his head. "No."

"So who was she?"

"What?"

"The woman in the tale—she's real, isn't she? I swear I could almost see her take form right there in the room, right there in your eyes."

"I don't know, truth be told," he said. He felt vaguely annoyed for he wasn't ready to speak of the woman who had risen in his hands just as she had risen from the sea in the tale. He had merely set out to tell the selkie tale, and he had told it true to the tradition of it, only the woman had become real there in his words and he had seen her so clearly in his mind that he thought for a moment he could reach out and touch her.

"I think you do know, somewhere in that head of yours. I think you know just fine who she is."

"I think," he said quietly, "I think maybe she was mine." He turned then and walked off into the night, where the darkness, unlike the darkness in his head, was sometimes his friend.

Part Five

A Glimpse of the World Before
August 1976-June 1977

Chapter Forty-nine

The House With Moon and Star Shutters
Summer 1976

THE HOUSE WAS LONELY, or at least that was his first thought when he pulled up on his bike to the old Victorian. It was tucked away amidst a bower of roses growing wild, their canes clambering up the walls around the cupola and scrambling thick across the roof. They might be the one thing still keeping the house upright, for it had seen better days, to be sure.

He stopped and parked the bike in the overgrown drive. There was a 'For Sale' sign hanging faded and crooked off a post, nearly hidden in a patch of bramble at the end of the lane. He wondered if the house actually was for sale or if the sign was merely forgotten.

He walked up the drive slowly, taking in his surroundings. There was lavender gone wild next to the house, thick with bees and butterflies on this sunny afternoon, the shutters hanging off the windows of the bottom floor, the porch with an ancient swing, near rotted from the depredations of weather and salt winds. It swung slightly in the breeze, as if a woman sat in it reading, one foot on the porch floor, pushing the swing just a little bit.

The stairs to the porch were a silver grey, though he could see the original traces of white paint on them. They needed replacing. The porch itself had boards half rotted away, home now to ants and squirrels.

His hand traced a worn shutter, fingers stopping where a crescent moon had been carved with no small skill into the wood. Beyond it was a star, five-pointed and marked out in flaking blue paint. Touching the wood had set off an echo inside him, like hearing a beautiful song, but only a note here and there, so that one couldn't quite recall the song in its entirety, only feel the ghost of it inside and the haunting of beauty half-forgotten by the mind, but remembered in some part by the cells and the heart.

He walked around it, eyeing up the house's lines, counting the windows and imagining the layout inside. He automatically started compiling a list in his head of the materials that would be needed to fix it up. It surprised him a little, that he had gone that far in his thinking already, that he felt some strange connection to this house as if he needed it as much as it clearly needed him. He could do the work, of that he had no doubt. That he wanted to do it, well that too surprised him in no small way. He wanted to fix this house, and it was a foreign feeling for a man who had not wanted anything in a very long time.

Bridget had given him the keys but the back door was open, the old brass door knob turned verdigris with time and the elements. He walked in and called out.

"Hello? Is anyone here?" He felt a tad foolish as his words echoed back to him in the dusty, sunny air. Who did he think he was talking to—ghosts? Well, he supposed it wasn't a bad notion to be polite to any that might be lingering. A man who didn't make friends with ghosts was a fool.

The bottom floor was in decent shape, despite clear evidence that birds and bees had made their homes here for a season or two. The floor was solid enough, and made from oak so that it would withstand the years. In the kitchen there was an ancient cast iron sink, coated in chipped enamel, and a wood stove with a bent chimney, which no doubt housed a variety of wildlife. The countertops and cabinets were a little hideous, a result of 1960s decorating, no doubt. He was certain the tin ceilings were original despite being buried under layers of dirt and grease. And the moldings, too, somewhat worn with paint peeling off in long strips, looked like the original article to him.

There was a large hearth around the wood stove, built of crumbling brick. He touched the upper arch and a cloud of dust rained down. The entire thing would have to be torn out and re-built, maybe with stone native to California.

The house was from the Queen Anne period, defined by a variety of characteristics that he recognized on sight—the octagonal tower, the small colored panes of glass in the doors and windows surrounding a large, clear pane. This house also sported three of the fluted chimneys that were popular in that era, as well as the siding—clapboard shingles on the body of the house with fish scale shingles on the gables and tower.

There was something about an old building in need of care which calmed him. He understood the ways of wood and stone, of leveling and rebuilding and restoring something step by careful step, staying true to its original lines and purpose. Each building had a spirit of its own, some good, some bad and some, like this house, slightly melancholy with the echo about it of having known happier times.

Money, Bridget had assured him, would be no object. She explained that her grandmother hadn't lived in the house for many years, but had been in a care home and had only recently passed away, leaving the house and her money to her only granddaughter. Bridget occasionally slept out here, though she had a room in the city too, where she most often spent her nights.

He started with the basics, for the electrical system needed an overhaul to bring it up to code and make it safe. The boiler needed replacing as well, and the house could use a new water heater. None of the fireplaces were functioning and much of the woodwork in the house was covered in black paint and grime; he would have to strip it all back to the original wood and sand it down and refinish it in a manner which better suited the spirit of the house. He didn't even want to think what he was going to find when he pried up some of the boards—he was certain he'd heard pigeons cooing under one of the bedroom floors and there were definitely bats in the tower room on the third floor. The defining feature of the house though was the grand octagonal tower that fronted the three stories. He could feel the itch in his hands to strip it back and restore it slowly to its original glory.

He began the work a few days later and continued to labor on the house whenever he had a chance—on weekends and in the evenings when he didn't have a fight scheduled or a training session with Eddy. As he worked through the days of that long California summer the peace of the old house surrounded him, sinking down into his bones and setting a rhythm which was instinctive to him. It was a rhythm which was slow and easy and exacting for it was that of wood and stone, angles and saws, hammers and nails, sandpaper and paint.

Sometimes as he worked he felt like there was another house beneath the bones of this one, another house that he had built and which his cells remembered the form and shape of even if his mind could not recall it. It was like a hum in his brain, that other house, the ghost house, the tracery of which sometimes rose—just there in front of him—where he could not quite see it, only feel it in the boards and struts and plaster and paint. He wondered for whom he had built that house—had it been his, had he shared it with others, had he loved it? Thinking about it always started a sharp pain in the side of his head, so that he pushed the house away when it rose phantom-like in his mind.

By August he had made significant strides on the list of things to be done. The new boiler had been installed and the piping all through the house had been replaced. The wiring was redone throughout most of the house, though there were still the bedrooms to be done as well as all the tower rooms. He'd stripped back years of wall paper on the walls and paint on mahogany posts and stairs and on paneling in the study which turned out to be a stunning purple heartwood. He'd rebuilt two of the three hearths in the house, using river stone to create both drama and a sense of continuity with the natural surroundings. Over the months of work he felt the house changing, warming in its bones, the light transforming as the energy of the house shifted and the spirit of it was brought back to life.

He had taken up the dreadful carpet in the third floor tower room and found a floor of beautiful yellow pine. All it required was sanding and staining to be brought back to a lovely sheen. The original plaster was in good enough shape in the room that all he had to do was patch and paint it the pale buttercream which Bridget had picked out. It gave the room the appearance of being lit with sunlight even when it was grey outside. Sometimes he slept there when he'd worked late on the house and was too tired to make the trip back into the city. He had no real home there anyway, just a room at Molly's. Here he could sleep with the windows open and spare himself the sense of claustrophobia which he often had inside buildings. The eight-sided tower was fronted by trees and the rustle of the wind through them at night was soothing and gave him the sense of being outdoors.

He was lying in it now, having spent a long day stripping the newel posts of the hideous black paint with which someone had coated them. He'd been sore all day; he'd fought the night before and the fight had gone long—forty minutes of brutal slugging it out. His opponent had been one of those thick browed sorts that didn't have a lot of grace in the ring but did have a rock-solid center of gravity and a native stubbornness that made it hard to knock him down or even move him around the pit a little in order to buy time to catch his own breath.

He had a bed here in the tower room, just blankets on a bit of foam but comfortable enough most nights. He was trying to read by the light of a candle, as the electricity wasn't hooked up in this room yet. Three moths hovered around the flame, causing it to flutter and dance in the warm August night. Bridget had given him a copy of *The Frenzy of Sweeney* by one J.G. O'Keefe which she'd found in a bookstore in the Haight.

"It's an Irish epic about a man driven mad by violence who lives in the trees," she'd said. He'd merely said thank you and taken the book from her. He was pretty sure she was giving him a rather direct message with the book. He was reading it through for the second time now and found himself struck by a few lines in particular.

'*I am haggard, womanless, and cut off from music… . Ronan has brought me low, God has exiled me from myself…*'

And that, thought Mick, was cutting it a little too close to the bone. He put the book down and sat up. The night was warm and the windows were open. A small bat flitted about in the beams above his head and the scent of oleander drifting in was like a distillation of moonlight, silver-white and aching in its smell. He was both tired and restless at the same time. He often felt this way after a fight. He couldn't help but wonder if his luck was going to run out some time soon. He was 18-0 right now and it made him a little edgy. A run of luck like that was bound to make a man nervous.

He got up from the floor and went to the window and leaned out into the night. The moon was just a sliver off full and it lit the yard below silver. He ached and not just from the fight. The ache was more of an interior one. It had been such a long time since he had been touched in tenderness. He pushed his fists into the window frame; he was frustrated and longing for a woman's touch, a woman's warmth to take away this need in him. There was only one woman he wanted, though, a phantom who might exist only in his mind. The doctors had told him it was possible his mind could manufacture trace memories of people and events which had never actually existed or taken place. The mind strained to make a story even if it had no material with which to write it.

The night breeze against his chest was like a caress from the hand of that ghostly woman. He wished his porous mind could summon her up and begin to fill the spaces where she had once been in his life. He sighed and leaned his forehead into the wooden frame. He hadn't replaced it yet and splinters of old paint drifted down to the floor around his feet. He pushed his head into the rough wood hoping a bit of pain would lessen his longing.

The top stair to the tower squeaked and though he could have replaced the board he preferred to give himself the warning the noise provided. He took a breath feeling more than a little frustrated. Bridget had let him be for a few weeks, apparently that time was up. He didn't turn at once but he heard the soft pad of her bare feet cross the floor and felt the disturbance of her body as it neared his.

She touched his back and he shivered, the feel of another's skin against his own without violence was electric. He moved away from her hand, and turned around only to be confronted with her completely naked body. The shock of it went through him, his body responding accordingly to the first naked woman he had seen in some time. He swallowed and closed his eyes seeking strength even though the scent of her was both sharp and hot in his nose. It was the smell of female desire and the male animal rose up in him demanding its due.

"I can't, Bridget, we've had this discussion. Ye know I cannot do this with ye."

"I don't see why you make such a thing of it. It doesn't have to be, you know," she said softly.

He shook his head. "Desire is a thing of little space an' then the mornin' comes an' with it regret."

"How can you be so certain we'd regret it?"

"Because I can give ye my body, but I can't give ye my heart an' I think, in the end, that's the thing ye really want."

He touched her face. There was no telling her what he truly felt because it wasn't kind to say it. She was the sort of person who was always going to try to fill the hole in her life with outside forces—men, drugs, wandering—and none of it would ever be enough. He was afraid of falling into the vacuum she held at her core. He felt a sadness for her because she could not help who she was any more than he could.

He looked down at her, his hand still cupping the edge of her jaw. Her hair was a soft, dull copper glow in the moonlight and her skin was as white as the oleander petals that glowed outside the window. She moved her face against the palm of his hand and he could feel the strain in her. She was a lost girl and he was a lost boy; they just weren't fated to be lost together.

"It doesn't have to be forever; I'm not really that kind of girl anyway and you, Irish, you are most definitely not that kind of guy. But for now, let me be your shelter, just until the storm passes." Her hands were on his chest, warm and soft. He put his own hands on her forearms to still her movement.

"I just can't," he said. He no longer cared how it seemed to her or if he appeared entirely crazy. His body had some decided opinions on the state of his sanity just now and none of them were flattering.

"You're an unusual man," she said, seemingly not angry at his latest rejection of her charms. "I find it interesting."

"Interesting?" he echoed, irritated.

"Yes. I don't know too many men who wouldn't have sex when it's offered, when they have no ties elsewhere, at least not ones they can remember. I don't see why you're so certain she exists."

"I just feel her," he said, knowing it sounded flimsy compared to the feeling he carried inside.

"If you don't know who she is, does it really matter?"

"Does it matter? Aye, it matters to me."

"Do you think she's waiting for you? Do you think she's staying faithful to a man who has been gone so long?"

"I don't know," he said softly. "It's not really about what she's doing, she may well think I'm dead." She most likely, he amended inside his head, did think him dead, if she existed. Always the damned *if* which haunted his entire existence. If she existed, if he'd had a life worth remembering, if he was a father —*if, if, if!*

"D'ye think maybe ye might have pity on me an' cover up?" he asked, because his body did want her to a terrifying degree and he didn't think he could stick with his morals if she didn't put some clothes on. Bridget laughed and shrugged into the shirt he had abandoned on the stepladder before he'd gotten into bed. It was covered in paint splotches and smelled of turpentine and sawdust, but it provided some relief to his overstrained principles.

She looked up at him as she buttoned the shirt, her blue eyes almost black in the candlelight. Without her usual costume of bangles, rings, makeup and gypsy skirt and blouse, she looked terribly young and terribly vulnerable.

"Can I stay up here with you tonight, Irish? I promise not to touch you. I'm just lonely and the house feels so empty downstairs."

He sighed. "No funny business, all right?"

"Cross my heart and hope to die, stick a needle in my eye."

He startled a little at her quoting of the old playground rhyme. It had always struck him as a little gruesome but that wasn't what bothered him tonight. It was that for a second it set off an echo in his head, one that floated out getting fainter and fainter but something he strained to hear all the same. She lay down on his simple foam mattress not bothering to cover herself with a blanket. It was too warm for covers, he felt the clammy prickle of sweat on his chest and saw the soft sheen of it on her upper lip. He lay down beside her and turned to blow out the candle by which he'd been attempting to read.

The moths were still fluttering about the flame. He watched them for a moment, mesmerized by their dance. They flew in tighter and tighter revolutions, one so close he thought it must surely ignite and fall into the heart of the fire. He didn't wonder why they took the risk, it was, he thought because fire was warm and beautiful, and he knew sometimes that was more than enough to risk immolation of either wings or self. And then one did fly too close and catch fire and for a second flame took wing, and just as swiftly there was nothing to know it by but a tracery of smoke curled upon the air. It was like his life before—a chimera of smoke and ash, there and then gone.

He licked his forefinger and thumb and then snuffed the candle not wanting the other moths to succumb to the lure of the fire. Outside were the usual night noises—the distant screech of a swift, the much closer and cacophonous call of tree frogs, and the occasional hiss of a car passing on the distant road.

The dark made it easier to talk as if all things could be asked and answered and then forgotten with the arrival of morning's light. He could still smell Bridget, the heat and invitation of her, but he knew she was like the flame and he was no more than the moth.

"Can I ask ye a question?" He could feel a moth fly over his face— one of the survivors, just a tiny displacement of air and space as it sought heat and light.

"Ask me anything you'd like, Irish. For you, I'm an open book."

"It seems odd, I suppose for a woman to be on her own as ye are. Isn't there a family somewhere that misses ye? Brothers or sisters?"

He could feel her shrug across the expanse of the damp and creased sheet on which they lay. "I left them behind a long time ago. It's better for me and them if I just don't go home. I was always the piece that didn't fit. I've been some bad places, Irish, and don't nobody back home want to know about that. You see stuff, you do stuff and you aren't the same person. You can't go home again, it's a mistake to even try, it just shows exactly how far you've traveled away from who you were. People change and they move on, their lives keep going. But when you're the one who left, it's like some part of you stays in stasis. You think the world is going to roll back for you, and then you realize it's like water 'round rocks in a river, for a little bit their lives parted and there's that space where you used to be, and then it keeps moving, closes back together and there ain't a place for you anymore."

"Are ye sayin' ye can't go home again?" The statement didn't sit well with him. He didn't like that idea. He supposed it was because he hoped that someday if he figured out where home was, he could go back and that someone there would be happy for his return.

"Not all families love in the right way, Irish, not all mommas and daddies want their babies to come home. Some babies just gotta make their own way in the world."

"I'm sorry," he said.

They were quiet for a time then and he thought she had fallen asleep when she spoke, her voice as soft as the dark that enfolded them.

"Irish?"

"Aye?"

"I feel less alone when you're around."

"Why do ye suppose that is?" he asked, though he feared he knew.

"Maybe it's because you seem even lonelier than I do."

And that, thought Mick for the second time that night, was cutting it too close to the bone. Unfortunately, it was no less true for the discomfort it caused. He turned over and put his arm around her. He didn't love her, but here in the dark, with the scent of oleander, silver and aching coming through the windows, it didn't matter. She needed someone and he was the only one here to hold the loneliness at bay.

He lay awake for a long time after Bridget fell asleep, both thinking and not thinking in the way that night thoughts were—a stream that meandered and rippled and the shape of which would disappear before morning. His last conscious thought before sleep came for him was that he could still smell the smoke of the dying moth.

He awoke in a shaft of sunlight, the scent of frying ham having tickled his senses into consciousness. He got up and pulled on his jeans and a fresh t-shirt. He felt groggy this morning though he'd slept so deeply he had neither dreamed nor moved much, judging by the stiffness in his body.

There was a narrow set of back stairs that led from the top of the tower down to the kitchen. He had managed to strip them but had yet to finish them, and the stairs were soft and powdery with wood dust under his bare feet. Sunlight filled the kitchen, touching the birch table and sideboard and gleaming off the tin backsplash he had installed behind the sink a few days before.

"I guess you didn't get much sleep last night," Bridget said and there was a curious tension to her voice. She was scrambling eggs on the camp stove he'd been using to boil water and make his meals. Her back was to him so he couldn't read her expression but he knew he hadn't imagined the tension.

"No, I slept well in the end," he said, pouring himself a cup of tea and sitting down at the table. He did feel a little bleary-headed still, despite the heavy sleep.

"Really? Because I would have thought that drawing took a few hours."

"What drawing?" he asked blankly. He was confused as to what she was talking about and even more so by why she seemed upset.

"The drawing on the table. I didn't draw it, so you must have."

He looked over the table and saw a large sheet of paper. It was from the pad he'd been using to rough out his plans for the house. He reached out his hand and pulled the paper toward him and then felt the bottom of his stomach drop out. "I...I don't remember drawin' that," he said, wishing she would quit looking at him so oddly, like he'd grown an extra head during the night.

"Well, you did," she said, stating the obvious. He saw his hand in the drawing, he knew the sort of lines he used, the pressure he put behind the pencil, the curves he used to indicate depth and perspective.

It was a lovely house. Two stories, with a well thatched roof that would keep out the rain no matter how hard it drummed upon the rushes. It looked solid, meant to weather the years and keep secure its occupants. It sat snug in a wee dell of trees and flowers, and had a stout door and deep windowsills. It was his ghost house, the one he had always felt beneath the bones of this one, the one that had always been just beyond his reach, here now, lined bold yet lovely upon the paper. An Irish house. The house was surrounded with greenery—a wee garden, roses clambering up the walls, bramble thick upon the low stone wall and a little wooden gate, and flowers everywhere. Bridget was right, this drawing must have taken hours.

He felt the familiar thump of pain on the right side of his head. The pain he always got when it seemed that a memory was trying to surface.

"She liked plants, all sorts," he said, and the pain in his head was like a knife cutting thin and sharp now.

"Who liked plants?" Bridget asked, her words wary as if she understood intuitively that they were on strange ground here.

"The woman who lived there, or maybe she still lives there for all I know."

"This woman—did you live with her?"

"I think so, once upon a time."

"Like in a fairy tale?"

"No," he said, feeling terribly bleak suddenly, "not like in a fairy tale, just a life, a real one."

Chapter Fifty

Stars Falling All Around
December 1976

HE HAD COME to the church to pray. He'd been drawn here tonight like an iron filing to a magnet, needing to speak to something; that greater presence he sensed from time to time. He had come to ask that power to give him back some small corner of his old life, a hint, anything that would tell him who he had been, and where he belonged. By his reckoning, as much as he could figure, he had been gone from the world before for more than a year now.

The church was quiet. It was late on a Sunday night and Christmas was only a week away. He had plans to spend the day with Father Jan and Eddy, helping out at a soup kitchen. He had no desire to celebrate the holiday; and even if he had, there was no family with which to spend it.

He picked up the box of matches that had been left by the small white candles and struck one. The flame sprang warm against the hushed dark of the church. He touched the flame to a candle and watched as the warmth caught and flickered, then held, swaying only a little where a draft from the body of the church caressed it. A prayer that was not words but merely longing, moved through his body, a rhythm of need and yearning flowing along with his blood. Suddenly the flame touched his fingers and he dropped the match, sticking the singed ends of his thumb and forefinger into his mouth to stop the worst of the burning.

He'd lit seven candles. He stared at them. He hadn't counted—he'd lit a bunch and then stopped. He wondered if the number had a significance. A woman and six children? He felt slightly dizzy at the thought. But no, surely he'd had a mother and a father and maybe even siblings in that life in the world before. And a wife. A wife, a child or two, two parents and maybe a brother and a sister. He shook his head; he had no bloody way to know why he'd lit all those candles or if they were people still alive or long passed from him.

Suddenly the silence of the church was shattered by a woman's shout. As he whirled around to see what was wrong, a silver-sharp needle of pain lanced through his head. He dropped to one knee, hands going to his skull, as if they could harness the agony somehow, keep it confined and control it.

He froze in terror, quite certain he was losing his mind for he had heard three words shouted at him and yet the church around him was still empty. The voice had come from somewhere else it seemed to him, somewhere distant as if a small portal had opened in the air, or a figure in a painting, static for years had suddenly come to life and cried out loud. The echo was still there, the repercussion moving the air around him.

A woman's voice. His woman's voice. He knew it, as he knew the shape of his own hands or the feel of his skin against his bones. She had an American voice. So had he lived here in the US when he had disappeared? He clenched his fists on his knees. So many questions and never any damn answers. It was like trying to hold snowflakes in his hand, a mere touch and they melted away to invisibility. But just the fact that he'd heard her voice and *knew* it was her voice gave him hope.

That small weed of hope shrank almost immediately. It was the way it often happened for him as the reality of his situation sunk in once again. He didn't know this woman, he didn't know if she was real or what she looked like. How long would a woman wait? If there were children they might not remember him, not to mention him remembering them. There would be other concerns and considerations for her and life would and did move on, it was just the nature of it. What if one day he found his way home, only to find there was no longer a place for him and that his empty spot had been filled by another man?

A rush of jealousy so primal that it took his breath away flooded through his body. He stood up and backed away from the candles and sat down on the nearest pew. He put his hands to his head and fought to take in a full breath. It had been a while since he'd had a rush of emotion this strong and it overwhelmed him.

He thought of his memory like a small black box which was bound with a padlock and fine chains and until he found the key to that lock, until he could break those chains he would remain lost. There was the fear, too, that if he ever did find the key and open the box, he might not like what came tumbling out. What if he had been a bad person? It seemed to him that most good men didn't get shot and beaten.

And yet, right now, in this moment with the woman's voice still echoing inside him he would have given anything to remember who he was, even if that man wasn't a good man.

Three words—still thrumming through his blood and making his chest tight—*wait for me*.

When he came out of the church the Banshee was standing on the stairs like she had been waiting for him. He smiled at her and she fell into step beside him. He was glad to see she wasn't barefoot. She had the warm wool stockings and boots on that he'd given her during their first meeting.

He offered her his arm and to his great surprise she took it and they walked for a little way until they came upon a bench which had been placed beneath an oak many years ago, for the tree had grown around it and swallowed parts of it. She pointed one of her long, bony fingers at the bench and he nodded. She wanted to sit, and his coat was warm enough to stand the chill of the night for a time.

He realized that the conversation he had begun in the church was still going on in his head. He wished he knew with whom he was conversing. So, to this stranger who seemed to dwell inside those dark spaces where his memory hid he said silently, *"I will wait for you. Wait for me too, if you can."*

As they sat snow began to fall, just lightly at first, delicate stars landing on their heads and shoulders and hands. The woman they called the Banshee looked up, the stars landing on her face, touching her lips and catching in her eyelashes.

"Magic," she said, her voice cracked from such a long time of silence.

"Aye, magic," he agreed, looking up into the airy pathways between the snow, pathways that ran all the way to the stars. He was startled a moment later when her hand touched his and then he held hers, one lost human being with another, holding hands while stars fell all around them.

Chapter Fifty-one

A Glimpse of the World Before
March 1977

"FIXING HER FLOOR? Man, I have heard it called a lot of things but fixing the floor ain't one of them."

"I really *am* just fixin' the floors," Mick said with some exasperation, though he knew Eddy was unlikely to believe him. Hell, he wouldn't believe him if he wasn't the one experiencing it. He lived with Bridget more or less full time at this point. Eddy knew what she looked like and didn't believe any man had the sort of fortitude required to stay out of her bed when it was so willingly offered. His relationship with Bridget was certainly complicated, but not in the ways that Eddy and any other red-blooded male might think.

He stopped as they came up over a rise and a small valley filled with redwoods revealed itself below them. The tall trees were wreathed in tendrils of the morning's fog and Mick took a deep breath of the cool air and then abruptly gasped.

"Ribs still bothering you?" Eddy asked, coming up beside him and looking out over the valley with the inscrutable look he wore most often.

"Aye, I expect they will for a bit. They aren't broken but they are most definitely bruised."

He'd fought a man out of Oakland three nights back and he had only won by a whisker, or a really lucky punch to the man's chin that finally took him out. He'd taken a fair beating before that and he was still feeling it.

"Man's spirit animal must be a wolverine; he was fierce."

"Aye, I don't need remindin' of it," Mick said. He sat down on a big rock that overlooked the valley. His knee felt like it was on fire and he knew he couldn't go any further for now. Eddy on the other hand hadn't even broken a sweat. He looked as cool as a cucumber and like he could climb for another twenty miles if he wanted to.

"You could give it up—the fighting," Eddy said, his tone casual though the look in his eyes was not. Mick knew what he thought of the fighting. Eddy believed he was either going to kill someone one of these days or get killed himself. He was probably right, but Mick wasn't ready to give it up just yet.

Eddy settled on the ground across from him, his back up against the trunk of an aspen and his legs stretched out in front of him. Wherever Eddy was he always seemed comfortable, like he could sleep on a tree bough and wake up refreshed the next morning.

"Have ye got a spirit animal?" Mick asked. He was hit with a sudden longing for a cigarette, and wondered if he'd smoked back in that life before. He couldn't remember ever wanting one prior to this moment.

Eddy sighed. "Yeah, I have a spirit animal. There's a story to it if you've got the patience to hear it."

"Oh aye, I've got the patience."

"Bastard," Eddy said, "you don't need to sound quite so gleeful."

"Ha, I knew it was a good story. Get to tellin' it, man." He moved down to the ground and put his back against the stone, easing his leg out in front of him.

"Throw me a beer, you know a story needs a wet throat."

Mick reached into the pack he'd brought up the mountainside and took out a bottle of beer and a wax paper-wrapped pile of sandwiches. He tossed the bottle to Eddy who caught it neatly out of the air. He took out a second bottle for himself and passed a sandwich over to Eddy.

Eddy took a bite and then a swallow of his beer as he looked out over the valley. Mick waited patiently, for it was a fine day and there was no hurry to anything.

"I always thought my spirit animal would be a wanderer, you know a lone wolf or a cougar, something that covers a lot of territory, the kind of animal that has itchy feet. Just like me, just four legs that keep on moving, instead of two."

"I'm guessin' that's not the case," Mick said.

"No, it sure isn't. I was up in Maine one spring, visiting an auntie. It was still a little chilly, everything wet after that big spring thaw, everything coming back to life. Maine is huge, but on the eastern side it is all about the water. And I am talking about *water*, man, the Mother of us all, that water, the water that wants the moon and surges through women's bodies.

The water that birthed us all and keeps us alive still. There's a pull there that's hypnotic, especially in the spring. We all move to the tides and the pull of this grand fucking world in the spring. I'm talking about *that* kind of water, that kind of night—you know what I'm saying?"

"Aye, I think I do," Mick said, because he did. He knew what it was to feel the earth surge with life beneath his feet, when it caused the blood to move quick and fleet as if it sparked with an interior fire which was fully connected to the outer world and the things that ran beneath that world.

"I could hear frogs everywhere. To me that's the real sound of spring, peepers singing their song, doing their thing in the ponds and creeks. Some nights it would get so loud a man couldn't sleep, just that crazy song they sing like they are gonna burst with it. A man can't sleep on those kind of nights anyway. I went outside, because since Vietnam I can't breathe inside so well and I need to get out and have the stars over my head and the earth between my toes in order to really get a lungful and calm myself.

"I just thought I'd amble down the road a ways, maybe until I got tired. The moon was high and on its half, like some big slice of peach up there in the sky, an' I could see my way just fine. I'd gone a fair way along when suddenly I feel this presence behind me, a big presence, not some little fox peeping out of the shrubs at me or anything, but something really big. You can tell the difference when a big apex predator has his eyes on your bag of bones. A bear, a mountain lion, or another man."

"Aye." He did know, he didn't think it was bear or mountain lion that had hunted him, but another man, or maybe men.

"And then I see a shadow crossing over mine, a huge shadow and it's moving. I feel like the shadow alone could swallow me whole, and man, let me tell you, I saw some bad stuff in 'Nam, but I have never been as scared as I was with that shadow behind me. I started to run, but it kept pace with me. When I picked up speed so did it. I could hear its feet slapping against the ground, in the way that webbed feet sound. It's a wet sound and it's unmistakable. I'm moving faster and faster an' it is too. I was terrified and exhilarated at the same time; it was kind of an uncomfortable mix."

"Did ye turn around an' look at it?" Mick asked, shivering like the shadow loomed over him, too.

"Hell no, brother, I did not turn around. There are some things a man just doesn't want to see. I knew if I looked it would change my world forever, it would take the struts out from under my life and leave me changed and maybe not in a good way. You know?"

"Aye," Mick agreed, "I know."

"I was on the wharf in a river before I realized this thing, this force, whatever the hell it was, was going to chase me straight into the water. I just stopped dead right there, with the old rotten wood of that wharf cold beneath my soles. I was half expecting something to hit me like a cannonball and send me straight out into those rough currents. But it just passed over and through me." He shuddered and Mick could smell the marshy scent of the night and feel the darkness that had chased Eddy down that country lane.

"And then there I was standing on the wharf and there's this huge silence, the kind of silence that exists in those hours after midnight and it's just me and a couple of tiny frogs hopping around on the end of the wharf. I tell you, man, I kinda wish I was doing drugs at the time because at least I could have chalked it up to that. I told my auntie about it in the morning, sort of an abbreviated version because I still wasn't sure if I'd hallucinated it or half dreamed it or something. She turns around from making flapjacks and says to me, 'It's your spirit animal, Edward.' And I'm thinking, seriously? Because first of all it would have been nice if my spirit animal had shown up a long time ago when it was supposed to and now that it does it's a damn frog? Then she says, 'Eddy, a frog's eyes are such that they can see two worlds at the same time.'"

"Yer spirit animal is a frog?"

"Hey, it was a really big frog—a fucking huge scary frog."

Eddy took a last swallow of his beer and then tucked the bottle back into the pack. Mick had long ago noticed that Eddy never left any trace of himself behind. He walked lightly in the world. He looked back at Mick, the dark almond eyes suddenly piercing.

"I'm just saying there is more than one world, there's what we see and that's one world and there's what we know in our bones and that's another world entirely."

"Aye, I suppose I agree with ye there. There are edge places in the world; ye can feel the intersections when you happen upon them." He was starting to get an uneasy feeling about just where this conversation was headed.

"If you're going to walk in that space you gotta be careful, you gotta go in prepared for it. Like a hunter who is after really big game, you have to have the right tools, and a plan. Because where those two worlds intersect, well, it's not necessarily a benevolent place. *You* know that, it's blood knowing. You know that where two worlds intersect the path between them is dark and lonely and populated with weird shit. You gotta have courage to travel that road, and there's no guarantee that what you find on the other side will be a good thing and won't scar you or even kill you. Because real belief, man, real knowing it tears you up, it makes you into something else, sometimes something more and sometimes something less. That's the risk of it."

Mick sat up straighter and gave Eddy a dark look. "Why is it ye're tellin' me this story? Because suddenly this feels like it has a bigger purpose to it."

"Because that place, that intersection, that's where your memory is, man, that's the land you are gonna have to travel if you want to remember who you were."

"How do I find that place? That's the problem, isn't it? Figurin' out where the ticket is to gain entry."

"I think I know where you can get a ticket."

"I'm not going to like this idea, am I?"

Eddy laughed, "Probably not, man, probably not."

As a witch doctor he didn't inspire great awe, Mick thought. The old man wore an overly large Hawaiian print shirt that had seen better days, baggy shorts and a pair of sandals made from tire rubber. On a small table beside him he had a bunch of feathers, a fan of leaves, a necklace of beautiful turquoise beads and a large, smooth quartz crystal. Beside these were two jugs of a dark and rather malevolent looking liquid. He hoped to hell that wasn't what he was expected to drink, though he rather suspected that it was, despite the fact that it looked like no tea he had ever seen.

They were sitting outside the man's trailer within the shelter of a ring of oaks. Overhead the night was thickly peppered with stars, and a soft breeze soughed through the branches above.

Eddy explained the paraphernalia upon the table. "The feathers are to sweep the shadows away, the beads are the land from which he draws his strength; the land is the source of his magic. The quartz is like a crystal ball, it is how he sees into your soul."

Mick swallowed. He wasn't sure what he thought about any of this, and he had a cold trickle of ice water running through his veins which was making his entire body shake.

Eddy had, after his first cryptic statement about an entry route into the deep murky well of his lost memory, explained it to him, and he'd been right—Mick didn't like the sound of it at all.

"I'm gonna be up front with you because it involves drugs." He held up a hand, knowing Mick's opinion on any sort of mind-altering substance. "I know, just wait a minute okay and then you can protest all you like. It's not anything you're familiar with—it's called yage or ayahuasca—it comes from a vine in South America. Well, only part of the recipe is the vine, there's a combination of things in it. I have an uncle who knows about this stuff, he's from Peru originally. I think I could get him to do the ceremony with you—he won't do it for just anyone, but I think he might when I explain your situation."

"Ye have an uncle from Peru?" Mick asked, as always confused by the vast and far-flung web of Eddy's relations. Eddy had drawn out his family tree one night and it had looked like the web of a spider on mushrooms by the time he was done.

"My Auntie Shirley has been married five times. This uncle from Peru is the fifth and it looks like he might stick, he's been around for fourteen years now."

"How does it work—this drug?"

"I don't understand how it works really," Eddy said, with one of his eloquent shrugs, "I just know that it does. You gotta be real careful what you eat the day before."

"Ye know how I feel about drugs. My head is messy enough without adding drugs to the mix."

"I do know that, and I understand why, but this stuff is different. My uncle just calls it 'the tea' and it's like it resets your head. I'm just thinking it might sweep the cobwebs from your brain, maybe allow you to remember something of what your life was, who you were before. If you want to remember."

Aye, that was the question, wasn't it? Did he want to remember? Did he want to know who he had been, or was he running from something, something terrible in his past that he would not want brought back to him?

"I'll do it," he said, and prayed to a God he wasn't certain he believed in that he wasn't about to make a terrible mistake.

This had brought him here, one month later, with sweat trickling down his backbone and ice water running through his intestines.

The old man might have been harmless looking but Mick revised that opinion rather swiftly when he got a whiff of the brew he had concocted for them to drink together. It smelled like someone had scraped a particularly moldy bit of forest floor together and boiled it, and then poured it in a cup without the bother of straining it.

The old man bent around the bowl, like he was trying to envelop it. A small breeze sprang up in the still night just as he began to chant. It was a soft lush sound, as if velvet had taken on a decibel, a note in the soft night air.

Mick stayed quiet, watching the old man, feeling detached from the scene before him, as he felt from so many things in his life. The rhythm of the words changed, and became something that sounded familiar, a prayer from childhood, something once spoken over folded hands against an altar rail. There was a strange low buzzing in his skull, an irritating sensation like bees had begun to move just a little above the nape of his neck. He resisted the urge to swat at the back of his head, or to just rub his scalp until the feeling dissipated.

Eddy touched his arm. "The words stir things up, the atmosphere, the shadows. He has to stir them up in order to sweep them away."

The old man picked up the bowl and drank several long, lusty swallows and then he gagged, spitting to the side. The chanting resumed then, building like a descant, multiple voices, a single voice, the voice of the night itself and the buzzing building inside Mick's skull until he thought he might go mad with the sensation.

Then the old man blew a single breath across the surface of the bowl, the dark liquid not even rippling in response. He said one last prayer.

"He's addressing the drug," Eddy said quietly, "it's the vine of life and it's what will bring the visions."

The old man looked at Mick and nodded slightly. Mick moved forward on his knees, and took the bowl. The smell was dreadful, but he had come this far, and drinking some foul brew was no great price if it brought even a sliver of clarity to his memory.

He took the bowl and drank, long swallows so that he might get it over with quickly. He gagged on the taste for it was even worse than the smell. He kept it down, which felt like a feat in itself.

He felt nothing for a good half hour, just a mellowness and a dying off of the buzzing inside his skull. Then he realized his lips had gone numb, and there was a spreading warmth in his stomach even as his legs turned cold. Vertigo suddenly overwhelmed him, and he shut his eyes. Behind his eyelids bright flowers burst open—crimson blossoms spilling amethysts, stars cascading like water rushing through a narrow aperture tumbling over each other in great silver streams, trees billowing with leaves pulsating with life, as though the universe ran through every vein, every green-sapped inch of them.

Suddenly he felt like he had been knocked to the ground and someone was hitting him, hard blows that took the air from his lungs. The pain was huge and spreading. It was the color of blood—scarlet and bursting. The ground beneath his hands was wet and the scent of decay rose thickly from it and then he was face down in it and the blows continued, driving his face into the earth.

And then he was no longer there. Instead he was back in the old man's yard, sick, violently retching into the dirt behind a tree, so dizzy he couldn't tell up from down. The nausea passed as quickly as it had swept over him, taking the vertigo with it. He sat up once the spasms stopped and took a long, shaky breath. Eddy was hunkered down in front of him, concern in his face and also a clear determination. The buzzing in his skull was back.

"He says you must drink more, he says what is in you has a powerful hold and that your body is so strong it fights the smaller dose. He says you must succumb to it and allow it to sweep the darkness from you."

And so he drank again, the taste not as bitter this time. He waited thinking the nausea must come, but it did not. What came instead was rage. It rose up, crimson as fire, burning the inside of his skull, killing the bees with a pain that seemingly knew no bounds for it felt as if his skull was splitting, leaking agony and dark thick viscous liquid like blood half-coagulated. He felt the wet of it, running through his hair, down the sides of his face, into and through his fingers. Just when it seemed he would have to die from the pain, that it would overcome him and kill him a voice, soft and soothing, spoke his name.

It was the dream and yet far more vivid than the dream had ever been. Except he wasn't in the boat, he was on the land and he was walking with the sea behind him. He could hear it and smell the salt of it, but his gaze was trained only on the land beneath his feet. Soft land, worn land, soil rich and loamy. He bent down to grab a handful and put it to his nose, breathing in its scents—growth and harvest and frost and decay. A small lane wound away over hills that were an impossible green, every shade of green from emerald to acid.

Without warning he found himself at the top of a drive, looking down into a hollow where a farmhouse sat in late afternoon sunlight. It was white and the doors and shutters were painted a deep and dazzling emerald. It seemed not quite real, as if a painting hung in the air before him, a painting that was peeling back layer upon layer of thick oils and colors—alizarin crimson, cadmium yellow, purple lake, sap green, and raw umber. And as each layer peeled back to hang raggedly at the edge of his vision, more of the house and its surroundings emerged. At first it seemed only a blur of figures and color but as the scene moved closer and the clarity increased he saw a wood, old trees, hardwoods—oaks, elms, ash. The ground beneath the trees was covered in a carpet of long grass and bluebells—bluebells thick with butterflies. A woman holding a child by the hand walked in the wood, gathering flowers. A small boy ran ahead of her and she bent down to the child at her side to take something from her. He could see the tiny one was a little girl, for she wore a straw hat with a ribbon on her head, dark curls rioting from beneath its brim. The woman kissed the upturned face of the little girl and when she straightened up, she was holding what appeared to be a clutch of weeds. The boy had swung himself up into the low branches of an oak, and Mick caught a glimpse of his face and drew in a sharp breath that drove needles through his lungs. The child looked so familiar—he looked like he could be his son, he was so like him in appearance and coloring. He followed them, though to his frustration he could not quite step inside the frame of the painting and could only bring its details closer by moving toward it.

The land seemed familiar to him, and the residue of pain clung to him, as though the land and the hurt were entwined and inseparable. The crimson pain threatened to overtake him again and he pushed it away through force of will. He could not let it cloud his vision of the woman and the children. His children—a boy and a girl.

And then the woman spoke to someone off the canvas, someone just off the edge beyond the ragged and thick edges of the peeling paint. He strained his vision, his hands clutching at the painting, trying to grasp at the paint to tear it away so that he might see the man to whom she spoke and yet he was afraid if he clutched it too hard it would dissolve. He knew she spoke to a man for there was a light in her face that spoke of love. He felt a surge of possession that was so strong it knocked him back down to his knees. He wanted to hit something or someone more like—the man she was looking at in that way for a start. He longed to touch her, to be touched by her. He longed to get up off this ground, and walk into the painting and join the small family there. Even if it meant spending a lifetime caught fast in a wood filled with bluebells.

Suddenly she turned her head, as if she sensed him watching and came toward him, the children still playing in the field behind her. It seemed to him that she could see him, but it was as if it was through a mirror tarnished by distance and time.

She put a hand up as if to touch him and he could smell her—want and need and strawberries and the sea coming forever into a receding shore. She smelled like desire and something more, something that made his guts clench and a silver shot of pain dart up his body. She smelled like home. And then she spoke to him and he strained to hear her, to know what she was saying and if she meant to speak to *him*. Her voice came to him through a long tunnel of echoes, just the remnants of what she said, whole syllables and half words making it to his ear. He put his own hand up to take hers and abruptly it all stopped. The peeling paint fell away and the picture itself—the woman, the children, the trees and the bluebells all swirled together and then vanished leaving only a trace of color and scent upon the air. And he was left with empty hands and an overly full heart.

He came back to himself to find that his shirt was off, his body clammy with sweat and the breeze prickling against every inch of him. He was lightheaded and light-bodied, like he was floating somewhere above, the ground no longer beneath him. The old man was touching the scars on his back, one finger tracing the pathway of each one and he could smell the woman again, as though it was she who touched him, ran her fingers soft as rain through the channels of his ruined flesh.

"The woman," he said, voice hoarse and broken, "where did she go?"

"What woman?" It was Eddy asking, and it sounded as if he spoke from far away, from another time, another country.

"I don't know," he said, shaking like a leaf, the sweat still running from his body though he was horribly cold. "There was a woman here, didn't you see her?" He knew even as he asked that they hadn't, only he had, she was simply part of his hallucinations. "I just know she was here, she was here," he said, and then felt the loss of it in his bones, for she was gone and his understanding of her had left with the vision.

"You called her wife," the old man said quietly and then walked away.

"Mick, man, I'm sorry, that was wild—are you okay?"

He sat up, dirt cascading down his chest, catching in his chest hair, the smell of it, dark and loamy, a comfort to his chilled, terrified self. He felt it on his bruised hands, earth, the thing that had always given him comfort and sustenance. One thing remained from the vision of the woman, one word he had heard through that strange echoing tunnel.

"My name's not Mick," he said, "it's Casey. My name is Casey."

Chapter Fifty-two

Taking the Dive

CASEY HAD SPENT the afternoon roaming the Marin Headlands and now was sitting on an outcropping of rock with the view of the bay stretching out below him. It was where he came to sit and think—high in the hills with the dark scent of pine wrapping around his senses and nothing but the wind and the gulls for company. He liked this city and felt as at home here as he expected he could feel at this point in his life. San Francisco was a brash city and always had been. It was the last wild outpost of the American Dream though it was a city that had seen a lot of dark days recently. He'd heard people say that the 70s in San Francisco was the graveyard of the late 60s. It felt all too apt in a city that had seen so much turmoil in just a few years' time. Patty Hearst's kidnapping by the Symbionese Liberation Army, the Zebra murders, the death of Janis Joplin, the wave of new and far more deadly drugs that hit the Haight and the people who inhabited its streets. But the lost and the forgotten still found refuge in the city by the bay: veterans and windy-foot children, gay men and women, musicians and vagabonds, gypsies and poets, wayfarers and renegades.

There were the dark threads that wove around the brighter ones—rumors that the CIA had run a human guinea pig farm in the Haight, testing hard drugs on the youth that filled its streets and rundown houses. Sometimes it was easy enough to believe when he saw the wreckage that roamed the streets, the hollowed out zombies and psychotics, and the boarded up store fronts where, Eddy had told him, a vibrant and colorful madness had existed only a few years before.

San Francisco was city as theater, city as pageant and spectacle. Even its setting was staged on a grander scale than most cities—the white-capped Pacific rolling into the bay, the beautiful dark hills falling down toward the water and the bridge spanning up like a golden arc of promise. It was the destination, but you didn't start the journey until you were already here.

Casey had made his own journey here but he thought he might be nearing the end of the road. Hale had told him to take a dive in his next fight. The odds on him were so high that betting against him and having him lose would result in a gold mine. He had expected this day to come; he just hadn't expected to feel quite so belligerent about it when it did. There were things to consider, though. Hale had promised him a handsome pay-out if he took the dive. It would be enough money to go to Ireland and see if he couldn't find out who he was and who he had once been. He knew he needed to stop fighting soon, because eventually he was going to take one hit too many and he was already dancing with the devil when it came to the odds on that particular issue.

Since the episode with the ayahuasca he hadn't felt the same about the fighting. He no longer seemed to need it and the rage which had fueled it was gone. Having his name had changed things for him too. It felt like a worn shirt which had long been lost, abandoned at the bottom of a box and newly come upon while searching for some other item. It fit, and it was comfortable, even if it took some readjustment. Somehow he felt more solid, less like a ghost and more like a man.

A gull landed on a rock in front of him and squawked, no doubt expecting some sort of food to appear.

"I don't have anything for ye, man," he said and the gull squawked again, seemingly annoyed by his lack of largesse. He had one of those echoes which had become more frequent since the night of the ayahuasca visions—an echo that made it feel that he had been in this moment before. The gull gave him one last beady glare and flew off, wheeling out over the bay until it was only a tiny arc of white against the dazzling blue of the water.

He held his left hand up in front of his face and looked at the narrow silver band. He twisted it around his finger wishing, not for the first time, that it could tell him its story and like a magic talisman lead him back to its matching partner.

He thought about the woman and children he'd seen in his drug-induced vision and wondered again if they were real, or if he had somehow wanted them so badly that he'd conjured them up with the assistance of the drug. He felt half-made of longing lately. Longing to know who he really was, longing for a history and a home that was his, rather than a house in which he and the woman who owned it both seemed more ghost than flesh and blood beings. He rose and dusted pine needles off the seat of his pants. Dream or not, he needed to find out for certain.

One more fight, and then he was done.

"You're fighting an Irishman tonight. Seems fitting," Eddy said, his voice muffled by the tape he was biting off to wrap around Casey's knuckles. "He's a Gypsy apparently. Didn't know the Irish had Gypsies."

"Aye, they're called Travellers," he said, putting up his hand so Eddy could apply the tape. When Eddy was done Casey jumped around a little to let off the excess energy before they went out to the pit. He was fighting at Molly's tonight and was glad of it; it was a good way to end his run.

His opponent was fierce looking. He strode into the lighted ring wearing a worn pair of jeans and a bright blue fedora with a red feather stuck in the brim. He flashed a smile at the crowd and it was blinding white, and winking with several gold caps. He had rings on all his fingers and a rather gaudy cross around his neck which he made a show of kissing before removing it. The rings took him a good two minutes to take off. He removed the hat last, doffing it to the crowd with a flourish and bowing, the lights gleaming off his shaved head. He knew how to put on a show, Casey thought. It was a good tactic; it would endear him to the audience. Casey just wanted to get on with it.

"You're a little tight tonight, man. You feeling fear?" Eddy was checking the tape on his right hand to make certain it wasn't going to slip at all once it got bloody. They were drawing interested stares from the opposite side of the ring. Casey knew people found the combination of a big Irish guy and an Indian interesting. "Balls and bowels, man, that's where fear always shows up. One's high and tight and the other is loose and rumbly. That's when you know you're afraid."

If those were the two indicators then Casey would have to assess himself as afraid. He usually got a huge hit of adrenaline before a fight, but this was the first time he could recall feeling scared. He wondered if it was because he suddenly felt there was something to lose if he was hurt, even if it was only a name.

"I'm fine," he said shortly. He didn't like to talk before a fight, though he never minded if Eddy talked to him and Eddy understood why his answers were always brief.

"Use the fear, and remember in through the nose and out through the mouth. Step back when you're tired and drop your hand to give it a rest whenever you can."

"Aye."

He met the man in the middle, feeling the rush of blood pumping hard through his fists. The referee was there to give them the rules. His hearing was heightened along with all his other senses and it sounded like the man was almost yelling in his ears.

"If one of you is down, the other lets you get up. Arms round each other is a foul. No fouling, no dirty punches—when you break, break clean."

They both nodded and backed off, assessing each other for strengths and weaknesses. Casey wasn't sure this man had any; there were no obvious tells in his demeanor or movement.

He saw the transformation come over the man, who went from smiling showmanship with the crowd to looking like he wanted to eat Casey's guts for breakfast. He knew the space you slipped into, because he did it himself with each fight. You could feel perfectly cordial about your opponent outside of the ring, but want to hurt him badly in it. It was necessary to winning, a man could not be squeamish about it or he was lost.

They spent the first few minutes taking short jabs at one another, feinting with one fist, throwing with another. Dancing in and out, eyeing one another up as wolves would confronting each other in a forest. He threw the first real punch just to get things started. Three minutes later he was starting to sweat, five and they'd both drawn blood. The man could fight. It might not be hard to take a dive because it was quite possible he was going to lose this fight without the need to cheat. The man was relentless and yet this was exactly the sort of fight he loved. There was a brilliance at the dark heart of it like nothing else. Something that was like rushing out and flying past the edge of things, touching it all—joy and dread, fear and fury, blood lust and blood exhaustion.

Ten minutes into the fight, Casey drove in on him hard and the man caught him out by telegraphing right and then catching him with a left hit to his head. His ear sang as the pain exploded and tiny stars danced in front of his eyes. Casey pulled back so that he could catch his breath. He dropped his right hand to give it a rest and brought up his left. He quickly checked his ear for blood, there wasn't any, though it felt like the side of his head had cracked open. He couldn't hear a damn thing out of his right ear and hoped to hell it wasn't permanently damaged.

Casey came back with a series of punches, pulling back a little on the really powerful hits—the uppercuts, the hooks. As a result he was taking a hard beating and his chest and stomach felt it. He kept moving his arms up and down to protect his head and watching the man's eyes to see where the next punch was coming from. He was a chancy bastard and caught him with a few misdirected punches to the jaw and shoulders. His knee felt like it was on fire and he could sense a slight wobble to it every time he put his weight forward.

It was here in the center of the fight that everything melted away. It was him and the man hitting him, the voices of the crowd outside the range of his hearing, everything drawn in tight, just the two of them in some primal embrace, locked in a dance to the death. A strange feeling would sweep him at such times that maybe this was purgatory and he was doomed to fight forever. Or at least until God forgave him his sins.

The man came in close and Casey tightened the space further so he couldn't sucker punch him. Then the man did something totally unexpected. He leaned in and whispered in his ear, the one that was still pounding with blood from the cracking great punch he'd given it.

"Listen, let's end this. Don't pull yer punches on me anymore, d'ye understand? Let's end this properly. Irish pride an' all that, right?" He winked at him, and Casey grinned back, splitting his lip and sending a bright spray of blood down his chin.

And then he just let it happen, instinct and the free fall right down to the essence of life—blood, bone and the fight to survive. It was time to be ruthless. He went in hard and fast, he had to end it before his knee gave out. Fifteen punches in sequence—head, sides, stomach, right, left, jab, uppercut, hook and then again and again.

The man who called himself Gypsy Boy had blood pouring from one eye and his grin was as red as a wolf's rising from a fresh kill.

"Now ye're feckin' talkin', boyo. Come on ye big bastard an' finish it if ye can."

He closed in fast and furious and took a blow to his stomach which telegraphed quite clearly to his legs that he was nearly done for. But the small break and few breaths had restored some of his energy and his focus. He put all of it into the last punch, the energy flowing like fire up his arm and exploding in a right roundhouse that drove the other man down to his knees where he gave Casey a bemused look before toppling over and closing his eyes.

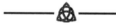

He'd been a fool, a great bloody fool. He tore the tape off his hands ripping the skin on his knuckles in the process. He should have just taken the dive, instead he'd allowed pride to have its way with him. It was, he suspected, one of his greater weaknesses from the life before. There would be no money now to flee the country either. He'd used up much of his prior winnings to clean up his hospital bills. He needed to get dressed and get the hell out of here and do it quickly. He pulled on clean pants and a shirt and bent down to put on his socks and shoes. He felt the air move rather than hearing anything. There was someone behind him. He'd been expecting it from the moment he knocked his opponent out. He just thought he might have an hour's grace before they came for him.

Ye're a stubborn bloody goat son, ye use yer pride instead of yer head an' it's goin' to get ye into trouble every time.

Thanks but ye're a wee bit late with yer advice, he said to the voice in his head, wondering why these echoes of his past life often seemed to come at inopportune moments.

He stood up slowly and turned. Hale had not come but Casey had not thought he would. He wouldn't handle his own dirty work; he had hired help for that. The henchman he'd sent was a small man, much smaller than Casey but he had a knife and Casey did not. He had long known not to underestimate small men, particularly the wiry ones who could often move as quickly as a snake could strike. Given a little more space he thought he could outmaneuver the man, but here in this tight little room which held a bench and a shower and lockers it was going to be far more difficult. If he could get himself over the bench and into the corner he might have a better shot at defending himself. He would have to take the chance as the man was closing in on him. Everything must answer—shoulders, wrists, elbows, legs, feet, eyes. He was tired and his knee was a blaze of pain. This was not theater, there was no crowd howling in the language of blood and sweat and pain. There was just the hope to survive and the stink of sweat and hatred.

He managed to hit the man a ringing blow to his head, but he got a cut across his arm for his efforts. It reaffirmed what he'd thought—the man was fast. Blood was dripping from his arm and he fought the urge to clutch it to his chest.

He was tired and the other man was fresh, he had his fists and the other man had a knife, he knew how this ended. He jumped up on the bench and that was when his knee finally betrayed him, giving out entirely just as he landed and sending him backwards in an arse-over-teakettle tumble where he struck his shoulder and head with bruising force on the edge of the lockers. There were stars exploding before his eyes and tiny birds chirping in his ears. He was on his back on the cold tiled floor. He thought blearily that it was a miserable place to die. He would have chosen the outdoors, stars overhead, wind in his face. Once his vision cleared, he looked up to see the man standing over him, a feral grin on his face.

"Mr. Hale says he never should have trusted a fucking mick. He also says goodbye."

Someone was pounding on the door, but it was too late. His last coherent thought was that he was sorry he would never know the man he had once been and then all was utter darkness.

———⟨☉⟩———

He awoke to the sound of rain drumming on the roof. Which was odd in itself because, like the song said, it hardly ever rained in California. There were voices nearby. They weren't speaking English, but the language they did speak was utterly soothing to him; just the sound of it was like mother's milk in his ears.

"Hey, Rip Van Winkle. Decided to join the land of the living again?"

Casey opened one eye and peered up to find Eddy, upside down, peering back at him. Beside him hovered another face, this one a little bruised and battered but with a grin that was filled with gold. The Irish Traveller he'd fought, and as he recalled, stupidly beat. He tried to sit up but found he was spectacularly dizzy, as though he'd just come off a whirligig at Coney Island. Had he ever been to Coney Island, he wondered? He was feeling distinctly muzzy.

"Where the hell am I?" he asked, supine again. He'd try sitting up later, maybe tomorrow. He looked around. He was lying on a bed in a caravan. It was a little lacking in décor, but was tidy and clean. He cautiously felt his head and found to his relief that it was still intact.

"Welcome to me humble abode," Gypsy Boy said with a neat flourish of his bejeweled hands. He wore a loudly-striped shirt, grey trousers, a leather jacket and a jaunty hat to match. "We're parked in a wee bit of forest as we felt it was a little hot in old San Francisco last night."

"Was I stabbed?" he asked, uncertain what was real and what he'd dreamed in the last day.

"Ach, it's only a scratch. We took care of that poxy fecker for ye. Ye've got ten stitches to remember it by though."

"Took care of it?"

"Aye, ye were bleedin' like the proverbial stuck pig an' passed out cold. Yer friend there," he nodded toward Eddy, "leaped on his back an' I gave him a few pokes to the head, an' one or two to the kidneys. He'll not be botherin' anyone soon."

"Or ever," Eddy added drily.

"Not feckin' goin' to let some sheisty fecker kill a fellow Irishman on me watch, now am I? 'Twas yer friend that saved ye. He took the knife off that bastard an' had it at his throat before ye could say Jack Robinson."

"Well, thanks for that," Casey said, meaning it quite sincerely.

"Ach, save yer breath to cool yer porridge, man. We'll take ye up to the state line or further on if ye care to travel with us for a time. Ye'll not be wantin' to go back or sure an' they'll kill ye this time."

He nodded, feeling slightly confused with the information coming at him. Gypsy Boy doffed his hat at him and ducked out the door of the caravan.

"Eddy?"

"The man's right, it's not safe back there. So I made an executive decision while your Irish ass was unconscious. We're running away with the gypsies."

"I can see why I need to but why are you comin' along? Ye have a job an' a life back there."

Eddy shrugged. "I think I'm done with San Francisco. I got itchy feet, man, it's past time for me to be moving along anyway."

"Are ye certain?" Casey asked, worried that Eddy had done something on his behalf that he was going to live to regret.

"Yeah, man it's time for me to go. More reasons than itchy feet truth be told, but that's a story for another day."

Eddy reached behind him and grabbed a canvas bag, which he then placed on the bed with Casey.

"Is that my stuff? How the hell did ye get it?"

"I was worried that Hale might send his men there once he realized you were gone. So I did a little reconnaissance and ended up climbing into the third floor tower, you know the place where you never had relations with Bridget." Eddy's skepticism was conveyed with the slight upturn of his lips.

"Aye," Casey returned the look with interest. "I'm familiar with the place."

"I grabbed your things, what there was, that is. You travel light, man."

He sat up then, despite the dizziness, panic coursing through his veins. "My ring, I always take it off before a fight."

Eddy fished in his shirt pocket and came up with the band of silver. "I knew you'd want it. Had to look a bit to find it. Got your rosary, too, didn't know you were a praying kind of man." He looped the beads over Casey's neck and they fell with a reassuring weight against his chest.

He collapsed back into the bed with relief. He felt better the minute he slid the ring onto his finger. It was as if the small bit of silver shored him up and made him aware of his purpose.

"When the gypsy offered I figured it was a gift horse whose mouth didn't need looking at too closely. We gotta hit the road, brother. You go back, you're dead. It's simple math really."

"I should say goodbye to Bridget, I owe her that much."

"She's gone," Eddy said. "She left yesterday. There's a letter for you. I found it sitting on your bed."

"Gone?" he said blankly.

Eddy handed him an envelope. It was a pale lavender and thick—old-fashioned stationery that would not have been out of place in a Victorian lady's home. He opened it and a trace of her jasmine scent wafted out.

Hey Irish – I'm selling the house, it deserves to have a family. And you were going to leave soon, we both know it. You were leaving the day I met you. It was nice to stop with you for a while on that dusty road. I hope you find her.

And that was it, she hadn't signed it. It was true to the windy-footed child which she had long been. She was right; the house deserved children and dogs and cats and noise and love. He felt sad at the thought of her drifting off across the country again. A woman could only live that way so long before something dark would catch her in its grasp. He had a pretty good notion just what was likely to snatch Bridget. He folded the letter up and put it back in the envelope.

"So it was you saved my life. Thank ye."

"You know what this means, man," Eddy said with one of his rare smiles that always put Casey on guard. He never smiled unless he was planning something.

"Uh no, I can't say that I do," he said.

"I saved your life, so you owe me a favor."

Casey sighed. "I suppose I should have seen this comin'. What is it that ye want?"

"When we part company with the gypsies, I want you to go on a walk with me," Eddy said.

"A walk? Ye want to go on a fockin' walk? I've just been stabbed, last I checked."

"It can wait until you are completely healed, but then I want you to come walking with me," Eddy repeated, a certain stubborn set to his chin which Casey had come to recognize over these last months.

"What sort of a walk are ye talkin' about here?"

"A long one, maybe uncomfortable sometimes, too."

"How long exactly? And how uncomfortable?"

"I want you to walk to South Dakota with me, so pretty uncomfortable."

"Ye want to do this for what reason?"

"Because there is nothing like a long walk to clear your head."

"Ye think walkin' a couple thousand miles is goin' to clear my head?"

"It's only fifteen hundred. And as to clearing your head, it can't hurt. Well, that's a lie, but we won't know unless we do it. So?"

Casey sat up, dizzy still from blood loss and the sound beating Gypsy Boy had ladled out to him.

"All right, you bastard, I'll take a walk with ye."

Part Six

The Far Side of Barsoom
May 1977-August 1977

Chapter Fifty-three

Roll Call of the Dead

MAY HAD BEEN a fitful month of sudden rains alternating with periods of sun. As a result, the fields and hedgerows were lushly green and filled to bursting with the chirrup of baby birds and the rustlings of hedgehogs and badgers.

Pamela and the children had come to Tomas' for the day along with Patrick and Kate. They had spent the afternoon happily roaming his land and having a picnic lunch amongst the ruins and brambles and blooming roses, both having long gone wild up tree trunks and over stile and wall alike. Patrick was walking along beside her, a vague tension about him that she knew was attributable to his work.

"Kate said Shura has left?"

Pamela nodded. "Yes, he literally ran away with the gypsies. He left with Yevgena when her visit was done. He is working in a small herbalist shop in Paris now and rents the room over it for his lodgings. I think he feels more useful there and he and Yevgena have become good friends. He's rather besotted with her."

"From what little Casey told me about her, I'm not surprised. Ye'll all miss him, though, I'm sure."

"We will, but we want him to be happy more than having him here. How is the case going?" she asked. She knew Pat and Tomas were still working doggedly on the Oggie Carrigan case and were slowly making headway. Both men had to keep up with their other work and other cases as well. For Patrick this was mostly composed of drawing up wills and land purchases and overseeing the details until all deals, whether that of land bought or sold or death disbursements, were concluded.

He smiled. "It's still a quagmire of paper an' snaky proposals, or as Tomas put it yesterday with much glee 'a serpentine imbroglio'. To summarize we're enjoyin' ourselves immensely, but it has been a deal of long hours. We've got an investigator lookin' into wee Jane's murder too. The coroner signed off on it bein' a suicide, so it's goin' to be hard to convince anyone to open it up as a possible homicide. Mind you, cases like this can take years of convincin' before someone agrees that it warrants a harder look. The wheels of justice turn slowly as the sayin' goes."

"You love it, don't you?"

"Aye," he smiled down at her. "I do." His expression turned serious then, like a dark cloud had crossed his face. "I assume ye heard about the killin' of the young man in Upper Donegall Street a few nights back?"

"Yes," she said. The scene had been a bad one and there was certainty in the community that it was a gang of men doing it, and that they were deliberately hunting for lone Catholics to catch and then murder in the most violent and terrible ways imaginable. The man was only twenty-four and had been out playing snooker for the evening. He'd met up with a girl he liked and offered to walk her home. At some point, after he left her at the door to her parents' home, he had been abducted and then beaten and tortured for hours before he was nearly decapitated with a knife and left like so much rubbish in an alleyway. An elderly woman whose house overlooked the alley found the body when she ventured out the next morning to put out her trash. She told the police that she'd heard the sound of a heavy vehicle which reminded her of the sound the black taxis made when they plied their trade along the Shankill Road. It was far too reminiscent of the scene Pamela had photographed shortly after Casey had disappeared.

"There's so much violence here, it's easy for a few murderin' deviants to hide their crimes under the guise of politics an' vengeance, but I think in this case these men are killin' for the sheer pleasure of it. Just be certain ye're not caught out alone in Belfast at night."

"I'll try not to," she said drily. She couldn't remember the last time she had been out after dark other than the dinner with Yevgena. Most of her evenings consisted of baths and books and getting small children to sleep at a decent time before collapsing herself on the downstairs couch.

Just then Conor launched himself off the garden wall he was walking on into his uncle's arms. Pat caught him deftly around the middle and swung him neatly up onto his shoulder, narrowly missing a low-hanging branch and causing Pamela to draw in a sharp breath. She was grateful to Pat and Jamie, because Conor got his necessary rough and tumble male play with them; the sort of things that made a mother go faint with all the thoughts of what might happen.

They had reached the edge of a small pond which was beautifully mossy about its edges with several nooks and crannies and wonders to explore. Isabelle squealed with delight and pulled her hand from her mother's and headed like a small tumbling drunk straight for the water's edge. Pamela grabbed her by the back of her sweater, causing Isabelle to shriek in protest.

Pat laughed, lowering Conor down so that he could explore. "That one has her daddy's temper."

"Doesn't she just," Pamela said, bending down to kiss her daughter's furious head of hair and letting her go, but keeping a wary eye on her at the same time. At twenty-two months of age, Isabelle was already a force with which to reckon.

"Da' always said Casey was goin' to be responsible for every grey hair on his head."

"Deirdre says the same. She says Isabelle reminds her of Casey in temperament, too."

"She's become a good grandmother, no?" Pat asked. Pat had made his peace with Deirdre in a way Casey had not been able to.

"She has. It's been nice for me, having her around from time to time. I never knew my own mother. I think, in some ways, she's trying to make amends for leaving you and Casey by loving Conor and Isabelle extra hard."

"Aye, I think so, too, though ye'd not get the woman to admit it in a month of Sundays."

Pat went off then at Conor's exclamation that he had found a beauty of a frog and Uncle Pat must come and see it. Pat was more appreciative of sticky amphibians than she was, so Pamela happily let him go.

Tomas came and stood beside her. "She's a wee beauty, that one," he said, watching Isabelle as she crooned softly to the frog which was now in her uncle's hands. It was true, even at her tender age, Isabelle was already showing signs that one day she would be in possession of a fierce beauty that was undoubtedly going to cause Pamela no little grief.

"When is James back?" Tomas asked, his tone so deliberately casual that Pamela rolled her eyes at him. He merely gave her one of his rather frightening grins and she sighed. She knew Tomas' thoughts about her and Jamie.

"Not for a few days yet, he's run into some snags with his business in Hong Kong." It was far more complicated than that and she had experienced no little worry over what she knew he faced in order to keep the business running smoothly. He had to barter with the triads every few years, and she knew he had not been relishing what lay ahead of him when he left. The world always felt slightly askew when Jamie was absent.

The five of them left Tomas' house in the late afternoon, sated by the warmth of the sun which had held all day. Isabelle promptly fell asleep in the car while Conor, sitting beside her, happily sorted through his treasures, of which there were many. His small pockets were stuffed to the brim with shells and bits of plant and what Pamela feared was a rather large snail.

It was easier coming home with other people. Pat's presence always took the edge off the hollow that existed in the heart of her house. She insisted Pat and Kate stay to an early supper and they agreed after one of those split seconds which passed between couples where volumes were communicated without a word spoken. It was one of the million things she missed about life with Casey. With his usual quiet intuitiveness, she thought Pat knew that she sometimes panicked at the thought of being alone. With Kate's help she made soup and sandwiches while Pat took Conor out to feed Paudeen, and Isabelle continued her nap on the sofa.

Supper was eaten in short order and there was talk and laughter around the table and a sense of ordinariness which felt a bit like grace, for the ordinary was rare in this country and Pamela had long ago learned to treasure it as it passed. Casey's chair still sat empty, for she couldn't bear the thought of anyone else sitting in it, other than perhaps Patrick. But Pat avoided the chair too, though she saw him looking at it now and again, dark eyes strained.

After supper, amidst the bustle of clearing the table and starting the evening routine with the children, she paused to call her neighbor, Lewis. He had not been well of late, and she checked in daily, especially just now as Owen and Gert were away. The telephone rang tinnily, with the strange crackle along the line that always made her wonder if her phone was tapped. She let it ring several times, as Lewis was stubborn about answering it for the most part. He would pick up normally though, for he knew she would show up on his doorstep if he didn't. It rang eight times before she hung up. She turned from the phone, feeling a pluck of worry along her spine.

"Would you mind if I ran over to check on Lewis? I want to take him some soup. He's been feeling poorly lately and he doesn't eat well at the best of times. With Gert and Owen away, there's no one to check on him but me."

"Aye, go," Kate said, "we've nowhere we need to be an' we love to spend any time we can with the wee ones."

Pamela packed up soup and bread for Lewis, as well as a few oranges because she knew he loved them but rarely bought them for himself. She put on her sweater and boots, for the ground was soft from several days of rain, and then set off through the quiet of the wood and field that separated their two homes.

She came out on the edge of the field, climbing over the lowest part of the stone wall which marked the property boundary, her boots sinking in the mud a little. She turned toward Lewis' house just as a dark cloud slid over the face of the sun, making it appear as though a spectral shadow flitted across the worn farmhouse. She walked forward hesitantly, the hair prickling at the base of her neck. Something felt off, but she knew her paranoia had become fine-tuned from living this long in Northern Ireland.

The yard around the small farmhouse was the same as it always was, littered with the things that Lewis was forever finding and fixing up: an old butter churn; a wringer washer; a Belfast sink with one corner chipped away and an Indian Racer, which when running blew out great clouds of blue smoke and made a noise like that of twenty chainsaws running all together. This last item was Lewis' pride and joy, and something he tinkered with almost every day.

The house was eerily quiet and most ominously the front door was ever-so-slightly ajar. She froze in place, breath caught hard in her lungs, everything around her sharpened so that the trees that lined the drive suddenly seemed like looming giants, the small crooked doorstep a crumbling ruin. She stepped up and over the doorsill, trying to stay as silent as the proverbial mouse. Her heart was pounding so madly in her chest that she thought she might pass out. She stepped into the narrow hall which led to the kitchen. The house was an old one and dark inside, mostly because Lewis kept the curtains drawn a good part of the time.

She saw movement in the corner and jumped, her hand flying up to her pounding heart. It was only Lewis' old collie though, tottering toward her on arthritic legs.

"Where's your master, Sotnos?" she asked. The old dog wagged his tail and whimpered. She rubbed his head in reassurance and he leaned into her legs. It was odd for him to be in the house this time of day, though it was possible the daily rounds of the small farm were getting to be too much for the old dog. He stayed at her heels as she looked around the rest of the house, his nails clicking loudly against the flagstones in the eerie quiet. She checked the bedroom. The bed was neatly made, Lewis' battered hat absent from the chair beside the bed where she knew he deposited it at night. So he had gone out this morning. She would have to check the outbuildings. Returning to the kitchen, she spied his rifle in the corner behind the door, where he always kept it. She put the food on the table and then picked up the rifle, checking to see if there was a cartridge in it. There was, so she snapped the barrel back into place and walked out the door, Sotnos still at her heels.

The breeze had picked up while she was in the house and the sun was now hiding behind the clouds making the landscape look dark and foreboding. The timothy heads in the field were bowing down before the wind, releasing their honey scent onto the air, but she thought she smelled something else below the sweet scent, something cold and coppery. She could feel her body draw up, her center of gravity high inside her, her muscles tightening in response to the possibility that she might need to flee in the next few moments.

She walked forward slowly, scanning the horizon around her for any movement, Sotnos glued to her leg. The byre lay in shadow and the cows were making noises of discontent. They ought to be out in the pasture grazing at this time of day.

She found him on the floor in front of one of the stalls. They must have come upon him when he was doing the morning milking. His hearing had faded in the last year, or they would never have been able to get the drop on him. He had, after all, once been a highly-trained killer. He was lying with the milking bucket overturned beside him. She took a breath and walked to where he lay, rifle still held to her side. The blood had congealed after it mixed with the cream and the byre floor looked like a gruesome painting by a drunken Surrealist.

Pamela propped the rifle up against the stall gate and knelt down by the old man, putting one hand to his arm. He was cold to the touch but she felt for a pulse anyway, hoping against hope. She couldn't find one and his flesh felt inert, as if he had breathed out his soul hours ago. Her heart sank and she wrapped an arm around Sotnos. The old dog was whimpering, his tail held tight between his legs.

She got to her feet, slowly, feeling achy all through her body. Achy and so very tired. She needed to think, to get help. Lewis had no one else, no family, no friends other than herself, Gert and Owen. This would break Casey's heart, he had been very fond of the gruff old man. Of course, Casey would never know and for that very small mercy she was grateful.

There were things she must do—return to the house, call someone, begin all the small acts which attended death. She stood just for a moment, though, for she needed to get her bearings. The echo of a gunshot seemed to hang upon the air, the fateful noise that was the border between pulse and breath and life and the dark gateway to silence and death. Had he been afraid she wondered? She thought not, he was a tough old bastard and he would have expected that death might come in this fashion—quick and bloody. He might even have wanted it so.

Pamela leaned her face into the stall gate, pressing her forehead into the slivered wood and seeking some semblance of stability from it. Just below her breastbone was a flood-tide of grief for the old man who lay dead at her feet, and for everyone else that had been lost along the way in this brutal country. It was her own roll call of the dead, a tattered sheet of paper she kept furled in her heart with the names written in the color of blood—Lawrence, Sylvie, Robin, David, the two babies she and Casey had lost. She had never added her husband's name to this list, for if ever she came to a place where she was certain he wasn't coming home, she knew that engraving in her heart would be something entirely different, both in depth and the color of its words.

She walked from the byre and did not look back, for whatever Lewis had been to her—friend, neighbor, protector—that was now gone and only the shell remained, only that and the sound of the wind grieving through the slats of the byre.

The police would have to come and so she did not want to involve Pat in this, being that he was not on their good side just now. She called Noah, even though she knew it wasn't likely he'd be in the house this time of day, for he would have a wealth of evening chores to attend to. To her surprise he picked up on the second ring.

She told him, quickly and without detail but he understood why she was using shorthand and merely said, "On my way."

She was standing by the byre door when he arrived, Sotnos still firmly attached to her leg, no longer whimpering, but still trembling.

He parked his truck and came to where she stood, concern written over his fine features. "Are ye all right?"

She nodded. "I know I have to call the police. I just wanted someone else with me when I did it."

"Aye, I think it's best if ye're not here alone when they arrive. I don't trust the bastards at all." And then, "Where?" he asked.

"The byre," she said, relieved that he did not expect her to go back in there. She wanted to banish what she had seen, and return to her last memory of Lewis alive, silent for the most part, gruff when he did speak, but he had looked after her and her family more than once. And he had been Casey's friend and she would have treasured him for that fact alone.

It was a relief to have Noah here, for his presence banished the echo of violence, though she was well aware of the irony of this feeling. He didn't hesitate at all, just went into the byre, in his usual business-like fashion. She supposed he had seen much worse than an old man who looked like he was merely in a deep and peaceful sleep.

It was only seconds later that he called her name. There was an urgency to the three syllables that made her step forward quickly. Noah was kneeling down by Lewis, Lewis' head braced between his two hands.

"Call for the ambulance," he said, "he's still alive."

"I can't believe I missed his pulse," Pamela said. "I might have killed him."

It was a few hours later and they had returned from the hospital to Lewis' farm so that she could retrieve Sotnos and lock the place up properly. Noah made tea while she did this and they were sitting together now, at the worn kitchen table.

"Strictly speakin'," Noah said, "it would be the four bullets in him that killed him."

"You're a bit of a literal bastard, aren't you?"

He laughed. "Aye, I am, but the fact of the matter is he's goin' to live an' he wouldn't have if ye hadn't gone to check on him. Now drink yer tea, ye're still shakin'."

She sniffed the mug in her hand, suspecting that he had slipped a little whiskey in to calm her nerves. She did indeed smell the hot peaty scent of whiskey but thought the man had a point. It would take the edge off her nerves.

The last hours were blurring already. After she had run in the house to call for an ambulance, she went back to the byre to find Noah doing mouth-to-mouth resuscitation on Lewis. If he made it through the surgery, the doctor had told her, he would most likely survive.

"He's a tough old goat," Noah said. His shirt was bloody from working over Lewis, but other than that he appeared entirely unruffled by the evening's events. Owen had been contacted in Kerry, and he and Gert were already on their way back. Noah had said he would arrange to have Lewis' animals looked after in the meantime.

"I probably took you away from your evening chores," she said, feeling suddenly awkward. "I need to get home. It's time to put the children to bed."

"I had one of my men finish up for me, I've naught pressing to do. I can drive ye home when ye're ready. But first finish yer tea, ye're white as a sheet an' tremblin' like a leaf in the wind. Drink up, ye'll feel better just as soon as the shock passes."

She shook her head. There wasn't a way to explain to Noah what she had felt there in that byre with the wind sighing through the walls. How to explain that roll call of the dead and what it meant to believe she was adding yet another name, what it meant to the girl she had once been but could no longer find within herself. Jamie would understand, because he had known that girl and he had changed along with her. He understood the missing parts as well as those that remained. She wanted to ask Noah what the cost was in the end, what it took from a human soul to live with such violence.

"I know how it is, Pamela," he said, as if he had heard her unspoken question. "Just when ye think this country can't take one more thing from ye, it does. An' I know there are times when ye wonder if ye'll survive it.

The hell of it is that ye do, even when it seems it would be better not to, ye do."

He drove her home after that and politely declined her offer to come in.

"No thank ye, I'd best head back home an' make certain all is shut up for the night. I'll come by tomorrow if I may an' check an' see what the news is on Lewis."

She nodded. "I'll see you then."

Inside the house there was warmth and noise, though only at a low level for Isabelle was asleep on Kate's shoulder and Conor was in his pajamas, insisting that his Uncle Pat stay to read him his bedtime story. The warmth and normality of the scene surrounded her and took some of the fear and tension of the last hours away. She took her first decent breath in hours.

"How's Lewis, then?" Pat asked, concern written over his face.

She dropped her coat over the back of a kitchen chair and sat down. Conor jumped up into her lap and she gave him a hug, relishing the wiggling energy of him.

"He was holding his own, last we heard. Apparently it is going to take more than four bullets to knock that stubborn old man down. The hospital promised they would call as soon as he's out of surgery."

"Uncle Pat is going to stay an' read to me. He promised," Conor said, this last with an emphasis that sounded so entirely Riordan in nature that she had to stifle a laugh. Pat heard it, too, and smiled. Conor gave her a smacking kiss then jumped off her lap and went over to his uncle, who swung him up in his arms.

"All right, boyo but I will *not* read more than four books to ye, that's the limit."

She watched as Pat carried Conor up the stairs, the two of them talking nonsense the way they always did together. Kate was smiling, her face turned toward the staircase, as if she too could see the tall, dark man with the arms of the small boy wrapped around his neck.

"Conor well knows that his uncle will fall asleep before he can get through one book, never mind four," Kate said, with a laugh.

"I'll spell him off before he's too tired to drive home. Thank you so much for looking after the children."

Kate waved a hand at her. "'Tis no trouble at all, ye know we love to spend time with them. I'm glad Noah was able to help Lewis."

"He saved his life, no thanks to me. I couldn't even find his pulse."

"Noah's good in a crisis," Kate said. "He's got the medic trainin' so no fault to ye, I'm sure I would have given him up for a ghost too. I'm very glad he's goin' to survive though, I know he's been a dear friend to ye." She continued on in her brisk manner, changing the subject to something more comfortable. "Miss Isabelle had a snack, an' she's a fresh nappy on her bottom, so she ought to sleep well for ye." She handed Isabelle to her, and Pamela held her daughter's sleepy body next to her own, feeling the sweet, warm weight of her. She leaned her cheek into Isabelle's cloud of dark curls and breathed her baby in—she had been bathed and put in fresh pajamas and she smelled sweetly of talc and the special chamomile soap she made for Isabelle's delicate skin.

She held her for a bit longer, and then carried her up the stairs, placing her gently in the crib. True to Kate's prediction, Pat was nodding off over the book he was reading to Conor. He opened his eyes at her entrance and stood, looking back down at Conor who was sprawled out, deeply asleep, with two books still clutched fast in his hands. Pat gently pulled them away and placed them on the shelf under the window, the one Casey had built and she had painted with crescent moons and stars.

They moved out into the hall, Pat manfully suppressing a yawn. He walked down the stairs behind her, pausing at the bottom to give her a quick hug. Then he and Kate put on their coats and shoes and readied themselves to leave.

"Are ye all right, then?" he asked, pausing on the doorstep, Kate's hand in his own.

"I'm fine, Pat. I think I'll just have a bath and go to bed. I'm exhausted."

"Aye, I would imagine ye are." The dark eyes met her own and she knew he didn't really believe that she was fine, but then she hadn't been for a long time. This was her new normal in life, and in ways she had never thought possible she had adjusted and learned to live with it.

The house was too quiet when they left. There weren't even dishes to tidy away, for Kate had left everything in apple-pie order, the way she always did every time she visited. Noah was the same, she realized; anything that required fixing he saw to it without even asking her, he simply did it because he knew it was necessary.

She drifted up the stairs, tired in body, but not yet in mind. She went to check on the children first, to make certain Conor was still covered and warm, and that Isabelle wasn't fussing as she sometimes did in the first hour of sleep.

The children's room was warm, for unlike her and Casey's room it only had one exposed wall, whereas the master bedroom was on the corner of the house, and caught the chilly winds that sometimes came sweeping through of a night. Both children were still fast asleep, Conor on his back with the covers already pushed off and away. She bent down and kissed his forehead, pulling the blankets back over him. He stirred slightly in his sleep, and then turned and clutched his old bunny to his chest. Isabelle was breathing deeply, making the soft cooing noise she made when she was completely relaxed. A slice of moonlight fell across her flushed cheek, her tiny rear end in the air the way it often was in sleep. Pamela missed standing in this room with Casey, watching their children sleep, exchanging soft talk, freezing into silence when one of the children stirred and then creeping out the door together and only releasing their breath when they were past the squeak in the hall floor.

She went downstairs and made herself a cup of tea, a brew with catmint and valerian to help her sleep. Then she took the old stone gin jar from the shelf above the Aga and filled it with hot water, screwing the cap on tightly so that it wouldn't leak in the bed. She paused at the bottom of the stairs, feeling a weight in her body like that of dread. She thought briefly about curling up on the sofa with Rusty for company and just pulling the old afghan over her. She shut her eyes and took a stair and then another, and then another. Before she knew it her hand was on the door of their room. She turned the knob and went in. The room smelled of dried rose petals and peat ash. She mostly used it these days to change her clothes and that was about it. Occasionally she would light a fire in the hearth, to get rid of the damp, but she had not slept in her own bed since Casey had disappeared.

The moon was just a sliver off full and it bathed the room in distilled silver, suspending every item and delineating their features—the curve of the tall dresser, the worn round of the chair back in the corner of the room, the stones of the fireplace and the graceful arc of the canopy over their bed. It was as if even time was frozen here and she might turn and find Casey in the bed, reading from the Farmer's Almanac and thinking out loud about which moon was best to plant kale beneath.

She undressed slowly, not bothering with the light. Her mind was caught fast somewhere outside that byre and she could still smell timothy laced with blood. She was too tired to take a bath, so she settled for a wash with hot water, sponging down her body and scrubbing her hands in the small basin she kept on the bedroom dresser. She combed her hair back from her face and put on an old jersey of Casey's; it was the thing she most often slept in. She could pretend sometimes that she still smelled him in it—wood and water and that dark note that always brought a flush through her body.

She stood for a time, looking at the room, at the empty bed. The sheets were probably slightly musty even though she did occasionally wash and change them, despite not sleeping in the bed. Tonight though, she wanted to be alone with her thoughts, and not crammed in beside Conor who, while generally an accommodating bed mate, did tend to kick off all the blankets several times a night, leaving her shivering.

She took a breath. "You can do this, Pamela Riordan," she said, her voice overly loud in the still silver night. She tucked the gin jar between the sheets. The soft linen was cold to her touch but the heat of the gin jar released the scent of the lime water with which she had pressed the sheets. She pulled on a pair of wool socks and took another breath, the trapped bird that lived inside her chest beating its wings a time or two. Maybe she couldn't do it. Maybe she should just go down the hall and curl up next to her son. Then as clearly as if he truly were there in the room with her, she heard Casey's voice from the last night they had shared this bed. She had been worrying out loud about Isabelle's temperature, being that it had seemed a touch high to her and the baby had been fussy much of the afternoon.

"*Come lie with me, darlin',*" he'd said, that look in his dark eyes that she knew so well. The look that said her worries would wait for the morrow, and for now she could just lie in his arms and let the world fade away.

She got in the bed, holding tight to the illusion that he was there, his body having warmed the sheets and that she could curl up to him and be instantly thawed. Just the touch of him was enough to bleed the tension from her usually. If not, there was always sex, which finished the job every time. Casey had caught on to this early in their relationship and had used it to his advantage many a night. Not that she had protested, for it was an effective cure for more than one ill.

She hugged his pillow to her chest, burying her face in the edge of it. She thought she could smell just the faintest trace of him there still. "Casey, I need your help, I don't think I can get through this without you. I know that's ridiculous, but you promised me once you would haunt me, you'd come to me if I needed you. Well, I need you, man. I need you so badly." Her voice sounded small, even in the great still of the night. Not a voice to summon either man or ghost. She knew her man, though; she knew the language which had always summoned him, the language they spoke with such ease to one another.

She stirred and stretched out, restless and wanting. She closed her eyes and ran her hands up her body, cupping her breasts through the worn cloth of the shirt. It was ridiculous this, thinking that by pressing her own bare skin against material his had once touched that she was somehow bringing him back, conjuring the phantom of his touch and his heat to her body once again. One hand slid down between her legs, touching the ache there. She remembered what Noah said, about sex being an assertion of life. It was indeed that, and with Casey it had been something more—something, as he had once told her, that was sacred. She missed him so, missed him in all the parts of their shared life, missed this at night, him next to her, inside her, missed the things he had whispered in her ears, the soft things, the smutty things, the romantic things and the moments of need which were so intense that only silence would do. She feared it would always be so for her, that even if she learned to move on in all the various ways of the world, she would still feel that dread hollow at the core of her being—both emotional and physical. She wondered sometimes if a man would ever touch her again with desire and love, if she would ever want and need again as she had with Casey.

She lay for a long time, her eyes watching the moon swim across the floor, trembling and silver-white, reminding her of other nights, nights that seemed as if they had taken place in another land and another time which was no longer her own.

Finally, long after midnight, with her feet wrapped around the gin jar and with Casey's pillow once again clutched tight to her chest she fell asleep.

She could feel him in the bed. The heat he always emanated, the heat that warmed her to the core and she turned toward it unconsciously, body aware of him down to her last cell. She felt his hand, a shock of heat and roughly callused ridges, against her skin, moving like water along her thigh, pushing up the shirt she wore. She gasped softly, arching so the cloth rose higher.

"I'll not leave ye," he said soft in her ear, and she could feel the warmth of his breath, the heat of that long body pressed against her own, so that she rose to meet it, opening to it, needing and wanting with a blinding heat that obliterated all thought. God, how she had missed him, missed this, missed the oblivion of it, the intimacy that went beyond the physical joining of the two of them, the thing that solidified the foundation of what they were. The ache which she had carried inside for so long now was for the fit of her to him. His hands took her hips, raising her for deeper penetration and she gasped, turning her face into the pillow, the feeling more than she could bear. But he moved relentlessly, driving her before him on a ceaseless torrent of sensation and she cried his name out loud, so that she awoke to the echo of those two syllables dying away against the bedroom ceiling. His name was there on her lips, her body rising up to meet him again, his scent heavy on her—that scent of wood and earth, and something deeper and darker, something that bound her to him even now through the barriers of time and space.

And then it was gone, and so was he.

Chapter Fifty-four

An Acceptable Level of Violence

Coming from the warmth and jollity of a wedding reception to the dark and rain of an unseasonably chilly night in Belfast was a jolt to one's system, Pamela thought, hurrying along the pavement and wishing she had been able to find somewhere closer to the hall to park her car. She had been hired to photograph a wedding party, and while it had been a pleasant afternoon and evening, she was now wishing she had departed a little earlier. She had left her equipment at the hall, locked away, having made arrangements to pick it up on the following Monday. Walking through the city at any time put her nerves on edge, it could hardly be otherwise with all the violence that was a regular occurrence here and she didn't want expensive camera equipment slowing her down. Not that the countryside in which she lived was in any way immune to the violence that regularly tore Belfast apart at its seams. Three days before a couple had been shot to death in their home out past Newry, their two-year-old toddler shot four times in the legs and left for dead. He had been found collapsed sobbing on his mother's dead body, covered in both her blood and his own. The story had horrified her even more than usual, not just because of the terrible tragedy of it, but also because it told her that children were not off limits in this wretched conflict.

Sometimes she felt numb to the tragedy, exhausted by yet another bloody tale. The fear and anxiety never went away, it couldn't in such a land, and yet she realized that she had become accustomed to it in ways

IN THE COUNTRY OF SHADOWS • 455

she would not have dreamed possible even a few years ago. When, she wondered, had all this become so damnably familiar? It was what Jamie had once referred to as 'an acceptable level of violence'. That grey area in which people could still function in a normal manner, despite inhumane acts occurring around them on a weekly basis. Her eyes turned toward the mountain upon which Jamie's house sat. She couldn't see the house from where she was, but she could picture it in her mind's eye, lit up, warm, golden and alluring, rather like the man who owned it.

Given her druthers tonight, she would have gone up to that fairy tale house on the hill and stayed there. Conor and Isabelle were safe and tucked up at Gert and Owen's house and she didn't need to be home for a few hours. But Jamie was away on business in New York and would be for the next several days. Without his presence the house wasn't the same welcoming haven that it was with him home. Though the truth was, things were still occasionally strained between them since that night in his study. She supposed it was naïve to expect anything else.

She realized suddenly that she had allowed her mind to drift, and that was a mistake she could not afford here in the dark streets of Belfast. She found, much to her horror, that between her hurry, the darkness and the rain, she was hopelessly turned around and wasn't entirely certain where she was now. One wrong turn was all it took in this city, one wrong turn and you entered through the portal of a nightmare. She stopped and checked around her as best as she could in the murk, but she didn't see a familiar landmark. Beside her rose brick walls topped with razor wire. The walls were far too high to see over and there was nothing here on the street by which to orient herself. Please God that she hadn't unwittingly stumbled into a Loyalist area. Up ahead of her there was a young man walking swiftly, head down, hands jammed in his pockets. Beyond him she saw the lights of a pub, or at least she thought it might be. She would head in that direction and pray it was a Republican establishment, where she could ask for directions, or at least stop for a minute to get her bearings.

She took a breath, pacing herself, and keeping the distance between her and the young man to where she could see him but not where he became too aware of her presence behind him. There was no way to know which tribe he belonged to and until she knew where she was, it was too great a risk to get close to him. She had walked two blocks in this manner when she heard a car moving slowly along the road behind her.

She glanced over her shoulder; there was no such thing as too cautious in this town. She moved in toward the wall, preferring to stay in the dark and the illusion of shelter which the wet bricks provided. Up ahead there was an open space of a block, where a bomb had gone off six months earlier and there was little but rubble left. The car would be gone before she had to cross that open space though. She put her head down, picking up her pace a little. The small action was a saving grace, for a spray of shattered brick hit the side of her face a second later. Before she understood what was happening, instinct drove her to the pavement. She felt her stockings tear, and there was a sharp pain in her knees. Her ears were ringing with a hot, red sound as bullets rended the air around her head. She scuttled closer to the shelter of the wall, though the refuge it offered was illusionary at best. She could feel the terrible strange energy that automatic weapon fire left behind on the air. She looked ahead, the car was a block up now and the young man who had been walking ahead of her was nowhere to be seen. It was ominously quiet. She thought she should make for the pub posthaste, in case the car came back around. She took her shoes off, not wanting the heels to slow her down, and ran crouched low to the ground and tight to the wall. She hadn't gone more than twenty feet when she realized that the young man hadn't disappeared, but was lying terribly still in the middle of the sidewalk. She dropped onto her knees beside him, and touched his shoulder, praying that, by some miracle he had survived the barrage of bullets. Then she saw his head, in the dim halo of light thrown down by a street lamp just up ahead, and knew that there was no way he was still alive. There was so much blood, dear God, it was everywhere. She was kneeling in it, the slick warmth of it in marked contrast to the chill of the rain and the cobbled stones beneath her knees.

There was a car coming up behind her again, long and purring, dark in tone, and sounding exactly to her panicked ears like the previous car. It was getting too close for her to outrun it and try for a mad dash to the pub up ahead. If she ran they would see her for certain, if she remained huddled here, they might well see her too, but it was the better of two very bad options. She lay down flat on the cobblestones, the young man's blood soaking into her clothes instantly. She was using his body as a shield, because it was all there was. She was counting on the fact that they wouldn't come to take the body; they would leave it dumped as a statement.

The car was moving more slowly. Her whole body was jumping with nerves, like electrodes were attached to every few square inches of her. She was certain now it was the same car—long and dark and made for prowling along the streets like a jungle cat seeking prey.

She chanced a look over the rise of the young man's chest, noting that he had mother-of-pearl snaps on his shirt. It was the tiny details that seemed carved out in a supernal dimension in such moments. Across the rain washed pavement, the car was almost stopped, and there was a man looking out the passenger window. His face had been covered with a balaclava, but now in the wake of the shooting, he had pulled it up and off his face, likely thinking both she and the young man were dead. He looked strangely familiar. The voltage on her nerves suddenly shot up, for she recognized the narrow grey eyes and the overly long chin. It was Constable Blackwood.

Everything slowed down, so that each second seemed drawn out fine as a thread as he looked right at her, and then brought the barrel of his rifle up, drawing sight on her like she was a rabbit caught out in a field, too far from the sanctuary of hedge or bramble. The entire world became that slice of gleaming metal, the mouth of the barrel invisible but seeming as though it held all of time and space in its maw. One shot, two, and then three. The young man's body jerked like a badly controlled puppet. Four. She felt a thunk near her ribs, and then a slice of burning pain. Please God let it just be shattered cobblestone cutting her.

The car was slowing further and she knew she was out of time. She was going to have to run and hope to hell she could somehow elude them. She waited until the car was slightly ahead of her and then jumped up and whirled around and ran hell-for-leather in the opposite direction. She didn't know exactly where to go, she only knew she needed to hide as quickly as possible. She heard the constable yell and the car took off with a squeal of its tires. Time moved so slowly that it was distorted, vision and hearing drawn out and drowning in a sticky muddle of adrenaline, terror and one single pinpoint of clarity that was yelling 'RUN!' in her head at full volume. She had hardly gone twenty feet when her right foot landed on a shard of glass. It bit hard into the arch, and she wanted to howl with the pain, but she had neither time nor breath for it. They would keep looping the streets until they found her. The pavements were empty, even the echo of the gunshots had not brought anyone out to see what was going on. These men could not afford to leave her alive.

Christ, Christ, Christ—it was half plea, half imprecation. If they caught her, she had a feeling they wouldn't kill her at once. Having been at too many death scenes, she knew just how preferable a quick death would be in contrast to the alternative.

There was a blind alley to her left and she dashed down it just as she heard the car come around the corner to the south of her. There were two long buildings which lined the alley and both appeared to be abandoned. She needed to find somewhere to hide and fast, it was only a matter of a minute or two before they realized she wasn't on the street anymore and would start to hunt her in a more organized fashion. She couldn't let her panic get the upper hand and miss a hiding spot through blind terror. She forced herself to stop and take a breath. Her eyes were adjusted to the dark and she combed the buildings for entry—broken windows, crumbling brick, an alcove—anything that might buy her some time. Dirty brick walls, slick with rain, towered up into the night. There were windows but far too high to present an escape route. Under the hiss of the rain, though, there was the sound of water gushing in a sizeable stream. She ran toward it, certain the car was going to turn into the alley any second now.

There was a window well, deep and old, with a pipe sluicing mucky water into its depths. The pipe was draining into one corner of the well. It looked as if it had been an actual well at one time which had been bricked over but with a spot left for drainage from the pipe. It could be very weak, and she might plunge right through it like Alice down the rabbit hole, with far less happy results. She was going to have to risk it, because she couldn't see anywhere else to hide. She stepped down carefully, testing her weight on one foot before bringing her full weight to bear with the other. The floor held. She reached a foot into the pipe and lowered herself as quickly as she dared. The pipe was narrow, but she thought she could just shimmy into it. She went in feet first. It was awkward and she was instantly soaked in the filthy water draining from the pipe. If she could push back far enough, she hoped she would be completely hidden. Her skirt rucked up as she slid in, and her thighs scraped against substances which she was glad she could not see. Her side was burning with pain, and there wasn't enough room in the pipe to reach her hand down and assess just how bad the damage was. She didn't *think* it was life-threatening, and frankly, at present, she didn't want to know because there was nothing she could do about it.

The car had pulled into the alleyway, she could smell the exhaust and feel the thrum of the engine reverberate through the pipe. She put her fist to her mouth so that even her breath was dispersed and hoped it would not drift out of the pipe and give her away. The odds of survival right now were probably about ninety to ten, and not in her favor.

Her ears strained for every little noise, the rain on the pipe pounding as loudly as a drum. Car doors opened, three of them—*click, click, click*. Three men. If they found her, she wouldn't stand a chance. Flashes of the scenes she had photographed recently flickered through her head. The sheer raw hatred, the pain and terror suffered by the victims seemed to thrum all around her. She would lose her mind if such a death awaited her. Being a woman would only make it that much uglier.

Forgive me, she said silently to Conor and to Isabelle. To Jamie and Patrick, too. And to Casey, wherever he was, because he would be furious with her for simply being in this fix. The footfalls were close now, soft and menacing. Somehow she knew it was Constable Blackwood. Like any true predator he would be the one to smell blood first. It was something she had learned over time, that such men could smell their prey, and seemed to almost have a radar that swept the area around them and told them where their quarry crouched, trembling in terror.

There was a narrow lip that hung over the mouth of the pipe, which should shield her if she chanced to look. She slowly rolled her head to the side and then tilted her face up just enough so that she could see. There was a man standing off a little way, she could only see him from mid-shin down, but she recognized his boots, those ugly bone-cracking boots.

"Any sight?" she heard another voice ask.

"No, not yet," the constable replied. He sounded perplexed and slightly excited as if he loved the hunt more than the actual catch. She had seen the results of previous catches and suspected he also loved that part all too well. She was certain the three men standing in the alley right now were the men who had been inflicting torture and death on all the Catholics killed over the last several months.

She didn't even dare to let out an ounce of her breath, despite the fact that her chest was a burning agony. Just then something brushed against the sole of her right foot. It took everything she had not to exclaim out loud. Her adrenaline was coursing so hard she was amazed the constable didn't hear it thudding and swooshing around her body, for he was standing only two feet away from her at most. A thin line of sweat was running down her spine, despite the frigid chill of the air. Something touched her again, on her leg. Her entire body was on high alert, making her skin extra sensitive so that she knew immediately it was whiskers brushing up against her. Dear God in heaven—there was a rat in the pipe with her. She felt the plump, sleek body trundle along beside her leg and then there was a sharp tiny nose sniffing at the back of her knee. There was blood seeping from the cut on her foot and soaking the side of her coat. Were rats attracted to the scent of blood? If the rat bit her she didn't know if she could stop from crying out. She had been bitten by a rat as a child, and had been possessed with an irrational terror of them ever since. She wondered wildly if there was a patron saint of rats to whom she could pray. Frankly, though, saints seemed a wee bit thin on the ground this night. And then she remembered that there was a specific prayer for the exorcism of rats. Casey had told it to her after she had seen a rat in the basement of the walk-up they had lived in while in Boston and flown up the three flights of stairs to their apartment in an utter panic.

We entreat you, Lord, be pleased to hear our prayers; and even though we rightly deserve, on account of our sins, this plague of rats yet mercifully deliver us for your kindness' sake. Let this plague be expelled by your power, and our land and fields be left fertile, so that all it produces redound to your glory and serve our necessities; through Christ our Lord.

She could hear Casey's voice in her head speaking it, his broad, rough tones, which had been the cadences of love to her for a very long time. A strange calm stole through her as though he were here beside her, his big hand holding hers, telling her everything would be all right.

Almighty everlasting God, the donor of all good things, and the most merciful pardoner of our sins; before whom all creatures bow down in adoration, those in heaven, on earth, and below the earth; preserve us sinners

*by your might, that whatever we undertake with trust in your protection
may meet with success by your grace. And now as we utter a curse on these
noxious pests, may they be cursed by you; as we seek to destroy them, may
they be destroyed by you; as we seek to exterminate them, may they be
exterminated by you; so that delivered from this plague by your goodness,
we may freely offer thanks to your majesty; through Christ our Lord.*

She clutched her St. Jude's cross in her hand, the chain she had worn
for so long, which also held the beautiful silver St. Bridget's cross Pat and
Kate had given her for her last birthday. She could use the help of every
saint in the canon just now.

Constable Blackwood dropped down into the window well, scattering her prayer to pieces. The blood in her veins turned to ice, while still
pumping so furiously that she could hear each thud in her ears of pulse to
vein wall.

"Come on man, the bitch isn't here."

"Just a second," he said and started to bend down. She wanted
to close her eyes, so she wouldn't see his face, and could be blind as he
grabbed her and pulled her into the living nightmare that would be her
last hours. Just then the rat poked its head past hers and reared up out of
the pipe. The Constable stumbled back out of the window well, swearing
and furious. The rat startled as well, scuttling back in by her neck, close
enough that she could feel its small, hot breath in her hair. Her mouth was
so dry with fear that she couldn't swallow and her eyes were stinging because she hadn't blinked for several seconds.

"It's no matter," Constable Blackwood said, "I know where the bitch
lives."

There was the sound then of the constable's hobnailed boots retreat-
ing toward the purring engine. She didn't move a muscle, just waited, no
longer worrying about the rat beside her. If he bit her, it would be a small
price to pay for the service he had just rendered her.

She waited until she couldn't hear the car engine before she let the
air in her lungs out a little at a time, not wanting to startle the rat, which
was still sitting beside her neck. She then counted out another five minutes
before pulling herself out of the pipe. She was soaked and so cold that she
couldn't feel her feet or hands, which she thought might be a blessing just
at present. Her legs were cramped and she rose unsteadily on them, frightened lest the departing car had been a distraction, and the man was still
standing in the street waiting for her to emerge. But the street was empty
as she pulled herself up out of the dank well, and she couldn't sense anyone about. The rain had died back to a mere drizzle and fog was starting
to gather in luminous clouds, hovering above the narrow alleyway.

She turned back to find the rat peering up at her from the edge of the
pipe, as if it was bidding her farewell.

"I think you just saved my life, so thank you for that and sorry about the noxious pest bit," she said as though the rat might have read her mind during the silent prayer, "you've been really rather decent." The rat fixed her with bright, beady eyes and tilted its head, before scampering off into the fetid depths of the pipe.

She walked as fast as she dared, not wanting to attract attention by running, sticking close to the dark shadows that clustered thick at the base of the old warehouse. Her entire body was prickling, and she startled at every noise or movement in the shadows. Within a few blocks she had oriented herself and knew where she was and which direction to head. She was certain she could feel eyes on her back every step of the way, targeting her through a rifle scope.

She made it back to the car without incident however, the streets deathly silent around her and the fog thick enough to limit her vision to a few feet in front of her. But if she couldn't see very far, neither could anyone looking for her. She had come to a decision on the journey back to her car. She understood only too well that Constable Blackwood would keep hunting her until he killed her, and so it was up to her to make certain he did not get another chance. His last words had made it clear that she was on borrowed time. She started her car and headed to the one place and the one person that made sense in this situation. South Armagh and Noah Murray.

The guard knew to let her in, and as befit someone who worked for Noah he didn't even blink an eye at her bloody, wet and bedraggled form. He merely nodded and put the radio to his mouth. He would let Noah know to expect a knock at the door.

Noah was standing in the door yard, the sodium light near the byre turned off, so that he was no more than a silhouette, but she saw his wary stance, and the rifle that was casually canted over his elbow. He gave her a swift and assessing glance as she got out of the car, his eyes sweeping her from head to toe.

"Come in, an' tell me what's happened."

He opened the door and she stepped inside gratefully. She stood on the mat, her clothes dripping, feet still bare, stockings in tatters, and utterly relieved for the moment to be somewhere safe and with the slightly hazy feeling that came after a massive dose of adrenaline.

Noah looked at her dispassionately. "Ye look like ye laid down in a pool of blood. Let's get ye out of yer coat, I need to take a look at ye. The blood—is it yers?"

"Some of it. I was shot at and I think one of the bullets hit me, but it's not bleeding anymore." In her determination to get here quickly she had ignored the pain in her side, but with Noah's words it came back full force, making her distinctly woozy. He took one look at her face and crossed the floor, stripping her out of the coat quickly. Then he picked her up and carried her to the kitchen table and laid her down on it.

She looked up, vision blurring a bit, so that Noah's outlines were fuzzy. She was trying to judge just how serious the wound was by the level of concern on his face. Then she remembered just whom she was dealing with—she could be dying and he would look as calm as a sunny day in May.

"Lie still," he said gruffly, "I need to look and see what's happened."

He pulled her sweater up and she winced as the air hit her wound. He gazed down at her, a look of chill assessment on his face. It wasn't the most reassuring expression and it didn't help that he suddenly went off into the depths of the house, leaving her alone on the table. She tried not to panic. He hadn't spoken a word of reassurance, though being that it was Noah, that was likely neither here nor there as to her actual condition.

He was back in a moment, a lantern in hand, which he set down on the table beside her. It cast a strong light and she was afraid of what it might reveal. He handed her a length of leather which looked like it had once been a belt.

"This is goin' to hurt, so ye're goin' to want to bite down on somethin', better this than yer tongue. I'm goin' to have to check an' see if there's an entry wound."

She put the leather between her teeth, feeling sick to her stomach in anticipation of the pain. He hadn't exaggerated either. He touched all around it, rolling her flesh a little and checking to see if there was a bullet entry. He looked down at her and nodded curtly. "Ye're not goin' to die. The bullet must have grazed ye, but it didn't go in."

She thought she might pass out from relief. She'd had a bullet graze her ankle once and had survived that just fine, other than Casey being in a rare temper about it for a good week.

"Don't move, a bit of material is stuck in yer side. I'm goin' to have to get the shirt off ye to clean this up properly. I'll get ye somethin' warm an' dry to wear once I'm done here. Can ye lift yer arms up? Otherwise I'll have to cut it off ye."

"I...I can lift my arms," she said shakily. The pretty lavender sweater was likely ruined with the blood but Casey had given it to her as a gift and she did not want it cut. Noah helped her to sit up and then drew the sweater carefully over her head. He was gentle but the mere movement of her arms sent a fresh trickle of blood down her side. She felt distinctly faint and still somewhat afraid.

"All right then, lie back down an' I'll figure out what I need to do for ye." He dropped her sweater on the floor.

She felt horribly exposed under his gaze, lying there as she was in only a bra and bloody torn stockings and a ruined skirt. He put his fingers to the wound and she sucked her breath in and closed her eyes.

"All right, ye can breathe. It's a wee bit deep an' needs a few stitches to close it up. I'm goin' to get ye a tot of whiskey."

She tried to take his advice and attempted a deep breath. The breath caught on her ribs and she gasped at the sharp stabbing pain. Noah came back with a glass filled almost to the top with whiskey in one hand and the bottle in the other. She wondered if he was planning to knock her out cold before he attempted cleaning up her side. He put the bottle down on the table, well away from her and then put his free hand to her back, propping her up so that she could manage the glass.

"Drink," he said harshly, "ye need to get yer blood sugar up so ye don't go into shock."

She sipped at the golden liquid without any real enthusiasm; she had never cared for the taste of whiskey, much to the chagrin of Jamie's master distiller who had been certain that given time and encouragement she would develop a palate for it.

"I said drink," Noah said with no small impatience, "sippin' at it like it's rat poison won't do ye a damn bit of good. Drink it, or I'll pinch yer nose an' pour it down yer throat."

She knew he meant it; he would have little compunction about pouring the entire bottle down her throat if she didn't do as he said. She took a breath and swallowed the entire glass in three gulps. It went down easily enough, but the whiskey hit her belly and sent up a strip of fire which singed the back of her nose and brought tears to her eyes.

"Ye're all right, then," he said gruffly, in what she thought was meant to be a comforting manner. "I can suture it for ye an' while ye'll be stiff an' sore for a week or so, it shouldn't give ye any bother more than that. What's goin' to hurt is washin' it out with the whiskey."

She looked up then. "Is that entirely necessary?"

"Aye, ye don't want to risk infection. Where the hell were ye that ye got so filthy?"

"In a pipe," she said, feeling nauseated now between the whiskey and the impending pain. He raised an eyebrow.

"Ye can tell me about it after I get ye sorted here. Holdin' yer breath isn't goin' to ease the pain, so let it out."

"I'm scared to let it out, because that's when you'll pour the whiskey on me," she said.

"No, it's not," he replied equably and poured the whiskey as he said it. It was like a fire had been lit along her flesh; the pain was absolutely searing. It was only Noah's hand on her shoulder that kept her from leaping off the table. She settled for cursing, volubly and inventively, rounding it off with a heartfelt, "Fuck!" before black stars began to burst in front of her eyes.

She regained consciousness to find that Noah was hunkered down on the floor, so that his face was level with her own. There was concern in the blue eyes, but a certain clinical calm as well that told her how mild her injury was compared with most he had dealt with over the years.

"Are ye all right now?" he asked and poured another tot of whiskey into the glass. "Here, a wee bit more internally will help take the sting out of yer ribs. Then I'll make ye a hot cup of tea with plenty of sugar."

"Oh yes, tea," she said with no small sarcasm, "the Irish cure-all— neither bullet nor stab wound can resist its curative powers."

He ignored her comment and after splashing a little whiskey over his hands, he picked something up and held it in the light. It was a needle and it looked, to Pamela's panicked eyes, wickedly large and wickedly sharp.

"Give me that bottle of whiskey," she said, "If I'm going to get through this, I'll have to be drunk."

In the end it was six stitches, a few undignified yelps and more whiskey than even Noah thought was wise. He took the opportunity to wash out the cut on her foot too, and close it neatly with two stitches, after stripping the ruined stockings off of her, along with her skirt. By the time he finished Pamela's head was swimming and she couldn't feel her ribs any more. She lay on the table, eyes tightly shut, knowing the room would float in a haze of alcohol should she open them. He covered her with a warm blanket then, for which she was grateful. The alcohol hadn't quite disposed of every shred of modesty.

"Do ye feel well enough to tell me what happened to ye?" Noah asked. He stood above her, blue eyes like slate, dark and impenetrable.

She nodded and began to tell him slowly, but then the panic and fear started to beat in her chest and the words tumbled out one over the next. He took her hand. "Slow down, Pamela, an' make sure ye leave out nothin'. Ye're safe. Ye needn't have any fears now that ye're here with me. I've dispatched a few men to keep watch over Gert an' Owen's place as well."

"What?"

"Aye, the guard radioed from the gate. When he told me what state ye were in, I felt it best to make certain yer children were safe, as he said they were not with ye."

She took a breath. "Thank you, I can't tell you how grateful I am."

"Never mind that now, just finish yer story."

She told him all of it: from getting lost, to being shot, to the men hunting her and the constable's words about knowing where she lived, to the rat and her return to her car. He said nothing throughout the telling, merely nodded now and again, to encourage her to continue.

When she was done, he said, "Give me a minute, will ye? I need to just tell one of my men something. I'll be right back an' then we'll get ye settled properly."

She closed her eyes. She was cold now that the fear had passed and was becoming aware of the smell coming off her skin and the discarded pile of clothes. God only knew what had been in that pipe. She only hoped she didn't get tetanus or something worse. She must have dozed slightly because it seemed Noah was back within seconds. She took a deep breath and attempted to ease herself up off the table, only daring to open one eye, under the theory that she would feel less drunk if she limited her field of view.

"Pamela, I really don't think ye ought to be up," Noah said.

"I'm all right," she said with as much dignity as she had left to her, which was—bloody, three-quarters naked and quite, as it turned out, inebriated—very little.

"Are ye, indeed?" Noah said drily.

"I'm a bit dizzy is all," she said and then swayed alarmingly. Noah caught her and eased her back onto the table.

"Stay there, I'm going to make up a bed for ye. Ye're not fit to go anywhere tonight. I think it's best if ye stay here until things are seen to."

He was right, she was in no fit state to go anywhere. She nodded, the contents of her head feeling somewhat liquid. She squinted at Noah, hoping to put a defined line around his image. He shook his head slightly and then went off to make up a room for her.

"All right, then," he said, returning a few moments later, "it's to bed with ye. Take my arm because ye'll not be steady on yer pins."

She took his arm because she didn't have the temerity to disobey this man and she was grateful for the support. He was right, she was not the least bit steady on her pins, though whether this was a result of blood loss or the large transfusion of whiskey into her veins was a point for debate.

The room was his, she realized as they crossed the threshold. It was spare in its lines, just a bed—luxuriantly large, which surprised her—and an old battered dresser with a few things on it: his wallet, a small crystal elephant, a syringe for sheep medicine and tweed cap. He sat her down on the bed and then went to rummage about in the small closet. It must have been an addition, for these old farm houses didn't have closets. She put a hand to the bed to steady herself; the whiskey had replaced her blood or so it seemed, for it felt like it ran in warm channels and then billowed out softly through her limbs.

Noah handed her an old flannel shirt, much worn, but soft and warm. It was the second time she had wound up in his clothes. It made her slightly uncomfortable even in her drunken state to realize this, though not so much as being partly naked under his rather clinical gaze.

"Thank you," she said, unfolding the shirt one-handed. He took it back and shook it out and then put it on her, sliding it over her arm on the injured side first and then putting it over the other and buttoning it up the front. She shut her eyes, it was an intimate act to have someone dress her like this, even though Noah did it with a business-like compunction that made it far less embarrassing than it might have been had he been a different sort of man.

He helped her settle into the bed, and then pulled the quilt up and tucked her in with a water bottle at her feet, like she was a child. She eased back into the pillows with relief. He was right, even if she could have navigated her way home, there was no way she could stay up all night to keep watch lest the constable decide to make good on his threat.

Noah left the room and she could hear him moving about in the kitchen. Between the hot water bottle and the whiskey, she was feeling suddenly very tired in body, though not ready to sleep just yet. He returned with a tray, the teapot still puffing steam from its spout and a pot of honey to one side as well as a wee fat jug for the milk. He put it down on the dresser and set to readying her a cup.

"You shouldn't have given me your own bed," she said. Each word seemed to require deliberate effort.

"Aye, I should have," he said, "it's by far the most comfortable one in the house, so I thought I'd best put ye in here. Will it do for ye?"

"Yes, it's fine," she said, thinking she did feel oddly comfortable despite the circumstances which had landed her here.

"It'll not be as comfortable as yer own bed, I know."

"I don't sleep in the bed much these days, or at least not the bed I shared with Casey. I sleep with the children mostly. They like it and I don't have to wake up alone in the middle of the night, wondering why their father isn't there beside me. I miss it," she said, with the meandering fluency of the inebriated, "having a man in my bed."

Noah continued in the act of pouring tea, as if she had said little more than she liked the color of his walls. He finished pouring, the purl of the tea into crockery the only noise beyond the crackle of the fire. She thought he wasn't going to respond and that it was likely best if he didn't, for even in the most flattering light it had been an indiscreet statement, at worst it sounded like an invitation. She should never have opened her mouth because whatever editor existed between her brain and her tongue always took a leave of absence when she imbibed anything more than a thimbleful of hard spirits. Whiskey was not her friend. She had only been drunk in front of Casey a handful of times and he had mourned the fact she wasn't given more to drink, being that he had found it an amusing experience each time. Not to mention, he had said, she lost all inhibition when drunk, which was merely another perk in his opinion.

Noah turned and handed her the mug, making certain that she had a firm grip on it.

"I don't expect you to fix it for me, what happened tonight," she said, feeling absurdly small and without any sort of moral authority, lying in the man's bed, drunk as a lord.

"Then why did ye come here, Pamela? Ye could have gone to yer friend on the hill, if ye wanted a less permanent solution to yer problem. But ye came *here*. Ye might want to ask yerself why."

Why indeed? The fact that Jamie was away was beside the point and she understood that. She had not thought twice about where to go tonight, nor about just whose help she needed in this situation. She knew what had to be done, and she didn't want the blood of it on Jamie. Noah was looking at her, his eyes cool and assessing like he was reading each thought in her head.

"I only meant that I have brought my troubles to your door, but if you don't want to be involved, I understand that." Like hell she did, she thought, but she had to give this man an out, because in truth her life or death was not his responsibility.

"It's what I do. It's why ye chose to come here, no? Because ye know if ye want rid of a killer, ye go to another killer."

"Maybe," she agreed quietly. "That's a bare bones summation of it, but I suppose there's a validity to it as well."

"Honesty as usual, Miss Pamela," he said. She had the odd sensation that he didn't mind and that he would rather she saw him for what he was, instead of building an alternate and more palatable version of him in her head.

"I don't have much else to offer you," she replied.

He gave her a long look, the blue eyes giving nothing away. "I wouldn't say that's exactly true, but that's a conversation for later."

"Is it? If you do this for me, what do you want in return?"

"Now is not the time, Pamela. I have business to take care of. Get yerself settled an' we'll talk in a bit." He turned and left the room, leaving her with the comfortable bed and her most uncomfortable thoughts.

She sipped the tea, hoping it would sober her up a bit. Her head was still spinning from the whiskey. She knew what business he meant. It was not the first time she'd had a man's blood on her hands, neither literally nor figuratively. It was the latter which troubled her more. She could justify what she had just done, what she had asked of this man without saying a word; she could come to terms with it because there were no other choices. She was all Conor and Isabelle had, the only parent left. She had to survive and she was not going to allow an evil man to orphan her babies because she was squeamish about mortal sin. Anything Noah might ask of her in return for this act, she would give him, regardless of what it was or what it cost her. It would be small in comparison to leaving her children alone in the world.

So thus reconciled to her decision, she drank her tea and waited for Noah to return.

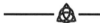

True to his word, he was back within twenty minutes, looking as unruffled as when he had left, despite the event which she knew he had just set in motion. He refilled her mug with tea, and then filled one for himself and sat down in a worn armchair which he had pulled over to the side of the bed.

Despite her earlier resolve, she felt dreadfully nervous. Noah was not a man to shy away from any topic, no matter how uncomfortable. And so, true to form, he picked up the conversation exactly where she had dropped it.

"What ye said about missing havin' a man in yer bed? I would imagine that ye do, though I warrant it's one man ye miss, not just a warm body, no?"

It was a rhetorical question in part, she knew, but it was also the opening salvo in their negotiation. She was going to have to take the bull by the horns, so to speak. The answer was flowing off her tongue before she could stop it anyway. For the truth was that she did miss the one man in particular and sometimes she felt starved by the need to talk about him, to speak memory into the air and so conjure up for an infinitesimal moment the man for whom she yearned.

"I do. I miss his touch, just the feel of his body sleeping there beside me, I miss the scent of him, I miss his body against mine," she said softly, the whiskey having set up housekeeping behind her eyes now and lending the room a subtle golden glow. "But it's not just the act itself, though I admit I miss the simple physical release of that, too—it's mostly the intimacy and the way it seemed to ground our relationship. There were times when we couldn't speak to one another for grief or fear, or even anger, but our bodies spoke another language and we could connect in that way when we couldn't in others. What we had was something rare, that I think maybe some people never have in their entire life."

She took a sip of her tea and felt the heat trickle down into her stomach, it seemed to fortify the whiskey's effect rather than dilute it.

"Aye, that's true. I did see ye with him, in the village one day. There was a deal of passion between the two of ye, apparent even to my untutored eye."

She didn't miss the slight sarcasm in his voice and looked over the steam of her tea at him.

"I don't know what your life has been like in that respect and I would never presume to know either. I hope you realize that."

"Aye, I know that, only I'm maybe a wee bit jealous, that ye had that, but then sorry that ye have it no longer."

"Thank you," she said, not certain what she was thanking him for, but then nothing really made sense right now.

"It sounds lovely, like a private world." She thought he spoke to ease her discomfort over having revealed herself so. "I think real love does that—creates a place, somewhere that's not quite of nor in this world, which belongs only to the two of ye, an' it's a world where ye retreat an' none can touch ye."

It wasn't the first time Noah had surprised her with his insight and sensitivity. That he was an intelligent man she knew well enough, that he was ruthless she also understood in equal measure, but this side of him always surprised her. Perhaps because he so rarely showed it.

"Yes," she said quietly and felt a soft rush of tears prickle at the bridge of her nose. "Yes, that's exactly how it was."

"Well, I see why ye would miss that."

"Sometimes," she started slowly, her eyes riveted to the brown and gold of the quilt on the bed, "I think sex can be just that—sex, just an exchange, a physical release for the two people involved."

"Erm—aye, it can be that. But have ye had that sort of sex yerself?"

"No, I haven't," she admitted. "But I imagine you have."

There was a tiny voice inside her head repeating rather insistently, "Shut up, Pamela, shut up, shut up NOW!"

"Aye, I have," he said mildly enough, considering. She squinted at him through the golden haze and saw that he was fighting a smile.

"And did you like it?"

He rubbed a hand over his face and sighed. "Well, aye, I suppose I did. But I'm a man, an' I think maybe we view sex just the wee bit differently than women do."

"You had to have had it with a woman, so did you mind if her expectations were different?"

"Well," he said slowly, suddenly looking like a man picking his way through a minefield. "I tend to be very honest about what I want, an' not sugarcoat it. I don't like the woman to believe I'm lookin' for a romantic relationship."

"What if there was a woman who felt the same—who wasn't looking for a romantic entanglement, but merely wanted the physical aspect of it?"

Noah's eyebrows were slowly rising in what appeared to be a rather large amount of consternation. "An' who might this mythical woman be?" he asked, inching slightly further back from the bedside.

"Me," she said, surprising even herself a little. "If it doesn't need to mean anything, you could have sex with me."

"I suspect ye've not had sex, solely because ye had the physical need of it. I would imagine ye've only bedded men ye loved."

"You'd be wrong there," she said.

"Would I?" He gave her a dubious look.

"Yes, you would. I've done some terrible things and sleeping with a man I had no wish to isn't the least of them."

"Well, if ye had no wish to, that's another thing entirely. I'm talkin' about havin' it because ye need the physical release or ye merely want the pleasure."

"That is what I am proposing to you," she said. Her blood seemed to have been replaced by pure alcohol but she had enough wits left to realize that she was likely going to regret this come morning. "Do you not find me desirable?"

Noah sighed; clearly she was beginning to tax his patience. "Pamela, listen to me, ye're drunk right now an' in pain, that's not the ideal circumstance under which to be makin' this sort of offer. An' as I stated before, it's one man that ye miss."

She took a ragged breath and gasped a little as it hit her ribs. "I can't have him, though, can I?"

"No, but it seems to me that's not the best reason to take another man to yer bed."

"So I should just go without sex for the rest of my life?"

He laughed. "I hardly think ye're in danger of permanent celibacy."

"It's not funny," she said somewhat offended by the brevity with which he was entertaining, or rather not entertaining her offer. She was beginning to have misgivings about her approach.

"No, it's not. I'm flattered, I truly am. But I'll ask ye a question—why me?"

She considered it as he had asked, and then answered truthfully.

"Because we don't love each other, so it won't be complicated."

"Sex is always complicated in one way or another, don't kid yerself on that score."

"I don't see why it has to be," she said.

"Because, it's just goin' to be with a woman like you."

"Are you saying I'm difficult?" she asked, feeling slightly stung.

"Aye, ye are, but I don't mean it in the way ye're thinkin'. Do ye honestly think ye could have sex with me an' not feel guilty about it in the mornin'? At the very least, we'd be awkward with one another. At worst ye're goin' to feel ye've betrayed yer husband on a profound level, an' then every time ye looked at me, ye'd feel that betrayal again. I won't be that man for ye, Pamela."

"I don't know," she said, "I think we might manage."

Noah looked at her, the gentian eyes mild but speculative, too. "Aye, it's possible we'd do just fine, but once ye've seen someone naked an' known them intimately, it's a wee bit hard to go back to purely business relations."

"Is that what we are—purely business?"

"Aye, what else would ye call it?" Noah asked.

"I thought we were friends," she said, feeling somewhat piqued.

"Are we? I've not had a friend in a long time. I'll not be certain just what that looks like. An' I've never had a woman for a friend. Particularly not one who looks like you an' proposes things that seem somewhat outside the scope of friendship."

"We've put a line around this relationship right from the start, so this is just another set of parameters," she said.

"As I recall," he said gently, "ye told me sex was most definitely not part of our dealins'. Ye made that clear right from the start, an' I thought ye were wise to do so."

"If I had offered it then, as part of the deal, would you have taken me up on it?" she asked.

"Aye, I might well have, but it would have been a mistake for the both of us an' for you in particular. Ye weren't ready to have another man in yer bed, Pamela, that wasn't yer husband an' the truth is, beyond physical need, ye still aren't."

"I know I'm not your usual sort," she said.

Noah laughed, and sat back in his chair. "An' how would ye know what my usual sort is?"

"Because I saw her here with you, one night. She was very blonde, and rather more built than I am," she said, flushing at the admittance.

"Aye, she an' I have an' understandin'. But it's purely sex, we're not friends."

"I only meant," she said, "that maybe I am not your type, physically speaking."

Noah's eyes met hers in the soft light of the lantern that spilled over the bed, creating a small circle outside of which the night with its violence and blood was banished. He looked down and rubbed his hand over his eyes, as though his head pained him.

"Pamela, ye'd best stop talkin' this way. When it comes to a woman such as yerself, type is a small word an' meaningless. I don't want to be a means to scratch an itch, do ye understand?"

"No, I'm not sure I do," she said in all honesty.

"It means that I won't have sex with ye just because the whiskey has gone to yer blood. Because as much as I'd like to be in yer bed, I know we would both regret it come mornin'. The truth is I'm not Casey Riordan, an' that's who ye really want an' that's who ye'd be pretendin' was makin' love to ye."

Even the whiskey didn't stop the shame from flooding up through her body. He was right. She wanted, her body wanted, but the one man she needed, needed deep in her cells wasn't going to be the one giving her the physical oblivion she was looking for. Only she had thought that for tonight, it might not matter to Noah, she had thought it was what he wanted.

She put her hand up and touched his face, her palm warm against the cool touch of his jawline and whiskers. She could smell him, the scent that was Noah—rain on the horizon, that clean almost searing scent of ozone as a storm rose in the distance. "I'm sorry, I'm being selfish."

He shook his head, chestnut hair a burnished auburn in the lamp light. "No, ye're not, ye've just had a very frightenin' experience an' now ye've more whiskey than blood in yer veins an' sex seems a grand idea. Under other circumstances I'd be more than happy to take ye up on yer offer."

"You're being very kind," she said.

"Am I? My body is of the opinion right now that I'm bein' unnecessarily cruel. Is this what ye thought I meant when I said ye did have somethin' to offer in return?"

"Yes," she said, "clearly I was mistaken."

"Yes an' no. Let me put it to ye this way—I'm not in the habit of blackmailin' women into my bed."

"I wouldn't see it as blackmail," she said, "only that I've asked you to do something very big for me and I would pay whatever price you asked in return."

He shook his head. "I don't know whether ye're crazy, or just crazy brave."

"It's what most men would ask for."

"Aye, well Pamela, it's not how I'd want to get ye into my bed. Ye'd hate me for it in the end."

"I think," she said, "I owe you an apology. I'm sorry for making such an assumption. Perhaps you could tell me what it is that you *do* want."

"There's no need to apologize, I'm flattered that ye'd consider it. The fact of the matter is," he continued, and she could have sworn he was holding back laughter, "I'm thinkin' about buyin' a colt from a dealer down in Wexford. If I do get him, I'd like ye to help train him."

"Oh," she said, feeling like an utter fool. "Well, of course, though I'm hardly an expert in that area."

"Ye know horses. Kate says she's never known horses to respond to a person the way they do to you. This wee horse I'm considerin' gettin' is high-spirited an' won't take easy to the bit an' bridle. I want him trained, but I don't want his spirit broken in the process."

"I'll do my best," she said. She had worked with Jamie's trainer, Jake, and with Jamie, who might have the best hand with horses of anyone she had ever known.

He nodded. "That's all, Pamela. I'm not lookin' to barter yer soul away from ye or anything."

"You could at least pretend you're not enjoying this," she said.

"Ah, no, ye're goin' to have to allow me that much—enjoyment of the offer, if not actually takin' ye up on it."

"I think," she said, with some attempt at pulling together her badly shredded dignity, "it's best if I go to sleep now and we pretend this conversation never happened."

"Whatever the lady wants," he said easily and left the room, closing the door behind him.

He checked on her an hour later. She was asleep, the day's terrors having taken their toll. She looked small and fragile in his bed, and he smiled as he thought of her offer. She had no idea how hard it had been to refuse her. Because, he knew, she would have done just as she said and given him whatever he asked for; she was one of the bravest people he had ever known. She was also heartbroken, and her offer had come from a place which was sad and lonely and believed she would never love again. She thought it did not matter where she gave herself, because it was not and never would be her husband to whom she was giving her body. But it mattered to him, and he knew one day it would, once again, matter to her.

He would have done it without any sort of barter. When he had left her the first time, he had gone out to the byre where a man who had been summoned waited. The man stood patiently, his head covered in a black watch cap, his features obscured by a dark beard and moustache. He was a small man in stature but big on talent and he had formerly been a sniper in the British Coldstream Guards. In his current incarnation he did the occasional bit of wet work for Noah. He had been slowly distancing himself from that end of his business and contracting it out. This one he wished he could do himself, because he would enjoy making the constable suffer a great deal before putting him down like the rabid dog he was. He knew it was best, though, if he hired someone else to do the job.

The man knew why he had been summoned and the business was done with a few simple words, and a piece of paper with the relevant details on it. The man would memorize the instructions and burn the paper. There would be no trace of anything to bring the blood back to Noah's door.

Pamela turned in the bed, muttering something under her breath, her skin lit gold by the lamplight. Yes, he would have done it without anything from her. For if this woman ever came to his bed it would be as a willing participant. Not as a form of payment.

He left her to her sleep and walked through his kitchen over to the window that sat above the old stone sink. The night outside was still dark, there were a few hours before the dawn. There was business he needed to attend to, details still to be sorted, ends that needed tying before the morning. By the time light rolled over these ancient hills, Constable Blackwood would no longer be a problem for Pamela.

For a moment he simply stood and enjoyed the echo of exultancy he had felt earlier, still there inside—a warm glow in his core. She had come to *him* in her time of trouble, rather than James Kirkpatrick. It was the first shift in balance; it would not be the last.

Chapter Fifty-five

Too Deep For Tears
June 1977

CONOR RIORDAN LOVED HORSES. He loved horses like other little boys loved baseball or hurling or football. He loved horses almost as much as he loved his mama, Isabelle and Uncle Pat. Jamie, too, he amended and of course his daddy.

He was standing on the paddock rail in Jamie's stable yard watching Phouka, who was eyeing him back with what Mama called his 'hotty glare.' Conor wasn't entirely sure what that meant, but Phouka was looking down his long nose and chuntering at him right now. Phouka never liked to wait. Conor understood that; he didn't like waiting either. Mama had promised they could go riding this afternoon, as long as Maggie didn't mind watching Isabelle for a bit. But Mama still had Isabelle with her and Kolya too. If those babies would just go nap he could go for his ride with his mama and Jamie.

He looked over to see if his mama was watching. She was talking to Jamie. He could see Jamie's bright hair and Mama's dark curls which were so short now, though not as short as they had been when she first cut them off. He hadn't liked that, she didn't look like his mama at first and it had upset him. Daddy would have hated it, her cutting her hair like that. He didn't remember everything about his daddy, but he did remember him stroking mama's hair sometimes and saying how pretty it was. It made him sad that he couldn't remember more things about his daddy. He did remember always feeling safe when he was around and like nothing bad in the whole world could touch him when his daddy was near.

Sometimes he wished they lived here at Jamie's all the time, the way they had when Mama got sick and almost died. Because he knew she *had* almost died, even if Jamie had promised him he wouldn't allow it to happen. He liked it here and Mama seemed happier here, too. Sometimes at home she got to looking out a window or just into the air and would seem awful sad. He loved their house too, and the woods that surrounded it, and his bedroom snug under the eaves. Sometimes he dreamed about his daddy in their house and it was like his daddy had come to visit him in the night. He would miss that if it stopped happening, so maybe it was best they stayed living there.

He clicked his tongue at Phouka. He'd brought him his very favorite treat—green apples sliced in thick chunks and one sugar cube. Phouka pranced over, snorting in anticipation and stuck his velvet muzzle into the curve of Conor's neck and blew out causing Conor to laugh. The only other person Phouka did that with was Mama and he knew it meant he was special to Phouka.

Whenever he dreamed about riding it was always Phouka he was riding, both in his day dreams and his night ones. He would imagine the two of them fighting bad guys together, just like Batman in the comic books he'd found in Jamie's attic. Phouka would have to be Robin, because Conor of course would be Batman.

"That's a pretty horse," said a voice beside him. He turned and looked up at the man who was suddenly standing next to him. He stepped away a little. It was the new man who worked in the stable. He had just started a week ago. He was a stranger, but not a stranger, because Jake had introduced him to the man. Conor couldn't remember his name though.

"He's my mama's horse," Conor said proudly. He loved Phouka and couldn't wait for the day his mama would let him ride her big silver horse. If his mama would have allowed it, he would have stayed in Jamie's big stable all day, every day. But she had said he mustn't get in the way of either the horses or the men who worked in the stable. Jamie always took him to the stable and let him have a ride on Danu, who was gentle and went slow. He liked Danu well enough, but he was far more excited by the big stallions—both Jamie's black devil of a horse (that's what Mr. Jake called him) and mama's silver beast (again, Mr. Jake's name for him).

"Do you want to ride him?"

"I can't," he said. "Mama says I'm not allowed until I'm older."

"Oh no, your mama said it's fine now. She said you've become such a good rider that you can ride the big horses now. She sent me down to help you get Phouka saddled; she said you're all going for a ride. But just so your mama doesn't get upset, we can ride together on Phouka."

The man put out his hand, and after a second's hesitation, Conor took it.

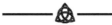

"Patrick tells me that Constable Blackwood disappeared a few weeks ago."

"What?" She startled a little, upsetting juice down the front of her pretty pale green blouse. The startle was genuine and she thought Jamie had brought the topic up so casually so that he might gauge her reaction to it.

"Yes, while I was away in New York. Pat said his sources told him the constable just disappeared like he was snatched up into thin air."

"So they don't know what happened to him?" she said, looking down and ostensibly wiping the juice off her blouse.

"No, but I did wonder, Pamela, if you might?"

"Might what?" she looked up blankly, all too aware that she had never been good at fooling Jamie.

"Might know how he disappeared so completely?"

"Why would I know?" she said, indignant. Jamie merely narrowed his eyes at her and gave her a knowing look. She swallowed, nerves getting the better of her. "I can't say I'll miss him if it turns out to be a permanent disappearance, but I don't see why you think I'd know anything about it."

She hadn't told anyone and never would. The deal between her and Noah was sacrosanct and quite literally sealed in blood.

"Because—" he began but just then Maggie came out of the kitchen door and waved down at them.

"There's a call for ye, Pamela. They say it's important."

She got up and brushed the sand from her clothes, glancing at Isabelle who was liberally coated in it too and would howl the house down if she attempted to remove her from the sandbox, where both she and Kolya were happily playing.

Jamie looked up at her from his seat on the grass. "Go on up, I'll watch them."

The phone was off the hook in the kitchen, so Pamela picked it up and said, "Hello?"

There was no response, just dead silence on the other end, as though someone listened but refused to speak. "Hello? Hello?" Still no reply. She frowned and put the receiver back in its cradle.

Maggie wasn't in the kitchen any longer so she couldn't ask her whether the caller had been a man or a woman. She walked back out into the bright afternoon and down the long slope of lawn to where Jamie was walking up, both Isabelle and Kolya hanging off his arms like limpets.

"Is everything okay?" he asked, lifting both children up high enough so he could swing them a little. Isabelle shrieked with joy and Kolya laughed his funny froggy laugh, which somehow sounded distinctly Russian.

"I don't know, when I picked it up no one answered and then they hung up. I suppose if it's truly important they'll call back."

Jamie gave her an odd look.

"What is it?" she asked.

"I could have sworn someone called me from the edge of the woods. I walked down there but there wasn't anyone around. It's almost as if someone wanted to distract us for a minute."

A prickle of unease put the hair up on the back of her neck and she looked over to the paddock where Conor had been admiring the horses only a moment before. Conor wasn't there now and neither was Phouka.

"Jamie, where's Conor?" she asked, the prickle of unease turning into a live wire of panic. Jamie looked around and then suddenly said, "*Christ.*"

She turned to look in the same direction and felt a thrill of pure terror go through her. Conor was on Phouka's back, his hands wrapped in the horse's reins and a look of terrified exuberance on his face.

Jamie stuck two fingers in his mouth and whistled for the horse. Phouka adored Jamie and would usually trot over to him, knowing he always had a treat in his pocket for him. He was already moving toward the horse when Phouka let out a high, panicked whinny and bolted in the opposite direction. Conor was clinging to the horse's mane, having dropped the reins in panic. The reins were dangling dangerously free around the horse's legs now. Phouka was moving like he'd been shot from a bolt and was headed straight for the great earthen bank beyond the old wall at the bottom of the garden. The drop on the other side of the wall was steep. If the horse went over the wall there, he would kill himself and most likely Conor, too.

She was running, moving across the ground swiftly and yet it was like that horrible dream where you ran and ran and yet stayed firmly in place. She would never make it in time.

Jamie ran past her, so fast he almost didn't seem human. He was running for the wall, and she saw what he meant to do. If he could catch Conor before Phouka attempted the jump, he might be able to save him from a deathly tumble. He might just break his own neck in the attempt. She ran, half-stumbling, because even though she wasn't going to get there in time, she had to try. She glanced back remembering the babies and saw Vanya running down toward them.

Jamie jumped, grasping the edge of the wall and pulling himself up. She stood frozen in horror, if Phouka so much as glanced against his leg, he could kill Jamie. Jamie crouched and then vaulted onto Phouka as the horse sailed over the wall, wrenching Conor up into his arms on his way. It seemed that the entire universe stilled, the horse beginning his long arc up to clear the wall, the panic clear in his frothing mouth and lathered coat. Jamie and Conor flew off his back and into the hedge near the wall, landing with an audible thump. And then it was just Phouka, dappled silver in the sunlight, arcing up and still panicked. She could not bear to watch and yet she could not look away.

He twisted just before he dropped, the great muscled body gleaming like quicksilver and then there was the sound of his landing and the long, piercing scream that tore the air apart.

She ran to Conor and Jamie, though she could not see her son at once, Jamie had taken the brunt of the impact and then rolled swiftly over so that Conor would not see the great horse fall.

Pamela dropped to her knees and took her son into her arms, careful to put his head to her shoulder as Jamie jumped up and ran to where Phouka lay, his screams vibrating all around them. Vanya ran toward them, his face ashen. Maggie had the babies, one on each hip and was moving up toward the house with them.

"Vanya, take Conor to the house now," Jamie said, his voice quiet.

Vanya nodded and grabbed up Conor, putting his hand protectively around the boy's head and half-running back to the house.

"Should I run and call the vet?" Pamela asked out of a sort of hopeless futility for she knew too well what Jamie would say.

"We can't wait for the vet, he's suffering too much. I have to shoot him, Pamela. I'm sorry, but it's the right thing to do. I'm going to get the rifle, say goodbye to him."

She nodded, face white and set as stone. She couldn't speak to agree with him, it was moot anyway because Jamie had no choice here and neither did she.

She knelt by the horse's head, so that his gaze could rest on her. He had quieted a little, as if he sensed the inevitable and knew that soon there would be no pain. She put her hand carefully between his ears where the beautiful silver blaze crowned his forehead.

"I love you, boy," she said, trying hard not to cry. She didn't want her agitation to upset Phouka. The great brown eyes blinked slowly at her as if he were acknowledging what she'd said. "Thank you for being my friend."

He let out a short sigh, and then a small whinny of distress. She stroked his head—the delicate muzzle, the silken ears which had always been alert and high with pride. A part of her heart would go with him and be forever lost. A breeze stirred his mane, and the sun caught in the hairs so that they blazed to life and made it seem as if he were moving.

Jamie returned with a rifle under his arm. She knew he kept one in a locked cabinet in the byre.

"Pamela, go. Go now."

For Jamie's sake she went, Phouka was beyond her comfort. She heard the shot when she was halfway up the long sloping trail to the house and felt like it had gone through her own heart. She took another two steps and then she stopped and crumpled slowly to the ground. She thought she might faint; her vision filled with dancing black spots. She needed to get up and go to Conor, but she had to pull herself together first.

There was a terrible silence behind her, no more horse screaming, just the strange echo that gunshot always left on the air. She bent over, her forehead almost touching the ground, unable to get a proper breath. And then there were hands, strong and capable, lifting her to her feet and arms that took her within their circle of grace.

"Oh, Jamie," she said, burying her face in his chest. His shirt smelled of blood and dirt and exertion, but it also smelled comfortingly of him— lime and leather and the scent that was simply Jamie.

"I'm sorry, Pamela, I'm so sorry." He held her tightly and she wished that she could just stay here, within his arms and not have to face Conor and tell him Phouka was dead. She took a shaky breath and let go of Jamie's arms and stepped back.

"I...I have to go to Conor."

"I know, I'll come with you."

She stumbled on the way up and would have fallen if it wasn't for Jamie's hand which shot out to catch her. She held on to his hand to make the rest of the walk. The warmth of his skin against hers was the one thing which felt real right now, a locus point in a universe gone awry.

Conor was standing in the kitchen, his small face stricken. He went to Jamie immediately. "Did you have to shoot him?"

Jamie hunkered down so he was eye-to-eye with Conor. "I'm sorry Conor, I did have to. His back was broken and he was in a great deal of pain. It was my duty to end that pain for him."

Conor nodded, small face set, but Pamela could feel the tears building in him. Jamie must have too, for he gathered Conor in gently and put the boy's head to his shoulder. "It's all right, laddie, he deserves your tears."

Conor threw his arms around Jamie's neck as the first sob broke out of him. Pamela knew he wasn't crying only for Phouka but also for the loss of his father, which he could not understand entirely but felt all the same.

Jamie patted his back. "Conor, it's not your fault, don't you think that for a minute. We're just glad you're safe, laddie."

"Mama," Conor turned his face up to hers, "I...I'm sorry about Phouka, I knew it was wrong to ride him but that man said..." Fresh tears brimmed up and spilled down his cheeks.

"What man?" Jamie's voice was low and steady. Conor still looked at him in alarm.

"That man," Conor repeated. "Not Mr. Jake. He said it was all right to ride him, that he wasn't as wild as he used to be. He said you told him it was okay."

Pamela took a breath, knowing Conor did not need to see her fury right now even though it was not directed at him. "Conor, I have always told you that Phouka is too dangerous for you to ride."

"I know," he said miserably, dragging his filthy sleeve across his eyes. "I's so sorry, Mama."

"I know you are, sweetheart. We will talk about this later, but for now I think maybe you need a bath and something to eat. Maybe a drink of tea, too."

Conor snuffled into his sleeve and then peered over the edge of his arm at her; tea was a rare treat and he knew it was a serious matter at hand when he was allowed to have it.

"Can I have it with two sugars?"

"Three if you like," she said and bent down to kiss him. "Come on, sweetheart, let's go run you a bath."

He looked to Jamie, as he sometimes did in moments of crisis, wanting a man's opinion on what was all right to do.

"Your mama is right, Conor—bath and food and tea."

She gave Conor a bath in the tub off her old room. He was quiet and didn't play in the water the way he normally would. His eyes were the deep grey they turned in moments of great upset—whether that of sorrow or fury.

"Mama?"

"Yes?"

"It's my fault Phouka died, isn't it?"

"Oh, sweetheart, no it's not. It was the man's fault. He is the grown-up and he knew better than to put someone as small as you on a horse like Phouka."

"Did it hurt him? When Jamie shot him?" Conor asked, tears now rolling freely down his face.

"No, he wouldn't have felt anything. It stopped his pain, Conor. Jamie did what was best for him."

She took him out of the tub and dried him down. There were pajamas left here from their long stay in the spring and he let her help him dress, despite the fact that he normally did all these things for himself now.

"Is Jamie mad at me?" he asked, voice trembling with worry.

"No, Conor. Jamie isn't mad at you. He was very scared you were going to get hurt and he's just happy that you're okay. He's mad at the man, not you."

She took him downstairs for his tea. Maggie had fried him up a sausage with some potatoes. He ate very little, though he did drink the tea she had promised him. He refused a story when she tucked him into the bed. She lay down with him, and held him, stroking his damp curls. He was still now, having cried himself out. Exhausted from the emotional turmoil of the afternoon, it wasn't long before his breathing became even and deep and she knew he'd slipped off to sleep. She longed to sleep herself. She felt hollowed out, the echo of Phouka's screams still in her head. Her horse, her beautiful high-stepping cantankerous bastard of a horse. He had been a beast for most people, but he had always been a perfect lamb for her and he had gotten her through some very bad spots in these last years. He had been a high-spirited boy from the get-go and she had always loved that about him. She left Conor deeply asleep, tear trails still visible on his small face, and made her way down to the kitchen.

The room was steeped in the sun as it climbed down the sky, rung by rung, changing color with each descent. Isabelle and Kolya were playing quietly together with a set of blocks, as if they sensed something was wrong and didn't want to add to the fuss and worry.

"Where is Jamie?" she asked Maggie, though she feared she knew the answer.

"He went to find the bastard responsible for killin' yer horse an' almost killin' our wee man," Maggie said, as she slotted plates into the sideboard, the china gleaming in the evening sun like it had been glazed with blood.

She started for the door, but it occurred to her that she had no clue where Jamie might have gone to find the man.

"Leave them to it," Maggie said. "Should Jamie find him he deserves everythin' comin' to him for what he's done this day."

Pamela waited an hour, spending the time readying both Isabelle and Kolya for their respective beds. They ended up sleeping together, head to toe, Kolya with one chubby hand clutched fast to Isabelle's wee nightie. She sighed; prying them apart when it was time to take her children home wasn't going to be easy. She hadn't spent the night here in Jamie's house since she'd left in the spring.

She made her way down to the byre. The old estate basked in the setting sun and the last of the light set fire to the land so that all the colors burned deep and rich, flaring here and there into tongues of flame which hovered in the trees and streaked in over the horizon in shimmering bands of crimson and amethyst and a pure and depthless blue. For so long now she had been numb to beauty but she suddenly felt like Phouka's death had punched a hole in the cocoon of that numbness. Feeling would enter now whether she wanted it or not. It frightened her.

Jamie was in the stable seated on a bale of hay, cradling his left hand in his right. There was blood leaking from his knuckles and dripping slowly through the fingers of his right hand. He looked up at her approach, his eyes a hard and brilliant green even in the low light of the stable.

"Jamie?"

"I'm all right," he said, knowing what her question would be.

She dragged a bale of hay across the stable so that she could sit near him.

"Did you find him?" she asked.

"No, more's the pity. I think he must have left the minute he got Conor on that horse."

"What happened to your hands, Jamie?" she asked, afraid of what the answer might be.

"I hit someone rather hard; I wanted to know who hired that bastard."

"Did you get an answer?" she asked, heart thumping painfully.

"I did, of a sort. After much persuasion, Niall admitted he'd been offered money by Julian to hire this man. Julian told him it had my express approval, that he'd had dinner with me in London, which was true enough, but I certainly didn't give him permission to recommend anyone for hire. I've only been back for two days, I had yet to notice a strange face in the yard."

"Oh God, I hired Niall while you were in Russia," she said, horrified.

"Yes, and who do you think put him under your nose just at the point when you needed someone on short notice?"

"I don't know," she said. "He just showed up one day looking for work. Stephen had retired and we needed an odd jobs man. Looking back, I guess he was a little too Johnny-on-the-spot."

"He's lucky I didn't kill him; it was a near thing. He swears he didn't know what the other man planned to do and I tend to believe him because he was inclined to tell all at that point. Still, he had to know it wasn't anything good. Not when there was bribery involved."

Pamela shivered a little, understanding just what Jamie meant by 'inclined,' but she could not find any sympathy in her heart for the man—his greed and willingness to turn a blind eye had almost cost her son his life and it *had* cost Phouka his.

"Are you sure it was Julian?"

"No, I'm not. Being that it was done over the phone, it could be anyone. Still, it wouldn't surprise me if it was."

"I still don't understand what upset Phouka so badly. He's always been a little high-strung, but he usually doesn't get spooked like that."

"There was a spur under the saddle," Jamie said wearily. "A small one, but it would have shocked the hell out of him as soon as there was any weight on it."

"Oh God—oh my poor boy," she said. Phouka had never known anything but love and kindness his whole life, pain like that would have shocked him and sent him into the terrible panic which had killed him.

She looked then at Jamie and saw the defeat in his face. His expression was generally so guarded that it surprised her. It was an indication of just how much this had upset him.

"I don't think Julian can be redeemed, Pamela. His mother has turned him in upon himself with hatred and lies. I can't undo twenty-one years of damage. I don't have that sort of power with him. After this…" he trailed off and put his head in his good hand, his left hand still lying palm up on his leg.

Her heart ached for him. It was his chance to be a father to a child of his own blood, and as fate and Diane would have it he would never be able to love this son and nor would the son be able to love the father. It was an irony so bitter that there were no words to comfort him.

"Jamie, I'm sorry," she said. She leaned forward and touched his hand lightly. He flinched and she knew she would have to call the doctor when they got back to the house. Like most males, Jamie was supremely stubborn when it came to seeking medical help for himself. His tolerance for pain was very high, and the flinch had told her he must have a broken bone in his left hand. She leaned down further to kiss his hand lightly, her lips barely brushing the bruised and bloodied skin.

He looked up at her, clearly startled.

"It's what I do for the children when they get hurt," she said in answer to his look.

"I know," he said, with a crooked smile, "but it's not quite the same when you do it for me."

She shrugged, feeling foolish. "I just wish I could take some of the pain away for you."

With his good hand he touched the side of her face. "You do, Pamela. It's because of who and what you are to me that I cannot let this pass with Julian. It's because of Conor too, an innocent wee child who I think my own son may have planned to kill."

"I don't understand why he would want to hurt Conor."

"Because to hurt you is to hurt me, that's why," Jamie said. "If Julian *is* at the bottom of this, then it makes sense. A twisted sense, but sense nevertheless."

"That goes both ways—the hurt," she said softly. "Which puts both of us right where he wants us."

Jamie smiled wearily. "It does but I don't see how we can change that."

"I wouldn't want to Jamie, even if we could."

"Nor me." He took her hand with his uninjured one and gave it a reassuring squeeze. "Let's go up to the house, I think we could both use a drink."

Two hours later the doctor had been and gone and Jamie had splints on two fingers. Pamela had lit a fire in the study as the room tended to get chilly once the sun went down, even on fine evenings. She had poured them each a stiff drink, trying not to think of her beautiful fiery-tempered horse. Jamie had already made the arrangements to have him buried on the estate as soon as the sun rose. She hoped Conor would not be damaged by this; it was a horribly traumatic event for a child who was still so young.

"I'd like to take you and the children to Maine for the summer," Jamie said, startling her out of her thoughts.

"What?" she put her drink down with exaggerated care, realizing the two swallows she'd had, had gone straight to her head.

"I have a house in Maine, as you know. I haven't been there in several summers. I would love it if you and Conor and Isabelle came along with us."

That was all he said, but she understood the subtext. She felt shocked that he would suggest she leave the country and yet she understood the sense of it too. She understood what he was offering to her and why. To go home for a bit, to wander the same shores she had walked as a young girl and not be in the space where she was waiting for a man to come home to her who might well never arrive. It would be good for the children too, to be away from this place in which their mother never truly relaxed and to live by the sea for a month or two. Far too much had happened in these last few months—someone trying to kill her neighbor, someone trying to kill her, and now her horse dying and her son having narrowly escaped the same fate. She was exhausted and nearing the edge of something she thought she might not be able to back away from.

There were practicalities to consider—work, her house, the animals and their care. Her heart gave a sick heave, for Phouka would no longer need care. The construction company only had a few minor projects going at present and she could leave those in Frank's more than capable hands. Gert would look after Rusty and Paudeen for her and Pat would drop by the house now and again to make certain all was well. For the first time in months she felt a longing that didn't contain Casey's lack. She wanted to go home to her own country and just be for a little while and breathe the salt air of the eastern seaboard.

"I'd like that," she said.

Chapter Fifty-six

The Dreaming Coast

JAMIE'S COTTAGE WAS reached by way of a narrow, sandy lane that ran between great tall old firs, the scent of which perfumed the interior of the car as they pulled up the lane. With that smell came a rush of childhood memory for Pamela, for all her summers had been spent in such places.

The cottage was a traditional Maine shingle, silver-grey with storm and time and surrounded by a tangle of thyme and lavender and wild beach roses. Cottage was, of course, a misnomer of sorts in the typical northeast tradition of downplaying all material possessions for fear of being thought grand. Grand wasn't how she would describe this house but rather elemental, as if it had grown onto those rocks, naturally and slowly over many years, like a seed from a fir tree had germinated into a dwelling. Across the front and sides was a huge wraparound porch which hung like an aerie over the rocky incline to the sea.

She wasn't prepared for the interior, but felt only a sense of immense light and wind when she put Isabelle down in the open entryway and let her scamper off across the floor behind her brother and Kolya. The entire inside of the cottage had been gutted and opened up to its beams so that the ceiling lofted overhead like a great honey-gold gull. The kitchen was tucked into one corner of this great room, fitted out with a deep ceramic sink and counters made from slabs of slate. It was into the living area that she was drawn. For facing out over the sea, the entire wall, floor to ceiling, was glass, and it had the effect of flight, as though one could step through the glass and sweep up into the limitless sky, wing above the waves, and never come to roost again. Two large chairs faced each other next to the windows, a small table between, heaped with books and paper. On the south wall was a vast stone fireplace, blackened with long use and an ancient hod filled with split pine to one side. A battered brass telescope gazed, three-legged, out to sea and books were crammed in the shelves—beautiful shelves, made from long shanks of driftwood and anchored invisibly to the walls.

She walked to the windows, a strange fear shimmering out through her veins, and yet an exhilaration as well that fizzed like a geyser in her blood. She never could maintain her defenses near the sea, here there would be no hiding from it, no cowering away from the sight of all that water so beautiful and entirely without conscience. She wasn't sure she could manage it and felt the bird of anxiety flutter in her chest. Jamie was opening a door, and she could hear the swell against the shore, the boom of the wind as it flew into the cove and flooded back out. The scent of ozone quickened her senses and she stepped onto the old porch, closing her eyes so that she would not panic. She had not been near the sea since Casey disappeared, she had not dared it, and for a moment she felt a white hot blaze of fury at Jamie for bringing them all here for if anyone understood what the sea meant to her it was he.

She took a breath and opened her eyes and felt as though the ground had disappeared from beneath her feet. The wind streamed at her here, rich with the scent of salt and marine life; it lifted her short curls clear up and fluttered them out with strong, silken fingers. It was like standing on the prow of a ship, with nothing to shield one from either sky or ocean, the planet no longer a fixed point in a chancy universe but rather what it truly was, a watery oasis in constant flux, spinning in a mad dance with a golden star.

She chanced a look below to a small beach, a crescent of sand, sheltered by large dark boulders rimed in salt and deep-green lichens. Dark-pointed balsam fir, mysterious and old as the rocks ran right down to the shore, wind-bent and salt-traced, heady with the scent of bleeding sap on this hot day. Low-slung schooners and gaily-colored dinghies slid past her view and further out, the blazing white sails of a clipper rode the round of the horizon.

Conor had followed her out onto the porch and stood now against her leg, her small stalwart son, his eyes straining out to sea already. She could feel the tension in his frame, the pull the water exerted on him. Moored near the small sandy spit was a blue dinghy, its sails a bright red, bobbing merrily on the light waves that rippled under it. Conor's sight was trained on it unerringly, and Pamela felt a sick lurch at the thought of her son out on the water and yet many of her best memories from childhood involved sailing.

"I thought," Jamie said, coming to stand on the balcony with them, "that if your mother approves I might teach you to sail this summer. Would you like that, Conor?"

Conor turned his face up toward Jamie, dark eyes filled with a wild excitement. He nodded to Jamie, made mute by the idea of his own boat and learning to ride upon the waves on his own power.

Pamela looked at Jamie, the fear and anger plain in her face.

"I'll be very careful, we'll go no further out than the point, and I'll tie his boat to mine. It will all be fine. At first we won't go in any deeper than I can stand to pull the boat around with him in it."

Conor looked up at her, dark eyes pleading. "Please, Mama? I want to go sailing."

She nodded at him, and then looked back at Jamie. He interpreted her expression correctly.

"It will all be fine, Pamela. You'll see."

She didn't reply saving her words for later when Conor was not present. Jamie continued, his tone light, as if she were not glaring daggers at him.

"The house is for you and Conor and Isabelle, there's a cottage down the laneway; it used to be an artist's studio, that's where Vanya, Kolya and I will stay."

"Jamie, I can't take over the main house."

"I asked you here, Pamela, with the express intention of you having the house for the summer. You'll want the privacy from time to time, and it's a good place to…" he hesitated, as though changing his words internally, before speaking them out loud. "To just be quiet, if that's what you want. When you don't, Vanya, Kolya and I will all be a little down the road. In fact if you yell, we'll hear you."

By the first night, Kolya was a permanent resident of the main house. There was no way he was going to tolerate being in such proximity to Isabelle and yet be parted from her for heaven only knew how long. Any absence to Kolya seemed one of permanence, for he stuck himself gamely to Pamela's leg and refused to be budged. At which point Pamela interceded on his behalf, pointing out to Jamie that both babies would be more likely to sleep if put in the same room together rather than in separate abodes.

The summer advanced on that note, with both households moving in a small migratory circle, back and forth, depending on the weather, the various moods, the meals and who was preparing them and that day's particular adventures.

Conor took to sailing as she had known he would, with a love for the ocean and the vessels that moved upon her which she understood all too well. True to his word, Jamie was careful with him and never let Conor out from under his watchful gaze. Still frightened and traumatized from Phouka's death, Conor wasn't keen to take chances and so slowly she found herself relaxing and realizing that Jamie, with his unfailing instincts about others' needs had realized the sea would help Conor heal from the experience with Phouka.

The days quickly took on a pleasing rhythm. She rose early to swim before the children woke. The water held an aching cold to it reminding her of her childhood summers along this coast and the freedom that only water could give her. The water was and always had been her natural element. When she was small she had dreamed of being a mermaid and had thought if she swam enough, that one day she would awaken to find scales, blue and iridescent, growing on her legs.

By the time she returned to the house each day, Jamie would have a fire going in the great hearth and coffee brewing. When the mornings were clear and achingly bright they would sit on the porch, coffee in hand and chat quietly, or merely watch the morning sailors slip by on the breeze. And so they swam and sailed and built castles in the sand and hunted seashells and other flotsam and jetsam of both sea and forest. At night, by the fire, they would tell stories and roast marshmallows and make blanket forts for the children, where Pamela occasionally found herself sleeping, quite uncomfortably, through the night with all three children gathered round her.

Often on the nights when she couldn't sleep she would wrap herself up in a blanket and sit out on the porch simply listening to the sea and watching the moon float high overhead, the firs dark sentinels against the backdrop of the stars. Jamie's light was usually on in the cottage down the lane, burning deep into the wee hours. He took care of business at night when it was quiet and he could work uninterrupted for long stretches of time. The time difference between Maine and Ireland made work that late at night a matter of practicality, he told her. The truth was Jamie found sleep just as elusive as she did. Nevertheless, it was a comfort, knowing he was there, just a stone's throw away.

Sometimes during those sleepless nights she would find herself uneasily replaying the last conversation she'd had with Noah.

"Ye're goin' where?"

"To Maine," she said. She felt she owed it to Noah to tell him, being that he had done a great deal on her behalf and because she wanted him to know she wouldn't be able to house any on-the-run men for the next two months.

"*With yer man on the hill?*" His disapproval was evident, and she bristled at it.

"*Yes, with Jamie and Vanya and the children. It's not a romantic getaway or anything, he's my friend. The truth is I want to be away for a while. I think it will do me good. It's along the same stretch of coast where I spent my summers in childhood, and I want my own children to experience that.*"

Noah nodded, his gaze narrow and shrewd as if he was hearing all the words behind what she was saying, all the things that were impossible to say. Now that she had made the decision to go, she was desperate to leave and be away from the darkness in this land.

"*Do ye think he's asked ye to go away for the entire summer out of the goodness of his heart?*"

"*Yes,*" she replied hotly, "*maybe you can't understand that, but it's how Jamie is.*"

Noah shrugged. "*Maybe, maybe not—but I'll tell ye this, he's still a man an' ye'd be served well to remember it.*"

"*He doesn't see me that way,*" she said, even though she knew it wasn't quite true. Noah had known it, too.

"*Ye're a fool if ye believe that,*" he said, and leaned toward her giving his words more emphasis. "*Ye spoke of not carin' to have men's desire, but ye have his an' I think ye know it. Question is, what do ye plan to do about it?*"

Sitting here now in her blanket with the sound of the sea at her feet she shivered. She had made a deal with him and he had not called her to account on it. There was, as of yet, no horse to train, and so she wondered what it was Noah would ultimately ask for as his due. A woman couldn't make a deal in blood and not expect to return it in like coin.

A little voice in the back of her head would always give her the same answer to her question.

"*It's what the devil always asks for, Pamela—your soul.*"

The stories of Barsoom began easily enough. Vanya had been caught up in a stash of old Edgar Rice Burroughs novels he'd found on Jamie's shelves and Conor, wondering what the story was about, had asked Vanya to tell him. Vanya's explanation had been simple, but the only word that stuck for Conor was Rice's rather baroque name for Mars—Barsoom. He had demanded that Vanya tell him all about Barsoom, right down to the particulars of its sand. Vanya did his level best, but Conor, having had the benefit of more than one natural storyteller in his life, was not satisfied with Vanya's rather terse descriptions. He wisely parked his small self at Jamie's feet that night with the request that *he* describe Barsoom.

Jamie had eyed the small boy and then had laid a finger alongside his nose and tapped it three times, as though weighing the gravity of his listener. Then he nodded, as if he had found what he sought and began… "On the far side of Barsoom, beyond the great Dunes of Karnam, lived a boy named Fledge who carried within him a warrior's heart, though his outside gave no hint of this for he was a tattery beggar of a child, with no home to call his own, and neither kith nor kin to ease his way through his world…"

So had begun a nightly ritual with Conor seated on the floor by Jamie's feet held rapt by both the timbre and rhythm of Jamie's voice and also by the trials and travails of Fledge, with whom Conor was very familiar from the hedge tales Jamie had told him throughout the winter and spring. For Fledge had many, many things in common with Conor, including his wild dark hair and his love for water—of which there was a great dearth on the far side of Barsoom. And though Jamie had started the tales for Conor, each one of them slowly entered the dark, enchanted realm where canyons went miles deep and three moons glowed in the evening sky. Pamela would sit next to her son, feeling the anticipation in his small body each time Jamie began with the words, 'On the far side of Barsoom…'

Isabelle began to climb up on Jamie's knee each evening, tucking herself into his side and gazing up at his face as he spoke, occasionally reaching up to pat his cheek as though to encourage the flow of his words. Kolya, never far behind Isabelle, took possession of his father's other knee. Vanya would slide his lissome form down beside Pamela, for they had come to find an ease with one another that was of great comfort to both. There was Fig, a nod to their absent friend Shura, Fledge's stalwart, if rather short, companion, who followed him through every adventure and fought at his side with great valor and a true heart. Fig also had a regrettable tendency to quote Roofi, the famed Barsoom mystic, at every possible and impossible opportunity. Each of them was woven into the story, though their characters were not always recognizable at once. The Sea Princess of Elysium, trapped in a thorn-encased tower at the mercy of an evil enchanter, was a regular feature of the story for more than two weeks before Pamela recognized herself in the remote and caged figure. Releasing the Princess was part of Fledge's journey, but the crystal key which would have opened her tower lay at the heart of a labyrinth guarded by a most dread monster that could change faces at will. Algea was the name of this monster, and while the rest of the audience was unaware, Pamela well knew that Algea had been one of the daughters of Eris, the Goddess of Strife and that her specialty was pain. Whether the infliction of it, or the relieving of it, Pamela did not know.

The night that Jamie had described Fledge's first encounter with the legend of the crystal key and the terrible frailty of said key which was the Princess' only hope of release, Pamela had left the small circle and gone to stand by the windows where the susurration of the sea drowned much of Jamie's words. She understood what he was trying to do—that in his own way, without confronting her directly, he was telling her there was a way out of this citadel in which she dwelt, where her heart was frozen in time, suspended, waiting for a prince no one believed could ever come back, except of course for the poor deluded princess.

Then came the night he told them of the Wandering Wastrel—the strange guide that Fledge and Fig hired, for he was rumored to possess a map that would lead the bearer through the labyrinth to the crystal key. The Wastrel had roamed from far to near in Barsoom and sang of the spheres of the Silk Road, that great arched pathway that ran through the stars and wound about planets and moons. The Wastrel had travelled it in a sailing ship, made from the wings of dragons and along the way he encountered all sorts of villains and vagabonds, but it wasn't until he met up with Fledge and Fig that he decided to abandon his lone wolf ways and join forces with other beings.

The Wastrel was both bard and minstrel, weaving spells with words and the silver notes of his magical lyre, which had come from a less than savory trade with a Saturnian camel shepherd. The trade involved many golden newts that had been left with the Wastrel by his father, a mysterious anonymous figure that the Wastrel had spent his life seeking, but never finding.

She understood that Jamie himself was the Wastrel. The Wastrel with his past that was a closed book, whose story was never told, and who deflected, with grace, each question that came his way. The Wastrel with his restless heart who wandered all the corners of the galaxy and yet had found no home.

All that summer they walked upon the carefully laid path of Jamie's words, the slipstreams of silver stars, the waste ground of the Great Darkness that lay beyond the River of the Milky Way. He became a divine enchanter each night, donning a mad scarf on his head, a pirate patch over one eye, staging a mock sword fight with Conor and Vanya while Isabelle and Kolya ran amok round and round his legs. He adopted each character as he told their story, becoming the dark Ceresian witch woman who kept some dread secret in her cauldron, (that night he wore a Medusian wig, or rather a mop stripped of its handle) the scholarly and horribly tall Ionian book trader, (an ancient monocle was dug out from an equally ancient dress-up box and stilts were fashioned) and everyone's favorite—the small drunken rug seller from Elysium, a character of sharp tongue and even sharper mind who wore gold hoop earrings and had a tatty stuffed parrot on his shoulder. Each one was a delicate thread in the overall design of this web Jamie wrapped them in each evening. All the denizens of Barsoom and beyond came to such vivid and full life that they lived and breathed with them, felt their pain, laughed with their joy and held their breath when they stood on the precipice of disaster. There was nearly a full-scale mutiny the night the rug seller contracted the Ganymedian Flu and was teetering on the brink of death. Jamie very wisely gave him a miraculous recovery the following night.

At Pamela's request the storytelling extended one night after the children had gone to sleep and Vanya had retreated to the cottage by the shore. She had left the large living room to make certain Conor had put his comics down and gone to sleep, and that Isabelle and Kolya still had their blankets on for the sea air was cool tonight and she did not want them catching a chill. When she returned, she found Jamie with his hands steepled under his chin, his eyes gazing out the windows to the swiftly approaching dark. The last of the day's light was caught in his hair and limned his profile so that he was bound in both gold and dusk, the emerald on his left hand flaring with green fire as it caught a last stray beam of sun. The planes of his face were in repose, for he was lost in thought, his lashes half spangle, half shadow, his mouth lined fine as though with an artist's brush. She stood for a moment, still, for to catch him unaware was a rare treat. He heard her though and turned and smiled at her, his face still caught in the web of that faraway place, the beauty of it imprinted in his expression, even as it flowed into something else, like sand running from one end of a glass to another—from enchantment to ease, from chimera to corporeality.

"Tell me a story, Jamie, something to chase the cold night away."

There was a quality to her voice, which caused him to look up and meet her eyes.

"Shall I spin you a dream?" he asked. "Shall I spin you a dream of stars and silks and Samarkand, or one of salted seas and talking walruses and a white-haired empress sitting atop a throne of ice?"

"Tell me a story about us," she said and sat down across from him, tucking her feet up under her.

He gave her a long look, which wasn't entirely comfortable and then he began, as if he had merely wandered down a hall in the storehouse of his mind and opened a door and found a story there to be told. "Once upon a time, there was a deck of tarot cards that belonged to a very old gypsy woman who had come from the darkest part of the deepest Russian forest. Now these tarot cards were no ordinary sort, for the backs of the cards were decorated most elaborately with vines and flowers and small wicked faces peeking out here and there and writing that was neither Latin, nor Greek, nor Russian but something far older. When the cards were turned over, though, the faces were entirely blank…"

It was the beginning of a ritual for them. On nights when the children slept and the sea murmured outside the windows, or when they sat late around a fire just the two of them. Vanya was a night owl who either read into the wee hours or disappeared on some adventure of which only he knew the particulars. There was an old deck of tarot cards which sat upon one of the driftwood shelves. Jamie would shuffle it and hold it out to her and bid her to pick a card. The card dictated which story he told that night. Each one was like a separate bead on a golden chain and yet they all linked together to create something more, something achingly lovely which could only have been created by Jamie's imagination. It was something for her to hold fast to as she made her way along this journey that had no map by which to guide herself.

It was also during these times alone with her that he began to speak of Russia, and of the people he had known and loved there. He told her of Nikolai and his Katya, of a small clerk named Volodya and how he had, in one last act of defiance, brought the angel of death to their camp. He spoke, too, of Vanya and Shura and their long trek with him out of Russia. He told her a little of Gregor, the *vor*, and the unlikely friendship which had grown between them. But he did not speak of Andrei or Violet and she, understanding, did not ask.

She saw that with the gift of this summer he had presented her with something more—a reminder of the thread that stretched back through all the summers of her childhood, the stars and lost beaches, the stories told by fires and the love found and lost. That strand stretched forward too though, through the fierce love for her children and her friendship with this man who had given her golden days which gathered like orbs of honey, one upon the next. Stars might shift and vanish, and earth might crumble before the onslaught of the sea, but the thread remained both gossamer and iron, for it was the glistening and tenuous fiber of life itself.

Chapter Fifty-seven

The Shape of Grief

A SUDDEN SQUALL BLEW up the coast for two days in early August. Shut in, they had resorted to games, books, puzzles and toasting bread and cheese over the fire and making blanket forts in the big main room. The children found it to be grand fun, and quite frankly, thought Pamela, so did the adults.

On the second afternoon when the little ones were napping and Conor was well occupied with his building blocks, she took out the photographs she'd brought with her to Maine in the hopes that she would find time to sort them into some semblance of order. She set them out on the kitchen table and began to arrange them by year and then by session.

Jamie came and looked over her shoulder. "What are you thinking of doing with these?" he asked.

"Doing?" she asked. "Nothing really, I just want to get them in some sort of order."

He pointed to the scrapbook she had placed in one corner of the table by itself. "That looks like more than sorting. Do you mind if I have a look?"

"No, go ahead," she said, though she felt suddenly nervous. The scrapbook had become a kind of project for her, something she worked on at night when she couldn't sleep and, as it turned out, something that she truly enjoyed. Jamie took it over to the windows where he could see better and spent a good half hour paging through it, chuckling here and there.

The scrapbook was different from any other work she had ever done. It owed its genesis to an afternoon when she had been taking pictures at a wedding and had gone outside for a bit of air. There was a group of young people out back of the hall playing football and she'd sat down on a keg to watch them. Finally she had asked them if she could take some pictures of them. They'd shrugged and agreed readily enough. Then one, curious about her camera, had come to sit down with her. His name was Finian Gold. He'd told her a bit about himself—mum single, he was the oldest of four, father fecked off to Liverpool to work years ago, and they'd never heard from him again 'an' sure as bleedin' Jaysus' had never had a pay packet from the man. Then there was the tiny but utterly fierce Bernie, a redhead of decided opinions and suspicions who looked like a being escaped from the borders of fairyland after a rather rough night of revels. And studious Ambrose with his big ears which were almost translucent when the light hit him from behind, and his three older sisters and his love of T.S Eliot's poetry. She had made a habit after that when she had work in Belfast to stop by the spots she knew they haunted and had met more of their friends, and taken their pictures too. After these hours of time spent with the raggle-taggle group of adolescents she would jot down notes about their lives and small anecdotes about their personalities. Sometimes she would sketch their portrait and put it in the scrapbook along with their photos and the notes. Bernie had an older brother in the Kesh, and another brother who'd been killed. Finian, the Pied Piper of the group, knew how to make Molotov cocktails and what routes were best to avoid soldiers, and how to hide from the local IRA when you'd managed to piss them off.

"Pamela, this is extraordinary. Have you thought about putting a book together? Publishers are interested in this kind of material."

"It's just some pictures and stories," she said, feeling suddenly embarrassed by the cobbled-together scrapbook.

"It's more than that. You've given these children a voice."

"Oh, believe me," she laughed, "they all have voices and aren't afraid to use them."

"Well, that's part of the beauty of this, you've allowed them to simply tell their stories in their own words. The sketches too—I didn't know you could draw like this."

She shrugged. "I didn't either. I'd forgotten how comforting it is— getting lost in the process of line and shadow."

She'd drawn Bernie as a fairy with flames for wings and tiny shoes made from tiger lilies. Finian, she'd cast as the Artful Dodger in checkered pants and a waistcoat from the Victorian era. Ambrose with his ears, she'd drawn as an owl, high in a tree surrounded by piles of toppling books and a pot of tea. There were more pages, more children, their stories, their losses, and the price which war, even an unofficial one, extracted from its smallest citizens.

"I know a publisher in New York who might be interested in this. Would you be willing for him to have a look?" he asked.

"I...yes, I suppose that would be all right," she said, flustered by the idea. "I would need permission from the children and their parents, if someone did want to publish it."

The next day Jamie, though it was still storming, drove into town, ostensibly for bread and milk. When he returned, however, it was with a clutch of books for Vanya and three pads of very good art paper, a box of charcoal pencils and watercolor paints for her.

"Keep drawing," he said, "you owe it to yourself."

And so that night while Jamie unfurled the latest installment of the Barsoom tales, she drew the words he spoke, sketching the characters he'd breathed into life. Over the weeks that followed she drew and drew in every spare moment when she wasn't out on the water or building sand-castles with the babies, or beachcombing with Conor. She drew all of them in the guises Jamie had given them within his stories: Vanya as a beautiful faun; Conor as the brave little warrior, Fledge; Isabelle as a fairy with missing teeth and a propensity to fall asleep in any convenient spot—tree branches, lily pads, or in the shade of toadstools; Kolya as a small Cossack, who was also half wood sprite and drew his strength from the vast northern forests of his ancestors. She never drew the Sea Princess though and nor did she draw the Wastrel. She couldn't capture Jamie on paper, some element of him always eluded her regardless of how long she studied his profile or attempted to pin down the shifting expressions of his face.

As she filled sheet after sheet of paper, she realized there was a small seed of contentment in her heart, which given time and nourishment might bloom into something that looked a lot like happiness.

Two days later the morning dawned fair and bright and stayed that way all the day through. Jamie and Conor took full advantage of the weather and went straight out to sea on Jamie's beautiful old sailboat, *Protophos*. Greek for 'first light' the name suited a vessel that belonged to Jamie as it suited the summer that unfolded around them.

Pamela and Vanya had spent the day ambling the cove with the little ones and running into town for the fresh milk and eggs and the bread Jamie had forgotten on his last trip. Jamie and Conor hadn't returned until the sun was well on its way down the yardarm and Conor had been so tired that he had fallen asleep at the dinner table, his hair stiff with salt wind and spray. She stood for a moment after putting him in his bed, just to watch his sleeping face. He was changing and it hurt her heart to see it at times. Time went so swiftly, regardless of grief and anxiety. Conor had lost the last of his baby pudginess a long time ago, but here he'd stretched out even more. This summer had given him firmer ground upon which to stand, and it was in no small part because of the man who had brought them all here. The sea had worked its magic on her little boy and she was utterly grateful to Jamie for what he had done.

When she returned to the living area of the cottage, she found Vanya curled up in a chair reading. Vanya loved the escape of a good novel, more he told her, than he loved almost anything else on earth. He was four books into the Barsetshire Chronicles and was utterly taken with the idylls of English country life as it unfurled in Trollope's imaginary county. He looked up as she walked past him, flashing her a quick smile before returning to the page. She and Vanya had solidified the foundation of their friendship this summer, until she realized that he had become so dear to her that she could not countenance the idea that he might well up and leave one day, just as Shura had done.

She spotted Jamie standing out on the verandah. The windows were open to the night air and he turned as he heard her step behind him.

"Come look," he said, voice filled with a quiet wonder. She stepped out onto the verandah, and gasped. The sea below was lit to a glowing blue haze under a sky so silted with stars that it looked like a casket of living jewels had been upturned and scattered thickly all across the horizon with an extravagant hand. Despite spending many of her summers by the sea she had rarely experienced the wonder of phosphorescence like this.

"Come," he said and put out his hand.

She glanced back at the still house, its dark gull wings spread large under the night sky. Only one small light burned steady, where Vanya sat by the picture windows reading.

"I've already spoken to Vanya, he will listen for the children. We're going out in the row boat."

The sea was entirely calm, though it appeared to dance with all the tiny lights sparkling within its depths and the boat slid out upon it with ease, like a fairy tale boat upon on a moonbeam sea.

"Oh, Jamie," she breathed as they moved out into deeper waters, and the light seemed to rise up and surround them with its unearthly glow. The water rippled silver then gold, cascading down the lip of each oar, lit from within with a pale green glow. Her father used to tell her it was mermaid lanterns deep below the sea that caused the phosphorescence. It was an idea which she still loved the romance of, even if she knew the facts. Jamie pulled on the oars again, and she had the feeling of skimming through light, the water dancing and alive beneath them.

She turned her face up toward the sky, though it was still hard sometimes to look at the stars without Casey, those still burning fires deep in the velvet reaches of the universe—all the great clouds of birthing stars, and the homely comfort of their own neighborhood, the Milky Way. She wanted to believe that her own pain could not amount to much under a dome of stars burning and dying, but that did not lessen its intensity.

"Making a wish?" Jamie asked. She looked at him; his question was light enough in tone, but she knew Jamie never asked anything if he didn't want an answer to it. So, because it was easy to be honest with him, she told the truth.

"I wish I could lose my memory sometimes," she said, trailing a hand in the water and watching the light limn her fingers, making them ghostly and beautiful at the same time. "I wish I could wake up one morning and know the children and all the other parts of my life, but that I could forget that my husband is gone."

"You might have a bit of difficulty in understanding just how the children had materialized into your life," Jamie said drily.

"I could have woken up pregnant because I'd eaten nettles or something, the way fair maids do in fairy tales."

He laughed softly. "Indeed, you could have. But I don't think you would truly want that."

"I don't know, Jamie, I might... for a while at least."

"I know," he said, and then was silent, for Jamie more than anyone in her life, understood when there weren't any words with which to comfort.

"I did make a wish on a shore near this one, long ago," she said, uncertain why she was telling him this. "I was only a child at the time, and didn't realize that the universe hears such wishes and shapes destiny from the words of a child's heart. I didn't know that there was a price to be paid for granted wishes."

"What did you wish for?" he asked.

"I wished that you would come back to me. I wished that somehow, in some way you would always be a part of my life. I've cost us both very dearly with that wish, Jamie."

"I would not wish you away from my life. If it saved you grief then yes, but for myself it has been a blessing—your friendship, the children, these weeks here."

He began to row again, skimming them along the light bridge of water; the only sound that of the oars dipping in and out and the soft lap of the water against the boat's hull.

"I owe you a thank you," he said suddenly.

"For what?"

"For saving my life while I was in Russia."

That silenced her. They had never spoken of that strange night, that night where they had been thousands of miles apart and yet had lain with one another in some other realm which she could not, to this day, explain.

"You saved your own life, Jamie," she finally said. "You had to choose that night, and you chose to live."

"It was you that led me to the place where I could decide," he said, "surely you know that."

"I don't know what I did, it was all very surreal and yet…" she paused, not certain how to explain her feelings around the events of that night.

"And yet, it happened. I don't know what exactly you felt at your end; I don't even know how I was so certain it was you."

"I knew because I felt *you*," she said quietly and then turned away toward the sea, unable to manage his gaze any longer.

"How did you know it was me?"

"Because I knew very well how Casey's body felt and it wasn't him," she said, "I knew it was you. Long ago you told me, Jamie, that it would be no ordinary thing if we were to touch in that way, and it wasn't, was it?"

"No," he replied. "No, it wasn't."

They rowed on some little way further, quiet and comfortable.

"It will get easier someday, Pamela. I know it's a cliché to even say it, but it's a cliché for a reason."

She looked up to find him gazing directly at her. He wasn't moving and the sea was so still that the boat barely rocked.

"I never forget but some days I can breathe without it hurting."

"The shape of grief changes, but it never goes away. You know this, you learn to live with it in a variety of ways, until eventually it is almost like an old friend, one who understands everything about you without you having to explain."

She nodded. Jamie had gone through more than his share of grief and so she listened when he spoke of such things. Below them a school of fish, incandescent, rippled through in a shimmering trail as though the Milky Way was both above and below them, a river of light within the sea and the sky. Beauty was becoming bearable once again, and part of her was sad to know it. She knew her grief would likely be with her all her life but she also knew that Jamie was right, the shape of it was slowly changing.

Chapter Fifty-eight

The One Searched For...

THE DAYS OF THAT SUMMER mounted one upon the next, each one a separate gem strung on the strands of water and long walks, of lobster stew and the scent of sun-warmed skin and peaches and sand each nightfall, of Vanya's novels and Jamie's stories and the children's delight in the unfettered freedom of this old shore.

Pamela wasn't certain just when it had happened, but at some point during these sea and sun-filled days, a bit of normalcy had begun to creep in around the edges of her soul. She found she had an appetite again and could eat without feeling sick, and breathe without feeling like she had glass slivers all along her airway. She thought maybe it was the proximity of the sea, of the days that were as clear as glass and the air that was thick with salt and summer wind.

Jamie stood on the deck above her just now, elbows resting on the rail, looking down to where she had been helping Conor and Vanya with an elaborate sand castle. He had changed out of this morning's sailing gear, swapping his unraveling sweater and worn jeans for a crisp blue cotton shirt and a pair of chinos. His hair was damp from the shower and it struck her suddenly what a strange intimacy this summer had given them—like a family, almost.

He held the truck keys in his left hand and he shook them at her as if in invitation.

"Where are you off to?" she asked, shielding her eyes from the sun to look up at him.

"Visiting a friend," he said. "Would you like to come with me?"

Both Isabelle and Kolya were napping, exhausted from a morning of playing in the cove and Conor and Vanya were still happily engrossed in castle construction.

She turned back to Vanya, who waved a hand at her before she could even speak. "Go, *moy podrooga*, we will be fine. I will listen for the babies."

"I'd love to," she said looking back up at Jamie, "but I ought to tidy up a bit. My hair's a fright and my clothes are sandy."

He looked at her and smiled. "The person I'm taking you to meet won't mind your hair nor a bit of sand. Come along before a child awakens."

She looked down dubiously at her cutoff denim shorts and the embroidered gypsy shirt made from patchwork squares which had taken her fancy in a tiny shop that had smelled rather strongly of pot. In fact, she thought she could still smell a whiff of it, despite the shirt having been washed twice.

"You look like the world's most ridiculously beautiful bohemian," he said, as if he'd read her mind. "So come along, you'll do fine."

She walked up on the deck, a sooty brow arched in his direction. "Is that your polite way of calling me a hippie, Jamie?"

"It's my polite way of calling you beautiful," he said and she faltered under his gaze. She felt flustered and so merely walked past him into the house. Despite Jamie's reassurance, she took a few moments to wash her face, and put on a bit of lipstick and mascara. Her hair had grown out to the point of a fine mesh of curls which were completely wild, so she tied them back with a scarlet ribbon that had adorned Isabelle's mad mop of hair earlier in the day. She glanced in the mirror to see if she was presentable. She looked tanned, healthy and slightly otherworldly, like a naiad who had found land for a day, but had no notion of earthly mores and customs.

Jamie was waiting for her outside, his hands busy with the wiring of an old radio he and Conor were rebuilding. He smiled as she came out and followed her down the stairs to the truck.

They drove north along the old coastal roads. The day was fine and the sea beyond dazzlingly bright, dancing with diamond wavelets. On the horizon lay Deer Isle, a green oasis afloat on the blue haze of the Atlantic. She took a deep breath and relaxed into the leather seat, happy to just be in Jamie's company with the coast slowly unfurling in wooded islets and small fishing villages with their clapboard houses brightly painted, and boats for both fishing and sailing skimming along the rim of the world.

She turned to look at Jamie while he drove. He was always a man comfortable in his skin, but she thought this summer had been good for him too. She was suddenly exquisitely aware of him. The sun and water had glazed him a golden brown, his hair bleached to platinum and a sparkling gold that turned the green of his eyes a brilliant jade. He looked healthy and relaxed and more beautiful than ever. He was, she realized, a man in the very prime of his life. It was with no small shock that she saw this and understood that while her mind may have been unaware of it, her body most certainly was not. She had long understood the effect Jamie's beauty had on those around him, she had long felt the effects herself, but this was something different. This was the heightened awareness, like a layer of skin had been removed, of a very desirable man, not just her dearest friend and protector.

Just as quickly as she felt the tug of desire, a quiver of guilt split it down the middle and left her feeling slightly sick with herself. How could she feel desire? She took a sharp breath and put a hand to her stomach, causing Jamie to cast a glance her way. She smiled in reassurance and then looked out her side of the truck at the sea and the land which was changing swiftly from the thickly-wooded dreaming sea isles to a starker broken landscape. As swiftly as the desire had warmed her blood, it fled, leaving her cold and shaken.

"Who is it we're going to visit?" she asked, when she was certain her voice wouldn't shake and betray her state.

"An old friend, her name is Pauline. She is someone I think you'll like which is why I asked you to come along."

"Well, you've got me curious now," she said lightly, though she had an odd feeling about the visit, as if there was more to it than a simple meeting of one of Jamie's friends with another.

They passed the rest of the drive in their normal daily chatter—the children, the novel Vanya had insisted all adults in the house must read this week—in this case, Harold Robbin's *The Adventurers*. She and Jamie had a fun evening taking turns reading the more lurid passages out loud, Jamie doing his in a stage voice worthy of Olivier which had left her and Vanya in stitches.

The house was reached by a long and winding green lane at the end of which was a weathered gate with a 'No Trespassers' sign affixed to it. They parked the truck and walked in to where the house sat in a small wilderness of maidenly white birches and long grasses sprinkled with forget-me-nots and crimson anemones.

A tiny garden fronted the small house. It was steeped in fragrance this hot afternoon, the scent of roses thick and heady, their canes netting the stone and beam house in a cascade of white and red and yellow. Geraniums bloomed profusely in tidy cedar window boxes and Virginia creeper clambered up the north side of the house all the way to the chimney.

Jamie knocked on the door, which was decorated with a wreath of sea holly wound about with a silver ribbon.

"Not home?" Pamela asked, half wishing the mysterious Pauline would be out.

"She'll be nearby, she's expecting us." He looked down toward the bobbing wharf where a sailboat sat, trim and well maintained. A look of something akin to lust crossed his face. She laughed and he turned toward her, a question in his eyes.

"Jamie Kirkpatrick, I swear you have seawater in your veins, instead of blood. Boats to you are like beautiful women are to other men, you've never met one you could resist."

"Said the pot to the kettle," he said, and then grinned, a heart-stopping flash of white in his browned face. "But for the record, I appreciate beautiful women too, some even more than sail boats."

And there it was again, that breathless awareness of him, the hot flush of desire moving through her like a jolt of quicksilver, bright and devastating. She turned toward the woods, dappled in the afternoon sunlight, so that Jamie would not see the telltale flush flooding up from her neckline. She saw the woman then. She emerged from a stand of young birch trees, though Pamela had the sense she had been there for a little while, as a deer might do, standing unnoticed while it observed and took a person's measure. She moved as gracefully as a deer, too, when she stepped toward them, a smile of welcome on her face.

She was tall, with the sort of bone structure that would leave her beautiful even when she was a very old woman. Her eyes were dark above high cheekbones, set off by a pair of silver bangle earrings and a cascade of snow-white hair that reached to her waist in a thick plait.

She held out her hands and Jamie took them. "Well, my friend it has been a long time."

"It has indeed," he agreed, gesturing to Pamela to come forward. She stepped up beside him, feeling a touch intimidated by the regal woman. She had the presence of a warrior queen, strong and straight-backed with an air of no-nonsense intelligence. She turned her dark gaze on Pamela and gave her a long assessing look before reaching out a hand to her. Her grasp was cool and dry, and her scent was green—something warm like sage.

"Welcome to my humble abode," she said. "I've been after Jamie to bring you to visit since I knew he was in Maine for the summer."

Pamela arched a brow at Jamie and he shrugged.

"Pauline this is Pamela Riordan, and Pamela this is Pauline Nighttraveller."

"It's lovely to meet you," she said. "How do you two know each other?" It was an innocent enough query, but the truth was Jamie did seem to have a plethora of striking female friends scattered around the globe.

Pauline smiled fondly at Jamie. "This one taught me how to sail one summer. He saw me gazing out to sea every day, looking longingly at all the pretty boats out there and he asked if I'd like to learn how to sail. It has been a long time since he has come to visit, or to sail for that matter, though."

"I haven't been to Maine in several summers," Jamie said, leaning forward to kiss the woman's cheek, "otherwise you know I would have come."

"Yes, I heard you had some troubles with an extended stay in Russia." She leaned back a little to better observe him. She brushed one hand along his jawline. "You are well again?"

"I am well again," he agreed quietly. "I survived after all, and that is no small thing in Russia these days."

"Surviving is no small thing, indeed," she said, but she looked at Pamela as she said it. Pamela felt the strange tingling along her skin, as she often did when first meeting a kindred spirit. It happened rarely in a life, but one felt it unmistakably when it did.

"Jamie, I replaced the cleat on my boat last week and the mainsail isn't running up as smoothly as it ought to. Could you run the boat out a little way and check it over for me?"

"Of course," Jamie said. Pamela gave him a narrow-eyed glance; he merely smiled and turned to head down to the sailboat that bobbed bright against the sunlit water and the weathered grey dock.

The woman gestured to her with one long-fingered hand. "Come inside, we'll get to know one another over a drink of some sort. He'll be occupied for a bit; I've been having trouble with the sails for a few weeks, so I'm grateful he's come to visit. I don't know anyone who understands sailboats as well as Jamie."

The house was lovely inside, spare in its lines, with well-chosen objects that spoke, Pamela thought, of a life lived in depth. The furniture was sparse and there were plants everywhere, many of them herbs which she recognized by the shape of their leaves.

There was a large picture window in the sitting room that looked out over the sea. It was a very private location, not quite as wild in aspect as Jamie's house and its environs, but lovely nonetheless. The main feature of the living room was the built-in bookshelves that lined two full walls and were chock-a-block with books placed higgledy-piggledy wherever they might fit. Pamela immediately felt more comfortable; shelves of books were an anodyne to her, and made her more apt to place an initial, if wary, trust in a person. Pauline saw the direction of her gaze and said,

"I collect stories from the various nations of my people and then I put them together in anthologies. They've proven fairly popular with the general reading public as well, enough so I can afford to live out here all year round and not need another job."

"You stay out here all year? The winters must be a little fierce."

Pauline nodded. "They are, but it's part of what I love about them. I had the house insulated and a big woodstove put in when I bought the place so that I could stay if I wanted to. About five years ago, I did just that. I make certain to have emergency supplies at all times in case I get snowed in or the weather makes it impossible to get to town for several days."

She looked at the bookshelves while Pauline made tea. The woman had been modest when she claimed she merely put her peoples' tales into anthologies. She had several books of her own on Native American myths and legends, as well as medicine, religion and rituals.

Pauline returned a few minutes later with a steaming tea tray, which held a knobby pottery teapot and mugs, a pot of honey in the shape of a beehive and chocolate chip cookies on a plate. Once the tea was poured out and distributed, Pauline sat across from her, curling her long legs up under her and smiling reassuringly.

"I'm going to be blunt with you, because there is a reason I asked Jamie to bring you for a visit."

"Oh, is there?" Pamela said, her tone slightly tart. She took a sip of her tea to steady herself. It was rosehip and had the bittersweet taste of the buds.

The woman gave a half-smile at her tone, but chose to overlook it.

"My daughter went missing a long time ago," she said, "and Jamie told me about your husband."

Pamela nodded, the bird in her chest which had been dormant for weeks suddenly giving a flap or two of its dark wings. She wanted to say something, but there were no words that stood in measure against that one hard sentence and no comfort to be found for that black hole in the middle of your universe. She did not have the sense that this was a woman who needed words of comfort, however. A small surge of anger flitted through her. Jamie might have told her why he was bringing her here, though if he had she wouldn't have accompanied him and the bastard knew it, which is exactly why he had sprung it on her in this fashion.

The woman was watching her and no doubt reading her like black print on white paper, Pamela thought, chagrined.

"Don't be too upset with him, he brought you here at my insistence," Pauline said. "You and I live in a world that few people, thank God, will ever understand. We live in a community that is formed by a terrible tragedy. And it is rare, and I say that with gratitude, to run into another member of this particular community. I wanted Jamie to bring you here so that you know there is someone who understands and will listen should you wish to talk."

"Thank you, but right now I don't think I want to talk about it—about him." She put her mug on the low table which was placed between the couch she sat on and the armchair Pauline was in. She clasped her hands together, the way she sometimes did when thinking about Casey, for there was the feeling that she might fly apart if she didn't hold tightly to something, even if it was only her own two hands. Somehow her awareness of Jamie earlier made it difficult to speak of Casey. She could never adequately convey him to a stranger—the big dark man who had been the safe place in her world.

"I understand, but if you change your mind, I'm a good listener."

"How long ago did your daughter go missing?" Pamela asked. It *was* oddly comforting to speak to someone who did understand the agony. At the same time she dreaded the story of this woman's child, because it clearly had not ended with her daughter returning. The hollow behind the heart was present here; she could feel it, as one did when one had the matching hollow in one's own chest.

Pauline took a swallow of her drink and looked out the window toward the sea. "You don't have to be polite about this, Pamela. I can tell you, or we can chat of other things—if there is one thing I understand, it's how hard it can be to either talk or listen on this subject."

"No, I would like you to tell me. I can listen, I just can't speak about Casey very often, even though I ache to most of the time. I see the looks on people's faces who know and I see the pity and I find that hard to bear. It makes me angry that they feel sorry for me, because they are so smugly certain they know his fate."

"I do understand that, I spent a long time being angry, rebelling against other people's certainty. In my case, the look I saw on other faces was that somehow she had gotten what was expected and that while it was sad, it shouldn't have been a surprise to her father and myself."

"I understand that," Pamela said, "my husband is—was a part of the PIRA for a bit."

Pauline nodded. "Then you know. My daughter was a prostitute, and though people will not often say it, they believe that women in that profession risk their lives and should know that they do. The truth is, Jenny was always missing in a way, it was only a matter of time before she went away forever. Do you know what I mean?"

"Yes," Pamela said. She did understand for she had spent a few hard years living in New York without money and it had only been by the grace of God and Hugh Mulligan that she hadn't wound up on the streets selling herself to men old enough to be her father. As it was she had done things to survive which she did not like to recall. She knew what it was to feel like you were not tethered to the earth, as if you could dissipate into the ether, and to fear that not a soul would notice.

"Jenny was troubled from a very early age. She was what my people called a 'lost one'. She would follow any wind no matter which direction it blew or how ill it might be. By the time she was in her teens we couldn't control her anymore, she had restless feet and she wouldn't stay put. I would search for her endlessly; I spent more time looking for her than I did anything else. She hitchhiked, too, which horrified her father and me. Her soul wasn't of the earth and so it drifted from here to there and back again. And while I know some say that all who wander are not lost, my girl *was* lost and like many of the lost she found bad company. There are always those who can smell the lost ones, and who slither forth from their lairs to wrap their slick coils about them. For her, it was heroin and then heroin's seemingly inevitable companion for a woman—prostitution.

"She didn't know her worth. It didn't matter that her father and I had tried to give her a view to another world, a different reality, to imbue her life with dignity and purpose. She was just lost. It was the hardest lesson of my life, finding out that you can't save some people no matter how much you want to, no matter how often you call on the gods it cannot be done. You never expect the soul you can't save to be your own child though. I spent years and a lot of money trying to track her down. It seemed like there was always a trace here, a scent there, some vapor trail that was just substantial enough to lead me down the next dead end road. The police were very little help, she was a known prostitute and an Indian woman, both facts which put her at the bottom of law enforcement's list of priorities."

She looked down into her cup, like it was a mirror that ran through time and could give her back a glimpse of the child she loved. Pamela knew what it was to long for such a scrying glass, but there was neither glass nor magic that gave back your heart once it was lost.

"It took us a long time to realize just how fragile she was and how deep her trouble had become. My husband and I were part of a grass-roots movement that eventually became the American Indian Movement, or AIM as it was known. He was a lawyer and I was a journalist with aspirations to one day write the great Native American novel. We got caught up in the movement and we were more focused on the injustice that in the end we could not change. Meanwhile we did not see, until it was too late, how far our daughter had drifted.

"The last time I saw her was one September when she came home for her birthday. She seemed a little better, in one of those small spaces in time where heroin retracts its claws just a little and allows the person to breathe again. It let us believe for a minute that there might be a way out, might be a life ahead that wasn't lived in an underbelly of darkness and addiction.

"We had a house out on Long Island Sound then and she would often go out on the shore in the mornings to watch the sun rise. That was where I found her, just as the dawn edged out in a narrow line between sea and sky. There was no wind that morning, so everything was still. It was one of those perfect days where everything is held in an autumn glass with its hues of crimson and gold and the deep blue you only see that time of year—a time that holds something sacred in its core. She looked so frail, she didn't weigh much at that point and she had always been tiny. That morning she looked translucent with the rising sun shining right through her bones. There was a weariness in her, too, just this terrible weight that someone as young as she was should never feel. I've only ever found it in combat veterans and prostitutes and children that are terribly abused.

"I went and stood by her and we watched the sun come in over the sea, setting fire to the land as it stole ashore. Then all that great stillness was broken by a single leaf whirling down in circles. It was scarlet with brown spots, already decaying. The rising sun caught the edge of it, rendering it translucent just before Jenny caught it. I still see her little nail-bitten hand cupping that leaf. She gazed at it for the longest time, that fragile leaf with its ghostly veins lying there in her palm.

"She said, 'This leaf is me, Mama, just drifting on the wind and waiting to land, but if I ever do land, someone will crush me.'

"She folded her fingers over the leaf and then opened them back up letting the morning air take the fragments, scattering them to the four winds. She left later that same morning, said she was going to head out to California to see her Cousin Eddy. She never arrived. Eddy had been waiting for her for a few days before he called me. I didn't worry too much at first, and neither did Eddy. Jenny was that way, always late, not showing up when or where she was meant to. So we didn't worry when we should have. I don't know that it would have made any difference in the end, still I feel such guilt over not being alarmed sooner."

She put her mug on the table, and when she spoke again the long line of her throat trembled.

"I never saw her again and I never heard that little girl voice on the other end of the phone again either. She always called on Christmas, it was the one thing I could count on. I lived for Christmas Day back then, because I could relax for a bit, knowing Jenny was still out there somewhere, even if it wasn't a good place, still it was somewhere. And somewhere is always better than nowhere."

"Yes, it is," Pamela said quietly. "Do you—" she faltered slightly, "have you ever found peace with it?"

"Peace?" Pauline looked startled, as if such a suggestion had never occurred to her. "No, I wouldn't call it peace, nor even acceptance. Resignation might come close and in resignation there is sometimes a strange sort of peace. It's not the sort of peace you would choose but life does not always give us choice."

She appreciated the woman's honesty, for she understood how dearly it was bought. She didn't want it, but she appreciated it, which was a conundrum all too common in her emotions these days.

"Your husband?"

Pauline shook her head, fine lines around her mouth suddenly visible. "He died a few years back. The official cause was a pulmonary embolism, in truth he died of a broken heart. The endless searching, the scouring every place she might have been and questioning every person who might have seen her, heard from her, calling the police every day and then once a week and then once a month. It took a terrible toll on us both, but it killed him."

Pauline rose from her chair and Pamela rose too, thinking perhaps they would go outside now and wait for Jamie to bring the boat back in. Instead the woman put up a hand and said, "Just wait a moment if you will, I have something for you."

She waited by the window. The sailboat was a speck but it was moving toward the shore. Jamie had timed things nicely, she thought wryly. Bastard.

When Pauline returned she held a necklace in her hands. Pamela recognized it as a Navajo design called 'Squash Blossom' for the silver flowers that lined the necklace from nape to drop. She had seen such necklaces before but not one quite like this, this one was barbarically beautiful, the coral near blood-red and the turquoise an oceanic and shimmering blue. What lent it the barbaric note was the bear claws that were spaced between the bottom three squash blossoms on each side.

"My nephew sent this to me. He told me that a woman gave it to a friend of his and she said it was for 'the woman with the ocean in her eyes'. The woman told the friend to give it to Eddy and that he should send it on to 'the woman who lives by the far coast' and I would know to whom it belonged when I met her. As soon as you walked in today, I knew it was your necklace. The coral is for protection and signifies long life and health. The turquoise, the Navajo say, is a piece of sky fallen to earth. It seems fitting that a woman with the ocean in her eyes should wear a bit of sky around her neck for balance."

Pauline fastened it around Pamela's neck and the weight of it lay like a fold of sun-warmed silk on her skin. She put a hand up to touch it, the stones smooth beneath her fingers. The necklace gave her an odd feeling, there was something unsettling about it and the silver had a strange heat to it that sent small shivers from her neck to her toes. It was unnerving but she didn't want to take the necklace off in front of Pauline, lest she hurt her feelings. The weight of the necklace and its strange warmth gave her the strength to speak.

"I tell myself stories sometimes," she said softly. "I think of him as 'away' in the Irish sense of the word, which gives me comfort. I weave tales in which he is safe and will return home one day. The more time that passes, the more I know my tales are futile, but in the dark of night, alone in bed, it's a comfort to imagine those stories." It was a huge admittance on her part, and one she knew she could not have made to anyone other than this woman who understood too well the pain of the smallest retreat or surrender to reality.

"You tell yourself the stories you need to, in order to allow yourself to move on and not feel guilty every time you're happy, every time you laugh or forget for a minute that part of your soul left a long time ago. We all tell stories to ourselves, those of us with the vanished in our lives. Stories are the first magic we know and we believe that if something is told often enough it takes on a truth of its own. In a way this is right, after all, you had a life with this man, you have his children which are all any of us leave behind on this earth in the end. So even if he does not come back to you in physical form, he is with you forever."

"I'm afraid that isn't quite the comfort it ought to be," Pamela said quietly. She heard the bitter note in her voice. It was like that always, even the clearest day and the cleanest water held a drop of bitter that rippled out in unexpected ways, particularly at moments when it seemed she might approach an understanding of the truth the rest of her life would hold.

Pauline reached over and took Pamela's hand in her own and there was something reassuring in the cool dry warmth of the woman's grasp. Beyond the window the sea was a great and fathomless blue under the early evening light. Far out the dark waited below the horizon, ever patient, ever there.

"There is an old tale from the Onondaga people," Pauline began quietly, "about how the Pleiades were formed. A group of children would gather to dance each day by a beautiful lake. One day while they danced an old man appeared to them in the chill autumn air. He was dressed in white feathers and his hair shone as silver as the stars in the night sky. He gathered the children about him and warned them that they must stop their dance, for they had attracted eyes high above that were very dangerous to them. Children are much the same in every time and every place and they were intent on their fun and continued to dance despite the old man coming to them again and again to warn them they must cease or suffer the consequences.

"One day one of the children decided they ought to have a feast after their dancing, and so each child asked their parents if they might take food—corn or beans, or the fat wild turkeys that roamed the forest that time of year. But the parents said no, saying the children could eat at home as they should, and not on the shore of the lake where they might waste the food that was so necessary for survival through the winter that even then was nibbling at the edges of autumn's gold.

"Regardless though, the children continued to dance and dance by the shores of that silver lake as the autumn progressed and the leaves turned from crimson and gold to dust. And then one day just before the first snow fell the children found themselves growing lighter and lighter, as light as the cotton from a dandelion in the early months of summer. They rose upon the air, higher and higher. A woman passing that way who had seen the children floating up toward the sky ran back to the village and then all the parents ran hoping to save their children, crying piteously and offering them food of all kinds and plenty of it, if only they would return home. But the children, excepting one, would not look back and continued to rise until the twilight came and they set upon the velvet darkness of the sky as a group of stars. The single child who looked back fell as a star through the sky, streaking the heavens silver and gold, but lost to his family and his people just the same. Those dancing children are the Pleiades and they will dance forever, or at least until man is no more.

"And that is the story *I* tell myself, that Jenny is one of those dancing stars. Her soul was the sort that would allow her to fly up there into the face of the moon and those big blazing fires that are only dancing twinkles from here. Because the stars dwell in a place apart, a place of no time and all time. A place where people are just a blink of the eye—stardust here and gone. And so, our lives do not signify greatly in such a place. It is," she finished wryly, "as I said, the story I tell myself."

They stood quiet for a time, watching as Jamie brought the sailboat into the dock and fastened it to its mooring. The evening light was advancing, heralding the night which would steal softly up from beyond the sea and swallow the world in an embrace of stars and a sliver thin new moon.

"Do you have a name other than Pauline?"

"An Indian name, you mean?"

"Yes."

"I do, it's Orenda, it's an Iroquois name. It means magic power. What a joke that is, for if I had any magic I would have used it all long ago to bring my daughter back to me."

"And Jenny?"

"Her name? Her name is the greatest irony of all. It took a long time for me to conceive. So long that her father and I had almost despaired of ever having a child. So when she arrived we called her Onida." There was a pause as she drew a breath that seemed to come from that place where the dark waited below the horizon. "It means the one searched for."

Chapter Fifty-nine

Heart's Truth

THE PUB WAS A SMALL ONE, old and intimate and rather down-at-the-heels. It reminded Pamela of many of the pubs back home. Ancient and scruffy, with regulars at the bar and wear marks where their elbows had rested for decades.

Jamie came back with a pint for himself and a shandy for her. The pub seemed to be a popular place for it was slowly filling up with laughing women and men with faces weathered by earning a living from the sea. There were summer people too, like themselves, accepted as part of a world that ebbed and flowed more than most with the seasons. Many of the locals earned the majority of their living from summer people and so had long ago learned to accept the change in their communities every year. Jamie had a different level of ease with many of them because some had known him as a young boy when he would frequently spend summers here with his grandfather.

They had stopped on their way back from Portland where they had met with the publisher from New York about her potential book on the children of the Troubles. The meeting had gone well and she was cautiously excited about the notion of publishing her book. The children had stayed back with Vanya and a local girl named Pru, who was of the sort that even at seventeen could make a grown woman feel wildly incompetent. The children adored her and Pamela had no worries about leaving them in her care for the day.

She took a sip of her drink and relaxed into the wooden back of the bench on which they sat. Jamie took a long swallow of his stout and sighed in repletion. She smiled at him, feeling happy. There was no longer any of the strain between them which had been so evident in the spring. It was a relief to her, though she wasn't inclined to be naïve about it either.

There was a shuffle and a stir and people stepped back to make way for the two musicians now wending their way through the crowd toward a makeshift stage, one carrying a penny whistle and a set of uilleann pipes, the other with a bodhran. Her heart began to beat a little harder and the bird in her chest stretched out its dark wings in warning.

The man with the bodhran had dark hair and somehow she knew he was Irish. He had the look of it about him. The black hair and the blue eyes 'put in wid a sooty thumb' as her old nanny Rose used to say about those thickly-lashed deep blue eyes.

Her throat grew suddenly tight as the first man drew a long note on the pipes, warming them for his performance. And then the man with the bodhran began to warm up, flicking the tipper back and forth, setting a rhythm, turning to say something to his fellow musician. The bodhran was the very heartbeat of Irish music. It had been Casey's instrument—the one he'd played most often when he'd been on the road with Robin, performing in pubs up and down the west coast. She had gone to see him one night in a pub on the coast of Donegal. They had conceived Conor that very night, in a field with the sound of a fiddle washing over them.

The duo played a few of the songs they knew would be familiar to most—*Whiskey in the Jar, Rocky Road to Dublin, Mo Ghile Mear* and *The Rising of the Moon*. A few rebel tunes of the sort that got everyone clapping and their blood thumping and then the inevitable laments meant to tug on heart strings and make the women swoon. Generally speaking it worked, it had always worked bloody well for Casey, even when she had known exactly what he was up to. That was when the dark-haired man with the bodhran looked straight at her, his drum at rest now upon his knee and began to sing. It was just what singers did—find a face in the crowd and play to it. It made the performance more intimate for everyone in the room and made the chosen audience member feel special. He couldn't possibly know that this song felt like a shard of ice to her heart. He couldn't possibly know that he reminded her of another dark-haired man who used to sing to her and make her feel like she was the only woman in the room and the only woman, for him, in the world.

Cold blows the wind to my true love,
And gently falls the rain.
I never had but one true love,
And in greenwood he lies slain.

> *I'll do as much for my true love*
> *As any a young girl may.*
> *I'll sit and mourn all on his grave*
> *For twelve months and a day.*

She could feel Jamie's gaze upon her face, but she didn't dare look back at him. The singer continued with only the soft ribbon of the penny whistle to accompany him.

> *And when twelve months and a day had passed,*
> *The ghost did rise and speak,*
> *"Why do you sit all on my grave*
> *And will not let me sleep?"*

> *'Tis I, 'tis I, thine own true love*
> *That sits all on your grave*
> *I ask one kiss from your sweet lips*
> *And that is all that I crave.*

> *My breast is cold as the clay;*
> *My breath is earthly strong.*
> *And if you kiss my cold, clay lips,*
> *Your days will not be long.*

She couldn't breathe, she was choking and thought she might get sick. She got up, nearly tripping in her haste to get away from the music. The place was packed and it was hard to get through the throng of people. When at last she made it to the door and stumbled out into the night, she had to bend over, clutching her knees and striving to get air into her lungs.

The fair day had turned and evening had brought a bank of fog with it. Her legs were still trembling as she walked over to one of the concrete blocks that edged the gravel parking lot. The cars were only glimpses of color and shape—a red-winged mirror here, a green-humped fender there. She dragged in a breath, feeling like a wheezy old man who had smoked two packs of cigarettes a day for the last forty years.

She could still hear the dark-haired singer. His voice was a bit like Casey's—a pure Irish voice, able to impart both agony and joy in equal measure to a song.

> *How oft on yonder grave, sweetheart*
> *Where we were wont to walk—*
> *The fairest flower that I e're saw*
> *Has withered to a stalk.*

She didn't even have the cold comfort of a grave to sit beside she thought with a small spurt of bitterness. And it might be that she never would.

> *When shall we meet again, sweetheart?*
> *When shall we meet again?*
> *When the oaken leaves that fall from the trees*
> *Are green and spring up again.*

And the answer to that final painful verse was, she knew, knowledge which she had fought now for almost two years.

Jamie, wise man that he was, gave her a few minutes to collect herself before he came out of the pub door.

"Are you all right?" he asked, his voice as soft as the fog that enclosed them here on this cold block of concrete.

"It's that song, I...it just hit a little too close to home." He sat there beside her until the breath returned fully to her lungs and she could stand without shaking.

As they walked toward the truck, he turned and the fog swirled around him, tendrils wreathing the bright glow of his hair.

"I'd like to go sailing tomorrow, just the two of us. Do you think you're up for that?" he asked.

"Yes, I'm up for it," she said. She had the oddest feeling, though, that what had just been asked and answered was far more complex than either of them realized.

"Do you believe that, Jamie? In the song that man sang last night—that the dead can't rest if we don't allow them to?"

Jamie looked over at her from his position by the bow of the sailboat, where he was running out the anchor chain. "I don't think there's an end date on mourning, Pamela. Perhaps that applies even more when you don't know if you're really mourning or not."

"Oh, I think we both know I've been mourning. I worry sometimes that I am holding him back. What if it's like the church teaches and we stay in purgatory until we do penance, or until whatever it is that still holds us to the earth finally lets us go?"

"I don't know, sweetheart," he said. "I truly don't. But I don't believe your longing for him is keeping him stuck fast anywhere, unable to move. It's you who is in purgatory, Pamela, caught in waiting and not knowing what happened to him."

"I know I have to move on. I'm just not sure how to do that and I know when I do, whatever it looks like, whatever that first step is, I will feel like I am betraying him."

He came over to where she sat and offered her a hand up. She didn't need him to respond. She had spoken the truth and they both knew it.

Despite being so far out on the water, it was still a hot day and she felt grimy with sweat and the effort of sailing so when Jamie had offered to anchor the boat so that they could swim, she happily took him up on the suggestion.

She skimmed out of her shorts and t-shirt, for she always wore a swimsuit beneath her clothes this summer lest the opportunity to swim presented itself. When she was little her father had called her his water-baby, and it was still true. The water was home and root to her, the place in which her body and soul felt most connected and at peace. She noticed Jamie looking at her and felt a flush of self-consciousness. He glanced away and she noted the fine tension along the line of his jaw. He got up then, pulled his shirt off and dove into the water. She forgot sometimes that Jamie was a man like other men because in so many ways he wasn't. She had so long been used to thinking of him as a being apart; special with his various talents, his beauty, his intuitiveness. But he was a man, one who had feelings and desires and she needed to have a care for that.

The water was a shock, so cold it was like needles all along her skin. She dove down and then flipped over, coming up with a gasp. She looked around, seeking Jamie's sleek golden head against the dazzling blue of the water. An incredibly strong swimmer, and even more at home in the sea than she was, he was already a fair distance away.

She dove down again and again, feeling clean and buoyant like she was a young dolphin. The water was freedom for her. The salt upon her skin, the slick slide of the water past her face and neck and breasts and thighs and toes released something in her. She felt strong again even as her muscles burned in the cold water, strong and buoyant as though the sea took the weight of her soul for those precious few moments while she swam. She felt nothing sometimes too, just gliding, not thinking, not feeling and grateful for the release of it.

The sense seized her suddenly that she could drift down soft as a primeval skeleton, here on the shelf of her own country, become weightless, drift with the tides and float soft toward the moon when it was full and turned the sea to a blaze of mercury. And feel nothing and ache for no one ever again. Maybe, maybe if she drifted down and away far enough, she would find her missing husband, somewhere in the depths waiting for her. She gave herself a mental shake, she needed to break for the surface and quit entertaining such morbid thoughts. She pushed in the direction she thought was up and then realized with utter terror that she was no longer certain which way was up and which way was down. It had happened before to her, once when she was a child and once in her teens. She had never forgotten the pure terror of either experience. The water was cloudy, and there was nothing to hint the right direction to her, no telltale gleams of sun pointing 'this way up'.

Don't panic, she told herself sternly, even as she felt her heart pounding wildly against her ribs. It was then she felt the first trickle of water in her lungs. She didn't remember breathing in and the panic hit her full force with just the thought of her babies orphaned because she had stupidly stayed under water too long. She started to frantically churn the water, trying to seal off her nose and mouth even though her lungs felt like they were on fire and might burst out of her chest.

And then Jamie was there, grasping her arm so hard it hurt, drawing blood to mix with the salt of the sea, dragging her relentlessly up toward the light, toward the pain. It felt like a terrible bubble inside her, a bubble that if burst, would flood her body with the poison it held inside. She could feel more water going into her lungs, threatening to drag her back in the opposite direction.

They broke the surface then and she gasped for air but her lungs felt both sodden and fiery at the same time and she couldn't breathe. Jamie dragged her to the boat and then pushed her up the ladder and onto the deck with no small force. She hit the boards with a thump that slapped her hard in the chest. Water sprayed out of her mouth, and she could feel Jamie pull himself up onto the deck behind her.

"What the fuck were you doing?"

She shook her head, lungs still heavy with water, unable to breathe, her chest on fire with the lack of oxygen and with pain dammed far too long. Jamie hit her on the back, flat-handed and hard. It hurt like holy hell and brought tears to her eyes. Then suddenly she was gasping, retching water, choking on it as it streamed from her nose and mouth, the salt stinging painfully. Suddenly she realized it wasn't just the sea, but tears pouring in an unceasing torrent out of her. Tears choking her, twisting up her windpipe, making her chest so tight that she couldn't get even a wisp of air. The panic had her in its claws and it was going to push her off the edge into the abyss. She put her head to the deck and felt the sobs tear open her throat, a high and horrible keening that felt like it might go on forever.

Jamie suddenly grabbed her and shook her, hard enough that her teeth clattered together. He was furious, green eyes incandescent with anger.

"You don't get to check out like that, do you understand? You don't get to leave your children, you don't get to leave me, do you hear me, woman!"

She nodded as best as she could, and he let her go. She collapsed back onto the deck, lungs burning, water still stinging her nasal passages and her eyes.

"I…I wasn't trying to drown," she said, in between pain-filled breaths.

"You weren't trying *not* to drown either," Jamie said grimly. He was white beneath his tan, the lines around his mouth and eyes sharp with distress.

The silence grew vast and deep, and Jamie's anger was palpable in the air around her. The tears still leaked out, silent now, but no less painful for that. When she finally spoke her voice was like ether, drifting out along the wires of tension between them.

"Oh God, Jamie—he's gone, he's really and truly gone, isn't he?"

He didn't answer, because it was not necessary, he merely touched her, gently now, because she needed something to anchor her in the midst of the storm.

She reached a hand back, and he took it, pulling her to him, understanding that right now she felt like little more than a scatter of atoms about to be blown apart permanently by the winds of pain. He understood that she needed someone who loved her to just hold her and not to tell her it would be all right because it never would be again.

He held her for a long time; rocking her there on the deck of the boat. Held her as she cried all of it out, the months and months of uncertainty, of staving off the idea of Casey's death, of wondering if he had been terrified, if he had thought of her, if he had called for her and she had not heard him. If he had needed her and she had failed him.

"I should have felt it, Jamie—I should feel that he's gone. I should have known the instant it happened, but I didn't. I still don't know it, but maybe—maybe the truth is I just cannot accept it."

"You'll accept when you can, sweetheart, or you won't. Only time can decide that for you."

She turned her face into his chest, too exhausted to move. They sat so for a long time, as the boat was carried on the wind and water, the day going down in a pearl-blue calm.

They were silent on the trip back to shore. Jamie knew better than to speak; he knew Pamela wouldn't be able to bear small talk just now. He watched her as he steered the boat in toward land. She looked hollowed out and exhausted but she also had a glimmer of something else about her—peace. Just a glimmer but it was a start. He had known if anything could grant her the release she so desperately needed, it was the ocean.

When they reached the shore and he was tying up the boat she turned to him. Her face was bleached of color, but was still starkly beautiful against its bones.

"Jamie, thank you."

He nodded, because there weren't words that fit, there might never be words for it, for them. But he had, he knew, helped her toward something she desperately needed.

He stood still, there on the shore, the soft lap of the sea behind him, the salt of it still drying upon his skin, and watched her walk up toward the house, her steps slow, but maybe stronger now.

Chapter Sixty

On the Far Side of Barsoom

IT WAS THE SCENT of ripe apples on the air that told her summer was almost over. That and the soft breath of cooler air that haunted the evenings. All their stories were told with a fire flickering in the background, and though the days were warm and brightly lit the nights required a thin sweater against the chill. No one of them wanted to be the first to admit that their time was over, and so they lived their days and dreamed their nights in a state of suspended animation, as if this summer could be held and kept permanently if only they handled it carefully enough, and spoke no word about it ending.

She knew Jamie felt it too and knew they all had to return to Ireland soon to resume their workaday lives, though she little understood what that meant anymore. The summer had become a sort of dividing line in her life, from the numb grief-stricken wife who yearned toward every sound at the door and every ring of the telephone only to be dashed with cold water when neither venue offered any glimpse of her missing husband, to this woman she was now, caught in a limbo where she could not go back, yet had no idea of how to move forward.

The tales of Barsoom had given Conor a firm grounding. Each tale, carefully constructed had, in itself, been a guide that brought her son back to himself, and given him the security to stand in a world where his father was no longer present. That and the sailing, which Conor had taken to the way wind itself rode upon the furled landscape of the ocean.

She stared into the flames as she listened to Jamie's voice weaving softly through what remained of the present night's installment. What he had given Conor this summer was a gift beyond measure and she would be eternally grateful to him for it. It did not surprise her. Jamie always gave of himself in ways that restored others, gave them back to themselves, and rarely did the man count the cost of it to himself.

She felt Conor suddenly tense by her side, and pricked her ears accordingly to the words that Jamie was saying.

"…and so Fledge took the key and raised it to the lock, the weight of it almost bearing him into the floor—"

"No," Conor said suddenly, voice rough with emotion, "Fledge wouldn't do that, Fledge would give the Wastrel the key. *He* has to unlock the door."

"Why?" Jamie asked softly, while Pamela froze to the spot, fearing that she knew what Conor was about to say.

"Because he loves the Sea Princess," Conor replied, as if it ought to be obvious to anyone who had listened to the tales.

"He hasn't even seen her yet." Jamie's face was a perfect blank.

"That doesn't matter, he knows her here," Conor thumped his chest, roughly over the area of his heart. He turned, dark eyes meeting his mother's head-on, "Right, Mama?"

She took a breath, and told the truth for the sake of her son and how desperately these tales mattered to him. "Yes Conor, he loves her."

"He should unlock the door, right? Tell him, Mom—the Wastrel *has* to be the one to unlock the door."

"Yes, you're right, the Wastrel has to unlock the door."

She did not dare look up at Jamie while she said this, nor after. It was far too dangerous, for the tales were no longer safely away in Barsoom, but had landed, without warning, right here in the midst of them. She ought to have known better, for Jamie, despite the raw tension in his eyes, still held to his nature, which was, and always would be, supple with grace.

"I think I got too much sun today, Conor-lad, because of course you are right—the Wastrel does love her and so it is right that he unlocks the door of her prison."

Because she too understood when grace was required, she rose and took Isabelle from her position on Jamie's lap carrying her to her small bed with its railing and laying a warm blanket over her, for the night was cool and Isabelle's fine skin was chilled. She returned for Kolya, who was curled, like a gloriously red-gold shrimp, on the rug at Jamie's feet. Both children were redolent of the scents of that summer; strawberries and peaches, jam and mint, the sharp tang of the firs, the brine of the ocean and the warm honey of sunshine on small compact bodies. She laid Kolya at the opposite end of the bed, and covered him, too. It was a vain effort, she knew, for he would gravitate like a satellite to its chosen sun over the course of the night, until the two of them were curled together, like tiny opposing quotation marks, head to small sticky feet. The thought of trying to separate them on the return to Ireland, didn't bear thinking about. She suspected both she and Jamie were in for an ugly week of it as they returned to their respective abodes.

She watched over the two of them for a few minutes, inhaling their peaceful dreaming aura, but tonight even Isabelle and Kolya could not soothe her pain for the man out there now, who spoke so patiently to the little boy who had just exposed his love in a very painful manner.

She walked to the window, welcoming the cool breeze that streamed through it. Somehow she knew that this would be the final installment in the tales of Barsoom. The summer was over, the enchantment was done, and reality had returned.

She heard Conor's voice raised in question a few times and Jamie's patient answers. Over these many weeks they had begun to behave as an organic unit, with its particular rhythms and peccadilloes, traditions and habits and yet amidst this rather cacophonous symphony of life, there was a discordant note. And she knew all too well who was responsible for the disharmony.

Suddenly Jamie was standing at the bed behind her, checking on Kolya as he did each night before leaving to walk alone the pathway to the cottage. He ran a finger over the round of Kolya's rosy cheek, and gently moved a curl which was tangled in Isabelle's long lashes.

Normally this was a peaceful time of night and they would often have a cup of tea in the kitchen after storytelling, before Jamie left. But tonight she knew there would be no lingering over tea, no chatting into the wee hours.

"You will excuse me, I'm tired tonight," he said, meeting her eyes as courtesy required, but obviously wanting nothing more than to be out of her presence.

"Jamie...I..."

He put his hand up to halt her words. "It's all right. I really am just tired. Good night."

He was gone out the door before she could say anything further. She spent the next hour giving Conor a quick wash before bed and then reading him his favorite books. After he drifted off she found herself rather agitated. She moved about the house, picking up the day's detritus—tiny, sand-caked shorts and sandals, cups and bowls smudged and still sweetly smelling of the blueberries Vanya had brought back from town and crumpled flowers, wilted from being clutched in small, warm hands.

Part of her longed to run down the path to the cabin, to apologize to Jamie, to take that darkness from his eyes. She knew what was required for such a thing and was frightened that she could even consider it. She bent to pick up a pile of wet towels that had been spilled in the wake of small, wet bodies, near the bathroom door. When she stood, she started a little for Vanya had materialized directly in front of her. She hadn't heard him come in from the deck, where he had very tactfully removed himself during the end of the storytelling.

He took the towels from her hands. "I will watch the children to-night. You go to Yasha, he needs you."

She looked at him, her face apparently as transparent as glass, for he smiled and touched her arm. The lucent cat eyes were dark with sympathy.

"There has been, I know, no woman since Russia," he said. "Don't think, just go."

When the man had a point he made it well, she admitted. She paused only to straighten her hair a little, and then gave it up as a lost cause. She had gone sailing with Jamie and Conor that day and had a mess of salt-tangled curls on her head as a result. It's not like Jamie hadn't seen her all day, or for that matter, all summer, and she had given little care to her appearance most days beyond a shower and running a comb through her hair. Still, she had seen his eyes in more than one unguarded moment and knew that he saw a desirable woman when he looked at her, though he had been excessively careful not to show it.

Outside the night was moonlit, every rock and needle on the path-way outlined, the path itself resembling a small stream that rippled directly down the hill to join the sea beyond, itself a swathe of rippling pewter through the gaps in the fir trees.

She was at the door of the cottage in what seemed like three steps, the nerves along her arms and legs jumping with anxiety. She knocked quietly, half hoping he wouldn't hear and she could run back to the safety of the main house. The man, however, had the hearing of a bat and quietly called out.

"Come in."

His back was to her, and he looked out the window through the thick stand of trees to the ever-lamenting ocean, hushing softly against the stony shore.

"Jamie, I'm sorry—" she began, but he cut her off swiftly, voice rough-edged.

"Don't," he said, "you have nothing to apologize for, I'm the fool here. I wasn't aware I was quite so transparent. Even a wee boy can see straight through me. I did not intend that any of this should make you uncomfortable or put you in an awkward situation. I only meant to give you this summer to distract you, to maybe even allow you to take a breath whole without Casey's name beating inside you."

She walked forward and put her hand lightly to his back. "Jamie, I...sometimes I feel like I live there, on the far side of Barsoom, but there is no Wandering Wastrel to come and lead me out, and I have no map to tell me which road to take back home. There's just shifting sand beneath my feet and I keep going in the same circle, thinking the journey will get less painful, but it never does. I want you to know that there were times this summer when it started to hurt less. And even though it felt like a betrayal later, in the moment it was a relief. There were even times I was happy, and I owe every moment of that to you."

The line of his back thrummed with tension against her hand.

"Jamie, will you please look at me?"

He turned and she caught her breath at the expression on his face. The cost of these magic evenings was suddenly there so clearly, tabulated in the dark fractured light of his eyes and the drawn lines of his normally mobile mouth. And yet...she shivered...and yet this man took her breath away and returned it with something that felt like she held a fiery star right there in the cusp of her hands. Impossibly beautiful, and utterly terrifying at the same time.

The moon filtered down along the firs outside, sifting amber scent along with silver light through the windows and outlining Jamie where he stood, clad in worn jeans and a t-shirt that said 'Billy's Bait and Tackle' across its salt-beaten front. His feet were bare and glinting with the gold dust of sand from that day's sail, his hair, so sun-bleached that it had streaks of near white in it, was still tousled from Isabelle's attentions, the vertical crease in his forehead sharp as a knife, as it always was when he was particularly upset.

Vanya's words echoed within her, each placed delicately as pearls on a string, the intent unmistakable.

"There has been, I know, no woman since Russia."

She knew, even if Jamie in all his wisdom did not, where this summer had always been leading them. It was for her to take the step across the abyss. Jamie could not be expected, nor asked to do such a thing. It was time for the Sea Princess to break her enchantment, as much as the breaking would cut her.

"There is nothing to apologize for, Jamie. I suppose we ought to have seen where this might lead. Conor is too sensitive to the currents running about him at times, even if he doesn't understand what it all might mean. And I'm sorry for saying what I did, only the story matters to him and he needs it to be true in his life right now. I couldn't betray that."

"This isn't your fault. What did your son recognize except the truth? I got so involved in telling the tale that I wasn't as circumspect as I might have been about what to put in and what to leave out."

She took his long, fine-boned hands in her own, sliding the warmth of his palms to fit against hers. "Jamie, you have the key, only you, no one else. You told the story true, I've never loved a man other than Casey and you. I would have you unlock this door. I want to feel something again, and only you can help me do that."

His breath caught hard, his eyes as black as unmined emeralds. "Pamela, are you certain of what you are asking here?"

"Yes," she said softly. "I'd like you to make love to me, if you'd like to that is."

"If I'd like to?" he said and smiled, though she could feel the fine tremor that strung itself taut between their hands.

"Well, would you?" She was starting to feel just a tiny bit ridiculous, because if he said no, it was going to be horribly awkward for the both of them in short order.

"Like a Barsoom trader lost ten days in the Infernal Wastelands, who suddenly sees an oasis on the horizon."

They laughed, the tension easing a little between them. But there was no laughter in his voice as he spoke his next words. "Be careful, Pamela, because it matters what you decide. The regret in this instance, and it *will* come, won't be of normal measures."

She owed him the truth as far as she understood it just now. "I'd be lying, Jamie, if I said I was ready for more than this—more than tonight, but for tonight I can let go of him. Just for these few hours."

He shut his eyes, seeking one last vestige of self-control and good sense, but she moved in toward him and touched her hand to his neck, drawing him down to kiss her.

Time unlocked itself for them that night. The last of Jamie's reservations fled with the touch of her skin under his hands, and the force of her own need, a need that pushed aside all barriers and gave to him a passion such as he had only dreamed before.

And though he knew it unwise, he opened all the reefs and corals of his heart in those hours and gave her rule of them. Until they were both as boundless with love and heat as the great dreaming ocean that called ceaselessly from beyond the window.

Once, long ago, he had told her it was no ordinary thing to touch her, and so he found the truth of his words in her and she in him.

They spoke little, but for once in the night when he quoted to her the words of his desire.

O lente, lente currite noctis equi!
O, run slowly, slowly, horses of the night!

The horses of the night galloped by on silent feet, silken-maned and dark and heeded no imprecations to slow their run, nor to unspool time and halt the traitorous world that spun on regardless of lovers who would wish otherwise.

Just for these few hours, she had said, and had intended the words to extend no further than that. It was his tragedy that he understood exactly what that simple statement had meant and yet had chosen to enter the fire anyway and allow it to burn him as fires will.

She left the bed with the dawn light, but first she leaned over him, looking long into his eyes, her own unreadable. Then she bent down and kissed him. "I love you, Jamie. I always have."

At some point during the night the fog had rolled in, relentless and thick as swaddled cotton. Anything could be made blind by it, even perhaps, love. And so he watched her disappear away up the hill toward the main house and knew that, in all the ways that mattered she had already set out on a journey that was going to take her much further. A journey on which he could not follow and could only hope that one day the path would bring her back.

He turned toward the bed and closed his eyes against the sight of the rumpled sheets. But then he opened them again and allowed the images and scents to flood his senses. Later he would lock them away, keep the memories somewhere that would not cause him to bleed inside at their very presence. But for now...for now, he would allow himself a moment of weakness and feel the pain and the joy of it, fully.

He recalled how afterwards, when desire was both sweetly abating and re-building, she had seen the dagger drawn sharp against his chest, had understood its message with the fine scrollwork of a folded lily at the base and had bent to kiss him right there above his heart, and he heard Gregor's voice in his head, as he had not in a very long time.

"To love another man's woman is a fool's game."

Part Seven

The Dark Man
Autumn 1977-Autumn 1978

Chapter Sixty-one

Solitude
October 1977

He came upon the wood late one evening as he walked under a waning moon the color of marigolds. He liked the night walking, liked the empty country lanes and the occasional cottages, inhabitants slumbering under their snug thatched roofs, unaware of the tall, dark stranger who passed by, silent as a wolf, scenting the turf smoke of their humble hearths. He had taken a turn just out of a small village this night at a country crossroads. He took the right hand road, a narrow track up a long hill, thickly bordered by hedgerows, the dwellers thereof asleep in nests and burrows, the last of the blackberries falling overripe from the brambles to be crushed beneath his booted feet. He stopped and gathered a handful from a branch sticking out into the narrow lane, the last of summer's sun and soft wind thick upon his tongue with the taste of them. There was an old superstition about picking them so late in the season, for after the end of September the fruit was said to belong to the fairies. He didn't know where he'd come upon that nugget of information, but it was there in his mind even as the taste of the berries lingered in his mouth.

The walk up the narrow lane was long, but so was the night and it was a rare time when his knee wasn't giving him overmuch grief. The weather was fine, just a soft wind sighing over the hills and through the trees. A man could manage many a mile in such conditions. When he crested the hill, he saw a narrow path which led into long grasses and a small wood. The light was bright enough that he could see to put one foot ahead of the other. Sometimes on such nights, if he walked far enough, he felt weightless, as though he might float away, become merely spirit and leave his flesh, battered and scarred, behind and become a part of the night and the wind, the wood and the water and drift upon such currents until he was just a bit of the sky or one of the smoke-soft stars. Sometimes he thought a man could just walk until there was no longer need in his bones, no longer want in his cells, no longer an ache in his heart for things to which he could put neither name nor form. And so he kept walking as the night spread like a mother's comfort over the land.

He was aware of a larger wood off to his right; it was kept somewhat invisible by its own dark nature and his need to keep his eyes to the path which he was on, for his knee couldn't afford a stumble. Then the path turned sharply to the right and upward and he had no choice but to enter the wood. The trees soared into the night and blotted out the face of the moon. The silence they held was eerie, like that of a cathedral or a place of worship far older, far wilder, a place for a moon that was as narrow and sharp as the blade of a sickle. He kept walking, despite the jolt that shot from the primal seat at the base of his brain down his spine to settle low in his stomach, leaving a prickling awareness of something behind, always behind him. Long ago, in that other life, he remembered a man telling him that the trees had eyes, and not just those of the birds and animals which dwelt in them, but eyes far older, things that peered out from that other realm, the one that was always a half-heard whisper away. He felt all those eyes upon him, as though from a strange distance, eyes that assessed and knew the measure of a man in a glance. They would bless or curse, those eyes, at their own whim and in their own time, which was the time of wood and water and the turning of the seasons.

"You walk until the land gives you back to yourself," Eddy had said to him as they stood in the grasp of a cold South Dakota morning. "Let the land heal you and when you find your woman, let her finish the job."

And so he had walked—walked off the freighter he had taken out of New York on a beautiful September morning, into the harbor of Cobh. He had walked straight out of the town, his canvas bag slung over his shoulder until he felt the roll of the countryside beneath his feet.

On that first day he walked until the light began to fail and then he stopped and looked around him. The sun was setting low against the backdrop of checkerboard fields, washing over the stone walls and setting the land all around on fire with the jewels of autumn: the ruby flush of haws spilling over a wall, the chrysoberyl of broken stone, the brown-gold topaz of the changing leaves and the amethyst shadows spreading out from the hollows of thicket and wood. He took a deep breath in and smelled the land, the cold chill of it on an October evening. He knelt down and took a handful and put it to his face. He touched his tongue to it, remembering a bit he'd read months ago about the Irish peasants eating dirt during the Famine in a desperate bid to stay alive. He swallowed a little of it, the grit lingering in his throat. He had the odd notion that if the land was inside him, it would somehow be the magic potion which would give him back his memory. It didn't and he snorted a bit at his foolishness and returned to walking.

The weeks of walking would be a time he remembered for the rest of his life. There seemed no separation between him and the land and he felt porous, as if everything he saw and touched went through him and became part of him. Everything from the vast limestone pavements he walked in the Burren, to the smell of the seaweed on western shores to the Icelandic swans he heard one afternoon coming in to roost for the winter—great grey swathes of them with their lonely trumpeting resounding over the barren rock on which he stood. The fields turned over rich and black and gone fallow and drowsy for the winter, the hedgerows edged in frost in the mornings, the woods he came upon thick with all of Mad Sweeney's trees—the hollies and the oaks and the yews from which Sweeney had embarked on his flight away from madness. All of these things were a part of Casey, and he suspected, always had been.

The voices which sometimes spoke in his head, those bells of his past, were more resonant here and lingered longer with him. He found a strange sort of peace and was aware of small pieces of the puzzle lodging within him, stopping to find their corner of the picture and to fasten themselves in place. He began to hope he might regain his memory, if not in its entirety then at least enough to know who he had once been.

All that walking had brought him here. To these dark woods in the foothills of the Wicklow Mountains. The last few days he'd been thinking he would need a place to see through the winter but the idea of staying in a town felt claustrophobic to him. He wanted quiet and solitude. He would need to make a decision soon.

He had quiet now—just a wee bit more than a man needed on a dark night. There was little undergrowth amongst the tall pines, as the light couldn't filter down through the dense plantation, and so it was easy walking, the ground soft with a thick layer of needles and the scent of them astringent in his nose. He was relieved when the stand of dark pine ended abruptly a few minutes later, cutting a straight line across the hillside. Forestry plantings were like that—they began abruptly and ended abruptly and formed no natural part of the landscape. He came out into the open, grateful to be out of the oppression of the woods and found himself in an old field, one that had not been cultivated in a very long time. Long grassed-over ridges stood stark in the moonlight, broken only by the occasional white of stone rising up and splitting the earth here and there.

He walked into the field and the scent of the pines, amber and cold, followed him as he walked the ridges, jumping over the crevices between and feeling the softness of the soil beneath the thick furze of grass. He walked all the way over to the far edge of the field before his knee complained in a way that meant if he didn't stop for a rest, he would be stopping here all night. He didn't want to attempt sleep with the dark wood still looming so close by.

He sat down on a ridge, and eased his leg out, resting it on a hummock of grass. This was an old potato field; he recognized the form of it. The ridges were lazy beds, so called by the English overseers who didn't understand the Irish method of cultivation. Each ridge was roughly a spade's length wide and was made by slicing and turning over rough sods, then spreading manure over the top into which the seed potatoes were set. He realized he'd done it himself, that he understood this method of cultivation because he'd used it. He wondered if this field had been deserted after the Famine. It seemed an odd place for it, so far away from any town. It was possible it was part of an old estate; many of those had been abandoned after the Famine and the small villages that depended on them had become ghostly places where only the occasional decaying cottage remained to remind a man of how fleeting and fragile life was.

He dug in his bag for his thermos and took a long swallow of the cold tea he'd brewed over a campfire that morning. He would love to be by a fire right now, one with a roof above it preferably. A fire, a roof and someone to talk to.

"Ye're gettin' greedy, man," he said, the sound of his voice like a shock wave in the quiet of the night. He was talking to himself more and more these days, and while it didn't worry him too much, he did think it would be nice to have someone else answer back occasionally. After all, he already knew his own opinion on most matters.

He couldn't remember the last time he'd had a proper conversation with someone—probably that last night with Eddy. He missed Eddy. He missed the wise-cracking and the talk, but mostly he missed the companionship of a man who spoke when he needed to and understood the want for silence as well. In the end they hadn't walked all the way to South Dakota—they'd bought used motorbikes in Wyoming and ridden after that—and the time, whether walking or riding, had done what Eddy had intended it should and cleared his head, creating a space between his life in San Francisco and the unmapped future which lay before him. They arrived on the Ridge on a hot September day. Pine Ridge to be exact, the most notorious reservation in the United States. It was then he realized Eddy's history was a whole lot more complicated than he had ever suspected.

They hadn't stepped a foot onto the reservation until after dark set in and then had holed up in a cabin high in the pines, a good distance away from the settlement. The cabin windows had been shot out at some point and the roof was falling in. Eddy had said they couldn't even light a fire until after dark.

"*Are we hiding?*" Casey asked. *He was certain Eddy must have people here that even if they weren't family, had been friends.*

"*I have some bad history here. I probably shouldn't have come back, but I didn't figure anyone would see us up on the ridge. This cabin has been deserted a long time. A guy was murdered here and people think his spirit hangs round it, so they avoid it.*"

"*It doesn't bother you?*"

Eddy shook his head and pushed his hair back from his face. "*No, it don't bother me, it's my brother after all.*"

"*Yer brother was murdered in this cabin?*"

"*Yeah, he was.*"

"*What happened?*"

Eddy shrugged. "*He was a throwback, my brother, to the days when men like Crazy Horse rode these plains. He had a warrior's heart and he couldn't help but fight. The goons—that's what people here call the tribal police—didn't like him, he was always stirring people up, wanting change, trying to remind the people of what we once were, of what we might be again. He was a leader and people listened to him. He went after the tribal council, it was run by this guy who was corrupt and pretty much lived in the white man's pocket. The same guy headed up the goons too. People were starting to turn against them, they wouldn't vote the way they were supposed to, they wouldn't go along with the tribal line. You'd have to understand how it was back then, how it still is really. It was terrifying to live out here, people armed to the teeth roaming around at night, goons coming in and busting up houses and people, just because they didn't like their politics. The murder rate on the reservation is seventeen times the national average. It's a place of no hope and it's dark man, the kind of dark that sucks your soul out and makes you want to drink yourself blind, so you can't see what's coming because it's never anything good.*"

"*So they killed him?*"

Eddy nodded. "*Yeah, they strung him up in the trees behind the cabin and then shot him full of holes. It was during my second tour of Nam. I was filled with a lot of anger when I came home. I went after the guys who I was certain killed him. Upshot of all this is that there's a warrant out on me and there were cops sniffing around in San Francisco—they were going to catch up with me any day. It seemed a good time to vamoose—for both of us.*"

"*Ye took a great risk coming here, no?*" Casey said quietly.

Eddy gave that eloquent shrug that spoke volumes.

"Everything is a risk, sometimes doing nothing is the greatest risk of all. I was told to bring you here."

"By who?"

"I asked the Great Spirit to give me a dream that would tell me what to do with you."

"Do with me?"

"Yes," Eddy grinned, "I said tell me what to do with this white bastard so I can get rid of him."

"So what dream were ye given?"

"I saw a wolf—big black bastard sitting on the butte, the one we're sitting on right now. He sat there for a long time, gazing off into the distance. You know that gaze that has no horizon to it, it just looks forever and you don't know if it finds what it seeks or if it seeks anything. Then out of the tree line came a she-wolf, silver, like she was made from moonlight. She had green eyes, just like you said—a woman who holds the ocean in her eyes—and she came and sat beside the big black one. The two wolves sat for a long time and then she turned and ran back into the tree line and I saw she had pups waiting there, one black and one silver and the big black got up and followed her. By the way, man," he added, "can I just say I'm a little pissed that you got a wolf while I got a fucking frog."

"I'm startin' to think it's no accident we became friends."

"It's not," Eddy said all trace of joking gone from him. "The wolf is my brother. Both of my people and of my actual brother, Will. I knew you were another because I could see the wolf in you, but also because my brother told me you'd come."

"He told you?"

"Yes, he visits me in dreams sometimes. He gives me advice, tells me what to do, just like he did when he was alive. He was always a bossy son-of-a-bitch. I dreamed about you before I met you. I saw you sitting in a field talking to my brother, and he looked up at me and smiled in the middle of this really intense conversation you two were having and I knew he had brought you to me for a reason."

"What was the reason?"

Eddy looked at him. "I think he meant for you to be my brother for a little while. I could help you and you helped me get my head straight again. Now I'm supposed to send you home."

A wolf, he thought, sitting now on an ancient potato ridge, the pain in his knee dying back to a dull fire. A wolf—fitting to be sure, wild and running the edge of civilization, reviled by town and homestead alike. Aye, there was a resemblance he thought, sniffing at his clothes. A bath, a haircut and shave wouldn't come amiss about now.

He stood up slowly, his pants damp from sitting so long on the soil. His knee was aching but it felt like it was going to bear up for a little while, at least until he could find a place to bed down for the night. He shouldered his bag and it was then he saw a trail leading up the mountainside. It sparked something in him, that strange electric jolt in the blood which he had come to believe signaled something from his past—an event, a person, a place.

The trail called to him in the way land called to a man—with no more than a glance, a scent of smoky earth, a rustle in the trees, a horizon over the hill, a bend in the path through the forest. And so he answered the call.

Chapter Sixty-two

Peace Comes Dropping Slow

IRELAND WAS A SMALL COUNTRY, but even small countries have their wild places where no man has set foot for many a year, where seasons pass and trees fall and stone shatters and there is none to witness it but God and the occasional beast straying off its normal pathway. It was such a place he sought, and it was, high in the passes of the Wicklow Mountains, such a place he found.

Casey came upon the hut the day after he had sat in the abandoned potato field. He had followed the trail all the way up the mountain and there it was, sitting in a small crook of great stone with a dark pine wood at its back. It looked to him like an old shepherd's croft, used only when the animals were brought high into the mountains to graze the summer grasses. Apart from a couple of old bird nests and a crushed wasp's nest it appeared that neither man nor beast had set foot here for some years.

He bought himself an old truck and then went about collecting the supplies he would need to make the hut habitable for the winter. He had money enough to get through a year, even two if he was careful. Eddy had made certain of that. Eddy, as it turned out, had bet on Casey during that last fight and walked away with a bundle. He gave Casey half. When Casey protested he said, "It was your fight, take the damn money."

It was the work of a week to repair the hearth and the chimney and then to remove the detritus so that the chimney might draw well. The work was easy for him. Wood seemed to obey the command of his hands, shaping itself to become something else, something more, function within form, grace in the grain. He lost himself to it, the scent of the wood and the unexpected beads of sap that smelled like a hot summer's day in a pine forest. He leveled the floor, for it was just hard-packed dirt. He laid large, flat stones and put down a vapor barrier, then built a floor of pine planking set on two-by-fours.

His needs were few—a simple bedframe, a mattress he found at a secondhand shop which had come almost new from the estate of an old woman who had died recently. He bought a pot and a frying pan, a bowl and a plate and a set of utensils. He made a table and set one chair at it, for there would be no one to share his meals or make talk with him in the cold winter nights.

His life in America already seemed distant, something he had put behind him with little trouble and no regret. He missed Eddy but he understood it had been time for them to part.

"Where will ye go?" he asked Eddy that last morning before they went their separate ways. Eddy seemed rather fatalistic in his view of the future, but Casey hated to think of him on the run for the rest of his life, or locked up in a prison where he wasn't likely to see the light of day ever again.

"I'll head for Canada. I have Cree relatives in Alberta. They'll take me in and if the long arm of the law extends that far, there's always the Northwest Territories and living with my Inuit second cousin."

"The array of your relatives never fails to stupefy me."

"Man, I told you long ago, we are a family that gets around."

"Ye've got no worries about gettin' over the border?"

"Longest, friendliest border in the world, man, with plenty of wilderness along the route. For a running man with two good feet, it ain't no thing."

He'd grabbed Eddy in a fierce hug then, a little frightened at the notion of being without the one person he knew from this life. They parted and looked at each other.

"May the four winds blow you safely home, brother," Eddy said and then he was gone with the rising sun at his back. Casey stood for a moment watching him, and then he turned toward the east and began to walk.

It snowed on the last day of November. It was snowing when he awoke with the dawn, big soft flakes that drifted like feathers lining the nest of mountain and wood. He sat for a while with his cup of tea, watching it pile up thick and soft, muffling the usual morning sounds. He had always found snow to be peaceful, it shut the world out and allowed a man space to just be and think his own thoughts.

His wee hut stood snug in its spot, with the clouds seemingly wrapped round the chimney. It was like the hut was suspended between snow and sky, the entire world a soft blue-white. Casey stood and took a deep breath of the clear air, so pure it almost rang like crystal. Something of himself had been restored here in this mountain fastness, but with that restoration had come a thing that stirred restlessly in his blood and bone marrow. He dreamed more often of the woman here, as if something in the land spoke of her at night when his defenses were low. In one dream he had seen her clearly, had even touched her, but couldn't recall her face when he awoke in the morning. He found himself out of sorts and frustrated all through that day, his axe hand clumsy and his feet not as sure as they normally were. He cursed himself for a fool much of the day, though he swore he felt the silk of her along his palms through to the evening. Finally he cracked the ice on the small pond which sat in a hollow just down from the hut, and drenched his hands in it until they were so cold that the pain was like burning and he could no longer feel the woman's heat upon them.

His days wore a rhythm, a measured beat that was soothing to him. He was up with the sun each morning, bathed and dressed just as the rosy light of dawn crept in through the east window. He had his breakfast out in the open air on fine days—porridge with honey and cream when he had it on hand. After breakfast it was time to gather wood. He had dry pine, five cords deep in a lean-to he'd built against the hut. He'd made a trip into the closest decent-sized town before the snow fell, where he bought flour, sugar, oats, potatoes and carrots in sacks. He stocked up on tea and bought two bottles of whiskey. He put together a medical kit and bought himself warm clothes to last the season.

As the days passed and he lost himself to the rhythm of life lived with the land he found himself humming tunes he didn't know, songs he could not remember the names of, but just the notes made him happy. He realized one day that peace had come to him, dropping slow as the poet had long ago said, but there inside him nevertheless. What remained to him now was to find the man he had once been, or to make a life and peace with the one he now was.

The clouds were shredding over the mountain pass, the low winter sun gilding the hilltops in the gaps between long, lingering ribbons of fog. The trees were dressed fine, the maiden birches silk-wrapped with snow, the firs frost-tipped, throwing their dark branches into greater relief. He shouldered his rifle and stepped out of the tree line. He'd had company while he was gone hunting for there were traces of a delicate-hoofed deer which had left its tidy prints, neatly spaced, with small drifts where the hooves had glanced off the snow.

He walked the long track in to his hut. It was going to be cold tonight, he would need to build the fire high and hot, and rise during the night to replenish it. He'd caught two rabbits today and he would make stew with them. It would last him a few days, if he rationed it out carefully.

Inside the hut he built the fire quickly, glad that he had split a box full of dry pine kindling before he left on his hunting trip. It didn't take long for it to build to a fine blaze and the heat of it felt lovely against his face and hands.

He grabbed the kettle from its wee stone shelf by the fire. A flicker of movement caught his eye as he stood up, kettle in hand. He went to the window, eyes narrowed against the fir-shadowed snow. It had been too big to be a hare, or even one of the shy deer that fed on the edges of the meadow at dusk. His eyes swept the long shadows, the pitch dark near the trees, where a man could hide. He tracked back, looking away from the tree line, across the meadow's open expanse and then froze.

It was a man and he wasn't hiding, he was standing out clear on the track, just standing and looking toward the hut. He was a big bastard, and Casey felt a thread of fear run through him like a red hot wire. He had a loaded rifle at his disposal and the skill to take the man out from his own doorstep and yet he felt afraid to go outside and confront him.

He grabbed his coat and shoved his feet into his boots. The rifle was still loaded and ready to go and he grabbed it up like it was an extension of his arm.

Outside it was already colder than it had been a mere twenty minutes before and the breath he sucked in had ice crystals in it. He cocked the rifle, looking down its sight line. He walked over the snow; his boots crunching so loudly that it sounded like pistol shots echoing in the night, his adrenaline making his ears overly sensitive. There was no way the man didn't see him, so the sound hardly mattered.

"What do ye want?" he said loudly, and the words cracked off the trees, shaking down a soft rain of snow along the edge of the wood.

The man didn't answer, just stood there like a specter from another time, the wind moving his hair a bit. Casey didn't like his silence, faced with the business end of a rifle most men would start to explain themselves quickly. This man seemed entirely unfazed by the possibility of getting shot.

Casey walked forward a few steps more, but the man did not move, though Casey could feel him watching with an intensity that was unnerving.

"Who are ye? An' what the hell do ye want? Speak up, man, or I'll shoot ye where ye stand." His voice sounded weak, sapped of its strength by the cold and the man's strange stillness. He fired off a shot well above the man's head and still he did not move. He almost seemed to absorb the atmosphere around, pulling in what little light there was near him.

How long Casey stood there, he could not have said, only it seemed seconds and an eternity at the same time. His eyes had begun to water from the cold and he blinked. The night and its shadows were playing tricks with his eyes. It seemed like the man was melting away at his edges, becoming less substantial, not so much a man as a collection of shadows. And then even that dispersed, getting murky around its edges, though maybe the man was just backing down the track, ready to turn and run at the first opportunity. Suddenly there was no one there, just the wind and the soft drifts of snow released from the tree boughs.

He walked all the way down to where he knew the man had been standing, for he'd marked the spot with his eyes as being right in line with a fir that had a distinctive bent top. He kept the rifle cocked and ready, in case the man was lying in wait for him somewhere just off the track.

There was no one there, not even a trick of the dark. He looked about wildly, but there was no sign of the man anywhere. Something moved just then right at the edge of the pine wood. It was low to the ground and fast. He walked toward it carefully and it froze under a gorse bush. It was too small to be a badger and not streamlined enough to be a stoat. He hunkered down after casting another glance over his shoulder.

"Jaysus Murphy," he exclaimed when he saw what sat in the bush, glaring up at him. It was a cat—a thoroughly disreputable looking cat with one eye swollen shut and bald patches where it was missing fur.

"What in the name of all that's holy are ye doin' up here?" he asked. The cat looked at him solemnly from one huge amber eye. It attempted to meow but all that came out was a nearly inaudible squeak. He reached a hand toward it carefully, not wanting to startle it. He got his fingers in under its belly and scooped it up just as it bit him sharply on his index finger.

"Ouch, ye wee bastard," he exclaimed, almost dropping it. The cat hissed at him.

He tucked the cat under his arm and strode off to the hut. When he reached it he turned back to survey the area one last time, his eyes sweeping from the curving side of the hill to the snow-laden scrim of trees. He shut the door behind him and bolted it immediately. He closed the shutters, glad that he had built them on the inside for he wouldn't have wanted to stay outside long enough to shut them all.

He set the cat down and then put a few more pieces of pine on the fire. He warmed a bit of milk over the flames and poured it into a bowl for the cat. It set to drinking without hesitation. He wondered how the poor wee thing had ended up here high in the mountains. Had the man he'd seen at the end of the trail dropped it there? And if so, why?

He opened a tin of sardines and mashed up a couple, making certain to remove the few bones he could find and then set it down before the cat. It ate swiftly, looking up at him every few seconds as though it expected the food to be snatched away.

"Ye needn't worry, I'll not steal yer dinner."

He looked the cat over. The poor creature was more than just a bit ragged-arsed looking and appeared to be on the verge of starvation. That might be expected, what with it living rough on a mountain top. He wasn't the one to be passing judgement mind you, being that he knew he looked a perfect wild man with his beard unshaved and his hair uncut for months now.

"Ye're a bit in the way of bein' a cat melodeon, aren't ye? Ye've taken the phrase literally, an' decided to embody it, have ye?"

The cat looked up from where it was now delicately washing a filthy paw and gave him a look which in a human would have been considered less than complimentary.

"Aye, it's a big word, it only means to be in a terrible state—it was a word my daddy used to use when I'd make a grand mess of things."

The words struck him seconds after he said them—he knew the word because his father had taught it to him. The thought had risen naturally within him, as though he did, indeed, somewhere inside remember the man who had been his father. He felt for a moment like he was choking and had to make a concerted effort to get in a decent breath.

He made his own supper then with the cat watching his every move. Once the food was ready he found he had little appetite. He was aware of his heart thumping hard beneath his ribs, though whether it was having an actual memory or seeing a man who had inexplicably disappeared which caused his agitation, he couldn't have said.

He settled into his bed shortly after he cleaned up the dishes and the cat came and curled up in the crook of his arm, purring loudly. He didn't have the heart to shoo it off the bed; he would just have to hope it wasn't hopping with fleas. He liked the sound of its purring, like a small motor chugging away in reassurance. It was comforting to have the small warm body curled up next to his. It pushed away a little of the fear which had sprung up in him at the sight of the man on the trail. It wasn't the man's presence there that worried him so much, people got lost in the mountains and people were foolish enough to set off hiking even in foul weather. No it wasn't that at all, for even though the man had unnerved him with his unnatural stillness even that might be explained away. What couldn't be explained was the complete and total lack of footprints in the snow where the man had been standing.

Chapter Sixty-three

The House of the Dead

HE STUMBLED UPON the building near twilight on a raw spring day. It reared up in bits and pieces—the remnants of stones in the outlying area, stones that had been shaped and carved for the purpose of building. He knelt down and ran a hand over one. It was well covered with moss and ivy, but the shape was still unmistakable. He knew what it was in his very cells to cut stone, to form it beneath your hand so that it retained its beauty and at the same time release it to another purpose. He stood then, the pain in his knee terrible but a pale echo compared to the agony in his head. He would have to stay here tonight, for he knew he couldn't go much further before the pain had him fast in its clutches.

He had driven north two days before. Instinct and common sense had told him not to try to cross the border at any of the official checkpoints. He had parked his truck at the end of a deserted country lane in County Monaghan and crossed the border on foot into South Armagh via a field where cows popped their heads up at him in curiosity, but no other living being was around to see or hear him. He'd roamed the area with care, he might not remember everything but he knew enough to be wary in an area bristling with British Army personnel and PIRA members, both of whom were likely to shoot first and ask questions of your cold corpse later. He had stayed to the wooded areas when he could and kept away from the towns and clusters of farms. He'd brought enough food to last him so that he wouldn't need to venture into a village. He truly was behaving like a wolf, lurking about the edges of the places where people gathered.

He let instinct guide his rambles. He wanted to see if the cell memory which seemed to play out in other parts of his life could help him here too, with the land and where his place upon it had been. He took in the area around him—all the tidy farms and well-kept stone walls, the small wooded areas scattered here and there across the landscape of well-worn squares of green. There was a heightened tension around here that he could feel all along his body.

He had changed during his winter sojourn—his senses, so accustomed to life on the mountain, were overwhelmed here amongst people and things—cars, machinery, domestic animals and just the sheer noise of civilization. His sense of smell had been sharpened by living outdoors so much and he was used to the dark aromas of the forest—the sharp perfume of the evergreens, the stygian scent of the forest floor, and the smell of other animals—scat and nests and food and danger. His eyes had become accustomed to the subtleties of life far from civilization, had learned to see small details—the delicate orchid that grew only in the rot of a fallen tree trunk, the dappled umber flash that was a deer's pelt flying on the hoof, the overspun spider web that meant high winds were on the way. This altered perception of the world made it hard to adjust to the rampant noise of humans going about their daily business. It also meant that he heard the big vehicle long before he saw it. It was rumbling up the narrow lane he walked, and he felt a ripple of visceral alarm from the root of his spine to the top of his scalp. He clambered up over the stone wall which bordered the road he walked. In his haste, he came down at a bad angle for his knee. He bit his tongue to keep from cursing out loud just as the truck rolled past.

He took a few breaths and chanced a peek over the wall. It was an army truck. He couldn't afford to get caught without identification, there would be far too many questions for which he did not have answers. He would cut across this bit of land he was now on and hope he didn't run into an indignant farmer who took exception to scruffy-looking trespassers.

He paused for breath a few minutes later. He needed to orient himself so he knew in which direction to head. It was then that he saw the little house. It was such a part of the landscape around it that had he not stopped to catch his breath he likely would have walked right past it.

It was a house for the fairies, he thought. The lines of it emerged from the woods around it—sticks and bark, stone and moss, feather and root. He was frozen to the spot just looking at it as one of those bells went off loudly in his head. So loudly he wished he could make it stop. He even put his hands over his ears, though of course it didn't do anything to stop the buzzing in his head.

He stepped toward it, not really understanding what he was doing, but allowing instinct to guide him. He reached forward and touched the bits of furniture—the little birch bark stove, the walnut shell cradle, the bits of leaf and lunaria which made up bed canopies and blankets. He touched a gentle finger to the small bits and bobs and slowly his hand floated up to the room which was a library, judging by the shelves and wee books made from leaves and flower-threaded paper.

His hand was suddenly shaking so hard he could barely move it into the tiny room. He pushed gently on one of the small bookshelves and it popped open under the pressure. He swallowed in an attempt to get his emotions under control and reached into the small space behind the shelf. The hollow was surprisingly deep. He reached down and felt paper, a solid wad of it. He grasped it and pulled it up. He held the paper in his hands for a moment, feeling guilty. This was someone's private hidey-hole and here he was pulling things out of it.

He dug in his pocket wondering if he had something he could leave behind. It didn't feel right to take the papers without leaving something in exchange. His fingers encountered a smooth warm object. It was an especially fine agate he'd found that very morning, glimmering like a solid bit of sun from the crevice of a stone wall. It fit perfectly in the little kitchen sink which was made from a seashell. He tucked the papers in his pocket, feeling slightly guilty about taking them and yet he had no compulsion to put them back.

He looked around. The sun was starting down the sky and he realized he'd lingered longer than he should have. He needed to move along before someone found him. His headache started while he was walking toward the back of the property. It was one of those intense ones that came out of nowhere and blurred his vision and made him feel sick to his stomach. He sat down, the ground damp beneath him but reassuring. He was a good distance from the house now and it should be fine to stop for a bit until he could quell the nausea and get back on his feet. He looked around him. He was under a huge blooming hawthorn which had small bits of faded cloth tied to it. It was a beautiful bit of land, well-treed and with a small stream cutting across one corner. He fished a pain pill out of his shirt pocket, hoping it would take the edge off his headache so that he could collect his wits and get moving again.

Something on the ground caught his eye—a small clutch of plants, or the skeleton of them at least, tied together with a bit of thread. It was an abandoned posy left here under this tree. He wondered if it had been an offering to the fairies as hawthorns had long been known as the 'fairy tree'. Curious, he picked it up, and that was when the pain slammed down like an anvil on him, and the branches and snow-white blossoms of the tree whirled round and round as he clutched the skeleton of an ancient posy in his hand, thorns pricking his palm.

He felt like the roots of the tree had grown up through him and were tangling in his brain. Surely his skull must split apart with this sort of pain. The scent of the hawthorn blooms was overwhelming, sickening him even further. He leaned over and retched, his entire body heaving with pain and nausea. There was little more than bile in his stomach as he hadn't eaten since morning and then it had only been a bit of bread and cheese. He hadn't felt this sick since he'd drunk the ayahuasca tea. Finally the sickness receded enough that he dared to roll over onto his back and gulp at the air. He lay there for a few moments, the blooms of the hawthorn white and thick above his head. The smell of them was still overpowering, but he could manage it now. There was still a strange thrumming fear in his bones—fear that smelled like blood and pain and violence.

He dragged himself to his feet and started walking. He was tired but needed to get clear of this bit of land before the dark of it reached up through the soil and grabbed him.

He walked a good two hours before he literally stumbled into the building. His foot hit a block of stone well hidden amongst the grass and low shrubs and he almost tumbled over onto the ground beyond. He looked up and saw the building through the trees which grew thick and tall right up against it.

It had once been large; his eye had always been able to see the outlines of a structure's original form. This place was buried so deep in the woods it felt like he had stepped through a portal in time and fallen back a hundred years or more. The size and age told him the building was one of two things—an old estate, long abandoned, or a workhouse for the poor left over from Famine times. The latter was the most likely, because if his eye was telling him true, it was laid out along the specifications to which most workhouses had been built. Many workhouses had gone on to other purposes once the Famine was over, some would become sad institutions that housed the poor or mentally ill. Why he could remember tidbits of history and architecture he did not understand, but much of the knowledge seemed innate and had been well fortified with books over these last few years.

Casey found a relatively sound part of the building, and entered a door there. Steps led up from a small landing, the wind moaning its way to the second floor. He tested the first couple of stairs and found them sound enough to risk. Fishing a torch out of his bag, he turned it on, playing it on the ceiling above. It was more form than substance and he could clearly see the stars through the holes in the roof. There were vines hanging down like great green clouds and near the stairs, where he stood, a tree grew, three times his own height and clearly undisturbed for many years.

Casey went up the stairs slowly, checking each one so that he didn't plunge through and break his neck. No one would ever find him here, and a man could linger on injured for a very long time before succumbing to death. He came out onto the second floor into a great room with corridors leading off it. It was a vast echoing space, the sound of his steps loud and unnerving, coming back to him multiplied so that it seemed as if a legion of ghosts was shuffling about the room. He shivered. Exhausted from the pain gnawing through his head, Casey just wanted to find oblivion for a few hours. Perhaps down one of these corridors he would find a room where he could lie down for a bit. He walked down the corridor that appeared the most sound of the three he could see. The branch he chose had small rooms spaced evenly along each side. He assumed this was where the workhouse staff would have had their quarters, as the person actually seeking refuge here would have slept in a long dormitory crowded with hundreds of people, most ill. Not unlike himself right now, he thought, as a wave of nausea swept through him. He needed to pick a room and lie down.

He chose a room which had a hearth, and prayed the chimney wasn't too decayed to draw the smoke up and away. This place was buried so deep in the wood that he didn't worry about anyone either scenting or sighting the smoke. He gathered bits and pieces of wood that had fallen either from the roof or branches that had made their way in over the years. It took about twenty minutes of scavenging so that he had a good-sized pile that would last him the night. He pulled his sleeping bag out as well as another of the pain pills the doctor in Dublin had prescribed for him. He needed two, but he didn't want to be entirely unconscious should someone come upon him in the night, as unlikely as that seemed.

He built the fire carefully, feeding it slowly as the medication took hold and blurred the outlines of both his pain and the room around him. It was like dousing a fire at the edges but without the ability to actually put out the hot heart of it. He was relieved to see that the smoke was going up the chimney. It was drawing well enough that he needn't fear choking to death on smoke while he slept and the warmth of the fire was a relief to his chilled, damp self. He changed his wet sweater for a dry one from his bag, and then crawled into the sleeping bag with what little strength he had left.

Casey lay awake, despite his exhaustion. His knee still hurt like a burning blade was stuck into the bone. The night around him was so still that he cleared his throat just to hear something. The sound was startling. He didn't frighten easily, but the place was bloody unnerving, what with the wind creeping into every corner to moan and make complaint and the dead leaves scuttling across the floor like tiny, spectral footsteps. It was in part, he knew, the purpose this building had served; it was a place people had fled to with great reluctance, with only a small hope left that they would survive the holocaust that was laying waste to the country around them.

Suddenly, he realized that he hadn't looked at the papers he had pulled out of the hole in the fairy house. He pulled his coat over to him and dug in the inside pocket. They were gone, the small bits of paper were gone. He searched through all his other pockets returning to the inside pocket again, in the vain hope he'd missed the papers due to the medication which was making him feel rather woozy. Finally, he put his coat down in defeat. He felt terribly bereft as if the papers had truly been his and he'd been meant to have them.

He lay back down, utterly exhausted and not just physically. He was tired in all sorts of ways he realized. He had sought isolation when he arrived here, wanted it with a longing like that of an addict craving his drug of choice. For a long time he had savored it, for it had brought a certain level of peace with it. But sometimes, like tonight, he wondered if the isolation wouldn't eventually drive him mad. He prayed before sleep, because the building and wind and the loneliness in his heart seemed to require it. It was a drifting prayer, half spoken out loud, half a slow stream of thought in his semi-conscious mind. He prayed for his pain to recede, he prayed for the people he could not remember but who lived inside him somewhere like ghosts that slid through his fingers each time he tried to touch them.

Sometime deep in the night, Casey thought he felt a hand touch him—a woman's hand, soft and sweet upon his skin, easing the ache in his knee. He turned toward her and felt the softness of her against him and her hands cupping his skull to draw it down to her breast, dousing the last of the fire in his brain. He thought he heard her speak too, just soft nonsense words of love, though he couldn't understand the individual sentences. Still, the meaning was clear to him and the comfort of that soothed him, pushing him down into the well of oblivion. His sleep was easy and deep. For tonight, with the phantom woman's touch upon him, he did not sleep alone.

Chapter Sixty-four

Smoke From a Far Distant Fire
September 1978

NEAR THE END of the summer, Casey came down out of his solitude with the plan of staying on the roads for a few weeks. He hadn't ventured down out of his mountain fastness since his trip into the North. In truth, that journey had frightened him, as if he had come too close to something his memory was not ready to reveal.

He walked through the last two weeks of August. McCool the cat came with him and either trotted at his side or curled up in his canvas bag and slept while they covered mile after mile. The weather was beautiful, the days golden and warm and the nights dry enough that he could sleep out in them with the stars for his roof. Around him the country unfurled as he walked, and with each mile he could feel the past rising in layers. History lived here in every atom of the land and every tree and rock and leaf were part of that heritage. It was the idea that his own father, grandfather, great grandfather, might have walked this way of a moonlit night with cares and fears and wants and yearning, and yet with the ground beneath their feet and their hearts aware of some great pulsation, of invisible roots that went down through the bottom of a man's soul into this ground, this land, this country bounded by sea and hedge and cliff and bog.

It was mid-September when he wandered back into Wicklow, his thoughts on his mountain hut and whether he would spend his winter there once again, or if he would need to find work of some sort and hunker out the season down here below with other people and noise and interference. The thought of company, even if it was merely that of shopkeepers and the odd farmer he did work for, had its appeals. A man's thoughts tended to go into dark places when he was alone too long, particularly when he did not have the rosary beads of story and past with which to comfort himself.

Casey came across the fair on a sunny Sunday afternoon. He had been ambling since the morning, his knee stiff and painful after a night spent in the hedgerows with just a sheet of canvas for shelter. The road he was on was one of those meandering cow paths that ran in a narrow ribbon through miles and miles of farms and fields. He'd walked a ways down it, unable to see anything beyond the high hedges that bordered the road along the sides, when suddenly the blackthorns opened up into a field golden and shorn from recent harvesting. The land was filled with people and horses, tractors and carts, laughter and music. He followed the sound of the music, as surely as a child would follow the Pied Piper.

He hadn't been to a fair in years. The thought made him laugh, for in truth he didn't know if he *had* ever been to a fair in his life. It was only that it seemed familiar to him—the scent of the horses and the hay newly mown and bundled into haycocks and bread baking and colcannon cooking in cauldrons over big fires.

He paid his fee and then ambled through the grounds. The people were country people—faces reddened by the elements and time, the women sensibly dressed, the men shy of eye and tongue, gathering in wee clumps as they spoke of horses and the weather, and horses and farm equipment and of course, horses again. Off to one end was a cluster of gaily colored caravans, for where there were horses there were bound to be Travellers.

He paused near the paddock where the horses were held, drawn to watch them in their innate beauty, the sun shining on coats of copper and ebony and bay and roan.

"If ye're lookin' for a good horse, I can set ye up." There was a man leaning over the paddock rail beside him, his cap set at a jaunty angle, a spotted kerchief knotted around his throat. Casey merely nodded politely at the man and then watched the bartering, as men ran their hands down long legs and over rumps and commented on 'the fine broad back of her'. The love of horses was near to sexual in nature, he thought, and the looks on the faces of the people there were those of love and obsession.

A flash of obsidian caught his eye as a colt ran past and he leaned over the paddock rail to get a better look at him. He was a gorgeous wee thing—coal black with a white blaze on his forehead and a gait to him that said he had plenty of spirit. He felt that strange sense of dislocation that he sometimes did when it seemed like he was about to remember something, as if he heard music from a great distance, a tune that was familiar but he couldn't grasp enough of the notes to follow the melody.

"He's a beauty, isn't he? He was one of a pair. Identical twins. His brother went to a man up Armagh way. His brother fetched a very pretty penny, an' this boy will too. I've also a couple of sound ponies, if ye want to come have a look."

The man must have thought he'd spied the lust of a horse lover when Casey's eye had been drawn to the colt. But the colt was like most things for him—an echo of something else, another horse perhaps, in that other life in the country behind him.

"I'm not in the market for a horse today," he said politely. He wasn't in the market for a horse ever, truth be told, but he thought the man might not be the one to understand just how intimidating he found the beasts, beautiful as they might be.

He moved on then to the small race track that had been set up for the day. Again it was just part of the field, cordoned off with temporary fencing, with a marked line at one end and string at the other for the starting line. The horses danced behind this string, the two currently in the offing a big bay with a white mane and a chestnut beauty that shone red in the sun. He stopped to watch, for he appreciated the strength and speed of the animals from a relatively safe distance.

It was almost time, for the horses were prancing with impatience, the big bay turning sideways and the chestnut coming up off its forelegs a time or two in its excitement to be off and away, streaking down the field.

He didn't know what made him look round just at that moment, but he felt like someone was tugging on his ear, trying to turn his head to the right. When he did, his heart rose up in his throat and his blood turned to ice water in his veins. A little girl, clad in a red dress that was just a tiny bit too long was stumbling out onto the field, the hem of her dress catching beneath her tiny sandaled feet. Her eyes were fixed on a flower that was growing, against all odds, in the midst of the field. He yelled, but the sound of it was lost in the blast of the starting pistol. He could feel the vibration of the horses' hooves even as he leaped over the fence and started to run. The horses wouldn't stop on time, they couldn't, the little girl would be trampled to death before anyone could catch them.

He didn't think, he just ran, everything around him a blur, the world reduced to the little girl on the field and the horses bearing down on her, foam flying from their lips. He was afraid he wouldn't reach her in time, for she was still wobbling toward the flower, entirely oblivious to death bearing down on her. He grabbed her and clutched her to his chest and then dove and rolled, arse-over-teakettle out of the way of the pounding hooves. He came up onto his knees, and felt the edge of a hoof glance against his back as the horses flew past. It winded him, and he saw stars for a minute, but he hung onto the little girl, who was too shocked to cry, her tiny face white as a snowdrop as she looked up at him with huge eyes.

"Ye're all right then, wee girl," he said, trying not to breathe in until he knew whether he had broken ribs. People were flooding the field now, the horses finally stilled near to the finish line. A woman swooped down on him, her eyes wild and hair coming out of its pins. The little girl started to cry then, and he realized the woman must be her mother. He handed the child to the woman, who swept her into her arms, hugging her tightly.

"Thank you so much," she said, "thank you, thank you."

A couple of men helped him up off the ground. His adrenaline was starting to die back and his knee was already complaining loudly. He didn't even want to think about his back, he wasn't sure how much more abuse it could stand.

One of the men said, "Come this way, there's a first aid tent, ye're goin' to need someone to look at that back of yers an' yer knee, too. Sling yer arm round my neck, ye'd best not put weight on yer leg until we know if it's damaged."

Another man brought his bag and placed it inside the tent flap and he was greatly relieved when McCool popped his head out of the top and let out an irritable meow.

There was a woman manning the first aid tent, which he hadn't expected. He suddenly felt shy, as the two men deposited him on a chair. The woman shooed everyone else out, and had him move to sit on a camp bed. She had a very no-nonsense air about her, which made it a bit easier to relax, despite the pain.

"They tell me ye took a horse hoof to the back, so we'll need to get the shirt off of ye so I can have a look. I'm going to unbutton it and take it off ye, because I don't want ye movin' yer arms about too much until we know the damage that's been done."

It felt oddly intimate, sitting here in the quiet tent, having a woman, no matter how no nonsense her demeanor was, take his shirt off him. He looked up into the corner, where the canvas was thin and the sunlight fell in bright lattices, in order to avoid her eyes.

She folded his shirt and laid it to the side and then moved around to his back. The silence was absolute. He could feel the prickle of her gaze on his ruined skin. The first view of it was always shocking. He waited, focusing his attention on the noise outside—the whinny of a stallion, the clink of horseshoes ringing a post and the laughter of a woman near to the tent.

"I'm a nurse," she said quietly, "I see plenty of things that would give ye nightmares, a few scars on a man's back aren't goin' to bother me."

She proceeded to check the area around the bruise, pressing here and there, he assumed, to see if anything was broken. He sucked in his breath and then let it out as she continued to prod the spot. Holding his breath wouldn't help, it was going to hurt like—well like a horse had stepped on his kidneys, in short.

"Ye've got a very big bruise, but I suspect it's not the first time ye've been hit hard. As far as I can tell, ye're good, ye'll be sore as hell for the next week or so, but nothing is damaged permanently. Mind now, if ye start pissin' blood, ye'll need to see a doctor. I'll need to have a look at that knee now, so off with yer trousers."

He stood with her help. There was clearly little dignity in being a hero. He fumbled undoing the pants, and then she eased them down over the knee and had him sit again, trousers puddled around his ankles. He was feeling increasingly ludicrous and hoped to God no one wandered in seeking medical attention in the next few minutes.

"This is an old injury, is it?"

"Aye, only I twisted it today. I don't usually run on it like that."

She looked up from the knee, which was swollen and hot but, he thought, hadn't sustained additional damage, beyond making him hobble for a few days. "No," she said, "I don't suppose ye do. I'm goin' to wrap it for ye because ye'll need the support. It probably wouldn't hurt to find ye a cane either, just so ye can take the weight off it for a bit."

She wrapped the knee in a clean length of bandage, keeping a good tension to it, so that the strain on the joint was greatly relieved by the time she was finished. He stood the second she was done and pulled his pants back up, for there was the sound of voices approaching the tent.

She went to the door, and came back a minute later. "Someone's hurt their back, I'd best go to them an' see what the damage is."

She turned back in the doorway of the tent, the autumn sun falling down around her like a shower of leaves.

"Have ye a place to stay? I'm at Leeward Farm, an' I've either a spare room or if ye prefer, a weather-tight byre with fresh hay in it. Ye're welcome to either, should ye need somewhere to lay yer head."

"Thank ye, kindly," he said. "I might have to take ye up on that, I don't think my knee will take me far tonight."

"No, it won't. Look, I'll wait for ye by the entry gate. I'm done here at nine o'clock."

"All right then, I will," he said.

He put his shirt back on and fastened his pants and then made his way outside and found a table nearer to the activity where he might sit and pass a few hours. By the time he sat his leg was shaking, his knee on fire. He never went anywhere without his pain pills and he fumbled in his pocket hoping the two he had stowed there hadn't tumbled out on the field. Thankfully they hadn't. He put them in his mouth, and swallowed them dry. A woman came up with a pot of tea just then, and a plate of colcannon fresh off the fire, as well as sausages and brown bread, the latter so hot that the slices steamed even in the warm autumn air.

"Here man, have a bite. I'm the wee girl's nan, an' we're right thankful to ye. I don't know how she got herself out on the field, but sure she'd be dead now if ye hadn't seen her."

"Ye're welcome, anyone would have done the same. I'm glad she's goin' to be fine."

She patted him on the shoulder. "No, not anyone, that took a rare courage, ye might have been killed yerself. Ye need anything else, I'm over at the food tent, don't ye hesitate to ask."

He nodded and smiled, uncomfortable with the woman's scrutiny. He tucked into the food, for he was hungry, and it wasn't often he was privy to this much food all at once. By the time he was done the pain medication had taken hold and he felt slightly drowsy. The smell of the turf fire near the cooking tent, the freshly baked bread and the scent of the horses all combined in a heady brew that was as familiar to him as the palms of his hands.

Later, he wasn't sure if he had been awake or asleep or maybe in that strange place that existed between the two lands, where things could come up out of the murk of the subconscious and a man might never know if they were dream or memory.

There was a woman kneeling at his feet, dark head bent over his knee as though she were inspecting it. Her hair was the color of a crow's wing, a true black of the sort that was iridescent with shades of green and violet where the light touched it.

She touched her lips to his knee, kissing it. Then her hands came up and she rested one over the knee, and her touch, warm and gentle, drew out the worst of the pain.

"Lord, don't stop, woman, that's bliss that is."

He wanted to reach out and touch her, feel her skin against his own, smell her scent and look into her eyes and drown. But she didn't look up, and he didn't dare touch her for fear she would be gone like a bubble borne away by the wind. He could feel the need of her in his hands and the ache for her in his heart, sharp as a fishhook caught fast.

She looked up without warning and he caught his breath, and then she opened her mouth to speak and someone cleared their throat, twice, politely.

He opened his eyes, feeling a wave of irritation. He felt the woman had been on the cusp of speaking, and that her voice alone might summon forth more shards of his memory, so that the broken glass that was his mind might begin to resemble a vessel that could one day hold something and keep it.

There was a man standing in front of him, wearing a peaked cap, his blue eyes set wide in a weather-beaten face. He smiled and a gold tooth winked out at Casey.

"Can I have a word?" he asked.

"Of course," Casey said, sitting up and making an effort to clear his head. He rubbed his hand on his thigh, the buzz of the imaginary woman's touch still there, like small zaps running through his skin.

"Ye'll pardon the bother, but me nan would like to see ye."

"Yer nan?" He squinted up at the man, wondering why on earth someone's grandmother had a hankering to meet him. Inside his head he was desperately trying to hang on to the image of the woman's face.

"Aye, she says she recognizes ye from another place, some other time. She's old, but she knows every face she's ever seen, an' she got right agitated when she spotted ye, when ye saved that wee girl from bein' trampled underfoot. She says come near evenfall, she's busy right now, but she'll be back at her wagon then."

Wagon, that meant she was one of the Travellers whose caravans he had seen when he'd come into the fair ground.

"Ye'll come then? We're the Ward camp."

"Aye," he said, "I'll come."

He closed his eyes as the man walked away, trying to summon the woman back, to see those big green eyes and the furls of dark hair, to feel her touch him again. He curled his hands inward, toward that elusive feeling in his skin. He took in a sharp breath of frustration, for inside his head it was dark, and when he opened his eyes, his hands were empty.

He went on the cusp of evening, as he had been instructed. The dusk gathered quickly this time of year, the air cooling along with it. It was a reminder that the season had turned, and the nights were about to get long and cold. He had been trembling since the man had come to him, wondering if this was where he found out who he was, who he had been in that other life that had taken place in the country of before.

The man with the gold tooth came up to him and escorted him to where the woman sat. Then he gave him a nod, and melted away into the shadows of the night. The woman was small, and sat in a chair near to a fire, her lap neatly covered with a red crocheted blanket. Most of the encampment was ringed with the aluminum caravans that the Travellers preferred these days. But here and there was an old style vardo, and it was near one of these that the old woman had her fire.

She looked up at him as he entered the firelight, as nervous as a boy sent off to school alone for the first time. She smiled and reached her hands toward him.

"Bring yer face down to me, man," she said. Her voice was soft, though gravelly, no doubt from the years of living on the road and the fact that she smoked a pipe. He saw one laid to the side, a fine thing, carved with wee flowers. He hunkered down in front of her, ignoring the immediate protest in his knee. She put her hands to his face, her fingers moving restlessly over the flesh and bone. She put her left hand on his head, stroking his curls, the fingers tremoring slightly. Nearby a fiddle started in on a plaintive note.

"There is a woman that ye miss," she said, her eyes bright within folds of weathered skin.

"Aye," he said and smiled, "I suppose most men could say the same, no?"

"No, lad, not all. Not many that have such sadness in them, as you do."

He drew back, not liking the woman's sharp assessment of his emotional state. She tilted her head to the side and gave him a shrewd look.

"I'm an old woman, boyo, an' I spent many a year on the road tellin' the fortunes an' so I became a sharper judge of humans than most. My children depended on my skills to keep the food comin' in, an' so I got very good at it. Ye needn't feel that ye're exposed to me any more than that. Sit in this chair beside me, that knee of yers isn't fond of the kneelin'."

He sat next to her, and straightened his leg as much as he dared. And that was when it came to him—a memory maybe, though it felt too diaphanous, too fleeting to be called such. Like a ghost hovering near the edge of the campfire, refusing to come into the light, knowing it would disappear altogether if it did. Perhaps it was only that the white smoke rising and curling into the night like a sinuous dancer recalled something to him, like he had known a night such as this one—the caravans, the fires, the fiddles and a woman who danced like the smoke and felt like fire in his arms.

Somewhere nearby a woman began to sing, an old lament from Scotland. The words came over him like chill drops of silver, shivering through his blood and making his heart ache.

By yon bonny banks and by yon bonny braes
Where the sun shines bright on Loch Lomond
Where me and my true love will never meet again...

"Yer grandson did say ye'd seen me before?" He kept his tone friendly but flat, he didn't want his nerves to be apparent.

"Not yerself, laddie, but a man who must have been yer grandsire, I believe. Ye look too much like the man for him not to be blood."

He felt a fine tremor set itself along his skin, raising goosebumps on his arms and hairs on the back of his neck. He wanted to get up and walk away, for he was afraid of what she might say and even more afraid that it might come to nothing, and that she would realize her mistake in a moment or two.

"It were a long time ago," she said, as if she had read his thoughts plain as day. "Though I remember it like 'twas yesterday. I remember because I were just a slip of a girl, no bigger than yer arm, an' I'd just gotten myself a fine red petticoat banded with a strip of black velvet. 'Twas the finest thing I'd ever owned, an' I've niver been so mad about another bit of cloth since. Funny how memories attach themselves to things in that way." She stopped to light her pipe and he sat patiently as she took a long draw of it and then breathed the fragrant smoke out onto the night before settling in to tell her story.

"It were a fine spring, soft rains, flowers bloomin' an' crops comin' up early. The stones had turned in the streams an' we were on the move the day after Saint Patrick's. I were still livin' on the road with me mam an' da. It were fifty year an' more past this very spring when I met the man ye put me in mind of. One afternoon, we broke a wheel an' got stuck in a boggy patch when we pulled aside from the road. We thought we might not get the wagon out ever again. A man come along then, an' he spent the entire afternoon helping me da pull that wagon out, an' then mended the wheel for us. We asked him to stay to dinner, an' so he did. The weather turned foul that night, so he stayed, curled up rough under the wagon with a canvas sheet for his cover. He were big an' dark, like you. Tall as you too, an' there's not many men that size runnin' about now, much less back then. He were on the run, there was men lookin' for him an' so he moved with us for a bit. A week maybe, went as far as the foot of the Wicklow Mountains with us, an' then one night he just disappeared, an' we never saw him again. When I saw ye today, after ye saved that wee girl, I thought I were seein' a ghost ye're so like to him."

"Ye remember him so well after these many years?" Casey asked.

She smiled, as though recalling something very pleasant. "Oh aye, I remember. He wasn't the sort of man a woman forgets. An' I was young then, an' pretty as a new sprung flower. He noticed me, men did then."

"I have no doubt of that," he said. "The man's name, do ye remember it?" he asked, not caring now if his voice shook. It mattered too much.

"His name were Brendan," she said, "an' his people were from Connemara, he'd a hand with the horses, were right gentle with them, could call 'em up like he were the wind. He were haunted by a woman too, just like yerself."

"I...I meant his last name," he said, not wanting to cut her off, but not able to bear waiting any longer for her to say it.

"It were Riordan, he become a bit of a legend later on. Was he yer grandda' then, lad?"

The night spun a little, the scents overwhelming him—burning peat, the haycocks, horses, the smell of meat cooking over a fire, and the raw smell of whiskey. He looked up to the stars that were strewn thick as if someone had thrown a handful of salt onto a round of black velvet, and used their distance to steady himself. Away over the fires and the moving wind, the woman was winding through the final verse of her song.

The wee birds sing and the wild flowers spring,
And in sunshine waters lie sleeping.
But the broken heart knows there is no second spring,
Though the woeful may cease from their grieving.

"Aye," he said, and found that his voice no longer trembled. "I believe he was."

Chapter Sixty-five

At the Crossroads

THE CROSSROADS WAS a strange one, buried deep in the countryside, the signs, denoting the various small villages, so mired in ivy and bramble that whatever directions had once been on them had long ago been engulfed. At one end there was an ancient stone bridge, once sturdy, that was now succumbing to ivy and time. There was a wee pub on the corner, smart looking and clean with flower baskets out front and an ancient petrol pump to one side. Even during the daylight hours the area surrounding it had the feel of something just slightly off. Some would call it faerie territory and advise him to pass through quickly and not pause for even a second no matter how great the temptation. But he was tired and his knee was sore, and right now a pint and a sit on a stool for a half hour or so sounded like his very definition of heaven.

Inside the pub it was cool and dim. The interior was as neat and clean as the exterior, but it still had the feeling of a place that belonged to something other than the human realm. The bottles on the shelves glowed like jewels—ruby and citrine and topaz and amethyst. The bar itself was a thing of beauty—a glowing length of well-polished mahogany. He looked about but didn't see anyone. The place was quiet as a tomb, or as quiet as one might expect the portal to another world to be.

Suddenly there was a man standing right beside him. He had seemingly materialized from nowhere and Casey jumped enough to bang his head on one of the low beams.

"Sorry young fella, I was out back feedin' the goat an' didn't realize anyone had come in. Ye gave me a start, thought a giant had come through the door when I saw ye standin' there."

In truth, Casey felt like a giant next to the tiny man, who stood barely higher than his elbow. He had curly white hair around the sides of his very round head, and a gleaming dome of immaculate baldness on top. While not terribly fairy-like in appearance he did bear a rather remarkable resemblance to a Christmas elf with his rosy round cheeks and smiling blue eyes.

"Will ye sit? Ye're makin' me nervous towerin' up by the thatch as ye are."

"Aye, I'll sit," Casey said and lowered himself to one of the neat little stools that were lined up at the bar.

The tiny man popped up behind the bar, though Casey could have sworn he hadn't seen him move through the hinged flap in the counter.

"What will ye have—no, no—let me guess—a pint for the thirst an' a tot of whiskey for the knee."

Casey opened his mouth and shut it. The man had said he was out back so he knew he hadn't watched him limp up to the pub.

"It's how ye lowered yerself onto the stool, lad, I know pain when I see it."

Casey felt a moment of sheer befuddlement, how had the man known what he was thinking?

"Now, there's a jot of the Connemara Mist for the knee an' a pint of the black stuff for yer throat. Are ye just passin' through on yer way to somewhere or were ye thinkin' of stoppin' for a bit?"

"I don't know," he said, feeling rather dazed. "My name is Casey," he said and put out his hand to the man, thinking an exchange of names might steady him and make the place seem more real.

The man took his hand and said, "Finn Egan at yer service. Ye've a Belfast accent on ye, no? I've a cousin lives up that way, miserable old bastard but a very fine solicitor, or so I'm told."

"Aye, I grew up in Belfast," he said, thinking it was an innocuous enough bit of information and true as far as he knew. Frankly, he was surprised that Belfast existed in this realm.

The man looked him over, pursing his lips as if making his mind up over some matter. Then he reached behind him and took down a canning jar from the top shelf of bottles. The jar held a liquid so dark that it bore a decided resemblance to tar. The man took the lid off the jar and poured a bit of the dark liquid into a glass and handed it over to Casey. The fumes that preceded it were so strong that Casey thought he might get drunk off that alone.

"Here laddie, try this, 'tisn't more than a thimbleful, but it will fix the last of what ails ye."

It was considerably more than a thimbleful, Casey thought, still it would be rude to refuse when the man had opened it especially for him. He drank it in two neat swallows.

"Jaysus Murphy!" The drink went down mellow enough, but once it had set up house in his belly it ventured out with streams of fire through his blood.

"'Tis tasty, no? It's a brew I make meself with the blackberries from the hedges. I call it Angel's Ether."

It was, indeed, tasty it was also, he thought, wiping the tears from his eyes, about seventy proof. He couldn't feel his head much less his knee at this point. It occurred to him that he'd had a very generous pour of whiskey, a pint and then this Angel's Ether in about ten minutes flat. The man was either trying to enchant him or kill him. Still he wasn't in pain, and he felt more relaxed than he had in months.

"Would ye like a sandwich? I make a mean ham an' cheese melt an' I feel like ye might need somethin' more substantial in your stomach than just alcohol."

The next hour passed pleasantly as he ate the sandwich the man made him and had another pint, which he wisely nursed over the full hour. Finn Egan was one of nature's naturally gifted talkers and he needed little encouragement to keep up a steady and entertaining patter about the area and the people who lived in it.

Finn looked at him speculatively. "Are ye lookin' for work, by any chance? I've need of a barman a few nights of the week."

"I'm workin' at Leeward Farm, but it only takes up the days, an' not all of them either. I could use the work, sure."

"Ah, Leeward Farm," Finn said. "You're the lad all the girls have been buzzin' about then."

Casey looked at him in surprise. "Me? I don't think so."

"Oh aye, you. There's about two hundred people all total in this village, an' that's only when everyone is at home. Trust me when I say ye've caused a stir. The housewives are all speculatin' on just what yer relationship is to Claudia."

"I'm workin' for her, that's all," he said abruptly, annoyed at being the subject of village gossip. Claudia was an attractive woman, though even had he been in the market for love it was clear to him she was still mourning her lost husband. It was part of why living with her was a simple and uncomplicated arrangement.

"That's as may be, but folk do love to make up stories if ye don't give them one yerself."

He sighed and took another swallow of his drink. There was the rub, for he had no story to share. He thought longingly of his wee hut in the mountains. There he need not have a past or a story, he could simply be. People wanted your story. They wanted to know where you'd come from, who you'd been and who your kin were. They wanted to be able to fix you in place, the way a photographer might use chemicals to fix an image to paper and so grasp a moment for all eternity. If you had no past, you didn't really exist for people. You were a ghost in walking form.

"Well, they'll have to gossip then," he said, "for I've got no story to give."

His life found a rhythm in the wee Wicklow village. He liked both the work on the farm and his evenings tending bar for Finn. He'd formed a friendship with the man which he quite enjoyed, and felt like civilization was returning to him slowly but surely. Living with Claudia was simple enough too. He had been a month now at Leeward Farm. Claudia, as it turned out, had been trying to work at the local infirmary unit and run the farm singlehandedly after her latest hired man had moved on to a bigger farm. He had at first said he'd stay a few days and help her out until she could find someone else, then one day had slid into the next and he had found he enjoyed the work and the company as well. He'd had to make one trip back up into the mountains to his hut, to pack up the few belongings he'd left behind. McCool settled in at Claudia's like he'd been born to farm life and abandoned Casey to spend his evenings by the woman's fire.

Claudia had been widowed two years before and it had been her husband who had kept the farm ticking over. It was a lovely stretch of land, at the base of the Wicklow Mountains near to the border between Wicklow and Wexford. The farm sat on a slope that opened onto a beautiful vista of rolling farmland looking like a great green quilt sewn together with thick hedges of hawthorn, blackthorn and bramble climbing its way through and over everything. It was a picturesque area, lush with vegetation and narrow twisting lanes, and steeped long in history. The farm was small, and beyond a kitchen garden the fields had been given over to hay. There was more than enough work, for the last of the hay had to be brought in and there were repairs long overdue on all of the buildings.

Life on the farm agreed with him, he enjoyed the work, the physicality of it, the routine of it and the tangible result he could see each and every day, whether it was the pile of firewood stacked deep or the repairs done to the tractor, or the mucked stalls and contented sheep.

He had a small room to himself in the loft of the byre, which was cozy once he had banished the resident spiders and bachelor squirrel. It was kept warm by the heat of the byre below and he had a little space heater and blankets enough to keep him comfortable. He hung his rosary on the wall above the bed and put his few meagre possessions away in the small, beat up bureau Claudia had dug out of her woodshed. A few sweaters, a few shirts, three pairs of working pants and one pair for dress were all he possessed, along with a coat he had bought the autumn previous, a thick oilskin garment that would keep him warm and dry regardless of the weather.

He'd gone back to the wee farm in County Down twice since the day he'd found the fairy house. He never did find the papers he'd lost, but he'd left a few more things for the owner of the house—just small things which might seem a treasure to a child who didn't know from where they came. He never saw anyone about, though he went at odd hours when he thought it was not likely that anyone would be around.

He had held the old Traveller woman's information about his name to himself, as if it was a precious object in a box, one that couldn't be looked at too often lest it tarnish from the scrutiny of the air outside. He had a name, but he had little else. What good did a name do a man if he didn't know the man behind the name? It wasn't like knowledge of his name had suddenly restored all the missing bits of his memory. If there was a life waiting for him, if there was a family and a woman who still waited, he had to be certain he understood who he was, before springing the shock of his resurrected person on them.

"Come down to the pub with me," Claudia said one mizzly night when Casey had been planning to curl up early in his bed with a copy of Robert Praeger's book, *The Way That I Went*. With her words though, he felt a sudden longing to be amongst people and lights and music, even just to sit and watch the village whirl of life and courtship and chat about livestock, bad roads, a worse economy and the wistful talk of maybe one day moving to America. In this wee village when someone said 'the pub', they invariably meant Egan's.

"There'll be dancin' tonight, so ye might want to wear your good clothes," she said and he noticed that she was wearing a very pretty red dress, which suited her dark hair and eyes.

He put on a crisp white shirt and his lone pair of good pants that he'd bought at what passed for the local haberdashery when he'd received his last pay. He tidied his hair as best as he could. He needed it cut, but barring that he would just tie it back and let the men think of him as that 'long-haired hippie Claudia has workin' for her', a description he'd heard from Finn. None would call him such to his face, for he had realized with some surprise and no little dismay that other men feared him, for something they saw in his face perhaps, or maybe they knew him for a man of violence and trouble and wanted to keep clear of it and him.

Despite the miserable weather, the pub was full. Men were shoulder to shoulder at the bar, hands coming out of the line of tweed and wool and Donegal caps, filled with pints of stout and bitter and porter as well as the occasional peat-gold flash of whiskey. One of the farmers, a man whose tractor he'd helped fix last week, put a glass of whiskey on the table in front of him and said, "Throw that back, man, it will take the chill from ye."

He'd already bought himself a pint of Harp and one for Claudia as well. He took a swallow of the whiskey, not wanting to offend the man and hoping to take the edge off his nerves. He wasn't used to this many people all at once. It was a little overwhelming.

He looked about him, mesmerized by all the activity. The village seemed to be in a mood for fun this night. There was music and dance and women coming out of their coats and rain slickers and boots and shawls and kerchiefs like a tree full of butterflies suddenly released from their respective chrysalises. The music had already begun and he could feel the thump of the bodhran right to his marrow, and it set up an itch in his hands. He thought perhaps he had played it, back in that other life.

Someone coughed lightly and he looked up. He recognized the girl from the local men's shop. She'd helped him pick out the pants he was wearing. She was pretty, with one of those round, rosy faces that would look weathered and ruddy in some years' time. She swayed a little in time to the music, hands clasped in front of her, as shy and uncertain as a deer in her green dress. He felt a bit of melancholy at the sight of her; her face was lit up like a candle glowed within and he supposed he would have to dance with her. It wasn't an unpleasant prospect entirely, so he wondered why it filled his chest with a weight of sand to contemplate it.

"Would ye like to dance then?" he asked, and she nodded, wordless but the glow in her face amped up another few notches, causing him no little worry. He had nothing to give this girl other than a twirl around the dance floor. He wasn't entirely certain he could dance though, truth be told.

Once on the floor, the steps came naturally though, and he moved with ease guiding her around the small space of the dance floor. She was uncertain on her feet and a bit slow to know which direction his hand was guiding her. He firmed his hand up on the small of her back, so she wouldn't trod on his toes and he felt the response in her body immediately. He left the hand as it was, to spare his toes, if not her feelings. He noticed that Claudia was watching them, and the look on her face was one of disapproval, though of what he wasn't certain, just that seeing him dancing with this girl didn't seem to please her.

There was a tarnished mirror above the hearth, an old one in a heavy gilt frame. He could see the various couples turning and whirling in the glass, the music tempo a wee bit melancholy, giving him that ache he sometimes got in his chest at the sound of a fiddle or the pipes. It was a timeless scene, for it might have been a decade or two ago, or even a hundred years before—dance and drink and courtship, and shy men and women with yearning in their hearts for more than this wee village or even the wider world could possibly give them. He was wise enough to know that all of human experience existed as much in this small village as it did in larger towns, and yet a person could be suffocated by the weight of that as well and blame it on the wee village and its invisible confines.

It was warm in the pub, the fug of damp wool and drink sitting thick in his lungs. He felt lightheaded, and noticed that the girl in his arms was as flushed as a ripe apple about to fall from the tree. He shouldn't have downed the whiskey, he knew better, but the temptation to take away his nerves had been too great. When the music ended he escorted the girl back to her friends, who were all giggling and flushed and giving her rather pointed looks.

He enjoyed the dancing, and found the steps came naturally to him, and he partnered one woman after another, some of the young girl's friends and then some of the older women of the village, who were married and happily so but didn't mind being taken about the dance floor by a young man. When finally he begged off for his knee was giving its familiar ache as it did when it felt it had moved him about enough for one day, he found Claudia waiting at the table for him. Once he'd sat for a bit and finished off his pint, she'd looked at him and said, "Dance with me," and then took his hand and led him out onto the floor before he could protest.

She moved well, and followed his lead smoothly. He looked down at her, suddenly aware that he was holding a desirable woman. One who was lovely and intelligent and kind and with whom he talked over the dinner table each night. The scent of her hair tickled at his nose and he was all too aware of the soft press of her breasts against him. He swallowed and tried to think of other things—how much feed was needed to see the sheep through the winter, whether he ought to turn over the north field one more time and if he'd remembered to feed McCool his dinner this evening. None of it worked and he worried that Claudia was going to notice his senses had been stirred by her proximity.

She looked up and gave him a small smile, a knowing one that clearly communicated that she was aware of his body's response to her and was pleased by it. He smiled back at her, though he was vaguely uneasy. Yet at the same time he was sorely tempted. Claudia was fond of him, and he of her, but she wasn't going to fall in love with him because she was still in love with her husband. He considered the possibility that it might work for the two of them. She moved slightly closer to him, an imperceptible distance to anyone observing them, but he felt it along every inch of him.

He understood just what it meant. His body wanted the solace of a woman's touch, a woman's warmth, and if he was entirely honest, so did his soul.

He took a breath and closed his eyes for a second, the heat of the woman in his arms overwhelming. When he opened his eyes again there was a strange aura around his vision and he blinked trying to clear the fog. His sight narrowed suddenly down to something strange, like he viewed a painting in the distance and the woman in his arms was suddenly no more than a figure from another time and no more substantial than the autumn leaves which stuck fast to the pub windows.

He turned, confused, the music sounding distant now, the fiddle playing an air that danced in and out of his hearing, like notes upon the wind. The people were like those glimpsed in a glass ball, the sort that would hang over a dance floor—tiny and distorted and moving slowly, as if the music were a stately pavane rather than the lively air it was. The old gilt mirror appeared to be moving, the surface rippling softly like melted silver poured slowly across an uneven surface.

A space cleared in the middle of it, smoothed by his brain's unreliable neurons, and a face appeared bit by bit—a jawline of such delicacy and skin the color of roses and opals and ivory. The face was alight with laughter, looking up into his own, so fiercely beautiful and so terribly familiar that he lost his breath. In some small part of his mind he understood that he had stopped, that he was somehow still in the pub, with dancers two-stepping around him, but the woman in the mirror seemed more real to his eyes just now, and he wanted to walk across the floor and reach through the mirror and whatever else divided them and touch her, let her draw him across the barrier that stood between them. She turned suddenly and glanced from the mirror, her expression as grave as that of a woman in a 19th century painting, all tints of cream and ivory, and eyes that took the breath from a man's soul. He saw her as through smoke or fog, glimpsed clear and then half disappearing like she was a mirage, something a man who hungered might see just to keep him going that last mile.

The vision kaleidoscoped down and she was distant, a figure so small he could hardly see her against the horizon the mirror set. Then there he was back in the pub, the low light too bright and the music too loud and everyone staring at him as he stood stock-still in the center of the low-beamed room. He had dropped his hands from Claudia and she stood looking at him, flushed scarlet with embarrassment. The familiar sharp pain sliced through his head, and he feared he would be sick in front of all of them.

"I'm sorry, I was just taken oddly there for a moment. Ye'll excuse me." He left the floor and Claudia and went out into the night through the pub's back entrance. He was sorry to embarrass Claudia, though with luck the brown-haired farmer who had been glaring daggers at him much of the night would take the opportunity to rush to her rescue and thus install himself into her good graces.

He ran to the edge of the small wood that sat behind the pub, he felt half sick to his stomach and didn't want to vomit within sight of anyone who might look out the foggy pub windows.

It took a few moments to get the nausea under control and then he sat on an old wooden wire spool that was out behind the pub. He took a few breaths and watched them drift off into the cold October night. He wished the memory hadn't left as soon as it had come, but it was always so with his patchy brain—a sliver, a side view, a glimpse in a funhouse mirror and then nothing.

He walked back to the farm unable to face the crowd of villagers again. Claudia had her wee car and would be fine on her own. He on the other hand might never be able to show his face in public again. He climbed the stairs in the byre to his room and lit the lantern, took off his good clothes and then lay down on the bed. The lantern cast a soft glow around the space. He could smell the hay, slightly dusty; the feed with its warm graininess, and the sheep, the scent of wool and lanolin, and he found all of it comforting. He was tired, the pain and nausea having left as he'd walked the two miles between the pub and the farm. The byre was warm, and it lulled him like a tincture of valerian so that sleep took him swiftly and softly.

He was dreaming, as though sleep had dropped him so deep into a well that he'd fallen through like a character in a child's storybook, arriving in another world so fantastical as not to be possible. But there was little fantastical about this world other than how warm he was, and that the woman of whom he always dreamed was, at long last, speaking to him. Speaking to him about, of all things, a bill for hay.

"Do you really think we need this much hay?" she asked, a wee line across the top of her nose as she looked over the piece of paper she held in her hand. "We only have the one sheep, after all." The paper unfurled suddenly, spiralling out from her hand and down across the polished pine floor until it touched his feet. He bent down to pick it up and the scent of strawberries and green growing things and something that smelled a bit like the wind off the ocean on a fine day filled his senses. He breathed it deep, and felt his body relax in the way it did after satisfying a long held back appetite. Hunger—both that of body and soul, satiated for a moment.

And then she looked up and laughed, her eyes the green of a spring in full flush, like the hills of his land. He laughed with her and suddenly she had tumbled him to a surface of some sort, grass or a bed, he didn't know, only that it was soft and she was warm, so warm and her hands were on him and he wanted her so badly he thought he might die if he didn't take her then and there. Then suddenly they were talking again, but she was still touching him and he couldn't really hear what she was saying entirely.

It seemed to him that he asked her a question, something to do with Claudia and the girl he had danced with in the pub, and she laughed and reached up and kissed him on the corner of his mouth.

"Casey Riordan, for heaven's sake, man, you know well enough the effect you have on women."

"I don't know what ye mean," he said, but he did know, he knew himself suddenly like his wholeness had flooded back at the touch of this woman. It was as if he could see it all, his history, who he had been, who he was, who he might be in the depths of those green, green eyes. He felt joy well up, as he grabbed at memory the way a child might plunge its hands into a bin of candy, with greed and wonder.

He ran his hands down her back, realizing with delight that she was naked. One hand touched the line of his jaw, thumb rasping sweetly over his stubble, the other hand drifting with intent down his chest and then over the plane of his belly, touching his cock so that it sprang eager to her hand, a delirious sort of joy fizzing through his blood. He was almost blind with desire and the need to simply join with her and feel her heat around him.

"Casey, please," she said in a voice of both surrender and demand all at once, "touch me, touch me now."

He wanted to say to her, "Tell me yer name, woman, tell me where to find ye. Tell me why it is ye haunt me in sleep an' in the waking hours, but ye never tell me who it is ye are."

It was the voice that brought him up through the well, reluctantly, like a swimmer who wanted the drowning and dreaded the rescue. The voice was all wrong, it wasn't that soft, grave, slightly throaty voice that tickled right there at the base of the brain, where his memory was locked up awaiting the key which would turn the tumblers and set his life in motion once again. That voice had set the tumblers, rusty as they were, to moving, like a clear golden oil poured between the iron pieces, washing away the detritus that kept him stuck fast, locked inside his own head. This present voice was different, it scratched at his consciousness, pulled his sleep off as though it were merely an autumn cobweb, and submerged the memories back down into that cold black water.

He was not in a bed with a green-eyed woman whose voice warmed him both in body and soul. He was in a byre, with a lantern lit low, and the smell of sheep and dusty timothy thick in his nose and Claudia was sitting on the side of his bed. He felt both angry and bereft, for what the waking had cost him.

He sat up, realizing the blanket had fallen off the bed at some point and that the underwear he wore were not doing much to hide the fact that he was as hard as an iron pipe with the memory of the dream woman's touch still lingering on him.

"Claudia—what's wrong?" he asked, leaning over and clutching up the blanket in an attempt at modesty.

"I came to check on you. You left so abruptly, I was worried you were sick."

"I'm sorry, I had one of my headaches," he said.

"I thought as much," she said and then reached forward and pulled the blanket from his hands.

"I could help you with that," she said softly and then touched him. He suddenly felt fourteen, awkward and certain he was going to go off like a rocket and embarrass himself. He knew he should protest, he knew it wasn't right even though he did desire her, and for more than just physical reasons. Touching him as she was, she could have little doubt about his ability or readiness. He wanted to have sex for the pure release of it and for the sake of a few precious moments of oblivion, of allowing his heart and mind to take a back seat to his body.

"No man has touched me since my husband died," she said and it was no more than a plain statement of fact.

He put his hand down and gently removed hers from his body. He ached with need.

"Aye, an' I know that seems reason enough," he said gently. "In the end, though, what do we have to give one another other than a few moments of warmth? Then tomorrow, if not sooner, we'll feel empty an' just the wee bit sadder."

"Maybe we wouldn't. Do ye have any notion of what it is to long for touch, to simply want someone to show ye some tenderness?" she said, anger and pain mixed in her voice.

He wanted to tell her just how well he knew, just how well acquainted he was with the taste of loneliness and that simple human need to touch and be touched; it was the very manna of life itself. A man or woman could die inside for want of it.

"Casey, if ye're goin' to leave—and I think we both know ye are—then it's best that ye do it now before it's too late."

He nodded. The fewer words he said the better, at this point. He felt like he would only make things worse by trying to give her any comfort.

"Did your wife die?" she asked. "You never speak of her, but you still wear a ring."

He took a breath and thought about explaining, but then decided it might be wisest to allow her to believe him a grieving widower.

"Aye," he said. It would have been closer to the truth to say *he* had died, he thought, weary.

"I'd like to keep McCool," she said, looking away from him. "He's grand company an' he's settled in here, it would be a shame to subject him to a rootless life."

"Aye, I'll go an' I'll leave ye the cat," he said bleakly. She watched him as he dressed, shrugging into an old sweater, pulling on the pants he had discarded only a few hours ago. He knew the effects of her hand and her soft skin showed clearly in the lantern's glow. Well, he was only a man, and a lonely one at that. Perhaps it would give her some comfort to know she had stirred him.

He packed his things, which only took five minutes.

"Thank ye, Claudia, for takin' me in. I didn't mean for…" he let the words die away, because he didn't know what to say without making the situation far more awkward than it already was. She nodded, her head still turned from him, but he thought he saw a glimmer of a tear on her cheek. She was right, it was best if he went now. He leaned down and put one hand to her chin, tilting her face up toward his own. And then he kissed her.

The night outside was cold and filled with mist, and he couldn't see more than a foot or two in front of his nose. He shivered, his clothes and boots feeling damp at once. He was tired but he gave his head a shake and shoved his hands deep into his pockets and started down the road.

Before he had thought of want and desire, and what those things were to a human. He only understood one want anymore—just one. He wanted to go home.

There was a light on upstairs above the pub and Casey heaved a sigh of relief. Finn answered his knock within a couple of minutes and giving him a shrewd look as he stepped in over the threshold, said, "I waited up, I did think ye might need a place to stay after tonight."

"Ye did, did ye?" Casey said, with no small sarcasm.

"Aye, a blind man could have seen the looks Claudia was throwin' at those young girls you were dancin' with. Ye can't play with the female hearts, lad, an' not get caught in the crossfire that results."

Casey looked at him blankly. "How is it my fault?"

Finn waggled one of his grizzled eyebrows at him. "Well lad I'll not say ye're to blame but the women of the village have been actin' up something fierce since ye arrived. Me sister says ye're one of them lads as turns the females soft in the head."

Casey snorted. "It's not like I encourage any of them."

"No, ye don't. Frankly that only seems to make ye that much more attractive to them."

"Well, I'm not sure how I'm meant to fix that. I'm only goin' about my business, livin' life as best as I can manage."

"Why is it that ye don't take up with one of them?" Finn asked.

"Ye're never shy with the questions are ye?" Casey said, hanging his coat up on a peg behind the door and setting his boots on the drip tray below.

Finn laughed. "No, I'm a nosy beggar an' not ashamed of it either, so ye won't sidestep the question quite so neatly there, boy. Truth is ye don't seem the sort to go without female companionship." He gave a delicate cough at this juncture, leaving Casey in no doubt just what he meant by companionship.

Casey considered not answering; as nosy as the man might be, he didn't take offense if a body didn't answer.

"There is a woman, or was, but for me I suspect it will always be a present thing. I suppose I am just a one-woman man."

"An' where is she, this woman?" Finn asked, lighting the gas ring on the stove and then filling the kettle. He indicated that Casey should sit down at the table. Casey sat and then answered the man's question.

"Well, there's the rub," Casey said, "I don't know." He sighed, for Finn was looking more curious by the moment, with a gleam in the bright blue eyes that said he wasn't going to get away from telling this story.

And so he told him, because it was quiet and there was no one about and because he felt the need, after all this time, to talk about it. He told it as well as a man could who still felt that his memory was as holey as a sieve. He told Finn his real name too, and it was the first time he'd said it out loud to another person. It felt good to acknowledge it as if by saying the name it became his once again.

"So ye came back here to see if the country would give ye back who ye once were?"

"Aye, I suppose I did."

"It hasn't done the job ye hoped it would?"

"Not yet, though I feel that I'm on more solid ground since I came home."

"An' what if ye don't find her?"

Casey shrugged his shoulders; the question was one that had haunted him many a night. What indeed?

"I've not given up on that happenin' just yet. I'm hopin' time does its work an' gives me back enough of my mind so that I can find my way home one day." Before it's too late, he added to himself, not wanting to say it out loud, for fear of bringing it into the light and making it fact.

"If ye don't go soon, man, ye'll end up breakin' Claudia's heart, an' she can't afford that. There are men around here who'd be happy to pay court to the woman, but she won't ever see past you to them, as long as ye're here."

"I know that, Finn. It's only that I've found a bit of a home here, an' I think I'm afraid to leave it without an' understandin' of where it is I'm headin'."

"Oh, laddie, we're all walkin' blind in the dark, that's just life. Somewhere, there's maybe a family that's missin' ye, ye have to at least find out."

"I'm afraid, Finn. No, that's not even true; I'm fockin' terrified. What if I never remember things properly, what if I get there an' they've moved on with their lives, an' there is no room nor place for me? I'm not sure I could bear it."

Finn gave him a long look, the blue eyes candid. "I think ye're not a coward, in fact I suspect ye're anything but, so quit behavin' like one. If ye want help, I can ask my cousin who is the solicitor up in Belfast to have a quiet word about, an' see if he can find out if anyone matchin' yer description is missin' in that area. It means ye'll have to stay on a week or two more. Ye're welcome to my spare room in the meantime. So what do ye say, boy? Will ye let me ask my cousin if he can find some information for ye?"

Casey felt a little sick at the notion, but it might be a start and maybe with Finn's help he could find a path that would lead him in out of the dark forest which was his absent memory.

"Aye," he said, "go ahead an' ask him. It's likely it won't lead anywhere, still, I suppose it's worth a try."

Part Eight

The Undefended Heart
September 1977-September 1978

Chapter Sixty-six

The Workhouse
September 1977

THOMAS WOLFE HAD ONCE famously said 'You can't go home again.'
Pamela had always thought he meant that after a long absence, one could
not go home again without finding it, and oneself, utterly changed. After
only two months away, she was finding a painful truth to the simple statement. She was irrevocably changed by her time away and by the things
she had come to accept in that time. Acceptance, she had found, was a
double-edged sword, and coming home without the hope of Casey one
day returning had made the house seem particularly empty and foreign to
her. It was like she was a visitor, here temporarily and uncertain of where
things were placed, and what the rituals were that had once made this
house a home. It wasn't uncommon to feel unsettled when a house had
been empty for some time, but she felt like this was a bigger shift than
merely recovering the normal rhythm of her daily life.

Gert and Owen had picked up the children early this morning, with
the plan of keeping them for the day and overnight. The children had been
very excited to see them and had gone off without a qualm. It would give
her the time to sort her paperwork and get the house in order, though
there wasn't much to do. The yard had been well tended, the garden free
of weeds and near ready to harvest. The byre had been cleared out and re-
stocked with fresh hay for the winter season. Gert and Owen had collected

her mail, and kept Rusty, Finbar and Paudeen with them for the summer. Gert claimed ignorance as to who had done all the work.

"Owen and me, ve vould have happily done the weeding and hoeing, but it is always done when we get here." Gert added a little *hmmphmm* at the end of this sentence, telling Pamela that Gert knew exactly who had done the work, just as Pamela did.

After cleaning up the detritus from breakfast, sweeping up toast crumbs and wiping away sticky golden handprints made with honey, she assembled her piles of paperwork. Pamela sat, trying to imbue herself with a brisk feeling of getting down to business. She had a longing to run outside and down to the sea, even though here the sea was distant and not an eternal lullaby out her windows. Her thoughts drifted to Jamie, as they so often did. She missed him already, missed his daily presence and their meals together and their talks late at night when the rest of the house slept around them. He had left for Brussels shortly after their return to Belfast, for he had an entire summer's worth of business meetings to catch up on.

She had only seen him once before he left and it had been strangely awkward, as if she were holding herself in check to keep from running into his arms. She had been a fool to imagine it could be otherwise, they knew each other in a different way now and could not just fall back into their old routines as if nothing had changed between them. She wanted her old Jamie back, still she could not find regret in her for that night in his arms, with the sea singing to them outside the windows.

Pamela sighed and turned back to her paperwork. The company had stayed afloat over the summer, but just barely. There were still outstanding bills to be both paid and collected, and she needed to go over all the invoices for various materials and work done. The sheaves of paper on her table lay thicker than the reaped hay in the fields that dotted the countryside.

She had worked her way steadily through two piles of paper and was just rising to make a pot of tea when there was a knock at the door. She went to answer it, her hand on the latch before she realized that her summer in Maine had made her far less wary. She stretched up and peered through the small peephole Casey had built into the door. Noah stood on the doorstep, nattily clad in a pale blue sweater and impeccably-ironed navy pants. She opened the door.

"Hello," she said, and found that she was pleased to see him, even though she felt suddenly nervous as she recalled their last conversation before she had departed for Maine. Noah was in some ways rather old-fashioned, and Ireland was still a very conservative country. To one who didn't understand the dynamics of her long relationship with Jamie, she knew it looked odd from the outside, the way they often lived in one another's pockets and functioned as a family. Though the truth was that dynamic had changed and shifted forever and she suddenly felt like that change was as clear as a scarlet 'A' on her chest.

Noah, however, was not here to discuss her tangled web of relations with Jamie.

"I've somewhere I'd planned on goin' today. Would ye care to come along?"

She looked at him blankly, she wasn't sure what she had been expecting, but a jaunt around the countryside had not been on the list.

"Go where?"

"Just a place out in the country. It will be a quiet sort of day but the scenery along the way is grand. I think ye might like to see the place I'm goin'. Ye'll want to bring yer camera along."

She understood that he was offering her an olive branch and knew it was wisest to take it while the offer was there. Besides, her head was beginning to ache and she knew she could sit here all day, fretting over the long columns of numbers, but it wasn't going to come out in a way that made her happy. The thought of being outdoors for a few hours and taking pictures of the countryside was greatly appealing.

"I'd like that. Just let me get a sweater and my camera."

Upstairs she collected her things. The sweater was a thick cream one she had bought a few years back and loved for its silky weight. The day was nice, but she knew the weather was likely to turn chilly as there was a stiff breeze blowing through the tree tops already, and that usually portended rain on its way. She took a glance in the mirror and gave her hair a cursory tidying. It had grown out so that it almost touched her shoulders now, the curls framing her face in a mad cluster. She sighed; there was only so much to be done with it, other than scraping it up into a tie.

The ride was a pleasant one through the winding green countryside, the sun playing fitfully across the pastures and through the trees and over the bramble-laden stone walls and hedgerows. It was a beautiful day and she shed her sweater and relaxed back into the seat. They talked a little, but mostly passed the drive in a comfortable silence. Noah pulled his truck over and parked it in a grassy field what seemed only a few moments later.

"We have to walk from here," he said, "it's a bit of a ways in, but worth the effort." He explained no further, so she got out of the truck, shouldered her camera bag, and prepared to follow his lead. The countryside was deep here with no sign of other humans nearby. Ireland, despite its size, had many such pockets, places where it could easily be the present or two hundred years ago.

It was an effort, too, for it wasn't long before the track narrowed to a mere trail not even a body's width across. The vegetation was so thick that the air was dank and heavy and slightly oppressive. She had the sense that there were eyes watching her from the cover of the woods, furtive and wanting something, something inexplicable that she did not have the ability to give.

She stopped a second later, startled, for there *was* a face there in the woods, looking steadily at her. It was a statue of the Virgin Mary, covered partially in moss and almost obscured in the rampant ivy that was smothering everything around. Good, if lapsed, Catholic girl that she was, the prayer started automatically in her head.

'*Holy Mary, pray for us…*'

A simple plea and it felt apt here, as if something was asking the universe for help. She crossed herself reflexively and moved on.

A few more feet down the trail and she stopped, a terrible cold enveloping her. She looked around but there was no one near, except Noah walking ahead of her, swinging the stick he carried. He turned back when he realized she was no longer right behind him.

"What is it?" he asked, narrowing his eyes to better see her in the thick gloom of this strange forest.

"I don't know. I just got a terrible chill there." She rubbed her arms and walked toward him. "It's gone now."

"This is Famine ground," he said, rather cryptically. Much of Ireland was Famine ground, and she knew some areas had been hit much harder than others, though most of those were deep in the Republic or far out west.

"Casey used to say he believed the Famine was one of the things that seeded the Troubles."

Noah nodded. "I wouldn't argue with the man on that, it contributed greatly to be certain. Ye don't speak his name often," he said, as they continued to pick their way through the long grass and undergrowth.

She shrugged. "It's hard to talk about him. History to him was just a part of his life. It's in the air here in a way it wasn't in America. My father taught me Irish history from the time I was just wee. He was Irish, too."

"Is that how ye ended up here—yer da?"

"No, I came here to see Jamie. I knew him when I was a young girl. He was a good friend to me when I was young and alone and, I admit, I had a terrible crush on him. My father died when I was sixteen. I stuck it out in New York for a few years and then made my way here. Then I met Casey and the rest is history."

He nodded, and turned back to the narrow track to continue walking. She followed along directly in his wake, for the trail was so overgrown and thickly hedged that Noah was holding back bramble and branches for her every few feet. It was claustrophobic and she wondered where on earth he was leading her. She put a hand to her throat, hoping to stem the rising tide of panic. It wasn't just the remoteness of the location nor the deep, thick vegetation, there was something dark about this land, about this path they walked upon.

Then suddenly the land opened a bit, and she saw that they were under a great stone arch which had been completely invisible from even a few feet away. As it was Noah had to push aside a curtain of ivy so that they could walk through. She took a breath, trying to will away the sense of suffocation she'd had inside all that vegetation. It didn't dissipate, though, and if anything she felt the weight in her lungs increase, like wet sand was moving through them rather than the oxygen she was straining for.

"Ye're sensitive to it, aren't ye?" he asked, a look on his face as if she had just answered a question for him to which he had known the answer.

"Yes," she said, "I'm sensitive to it, though if you'd tell me just what *it* is, I'd appreciate it."

"'Tis the *cosan na marbh*," Noah said, his voice quiet but as startling as a shout in the still atmosphere, "the pathway of the dead. A third of the people who took this road in, would come back down it in their shroud."

The sense of dread was like a snake gripping her belly now. She had always had this strange sensitivity to such places. Casey would have said it was because she could sense the ghosts that lingered and all their longing and sorrow.

"Have I made a mistake bringin' ye?" he asked. "It's only that I wanted ye to see it. I stumbled across it long ago, an' though it spooked me, I felt peaceful here. I know ye like old places that no one knows anymore, an'," he shrugged, "I just felt I should show it to ye."

"No, you haven't made a mistake. It's just that," she took a breath into lungs that still felt constricted, "there's so much sadness in the air."

"Aye, there is. Life is such a mix of both, more joy at times, an' then, as ye know well enough, sorrow will come in a heavy dose. Ye're the sort who understands that better than most, an' it's made somethin' both stronger an' yet finer of ye. Come, the buildin' is this way." He reached a hand to her and she took it, needing to feel the solidity of warm flesh which still held coursing blood beneath the skin.

She might have missed the building all together if he hadn't led her to it. Ruined walls were thick with brambles and ivy and ferns and moss. Even the windows were shrouded, small openings here and there in the ivy like sly eyes peeking out, eyes that belonged to no earthly being. Buildings held to their spirit, buildings were the energy of those who had passed through them and had lived and loved within their walls. This building had held only sorrow and pain, only anger and fear.

She followed Noah in by a narrow door with a low-beamed lintel. Inside, there was no sound, no movement, and yet the silence had a weight to it, as if someone listened and waited. Fear feathered down her backbone, light as an early frost creeping outward along her nerves. She felt oddly weightless as she climbed the stairs behind Noah, as though she belonged to the ghosts that dwelt here and not the solid realm of humans. It was like she was drifting through both time and space and when she finished the climb she would have made the transition from flesh to spirit entirely.

They came out onto the top floor a few moments later and she took her camera bag off her shoulder and set it down as she looked around. The window sills were deep and vines and moss grew over the faded paint. The window panes had been broken out a long time ago, and a breeze blew through the empty spaces. She could feel the sadness of the place, though knowing the history of the workhouses in the smallest part would give a person that understanding. But here it was as if the despair and pain were soaked into the very stones. The things that had happened in this place were beyond human ken. Husbands and wives separated and not allowed to speak to one another, small babies ripped from their mothers' arms and their mothers never allowed to touch nor see them again and never to know the fate of their child. Many of those children would have been carried down that road—that pathway of the dead of which Noah had spoken. It made her own arms ache for the feel of her babies, of Conor, solid and warm, smelling of plants, earth and water and crayons and humbugs and of Isabelle, wiggly and running at a higher temperature just like her daddy always had, her scent that of sunshine and jam and talcum powder.

To come to a workhouse at all meant the end of something, it was clinging to a vain hope that a family might survive by surrendering everything that had kept them together—home, land, love, dignity and the simple autonomy of living together as a unit, as a family. Of course the crowded quarters of workhouses and the subsistence diet which was doled out each day meant that if fever took hold, it swept through the houses like wildfire. Smallpox, dysentery, typhus and the most dread disease of all—cholera. It had been estimated that ten times more people died of famine diseases than of actual starvation. It was likely that within these haunted stones hundreds, if not thousands, had died terrible deaths.

She shivered again, rubbing her arms as if she could take away the atmosphere of the building with the solidity of her own touch. "The ghosts are thick in here," she said, "and not particularly welcoming."

"Ye believe in ghosts?" he asked, giving her a hand to help her over a gap in the floor.

"Yes, even if it's only a certain energy that's left behind, we are always haunted by past events and people. Great tragedy resounds in the places it occurs, I believe, forever.

"An' personal tragedy too?" he asked.

"I think that, too, resounds forever, only the place it echoes is in our own hearts."

Noah had a strange intensity to him today and it burned in the midst of this sad, shadowed room. She was more afraid of what his intentions were in bringing her to the workhouse, than she was of the ghosts that moved against the vines and eyeless windows, sighing and waiting for something that would not return. She understood such ghosts, and the sort of longing that would hold you in place for hundreds of years. She did not want to understand what was causing the flame in Noah's eyes. He opened his mouth and she willed him to stop, not to say whatever it was he had wanted to say all this day. Just then something moved in the ancient hearth that stood guardian along one wall, and a small puff of ash and smoke was released into the air. There had been a fire in the hearth recently.

Noah turned at once, his eyes taking in every corner of the room and searching the shadows behind her. She moved toward him out of instinct, even though he was likely more dangerous than any stranger who might have stopped here to light a fire and seek shelter for a night.

"The ashes don't look old," Noah said, his eyes narrowing as he looked down at the hearth. "Someone has been stayin' in here."

He knelt down and put his hand to the ashes, poking them around with one finger. A fine mist rose on the air, like a ghost had breathed out from the spent fire.

"It's still warm," he said, and now she knew she wasn't mistaken about the upset in his voice. The question was why he should be upset about someone trespassing here? Unless this building had a larger meaning to him than just some abandoned point in the long road of Irish history.

She looked back across the long room to where the door yawned into darkness. Someone could be standing there right now and neither she nor Noah would be any the wiser. She wanted to leave. She wanted light and a warm fire and something hot to drink. She wanted Isabelle asking her to read the same story for the twelfth time, anything to banish the chill this place had put in her core.

She turned to say so to Noah, and knew with a sudden certainty that someone *was* standing in the shadows of the door, someone was watching the two of them. She turned back and walked slowly toward the top of the stairs, certain now that there were eyes in the dark which could see her as clearly as if she was outlined in ink against a white sheet. She didn't feel fear, only a strange pull, as though she were a thread drawn fine through a needle. It was stupid, it could be a wild animal or a dog gone feral and here she was walking toward it, she might just as well bare her throat and invite it to taste. She stepped closer, a raw ache in her chest, a wave of something coming at her from the stairs as if longing had been transmuted into corporeal form, the force of it so great that it had crossed the divide between the realm of pure emotion and that of the physical. She had the odd sense that time didn't exist here, at least not in the normal fashion of the workaday world.

"Pamela, where are ye goin'?" Noah's voice broke the spell, shattering the strange web that had been woven around her. She felt both relief and anger in equal parts. She turned back, the strange sensation gone as abruptly as Noah's words had been uttered.

"I just thought I heard something," she said quickly. She felt oddly worried about the entity on the stairs. She didn't want Noah to know someone had been there. "Probably just a fox," she said, though she thought it had been a man standing there. A man swift and light on his feet and now gone. But she did not want Noah chasing after him for fear of what might happen. She wondered who he was—some homeless wanderer, a wraith that lived in the spaces in between this world and that? She had felt something strange, like a silent communication was taking place between them, but she did not know the words of it, could not translate what it was the silence was saying. She stood at the top of the stairs looking down. There was a strange scent, a little like something burning with just the ghost traces of it left upon the air. There was something both disturbing and familiar about it at the same time.

Noah went down the stairs first and she followed carefully in the spots he had used. She had the odd sense that something had been ruined for him up in that room, only she didn't know what and was hesitant to ask him.

She was relieved to be out of the claustrophobia of the building, and took a long breath in. It was relief and regret both to leave the grounds, for she had the sensation that she had left something behind, something that belonged to her.

"Horse feathers," she said out loud, as if uttering the word would dispel the disturbing enchantment which had settled around her like a coating on her skin.

"What?" Noah turned to look at her, a bit of ivy casting shadow over him, so that she could only see one side of his face.

"Nothing," she said, flushing, "just talking to myself."

She turned back and looked up at the windows just before they ducked under the last fall of ivy that would separate the workhouse from their view. For a moment she thought she saw movement there, on the second floor, where the coals of a recent fire had still been warm to the touch.

On the drive back, Noah slowed his truck some distance from her home, in an area she wasn't familiar with. It was the sort of beautiful, bucolic countryside that could lure a person into thinking that this was, indeed, the land of myth and legend, the green land rich with fairies and tales and mysticism. It was the first great lie she told, this country, for beneath that lush green beauty was an unending wellspring of blood. Noah pulled to the side, in a lay-by cut into a hedgerow.

"Are ye in a rush to get back? I brought some lunch along an' I know a nice spot to stop an' sit a while."

"All right," she said, in no hurry to return to her columns of numbers and her empty house.

He pulled down a narrow track and they bumped along until the lane ended in a small meadow ringed in huge old oaks interspersed with ash. The meadow was green still, the dusty deeper green of late summer, but the trees knew it was truly early autumn, for the light and shade they cast held tinges of gold and crimson, as though those colors were the blood that ran beneath the green which still infused the skin of the leaves. A narrow stream, the color of peat in its depths, cut across the field. They sat down beside it with the water running dark and murmurous past their feet. Noah doled out the food—ham sandwiches and a flask of tea and some of Kate's molasses cookies.

"Ye look well," he said. "Yer summer did ye good."

She nodded, and swallowed a bite of sandwich before replying. "It did. How about you, how was the summer for you?"

He laughed. "Oh, ye know, gun runnin' an' terrorizin' the countryside is always good for relaxation."

She laughed, slightly shocked that he was joking about it.

"Ye needn't look like that, Miss Pamela. I behaved myself all summer, spent a week in the Canary Islands, an' worked the farm, didn't even smuggle so much as a pig over the border."

"Not even one pig?" she said teasingly.

"Not so much as a rasher of bacon," he replied.

The day had turned hot and she skimmed off her shoes and socks and put her feet in the water. It was cold, but not unpleasantly so. Noah followed suit, and they sat quietly for a time soaking up the sun and pleasant chill of the water.

"I hope ye don't mind if I make an observation," he said suddenly.

"Go ahead."

"Ye seem less anxious, less strained maybe, like ye crossed some divide these last few months an' ye're maybe more able to move forward now, even if ye will always want to look back as well."

"I just came to a realization that Casey is not coming back to us. Logic told me it was the reality before, but I think my heart is starting to understand it as well."

It was a very weak explanation compared to the reality of what she had felt that day on the sailboat with Jamie, like her very heart was being torn from her chest and she might actually die from the acceptance of what her mind knew and her heart could not bear.

"I'm sorry for that, Pamela. I know it's a step ye were goin' to have to take eventually but each step away from who ye were with him is a painful one."

She nodded, unable to speak. It might be knowledge she now had, but it was still too hard to put words to it most days.

"Do ye wish me to keep lookin' an' askin' questions then? Or would ye rather I stopped?"

"I wish I could give you a straight answer, Noah. Part of me feels like the hope I cling to isn't healthy any more—not for me, not for the children. But the other part of me—that part will always want to know what happened to him, good or bad. I don't want to come to the end of my life and still be haunted by not knowing his fate. So yes, if you ever find out I would want you to tell me. Even if it's something you think I can't bear, I still want to know."

"Aye," he said. "I thought ye might feel so."

"Now it's my turn to ask you something."

He smiled. "Ah, ye're scarin' me now, but ask away."

"How did you get started down the path that landed you where you are now?"

"D'ye mean bein' the godfather of the South Armagh IRA?" he asked drily.

"Yes, that's what I mean."

He shrugged. "I was young, really young when the farm landed on me with my mam an' da' dyin' within months of each other. I don't know what ye know of Kate an' my lives at that time, but it wasn't easy for us an' suddenly there I was responsible for the land an' my sister's survival."

Kate's words from long ago echoed in her mind. 'After we lost our entire family he changed, he became someone I didn't always recognize, someone who frightened me.'

"I was angry for a long time, so angry that there were times I thought I'd explode with it. I was like a bomb waitin' to go off an' just lookin' for the opportunity to explode in a very bad way. Fortunately, there was a man in my life who saw that an' taught me how to funnel it properly, how to channel all that energy into a long game."

"And is that what it is, a long game?" she asked.

He turned to look at her, shading his eyes with his hand. "Aye, a long war, a long game, a long campaign. Don't mistake my wordin' to mean that I take it anythin' less than deadly serious."

"Noah, I think I know you better than that by now. I wouldn't underestimate your dedication to your cause or country. Who was the man?"

"Mickey Devine," he said. She knew the name, Mickey Devine had been legendary as much for his ruthless leadership as for his cold-blooded ability to offer up his own men when the cause demanded blood sacrifice as its due. "He passed the command down to me when he got lung cancer. He was an honest man, and he saw me for what I was, an' didn't hate me for it."

"You sound like that surprised you," she said quietly, aware that some small crack had opened in the ground of their friendship, and that the narrow chasm of it was both dark and alluring at the same time.

"It did. I had little experience of anythin' else to that point in my life. Other than Kate, but she was my wee sister an' there were times I thought she loved me out of duty an' necessity, not just for myself."

"She understands you far better than you might believe, Noah. She does love you for yourself."

"I know that now, but a young man can be short-sighted about others at times." He cleared his throat as if he was slightly uncomfortable. "I think that about you, that ye like me for myself an' not only what I might do for ye."

"I do," she said.

They sat quietly for a bit after that, watching the sunlight play through the trees and onto the surface of the stream, dancing in diamond bits and then skittering away, much like the summer that was now past. The water held a cold in its deeps which heralded the turn of the planet. Waterweed, soft as fairy down, tickled the soles of her feet and she felt slightly drowsy. The strange atmosphere of the workhouse had washed off her, though the yearning she'd felt so strongly there still ached a little in her chest. It occurred to her that she hadn't taken so much as a single picture. She thought she might like to go back and photograph the place properly, if she could find the courage to do so on her own.

She looked over at Noah. He was in profile to her, his dark hair flickering with notes of red in the sunlight, lean face relaxed. A smile played about his mouth and he seemed rather lighthearted suddenly with no trace of the strange intensity that had fairly crackled off him in the workhouse.

"Penny for your thoughts," she said. She was curious as to what had him looking so pleased.

He smiled and flicked a droplet of water in her direction. "It's only that it's pleasant, bein' here with ye. I missed yer company," he said, "an' don't think that doesn't surprise me."

She laughed. "I'm not sure how to take that, Mr. Murray, but I missed your company, too."

It was true, she had. There was a simplicity to being friends with this man which was both reassuring and easy.

"I didn't know that I'd see ye again once ye came back from Maine."

She looked at him, surprised. "Whyever not?"

He gave her one of his extremely candid looks and said, "Because, I expected that ye might find somethin' while ye were gone that would make our relationship unnecessary."

"And what would that be exactly?" she asked, voice tart.

"Only that I thought perhaps ye may have found yerself closer with Mr. Kirkpatrick, an' I daresay the man doesn't like my relationship with ye."

"He doesn't," she said bluntly, "but I am in charge of making my own decisions about just whom I associate with."

"Aye, I suppose that's true enough. I've rarely met such a willful woman."

She raised an eyebrow at him. "Really? I've met more than a few Irish women and I know how feisty most of them are."

Noah gave her a wry look. "Ye're quiet about it, Pamela, but ye're incredibly headstrong. Yer husband was clearly a man of some fortitude."

"Casey appreciated a strong woman, though he often didn't appreci-ate what he viewed as my 'fockin' reckless disregard for the well-being of my own neck,' or words to that general effect."

Noah laughed and then, like quicksilver on a flat surface, his mood changed direction again.

"What are we exactly, Pamela?"

The question surprised her a little, though Noah seemed to be in an odd mood today.

"Friends, I would have thought. Aren't we?"

"Aye, we are," he said, "but will that serve ye well enough when I don't have anything to offer ye?"

"I don't expect anything from you other than your friendship," she said.

"Don't ye? Do ye not want any sort of protection anymore?"

She hesitated before she gave him an answer. The truth was she was still afraid, and with good reason. There had been two letters waiting for her upon her arrival home. They were not any kinder than the several that had preceded them. In fact, she was worried that she was dealing with someone who was mentally unstable to a terrifying degree. But did she have the right to ask this man for anything more? He had killed on her behalf already. He had told her at their first meeting there would be an expectation of a return for whatever he did for her. She wasn't naïve or vain enough to believe that he would continue protecting her without her giving him something back.

"I want to be fair, Noah," she said at last. "I don't take for granted all that you've done for me these last two years. Would I like your protection? If I'm being totally honest, yes, I would. Too much has happened in our little corner of the world, and most of it has been random. There's no way to anticipate or prevent such a thing happening to me and my children. I have been able to sleep at night and occasionally relax my own vigilance because of you. But what can I do in return? You've only put men up at my place a few times and that hardly seems like a fair exchange."

"Is it that ye don't want to be indebted to me, an' so ye feel ye must always balance the scales between us?" he asked quietly.

She shook her head. "Noah, if I were worried about that, I would have ended our arrangement long ago. It's only that I feel the parameters of my life have shifted a little, and I want to be certain you don't feel the account between us is out of balance."

His gaze was intent, the gentian eyes mild but, she had no doubt, taking in every bit of her face, every telltale emotion or thought that crossed it.

"Perhaps, one day, I'll need somethin' that you can provide. Until then, consider yerself paid up in full," he said.

He stood and then gave her a hand up, and they walked back to his truck in silence. She had the oddest feeling that a deal *had* been struck, only she wasn't aware just what the terms might be, nor who would bear the greater cost.

Chapter Sixty-seven

A Kirkpatrick Christmas
December 1977

SINCE CASEY'S DISAPPEARANCE Pamela had found, to put it mildly, that Christmas was a time to grit her teeth and get through from one side to the other. She had made certain there were the things the children expected—stockings, good food, presents and decorations, but for her the season had been a blur each year. The first year, Casey had been gone only a month at Christmas and she could not remember the time at all now. Deirdre had made certain there was a meal and wrapped gifts and a stocking for both Conor and Isabelle, though only Conor had been old enough to take any sort of note.

This year, Jamie had invited everyone to his home for the day. Pat and Kate, Gert, Owen, and Lewis, Tomas, and Finola and of course, her and the children. When they arrived the house glowed with well-polished floors and furniture and lit fires and candles and Christmas lights. The scents of ham and turkey and chestnuts and plum pudding filtered out fragrant and festive. Maggie was away spending Christmas with her sister and so Pamela had come up the day before to help Jamie with some of the preparations. Finola had been here since early morning helping him with the rest of the cooking.

Coats and boots and scarves and mittens were removed and everyone gathered in the great room which was lit with hundreds of fairy lights and had a huge tree in one corner. The children scampered in delight to the lights and tree and gaily-wrapped gifts which lay beneath spreading pine boughs. Patrick and Kate had already arrived and Kate was flushed and lovely in a periwinkle dress and Pat looked terribly grown up to Pamela suddenly. He had come into his own in these last few years and wasn't the boy she'd met one day in a university class. Gert, Owen and Lewis arrived shortly after—Gert with a platter holding her famous *krustenbraten* along with red cabbage and dumplings.

Tomas came in smelling of snow and whiskey. He kissed Pamela on both cheeks and then gave her a searching glance. "Ye look well, girl. It's nice to see." He then ruined the sentiment by casting a significant glance in Jamie's direction.

"Tomas, give over," Pat said, coming up and giving her a hug. "Merry Christmas, Pamela. And he's right, ye do look well."

Patrick knew it was the first Christmas she had felt like celebrating, and he of all people understood that it also came with a grain of bitter sweetness at its core, because it was yet another change in this long road she was traveling.

Jamie, with his understanding of children, told them to unwrap their gifts first and they would have dinner afterward. There was a beautiful shearling coat for Conor which was a miniature copy of one Jamie had that Conor loved, and a dollhouse for Isabelle as well as skates for both children. Kolya had a new train set which had whistles and bells and a small town for it to chug around. Vanya, whose feet were always cold, was the recipient of a plethora of socks and many novels. Patrick, a beautiful leather lawyer's bag. Kate, a set of French baking dishes. Tomas, a gentleman's walking stick made from blackthorn. Owen and Lewis each got a bottle of the special reserve single malt from the distillery, Gert, a Hummel angel to add to her collection and Finola, a leather-bound herbal with which she was clearly very pleased.

"This is for you," Jamie said and handed Pamela a small packet, wrapped in thick cloth.

She unwrapped it carefully, a fine tremor running through her fingers, as if they sensed what lay inside that soft cloth wrapping before she did. It was an old book, well worn, covered in fine leather, the papers rough cut and a soft grey. She opened the cover carefully and gasped.

"Jamie!"

He smiled, clearly delighted with the effect the book had on her.

"What is it, *moy podrooga?*" Vanya asked, leaning over her shoulder in interest.

"It's a first edition of Shelley—it has his handwriting inside." Her fingers trembled as she touched the old writing, the loops and lines of the long dead poet's hand. The ink was faded, but the words were still legible.

"Where on earth did you find this, Jamie?"

"From a dealer I know. I asked him to look out for such a thing some time back," he said casually.

"Thank you, thank you so much," she said, blinking back tears. He could not have found a gift that would have touched her more, and she was quite certain he knew it.

She gave him his gift then. She had made him a sweater in deep blue because it was the color she liked best on him. He put it on right away, despite the fact that he'd been impeccably dressed in a beautifully tailored pale green shirt.

"When did you find time to do this?" he asked.

"At night when the children were sleeping."

He smiled, but it was an expression of understanding because he knew how often she was awake into the wee hours, unable to find the simple comfort of unconsciousness.

Dinner was served in the formal dining room. The long table was lit with tapers on a background of rich red and gold. The good china, which had been in the Kirkpatrick family for more than a hundred years, had been brought out and washed and now gleamed beside holly and silver and the sparkle of Waterford wine glasses.

There was talk and laughter and ambrosial food and wine poured without stint. By dinner's end Pamela felt slightly tipsy and very relaxed. She caught Jamie looking at her more than once, his eyes warm but also with a question somewhere in their depths.

After dinner, Jamie had a surprise for them. Two sleighs pulled up outside the front door, bells jingling merrily. Danu and Naseem, both sporting festive red blankets, were harnessed and snorting with impatience. Filled with good cheer and with the adults well-fortified with alcohol everyone tumbled into their respective sleds. Pamela, Conor, Isabelle, Kolya, Tomas and Lewis all with Jamie, and Kate, Gert, Owen, Finola and Vanya with Patrick as driver of the second sleigh.

Pamela sat up front with Jamie who was driving the first sleigh, with Kolya, looking like a proper little Cossack in a blue wool coat, tucked between them. Isabelle, pink-cheeked, hair tumbling riotously from her red wool hat, candy cane held aloft in one sticky hand, was seated upon Jamie's knee, the only place, in her opinion, for her to sit in the sleigh. Jamie had one protective arm about her, and Conor was standing, leaning over the lip of the sleigh, fascinated by the sight of Danu and her harness bedecked with bells and holly. Her children looked happy; her children *were* happy and she realized, so was she.

They drove off under a quarter slice of moon, as twilight stole over the land, the sun going down in thick amber, scented with cold oak bark. Jamie took them along the trail toward Finola's cottage, as it was a long stretch and utterly picturesque. The boughs formed a snowy canopy over their heads and the runners of the sled whisked with a frothy hiss over the snow. She leaned over to kiss the top of Conor's head, feeling the excitement thrum through his small body as they skimmed over the silver snow.

Her eyes met Jamie's over the top of Kolya's shimmering red head. Jamie was still wearing his crown from the Christmas crackers they'd popped after dinner. He grinned at her. She smiled back feeling that rush of euphoria in her veins that she often felt around him, like her blood had been replaced with champagne.

They came in from the chill to find cocoa for the children and mulled wine for the adults. They played games and Tomas surprised everyone by playing the piano with great vigor and producing from his chest a lovely baritone voice that led everyone in singing. There were roasted chestnuts after that and popcorn for the children and whiskey for the men, and a lovely golden Sauterne which Jamie knew she loved, for the women.

It was Conor's idea to play Blind Man's Bluff. It was a mad scamper around the bottom floor, with the big people assisting the small to elude the Blind Man, at which the adults took turns. There was much laughter and stubbed toes and the delighted shrieks of the children. She stopped for a moment and looked around as the hubbub proceeded about her. Tomas was currently the Blind Man and was chasing Isabelle, his hands making clapper-claw motions and Isabelle was squealing with glee. Kolya was creeping up behind him and Conor was hiding behind his Uncle Pat. Lewis was sitting, sipping parsimoniously at a tumbler of whiskey. He had never fully recovered from the shooting and had told her the week before that he would be selling his farm come spring. The smell of gingerbread wafting from the kitchen told her where Kate and Gert had disappeared to.

All of these people had closed ranks around her after Casey's disappearance, and sheltered her in what ways they could. No one, of course, had the power to take the pain from her but they had done their best to help her through it and keep her safe as she had at first stumbled along the pathway and then begun to walk with more confidence. She looked over at Jamie. He was laughing as Isabelle scampered up to him, still shrieking. She jumped, arms outstretched in the perfect trust that Jamie's arms would catch her. Just as they had from the day he'd returned home from Russia and taken them all under his care. She loved these people in all the various ways of friends and family, but what she felt for Jamie was something apart and with a depth to it that sometimes frightened her.

She realized then that Pat was watching her, his dark eyes both thoughtful and a little sad. He smiled at her, but she understood the look in his eyes. Regret for what was lost and could not be again and understanding for the fact that she was moving on without his brother.

It was Jamie's turn then to be the Blind Man. Pamela scooped up Isabelle and ran off toward the kitchen, her little girl wiggling in her arms. She tiptoed down the back hall which ran behind the kitchen and they crouched at the bottom of the stairs there, Isabelle's eyes alight with unfettered joy in the day. It made her throat a little tight, realizing how uncommon these sorts of times were in her children's lives. While she tried hard to hide her fear and stress at home, she was certain the children felt it on some level, nevertheless. Certainly Conor did.

Jamie came into the hall then and Isabelle said in a whisper loud enough to wake the dead, "Mama, is Jamezie!" and then buried her head in Pamela's shoulder.

Jamie came down the hall making growling noises that turned Isabelle into a live eel in Pamela's arms. He came within touching distance and then said, "Fee fi fo fit, I smell a little one named Isa-bit."

"Dat's me!" Isabelle said and popped down out of her mother's arms to wrap herself around Jamie's leg, almost sending him tumbling over onto the flagstones. As it was he landed on the stairs beside Pamela, knocking his head against the wall on his way down.

"Isabelle!" Pamela admonished. Isabelle's lip began to quiver immediately. Jamie, sensing this sea-change in Isabelle's mood, took off the blindfold and gave her a hug.

"I think Gert has some gingerbread men in the kitchen for you, Isabit. Why don't you go see?"

Isabelle scarpered for the kitchen, hurt feelings forgotten with the balm of promised treats.

"Are you all right?" Pamela asked, checking the side of his head where it had glanced against the wall.

"I'm fine, don't worry about it. She's just in high spirits. I think they've had fun, though I imagine they'll all drop soon."

"It has been a perfect day, Jamie. Thank you."

"You're welcome," he said. She was suddenly aware of how closely they were sitting. They hadn't touched since that night in Maine. He was looking down at her, his face shadowed in the dim light of the hall.

She met and held his gaze which was the gaze of the man who had reawakened her body months ago by the sea. She had missed his touch. Just how much became clear as he leaned down and kissed her. His mouth was warm and sweet against hers and she felt herself swaying toward him and uttering a small prayer that all the children would stay where they were for at least a minute or two.

She touched her hand to the side of his neck, the skin smooth as water beneath her palm. She could feel his pulse leap to her touch and felt her own speed up in response. He put his hand to her face, drawing her forward without needing to exert the slightest pressure. She put her face to the crook of his neck, breathing in deeply. He smelled of lime and sandalwood, of horses and leather and snow. It brought tears to prickle at the back of her eyes and flooded her entire body with desire at the same time. She put her hands flat against his chest, feeling his heart and just breathing him in and out.

"Stay," he said softly, his hands covering hers. "You and the children. Stay for the night."

She nodded, wordless, her entire body lit from within by the white heat of desire.

"Pamela." A voice from the end of the hallway interrupted their reverie. It was Finola. "There's someone askin' for ye on the telephone."

She took a breath to steady herself, and then released Jamie's hands with regret. She hadn't even heard the phone ring.

The light in the kitchen seemed terribly bright after the dark of the hall. "Hello?"

"Pamela, it's Noah. I'm sorry to disturb yer Christmas but I need to meet with ye as soon as possible."

"Why?"

"Ye know I'm not goin' to say much over the phone. I wouldn't ask on this night if it wasn't important."

"All right," she said, uneasy. He wouldn't call unless it was an emergency.

"It's to do with our original discussion, the very first one we had. D'ye understand?"

Her heart started to thump so hard it hurt. "Yes, I understand."

"Do ye have a pen and paper? Ye'll need to write down the directions. An' Pamela, ye can't breathe a word of this to anyone, d'ye understand?"

"Yes," she said. He gave her the directions then, and she scribbled furiously, her heart in her throat.

Jamie was standing behind her when she got off the phone and judging by the look on his face he had a good notion of what she was about to say.

"I…I have to go," she said, a furious rush of color flooding through her skin.

"That was Noah Murray on the telephone, wasn't it?" he asked, his voice deceptively amiable. She knew better than to be fooled. That particular tone meant he was in a cold fury.

"Yes," she said. It was like having cold water thrown in her face to go from the moment in the hallway to this. She had to go, even though she feared leaving just now was going to cost her dearly with Jamie. She couldn't blame him either.

"What's so important that he needs you to leave and run to him on Christmas Day?" Jamie's arms were crossed over his chest and the green eyes were narrowed with anger.

"I can't explain that just now," she said.

"You can't tell me why you're leaving?"

"No, I can't," she said miserably.

"I see," he said, and she shrank a little from the chill in the two simple words. "Well, you're a grown woman and I can't prevent you from doing as you please but I'm damned if I'm letting you take the children to go to a meeting with that man."

"I'm not taking them. I'll ask Pat and Kate to bring them home when they leave here." She sounded conciliatory, she knew, and hated herself a little for it. It had been a perfect day and now it lay about her in ruins. It was no one's fault but her own.

"Well, then go. Please don't let me detain you any longer," he said.

She left after speaking with Pat, who looked little more pleased than Jamie concerning her departure. She was shaking and it took three attempts to get the keys in the ignition of the old Citroën. Her mind had been wiped blank with anxiety after Noah's call, but she could still feel the touch of Jamie's lips on her own and the heat of his hands on her skin. She looked in the rearview mirror and her heart felt heavy in her chest. The house looked suddenly insubstantial as if the joy of the day had merely been a temporary illusion, like a candle set inside a paper house that had suddenly gone out.

She sighed, put the car into gear and drove away.

It wasn't an easy task to find the place where Noah had instructed her to meet him. The cold though had produced a clear night and visibility was good. It was a bit of a drive for the location was out beyond Newry and then down a series of old country roads, some of which appeared to have been unused for years. The last road he'd instructed her to take was little more than a track which petered out into a field long abandoned; judging by the shrubs growing in profusion across what had once been tilled land. There was a stone byre, narrow and high, at one end of the field. She got out of the car and walked toward it. She recognized one of Noah's men. He nodded at her and said, "He's waitin' in the byre for ye."

She nodded in return and walked into the old stone building. Three lanterns hung from the beams, and the space was lit for the purpose it had been put to. It was bright enough to see the man in the chair, arms tied to the chair back, ankles bound to the chair legs. His face was swollen on one side and his lips were bloody. She had been prepared for this, but it was still a bit of a shock to see him. It was the man who'd tried to recruit her as an informer—Mr. Davison. A flood of adrenaline rushed out through her blood in jets and she regretted the wine she'd drunk earlier in the day.

She looked at Noah. He stood beside the man, his hands gloved and his face impassive above a dark sweater. "Can I have a word with you outside?" she asked.

"Aye," he said, and walked out with her, heading over to a low stone wall to the left of the byre. The old rock was thick with frost-gilded ivy. "What is it?" he asked. There was no impatience in his voice, just a removed calm which was chilling to hear.

"That man in there," she said, calmly, even though her heart was banging against her ribs like Thor's hammer, "that man in there is Special Branch."

"Aye, I'm aware," he said, as if he'd just admitted to preferring one brand of tea over another. "What I'm goin' to ask you is this—what was Special Branch doin' in yer house riflin' through yer cupboards? We caught him with a bundle of money in his hand, an' a pile of letters. I see by yer face ye know exactly what it is I'm referrin' to."

"Are you accusing me of something?" she asked, not liking his tone in the least.

"No, I'm merely askin' ye if ye know why these things might be of interest to a Special Branch officer? So much so that he felt the need to break into yer house."

"I found the money one day while I was putting something in the cupboard. It was in a paper bag, I have no idea where it came from. He wants me to believe that it was pay-out money to Casey from the British. For all I know he planted it there, being that my house seems to be some sort of central station for spies and soldiers to come by and either terrify or blackmail me."

"Aye, he says the money was there an' he only knew it had to be hidden in the house somewhere. The letters, I take it, were hidden near to them."

She nodded.

"Ye ought to have told me about the letters, Pamela. I cannot protect ye properly if I don't know the threats ye have against ye."

"Can we talk about that later? I want to know what he told you."

Noah put one gloved hand into the other. "Here's the thing, it may be true or not because he was afraid we'd kill him, I think, so he was desperate when he said it. He might have been just buyin' time, an' maybe thinkin' ye'd be able to sweet talk me out of hurtin' him. He's barely been touched, but I don't think his tolerance for pain is all that high. Ye'd think they'd train them a little better to withstand this sort of thing, but apparently he's not the bravest soul."

She felt oddly remote, standing here in this frosty field with a man who was feared country-wide for his ability to find a man's breaking point, calmly discussing beating a man.

"He says he has information to do with Casey. He says he knows what happened to him."

She nodded. The lovely day at Jamie's had evaporated as if it had never happened. Here, she thought, was the truth of her life—blood and hurt and weighing the cost of truth and lies.

"Sometimes it's easier not knowin', Pamela. It's for you to decide where your limit on that is. Ye have to ask yerself how he knows what he says he does about yer husband. An' if so, how high a price would ye put on extractin' that information."

That was the million-dollar question. How badly did she want to know exactly what had happened to Casey? Would having an answer or details allow her to sleep better? Would it lay his ghost to rest eventually, both for his sake and her own?

"So, knowin' that, what is it ye'd like me to do with him?"

"Do with him?"

"Aye, it's not a euphemism, Pamela. I'm askin' do ye want him dead or just beaten to see if he has any more information to offer?"

"Can I just talk to him before I make any decisions?"

"Aye, as I said it's yer call here tonight."

She walked into the byre. "I want a moment alone with him," she said to the man standing guard. Noah was behind her and nodded to the guard and they went out together leaving her alone with the man she knew only as Andrew Davison. She wondered if that was his real name. He looked at her, one eye swelling shut, and a certain defiant anger in the other.

He started the conversation. "Is this your Christmas present from your man out there? Deliver you a Brit on a silver platter? Tenderize me a little before he kills me?"

She sat down opposite him on a wooden chair and then wondered uneasily if this was where Noah had sat to begin the interrogation.

"You were in *my* house, stealing both money and personal items so please don't play the innocent victim in this. I want to know what it is you claim to know about my husband."

"And if I don't tell you?"

She shrugged, feigning a nonchalance she most certainly did not feel. "Then I don't care what he does with you tonight."

"You like the bad ones, do you? Are they good in bed? Is that the attraction? Does that turn you on—the thought of all the blood they have on their hands?"

"You want to bait me, Mr. Davison? I wouldn't if I were you. I don't think you can afford to antagonize me too much. I suspect what you were doing—stealing from my house, on Christmas night no less—wasn't sanctioned by your bosses, was it?"

"Oh, it's not the first time we've been in your house. And we're clearly not the only ones who've crossed the threshold. Those letters were very interesting. Someone certainly hates you with a certain vigor, no?"

"You said you knew something. Do you want to tell me or not? Because I'm happy to call Mr. Murray back in here to deal with you."

"Ah, yes, Mr. Murray. This whole thing comes back around to him."

"I'm not here to talk about him. I want to hear what it is you claim to know about my husband."

"Are you familiar with the Nutting Squad, Mrs. Riordan?"

"Yes," she said. The Nutting Squad was the IRA's internal security unit. They investigated breaches of discipline and enforced rules and regulations. They were also responsible for vetting new recruits, but everyone knew their real role was to collect and collate information on suspect or compromised individuals. How they 'collected' this information was left to them. Casey had once told her he'd rather face a lifetime of incarceration than spend a day with the Nutting Squad. He'd said the man who ran it could make a man confess to things he'd never even dreamed of much less done.

"This is what I know, *Mrs.* Riordan. Your husband is dead and he was killed because he found out about an informant who was higher up the food chain than he was. An asset so powerful and in so deep with the IRA that his handler would throw your husband to his own side, knowing they would rip out his throat like the wolves they are." He smiled, and the gesture split his lip causing blood to run down his chin. "It's a long seven days with the Nutting Squad, and those boys revel in the infliction of pain. Do you know what they did to your husband, do you know how he would have been choking on the smell of his own fear and piss by the time they put a bullet in the back of his head? He died as he lived—by violence and crime."

She had a knife in her pocket. Casey had insisted she get one years ago. It was a pretty pearl-handled thing, with a blade that was as sharp as a razor. She stood up and walked over to the man and stuck it to his throat.

"How is it *you* know this?"

"Imagine that there's an informant for the British Army and he kills Special Branch's informant to protect himself from being exposed."

"Casey never had anything to do with Special Branch," she said. She felt suddenly so tired as if her legs couldn't possibly bear her up any longer. Certainly her heart could not.

He reeked of fear. He was trying to buy time but antagonizing her seemed a poor way to do it.

"You don't actually know do you? You're just guessing, aren't you?"

"Am I?" he said and smiled again.

"Is there something about this that amuses you?" A trickle of blood ran down the man's neck and there was a fleeting second where she wanted, very badly, to just shove the blade in. She threw the knife to the floor, frightened by the overwhelming urge to hurt the man.

"I'm just telling you how it is—you wanted the truth and now you find it unappetizing. It's hardly my fault your husband died in pain, probably screaming or drowning in his own blood."

Her vision pulled in so that all she could see was a narrow field. She thought maybe she was going to faint when suddenly she realized she was hitting the man over and over in a blinding wave of fury and anguish. His arms, his face, his shoulders and he was laughing. The laughter was the last straw; she picked her knife up from where she'd thrown it. She would stick it in his jugular vein and just have done with it. Anything to shut him up, anything to make the pain stop. She raised her hand and the light from one of the lanterns flashed along the blade like a flame. Her arm came down and then other arms came around her from behind and pinioned her. It was Noah.

"See to him," he said shortly to the man who'd run into the byre with him. Awareness of her own state came to her. She was breathing hard and could feel tears building up, the pressure nearly unbearable behind her eyes. She still felt a blinding red rage; her whole body throbbed with it.

"You can't just leave me here. Pamela!" Davison's voice had risen to a high pitch, a screech of real fear as if he only realized his mistake now.

She turned back, even while Noah still held her in a firm grip, and looked Davison square in the eyes. "Don't you *ever* say my name again. I don't care what they do to you. No more than you care that my husband was tortured for days and then dumped in some shallow grave so that I will never even have the comfort of finding his bones. I truly don't care if you suffer or if they kill you quickly."

"Pamela, come on," Noah said and gently led her out into the night. She half-stumbled, half-ran to the wall and then bent over the top of it and was sick, more than once, in the snow. Noah gave her a few minutes alone. She slowly sank down to the ground, too weak and dizzy to stand any longer. She had almost killed a man. A silly, weak man.

Noah came and sat down beside her on the frozen ground. "Ye all right now?"

"You did warn me," she said, weary. "I have only myself to blame."

"Aye, I warned ye, but there is some knowledge that no amount of warnin' can prepare ye for."

"I already knew," she said, wearily. "It's just another step down the road to where I finally truly understand it, that's all."

"He pushed ye because he thinks he's goin' to die tonight anyway. He thought a woman would give him a quicker an' more merciful death."

She wiped a hand across her clammy brow. "He almost got his wish."

"One way or another my men an' I have to deal with him. What would ye have done?"

This moment was her Rubicon. If she crossed it there would never be any returning to the girl she had once been, there would be no pretending that she was somehow different than these men in the field or the dirty players on either side of the divide. This was different than asking Noah to kill a man for her, because the constable had been a direct threat to her life and her children's well-being. This blood would be on her hands and there would be no rationalizing it away. Right now, she wasn't certain she cared. She knew later when rationality returned and took a higher hand than emotion, she might feel very differently.

"Am I a coward if I don't want to see him killed?" she asked, and wondered if she was asking Noah or herself.

"No," he said. "He has a gamblin' problem an' a wee issue with prostitutes as well. He's got a family back in England; he'll be amenable to blackmail. If not, we'll finish it."

"Thanks for stopping me in there," she said after there had been a long silence between them.

"Aye, I wouldn't let ye do that. Ye don't need that sort of thing on your conscience. It might not weigh on ye tonight, but later on it would haunt ye."

"I need to go home, Noah," she said. He nodded and walked her back to her car.

"Are ye certain ye're all right to drive?"

"Yes, I'm all right," she said, and found oddly enough that she was. She felt vaporous, as if she was so tired she was near to invisible. The anger was gone leaving behind a dull ache in her chest.

He nodded and turned away, walking back toward the byre. She had no idea what they would do to Davison. And as long as they didn't kill him, she could not find it within her to care.

She turned the car on and let it warm enough to thaw the windscreen so she could see to drive. She drove partway down the track and then stopped. She sat for just a moment, trying to remember if she needed to turn right or left when she came to the larger road. She wasn't quite certain how to get home from here.

And then she thought there really was no set of directions, no map and no guide by which to find her way home. It was a strange word— home, and one she thought no longer meant to her what it once had.

The Christmas festivities wound up shortly after Pamela left. Jamie's temper was well disguised but the tension emanating off both him and Patrick was not. Pat and Kate bundled up Conor and Isabelle and left an hour after Pamela. Gert, Owen, and Lewis went too. Before Tomas departed he took Vanya to one side.

"Keep an eye on him tonight," he said, nodding toward Jamie who was helping his grandmother into her coat. "He's been on a fine edge all day, only I thought it was goin' to be all right as long as Pamela was here. I saw them in the hall earlier, an' I think you did, too. He'll be like a bee trapped in a bottle, an' I can't say I blame him. I don't know what that woman is thinkin' sometimes."

"I think," Vanya said quietly, "the only thing that would make her leave on such a day is information about her husband. She was very agitated when she left."

Tomas nodded. "That might well be part of the problem. Jamie is a patient man, but even he has his limits. A blind man could see things had changed between them after they came home from the summer, an' now they're back to walkin' around each other like two porcupines with their quills up. We all know who she left to see."

It was true. Vanya had been coming through the upper hall and both Pamela and Jamie were unaware of him, invisible in the shadows at the top of the stairs. He had seen Jamie bend down to kiss her. And he'd seen her body melt into Jamie's and heard Jamie's whispered question and seen her response. Yes, Jamie's senses had been primed for something else altogether tonight. And Vanya thought it was a pity it hadn't happened, even though the thought hurt him in myriad ways.

Long after the guests departed and Kolya was asleep, Vanya went in search of Jamie. The dark was thick and stranded with narrow silver threads of rain. The snow was melting away, opening up raw patches of earth here and there. It was hard to believe they had all been out in the sleighs only hours before.

He found Jamie by the paddock, sitting on an upturned barrel. He was braced against the paddock rail as a chilly mist of rain fell all around him. His fingers, tensile and strung like wire over his face, ran with silver beads of water, the emerald he wore a cascade of fire against the translucent gold of his hair. Vanya stood beside him, quiet.

"Yasha?"

"It's all right," Jamie said, though he was shivering hard, his sweater soaked through with rain. "Just one of my headaches."

"Not only the headache, I am thinking," Vanya said.

"No, not only the headache. Percipient as always, Vanya." Jamie said, a long shudder rippling through his body.

He put a hand to Jamie's shoulder. "Yasha, we need to get you in the house. You're freezing."

Jamie spoke as if he had not heard Vanya's words. "When I first came home," he said quietly, "I thought it was enough, this friendship, this strange love she and I have always shared, but now even friendship has become insupportable."

"I think this is not entirely true. I think you cannot have it now. I think if you are patient, the day will come when she will have a whole heart to give to you. It is already partly yours and has been for a very long time, no?"

"I know this, but some nights half a heart is worse than no heart at all."

"You have known this for a long time so what is different tonight?"

Jamie laughed, a hollow sound and turned his face up to the rain, his eyes dark.

"Good old-fashioned jealousy, I suppose. He called and she ran. I know there was probably some emergency on the other end which she felt could not be ignored. I do wonder how often he manufactures something to keep that chain he has on her in working order. I'm afraid for her, and I'm angry with her. It's not a comfortable mix. There's a side of Pamela that's ruthless, and it's due to everything she's had happen to her here and the losses she's suffered, which have been too many. I believe Noah sees that ruthless streak in her as well, and he exploits it. I think he believes it brings her closer to him, and I fear he's right."

"You think he is not truthful with her?"

"I think he mixes small bits of truth into a larger fear, the one she carries with her always that she will never know what happened to Casey. He lets her believe he might know things, or find something out and it's enough to keep her coming back and to keep her hope alive."

"It seemed like something more tonight," Vanya said.

"I know and that worries me." He looked at Vanya, meeting his eyes through the drizzle. "I'm sorry. When I am like this I'm stripped bare of my usual defenses. I have been reckless today and others have paid for it."

"Do not apologize to me, Yasha. I do not require it from you. We need to get in out of the cold or both of us will have the noo-munny, as Shura would say."

Jamie nodded, a movement that was almost imperceptible.

"Come, my Yasha, let us put you to bed and then we will send you off to your elephant dreams."

They walked back to the house in silence, Jamie shivering hard enough that Vanya could feel it in the space between them. He knew what plagued Jamie was more than a headache. He knew there were pills prescribed by a doctor, which Jamie never took. Jamie had, one night, explained it to him.

"There are times when I can't control the stimuli coming in; it's like there's a gate inside my head and my soul that is stuck fast in the open position, and it allows a flood to come through—sound becomes color, and color becomes texture, and texture becomes sight. It feels like this amazing rush when it's happening but then after, on the down-swing, everything is so grey in comparison. Nothing feels right or good. And sometimes, during the grey patches, the nights are particularly long."

An hour later, Jamie was asleep, rendered unconscious and set adrift to dream elephant dreams by the small bottle of yellow powder he kept under lock and key in a cabinet in his bedroom.

Vanya sat by the bed as the night gathered weight in the corners of the old room, and watched as it slowly rolled up from the floor, softening the outline of the man on the bed. He could feel his pain, as he felt other things with this man—his joy, his love, his anger. It was, for Vanya, both a blessing and a curse all at once. But to sit here, while Jamie was peaceful, even if it was a drug-induced peace was, in the moment, all he could ask of the universe.

He, perhaps more than any other person living, understood what Jamie had endured in Russia, both in the gulag and in the weeks that preceded it. Lubyanka released no man without inflicting its particular whiplash upon both skin and spirit, both bone and blood. And yet, he thought, the greater torment for this man was here in this country, for reasons both public and personal. He had not expected it to be so but then he had not understood the love Jamie had carried for so very long. He understood, too, that a life lived in such a fractured way would eventually tear a man like Jamie apart. The headaches alone were proof of that.

Sometimes, when he was like this in the extremities of pain and emotion, and under the influence of this particular medicine, he would talk and despite the heartache it caused, Vanya listened and took in his words, knowing that he saw a side of Jamie that others did not. Not even, he thought, Pamela, and she saw more than almost anyone with this man.

Being Russian had given Vanya a certain harsh practicality. He would survive and so would Jamie, for a broken heart, after all, still kept beating.

Chapter Sixty-eight

The Unbounded Ocean
February 1978

THE BUILDING WAS ONE of those strange little three story constructions that was jammed in between two larger buildings and yet somehow still seemed to appear as if it were leaning, a bit drunkenly, to one side. It had a beautiful slate roof and was wreathed in delicate scarves of fog. The bottom floor was occupied by a law firm, the second floor by a millinery shop and the top floor by a very old and venerable Parisian publisher. Pamela took the wrought iron lift which she had to hand crank herself in order to rise to the third floor.

She was in Paris for two reasons, one was to meet with Monsieur Bellerose of Bellerose Books, who knew the American publisher who had bought her book last month. Monsieur Bellerose wanted to discuss the possibility of publishing *Children of the Troubles* in France. The other was to do a magazine interview about said children of the Troubles for a small politically-minded publication. After that she had arranged to visit with Yevgena. She had three full days to herself in the City of Light and she planned to enjoy every minute of it.

Monsieur Bellerose was a slightly tuberculotic-looking man who chain-smoked Gauloises and smelled of smoke and brandy. He was also one of those perfectly lovely souls whom Pamela liked from the moment he greeted her and kissed her hand. Their meeting went well and spilled over into a scrumptious lunch with an even more scrumptious bottle of wine to go with it. She parted from him, slightly tipsy and with a contract in her hand for the French rights to her book. She stopped at a café and bought a very strong coffee so that she would arrive sober for the magazine interview. The interview took place in a small grotty office building on the Rue Béranger but the man who interviewed her was kind and allowed her to practice her rather rusty French in some of her answers.

Thus, having had a rather successful day, she arrived at Yevgena's beautiful apartment in good spirits. They settled in her parlor, a lovely room decorated in the bright colors and bohemian style that Yevgena, a true gypsy, preferred. Seated with a cup of chamomile tea with bright bits of golden flowers still floating in it, Pamela sighed, feeling content as she had not in some time.

"You had a good summer in Maine?" Yevgena asked, breaking a corner off a wafer-thin almond biscuit and popping it in her mouth.

"Yes," Pamela said, "very good." She wondered how much Yevgena had guessed about their summer. She knew the woman had a very well-honed sixth sense, particularly when it came to matters concerning Jamie. Jamie, whom Pamela had not seen since Christmas. She had spoken with him on the phone one day and he'd been rather short with her. It was to be expected but it still stung. She had never been comfortable being on the outs with Jamie, but she knew this time was different.

"Do you ever stay in the house in the Marais?" she asked. She knew the house had been where Yevgena and Jamie's grandfather had once lived together.

Yevgena shook her head, her dark hair catching the light from the red lamp next to her and glowing like a crow's wing in the sunlight. "No, it is properly Jamie's house now. He always tells me to use it when I like but I have not wanted to be there since my James died. Besides, Jemmy is using the house right now."

"Jamie's in Paris? I thought he was in Vienna."

"He was, and now he's in Paris," Yevgena said, sipping her tea daintily.

"Oh," she said, uncertain why the news had disconcerted her, but it had. She felt a flush race up from her neckline through her face and was fully aware that Yevgena was noting her every expression. She coughed; she had a flower petal stuck in her throat.

"When is the last time you had an evening out, darlink girl?"

"I don't know," Pamela said honestly. "I don't go out any more; there isn't time for it."

"Well, tonight," Yevgena said decisively, "there is time and it is Paris, so you can hardly imagine you would stay in. I'm invited to a party, and I want for you to come with me."

Pamela raised an eyebrow. She had the sense there was more to this than a simple outing.

Yevgena spread her hands, rings winking in the light. "Darlink, that is a look you have learned from Jemmy, do not be using it on me. It is bad enough when he does it. I am only wanting you to have a little fun. Tonight, you wear a pretty dress and go to a nice party and maybe drink a little wine. Now does that sound so very terrible?"

"No," Pamela said, still suspicious, though of what she wasn't exactly certain. In truth, Yevgena's offer did have appeal. It had been a very long time since she had worn something pretty and went somewhere just for the fun of it. One could hardly, she thought, count cleaning Tomas' house and talking to the badger as an evening out in society.

"I don't have a party dress," she said. Yevgena looked her up and down, her eyes assessing in a way Pamela had only seen before in French dressmakers. She left the room and returned a few minutes later with her arms filled with folds of delicate silver-green material.

Pamela took it and shook it out. It was a beautiful dress, made of layered silk voile which flickered from a silver-grey to shimmering green as it caught and moved in the light of the late afternoon sun.

"Try it on," Yevgena said, with a rather determined light in her face which told Pamela she was going to a party whether she wanted to or not.

She came out of Yevgena's bedroom a few minutes later feeling wildly self-conscious. The dress was gorgeous but it also left her with a quantity of bare skin on display.

"You look fabulous, darlink." Yevgena stood back and surveyed her handiwork, and clapped her hands together with satisfaction. "Go look in the mirror; see if I don't know my business."

"It's a bit revealing," she said nervously. Her entire back was bare, down to the top of her buttocks.

"You're young, and you can carry it off." Yevgena said, tapping her lips thoughtfully with an index finger. "Perhaps we do need a wrap for you; I don't want you catching cold. First, let's deal with your hair. I think we will just pull it back, no? Your face does not require concealment after all."

Her hair was just long enough to slick back and fasten in a low knot at the nape of her neck. She put on her make up while Yevgena went to get dressed. She felt a quiver of excitement at the idea of going out amongst adults for an evening of conversation and music.

When Yevgena returned she had transformed into the exotic Russian Gypsy who was more than a little intimidating to Pamela, even after knowing her for many years. She wore a scarlet silk dress with an oriental collar and a black shawl that shimmered with sequins. The wrap she had brought for Pamela was a gorgeously filmy silk, of a green even paler than the dress Pamela wore. It was embroidered all over with tiny silver butterflies. Yevgena placed it around Pamela's shoulders; it was softer than swansdown and yet had a comforting weight to it. The ghost scent of perfume rose from its folds, wrapping her in notes of jasmine and hyacinth.

"I wore it to a wonderful party that was held at the Hotel Lambert. James brought it home for me from one of his yearly trips to Hong Kong. It's gorgeous, yes? And perfect for this dress."

"The Hotel Lambert?" Pamela asked, feeling her nerves come to full and vigorous life.

"Yes—James was friends with the Rothschilds—Guy and Marie Helene that is. Her parties were legendary. It was quite something to be invited. James knew everyone and everyone loved him, he was invited to every bloody social occasion in the city, I swear."

Which sounded rather a lot like the current James, Pamela thought, mouth dry. She did not feel up to the glitter and glamor of Paris' current aristocracy.

"Not to worry, darlink, the hosts are not of that sort," Yevgena said, having apparently read her mind. "And now for the jewelry—don't protest—this dress absolutely requires it."

A rope of rough cut aquamarines, bound with freshwater pearls and anchored by a glimmering moonstone was looped around her throat with teardrops of the same stones gracing her ears.

"It's beautiful, Yevgena, but I'm terrified I'll lose it."

Yevgena flapped a beringed hand at her. "I do not wear it anymore, darlink. Do not worry yourself."

A car arrived at seven to pick them up and Pamela settled back in the luxurious leather seat and took a deep breath to settle her nerves. "Is Jamie going to be at this party?" she asked.

Yevgena shrugged, a gesture that sent alarm bells to ringing in Pamela's head. "Maybe, I do not know. I am not always aware of the man's social calendar."

Pamela thought that probably wasn't entirely true but forbore to say anything else. When she chose to be, Yevgena was about as forthcoming as a sphinx.

Yevgena reached over and took her hand, giving it a reassuring squeeze.

"Just relax, darlink. Trust me, it will be a night to remember."

The chateau was set well back at the end of an avenue of lime trees, barebranched and black this time of year. The house itself glowed against the chill winter night, tall and built of white stone, which was luminescent in the moon-filled night. The windows were flame-lit, candles shimmering in each and every one. With her limited knowledge of Paris Pamela thought they were in the Hauts-de-Seine département, which was part of the greater Île-de-France region. Not that she would know her way back into the city, even with a map and a compass.

A winding marble staircase led to great front doors out of which spilled music and the sound of voices raised in laughter and talk. She resisted the urge to clutch at Yevgena's arm like a frightened child. Inside there was light and the scent of orange blossoms and the sound of water tumbling into water.

Yevgena touched her arm. "Darlink, I need to go powder my nose. I will meet you in the ballroom." And with that she was gone, leaving Pamela staring suspiciously after her.

She felt someone's regard, turned and saw Jamie, his bright hair a point of light against the dark paneling behind him. Unerringly, across the marbled expanse of the foyer, despite the milling crowd between them, he met her eyes. There was surprise in his face, and then just as quickly it was shuttered behind his polished courtesy. He came forward, through the throng of people and she fought with the desire to turn on her heel and run back down the wide marble staircase. Yevgena had tricked her, but to what end she could not fathom. It was too late to run, for Jamie was in front of her.

"Pamela?" He was not going to bother with the social niceties she saw, nettling slightly at the look on his face. It wasn't as if she had taken it upon herself to come here, uninvited.

"Jamie."

He raised one eyebrow at her, in what might have been her least favorite expression in his repertoire.

"I thought," she said tightly, "I was invited."

"You just happened to be in Paris?" He smiled, but it wasn't the sort of smile that took the sting from his words.

"Yes, I did, as a matter of fact. I had a meeting with Monsieur Bellerose of Bellerose Books and I had an interview with a magazine. So, if you must know, I was here for work reasons. Yevgena invited me to come here with her tonight."

"Ah, now I begin to understand. Where is Yevgena?"

"I don't know, she melted away the minute we came through the doors."

"Well, allow me to take your wrap," he said and removed it from her, handing it off to a man who seemingly apparated out of thin air, ready to serve. She felt suddenly awkward and exposed in the beautiful dress.

"You're exquisite," Jamie said, correctly reading the expression on her face. Then he offered her his arm. "Shall we?"

A server in a flawless black and white uniform arrived with a tray of wine and champagne. Jamie plucked a golden wine from the tray and handed it to her. She took a nervous gulp and the taste of cold apricots and white flowers flooded her tongue.

He took her through to a long formal drawing room with high frescoed ceilings and gilded plasterwork. Long and narrow Oriental rugs woven in pale blues and greens covered the marquetry floor and plush divans and chairs were placed here and there in the room so that one could sit if one so wished. A fire burned in the vast hearth, giving the room a cheery air.

"I have a few people with whom I need to speak," Jamie said. "Will you be all right on your own for a few moments?"

"Of course," she said, still flustered and feeling like a wallflower at a grand ball. She cursed Yevgena under her breath for leaving her alone. The glass of wine she was drinking had gone straight to her head and she found a chair to sit in so that she could catch her breath and observe the other guests.

Around her was a veritable polyglot of languages. She caught snippets of Arabic and Hebrew, Spanish and Italian, though of course the majority of people were speaking in either French or English. She spoke to a variety of them as they passed her chair and politely engaged in small talk. She realized there was an impeccable mix of guests—cabinet ministers, artists, musicians, religious figures, military leaders, philosophers, scientists and a particularly lovely Italian man named Pietro who was an amateur astronomer and said he had known Jamie since he was a schoolboy at Oxford. He sat down in the chair near her and began a conversation in French which thankfully she could follow quite well.

Dinner was served shortly thereafter. Set at round tables, the meal was a work of art in itself—Limoges china, Waterford crystal, snowy white linens and delicate sprays of freesia in narrow jade vases at each place setting. The food was perfect and there was a dizzying array of it—delicate soufflés to start and then a fish soup partnered with a sumptuous rosé, wild salmon and braised beef, poached turbot, coquilles Saint-Jacques, moules marinières, small savory asparagus tarts, artichokes in brown butter and the perfect wines to accompany each entrée. There were mint and rosewater sorbets between each course to rinse and prepare the palate. Pamela drank more wine than she ought to and ate less than was wise. She could feel the warm blush rise in her skin which wine always caused in her. She saw Jamie glance over at her more than once, concern written clearly on his face. Feeling defiant she drank more wine. She made small talk with the man seated next to her, though later she could not have said what they talked about. There was a woman sitting beside Jamie at his table. A woman who was—to apply the word Jamie had used on her earlier—exquisite. She was Chinese, with all the purity of bone and skin her race was famed for, but there was something of the Caucasian in her as well, despite the grace and flawless etiquette that were purely Oriental in their forms. She suddenly realized just who the woman was. Sallie O'Rourke—Jamie's lawyer in Hong Kong and the person who helped him with all legal matters in the Far East. Pamela had dealings with her while Jamie was in Russia and had enjoyed the woman's quick wit and formidable business acumen.

After dinner, the entire company moved to the ballroom. She retreated to the shadow of a potted palm and watched the party unfold around her like a paper chrysanthemum thrown into warm water. It was well organized, but in such a way to make everything seem perfectly natural and spontaneous. The ballroom was large with a floor of polished marble that glittered in the light of a string of chandeliers which were strategically spaced the length of the ceiling. The walls boasted gorgeous frescoes of ladies and gentlemen in scenes of bucolic splendor which spoke of work original to the chateau. She estimated it to be of the 18th century. Living with Casey had given her an education in dating buildings.

The wine flowed like a fountain in full spate, and there was whiskey—she could smell the heady smoke of Scotch and the velvet peat of the Irish malts. Candles, still sweet with the labor of bees, burned in sconces all around. It was light expressly for flattering skin and hair, and profiles that were no longer in the first flush of youth. There was music too, played softly, beautiful music designed to put people at ease, and also an ache in their hearts. She could hear uilleann pipes ribboning through the loftier instruments, wounding with its airs. People milled about, animated in conversation, or merely watching, as she was, the activity swirling around the room. Everything was beautifully coordinated, food and wine and spirits delivered faultlessly, the servers moving through the guests as if performing a dance. Guests were introduced, encouraged to mingle, and found themselves in small groups of like minds, or if inclined to debate, were moved along smoothly to the next group, where spirited opposition was the theme. It all, she realized, felt very familiar, and so it ought to. She had been at such gatherings before; she had hosted one or two herself. This party was Jamie's; it had his touch all over it. Why he was hosting it here she was less certain about.

He was not, however, hosting it alone. He was doing it in concert with Sallie O'Rourke. Between them, she and Jamie created an evening of wit and entertainment, of music and laughter and attention to each guest and also to one another. They rarely spoke and barely looked at each other, and yet Pamela sensed they were in accord on who might need to be gently extricated from one grouping and moved to another, who needed their glass refilled, and who most assuredly did not. In the few times they passed one another they would pause, chat briefly and Sallie would inevitably touch Jamie on his arm or shoulder as she leaned in to whisper in his ear. Each time she did it, Pamela felt a white-hot jet of jealousy shoot through her. It was ridiculous and while it was not the first time she had been jealous of a woman in Jamie's life, this time it felt different. This was a woman who fit Jamie perfectly, in looks, comportment, intelligence, ambition and wit.

The lovely Italian astronomer had rejoined her and he deftly talked to her of everything from the stars to his grandchildren and her own children. She appreciated his efforts to distract her but she found she was only half listening to his conversation as her eyes followed Jamie around the room.

"In Italy we have a saying—*Sei la luce dei miei occi*— it means, 'you are the light in my eyes.' I think if you look closely you will see that light in Jamie's eyes and perhaps also in your own. And now, lovely Pamela, I will take my leave of you. The hour is growing late and I am an old man. I am off to my bed and my books." He bent over and kissed her hand and gave her a small salute in parting. She sighed, envying him. Bed and a good book sounded perfectly lovely to her right now.

Jamie was bringing Sallie over. She had wanted to meet her for a long time and yet, tonight, she did not want to speak to her at all.

"Pamela, I'd like to introduce you to a very old friend of mine—Sallie O'Rourke. Sallie, this is Pamela Riordan, also a very old friend of mine."

"Pamela and I spoke on the phone many times during your Russian holiday," Sallie said.

"We did, indeed," Pamela said, extending her hand to the woman and smiling.

Instead, Sallie hugged her and Pamela felt both the delicacy of her bones and the force of her character in the simple embrace. Her scent was light and reminded Pamela of a teahouse she had once visited where they had washed the tables and the floors with a fragrant oolong each morning.

"I feel I know you already. If you are in Paris for a few days we should have tea together."

"I'd like that," Pamela said politely, quite certain that she would rather pull her own fingernails out with a pair of pliers. Under any other circumstances she thought she would like the woman a great deal, but tonight jealousy precluded any friendly warmth.

"Well, tell Jamie to call me if you'd like to have a visit. You'll forgive me but I need to check in with the kitchen staff. Jamie, can you attend to the finance minister? He's had too much to drink and has been making passes at the interior minister's wife."

"Of course," Jamie said. He turned then to Pamela taking in the flush in her skin and correctly interpreting it. He treated her to a rather stern glare. "You stay put, I'll be back in a few minutes."

She watched as Sallie walked away, one long elegant leg flashing out of the slit in her dress. Men turned as she passed, all of them looking rather like sheep with their tongues hanging out. 'That, Pamela, is completely uncharitable,' she said sternly to herself. She knew her every thought right now was filtered through the green-eyed monster of envy.

She wasn't a fool, she didn't think the man was celibate. She had thought, naïvely it now appeared, that since their night in Maine, he would not have been with another woman. She felt dreadfully unsophisticated, for she understood there was a separate world in which Jamie lived, and it was not the one where he belonged to her. It was one in which she did not truly know the man who moved with such ease through a throng of politicians and poets and world-class raconteurs. She had long found this side of him intimidating.

She situated herself in the shadow of a potted palm once again and watched, and took another flute of wine each time the server offered her one. Good lad that he was, he came by often.

The palm, despite its largesse, couldn't protect her from the more predatory males and one in particular became intent on pressing his case—which seemed to consist of whisking her off to St. Tropez this very night to spend two weeks of carnal delight on his yacht, an experience, he assured her, that was not to be missed. He was, he claimed, a prince of a minor Arab principality.

It might be true. His clothes were most definitely made on Savile Row and he had a gloss about him that only came with great wealth. He ran a finger down her cheek. "Such skin, like an orchid, but flushed so prettily. I wonder do you blush all over when your blood is hot?"

"Yes, I do," she said tartly. "As for your kind offer I will have to say no. I'm flattered, but I have to get home to my children tomorrow."

"Oh, children? How many do you have?"

"Six," she replied, straight-faced, "all of them girls."

"My apologies," he said, "I did not realize you were a mother." He then beat a hasty retreat to the opposite side of the room.

A woman with an immaculate blonde chignon who rather reminded her of an older Catherine Deneuve walked over to her. "That was an Arab prince you just turned down. He really does have a yacht anchored off St. Tropez. They say he is very good to the women he woos. They never leave the yacht empty-handed—jewelry, by the bagful I've heard, and money enough sometimes to buy a very nice apartment in the city of your choice. He looked very taken with you; he might have kept you in comfort and luxury for several months."

"I have children at home. I somehow doubt he'd want them on his yacht for two hours, much less two weeks."

"Not, I am thinking, six girls though."

She laughed. "No just two—a boy and a girl. Probably still enough to frighten him."

"You turned him away and yet you do not seem offended by his attentions."

"No," Pamela said. "He seemed a little lonely. I can understand that."

"Oh, lovely girl, men are always lonely. They believe a face like yours can still that ache in their heart, and also," she laughed, "other parts. Truthfully I think most of them want some sort of cross between their mother and a sex goddess."

"And what about lonely women?" Pamela asked, feeling the buzzy hum of the wine throughout her body. She really ought to have stopped at least three glasses ago and yet, when the obliging boy came by, she plucked another glass off the tray.

"We women are born lonely and meant to stay so. It is how the world works. Men seek their solace in us, and we sometimes find it for a fleeting time in the children they give us. Then once the children are grown and gone, we are lonely again. It is best to come to terms with that. It is just how life is."

"It doesn't seem fair," Pamela said, "that they should find solace in us and we none in them." This was patently not true in her own life and had she not been in the grip of jealousy she would not have said it. Both Jamie and Casey had offered her solace in a variety of ways, but she wasn't inclined to have a just and fair memory at present.

The woman laughed again and toying with the triple strand of black pearls at her neck, she said, "You make them pay for the solace they find, sweet girl, that way when you are old and the men are gone, you will still have the comforts of life."

Jamie returned to her side in time to hear the woman's last statement.

"Excuse us," he said, the very picture of the cordial host and yet she could feel the tension in the hand that held her elbow as he led her away.

"Of course," the woman said, and inclined her head a little, an amused smile playing about her mouth.

"Who was she?" Pamela asked, looking back over her shoulder at the extremely soignée woman who was watching them go.

"Paris' most famous madam, therefore the world's most famous madam," Jamie said, still hustling her unceremoniously from the room. "If you'd stayed another minute she would have recruited you."

"Really? You think she would have recruited me? Hmm. That's rather flattering."

Jamie sighed and said, "Women."

"Where are we going?" she asked, for they had left the ballroom and were in a long and quiet corridor with several closed doors lining its gleaming marquetry length.

"Out of there, away from lechery and debauchery."

"Is that the couple in the corner who looked like they could be twins?"

Jamie gave her a rather stern glance. "Are you drunk, Pamela?"

"A little," she admitted. "The wine seemed awfully strong. Mind you, I could run for the head of the Temperance League these days and get voted in on abstemiousness alone."

"You *are* drunk," he said. "You always use big words when you're tipsy. And while I'm running down your laundry list of sins here, I might add that dress is positively indecent."

"Is it? I thought it was rather lovely," she said, attempting to give him a flirtatious look but failing due to rather numb eyebrows.

He laughed. "It is lovely, but sweetheart, I can see the dimples at the top of your arse."

"Can you really? Admittedly it feels a bit airy."

"Airy, is it?"

"Jamie are you laughing at me?"

"Maybe a little. You're a very charming drunk."

"Am I? Casey always said I lost all inhibition," she hiccoughed, "and that he'd keep me in drink permanently were it left to him." She flushed, realizing what she had just said. "Sorry, apparently I am also indiscreet when in my cups."

"No apology necessary. You're lovely when you're indiscreet."

"Jamie, I believe I *am* drunk."

"The possibility had occurred to me, Pamela," he said. He opened one of the many doors then and guided her into a softly-lit room. It was a small space, intimate, a gentleman's study or a library. The walls were painted a deep burgundy and gold leaf molding stood out bright and rich against the background of reds and deep greens and dark polished wood. There were candles burning on the window ledges as well as the low light of a banker's lamp on the large desk which sat beneath the shelves that housed rows and rows of gilt-edged books.

Jamie stood beside the large marble hearth, away and apart from her. She wondered if she was about to receive a lecture.

"So this is *your* party?" she asked.

"Yes," he said easily. "Please sit down, Pamela. You seem a little unsteady."

"I'm fine standing," she said, feeling a twinge of annoyance.

Jamie raised one gull-winged brow at her. "Oh, I see, it's to be that sort of conversation, is it?"

"I don't know, do I? You're the one who dragged me in here."

"Because, as usual, you managed to attract some of the least savory people in the room. The biggest playboy in Europe and a woman who runs the most successful brothel in the world."

"I apologize for my lack of social élan," she said, voice as haughty as she could summon up on a raft of wine.

"There is no social situation to which you are not equal, Pamela, and you know it. So why don't you say what you really want to say?" His voice was chilly, but she noted how he put one hand to the mantelpiece as though to steady himself.

"What is tonight's purpose?" she asked, afraid she knew the answer.

He shook his head. "I had hoped not to talk to you about this, until I was certain, but as you've asked, here it is—I am considering making a life here in Paris, at least part of the time. I am merely making connections and testing the waters."

It was the answer she had not wanted to hear. "Oh," she said, and sat down, clutching her elbows tightly to her stomach. It felt like she'd been hit, hard and without warning. "How part time, exactly?"

"Six to eight months of the year. Possibly more when Kolya is of an age to attend school."

"When were you going to tell me? Or were you?"

He looked down, his hand tightening around the glass he had carried out of the ballroom. "I did not expect you tonight, Pamela, and am not quite ready to have this conversation."

"Is she part of it—Sallie?" She felt as if all the blood in her body had flowed out through the bottoms of her feet.

"And if she is?"

"Aren't you a little busy already? What with a wife in Russia and a—"

"And a what, Pamela? Please finish your sentence."

"And a nothing in Ireland," she finished, half-sick with misery and shock.

"That's by your choice. For the record, you could never be 'nothing' to me. I'm insulted that you would even say it."

"I'm sorry, I'm just jealous and I know how ridiculous that is."

"No, not ridiculous at all. I'm jealous as well, only I'm jealous of—" he halted, but she knew what it was he had been about to say.

"It's all right, Jamie, you can say it. You're jealous of a ghost."

The light of the fire lay on his hair and lashes and touched flame to the emerald on his left hand. The hand on the mantelpiece was white with pressure.

"Pamela, what is it you want to say? Spit it out and save your spleen as you once so succinctly recommended to me."

"I just…I…well it's clear that you and Sallie—who is lovely and no fault to her, it's clear that you and she…" she trailed off, uncertain if she should continue. But it was far too late for caution.

"Do you really think, Pamela," he said, and the amusement had been wiped from his voice entirely, "that after Maine, I could just move on as though nothing had changed?" His eyes, those beautiful light-spilling eyes had gone dark.

"I don't know, could you?"

"Could you?" he responded.

"I asked first," she said aware that she was rapidly descending into adolescent retorts.

"Pamela, I think perhaps it would be best if we stopped this conversation here and now. It can only do damage to us both if we continue."

He turned, his profile stark against the gilt spines of the books on the shelves behind him. He smiled at her, but it was a pained expression. She had gone too far to stop, and so had he.

"You know full well I haven't so much as touched another man, Jamie."

"Not even Noah Murray?" he asked, a hectic light suddenly flaring bright in his eyes.

"Noah? What on earth would make you ask that?"

"It's my understanding," he said, with a deadly calm that did not bode well for the direction of this conversation, "that he gave you a rather large sum of money. He doesn't strike me as the sort of man to do something of that nature without extracting his pound of flesh."

"Damn Patrick! You and he are like a couple of gossiping old pensioners. Can I even sneeze without him telling you?"

"What the man does tell me, he tells me out of concern for your reckless disregard for your own well-being. Is it true, did you take money from him?"

"No—well, yes, in a way I suppose. He gave me a check long ago, to cover my mortgage should I need it."

"If you needed money, you should have come to me."

"I didn't use it," she said, knowing it sounded feeble.

"But you accepted it. What else has he given you? And what has he asked for in return?"

"What are you implying, Jamie?"

"Implying," he said heatedly, "I'm not implying, I'm flat out asking."

"I'm fully aware that you don't like my association with him."

"Not like it?" he laughed, "I fucking hate it."

"Oh," she said stiffly, "I don't see why—"

"You don't see why?" he said furiously. "This is why." He crossed the room in three strides and then took her by her arms and pulled her up on her feet and kissed her hard and thoroughly—thoroughly enough that her knees turned to water and her head was spinning by the time he stopped and let her go.

"Does that explain it to you well enough?" He asked, green eyes still simmering with anger.

"Ah, yes, I think so," she said, still lightheaded from his explanation. "I'd best sit down before I need smelling salts." She was only half-joking, for he had taken her by surprise and the kiss had both shocked and aroused her. "For the record, I've never slept with him nor did he ask me to." She thought it best to refrain from mentioning *she* had offered to sleep with Noah, in return for him killing a man. "Can you say the same?"

"I have most definitely not slept with Noah Murray," he said, and laughed.

"It's not funny, Jamie."

He put one long-fingered hand back on the mantelpiece. "No, I don't suppose it is. I apologize."

"Well?"

A candle fluttered, dark and then light, as though a moth had touched it and burning, flown away. It was a moment before he replied. He looked at her with faint reproach.

"No. And just so you know and won't wonder, I have never slept with her. We have long been friends and knew that sex would damage the relationship, and so we chose the wiser course."

"While we," she said, "did not. Do you regret it—that night in Maine?" She felt like the words might choke her.

"Why would you think that, Pamela?"

"Vanya told me what happened that night at your house, after I left."

"That was indiscreet of him," Jamie said, face suddenly pale and his pulse visible in the hollow of his throat. "I have Patrick, and you, it appears, have Vanya. He's a charming boy but imprudent with his tongue."

"He cares about you, a great deal, what hurts you also hurts him."

"I had one of my headaches. I had taken something for it. It was unfortunate that he found me when he did. I said more than I should have, and that is what hurt him."

"Is it, Jamie?"

He looked at her, eyes dark and face pale in the dim light, with a streak of fine color on either cheekbone.

"You hold the knife, Pamela, it would perhaps be only kind if you wielded it less often."

She went toward him, aware that she was still trembling. She opened her hands as she came near to him. "There is no knife, there is nothing here but a woman and a friend."

"Friend, you say, and yet you claim to wield no blade."

"Jamie, I—" she choked on the words, afraid that if she began crying she wouldn't be able to stop. She reached out to touch him, but he put out one of his hands and caught hers before she could.

"I'm only a man, Pamela. I love you and I've long desired you, you know that well enough, but since that night in Maine…" He shook his head, the light from the candles tremoring on his hair, and echoing over and over in the windows of the room. "Don't come near, not right now."

"Do you think it's any different for me? I miss you even when you're in the same room."

"Oh God, woman, you and that brutal honesty."

She pulled his hand aside and stepped inside his defenses, insufficient as they were this night.

"Jamie, I love you, I have from the first day I saw you all those years ago. It has been a love of many facets, and it still is. I made vows to Casey though, and I believed I would keep those vows for the rest of my life. Somehow that night in Maine with you only felt inevitable, and not like I had broken a promise. But if you regret it, if it has caused you pain, then I—"

He stopped her by the simple expedient of taking her face in his hands and kissing her. When at last he stopped, he gave his answer. "There is no room within me for regret, not with you."

And then, his breath warm against her mouth, "Come home with me."

Long ago, another woman, a stranger to her now, had been in this house. It was here that she had learned the story, long hidden, of Jamie's twin sister, Adele. Here that she had come to understand and know him better and here that she had found the allies she needed to save his companies. She had also been newly pregnant at the time, so newly she hadn't even yet realized it. She had lived in this house for a week, worried sick about the man who now walked up beside her, and took her hand in his.

She waited while Jamie got out the keys, looking up at the house as it sat in the white light of the moon, sentineled by ghost-lit lime trees, their branches snow and shadow. The garden walls were steeped in the pale light as well, blotted with thick swatches of ivy. From the dormered window of one of the upstairs bedrooms, a single light shone. Jamie unlocked the door and then stepped aside for her to walk through. She thought for a moment she heard someone whisper behind her, just a sound, which might have been her name, but was surely only the wind murmuring through the ivy.

Inside, the scents of sandalwood and roses hung upon the air. Moonlight traced the gilt edges of an old chair and limned the lines of poetry engraved over the mantelpiece, which she remembered from her last visit.

> *And the sunlight clasps the earth,*
> *And the moonbeams kiss the sea:*
> *What is all this sweet work worth*
> *If thou kiss not me?*

Shelley, of course. His words were inevitable here.

The hush of emptiness was around them. She looked up at Jamie, and he said, "She's away for a week, visiting her sister in Brittany. It is only us." He was referring to Madame Felicie who had once been his sister's nurse and now looked after this house for him.

Her hand still in his, she followed him through the kitchen and up the stairs of the old and beautiful house which had once held other lovers, long ago. At the bend of the stairs he kissed her, the moonlight falling through the long casement windows above them, fretting through the strands of his hair. It was a kiss which held a question at its core, and she responded with an answer made of many years and long desire stirred to wakefulness beside a dreaming sea.

The bedroom looked out over the garden and the moon dipped in, wicking through the curtains, shimmering them to silver. Jamie took the wrap from her shoulders and laid it over a chair. He turned back and held out his hand. She took it and stepped into his arms.

He leaned his forehead against hers, and she could feel the pulse of his blood, swift and warm, her own speeding up in response. She knew this man and understood his constraints all too well.

"I—" he began, because it seemed, once a Jesuit acolyte, always a Jesuit acolyte. She put her hand up to his lips and said, "Tell the Father General in your head to close his eyes and look away, because he really shouldn't see what's about to happen."

He laughed and she reached up to kiss him. And still she felt the reserve in him, the hands that held her lightly, the breath that stuttered and paused. It was for her to unleash what held him in check.

"Jamie." Her voice shook, but it wasn't from nerves. "I need you."

On that his hands closed, the hesitancy gone from him. The dress drifted down her body, her skin glowing as softly as pearls in the dim light. She shivered as he smoothed his hands along the glow. Her hair had tumbled from its pins and he pulled it aside to kiss her neck there in the hollow of her shoulder. She was trembling and so was he, the fire between them arcing back and forth, enveloping them, telling her that this time would not be like the last, this time would hurt more and damage them both. And yet, she did not want to stop, she only wanted this night to last as long as it might. In a moment she was completely bare to his hands, and she felt as if fire coursed through every cell in her body.

A cask of moonlight had been poured, silver and thick, across the bed. It was light enough that she could see into his eyes, and far beyond that as well, it seemed. Yes, this would hurt more, but she no longer cared. It was clear he did not either. He lay her down across the bed, covering her with his body, even as she arched toward him in need. And then it was as she remembered and yet not at all the same. It was both cascade and deluge all at once, as she opened to him, welcoming the plunder, the bruising blood tide that rushed to every last cell, the greed that grasped and demanded and knew nothing other than its own want.

Yes, this was not like Maine, for that love had been healing, had been both tender and wild in its consummation, had given and taken equally. But *this* was not that love; this held within it something darker, an emotion akin to pain and a passion so bruising that she knew neither of them would recover from it, and yet nor could they walk away from this dark, intoxicating fire, much as it might have been wise to.

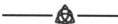

After, Jamie left the bed to light a fire in the bedroom hearth. She sat up in the welter of sheets and blankets to watch him as he moved about the room. Even now his beauty could stop her breath in her throat and make her ache. He looked like a different man than he had a few hours ago, like he had been newly made and forged fresh from some fine metal. He was still her Jamie though, still the man who had helped her through every painful day since she had lost Casey.

She felt a wave of guilt that she should think of Casey here and now, and with it came confusion whether the guilt was for what they had just done, or guilt that she should think of another man while in Jamie's bed. Casey would always be a part of everything for her, though. She supposed this particular situation was no different because Casey was the only man she had ever had this sort of intimacy with.

She realized Jamie was watching her and she looked away from his gaze, feeling suddenly too exposed and too naked, both in the literal and the figurative senses of the word. Jamie came back to the bed and got in beside her. He took her hand and gave it a gentle squeeze. She looked up at him.

"I wouldn't want you to feel like you had broken faith with Casey," he said. Never a coward, he looked her in the eyes as he said it.

"I don't," she said, softly. It was true, she didn't feel she had cheated on Casey. He had been a man of some understanding and he had not expected her to live like a nun should something happen to him; he had told her as much long ago.

"If you did feel that way, I would understand," he said. "I know in your heart, he is your husband."

"Jamie, I—"

He shook his head, forestalling her words. "I would be a fool to think otherwise, Pamela."

"It has been," she said quietly, "more than two years. I'm not a fool, if he was able to come home he would have. That he has not, tells me he never could."

"It is only natural that you would think of him. He is the love of your life. It would not be in your nature to forget just how that feels."

"He is the love of my life," she said, "but you are my soul, Jamie."

As he sometimes did with her, he replied in poetry, because he knew she understood the further meaning of the lines he spoke.

"This isle and house are mine, and I have vow'd
Thee to be lady of the solitude.
And I have fitted up some chambers there
Looking towards the golden Eastern air
And level with the living winds, which flow
Like waves above the living waves below."

Shelley's soul within a soul, one spirit, divided between two bodies.

The burnished glow of the fire moved over Jamie, casting shadow and light in equal measure. Her fingers were twined through his, as if they had always rested there. For this moment, she felt entirely at peace. The fire played with the aureate beauty of his hair, strands of platinum and amber glittering amongst the disheveled gold. She traced her hand over the tattoos that spanned his chest and ran down his arm. He had never told her the significance of each one, so she did not know the story behind the tiny field of skulls, the violets that grew delicate upon each prick of barbed wire—though she thought perhaps she understood those a little—and the wolf's head that gazed out at her from the inside of a shattered star. His right hand rested on the curve of her hip, softly possessive. He spoke when her hand paused, feeling the question though she did not voice it out loud.

"The wolves are to remind me of what an unpredictable animal is man. The lily is you," he said quietly.

"What?"

"I told Gregor about you while he was tattooing me. He understood you were an integral part of my story, so he put you there on my chest, permanently."

"He sounds like he was a complicated friend."

Jamie laughed wryly. "You could say that."

She touched him carefully, just there where the lily was etched over his heart, and heard his breath catch in his throat.

"And what did you tell him about me?"

"The truth."

"And that is?"

He put one finger to her chin, a gentle insistence there forcing her to look up and meet his eyes.

"I told him that you are my dearest friend, and that I loved you, as a man loves a woman, but that you belonged to another man and I had made peace with that."

"Had you?" she asked, sad that she had ever caused this man a moment's heartache.

Jamie smiled at her. "I thought I had at the time, or as much as I was ever going to be able to put my feelings for you aside."

"I'm sorry, Jamie," she said.

He brushed the pad of one thumb over her lips to halt her words.

"I'm not, sweetheart."

She put the tip of a finger to one of the tiny violets. "You can talk about her, it's all right you know," she said. "I would rather you told me about her than to have you feel you couldn't."

Jamie shook his head. "I would rather not talk about her just now, Pamela."

"Jamie?"

"Mmhmm?"

"You moving here to Paris, is…is it because of me? Do you need to be away from me?" The idea of him living so far away and of not seeing him anymore made her feel physically ill.

He was silent for a moment. "In part, yes, things have been terribly strained between us, sweetheart. It's become difficult for the both of us and I don't want things to get any more confusing for the children."

"And you think leaving won't confuse them? They love you, Jamie."

"I love them too, Pamela, but as time goes on, they are going to want a real family life."

"You think you can never have that with us?" she asked.

"I would love nothing more than that, you know that. I also know that right now you don't have it to give."

She put her head down, shutting her eyes tightly, trying to dam the flood.

"Hey," he pulled her to him and held her tightly.

"I can't bear the thought of you being gone. I can't imagine my life without you in it. And yet," she tried to take a breath, her chest tight with anguish, "if you need to go, if you think living here would make you happier, then I understand."

"Do you?" he asked.

"Jamie, your happiness matters to me more than my own. So yes, if you would be happier here, then I would understand it and I would wish you well."

"Oh, Pamela," he shook his head. "You mean it, don't you?"

"Of course I do." She reached up and kissed him, and he replied with the silent assurance of his body and she, made helpless by this thing that rose up between them when they touched, responded in kind. When they at last lay quiet again the fire had burned down to coals. Beyond the windows the light had turned ashy, morning would soon be on its way.

"Will you tell me a story, Jamie? One more from *The Faceless Tarot.*" She wanted to simply drift to sleep in his arms with his voice soft in her ears.

"I think I might have one or two left in my storytelling bag," he said, smiling down at her. "Aren't you tired of these tales yet?"

"No, never," she said.

From the threads of the night he created something which was solely for the two of them. Something fleeting and gossamer and yet anchored in their history together. From the lost girl he'd found on a shore so long ago, to the lost man she had saved that summer, to the two adults who had journeyed together and apart to arrive here on this night.

"You need to sleep," he said at last, words soft as smoke in the deep of the night. "I think that's enough of the story for now."

"I don't want it to end," she said quietly, "it's a tale that should just run on forever."

He stroked the line of her back, his eyes meeting hers. "Then I will keep telling it to you, as long as you need."

"I love you."

He touched the side of her face, fingers as soft as a trace of falling snow. "I love you too."

Chapter Sixty-nine

And Still, And Always

PAMELA AWOKE TO FIND Jamie gone, though in his place on the pillow next to her was a note, which informed her that he would return soon. Sitting neatly by the closet was the suitcase she had left in her hotel room the day before. She got up and had a bath and, not yet able to decide what to wear for the day, she wrapped Jamie's robe around her still-warm, damp skin and went downstairs to see what there was to eat. The answer turned out to be one egg, a wedge of cheese that had seen less moldy days and a glass bottle of milk. Clearly Jamie had not been eating in while he was here.

In lieu of food she wandered around the bottom floor of the house. She had fallen in love with it the first time she'd visited, for it was a house of great charm as well as beauty. Every piece of furniture—from the Joubert writing table to the reading chair that looked like it had come from a very down-at-the-heels flea market; to the pottery and china and old silverware and crystal; to the damask curtains which covered the casement windows and the beds hung with curtains of pale brocades in lavender and celadon and the sheets fumed with violet or rose water; to the potbellied Chinese jars in the kitchen and the bright Provençal pottery in its brilliant hues of orange and yellow and cobalt—had been chosen with care and love.

In the study she opened a window and leaned out into the pale morning light. A few snowflakes were drifting down, laying a light blanket over the ivy and stone walls and frosting the dark boughs of the lime trees. On the desk there was a sheaf of papers and on the top of the pile there was one blotched with ink and filled with Jamie's distinctive, yet fine, scrawl. Left-handed, Jamie always had smears of ink on his papers when he wrote swiftly. The paper held a poem which had clearly been dashed off, and was like so many of his musings and thoughts—a strand of webbed beauty, spun and discarded.

In the autumn, he says
He will go back to Rome
To London and Amsterdam
The winter cities
He will not outlast
The gardenias in Venice.

He came to write Venice,
But found he was too grandly preceded.
So instead followed ghosts
In the thick amber twilights of July.

She heard the door open then and ran out to meet him, feeling vaguely guilty about reading his poem. There was snow in his hair, melting into bright droplets which glimmered before evaporating in the warm air of the kitchen. He had an armful of paper-white narcissi, as delicate and translucent as the snowflakes in his hair.

"Beautiful and rare, like you," he said and leaned down to kiss her as he handed her the flowers. The delicate scent wafted up and the snow-flakes turned to dew on the fragile petals. She stuck her face in them, her throat suddenly tight and tears gathering in her eyes. Jamie kissed her fore-head and then set his other parcels on the table.

"And food, too," she said, sniffing the air.

There was a bag with sugar-dusted croissants and some pears and cheese, the latter of which she put in the fridge. She poured him a cup of coffee and then put the croissants out on two plates, along with butter and jam, sliced pears and cream for the coffee, while he put the flowers in a beautiful old jade vase with almond flowers painted on it.

"I had a meeting," he said and smiled. She reached across and re-moved a bit of sugar from the corner of his lips and he caught her hand and kissed the palm of it.

"I didn't ask," she said and laughed, because of course she had been thinking it.

"No, but I could see you wondering."

"Jamie, if you have business you have to attend to, I'll be fine on my own. I know you didn't expect me, after all."

"While unexpected, it doesn't follow that your arrival is in any way unwelcome. I have already cleared my schedule for the day. I intend to spend it with you in this loveliest of cities, right after I make love to you and allow you to get dressed."

An hour later when he'd made good on his first promise and was lying back on the bed watching her dress, he said, "Wear something warm, sweetheart, it's chilly out there. However, I promise you there is no city as beautiful as Paris in the snow."

It was true. What followed would always remain for her a day of perfect enchantment. It was a day—literally—of wine and roses. Small sugared roses which they ate while walking the cobbled streets of Montmartre and the wine they had with lunch in a small café on the Rue Poulbot. Once a village of windmills and vineyards, Montmartre had become the mecca of artists, both those established and those struggling to become so. The ghosts of the Belle Époque still lingered in the narrow streets and between the old buildings—Renoir, Degas, Moreau, Van Gogh, Toulouse-Lautrec and all the other artists and writers and dancers and the echo of the cabarets, theaters, music halls and circuses.

Late in the afternoon, as they stood looking down over the city from the steps of Sacre Coeur, she became aware of a small tingly spot in the middle of her back.

"Jamie," she reached up so that it looked like she was kissing the side of his face, "is someone following us?"

"Yes, it's the short man with the terrible hat, the other one with the neckerchief who looks like a pirate and the one with the scar," he said casually and then did kiss her as though he hadn't a care or thought in the world beyond the two of them, wandering idly through the steadily thickening snow. He smelled of beeswax and so did she; they had both lit candles in the cathedral.

"What do you think they want?" she asked, her face pressed to his. To outward appearances they were no more than besotted lovers, a role that wasn't a stretch by any means.

"Can you run in those ridiculous boots you're wearing?" Jamie asked, looking like he was whispering something extremely suggestive in her ear. An old woman in a black shawl passed by and gave them a disapproving look.

She looked down at said boots with some measure of doubt, they had rather high and delicate heels and had been bought for their aesthetic value and clearly, she thought wincing a little, not for their comfort. "Yes, I can run," she said, stoutly.

They picked their way down the stairs from the cathedral. At the bottom, Jamie looked at her, smiled and said, "Run!"

Like gulls on the wing they flew down the street, running so fast it seemed like it was impossible to fall. It was the way she remembered feeling as a little girl flying down a hill, out of control and perfectly free. Near the bottom of the street Jamie darted to one side, ducking into a doorway. He emerged holding a bucket.

"Up these stairs," he said and caught her by the arm, pulling her up one of the narrow staircases which served as the alleys of Montmartre.

"What is that? It reeks."

"Fish guts," he said and then threw the contents of the bucket onto the stairway below them.

The first man made it up ten stairs before he slipped and went careening backwards, his arms wind-milling madly. "Man with the funny hat," she said.

"One down and two to go," Jamie replied and then they took flight again. This time across a small courtyard, thick with trees and a tiny bench with an angel's head gathering snow. It became a blur after that of feint and counter-feint and running and ducking into doorways, and dashing through a café and out the back through a kitchen thick with steam and the scent of frying tripe and garlic, with startled chefs glaring at them and waving spoons and ladles and knives in indignation. Then under an archway and into a narrow alley and up stairs and down stairs, until she had no idea if they were merely running in circles. Her feet were soaked, her lungs hurt from running and she felt wildly, joyously alive. At last they spilled into a courtyard which had a high fence on three sides and the only open space was at their backs. They could hear the footfalls of the men already. They were trapped and Pamela wasn't sure what they were going to do, barring sprouting wings and taking actual flight. Jamie glanced back and then withdrew a bottle from his coat pocket, uncorked it and flung the contents across the snowless cobbles under the entry. And then he seized her by the hand and ran for the corner of the courtyard which was most thickly dressed in shadows.

Jamie had the reflexes and strength of an acrobat. He pulled himself up on the fence in a series of moves too quick for her panicked eyes to take in. The men were in the courtyard now.

"Pamela," he whispered urgently, "take my hand. I'm going to pull you up."

How he was balanced there she did not know. The top of the fence was no more than half an inch wide and of rounded iron. If he fell, there were iron spikes dotting the top of it which would quite neatly impale him. Or her, she thought grasping his hand and scrabbling up the fence. He was right, her boots *were* ridiculous. But she was upright on the fence, balanced like the dancer she had so long ago been. They inched along the fence and she saw his goal. There was a stone balustrade just beyond the fence, which in turn was capped with a massive stone gryphon and the gryphon in turn sat just below the roofline of a large house. It was going to be a stretch—literally—to cross the divide between the fence and the balustrade. She looked down and realized the fence was on the side of one of the butte's steep drops. If they fell—no, she mustn't think about that or she would lose her footing to an attack of nerves. Jamie moved like quicksilver ahead of her, in and out of the spikes, keeping his balance as though he was a child on the broad level of a stone wall. His hand still gripped hers, though, and she put her faith in his ability to keep them from a rather bloody fall or a gory impalement.

They reached the corner of the fence and Jamie let go of her hand. He stepped forward and then jumped. If he missed on this first try, there wouldn't be another. He jumped and grasped the gryphon's beak and swung himself up and over so that he sat astride it. "Come on, jump!"

It was a command and she obeyed, because there was no other choice and because she trusted him to catch her. He would have to catch her or she would tumble to her death down the long drop or be caught by the men, both of whom were in the courtyard now, one attempting to scrabble up onto the fence. She jumped and for a split second she thought she'd miscalculated and was going to pay for the mistake with her life. But he grasped her hard just above both elbows and pulled her up so that she caught a startling glance of beak and fierce eye and then she was up and over the gryphon's back. She pressed a hand to her chest trying to catch her breath. There wasn't time, though, for Jamie was beckoning to her now from the roof of the house. She caught at his hand once more, and rose, part of the air for a fleeting second and then was there beside him and the roof was blessedly beneath their feet. They scrambled up to the peak where there was a dormer window. Jamie pulled out a pocket knife and slid it between the frame and the window. It took a fair bit of jiggling but he finally got the hasp to give and the window swung open.

Inside it was so dark that it was like stepping into a black velvet bag and having the top cinched shut over their heads. They stood for a moment, catching their breath and letting the darkness settle around them. Far off there was the sound of music, something beautiful and light. They walked toward that sound. They were in an attic, she thought, where old furniture had been stored, for as her eyes adjusted to the dark, she caught the stray gleam of a brass headboard and felt the looming bulk of an armoire. They found a door after some groping and stepped out onto a landing above a steep set of stairs. Far below bright lights were shining and there was the savory smell of cheese and meat and fish. Her stomach rumbled loudly and she pressed a hand to it, willing it to stop.

"I promise to feed you soon," Jamie said and kissed her before leading the way down a winding set of stairs. They stopped on the second floor which was hushed, though the noise from downstairs was getting louder. It was much warmer on this floor, the heat having risen by degrees as they made their descent. They located an elegant powder room, tiled in palest green and well stocked with soap and combs and towels. Pamela looked in the oval mirror over the sink and gasped.

"Jamie, I can't go downstairs like this."

He plucked an oak gall from her hair and rubbed a smut of soot off her cheek. "Just tidy your hair a bit and it will be fine."

"Typical man," she said.

Someone tapped on the door just then and Pamela felt panic shoot through her.

"C'est occupé," Jamie said shortly and the person moved away.

She pushed her hair back behind her ears. "Here," Jamie said, rummaging in a basket beside the sink, "here's a clip."

He handed the clip to her, it was a beautiful silver butterfly set with amethyst and tourmaline stones. She thought they were paste, but wasn't entirely certain they weren't real.

"I can't use this, it's an antique."

"We'll mail it back to her."

She did her best to scrape her hair back but the curls were madly knotted and refused to lie flat against her head. She put the clip in and hoped it would hold. Otherwise she was going to look like an inmate freshly escaped from the asylum. She sighed. Jamie had quickly run a comb through the bright strands of his hair and straightened his shirt and was ready to go.

"It's hopeless. If I had known you were taking me to a party, I would have packed an evening gown in my pocket. My stockings are an utter ruin."

He gave her an assessing eye and then tugged down her sweater so that her shoulders were partially bare. "There, no one will notice your stockings now."

"You can tell Yevgena had a hand in the raising of you," she said tartly. She followed him down the stairs. The bottom floor was brightly lit and the sound of laughter and chat and music grew louder as they descended. It was a beautiful house and paintings lined the walls of the stairway with discreet and muted spotlights beneath each one.

At the bottom of the stairs Jamie offered her his arm with a flourish. "My lady, our party awaits."

A few heads turned as they entered the main room where the party was being held.

"Champagne?" Jamie lifted two glasses from a passing tray and gave one to her.

"Yes please," she said. He clinked his glass against hers and then they drank, the geysering fizz of the champagne on her tongue mirroring that in her blood. They were in imminent danger, there were still two men chasing them, and all they had for their defense were Jamie's wits and his rapid-fire daring. He moved through the room as though they were invited guests and she held onto his arm moving with him. He chatted with a couple of people on the way through, his French flawless and his self-assurance such that no one dared to suggest they didn't belong here, though they did draw a few odd looks. They were, despite their ministrations in the upstairs bath, both disheveled, bruised in spots and somewhat grubby.

Jamie grabbed a handful of food from a passing tray and split it between the two of them.

"I did promise I'd feed you," he said, popping a crab puff in his mouth and swallowing it down with the last sip of his champagne. She ate her food—two crab puffs and three small rolls with spiced sausage in the center that were divine—as they continued to wend their way through the company.

A woman with perfectly-coiffed white hair and wearing a simple blue dress, which Pamela knew meant it was terrifically expensive, turned toward them, surreptitiously sniffing the air and wrinkling her nose. She then looked down at Pamela's boots, which were wet and not nearly as pretty as they had been this morning and made a small horrified sound of Gallic disapproval, which was, Pamela thought feeling a tad shriveled, like no other disapproval in the world.

"There's a distinct whiff of sardine on us," Pamela said, stifling her laughter though it was making it hard to breathe. "And despite my cleavage that woman definitely noticed my stockings."

At last they made it to the big double doors and walked out through them sedately, despite the butler's look of disapproval. Once outside they ran down the front stairs pausing only to put their coats back on. Then they both exploded in laughter until they were weak with it. The snowy street around them was quiet and there was no sign of their pursuers. Still, once they regained their composure, they moved swiftly down the cobbled streets toward people and light and hopefully transportation to take them home. Had a mule come along right now, emerging out of the snowy wastes of Paris, Pamela would have gratefully hopped on its back.

Jamie stopped halfway down the hill. "In here," he said and pulled open the door of a little café which was almost hidden behind a snowy drape of ivy.

It was dark and she had to blink a few times to adjust to the lack of light. But there was warmth and the scent of food making her stomach rumble as though it had not taken notice of a couple of crab puffs and bits of sausage in pastry.

Jamie led her to a table in the corner which held only a fat red candle in a jar to light the area around it. It also, she noted, had a clear view of the door so that Jamie could see who came in behind them.

"Do you think I can safely go to the washroom, without you disappearing or getting assassinated in my absence?" she asked.

"I can't guarantee anything," he said and grinned, a flash of white in the gloom of the corner.

There was a tiny, cracked mirror hanging askew over the ancient hand basin. She looked in it and a stranger looked back. A flushed stranger with eyes shining brightly, and a slightly giddy look to her countenance.

When she returned it was to find that Jamie had ordered food and, this being Paris, also wine. He poured her a glass as she sat down, and the exotic notes of lilacs and pepper reached her nose. The wine was a Valtellina, warm and velvety and redolent of the sunbaked hills from which it had originated. It warmed her blood nicely, sending a flush through her skin.

"I think we either lost them or they're waiting outside in the snow," Jamie said. "Either way, I need food if we're going to continue."

The food was divine, and she ate with an appetite born of the day's adventures. They shared a well-spiced cassoulet and she was entirely full before she even managed half a serving. No one had followed them into the tiny café for the snowy night had kept people off the streets and it was only them and three other tables of patrons.

Despite the lack of an audience, however, a man got up to play an accordion. The café had a microphone and two stools at one end. He was joined by a man with a Spanish guitar. They played Gypsy music of a sort both she and Jamie were very familiar with.

She turned to look at Jamie and he smiled, green eyes soft in the candlelight.

"Dance with me," he said and she took his hand and followed him out onto the floor. He took her in his arms, and she moved with him as the guitar player began a slow Gypsy ballad. So near to him she had the heightened awareness she so often felt with him, brought into the full sunlight of knowing him as a lover and the heady anticipation of the night that lay ahead. Providing, of course, they actually made it home intact. The thought had the effect of sobering her a little.

"Jamie, do you think we should involve the police?" she asked, quietly.

"No, the man with the scar is a gendarme," he said. "It's too risky. I'll get you home safely, I can promise you that much." He pulled her closer and she took a deep breath. She believed him, he never made a promise he didn't keep.

Her fingers were brushing the inside of his collar, feather-light, but she knew the message was sent and received as it was meant to be.

"Pamela, if you don't stop that…"

"Yes?" she turned her head so that their eyes met through the hazy light. She leaned in and put her cheek against his and said his name soft in his ear, "Jamie." It was both question and command. The two syllables were all the man needed, for he took her hand and pulled her with him off the dance floor.

"Let's go. Out the back."

They went through the kitchen, where a woman was cleaning a large pot. She stopped and clapped her hands together and then hugged Jamie, exclaiming away in Spanish. Jamie replied in the same tongue and the woman's expression became serious. She looked down at Pamela's feet and nodded. She then bent down and took off her own shoes, a rough looking pair of flat-soled leather loafers.

"Give her your boots," Jamie said. He took in her look and added, "I'll buy you ten pairs to replace those, now trade her. You need to be able to run and you can't do it any longer in those boots."

She sighed and took them off. The other woman's shoes were a tiny bit big on her and had decidedly not been worn for aesthetic reasons. Jamie said goodbye to the woman, and she said something to him which sounded rather like an admonishment to Pamela's ears. Then they were out the back door and into the night where the snow was falling more heavily, the air hushed and still.

Jamie offered her his arm and she took it and they set off through the snow at a brisk pace which had the overly large shoes flapping against the soles of her feet.

They hadn't gone more than twenty yards when behind them two dark figures emerged from the shadows. Pamela felt an arrow of fear dart up the length of her spine. She was certain she had seen a glint of silver in the hand of one man. They were well back but the streets were empty and she knew they could close the gap quickly if they wanted to.

"Jamie," she said, breathless, "there are two of them and at least one has a knife."

"I know," he said and then suddenly stopped at the back door of a small building. "I'm going in here for a minute. If they get any closer just scream."

She watched, nerves jumping in her hands and feet as he jimmied the window of the little dark building with his handy pocket knife and was in before even a minute had passed. He emerged two minutes later, his coat lumpen and positively clanking. He dug in one pocket and pulled out two spherical objects. He handed them to her. "Take them, I have four more."

She looked down into her hands to find a ball in each. They were the hard wooden ones used to play *boules*.

"Weaponry," he said, before she could ask.

The snow had lit the night so that the street ahead was visible. It was cold enough to see their breath in white ribbons which curled off and dissolved into the greater air around. Small lozenges of light lay on the snow here and there—lamps in apartments and cafés, candles lit in windows on a cold winter's night, small beacons by which they flitted from point to point.

She looked back as they flew along and saw that the men were gaining on them. Her fault, no doubt, Jamie could move like the wind when he needed to.

"Come on, up the stairs," he said, and she followed up the narrow staircase set between two tall white apartments, each one with a tiny wrought iron balcony, frosted with snow like elaborate wedding cakes. Halfway up, he halted.

"That way," he whispered and pointed to one of the balconies. The window that looked over it was dark and Pamela prayed the owners were not home at present because she knew exactly what he intended.

He swung himself up over the railing and onto the balcony. She scrambled up the wall, finding a toe-hold and a belated gratitude for the sensible shoes. Jamie reached down and pulled her up once she was within his grasp. She hopped nimbly down from the railing and in beside him just as the men came around the corner.

The men clearly didn't know where they'd gone, though they would see their tracks in the snow soon enough and put it together.

Beside her, Jamie stood slowly and then fired off the balls with deadly accuracy. The kerchiefed man went up off his feet like something in an old Hollywood movie, one of the Three Stooges playing slapstick physical comedy for laughs. He let out a furious howl as he landed, whether it was of pain or outrage, Pamela could not tell. The man with the scar did a jig worthy of a vaudeville tap-dancer, the balls raining around his feet though one made contact with his stomach and doubled him over. Not enough to stop him from calling them some very colorful and unflattering names in French, though.

"This way," Jamie said, and she realized he'd opened the window to the apartment at some point, and had already slipped in. He offered his hand and she took it and stepped in beside him. The apartment was quiet around them. Perhaps they'd caught a bit of luck, and the owners were out for the evening or away. It soon became clear that whoever lived here liked to live in rather crowded quarters. Chairs, a chaise, tall vases, plants everywhere—one with truly impressive and vicious thorns—and what she thought was a spinning wheel, which Jamie just saved her from falling over in the dark. There were numerous ornaments, too, which she discovered by accidentally brushing up against a few and sending them over in a dominoing cascade. In the quiet it sounded as loud as a crash of cymbals and they both froze, not even daring to breathe.

A light clicked on partway down the narrow hall which was their only route out of the apartment. She could see the door leading out and it seemed several miles away, though in reality it was about twenty feet. She clutched Jamie's hand, fearing that some enormous man would emerge in the lit bedroom doorway with a bat in hand.

"We'll have to make a dash for it," Jamie hissed, and pulled her along behind him. Pamela hazarded a look into the room as they passed the glowing doorway. A woman with lavender-rinsed curls sat up in her bed, her wrinkled face incandescent with outrage. She was eighty if she was a day but, despite her dentures being in a glass on the bedside table, she had a look of righteous fury which might have put a Valkyrie to shame.

"*Touts mes excuses,madame,*" Jamie shouted over his shoulder, moving Pamela around in front of him and hustling her down the narrow hall and toward the door. The woman, much swifter on her feet than one might have credited given her lack of teeth and venerable age, emerged from her bedroom to thwack him over the head with an umbrella. Pamela tripped and Jamie swore as the umbrella made contact.

"*Tiens, prends ça voleur!*" The old woman shouted with some satisfaction. Jamie sustained two more hits as Pamela scrabbled with the locks on the door, of which there were three. They fell out into the narrow hall and half-stumbled down the stairs bursting out into the night with the old woman halfway down the stairs behind them still shaking the umbrella at them and swearing vociferously. French, Pamela thought, was a most descriptive language.

It was then she realized she had lost a shoe in the old woman's apartment. There was, however, no going back for it. For at the top of the snowy street was the man with the scar, upright and no doubt far more incensed than he'd been before Jamie had hit him with the ball.

"Two down, one to go," Jamie said and they fled through the small courtyard of the apartment, which was ankle deep with snow and featured a fountain with a naked satyr in its midst. Then it was up yet another steep staircase and down a winding street, skidding sideways and then swooping off to the right and up a narrow space between a bakery and a cabaret—jazz music poured out in notes of liquid silver and the snow was lit here and there with lights both golden and red, casting rectangular shadows. Shutters opened overhead and someone shouted, and a dog barked angrily behind them.

From a doorway Jamie grabbed something and then he turned and waited for the man to come around the last corner they'd rounded. He hurled the items with his usual precision. One made contact with the man's head and exploded in a shower of clay and dirt and the other hit his shin causing him to go down like a felled tree.

"What was that?"

"A flower pot from the house back there and the little grape-munching cherub I took from the old woman's apartment," he said. "I think the cherub cracked his shin—it weighed a good bit, probably worth a good amount, too. He won't be permanently injured but he won't be able to walk for a few days."

They ran on a little further until Jamie stopped and looked about to get his bearings. Neither of them needed a map to realize where they were, though, as it became clear with one look down the street. They'd crossed into the Pigalle. Ahead of them stretched all the vices and delights of France's most famous red light district. They slowed to a walk, for despite the snow and the cold the district was busy and there were several people out on the streets.

They passed two women shivering outside a night club door who were wearing such insubstantial clothing as to make their occupation quite clear even to the untutored eye. One was tall and dark-haired with a generous quantity of navy blue eyeshadow above her dark eyes, and the other was a small curvy redhead, with big blue eyes and breasts that were close to spilling out of her sequined top.

"Monsieur, you ought to buy your woman some shoes," the tall one said and both of the women laughed. The redhead then made a suggestion which Pamela thought was only *just* physically possible.

Jamie inquired as to how much such an act cost and Pamela gave him a sharp poke in the back.

"Both of you for half the price we usually charge. I like the look of you and my friend here likes your lady."

Jamie appeared to give it some thought and Pamela poked him harder this time.

"How much for your boots?" he asked the tall one.

The woman looked him over with the glint of a practiced grifter in her eyes and then named an exorbitant price which was more, Pamela thought, than the aforementioned act would have cost. Jamie pulled a wad of *franc* notes from his pocket and handed them over. The woman tucked the money into her bra and bent down to unlace her boots, which rose well above the knee and were made of red patent leather. They were not boots for walking or even, Pamela thought lacing one on after the woman handed it over, standing upright.

"*Merci mes chère dames, je suis désolé que nous ne puissions nous attarder, plus longuement!*" Jamie said in parting and then bent over each of their hands and kissed them.

Then they were off, she tottering a little on the heels, which were also not made for snow. Thankfully they found a cab a block further down. Pamela collapsed gratefully into it, the night's adventures suddenly taking their toll.

It was a relief to return to the house. The morning seemed weeks ago, instead of the hours it had been. Jamie made her sit down in the kitchen where it was gorgeously warm and unlaced the boots for her. He'd put a pan of hot water down for her to soak her feet. Before she put her abused appendages into the much-needed warmth, she checked Jamie's head over. There was a small cut where the tip of the umbrella had made contact but not anything that should require stitches. She did, however, insist on cleaning it out with a bit of brandy.

"That brandy is rather expensive for a head wound," he said, wincing and blinking as a few drops of the liquid rolled down his forehead. When she sat down to soak her feet, which felt rather like pinched blocks of ice, Jamie made hot toddies with lemons and sugar and a very generous pour of Calvados into each mug. She eyed him over the steam of her cup and found him looking back. They both burst into laughter at the same time.

"I had a wonderful time today," she said through her laughter.

"The bar is rather high with you, isn't it? I won't be able to conjure up scurrilous gangs of men intent on killing us and prostitutes with such gloriously vivid imaginations all the time, you know."

"You?" she smiled. "This was probably a low key day for you."

"No day with you is low key," Jamie said, his eyes meeting hers. He set his toddy, unfinished, to the side and then took hers and set it beside his. And then he put out his hand to her as he had all day and, indeed, as he had for the last two years. She took it and stood up, stepping daintily out of the water. Then without either of them speaking, they went upstairs. The silence between them felt both comfortable and necessary. In the bedroom, everything was forgotten, the day's fears and adventures and the resultant cuts and bruises banished by the beautiful madness that lit her blood and nerve endings as soon as he touched her.

He brushed his lips against her brow and then kissed the line of her cheekbones, her chin and neck and then her mouth, which yielded to his immediately. His hands on her skin drifted feather-light and yet the demand, the desire in them was clear and echoed through her own blood, her bones, yielding her up to him without hesitation.

The words were soft, but said with ease, because what was true between them this night had been true for countless nights. "I love you."

It was within this place that they moved, sought lips and skin and curve and hardness, sought breath and blood. This love, this love that came from they knew not where, because there was no knowing where something seemingly without limit had its genesis. Because there did not seem to be a time before now, before each had loved the other, before their lives had become as two threads, one gold, one dark, twined round each other until the colors were blended in the harmony of light and dark, of day and night, of friends and family, of lovers.

It arrived all too soon, that high sweet aching place from which there seemed no release, no want for release and yet release was all, was the finite, burning point of this universe of limb and breath, of linens and the soft, enfolding darkness.

It wasn't like the night before; it wasn't like anything either of them had ever known.

And still, and always, "I love you."

"Did they mean to kill us, do you think?" she asked, the mad dash through Montmartre seeming very distant now that they were tucked up in bed, warm and safe.

"I don't think they wanted to take tea with us," Jamie said. "Someone has been following me since Vienna. It's been a bit of a relay with the faces changing, but I'm sure they've all been hired by the same source."

"Does this happen to you often?" she asked, only half joking. "Strange and sinister men following you around foreign cities? And just how did you know the scarred one was a policeman?"

He laughed. "More often than you might think. I've gotten pretty good at evading pursuit over the years though. As to your other question, I've had troubles in Paris before and I've come to know certain faces. His is one."

"I thought you were leaving the spy business," she said. He never talked about it, but somehow she'd thought he'd left it behind and that his time in Russia had played a large part in his decision.

"I'm trying; it's proving to be a somewhat more difficult task than I'd hoped." He didn't say anything more than that and judging by the line of his jaw it was a subject best left alone.

"Have you seen Julian lately?"

He propped himself up on one elbow and looked down at her. "What is this, Pamela—twenty uncomfortable questions? I feel like all we're missing are the hot lights and the electrodes to apply to my skin." He smiled as he said it though, taking any sting from the words.

She merely looked at him. He sighed, interpreting the look correctly.

"I don't know what to do about Julian. It's a strange thing to be presented with a fully-grown child at this point in my life. He vehemently denied having anything to do with hiring the extra groom. Strangely, I was somewhat inclined to believe him. It could have been anyone speaking to the man as the whole deal was conducted by phone. I just have the sense that he is more puppet than master, though I'm not fool enough to let down my guard with him."

"I wish it was different for the two of you. I wish he was more like you."

"That would be a very mixed sort of blessing. I wouldn't wish my rather unstable mind on anyone, not even," he said wryly, "Julian."

"I wouldn't change a thing about you—I would only change the things that hurt you."

He looked down at her, the green eyes tender. He stroked the side of her face from temple to chin as though he were intent on fixing this moment forever in his mind. "You look happy," he said.

"So do you," she replied.

"That's because I am."

"May I ask one more question?"

Jamie raised one eyebrow, a golden glimmer in the low light of the lamp. "Has my saying no ever stopped you before?"

It was her turn to arch an eyebrow at him.

He bowed his head in mock capitulation. "I'm at your mercy, madam, ask away."

"Is it hard for you to be here? I wondered about that when Madame Felicie told me about Adele."

His expression changed in the way that light moving over water changes water but leaves it the same as well. "No, because I still feel her here in many ways. She had a butterfly soul and when it emerged fully from the chrysalis it was time for her to go. Something of her always lingers with me. I only wish I'd known about her sooner so we might have had more time."

"Madame Felicie told me you and your grandfather had an epic fight over it. I believe her expression was 'anvil and tongs'."

Jamie laughed. "That's one way of putting it. I've rarely been that angry in my life. I took off and lived in the streets of Paris for a few days. I had about five *sou* in my pocket and I was pretty hungry, as you might imagine, by the third day. My grandfather was wise and just waited me out. I showed up at a little café where we knew the owner. You met her tonight, and gave her your boots. I knew she would feed me even if I couldn't pay. My grandfather was waiting there for me when I walked in. He said, "Jamie, you need a bath, you're going to have to come home. And that made me laugh, and you know once you laugh the battle is done. Then he said, 'Come home and meet your sister, Jamie.' And that was that."

"I wish I could have met her," she said, softly. "Just because she's part of you."

His eyes rested upon her and she put her hands to his face. His stubble rasped pleasantly against her palms.

"There's a line of poetry," he said, softly, "from Wendell Berry which always makes me think of Adele. *I rest in the grace of the world, and am free.* That was how she was, at rest in the grace of the world and therefore free. I felt peaceful around her in a way I can hardly describe. I guess we had a strange bond being twins despite not even knowing about one another for so many years."

"Have you ever felt that sort of peace again?" she asked. She knew what his life had been and how much the burdens of others weighed upon him, her own not being the least of them.

He leaned down so that his mouth was next to hers and his breath became hers as she felt their respective pulses beat together. He tasted warmly of apple brandy. And then when they paused for breath, he answered, "Yes, here and now with you, *I rest in the grace of the world, and am free.*"

They had arrived at their last day. Pamela was returning home the following morning and Jamie was going on to business in Berlin. He'd promised to be home by the following weekend. She missed Conor and Isabelle and would be happy to return to them, but she was going to miss Jamie even for such a short time. They had come to a place with one another in these last days she would not have imagined possible even a week ago.

She was in the kitchen making coffee with the scent of pastry tickling her nose. She hoped Jamie finished dressing quickly as he'd promised to take her somewhere perfectly wonderful for lunch. He'd also promised her a bottle of Sauterne which tasted, he swore, like angels' tears. It was more likely to be dinner by the time they were both ready though. They'd slept until noon, both exhausted from the previous night's adventures. Jamie had woken her just as the sun rose and made love to her slowly, both of them silent, the sun gilding him in morning fire above her. They had gone straight back to sleep without exchanging a single word and she had slept more deeply and soundly than at any time since Casey had disappeared.

The sun glanced off her ring, sparking silver fire and she had a sudden vision of Casey the last morning she had seen him. He had been moving around the kitchen, Isabelle in the crook of his arm, and Conor had been on the floor playing with his trucks. She had been making oatmeal and eggs, Casey tending to the toast and making himself a flask of tea for the day. Their eyes had met for just a moment but between them had passed a bolt of pure contentment. She put her hand to the counter to steady herself. For just a second she felt out of step, as though she had only imagined the last three days and the last two years. Perhaps it was only that a woman's heart was always so—a piece here with Jamie, a piece always with her children and a piece forever belonging to their father. Over these last two years, she had found a happiness with Jamie which she had only begun to realize. It frightened her a little, as if she stood on the precipice of some strange new land for which she had neither map nor guide.

A knock at the door interrupted her reverie. She tightened the belt on Jamie's robe and went to answer it. She opened the door and found a woman standing on the doorstep. She was small in stature with red-gold hair and striking dove-grey eyes.

"I…I'm sorry," she said, "I was told James Kirkpatrick was here."

Like Vanya, her English was flawless and like Vanya it was heavily accented. Pamela backed away a little, realizing how she must look after spending half the day in bed with Jamie and now wearing nothing more than his robe. The woman's hair was the same beautiful red-gold as Kolya's.

"He is," she said. "May I tell him who is calling?"

"*Da*," said the woman, suddenly frostily polite. "You can tell him it's Violet. His wife."

She had begun to pack her bags while he was gone, having managed to rebook her flight to Dublin so that she could leave tonight instead of tomorrow. She had called for a car to pick her up to take her to the airport. Probably because she didn't want to prolong the agony by having him drive her.

"You're going?" He needed to ask, even though the answer was obvious. He was sitting on the bed. He felt exhausted. The last few hours had been stress of a rather high order. Jamie had come back prepared to face anger or for her to have fled in his absence. He hadn't expected this white-faced resignation. It made him a little angry, though he knew his anger was misplaced.

"I think it's best." She turned to look at him then and he saw that she had been crying. "It's all right, Jamie," she said, and he could see that she was forcing a smile. "I know, after all, that this is a Russian tale. I wasn't expecting a happy ending. I understand you need to see her and this is a shock to you as much as it is to me. I know you loved—love her, and she is, after all, your wife."

"It's not entirely coincidence that she is here now," he said. "I've been looking for her, or at least looking for answers, since my return from Russia. I thought one day there might be a phone call or Sergei would arrange a meeting and tell me she was either dead or had been promoted through the ranks of the KGB. I did not think I'd ever see her again."

"But you're happy that she is safe, surely?"

"Yes, of course. The rest of my feelings are not so straightforward. And the coincidence seems too great. We've had two days, Pamela. Two days out of all the years we have loved one another and suddenly she's here in Paris at the same time we finally find our way to each other."

"What do you mean?" she asked, holding the beautiful dress she had worn to the party in her hands. "Will you see that this gets back to Yevgena?"

"Yes," he said gently and then took the dress from her hands and laid it to the side. "What I mean is just as Yevgena meddled to bring us together I have sensed another hand in my other affairs for some time."

She nodded and they looked mutely at one another for several moments. The lamp glowed softly in the corner. It was twilight and would soon be full dark, and with the dark she had to go. In the light which remained, he could see the curve of her eyelashes and all the delicate tints of skin and hair, the deep water eyes, with their quiet observance. The soft mouth that asked to be kissed and also held within it a quick humor and wit. The line of jaw and cheekbone, perfect in their lofted fragility. He felt it as though a bell had struck somewhere deep inside, and a shaft of pain accompanied the knowledge, because it went bone-deep, as such knowledge will. He would never love another woman as he did her. It was as if all his life there had been a waiting in his heart, a piece of it put aside, for something and someone he had not known. But now it no longer waited, for it had found what it sought in this woman. She had possession entire of him.

"Julian's mother?" she asked, putting the last of her clothes into her bag.

"Yes, only hatred such as she seems to bear me would connive at something on this scale. She is still part of the Circus and she can pull strings. She clearly has contacts who owe her favors within the KGB."

"I suppose it doesn't matter how it happened," Pamela said bleakly, "only that it has."

"I don't want you to go," he said, aware that his tone bordered on desperation. Everything was flying apart so quickly, just when it seemed it might actually come together.

She shook her head, lips tight. "I have to go, Jamie, you know that."

He watched her as she zipped up her bags, her face set and white.

"I wanted more, I wanted everything." He blurted it out, the pain in his heart too great for subtlety or the kind parting words she needed.

She turned, and he saw that she just barely had a grasp on her emotions. The light had faded further, the lovely little gables across the road lit with lavender blankets of snow and embroidered with casements of gold. Paris in the snow; there was no place more lovely. There was no place more heartbreaking.

"Jamie, you are bound by honor and as old-fashioned as that concept seems to some, it is one of the things I love best about you. We didn't make any promises to each other."

"Didn't we?" he asked. "Was it my imagination, or did things change for us these last few days?"

She shook her head. "No, it wasn't your imagination. I felt it too. It felt like we might be ready for something more, something permanent. You need time and space to figure this out, though, and to talk to her. She is Kolya's mother and she is your wife. I do understand that you have commitments beyond this world we've lived in for the last few days."

She came to him then and knelt at his feet and took his hands in hers. She was cold and he longed to pull her into the bed with him and pretend none of this had happened.

"Jamie, I think we should not see each other for a while, and perhaps not even talk. It will only muddle things for you. I want you to have a clear head and for there to be no dividing loyalties. I know you loved her once, and perhaps you could love her again."

He stroked one hand over her hair. They had begun something these last days, which could not now be undone, but would change their friendship forever. He felt as though he had cheated her, by giving in to something which had been inevitable for so long now. There was no regret in him for what they had done, but there was regret for the damage it might do to her going forward. The damage it might do to him, he thought perhaps he deserved, all things considered.

"Pamela, what are you suggesting exactly?"

"We just stop it, here, leave what we've had these last few days, here in this house." Her eyes were the deep and aching emerald they were when she was trying to hold on to the extremes of emotion.

"No," he said. "What has begun here has barely been touched; this is the thin end of the infinite ache, Pamela. Do you really believe we can go back to who we were just a few days ago?"

"No," she said, and her voice broke on a sob, "but we can't go forward either and that leaves us in no man's land."

He gathered her to him and held her. There were things he wanted to say but knew he had no right. Things like—*for the rest of my days there will be only you and no other. It will not matter in which city I live or what I am doing or who I am with, there will still only be you. There will be nights of infinite skies filled with stars, but if you are not there to see them with me, they will be as dust. There will be poetry and music, but I will be blind and deaf to their seductions if you are not there to see and hear with me.*

A bell sounded discreetly from downstairs.

"The car is here. I have to go."

He nodded, then stood and picked up her bags. He had said what he must and so had she. Words had limited power and could not fix what they now faced. And then at the last moment she turned and put her arms around him and he felt the grace and pain of it, as they were both shackled and torn loose at the same time. She kissed him, hard enough that he could taste her tongue on his, and then she was gone, into the car, vanished like smoke from the fire in which they had burned for days.

And Shelley again, inevitably.

Joy, once lost, is pain.

Chapter Seventy

Lost Things
April 1978

SHE CAME HOME one day in late April to find a package on the table for her. It was bound up in beautiful grey paper, and she recognized Jamie's writing on the label. The return address said Paris. He was still there then. Perhaps he would choose to live there now with his wife and son. He had taken her at her word, and not contacted her since the day in February when she'd left him in Paris, standing on the walk in front of his beautiful house, watching her drive away. Vanya had told her that he'd arranged to have Kolya brought over to France. He'd hired the dependable Pru from Maine as his nanny. Pru had a yearning to see Europe and was probably the best nanny possible for Kolya.

She sat down at the table, tired and feeling a tightness in her throat. She looked over at the children. Conor was turning five in a couple of days, and Isabelle would be three in the summer. When Casey disappeared they had both been babies. He would be a stranger to them now. It hurt like a knife to her heart to realize that he was only a memory to his son, and no more than a notion to his daughter, the hero in a fairy tale, a hero who wasn't ever coming back to the castle.

She set the package in a cupboard, unable to open it just yet. Vanya must have brought it in with the rest of the mail earlier in the day. Vanya had shown up on her doorstep with a knapsack in hand one day, and announced that he had come to stay. And so she had stood aside and let him come in. It was nice to have his company and help and he had settled in nicely to the area. He was tending bar at the Emerald during the afternoon and evenings, and helping her out at the company in the mornings. It was a wonder there was still a company to tend to, though she suspected that Noah had something to do with that.

Later, after dinner and baths and stories and a short nap in Isabelle's bed where Pamela fell asleep reading *Green Eggs and Ham* to her, she went downstairs and took the package out of the cupboard and went to the table with it. She sat with her hand upon it for a moment, wondering what it was that Jamie had sent to her and perhaps more importantly, why. She smoothed her hand over the paper, her memory conjuring his scent, his step, the touch of his skin against her own. She pushed the thoughts away, feeling the prickle of tears behind her eyes. During the day, she told herself all kinds of pragmatic lies, but sometimes like now, she just let the truth rise up through the ashes of the last few months—she missed him horribly, missed his smile, his voice, his touch, she just missed *him*.

She carefully took the paper off to find two books. It took a few seconds to understand what they were. The first volume was their fairy-tales—Jamie's words, her illustrations—beautifully bound in lavender cloth with silver lettering across the front and down the spine. It was a London publishing house, a smaller one which had a reputation for only taking on very few books each year, but doing a marquee job on those that they did publish. She opened it to the table of contents, and found all their stories from that enchanted winter, spring and summer—*The Parliament of Owls, Selkie Jane, The Adventures of Bear in the Grim Forest, Trader in Barsoom* and of course, the story that had changed everything—*The Wastrel Among the Stars*. It brought back the time-stopped moments which had existed for all of them: Conor's healing by the sea, Isabelle and Kolya curled head to toe each night in the bed, Vanya's endless novels, and the tentative steps she had taken back toward life. And last, the starlit night in Jamie's arms.

The second volume was, she realized at once, a different matter. It was likely the only copy in existence. For it was private, a world Jamie had created solely for her. It was *The Faceless Tarot*, bound in dove grey and soft as a kid glove to the touch. It was, she saw in retrospect, a love song which he had sung to her through the months of its creation. Something indestructibly beautiful, made painful now by recent events. But it had been and would remain, a golden filament to which she had first clung and then felt her way forth from the dark, using his words as a guide. She could not regret that, nor anything which had culminated from it, not even the baby which she was now certain she carried.

She opened the book and saw it held a dedication. '*For Pamela, For always.*'

And that was when, after all these long weeks since Paris, she finally cried. Because he had loved her and she loved him, and it was all too horribly late.

Vanya was the first to know about the impending child. He had been overly solicitous of her which had made her wonder if he suspected, and when she threw up in the kitchen sink in front of him, she knew the jig was up. Vanya didn't say anything, merely set to making tea after handing her a towel.

He sat down at the table with her after the tea was ready. He put a cup in front of her, and she looked up to find a deep sympathy in the amethyst eyes.

"You are pregnant?" he asked, tone soft.

She nodded weakly. There was little use in denying it at this point.

"Have you told him?"

She shook her head. "No, not yet. I know I have to, Vanya. But I feel like I am just adding yet another complication to his life. We haven't talked since Paris. Well, you know that."

"He is home now, he got back two days ago," Vanya said quietly, and she felt a pang of unpleasant surprise. She was completely out of Jamie's circle now. It was hard to imagine that just a few short months ago they had been like family, they had been lovers.

"You're going to keep the baby?"

"I...yes," she said, shocked that Vanya would think otherwise. The thought had not even occurred to her. "It's Jamie's baby, I can't...the thought of..." she took a shaky breath. "No matter how things stand with us, I love him, Vanya. I can't imagine not having this child now that I know it's a fact."

"You are afraid though?"

"Yes, a little and," she laughed, "for a rather wide variety of reasons. You know that Jamie lost three sons?"

Vanya nodded. "Yes, he does not speak of it willingly, but he was very sick in Russia as you know and one night while he was still feverish and we thought he might die his words were—how to say—rambling about and that was when I found out about his babies."

"They all died because of something called hypoplastic left heart syndrome. The odds should have been against more than one of his children having the heart defect, and yet all three had it. It's possible this baby could have it as well. Then again, Julian is healthy and whole."

"And the other reasons?"

"I'm unwed and I already have two children. I might well be raising all three alone for the rest of my life. If I think about it too much, it overwhelms me. Ireland is, in case you haven't noticed, a fairly conservative country. Having a baby out of wedlock isn't unheard of but it's not an accepted thing either."

"You will have to tell him, Pamela, complicated or not, he should know."

She nodded. "I will. Now that I know he's home, I'll arrange to see him. Did Violet come back with him?"

Vanya nodded. "Yes."

"Do you think he loves her, Vanya?" she asked, not sure she wanted to know or what she wanted the answer to be. Jamie deserved to be loved and to love without reservation, but she had to admit the thought of him with another woman made her feel sick.

"I don't know," he said. "He loved her once but it was camp love, which is different because there is little freedom to choose and one snatches at love whenever one can. But he never loved her as he loves you. You must know, Pamela, he has never loved anyone as he does you."

"I'm not sure that matters at this point," she said. "But I will tell him as soon as he can manage to see me."

"Don't wait too long. He deserves to know as soon as possible."

"I tell him, and then what, Vanya?"

He reached across the table and took both of her hands in his and smiled. "Then we will just do what people do and wait for this baby to arrive."

"And after that?" she said, smiling wearily, relieved to have someone other than herself know about the baby.

"Then we love it, my friend, because that is the one thing that is easy."

Chapter Seventy-one

Lost Things, Part 2

DESPITE AN ATMOSPHERE which would have given a polar bear pause as to the suitability of its climate, Jamie found he was quite relieved to be home. At least here he could close a door and think in relative peace. There was little enough of it to be found once he ventured outside his study doors, however. Judging from the chill in Maggie's kitchen, he would be lucky if his tea didn't contain some sort of mild poison. While she had liked both Vanya and Shura from the start, and had become so fond of them both that he'd caught her crying over a pot of soup after Shura's departure, it appeared she had now found a Russian for whom she did not care.

He understood that Maggie had long considered Pamela the rightful mistress of this house. He supposed he had too, but Violet needed a home and he had hoped she would feel welcome enough to relax here until they could come to some sort of consensus over their marriage.

Violet's reappearance in his life had been like an atomic bomb, scattering him into particles too small to be seen so that there was no visible difference to his outside, but inside everything was in chaos. He didn't trust her and with good reason. But he was careful and kept nothing in the house which would be of value to her if she was a double agent. The ludicrousness of his situation impressed itself upon him with regularity.

He had loved her once. But it had been emotion formed under extreme circumstances. There was also the small matter of whether he had ever truly known her. So set aside love—what did honor demand of him?

While at times it seemed an old-fashioned notion, he had long lived his life by its principles. He had married Violet, he had made vows to her and he had meant it at the time. If he broke his promises because he was in love with another woman, then what did that make him? He was also well aware that while Pamela loved him, there was still a part of her that was married to Casey, and likely always would be. What he was giving to Violet was no different; however, he could not give her something that had been given fully elsewhere. That none of this was her fault did not help. He felt like his mind had been little more than a hamster on a wheel over which he had no control ever since he had come downstairs in the house in Paris and found Violet and Pamela staring at each other across the expanse of the foyer.

Kolya, normally a loving child, shied away from Violet every time she tried to touch or hold him. It was the normal aversion a child had for someone who wanted something from them too much. She in turn became frustrated and Kolya, sensing that, clung to Jamie if Violet so much as looked at him. It had made for less than convivial living conditions for all of them.

He found himself haunted by those few days in Paris. He and Pamela had crossed a line and there would be no returning from what they had experienced and the ways in which it had changed things between them. There had been little hope of turning back after Maine and now there was none at all. What had come to fullness there had been a harvest slow to ripen, and they had partaken of its fruits for only a few days and then had it snatched from their hands before either of them could tighten their grasp upon it. And now his hands were empty and so were hers. He often found himself sitting at his desk, as he did now, reliving moments of their time together. Remembering how she felt beneath his hands, and how she had looked as she said *I love you* with joy and abandon.

When Maggie announced Pamela, Jamie thought he might be hearing things at first. They'd not had contact since that last day in Paris and he had not expected any. It had been hard to respect her wishes, but he had felt he had to for both their sakes.

"Aye," Maggie said, in response to his look, "it's her. She looks a wee bit done in, so be kind to the lass."

"I'll try," he said drily. "She could have just walked in; she's never stood on ceremony before."

"Aye, well things have changed, no? I think she can be forgiven if she's a bit uncomfortable here now."

"Please just send her in," he said shortly. Maggie had more than made her discontent clear over the issue of Violet.

Pamela came in a moment later. Despite Maggie's words she did not look the least bit 'done in' but rather looked particularly beautiful—softly flushed, healthy, hair a tumble of curls tied back with a shell pink ribbon. She wasn't wasting away for want of him anyway. He felt a frisson of shame that he should want such a thing. He rose and moved around the desk, clenching his hands in an effort to squelch the urge to touch her.

"I'm sorry to barge in here, Jamie, only I've called to try and set up an appointment with you a few times, but I never heard back."

"I apologize," he said, "I didn't get any messages. We've only just arrived back a few days ago."

"I know that," she said, and he could see that she was nervous and hated that it had come to this between them. He thought of the last time he had seen her, in the house in Paris, fresh from his bed and cut the thought off as quickly as it rose in his mind.

"Please, Pamela, sit down. Would you like tea? I can have Maggie bring some."

"No, I think it's best if I just say what I have to say and then leave before your wife gets back home."

He sat down across from her in his grandfather's old chair. He had a sudden feeling he was going to need the moral support of it as well as the physical.

"That's not necessary, Pamela. I am still master of this house, after all, and no one dictates who is welcome here other than myself. You will always be welcome." He couldn't believe the words coming from his own mouth, considering that only a few short months ago he had hoped this woman would be mistress of his home and heart one day, and just how close it felt like they were to that during those days in Paris. And now she clearly felt like an unwelcome intruder. That this was his fault did nothing to assuage the pain of the situation.

She folded her hands in her lap and smiled at him, though it was a strained look. "I'm going to do what I usually do and just blurt it out—I'm pregnant."

"I...oh...I see." He had been hit many times during his boxing years, but he didn't think any opponent had ever flattened him quite as effectively as the simple statement he had just heard.

She gave him a tremulous smile. "I considered not telling you, Jamie, but I knew that wasn't the right thing to do. Whatever else has happened, you are this baby's father and I wanted you to know. What you choose to do about it, I will leave up to you. I want you to know that I have no expectations of you, I just felt it was your right to know."

He tried to take the information in and found that he couldn't quite manage it.

"Pregnant?" he croaked.

And then he did what he had not allowed himself to do before; he really looked at her and saw that she was, indeed, pregnant. She wasn't showing just yet in the obvious ways, but she looked softened in outline, and yes, fuller in the breasts and belly. She looked ripe and warm and soft. She looked like a place a man might find sanctuary of the sort that would last all his days.

It seemed to him, suddenly, that the entire life they might have led hovered there in the air between them like a shimmering fairy castle, glimpsed and then swiftly discarded as illusion. And yet the pain the vision left behind was all too real.

"There are practicalities which have to be thought about here, Pamela. You know that."

"This baby will be fine, Jamie, I know it will."

"There is absolutely no way to be certain of that."

"Yes there is," she said stubbornly, two spots of pink appearing high on her cheekbones, and her eyes lowering to the table which sat between them. "Look, I didn't come here to argue or make things difficult and I don't expect you to do anything. I did feel, however, that you had to know."

"Pamela, please don't say that. It's my child, and that is not a thing I could ever take lightly. You, better than anyone, know that." You better than anyone, he added in his head, know me.

"I do know, Jamie. I also know things are rather complicated for you right now, I don't want to make them worse." She was blinking rapidly and he knew she was on the verge of tears.

"There are things I would say, but I no longer have the right." Everything in the study seemed surreally bright, outlined so harshly that he could feel the beginning of a headache stabbing at the back of his eyes.

She nodded, tears trembling on the cusp of her lashes. "It's best if you don't, Jamie. This has been difficult enough for both of us, I think."

"If you need anything…"

"I know how to look after myself. I will be seeing a specialist in Dublin once a month. If there's anything that crops up, he will send me to London. I don't want to cause trouble for you. I just felt it was your right to know about the baby."

"I wish…" he swallowed, "I wish I could hold you and tell you that everything will be fine." The few feet of study floor between them felt as if it was a twelve-foot-high barbed wire fence.

"I think if you touched me right now I would fall apart. Just let me take what dignity I have and go."

He stood and walked her to the door. She looked up at him just before she crossed the threshold to the hall. The green eyes were filled with sympathy. It took every fiber of willpower in his being to not take her in his arms and beg her to stay.

"It's all right, Jamie. We'll manage somehow. No, please don't walk me out. I believe my composure has found its limit."

He nodded, mostly because he did not feel that he could speak just now. There weren't words to reassure her, because the one thing she truly needed was him and that he could not give her much as he longed to.

He sat for a very long time after she left, staring at the space where she had been. He could still smell her scent, that light soft green scent which was, since Maine, an utter aphrodisiac to him.

The situation was ludicrous. Here he was married to a woman he did not love, while the woman he did love was carrying his child and he could not go to her; could not do that which he most wanted in this world—to bring her and Conor and Isabelle, here to his home, to live under the care of his love. This should be one of those moments in life they celebrated, a moment held still in memory, so that years later they would be able to recall the details of it.

Their child. It hit him forcefully and he braced his hands on his knees, his whole body feeling as wobbly as jelly. Pamela was having his child. His child. He who had not fathered a living child other than Julian. He was frightened and rather stupidly elated at the same time. Because if he was to have another child in this life, he only wanted Pamela as the mother. And that he told himself sternly was the stupidest and most selfish thing he could possibly feel. And yet, he felt it, like a soft fizz in his blood that this was fated, had always been meant from the time he had seen that beautiful girl-child dancing on the shore so many years ago.

There were the obvious issues—the medical ones, and that gave him no small pause, for he did not think Pamela could possibly survive the loss of another child, life had already been terribly harsh to her in that regard. It had been so with him as well, and he did not think he could manage such a loss either, not with a child who had been made with such love. The most obvious issue was, of course, that he was married and his wife lived here with him and was the mother of his adopted son. His beloved son whom she had threatened to take away from him if he refused to stay married to her.

He needed time to make things right. He sighed; he also needed a damn good lawyer.

Chapter Seventy-two

Decisions
June 1978

FROM HIS VIEWPOINT up on the hill hidden in a patch of ferns, the scene laid out below Noah seemed like a child's diorama with moving parts. A miniature lake, spread out blue and rippled like the cellophane a child might use to indicate water, sprinkled with sparkles to make it appear as if it moved. A miniature castle tower of grey papier mâché, carefully painted to make it look real, backdropped by the sweeping vista of mountains—those built of cardboard maybe and covered in rolls of emerald velvet. The islet upon which the tower sat, blazing green on this fine summer afternoon, might have merely been constructed of rocks and grass, glued together painstakingly. The army trucks rolling through, child's toys from a Cracker Jack box. And the farm lorry, spilling with fragrant mounds of barley straw, placed innocuously in the corner of the parking lot near the castle tower—a toy of a little boy, forgotten in a corner of a grey bit of paper. But of course it was not a child's toy with moving parts. The lake was Carlingford Lough, the mountains were the Mournes and the castle tower had once been an Elizabethan stronghold—one of many which had guarded the east coast of Ulster. And that rather bucolic looking lorry filled with straw was packed with 700 pounds of explosives tightly wedged into milk churns and surrounded by petrol cans.

Trundling along the narrow road toward the neck, which was created by the point and the tower, was a Land Rover and two four-tonne trucks containing twenty-six members of the Parachute Regiment's Second Battalion. It was the Paras that had killed thirteen innocent civilians during Bloody Sunday. Six years later the bill for that tragedy was about to come due.

The line of sight they'd chosen as the point of no return was an old Victorian navigation tower. When the trucks passed that point it was time. A bee was buzzing around his head as he looked through the binoculars, probably wondering if he was some fantastically large insect with great goggling eyes.

The trucks seemed to move slowly from this distance, army vehicles did at times, particularly when they moved in convoy. The slowness was a weakness. When the last truck passed by the sight line he turned to the young man who lay in the ferns beside him.

"Now," he said.

The explosion was enormous, a ball of flames engulfed the lorry and blew the convoy into the air. In half an hour a receiver/decoder in a plastic lunch box would be activated setting off 1000 pounds of explosives lined up along the gatehouse wall in milk churns. The gatehouse was where the soldiers would seek cover after the initial attack and attempt to regroup. He would be well clear of the area by then. Within minutes it would be crawling with soldiers and helicopters, and he needed to be gone, every man involved in this operation knew where to scatter. By nightfall most would have made their way across the border into the Republic to designated safe houses where they could lie low for a time. Someone would bring him the information later with the final body count.

He went to Slieve Gullion to wait out what remained of the day. He would walk it until his blood cooled. As he drove up the mountainside the sun was beginning its descent down the sky and the world was lit gold and crimson and the day still held a fine heat to it. He got out and walked the last bit, up a narrow trail to a spot where he liked to sit and do his thinking. Below him the six counties steeped in the setting sun. He could hear the dull *thunk, thunk* of helicopters and all the other sounds of this country when yet another atrocity had taken place.

He sat down on a fallen tree, the roots of it fragrant with spilling dirt, the bark rough beneath his hands. Looking over the land below, he watched the sun recede like a slow tide across field and stone and water. He realized he was barely seeing it.

His network spread through all six counties. From here he could imagine that he could pick out the byre on a piece of land he rented under an assumed identity. Concealed in the loft of that byre was a virtual command post of radios and descrambling equipment tuned into the frequencies used by undercover police and soldiers. There were military-style transmitters and position-fixing devices and telephone taps routed through British

Telecom by people he had who knew how to break into the system. He had connections within the Ulster Polytechnic and an audio company factory, both of which had the equipment to produce the latest in electronic and radio detonation devices. It was how he had known to call off the bombing operation he'd planned for the Glasdrumman watch tower. This listening post was how he knew that the security forces referred to him as 'The Falcon' in their coded messages. Every PIRA commander was named after a bird, and in his view a falcon was far preferable to a chicken, which was what one Belfast commander who had long fancied himself quite the hard man, had been called. It told him that the army understood what he was and that he must be dealt with accordingly.

He had everything he needed—the weaponry, the well-trained men, informants within both the police and the army—to start the kind of war the IRA had long dreamed of, and the kind of war the British had always feared might one day blaze up from the ashes of their history here in Ireland. Only sometimes, lately, he wasn't sure he wanted it—that long dreamed of war. Long ago his British medic friend had told him when a man started seeing his own ghost it was time to get out. He said go while the ghost is still just a flicker in your peripheral vision because if you see that sucker walking in front of you one day, it's already too late.

He had found himself thinking about his childhood of late, an exercise in futility for he was a practical man and knew nothing had the power to change the past—neither praying nor wishing could change the pain of those moments which stuck fast with a man and made him, in part, who he was. He thought about the boy he had once been—the one who loved poetry and could be struck dumb by the beauty of the world around him. The one who'd had a Romantic's heart. He'd once heard Romanticism described as '*a search for a means to express an unappeasable yearning after unattainable goals.*' He'd quenched that young boy so thoroughly that he hadn't heard so much as a whisper from him in years. He'd pursued goals that were attainable and let the unappeasable yearning go. Some days he felt like Rip Van Winkle having woken to find himself a hundred years old, body and mind scarred beyond recognition. A life like this was like having hundreds of fragments of shrapnel lodged in your body and never knowing when a piece might work its way out and cause the sort of pain a man could not ignore.

He had always been harshly honest with himself; he preferred to live his life in black and white, always certain of his decisions and his next move. This had not been so the last year. He understood why. That he enjoyed Pamela's company, he had long acknowledged, that he desired her also, he knew all too well. But those were simple things in comparison to what he now understood about his feelings for her. It was the sort of knowledge which brought some of that shrapnel up to the surface of a man's skin.

He'd had his weekly dinner with Kate a few nights before, and she had let slip a piece of news he wasn't supposed to know, and yet he thought perhaps he had known it, after all, because he wasn't shocked by it. He had mentioned that Pamela hadn't been by to go riding of late. She sometimes came and borrowed a horse for an afternoon and he thought it was healthy for her and a way for her to move on from her beautiful silver horse which she'd lost last year.

"Well, she can hardly be expected to do that in her condition, now can she?"

"Condition?"

Kate turned from the stove where she was stirring tomato sauce, and her blue eyes were dark with dismay. "I shouldn't have said that, I wasn't thinking."

"It would have become apparent soon enough, I imagine," he'd said. "Mr. Kirkpatrick is the father, I assume?"

Kate sat down across from him, clearly stricken by revealing information she hadn't meant to.

"Yes, he is."

"So, is he marryin' her?"

"No, he can't. He's already married. The situation is difficult," Kate had said, but didn't explain further. Though she didn't know it, Kate didn't need to say anything more, for as much as James Kirkpatrick had kept an eye on him these last three years, so too had Noah his spies and informants who kept him aware of the man's comings and goings, and occasionally his personal affairs. He knew exactly why James Kirkpatrick wasn't able to do what was right by Pamela just now. He knew what the particular difficulty was. And so one man's difficulty became another man's opportunity.

It seemed to him that here was one of those crossroads in life where two things met—in this case want and need. He had a decision to make. And he realized, as the sun sank down to the tops of the mountains creating the illusion that all the fields around had turned blood-red, that the decision to be made, was indeed, no decision at all.

Chapter Seventy-three

The Proposal

SUMMER ROLLED OVER IRELAND in all its abundant and lush green glory, and with the surging growth in the fields and the abundant evidence of new life all around, a sense of well-being returned to Pamela. The nausea had passed about a week ago, and in the quixotic manner of pregnancy she now felt a sense of vigorous energy and purpose.

Pat and Kate had left for Donegal this morning to spend three days at the shore, bringing the children with them. Both Conor and Isabelle had been wildly excited to be spending three days away in a cottage by the sea. She, on the other hand, had been teary-eyed watching her babies drive off, even though she knew they could not be in more trusted hands. Even Vanya was gone, pulling a double shift at the pub, and sleeping overnight in the wee room over the Emerald, as he sometimes did when he worked especially long hours. She had come inside from waving the children off and had herself a bit of a cry and then dried her eyes and squared her shoulders, deciding to use her time wisely. She had a long list of things that needed to be done around the house, and decided she would tackle a few of those items while she had this surfeit of time. She would start with the floors, for the pine planks needed to be oiled and she had put off the task for far too long now. This was the perfect time, when there were no little feet to run across them.

She tied her hair up in a red and white kerchief, put on a holey pair of jeans that had seen far better days and an ancient work shirt of Casey's that he'd tried to toss in the charity pile but which she had rescued for painting and other messy work. Now wearing it was a comfort and like having him with her for the day as she attended to rubbing out all the marks on the boards he'd laid with a craftsman's precision and attention to detail.

In the quiet thoughts of Jamie and their situation intruded. He had attended most of her doctor appointments with her and had also set up a bank account in her name and given her the pass book for it, telling her to use the money for anything she might need. When she had protested he'd simply said, "It's my baby, allow me to do at least this much." There was a ludicrous amount of money in the account and so far she had not touched it. Their time together had been strained, though that was to be expected. He was doing his best to look after her but he was severely constrained by his current circumstances. Pat had told her what he knew about the situation with Violet, and Pamela had felt heartbroken for Jamie. Because Kolya was not his blood son, he stood a good chance of losing him, despite the fact that Violet was a spy with a dubious history. She sighed, and pushed thoughts of Jamie away. It was a path to frustration and upset and today she refused to walk down it.

She worked with a will and once she was done with the floor she moved on to beating out the quilts on the line outside, only to have one burst a seam in a perfect storm of feathers, much of which got caught in the folds of her kerchief and on her clothes, helped along by a brisk breeze which had sprung up along with a smattering of rain.

Back inside, with the quilts spread out along the sofa back and over the table, she eyed the hearth owlishly. She really needed a proper chimney sweep to come out and give it a thorough cleaning. She could probably clean the lower portion a bit as she had a chimney brush and a large bucket to catch the ash in. She tied another kerchief around her mouth and nose so that she wouldn't breathe in the ash, and set to cleaning the bottom portion with gusto.

There was a distinct thump somewhere higher up in the chimney. Casey had built it from river stone and while it made for a very beautiful chimney, it also appealed greatly to nesting birds with its convenient rockery and built-in heating system. She peered up the chimney with a gimlet eye, wondering if the family of blackbirds had come back to rebuild their nest. Vanya had removed it a week ago, placing it in sight of the distraught and screeching mother. A puff of soot fell down just then and billowed back up into her face. She dissolved in a fury of sneezes, blinking the dust from her watering eyes while groping in her pockets for a tissue.

At this inopportune moment there was a knock at the door. One of the local farmers was supposed to drop off a load of hay. She was a dreadful mess, but the man was always in a hurry and she didn't want him to leave before she paid him. She pulled the kerchief from her face, but left the one binding up her hair.

She cast a hasty glance in the mirror in the boot room, only to see bright green eyes staring back at her out of a mask of soot, so that she appeared rather raccoon-like. Not to mention there were feathers stuck in mad profusion to the kerchief on her head. Oh well, there was no time to fix it, the farmer would just have to take her as she was.

She opened the door to find, somewhat to her horror, Noah on the step. He looked oddly nervous, which was so completely foreign to his nature that she was immediately nervous, too. Frankly, she did not want to know what it took to touch this man's nerves.

"Come in," she said, wishing she had taken the time to at least rinse her face before opening the door.

He came in and then stood on the mat as if he had never been inside the house before.

"Are ye alone?" he asked. He was apparently unperturbed by her odd appearance; in fact she wasn't sure he was seeing her at all.

"Yes, the children are away with Pat and Kate. Here, give me your coat." His jacket was shiny with raindrops so she hung it over the chair nearest the Aga so it would dry.

"I was about to have a cup of tea, would you like one?"

"Aye, that would be grand."

She wet the tea towel while the kettle was heating and wiped her face down, and then shook her head over the sink to get rid of as many feathers as possible. She left the kerchief on, deciding it was better than the mess her hair was likely to be.

He'd followed her into the kitchen, and sat down at the table while she poured out the tea into two mugs, a prickling tension all along her skin, which she could have sworn emanated from him. When she brought his mug to the table and put it down in front of him, he looked her in the eyes and began to speak.

"I have somethin' in particular about which I would like to speak with ye."

"Okay," she said slowly, feeling like she was made of loosely-knitted wool and someone had found a trailing end and was slowly unraveling her joints.

"Will ye sit down?" he asked, "Only I think it's best if ye're not standin', when I say what I've come to say."

"Noah, you're really frightening me now."

"Just sit, it's not bad news or anything of the sort."

She sat, sneezing three times as she did so. He handed her a perfectly starched handkerchief and then plucked a feather from her collar, setting it politely on the table. She clutched the handkerchief in her fingers, feeling she needed its starchy support just now.

He smiled at her and then clasped his hands together on the table's worn surface. "I'll just go straight to the point, I think that's best." He cleared his throat and then proceeded to shock the hell out of her.

"I'm goin' to preface what I've come here to say with the fact that I know ye're pregnant with Mr. Kirkpatrick's child. Kate told me, she didn't mean to, it just slipped out, though truth be told, I realized ye've the look of it about ye."

"I—" she began, but he held up his hand to halt her.

"If ye'd just hear me out for a minute or two, I'd appreciate it."

She nodded, stunned by his words.

"Pamela, ye need to realize that it was one thing to live as a widow with two children. But to carry an illegitimate baby—that's another thing all together. The women of the village will not take it kindly. If ye marry me, they'll presume the child is mine an' none will dare to give ye guff over it."

"You're...you're asking me to marry you?" The words sounded so preposterous that she had to stifle a hysterical laugh as she said them.

"Aye, I am," he said, and though he looked serious enough, she kept waiting for him to laugh, to say he was taking the piss. "It seems to me ye're in a position where acquirin' a husband is a good idea. Kate said," he added, "that Mr. Kirkpatrick is not in a position to do right by ye."

"Do right by me?" she echoed, feeling like she had a scarlet 'A' tattooed to her face rather than a smattering of soot and feathers.

"Aye, so as he cannot, I thought perhaps ye'd consider marryin' me."

She wasn't quite certain there was a term adequate to describe her current state of shock.

"Look, Pamela, I know ye had a marriage of great love an' passion, an' clearly that is not what I'm offerin' to ye here. What I am offerin' is security an' safety, for yerself an' yer children."

"So that disposes rather neatly of me," she said, tea tasting suddenly sour to her tongue. "What about you?"

"What's in it for me, is that what ye're askin'?"

"Aye," she said, "that's what I'm asking."

"I'm fond of ye, Pamela. I'm sure ye know that by now."

She nodded. Yes, she had known he was fond of her, that he considered her a friend, that he desired her, but marriage was not something she would have anticipated.

"It's not the sort of thing I say lightly, so take it as such. I'm askin' ye to marry me an' that's not somethin' I've been compelled to do before in my life."

"You're serious?" The man was certainly not one for the soft pedal approach.

"Aye, I am."

He was too, she could see that clearly. She had not noted it before, but he was nicely dressed in dark wool pants and a clean blue shirt that sharply highlighted his eyes. He smelled of expensive cologne and his hair was freshly cut.

She took a deep breath and tried not to look like someone on the verge of hysteria.

"It's not the most romantic proposal," she replied.

"No, but I figure ye've had romance, an' it would be suspect comin' from me. I'm not a romantic man, ye know that well enough. I will keep ye safe an' fed, an' do right by the children. If they've a notion to go off to university one day, I'll fund their educations. It would allow ye to keep the construction business as well, an' I know that means something to ye. I've money, Pamela, ye could quit work all together, stay home an' tend to the babbies if ye'd like. I'm offerin' ye the protection of my name an' person, forever."

She thought about the small pile of letters that she kept tucked away, fearful of letting them go, though each one felt like it soiled her skin and mind as she read it. She thought of the threats and how they seemed to be building and building, and how the writer appeared to be losing his grip on reality. There had been four in the time between Paris and now. She was pregnant and about as vulnerable as possible between that and the children she already had. Running to Jamie, as she so often had in the past, was no longer an option. The police would be of limited help and could not rescue her in the wee hours of the night if that was when this mad person decided to come at her. There was, in truth, only one man who could keep her safe. Somehow she thought he knew that and had sensed her fear.

"What sort of a marriage are you talking about? Beyond seeing to the needs of the children and myself?"

"I assume ye're askin' about sex? Ye could come to my bed or not as ye saw fit. I'd prefer it if ye did, obviously, but I've no interest in havin' sex with a woman who has no desire to be with me. I think ye're not a woman who can live a life without it entirely. There are some who can, an' do, an' see themselves as none the worse for it. However, I think yer blood runs hotter than that." He said it almost fastidiously, but she didn't mistake his meaning. "Should ye choose to lie with me, I would make certain to keep ye satisfied."

She was too surprised to even blush. She wasn't even certain there were words fit for such a statement.

"Could I take a bit of time to think about it?" She was surprised to hear the words coming out of her own mouth, but realized as she said them that it wasn't the worst idea she had ever heard. Marriages had been made of less and flourished.

He regarded her with those cool gentian eyes for a long moment, during which she felt as if every thought that flitted through her head was as plain as rice on a black sheet to him.

"Aye, take a bit of time. But not too much longer, because yer belly is beginnin' to show an' tongues are goin' to wag. I can put a stop to that if we announce the banns. There's little I can do to stop it otherwise."

She didn't reply, for he was right and there was little point in arguing with the man. She didn't think she had the fortitude for it just at present.

"I'll go then, an' leave ye to think on it," he said, standing up from the table.

She walked him to the door, somewhat lightheaded, though whether it was her normal pregnancy lightheadedness, or shock from Noah's most unexpected proposal, she could not tell.

He surprised her by taking her hand, and putting it to his mouth. He kissed it briefly and held it as he said, "We're friends, an' that's more than many marriages begin with."

After he left, she looked at the clock. She thought about the various chores she had planned to get done today and gave them up as a lost cause. Noah's proposal had knocked the wind from her sails. She was still shocked to realize she was considering it.

Her mind was blank as she walked back to the table and sat down, putting her hands palm down on the table in an effort to keep the world on its axis. She would consider his offer, as he had made it—in a cool, calculating light. Seen in that fashion it was a good idea. He had presented it bluntly and she considered it thusly. It would save the company and it would keep her safe so that her children wouldn't end up as orphans. She could stay home if she chose, which sounded like a bloody relief at this point. She would still have money coming in, though it wasn't likely to be a great deal, once her book on the Troubles was published.

She was not a woman to accept an offer of marriage without knowing it would have to be a full marriage, or as full as the two of them might manage. It would be patently unfair to live under his roof, accept his care and protection and not go to his bed at night. It wasn't something she could comfortably live with and so would not. So that decided, she considered how palatable she would find sex with Noah. He was an attractive man, fit, well set up as the country parlance went. Viewed from an entirely physical aspect, yes, she could imagine going to bed with him. He was right, her blood did run hotter than that of a woman who could do without sex permanently. Viewed from an emotional aspect, well, she supposed she could close her eyes and think of Ireland if necessary. There would not be the desire that came with love, there would not be that terrible longing that possessed her every time she thought of Jamie, nor the ache she still felt and always would, from Casey's absence. It would be the stuff of comfort, perhaps some nights merely duty. She could do that, she had done worse and survived it. It would not be that bone deep need that went right to the marrow of her, to take her man to her and have him helpless in her arms, to be helpless in his arms too, and know it to be the most utterly right thing in the world. But she'd had that, and fat lot of good it had done her—here she was unwed with two children and a third on the way, the father of whom was married to a Russian spy. She laughed out loud at the ludicrousness of it, the sound echoing hollow beneath the thick exposed beams.

Noah had not said he loved her, and it was a relief that he hadn't, it made it easier to keep this as an exchange and something simple in its terms. His desire in trade for the security of her children and herself. His bluntness had kept it clean in that respect. She did not love him, did not fool herself into thinking she would grow to, either. He was smart enough to know that.

Unbidden, an image rose up in her mind of the bed in Paris, the sweet unending heat of it, the love and the laughter and how she had thought for a moment, a brief bittersweet stop of time that she would have it again—desire, passion, and love, most of all, love. But if she were honest, painfully honest with herself, she knew she had not been ready, Russian wives notwithstanding, to let Casey go entirely in the way that would be necessary to love Jamie as he deserved, as indeed, she too deserved. She might never be able to let Casey go and it was this fact that made sense of Noah's offer more than any other. Because for a man to whom it did not matter, half a loaf would be enough.

"Oh, man—why?" she whispered. She did not know if her words had been spoken to Jamie or to Casey, but knew also that it no longer mattered. Then she very sensibly dried her tears, stood up and went to finish cleaning the chimney. She would give Noah his answer, but she would take a little more time to consider, and time to remember what she'd once had, before she put it, very sensibly, from her mind forever.

Chapter Seventy-four

The Answer

PAMELA TOOK TWO DAYS to make her decision and during that time she did not see Noah, nor hear from him. She appreciated that he had given her time to make her choice without any pressure from him. She spent a sleepless night before she set out on what was an uncommonly fair morning to give him his answer.

The farm drowsed in the warmth of the morning, lambs small balls of wool on the horizon and a new dappled colt running the length of the stone wall beside her car. She slowed and watched him. His long legs were still uncertain, but he ran like the wind, his coat so black it shone blue under the sun. He had a blaze on his forehead that looked almost like a lightning strike. He ran full tilt along the thick green grass of the field as the shadows of leaves flickered across him, light and dark. She stopped the car and pulled it over to the stone wall and got out to watch him. He halted watching her approach. She leaned onto the stone, the moss that grew there in patches damp on her forearms. The colt tossed his head at her, and whickered softly.

"It's all right, wee man," she said softly, "I mean you no harm."

He tossed his head one more time for good measure and then walked toward her cautiously. She put out a hand carefully, giving him the back of it so he could smell it if he chose to. He nudged the hand with his nose and then butted it with his head. She laughed and he backed up a little at the noise. Then he came forward again and she breathed in his scent—hay and sun-warmed coat and sheer health and vitality. It brought tears to her eyes. She still missed Phouka every day. The colt nibbled her cuff with dainty little bites and then looked up at her with big velvety eyes filled with hope.

"I don't even have so much as a sugar lump in my pocket," she said, smiling at the horse through her tears. "I promise not to be so remiss next time we meet."

The colt looked at her as if he was making a mental note of her promise and then he took off at a kicking trot which swiftly turned into a gallop. She watched him go, gleaming coat and long legs and nothing in the world other than movement and sunlight and the green grass beneath his hooves. She envied him that. Near the end of the field he flung back his head and let loose a long and joyous whinny which lifted her heart with the pure fierce spectacle of his joy.

The horse felt like a sign, a good omen, and it calmed her nerves a bit.

Noah was in the biggest byre, moving straw bales onto a trailer. He looked up as she came in, his face perfectly neutral, though she sensed a wariness in his body.

He wiped his arm across his forehead, hair rumpled with bits of straw in it. It seemed best to get straight to the point and not even attempt talk about the weather or farm work or the beautiful colt.

"The answer is yes," she said, aware there was a slight tremble in her voice.

He gave her a very direct look. "Can we be clear about just what question it is ye're answerin' here?"

"Yes, I'll marry you," she said, feeling like she had a silver needle wound through her vocal chords which the words snagged on before making their way out of her mouth.

"An' have ye decided then what sort of marriage this is goin' to be?" he asked, something dark in his voice that made her shiver slightly.

"I am, as you pointed out," she said with some asperity, "not one to go without easily. Nor do I think it would be right to enter into that sort of marriage, so I won't."

"Ye did accuse me of not bein' terribly romantic when I proposed to ye, an' I admit ye were right about that. However, I think I could accuse you of the same just now."

She laughed. "Fair enough, Mr. Murray. How would you like me to put it?"

"Now, Pamela, that's maybe not a can of worms ye'll want to open just yet."

"A can of worms?" she raised an eyebrow at him in question.

"Because I am a man, an' men, though ye may not realize it, are sometimes filthy-minded creatures. So, suffice it to say I've thought about havin' ye in my bed a fair deal."

"You have?" The words were out before she could think about what she was saying.

"Aye, I have. Have you?"

"Have I what?" she asked, wishing she had kept her mouth shut.

"Thought about havin' me in your bed?"

"Since you asked me to marry you, yes, I have."

"An' what conclusion did ye come to?"

She looked down and took a breath; honesty had always been their natural bent in this strange relationship, she didn't see why this should be any different.

"I find you physically attractive, and I think I could come to desire you."

He laughed, a light sound that startled her. "Oh, Pamela, I do love yer honesty. I shall give ye a bit of my own. Give me time, an' I swear ye'll come to want me just as I want you."

If nothing else, she thought wryly, as the hot tide of a blush rose from her neckline to her face and scalp, they would always have the truth between the two of them. And that, all things considered, was no small thing.

She took a minute to gather her composure and when she looked up, it was to find him smiling at her. The expression on his face was almost soft, and it gave her an uneasy feeling in the pit of her stomach.

"Come with me for a minute, would ye? I won't make any more suggestive comments to ye, I swear. There's somethin' I'd like to show ye."

She followed him out of the byre, across the field, the sun warm on her shoulders. There was a sense of relief at having accepted his proposal, it felt like something solid and to a degree, safe. She would not have to lie awake at night worrying about every little noise, fearing that she and her children would be slaughtered before the dawn arrived.

Noah put two fingers in his mouth and whistled, three quick notes. She heard the colt before she saw him. He burst from the far pasture and ran toward them full gallop, thunder given fleet form on four spindly black legs.

"I know most women like a jewel on their finger, but I thought ye'd prefer somethin' a wee bit more lively. He's yers."

"Mine?" If her jaw could have dropped it would have. She had given the colt a good once over earlier and knew he was likely worth a very pretty penny. Certainly much more money than a ring would have cost the man. She found it slightly worrisome.

"Aye. Ye can leave him here if ye want until ye come to live here as well. I know ye still miss that great silver beast ye had, but I thought—I hoped enough time had passed that ye might have room in yer heart for a new beastie."

She found herself speechless. The colt was gorgeous and she was surprised at the gift of it, it showed an understanding of her that she might not have credited to this man once. It recalled the Christmas morning when Jamie had given her Phouka in the hope that the horse would help her heal from the loss of a baby. Wee Grace, who had been lost when Casey was interned.

"He's beautiful, Noah. Thank you."

"Just for the record, it's not that I thought ye would say yes, in fact I was near to certain ye'd say no, but I saw the horse last week when I was down in Wexford, an' I bought him on the spot."

The colt trotted up to her like they were old friends. He put his muzzle directly in her hand, and the feel of it, delicate and as soft as silk, brought tears to prickle at the back of her eyes once again. Noah produced a couple of carrots from his pocket and gave them to her.

"He's a mad little thing. I've no doubt, though, ye can tame him given time."

She felt that hollow low in her belly which she was all too used to. It had been the words 'given time'. She had a funny feeling it wasn't just the horse about which he spoke. The colt pushed his head into her stomach and let out a soft whicker of content. Then he flicked his silken black tail and trotted back off to the field to run.

"I should like to tell Patrick, so if you could just wait a bit to tell Kate," she said.

"Ye think he's not likely to take the news kindly, I suppose."

"No, Pat's reasonable, but Casey is—was his brother and he deserves for me to tell him myself. Outside of my children, he's the only family I have."

Noah nodded. "I'll wait then. I don't imagine Kate is goin' to be thrilled by the news either."

"Are you certain you want to do this, Noah?" she asked. He was right; they were going to upset a lot of apple carts with this news. She didn't care for the opinions of strangers, and people could go right ahead and gossip as they liked, but she did care what Pat and Kate thought and felt. She loved her quiet, stubborn brother-in-law like he was her own brother, and his opinion would always carry a great deal of weight with her.

"What we build between the two of us will be our business an' no other's. It may be the news will upset them at first, but they love ye an' they'll accept it for yer sake, if not for mine. Beyond that, Pamela, yes I am certain. I wouldn't have asked ye if it were otherwise."

"We need to talk about the baby, Noah."

"Aye?"

"This child will grow up partly under your roof and Jamie will always be a big part of its life. I need to know if you're going to be able to deal with that."

"I can be civil to the man, aye. Beyond that it will be up to him, won't it?"

"Yes, of course," Pamela said. It *would* be up to Jamie and that was causing her more worry than anything else in the matter of this engagement. Jamie was not going to be pleased about this at all and that, she knew, was putting it mildly. The thought of the interview which lay ahead of her made her more than a little nauseous. Casey and Jamie had always had a grudging respect for one another, despite a few altercations between the two and a certain amount of jealousy. They had even had, she believed, the beginnings of a friendship. They had trusted one another, too, and for both men that had been a big deal. She wasn't fool enough to believe that would ever happen between Jamie and Noah, despite the fact that Noah would be stepfather to this child. She would have to arrange to speak with Jamie soon, though frankly she would rather put bamboo shoots under her own toenails. It would have to be done despite her fears, for she owed Jamie at least that much for what they had been to one another, and for the sake of this child she carried.

Chapter Seventy-five

Patrick and Kate

PAT CROSSED THE THRESHOLD of his home and sighed with relief. It was the best part of his day this, arriving home, the smell of dinner on the air, and Kate's expectant face turned up to his for a kiss. Despite the worries that came with his work, and the other concerns in his life—his missing and most likely dead brother and the wee family he had left behind, and the threats he and Tomas faced on a daily basis—for this one bit of the day he felt like a lucky man.

One week ago the firm of Tomas Egan had a victory which still felt sweet. A judge had granted Oggie Carrigan his freedom. It was a huge success for them professionally. Privately, judging from the uptick in their hate mail, it might not be so advantageous. But when he remembered the look on Oggie's mother's face when she hugged her son, free for the first time in years, he thought it was well worth the personal discomfort.

They currently had two cases on the books with clients suing the RUC for brutality during interrogation. He sighed, they were getting a reputation as crusaders for justice and police reform. It was a little like sticking a sign on your back that said 'Please shoot me.' Tomas felt they should push for real reforms rather than just going on a case-to-case basis such as demanding that the interrogation rooms be equipped with closed-circuit cameras and having defined limits on how long a suspect could be questioned without a break. Limiting the holds, too, and having a doctor on site to examine the suspects both before and after interrogation.

They were still pursuing the case of Jane as well, the young woman Pamela had photographed in a field so long ago. It was a difficult one. The coroner refused to reverse his judgement that she had committed suicide. He was an older man, and Pat knew, a member in good standing of the Orange Order. He wasn't likely to help them pry the lid off what was going to be a veritable viper's nest of problems for the police. Providing they were ever able to bring the case to a point where charges could be laid.

He sniffed appreciatively. Something ambrosial had just come out of the oven. He changed out of his suit into a pair of jeans and a rugby jersey, washed up and returned to the kitchen.

"Sit," Kate said, "dinner's ready to go on the table."

He helped her carry the dishes over. They were having *coq au vin*. His gustatory horizons had been considerably broadened since meeting Kate. There was bread hot from the oven, too. He was famished and eager to dig in. He sat down and then realized Kate was still standing. She appeared, he thought, rather nervous. Her face was flushed from the oven's heat, and she looked especially lovely tonight. He wondered at times if the woman knew just what a hold she had on his heart.

"Patrick," Kate said, "I think we should get married."

He hadn't been expecting that. "What? I believe I asked ye to marry me for the third time hardly two weeks ago, an' ye turned me down, for the third time as well, I might add. I am not a vain man, but I will say it's gettin' the wee bit hard on my ego, all these refusals."

"Aye," she agreed, "but I have always intended to marry ye one day. Only it's become a matter of some urgency. Also, ye were just the bit drunk the last time ye asked, an' I'd prefer ye were in yer right an' sober mind when ye suggest marriage."

"So what is the urgency?" Pat asked, his mind not quite keeping pace. It wasn't an uncommon feeling for him with Kate, mind you.

"Well, because I'm pregnant as it happens, an' I should like the child to be born into a family where his mammy an' daddy are married."

Had she pole-axed him on the spot, he could not possibly have been more stunned.

"How...how..." he sputtered. They always took precautions and they hadn't so much as talked about having a baby.

"In the usual manner," she said, tartly. "If ye remember ye were there. 'Twas that night after the openin' arguments in the Bledsoe case an' ye would insist that I celebrate with ye, though ye know the drink goes straight to my head an' so we weren't as careful as we usually are."

"Aye, I remember," he said. It had been a lovely night, and as he recalled, a very passionate one. Why on earth hadn't it occurred to him that the woman might get pregnant? Then again, it was the one time they hadn't used birth control of one form or another, so he wouldn't have felt the odds were highly in their favor for conceiving. He had a sudden and vivid memory of his father saying, rather sternly, 'Once is enough to do the trick, an' when ye're eighteen and stupid with hormones the odds go up substantially.' Well, he wasn't eighteen, but the stupid bit possibly applied.

He stood and went to her, for she was still standing in the middle of the kitchen floor, flares of deep pink in each cheek giving away her distress. He put his arms around her and held her.

"Are ye happy? I know it's not what we planned, an' that this news couldn't come at a worse time."

"Hush," he said softly and kissed the top of her head, as she still wouldn't look at him. "I am happy, only a wee bit surprised is all."

"Imagine how I felt," she said, voice muffled in his shirt front, but he heard the relief in her tone at the same time.

"Ye might have told me all it took to make ye say yes was gettin' ye pregnant. I'd have done it ages ago."

She gave him a look and shook her head. He kissed her for a long moment, his entire being filled with gratitude that she had made her way into his life. Kate insisted on sitting down to dinner then, before it was ruined. He had trouble eating, though, despite being hungry and the food tasting divine.

He realized he wanted to tell his brother, he wanted to tell his da'. He wanted advice on how to be a father and keep up with his legal work at the same time. He wanted someone to tell him everything would be fine and that he would live to see this baby grow up. He wanted to reassure Kate that he was as likely as the next man to be here for the raising of their children, and to grow old with one another, but he knew it would be a lie and she would know it as such. She was a realist, and yet she had chosen to love him anyway. Mind, if she felt as he did, there had been little choosing about it, it had been a thing bigger than either of them. He'd loved this difficult, lovely woman from the minute she had taken his arm and allowed him to lead her in out of the snow one afternoon at his brother's house.

"What is it?" she asked looking up, the beautiful gentian eyes worried. "Ye're not eating."

"Oh, I'm just sittin' here thinkin' what a lucky bastard I am," he said softly.

"Ye are," she said, smiling, "now eat yer dinner before it gets cold."

Chapter Seventy-six

Give Up Your Ghost for Good...

"I AM NOT GOIN' THERE, an' that's that." Her son, small face as dark as a storm cloud, faced her across the width of the kitchen, his eyes a deep and angry grey. They were invited to go to Noah's the following day to see the colt and all the other young animals which had arrived on the farm along with the early summer. Noah had felt it was a way to introduce the children to the idea of living there and to take the first steps in establishing a relationship with them.

"Conor, sweetheart, you know you have to come. Mama agreed to go, and Isabelle is very excited about seeing the new horse. Auntie Kate will be there, too." She thought perhaps this would sweeten the notion, being that Conor adored Kate unreservedly.

He crossed his arms over his small chest and said, with a stubbornness that sounded like an echo of Casey, "I am not goin', I'll go stay with Uncle Pat. He said I can come visit his office one day."

She sighed. Conor was about an inch shy of staging a full-scale mutiny, or just detonating in spectacular Riordan fashion. She was all too familiar with the signs. "Uncle Pat can't take you tomorrow, he's in court this week. I promised Noah we would come visit. He said he'll bring the horses in from the pasture so you can ride. Just wait until you see Khamsin, he's beautiful, and he's *our* horse, Noah gave him to us for a gift."

Noah had left it to her to name the colt and she'd chosen the name Khamsin, which was the Arabic word for a warm wind which blew through the desert in the spring.

"He gave him to you," Conor said, still mutinous, though with a small gleam of curiosity in his expression. Like her, Conor had a great weakness for horses and was hard-pressed to resist such riches as an afternoon of riding.

"Yes, he did, but he meant the horse to be for all of us, as a family."

"He is not *my* family," Conor said, the stubborn fury back full force.

"No, not yet, but he will be once I marry him," she said. "He will be your stepfather."

Conor just shook his head. "No, he won't. I have a daddy."

She took a deep breath and marshalled her patience. Conor had a right to be angry, but right now she did not have the time to deal with it. When she had explained to him that she was engaged to marry Noah, he had glared at her and then went up the stairs and shut his bedroom door with a resounding thump. He had refused to talk to her about it since.

"Yes, sweetheart you do have a daddy. Me marrying Noah will never change that. You can only have one daddy, but as he's not here to be with us any more, I have decided to marry Noah."

There was a long silence, during which she kneaded down the bread she had rising and separated it into its loaves, then covered the dough for its final rising before Conor deigned to speak.

"Can Vanya come with us?" he asked, still clearly angry, but willing to make the sacrifice if he could have the comfort of Vanya with him. His arms were crossed over his chest, and his eyes were still a bit grey, though she could tell he was no longer in danger of going off like a pressure cooker with a loose bolt.

"You can ask him if he would like to, but he might say no, Conor."

Much to her relief, Vanya agreed to come along with them, though he wasn't in much better spirits about it than Conor. "I am not," he said, looking down his beautifully patrician nose, "liking him, as you know, but I am loving you and the children, so for that reason only, I will go."

She threw her arms around him in gratitude. "Oh Vanya, I am loving you too, thank you for making this whole thing easier."

"Just be certain of what you are doing, *moy podrooga*. I wish for you to be happy, not just secure."

"I'm sure I will be happy," she said, with a forced jollity to her tone that didn't fool Vanya in the least. If anyone understood that what a person wanted and what a person got were two totally different things, it was this sweet friend of hers, whom she was going to miss terribly when she moved into Noah's house.

"We have a saying in Russia, *Happiness is not a horse; you cannot harness it.*"

And that, thought Pamela, was only too true. Damned Russians and their honesty.

The next day dawned sunny and bright, and she was grateful for the fair weather, because the idea of all of them being penned up together in Noah's house didn't bear thinking about. She tried not to think about the fact that in a couple of very short months, they would be living there as a family. Conor's mood had been somewhat ameliorated by Vanya accompanying them. Vanya kept everyone distracted with silly tales and songs in the car, while she drove. She looked at her baby girl in the rear-view mirror. Isabelle's dark curls were bouncing madly around her tiny face and she was singing to herself, blissfully out of tune as she kept time with tiny thumps of her hand on the car window. Conor was sitting beside her, quiet, a carved horse clutched fast in his hands. She frowned; she hadn't seen the carved horse before, even though it looked vaguely familiar in some way. She turned her attention back to the road, as it didn't do to get too distracted when traveling on such narrow roads where people drove like they were on a six-lane freeway.

Noah was outside with the horses when they arrived. She appreciated that he had chosen to greet them in this way, casually, as if they dropped by often and it was not the sort of visit that made her stomach feel as though it was rife with angry butterflies.

It was an idyllic day to be here. The land unrolled around them in a blanket of stinging green growth and the sheep were out of their paddock and in the pasture with wobbly balls of white wool at their sides. The horses were milling around near the stable, sun gleaming off their coats. Ruby, a beautiful chestnut which Pamela had ridden a few times, gave a long whinny at the sight of her and trotted over to them.

Noah dug in his pocket, where he always kept a few sugar cubes for his horses. He held them out to Conor.

"Would ye like to give these to the horse? Her name is Ruby."

Conor gave Noah a wary side eye, but took the sugar cubes and held them out in his hand. Ruby took them gently, her lips just barely grazing Conor's palm.

"When ye live here, laddie, ye can ride her every day if ye care to, she's nice an' gentle."

"I don't want to come live here."

"Conor," Pamela said, voice stern.

"'Tis all right, Pamela, the laddie is allowed his own opinion."

"Don't call me laddie! Only Jamie can call me that," Conor said hotly and Pamela opened her mouth to reprimand him for his rudeness, but Noah shook his head. They were all saved then by the arrival of Khamsin trotting up, beautiful neck arched and his coat as bright as freshly-polished glass. The colt went straight to Conor and nosed his velvety little muzzle right into Conor's neck, and Conor laughed out loud. Pamela breathed a sigh of relief. Noah smiled at her over the heads of the colt and child, and shrugged as if to say, 'It will take time.'

Kate took Isabelle by the hand, and Vanya said, "Come, Conor, your mama tells me there are new lambs in the byre, let's go see them." Khamsin trotted quite happily along with them, clearly as taken with Conor as her son was with him. She was about to follow, when Noah spoke.

"Pamela, can ye stay back a minute?"

She turned in surprise, halted by the tone in his words. Conor and Isabelle were already halfway down the path to the byre with Kate and Vanya. They would be fine for a few minutes without her.

He had something in his hand, and when she realized what it was—a tiny blue velvet box—she felt a rush of panic. Noah stepped toward her and opened the box.

"I wanted to get ye a ring, because without it this doesn't seem entirely official, an' I would just as soon that it did. The ring will formalize things."

"I...but you gave me Khamsin instead of a ring," she blurted out, her throat dry.

"Aye, the more I thought on it, though, the more I felt a ring necessary. It's maybe more for me than you, come right down to it. Will ye wear it?"

She found she couldn't respond, the panic that had started in her chest washed through her body down into her legs which felt like they might give out at any second. Noah opened the box and held it out to her.

It was a tear-drop sapphire, a deep and glowing blue and it was rather shockingly large. She swallowed. Casey's silver band was still on the ring finger of her left hand. The thought of taking it off made the bottom of her stomach drop out and she clenched her hand around the narrow band, knowing that if she was to find the courage to take it off, it would have to be done privately. Noah closed the lid and handed her the box. Clearly, he had seen the reflexive clutch of her hand.

"When ye're ready," he said gently and leaned over to kiss her on the cheek.

"Thank you," she looked up at him. She appreciated that he understood, she only hoped that he wasn't hurt by her inability to put his ring on this minute.

"Pamela, I know this is not a love match for the two of us, but we can make our own rules as we go along, aye?"

She nodded. "Thank you for being patient with me, Noah, it means a great deal."

"Ye're welcome," he said gruffly. "Now let's go out an' see those lambs."

Viewing the lambs, and even having Noah tell him he could choose one for his own, had done little to soften Conor's attitude toward the man. He had eaten his supper when they arrived home, but he hadn't spoken much, not even when she tried to draw him out about Khamsin with whom he was in fast and furious mutual love. When it came to horses and the ocean, Conor was her son; when it came to pure undiluted stubbornness, he was his father's through and through. She allowed him his space and let him go about his business in silence for the evening. He told her he didn't want his bedtime story, but he said it politely, if a touch frostily. Like his Uncle Patrick, Conor needed time to think things through in his own manner, without being pushed to an opinion or answer. She understood his anger, and his confusion, she felt a bit that way herself most days. She wasn't certain how to fix it for him, but she did want to speak with him before he went to sleep, so that there was peace in the house tonight. Both for his sake and for hers.

It was cool in the children's room and Isabelle was snuggled up under her red quilt, her curls a wild halo around her tiny face. Conor's eyes were shut but she had long known the difference between her sleeping son and her awake son and knew he was pretending. He was lying on his back with his blankets clutched firmly under his chin. She raised an eyebrow, if he was truly asleep the blankets would have been on the floor and he would be sprawled on his tummy.

She leaned down and kissed his forehead. His eyes remained firmly shut.

"Conor, I know you're awake, sweetheart. Sit up, mama needs to talk to you."

She sat down on the side of the bed as Conor sat up and looked at her with the familiar stubborn set to his chin that he'd had since birth.

"We have to talk about moving, Conor. We have to talk about me marrying Noah."

"Uncle Pat talked to me about Noah." His little face was flushed, and she could tell he was using all his resources so that he would not cry.

"Did he then? What did Uncle Pat have to say about Noah?"

"He told me that my daddy would want me to be good, an' to be s-sup-su-"

"Supportive?"

"Aye, that's the word he said. He told me what it means, too," Conor said, somewhat defensively lest she was about to cast aspersions on his understanding. "I don't think Daddy would like Mister Noah, an' I *know* Jamie doesn't like him," he added, as if the mention of Jamie ought to underscore his own opinion as being true and just.

Pamela sighed. Certainly that was true. Conor remembered Casey well enough to know that, and he didn't need to be extra sensitive to know how Jamie felt about Noah.

"No, Jamie doesn't like him, but I do and I think, Conor, if you give it time and are fair with him, you might learn to like him, too. I don't expect you will right away, but you do need to give him a chance. He wants to have a good relationship with you, and so you need to meet him at least part way—do you understand what that means?"

"Aye," he said, small face still troubled. "It means you want me to be nice to him. If you *have* to get married, I wish you would marry Jamie. He loves all of us, not just you."

"Jamie is already married, Conor, he can't have two wives."

He swallowed, looking down at the blue squares of his quilt. "I know that, Mama, I just miss him."

"I do too, Conor. I think we might always miss Jamie. We're going to be all right, though, we have each other and that's enough." And it would have been enough, had she not been terrified of the letters that continued to come to her home. She would have married Beelzebub himself to keep her children safe. Noah was hardly Beelzebub, though she supposed Jamie and Conor might dispute that. No one really understood it, but she was fond of Noah and she did enjoy his company. It was enough to begin a marriage.

"Mama, I love you," Conor said, his eyes bright with tears. He threw his arms around her neck, squeezing her hard, his little body straining with emotion. He'd had to face so much for someone still so young, and he had already shown a depth of character which told her that one day he would be a very fine man.

"I love you too, baby, so much," she said, burying her face in his hair and holding him as tightly as she could to her. He smelled of all the things that were home to her—green growing things and horses and baking bread and the rough and tumble little boy that he was.

She stayed with him until he fell asleep, too troubled in mind herself to rest. There was something she had to do, and until she did there would be no ease for her. She had put the ring on the mantle of the hearth, hiding it behind the carving of a bird. Hiding it had done little good, for through dinner and baths and bedtime routine, the ring had been a small coal burning through her consciousness.

After Conor fell asleep she went downstairs and tidied up the kitchen and turned off all the lights, except the one over the stove that she had left burning every night for nearly three years. She went upstairs with Noah's ring, beautiful and shimmering in its velvet bed. It was ironic that he had chosen a sapphire because it was a long ago memory of seeing a sapphire in the window of a jewelry store in Dublin which had caused Casey to call her Jewel.

She sat on the side of the bed and took a long and shaky breath. She had a dull headache setting up house behind her eyes. Sometimes it felt to her like her life had assumed a strange shape she was never going to fully understand. Because things had been so natural with Casey, because she had loved him so, their daily life had possessed a fluidity where the borders moved and changed, but it was a natural movement. Now, it felt as if she moved from fear to sorrow to anger and then back again. This was not a natural country to live in, though, and therefore different rules applied. Everywhere in the world people married for all sorts of reasons, and love wasn't always part of the equation.

She put her hands on her knees, the low flame from the hearth sparking off her wedding ring. She remembered the day Casey had put it on her hand, and how hard he had worked in order to buy it. They hadn't had two pennies to rub together at the time and so he had put in extra shifts so he could get it for her. Their wedding had been such an impromptu affair that he gave her the ring two months later. In bed, no less. She smiled at the memory. She had been lying in the crook of his arm, while they chatted about the day, the night as soft as navy silk around them.

"Give me yer hand, woman," he said, just when he had been quiet so long that she thought he must have drifted off. "Not that one, the other."

She had given him her left hand then and he had held it up so that the light that drifted through their bedroom window outlined it in a soft ivory-blue. And then he had slid the ring over her finger and kissed her hand, softly.

"We've been married the two months today, I thought it was past time I put a ring on yer hand."

"It's beautiful," she said, tears pricking at the back of her eyes. They had very little money and she hadn't thought about a ring.

"No, it's not, Jewel, it's a plain little band, an' one day I hope to replace it with somethin' much nicer an' fittin' for that lovely hand of yers."

"I won't ever take it off, you'll just have to add on to it."

"Aye, I can do that," he said and kissed her. "For now I just wanted ye to have somethin' tangible about ye each day to remind ye that I am yers an' ye're mine, for the rest of our lives."

"I don't need reminding of that, Casey. I know it in my cells, you're my mate."

The words came back to her now. They had been true when she had spoken them, and they were true now. His absence did not lessen the veracity contained therein. Sometimes love seemed like a luxury which her present life could no longer afford. Noah had said when she was ready, but she would never be ready, not really, so there was no use in putting it off for a day that would not come.

She looked at the small blue velvet box. The ring was beautiful, even if it would never look as right on her hand as this narrow silver band. She put her fingers around Casey's ring. It was just a little piece of metal and yet it felt like she was about to rip away some vital part of her own body. She tightened her grip and pulled it up the finger and off. The pain of it was visceral and it took her breath away for a moment. This longing, this wanting more and all of a man who had long been dead—yes, she had to admit it—dead, was akin to slowly bleeding to death. Except that if she were actually physically bleeding she would eventually die from it, whereas this figurative bleeding would never end. It might, one day in the far future, slow to a trickle but it would never fully stop. She had to live with that and accept it was part of who she now was.

She got up and put the ring inside a scarf that Casey had given her when they lived in Boston, because he said it matched her eyes. And then she sat back down on the bed they had once shared and cried until, exhausted, she fell asleep.

Part Nine

Cosan na Marbh
August 1978-November 1978

Chapter Seventy-seven

The Country of Shadows

"I SHOULD LIKE TO KNOW what the fock ye think ye are doin'?"

"Please come in, Patrick," Pamela said and stepped aside. He came in, the steam fairly puffing from his ears, despite the rain running in rivulets down his face and his coat. He took his jacket off, and hung it on a hook to dry. He followed her into the kitchen and she could feel him behind her, like a steaming kettle about to go off in an eruption of boiling water. She had a good notion why he was here, for Gert had seen the ring on her finger the day before. She had hoped to tell Pat about the engagement in a much gentler fashion, not that it was likely to help.

Conor was out in the byre, playing, being only slightly less upset with her than his uncle appeared to be. Isabelle was upstairs having her afternoon nap, and so now she supposed, was as good a time as any to have this conversation.

"I take it you've heard about the engagement," she said, turning to face him, though her stomach was tied in knots. Other than Jamie, Pat was the person she had most feared telling. "I don't suppose you've come to offer your congratulations on my forthcoming nuptials?"

"No, I goddamn well have not!" Pat said heatedly. It was an indication of just how strongly he felt that he had sworn twice in the last two minutes. "I can't imagine what ye're thinkin', Pamela."

"Do you expect me to be alone for the rest of my life?" she asked, her tone flat.

He shook his head. "Of course not. Ye know that isn't somethin' I would ever wish for ye."

"Then what should I do?" she asked. "I am not going to love another man. This is it for me. So I should never even hope for companionship, or someone to talk to over the dinner table or have a cup of tea with at night? I like his company, as hard as that is for everyone to understand. I'm comfortable with him, as he is with me. It's that simple."

"Lord, Pamela, do you hear yourself? Ye sound like some tragic old woman resigned to her fate."

"That's exactly what I'm *not*," she said firmly. "Patrick, tell me the truth, do you really believe I could ever love another man the way I loved your brother?"

He sighed. The look on his face was very familiar. It was the look Casey used to get just before telling her how incredibly stubborn and difficult she was.

"I do think ye could have somethin' rare an' fine with Jamie, given time an' the chance of it," he said.

"That's a weak argument for a lawyer, particularly given Jamie's current situation," she said. "It's partly because of Jamie that I said yes to Noah's proposal."

"What? That makes no damn sense at all."

"Don't you see, Patrick? It will free him. When I marry Noah, Jamie will be able to get on with his life in a way he could not if I were on my own with his child. He will always be this baby's father, but I need to break the chains that bind him to me."

"And you think marrying Noah will do that for him? It won't, Pamela. The man will always love you, and I suspect you will always love him."

"I will," she admitted calmly, "but it doesn't matter. He's married and has to remain so in order to keep Kolya; it would break him to give up his son. I would never put him in the position of making that kind of choice, Patrick. Once I marry Noah, I won't see Jamie anymore, other than when I need to hand over the baby for visits. I know you've been worried that I would never be able to move on from Casey's disappearance and I admit, I don't know sometimes that I ever will. But I am learning to make a life for myself and the children without him. I have given it a lot of thought; I'm not making this decision lightly."

"I think Noah loves you, Pamela. Do ye really believe what ye're proposin' is goin' to be enough for him?"

"I don't know. I am very fond of him, though I don't expect you to understand that. There are many forms of affection and what I feel for him is very different than what I felt for Casey. If I had a choice I would always want what I had with your brother, but I don't have that choice anymore. I am making the best of a bad business."

Pat threw up his hands, she knew, however, it was in frustration and not surrender to her argument.

"Have ye told Jamie yet? The man is not going to be pleased by the notion of Noah bein' a stepfather to his child."

"I know. I do have to talk to him, though it's a bit awkward these days going to his house. It's not something I feel I can say over the telephone."

"No, I don't imagine so," Pat said, an edge still in his voice. The truth was that she was avoiding telling Jamie because she knew it wasn't likely to go well, and also because she knew this entire situation was difficult for him. He was stuck between a rock and a hard place with no room to move.

"Ye know he's retained Tomas as counsel? Tomas loves ye like ye're his own daughter, Pamela but he will advise Jamie to seek full custody of the child if ye marry Noah. I can't say I blame him either."

She nodded. "This is real life, Patrick. And in real life there are no guarantees of happiness. We both know that. I'm not the girl who came here all those years ago. I've had a lot of stars taken out of my eyes. I think I can actually build something decent with Noah. Not the stuff of love songs and epic novels but something that will be enough for the both of us at the end of the day. I don't have expectations of anything else, nor does he."

Pat shook his head and took a long breath in, before responding. "Pamela, ye know if ye need anythin', or if ye should change yer mind— I'm still yer family, I always will be."

"I do know that and I thank you for it." She leaned up on tiptoe and kissed his cheek and then laughed, rubbing at her lips. "You're just like your brother, well stubbled by noon."

"Aye," he said, "Daddy was the same. Said it was the curse the fairies had put upon the Riordan men at birth, an' that we'd need a magical razor to ever keep up."

"I suppose Conor will be the same one day."

"Aye, I imagine he will. I want to be there for the children too, Pamela. I want them to always know they are Riordans, an' what their history is. I want to tell them about their daddy, an' give them all those stories about him when he was a boy. I want them to know the man their grandfather was, and for Conor to know how much he looks an' behaves like him."

"I want those things for them, as well. I won't let Casey become a memory to them, Patrick. He lives inside them after all, he lives inside me too."

"I know," he said and sighed. "It's only it feels like somethin' is endin' that began on the day my brother walked in to that kitchen and saw ye for the first time. I'm feelin' sad an' sentimental, Pamela. I only want what he wanted for ye, that ye should be happy an' loved."

"I know that, Pat. It will be all right, you'll see. Give it another year or two and it will seem perfectly natural—Noah and me."

"To be perfectly honest with ye, I doubt it will ever seem natural to see ye with anyone other than my brother. I know yer mind is made up, an' in certain respects I do understand. It's just that when I think of Casey an' what he would have wanted for ye, it breaks my heart to see what ye now expect of yer life. It's true that we're all havin' to adjust to things we couldn't have imagined even a year ago, much less the three that Casey has been gone. There are times it takes everything in me not to storm into Jamie's house and tell him to get some damn sense. An' there are times like right this minute that I want to curse my brother to hell an' back for ever puttin' himself in danger."

She squeezed his hand and smiled in what she hoped was a reassuring fashion.

"Will ye be sad to leave the house behind?" he asked.

She nodded, leaning back and rubbing her knuckles into her spine. "I will miss it, but in truth, Pat, I haven't felt safe here since Casey disappeared. And now, with Lewis selling up his farm, I won't even have a neighbor nearby who I know. Without your brother," she shrugged, "it doesn't matter so much to me where we live, as long as the children are safe and comfortable."

"Aye, I understand that. I don't like ye bein' out here all on yer own either. It's just the wee bit too isolated."

"I wouldn't have thought so at one time, but now it does feel too out of the way most days." She walked over to the windows, to check on Conor. He'd been quiet for a couple of minutes, and like all mothers, she knew when a small boy was quiet it didn't bode well. He was just digging a hole, which would have to be filled back in, but she would worry about that later.

"Do ye ever regret it, comin' here to this country?" Pat came and stood beside her, looking out over the yard.

"No, of course not. If I hadn't, I wouldn't have had the time I did with your brother, and I wouldn't have my children, either. And," she tucked her arm through his, "I would never have met you and that, as far as I'm concerned, would have been a great shame."

He smiled down at her, and patted her hand. "Aye, it would have been, indeed. Only ye've seen a great deal of darkness since ye've been here, particularly these last few years, none could blame ye if ye wished that away."

"This land," she said softly, "it's like living in a country of shadows, isn't it? Just when you think you've found a patch of sunlight to bask in, it's gone and the shadows roll over you again. Or maybe the shadows are always with us, biding their time, waiting, and our time in the sun is just a brief respite. There have been days since Casey disappeared that I feel like I'm a shadow myself, like I no longer have substance enough to be real. I feel as if I drift over the land and through the house and the only thing that tethers me to this world is the children. And then there are other days that I feel far too real."

She looked up and saw the worry in his face. "I'm sorry, I don't mean to sound so maudlin."

"I don't like to hear ye speak so, Pamela, but I would rather ye were honest with me than tell me lies to make me feel better."

"Thank you for that, Pat."

"I'll have to head home soon, but is there anything that needs doin' while I'm here? Ye can't be findin' it easy to tote about hay an' feed these days."

"Noah sees to it, either he or one of his men comes round in the morning and at night to do all the heavy work."

"Well, that's good," Pat said, though he sounded slightly reluctant to admit it.

"Yes," she agreed, "it is." Truth be told, it *was* good. Noah had taken over all the outside work, as well as bringing in groceries the day before and seeing to all the things that needed doing that she now found awkward or exhausting. He'd had dinner with them last night after helping her cook and it had been pleasant to have the company, even if Conor had been less than appreciative of it. Noah had noticed that she was wearing the ring and she had seen his eyes light up at the sight of it on her hand, before he had turned away, busying himself with putting a chicken in the oven.

"How is Kate feeling?" she asked, thinking it was time to steer the conversation on to less rocky shores.

"She's good, she's managin' pregnancy as she manages everythin' in life, with complete efficiency an' minimal fuss, so I do the fussin' for her." He smiled and she was happy to see he was excited about this impending child. "We've set a date for August."

"I know, she's already asked me to be her bridesmaid." She looked down at her burgeoning belly. "Hopefully I'll actually fit the dress when the day arrives."

"She wouldn't want anyone else, regardless of how pregnant ye are. Ye're her dearest friend, an' soon will be her sister-in-law."

"And how about you, Patrick? Who is standing up for you?"

"Jamie," he said. "I'm hopin' that's not goin' to be too awkward for the lot of us, but if it can't be my brother, then Jamie is the only other man I want standin' at my back that day."

"I understand that." Her mouth twitched and she bit the inside of her cheek to keep from laughing.

Pat gave her a sardonic look. "Oh, aye, I know what ye're thinkin', Pamela. It's got all the elements of a French farce—what with my pregnant sister-in-law as bridesmaid, my best man bein' the father of that baby, an' the fiancé likely glarin' from the front pew, who also just happens to be my future brother-in-law." He laughed. "Well, as they say, ye can't make this stuff up. I'll be fortunate not to have to break up fisticuffs over the punch bowl."

She laughed. "I'll behave myself beautifully, I promise. I'll speak with Noah, if you talk to Jamie. We're all grown-ups, we can manage to be civil for a day for the sake of two people we dearly love. I'm thrilled for you and Kate." She meant it sincerely. Patrick deserved this happiness and Kate was more than a match for him. She would be able to keep his home life happy and well organized while he tried to wrest justice from the heart of the maelstrom that was the court and policing system in the six counties.

"Thank you, I know ye mean it. I want to be happy for ye too, Pamela."

She shook her head. "You don't need to be, Pat. I understand this is difficult, Casey was my husband but he was your brother. I wouldn't expect you to be overly excited no matter who the man was."

"I'm here for ye, regardless, Pamela. Always."

She nodded her head, afraid she was going to cry. Pat wrapped his arms around her and gave her a long hug. His strength was a tangible thing that shored her up, and had done so more than once over these last few years.

She watched him as he stopped out in the yard, bending down to speak with Conor. She was grateful for the relationship Pat had forged with her son. He was such a steady presence that Conor would always be able to rely upon him, and she knew Conor already sensed that and so had implicit faith in his uncle.

Pat turned back just before he got into his car, and waved at her. Even at that distance the worry in his eyes was clear. She smiled reassuringly and waved back, hoping that her expression would ease his worries a little.

She could hear Isabelle stirring upstairs. She would go up and get her before she got into something she wasn't meant to. Then it would be time to start dinner. She was tired, but grateful for the small things that made up the round of each day, every task like a bead on the day's rosary, each one taking her to the next thing that needed doing, and giving the hours a foundation.

She stopped for a moment on the landing, and looked out the window. Conor was using a hammer and nails to build something, and Finbar and Paudeen were looking on patiently while Rusty observed it all from the top of a pile of wood. The sun had re-emerged as it had done fitfully all day and light rippled over the yard, casting green through the edges of the copse and the long grass that grew knee-height near to it. With the light came the shadows, always behind, but never far away. The dark of them sat deep in the grass, and lived beyond the edge of the wood, where light could only penetrate so far.

What she had told Pat was true, she did feel like she lived in a country of shadows. Her fear was that she might never find her way out of it, and that she no longer possessed the passport to cross the boundary back into a world where the sun shone upon her.

Chapter Seventy-eight

Of Ice Cream and Men

THE AIR WAS SLIGHTLY CHILLY, the scent of peat smoke enticing from some distant hearth. Pat had gone by Pamela's to see if she needed anything and had found her in a welter of boxes, newspaper smudges on her forehead and chin, and a look of exasperation in her eyes. When he realized his wee nephew was unpacking a box and surreptitiously hiding away the contents, he wisely asked him if he wanted to accompany him on an errand or two. Pamela had shot him a look of immense gratitude and given Conor a kiss on the top of his head before they left.

He'd taken the lad along with him while he picked up a couple of things Kate had asked for and dropped off some legal work with a client who was fighting his village council over housing allotments. He had offered ice cream, but at Conor's mumbled, "No thanks, Uncle Pat," he had realized the situation called for more serious measures.

He drove to an area he often came to when he needed to think his way through a particularly vexing bit of legalese, or when he needed to walk and not think at all. He had nearly worn a path through this wood during the months following Sylvie's death.

Conor walked along beside him, Pat keeping his pace slow so that Conor didn't need three steps for each of his own strides. His nephew wasn't given to a great deal of chatter, but he was especially silent today, small fists jammed deep into the pockets of his corduroy coat, and an air around him like that of a small but particularly dark and dense storm cloud.

"Is there somethin' troublin' ye, man?" he asked, careful to give the question the proper gravity so that Conor wouldn't feel he was making light of him. He had a good notion what, or rather whom, was bothering Conor but he felt it was wisest to let the laddie get it out with him rather than having an explosion in the future.

Conor stopped, scowling down at the ground near his feet. Pat stopped too and hunkered down in front of his nephew. He knew the look on Conor's face all too well. It was the look of a Riordan male in the full grip of a temper. Conor's eyes did the same odd thing Casey's had always done when he was in a fury—they turned a deep smoky grey, rather than their normal black-brown.

"Do ye need to hit somethin'?" he asked.

Conor looked at him, startled. "Daddy used to let me hit things when I was angry. Usually just my pillow."

"Well, I think a pillow might not be quite enough this time. I think maybe ye need to hit somethin' a wee bit bigger an' harder. Ye can hit me, right here in the stomach."

Conor gave him a look of profound dubiousness. "Mama doesn't allow me to hit people, she says it's not nice an' I'm not to do it."

"While yer mammy is right most times an' ye need to listen to what she tells ye to do, she is also a woman an' they don't always understand that sometimes a man has to hit somethin' to get his feelins' out. So hit me, laddie, I can take it." Pat stood and braced himself.

Conor took him at his word and hauled back then let fly, hitting Pat with a solid 'thwack' to his belly.

"*Whoof!*" Pat stepped back from the blow, slightly winded.

"Uncle Pat, did I hurt ye?" Conor asked, his wee face worried but the grey slowly fading from his eyes.

"No, laddie, but I will say this, ye've yer father's fists on ye. He was a fighter, ye know. He boxed in his teens an' all the boys around were frightened of havin' to take him on, because they knew they would lose."

"Really?"

"Aye, really."

"Did ye ever fight with him?"

"No, we got along well, yer daddy an' me. Now an' again he'd get frustrated with me because I'd follow him somewhere I wasn't meant to be. I never told our da', so for the most part he put up with his little brother trailin' him around."

"I miss him, Uncle Pat. I miss my daddy." Conor's lower lip was trembling ever so slightly and Pat kneeled down and put his arms out to the boy. Conor ran forward and threw his arms around Pat's neck. Pat hugged him close, knowing Conor needed reassurance from a man in his life right now. He held him as the little boy sobbed, and felt his heart break a bit with each cry from his nephew's throat.

"Oh, laddie, I miss him, too."

"I love you, Uncle Pat," he said, still sniffling but having loosened his grip a little on Pat's neck.

Pat pulled back so that he could look Conor in the eyes. The boy needed to know that he meant every word of what he was about to say. "I love you too, Conor. Ye know no matter what happens or where ye live, I will always be yer uncle. I'm yer daddy's brother an' that means I'll do for ye whatever he isn't here to do. But ye need to stop bein' angry at yer mammy for somethin' she can't fix for ye. I know ye don't like Noah, but ye're goin' to have to give him a chance. If ye want to talk about it, or ye feel so angry ye need to hit somethin' again, then ye call me an' I'll come get ye and we'll deal with it together, all right?"

Conor nodded. "All right."

He held him for a bit longer. His wee nephew was having to grow up faster than he would have liked but with all that had happened to Pamela in the last few years it couldn't be helped. There was only so much from which she could shield her children. It was her desire to protect them that had led, he believed, to her agreeing to marry Noah. He was only afraid that she was bartering part of her soul to the devil she knew rather than risking the devil she did not. It stuck in his craw to speak kindly of Noah to Conor, but if the lad was going to be living with the man, it would be best if they started out on good footing. There was no way to explain to someone so young why his mother might choose to marry for reasons which had nothing to do with love. He would just have to be here for his brother's children in the years ahead, come what may.

"Uncle Pat?" Conor was looking up at him, as they began the walk back.

"Aye?" Pat steeled himself for one of those unanswerable questions children this age were wont to ask.

"Can we get ice cream now?"

Chapter Seventy-nine

The Infinite Ache
August 1978

THE MORNING OF THE WEDDING dawned fair and bright. Pamela was up to see the sun rise, spilling rose-gold over the hedgerows and painting the blackberry brambles and roses a glowing pink. There was a little breeze, and no sign of rain on the horizon at all. Pat and Kate would have a lovely day for their wedding. She stood by the octagonal window on the staircase, which had become both a confessional and a comfort over these last three years. Conor and Isabelle were still asleep and the house was hushed and peaceful around her.

She spoke softly to the morning, its rosy hue staining the window. "Patrick and Kate are getting married today and they're going to have a baby. You'd be so pleased and proud if you were here." It had become habit of late—this, stopping to have a chat with him by the window, letting him know the day's events, as if somehow the octagon was a magical bit of glass where neither time nor space held sway. She realized, especially on days like today, that she had kept some part of Casey locked away in a vault in her heart, where his disappearance had been the stuff of fairy tales, and he might reappear again if only she could remember the magic spell to release him from his banishment. She was just a woman, though, and did not have words of magic at her disposal. But even if it was only a bit of glass, she could not bring herself to tell him that she, too, was getting married again, and that she, too, was having a baby.

She touched the window, pressing her palm to the warmth of the rising sun washing through it and closed her eyes for a moment, as if she could reach Casey through it, and have that big hand grasp hers and reassure her that all would be well. She opened her eyes and turned away from the window; it was time to get ready.

The wedding was at one o'clock, and by eleven that morning, Conor was washed and pressed into his new suit. He looked like a little man in the navy suit, straight-backed and assured even if the expression on his face was that of a choking goose.

"Come here, sweetheart," she said to him and he walked over to her, his fingers still plucking at his collar. She knelt down in front of him and undid his top button, rearranging his small blue tie neatly over it.

"Is that better?"

"Aye," Conor said, nerves in evidence. His uncle had asked him to be the ring bearer, and Conor was anxious about doing his duty with the gravity required by the ceremony. She smoothed his hair back, it was still damp from the bath, but his curls were already fighting to escape the careful combing she had given them.

Isabelle, on the other hand, was perfectly happy in her tiny pink dress, with a circlet of pink roses nestled in her abundant curls. She looked like a perfect wild wee fairy. She was going to scatter the same pink rose petals down the aisle in front of her Auntie Kate. Pamela hoped she could resist skipping or dancing in the church. Isabelle was a child of exuberant temperament. She glanced at herself in the little mirror in the boot room. She was pale but the soft pink Kate had chosen for her wedding party, which consisted solely of Pamela and Isabelle, put a soft flush in her cheeks. Her hair was up, tidied away as best as she could manage, though wayward curls had already escaped the two dozen pins she'd fastened them with and were spiraling up around her face and neck.

Noah had offered to pick her up, but she had demurred and said his main priority was to get Kate to the church on time and she would meet them there. Pat would ride with Jamie, and then he and Kate would have Noah's car afterwards. So it was that she and Conor and a much excited Isabelle drove up to Father Jim's simple church in the beaten Citroën, which chuffed everywhere like a smoker on its last wheeze but got them there in due time.

Noah must have heard the sound of her car, for he stepped out of the church just as she pulled up. He looked handsome in a dark grey suit and crisp white shirt. He opened the car door for her and then stepped back to help Isabelle out of the rear seat. Isabelle took Noah's hand without hesitation, tumbling out in a welter of pink frills and falling rose petals, held firmly by Noah's hand. Isabelle did not share Conor's reservations about

Noah, though she still asked after Jamie what seemed like fifty times a day, to Pamela's beleaguered ears.

Noah looked up from Isabelle to Pamela and smiled. "Ye're beautiful, even more so than usual, an' that's sayin' somethin'," he said. The look that accompanied his words made her nervous and she flushed hotly, color flaming up from her neckline to sting her cheeks and hairline. He offered her his arm and she took it, raising an eyebrow at Conor's scowl and giving her other hand to Isabelle.

Kate was waiting in the tiny room provided for the bride, her bouquet set to one side. She had gone with a simple arrangement of violets tied with dark green ribbon. She looked up nervously as Pamela came in, her hands clenched together.

"He *is* here, isn't he?" she asked.

"Of course he's here," Pamela said, laughing. "I'm going to go see him for a minute, and then it will be time."

She went and put her arms around Kate carefully not wanting to wrinkle the lovely silk gown she wore. "Oh Kate, you look absolutely exquisite." The compliment was not an exaggeration, for Kate did look exquisite. Her dress was simple; the veil an antique which she had wisely left in its original state. The dress brought out the purity of her beauty. Her chestnut hair was pulled up in a simple knot, and her remarkable gentian eyes were alight with joy.

"You look beautiful too," Kate said. "I know because my brother hasn't taken his eyes off ye since the two of ye came in."

"Now, how can you know that?" she asked, feeling strangely nervous.

"Pamela, there are more ways to see than just with the eyes, ye know that well enough."

Noah's gaze wasn't the only thing making her nervous just now for the thought of being in the same building with Noah and Jamie, was giving her a nasty case of butterflies. She would have to trust that both men cared enough for Patrick and Kate to rein in their hostility toward one another. That dubious faith hadn't prevented a nervous rash from breaking out on the back of her neck, however.

She slipped into Father Jim's office which was where the grooms waited for their turn at the altar. Pat was just putting his suit jacket on. She realized suddenly what a handsome man he had become, certain in himself, no longer Casey's little brother or the boy she had met in a history class some years ago. Her throat was tight with tears and she wished that Casey was here to adjust Pat's tie and impart marital wisdom to him. She wished Brian Riordan was still alive to see the fine man his youngest son had become.

Pat smiled at her, the lovely smile that lit up his whole face. If he had any nerves today they were well hidden. Pat had long been a man of certainties, he had understood for a time now that Kate was the woman with whom he was meant to spend his life.

She adjusted his tie, which was slightly askew, he wasn't any fonder of collars and ties than his brother and nephew were. "Wait until you see your bride, she looks so lovely."

"I can't believe the woman finally agreed to marry me," he said. "I feel a wee bit superstitious about bein' this happy."

"It will all be well, Patrick. She was meant for you and you for her. I knew it the first time I saw the two of you together—remember when you brought her down to the cottage in Kerry that summer?"

"Of course I remember." They were silent for a moment for they were thinking of the man who had been there but was not here, and without whom this day could not be quite complete.

"I just wanted to tell you that I wish every joy for the two of you. I'm so happy for you, Patrick and I know Casey would be, too. I wish he was here, you deserve to have your family with you."

Pat reached down and squeezed her hand. "I do have family here today. You an' the children are my family."

Jamie came in then. He had his head down as he adjusted his cuffs and didn't see her at once.

"Father Jim says five minutes, Patrick. Are you ready?"

He was clad in a beautifully-cut suit and his hair was freshly trimmed and gleaming in the sunlight that fell through the office window. He looked up, and halted in his tracks like a hand had come up and hit him in the chest. Being Jamie he quickly recovered, but he had never been able to dissemble swiftly enough to disguise himself from her. She had seen the look of naked pain in his eyes for a flash second and knew the echo of it was there in her own eyes. She put her hand behind her back not wanting him to see her ring. He had to be told about her engagement, and yet she had not found the courage to do it yet.

"Pamela," he said, grace coming to the fore as it always did with him. He was never less than a gentleman, except, she thought, in bed. And then flushed, knowing how easily the man read her mind.

"Jamie, it's good to see you," she said, because, despite feeling as if someone had punched her just from the mere sight of the man, it *was* good to see him. Like drinking a long draught of cold water after walking for days without.

"Likewise," he said, and smiled. It didn't reach his eyes, though, and the dreadful constraint rose between them like a cloud of sand, cloying and hard to breathe.

"I need to get back to Kate," she said, heart thumping miserably in her chest. She felt a sudden deflation of spirits and turned before Pat or

Jamie could see the tears that sprang to her eyes. Pregnancy always made her feel as fragile as Chinese porcelain, and right now she felt as if she were hovering at a great height and the slightest gesture would cause her to fall and shatter into a thousand pieces.

The two men were quiet behind her. Pat touched her shoulder and the feel of that big hand shored her up a little.

"I'll see you both at the altar," she said gaily and went out the door. She stopped in the tiny vestibule, took a deep breath, wiped her eyes and sallied forth with a smile for Kate and Noah.

The ceremony was beautiful and also long, as Catholic ceremonies were wont to be but lovely because of the two people making their vows to one another. Pamela's heart lightened just watching them, as they each said the words that would bear them through this life together and into the one beyond. She could not help but think of her own wedding day, and how intimate it had been. She had been nervous until Casey had taken her hands in his own and smiled down at her and she had known the adventure they were about to embark upon was the most right thing in the world. Pat and Kate would have their own story, but she remembered well how it felt to set out on a life together, knowing you were no longer alone and had someone that loved you at your side and whom you loved in return.

She looked down and smiled. After Conor had done his duty as ring bearer he had come to stand beside her, as if he instinctively knew his mother needed his solid reassurance. He had tucked his small hand in hers and left it there throughout the ceremony. Isabelle, too, had done her work as flower girl well, skipping up the aisle to the laughter of all assembled and shrieking 'Jamezie!!' in the excitement of seeing her favorite man after what she deemed an inexplicable absence of such a long duration. Jamie knelt down and swept her up and that was where she had stayed—in the crook of Jamie's arm—for the length of the ceremony. Pamela had not even dared to look at Noah, but she could feel his gaze from where he sat in the front pew.

After, she signed the papers as a witness and then handed the pen to Jamie. It felt oddly intimate, the two of them bearing witness to a marriage, putting their signatures side-by-side and standing back together watching Pat and Kate sign. She could smell him—leather and lime and sandalwood and the comfort of these last three years, the scent which had told her she was secure for the moment, that she could relax her vigilance because Jamie would look after all of them. And he had, just as he had done from the moment she had first arrived in his house, unannounced, uninvited and welcomed just the same, all those years ago. Her throat was tight with tears, though thankfully no one would question it if she were to cry during a wedding ceremony.

There were pictures taken and then they all retired to the Emerald Pub as Gallagher's wasn't big enough. Pat and Kate had wanted the day kept simple; a few friends, their family, a nice meal and a cake. It was a lovely day, and she thought it was likely no one outside of her, Pat and Kate, could feel the tension which strung the air tighter than a freshly-tuned fiddle, between Jamie and Noah. Generally, Jamie could finesse any social situation to his advantage, or at least put everyone else at ease in the light of his charm and conversation. This particular situation seemed to be beyond him, though, and she felt as if she were walking a high wire each time the two men locked eyes across the room. They were, at least, smart enough to keep their distance from one another.

It was an effort of will not to gaze at Jamie, to just drink in his presence and ease, a little, the ache that sat below her breastbone. Contact was unavoidable, however, as they were both seated at the same table with Patrick and Kate, their chairs only feet apart.

They spoke, it seemed, of everything except that which mattered between the two of them.

At one point, unthinking, she had put her hand upon the table, resting it on the white linen. Jamie glanced down at it, and suddenly her ring felt horribly conspicuous, as if instead of the tasteful sapphire it was, it had become, through the alchemy of Jamie's glance, enormous and gaudy. He looked away quickly, responding to a question of Patrick's.

Dinner passed swiftly, and Jamie rose near the end to toast Patrick and Kate, in words so lovely that even Pat had a suspicious gleam in his eyes when he was done.

Noah came to sit with her when Jamie's toast was done. It was, of course, his right as her fiancé and Kate's brother but she felt her blood pressure go up a couple of notches as he settled in beside her, and she noted Jamie's hand whitened with tension around his glass. It was his second glass of wine, of little note with most people, but Jamie was normally so abstemious that it surprised her. It didn't bode well.

The tension was so palpable and overwhelming that it rendered her temporarily deaf. The chatter around her suddenly seemed as if it were occurring at a great distance, and she thought maybe she was going to faint. Such was her stress at sitting between these two men, that she found the idea of lapsing into a swoon quite attractive. Alas, she was not so fortunate and found to her horror, as her hearing returned to its normal level of function, the aforesaid two men were talking to each other. Coming into the conversation partway, she didn't know how it had begun, but she could tell already it was headed down a pathway which was a well-stocked minefield.

"It's the world we live in," Noah was saying, "that's just the fact of it."

"It's not a world I want my children growing up in," Jamie replied coldly.

"Children? I didn't realize ye had more than the one," Noah said casually, like this was a normal conversation between two men at a social event.

"I think," Jamie said with the drawl he only used when he was furious, "you're very well aware that I will soon have two. For the both of them I would like us to find another answer to the age-old Irish question."

"What other answer is there right now? Theoretically it's sound thinkin' to want peace. But at what cost? Puttin' down guns on the republican side isn't goin' to guarantee the other side doin' the same. Ye know that well enough, I'm certain."

"We will have to turn away from violence as a solution in this country at some point," Jamie said. "It's either that or what—continue with the politics of blood and gun until another generation is decimated?" He lifted his wine glass to his lips, and took a good-sized swallow.

"Easy enough said when ye're immune to it, livin' on yer lofty hill away from the hoi-polloi who only have to walk out their garden gate to lose their life. Or be sellin' milk an' bread in a mobile shop. Are we to lie down an' let them keep slaughterin' us? Is that yer high-minded solution?"

"No, I'm not fool enough to believe that peace will be anything but very slow in coming. We have to start on the process one day, why not now? After all, tit-for-tat revenge killings just perpetuate this unending cycle of violence, and that isn't going to get us anywhere except a whole lot more headstones in the cemetery," Jamie said, the heat in his voice intensifying. She glanced rather desperately toward Pat, but he and Kate were turned around talking to his Aunt Fee, and were not aware of the conversation between the two men—which was a blessing of sorts, she supposed.

"Tell that to the families who have lost their loved ones to armed thugs breakin' down their doors at three of a mornin'. Tell that to Pamela, with a gun near to hand all the time, just so she can sleep at night. A woman with wee children, an' ye know as well as I do that they would kill her without a second's hesitation. You tell me how we build peace on the back of madmen."

"Pamela," Jamie said quietly, "is this true?"

Noah answered for her.

"Ye need not worry for her, her well-being is my business now, an' I take it *very* seriously."

Jamie leaned back in his chair, a look of cool bemusement on his face. "Do you, indeed? Perhaps then, *you* should have kept away from her."

"An' what has proximity to you done for her—other than leave her pregnant an' unwed?"

"Noah, please," Pamela said, hoping the desperation in her tone would penetrate at least one man's anger. Her chest was tight with anxiety, because she knew even the most harmless argument between these two was going to escalate swiftly, and this argument wasn't harmless in the least.

She hiccoughed, which was one way insurmountable tension tended to manifest in her. Jamie shot her a sidelong glance.

"I think we need to cease and desist," he said smoothly, "as I believe we're upsetting Pamela. She only gets hiccoughs when she's especially nervous." He had the silken smile on his face which could be found in portraits of certain of his ancestors, and which he only assumed when he wanted to annoy the other person.

"Does she, indeed?" Noah said, not rising to the bait, though she noticed his foot was tapping an incessant beat on the floor. She thought she might, indeed, have to swoon in a moment if the two men did not stop.

Hiccough. Hiccough. Hiccough. Pat was now looking at her in alarm, as was Kate.

"Noah," Kate said, and there was a warning in her tone, as if there were a prior agreement which her brother was now breaking.

Pamela's hiccoughs were rising steadily in both intensity and frequency. She drank the glass of water Noah poured her, to little avail however other than spilling half of it down the front of her dress. Jamie offered her his napkin at the same time that Noah whipped a freshly pressed handkerchief out of his suit pocket and handed it to her. She took both napkin and handkerchief, burying her face in the starched depths of one, and flapping the other like a white flag of truce, indicating that they should stop hovering. Rescue came in the form of Aunt Sophy, who arrived in a rustle of taffeta, wafting Shalimar over all assembled.

"Come with me, Pamela, and we'll get ye sorted. The two of youze," she looked pointedly first at Jamie and then Noah, "ought to be ashamed."

Jamie looked up, green eyes still hectic with anger. "I am. I apologize, Pamela."

"I'm sorry," Noah said, and stood to help her from her chair.

"Men," Sophy said, with no small amount of disgust.

She hustled Pamela into the small pub kitchen. The windows were open and a small breeze blew through from the twilit woods beyond.

"Here, bend over the sink as best ye can, an' drink from the wrong side of the glass."

Pamela looked at her in surprise. "That's what Casey always got me to do."

"Aye well, he would, 'twas his daddy taught me to deal with hiccoughs that way."

She obediently drank from the wrong side of the glass and within five minutes she was leaning back against the counter, hiccoughs gone. She took a deep breath, and smoothed her hair back with the droplets of water left on her hands.

"Hard day for you, lass," Sophy said, and it wasn't a question.

"Yes, it is. I'm very happy for Patrick though, he deserves every bit of joy that comes his way."

"Aye, ye can be happy for him, an' still have yer own hurt. I know ye miss Casey every day but I would think days like today are especially difficult. Because he ought to be here by yer side, celebratin' his brother's weddin'. He ought to be the man takin' ye home at the end of night."

"He ought to be, but he can't be any more, and I think I'm beginning to truly understand what that means to my life."

Sophy reached over and squeezed her hand. "I'm that sorry, girl."

"I know," she said, "thank you."

They returned to the table to find that Noah was gone.

"He had a phone call," Pat said, noting her glance at the chair where Tomas now sat. Jamie rose and pulled her chair out and she sank into it gratefully. She knew she and the children would have to leave soon, so as to put a halt to any further contretemps between Jamie and Noah.

Sophy settled into a chair and grinned at her nephew.

"Will ye want me to talk to wee Paddy about the birds an' the bees, just so ye're certain he knows what's what tonight?" Sophy asked Kate.

"Oh, he knows his business well enough," Kate said, smiling, "bein' that I'm three months pregnant."

"Those Riordan boys have always been a precocious lot."

Long accustomed to the bold women in his family, Pat merely laughed. "Ah, but you'd be the expert in this area, Aunt Sophy. I do remember the drawins' ye showed us. Scarred the lot of us for life, an' it's not likely we'll ever forget."

"Ah, boyo don't force me to tell the story about yerself an' the nunnery," Sophy said, blue eyes alight with mischief.

Pat colored up and gave a rueful laugh. "That's not fair Aunt Sophy, ye know all my secrets."

She reached over and patted his cheek. "Ach, I'm only teasin', man. Ye're a lucky lass, Miss Kate, an' make no mistake of it. He's goin' to make ye a fine husband."

Kate smiled and leaned her head on Pat's shoulder. The look on her face was a lovely thing to behold. Pamela felt a small ache of envy in her own chest. She knew what it was to have that glow and she knew what it was to lose it.

"Is every woman in yer family a contrary bit of baggage?" Tomas asked Pat. He winked at Pamela, and she sent a silent thank you his way for lightening the mood at the table.

"Aye," Pat said, leaning over to kiss Kate, "they are, but we men wouldn't have them any other way."

"Ye don't see the men complainin' now do ye?" Sophy said.

"Ye have a husband? I'm surprised there's a man with the fortitude," Tomas said, with a wicked smile.

"Aye, there is, an' there was another before him," Sophy said easily, one well-plucked red brow arched in Tomas' direction.

"Did ye wear him down—the first one?"

"He died in bed," Sophy said pleasantly, "ye may apply yer fine legal mind to that an' draw yer own conclusions."

Tomas' eyebrows shot up and it was clear that he couldn't decide whether Sophy was in jest or not. Pamela suspected not, but made a mental note to ask Patrick later.

"I concede the floor to ye, lady, ye've rendered me speechless an' there's not many can say that."

The entire table dissolved into laughter, which owed as much she knew, to Noah's absence as it did to the sight of Tomas surrendering to a woman.

She stretched a little and leaned back in her chair, stroking her belly instinctively, for the baby was kicking, small thumps against her hand, barely felt on the outside but strong on the inside. She became aware of Jamie's regard, and stilled her hand, turning toward him before she could think to stop herself.

His gaze was utterly naked, and held within the green eyes was a longing so pure and piercing that she could not bear to see it. She turned away, feeling like she had seen something she was not meant to, something terribly private and painful. She clutched her napkin in her fingers, the band of the sapphire ring cutting into her flesh. The chatter and laughter around the table had not abated, and she was glad of it, praying that no one had noticed what had passed.

"You will excuse me," Jamie said quietly, and rose from the table.

Tomas was chatting with Sophy and Kate, and for a moment it was just she and Pat. There was a sympathy in the dark eyes that she could not bear to see. She was near tears as it was and Pat had always seen things too clearly. She had a transparent face at the best of times, and today, feeling particularly vulnerable had left her, she suspected, as easily read as a large print book.

"Pamela—"

She cut him off before he could say the words. "No, Pat, not today, please."

Sophy took in the situation in one glance and pulled Pat's attention away, giving Pamela the opportunity to leave the table.

She walked over to Noah, who was standing by the bar, a drink in his hand, which he had not touched. He looked at her and smiled, gentian eyes warm. One would think the tension between he and Jamie had never occurred.

"Ye look tired, it's been a long day, no?" Noah said.

"Yes, it has been. Lovely, but long. Would you mind taking us home soon?"

"Whenever ye'd like," he replied amiably.

"We can say our goodbyes to Pat and Kate, and then I'd like to go."

He nodded. "I'll go fetch the coats an' meet ye out front."

She breathed out with relief. She wanted to go home and take off her shoes and stockings. Her feet were swollen and her back was aching. Isabelle was tired, and from past experience Pamela knew she needed to get her home and in her pajamas before she went past the point of no return.

Isabelle, however, was having none of it. Stirred from a half doze on Gert's ample lap, she discovered that her roses had disappeared.

"Me needs a' find my cwown," she said stubbornly.

"Sweetheart, the roses were wilting anyway," Pamela said, knowing it was futile even as she said the words. Once Isabelle got a notion in her head there was little dissuading her.

"Me needs my *cwown*," Isabelle repeated, adding emphasis with a stomp of one tiny patent leather clad foot. She set her chin in an expression Pamela was all too familiar with. She sighed, she was going to have to find the tiny wreath of roses before they could leave, or suffer the indignant wrath of an exhausted three-year-old.

Pat, always able to sense another Riordan on the brew, came over to them and took Isabelle up in his arms, distracting her with a small ashtray which was filled with marbles. He nodded to Pamela, who cast about for the roses to no avail. Sophy came over and said, "If ye're lookin' for the wee lass's wreath, I saw her scamper back into the store room at one point."

The storeroom was dark. Dark, but not empty. Jamie stood, gazing out at the swiftly-gathering dusk, his arms braced on the deep window-sill. The window was open and looked out over the wooded lot which sat adjacent to the pub. The air was still and the dusk touched his bright hair with shadow, outlining his form in a pellucid blue. She halted, feeling like she was intruding on a private moment, knowing he had likely come in here to catch his breath and marshal the forces of will that maintained his manners and his façade. They were both wearing masks today that did not fit their faces.

A glimmer of pink caught her eye. Isabelle's wreath lay in a corner, wilted and forlorn amongst the dull gleam of kegs. There was no way to retrieve the circlet without coming to his attention, and yet there was no way Isabelle was going home without it.

"Jamie."

He turned abruptly, the utterance of his name shattering his peaceful reverie.

"I'm sorry to startle you. I just came to retrieve Isabelle's roses."

She hunkered down to pick up the roses because she could no longer bend over with any grace. Jamie beat her to it, picking up the small circlet and scattering rose petals around their feet. Their eyes met as he handed her the wreath. It was the first time they had been alone in one another's company all day. They had avoided this exact moment for good reason.

"How are you?" he asked, and she knew the question was much larger than the homely three words could possibly convey.

"All right," she said, because she always told Jamie the truth, and good would be a stretch today and he would know she was lying. She had felt his eyes on her face often enough today to know he had a fair notion of just how she was feeling.

"And the baby?"

"She's fine, Jamie. I had an appointment with the doctor last week, and everything is just as it should be. I left a message with Maggie to tell you."

"Yes, she told me, it's not the same as hearing it from you, or as reassuring as seeing you for myself."

He looked at her left hand then, where the sapphire glowed a lambent blue. "So it's true," he said quietly, "you're engaged to Noah Murray."

She nodded, her lashes sweeping down to hide her eyes. "Yes, it's true."

Beyond the room there was the sound of laughter and through the window came the scent of hawthorn, blooms long fallen to dust.

"Why, Pamela?" There was such bleakness in the two words that she wanted to back away from the question and not answer him. She felt a flash of anger which had jealousy at its core.

"I could ask you the same question, Jamie."

"Yes, you could. But Pamela, you know my situation, I have no choice at present unless I wish to lose my son. You know this is not what I want, not in the least." He sounded angry, maybe as angry as she had ever heard him, but she knew his anger wasn't toward her, it was aimed inward at himself. It was an untenable situation and her heart ached for him.

"I'm sorry, Jamie. It's none of my business and I shouldn't have said that. How is Kolya adjusting?"

Jamie shook his head. "He's a resilient little soul, but he asks about you and Conor and Isabelle twenty times a day, I swear. I can't explain to his satisfaction why we don't see you anymore."

"It's the same for us—Conor and Isabelle ask about you and Kolya all the time. Isabelle cried herself to sleep the other night, wanting her Koly." She shrugged. "Well, I hardly need tell you. It was clear how happy they were to see you today."

"And now it's my turn to apologize, because it's bad enough that I hurt you, I certainly never wanted to hurt the children as well."

"What of Violet, is she happy with the deal she has struck?" It was a foolhardy question, but she could not stop herself from asking it.

"She is not a fool, she knows what sort of a poor bargain she has in me. For here," he spread his beautiful hands, "there is nothing but the wasteland of the infinite ache. She is wise enough to know that ache is not and can never be, for her."

He stepped forward and she fought the instinct to go toward him, to touch him, to put her head to his chest and allow the tension to drain from her body. She was quite certain, though, that tension was the only thing holding her up at this point. And then he took her hand, the one that held Noah's ring and clasped it between both of his. Her skin prickled at his touch, her body acknowledging this man for whom it yearned.

"Don't marry him, Pamela, whatever happens, do not marry that man. You will destroy your own life and that of the children."

"Jamie, you have your own affairs to tend to, allow me to tend to mine."

"Is that what you call it—affairs? Jesus Christ, Pamela, you know what he is. Right now he's the biggest and baddest in the land but some day he won't be and then what will you do? There will be no safe bolt-hole then, no security to shield you from the men who will hunt him down and kill him like he is no more than an animal—which is no less than he will deserve."

She shook her head; she was desperately exhausted and didn't want to talk about this with anyone, least of all Jamie.

"I know who he is. I know what he has done, perhaps not the details but the broad strokes are more than adequate in this case. It's about as relevant though, as a pair of mittens on a hot summer day, isn't it?"

"No, it's not, that's *my* child in your belly, Pamela and if you think I will stand by and let Noah Murray play father to it, think again."

"Are you threatening me, Jamie?" She tried to pull her hand from his, but he held it tighter, the sapphire digging into her skin.

"No, I am not threatening you. I'm stating plainly that I will not have my child raised by that man."

"I would never keep you from your child. She will always know who her father is. How large a part you play in her life will be up to you."

"You keep saying *her*."

"I just think it's a little girl," she said. "I don't know why exactly, just that it feels like a girl."

"I've never fathered a daughter before," he said.

"You've never gotten *me* pregnant before," she said tartly. "It's why I don't think the heart syndrome will affect this child."

Jamie's eyes narrowed in exasperation. "I would dearly love to shake you right now," he said and she could see he meant it.

"Jamie, the baby will be fine. We will worry about custody arrangements after she's born."

"But you don't love him," he said it as fact, flatly.

"Does it matter? I am very fond of him though, if that gives you comfort."

"No," he said tightly, "it does not give me comfort. Fond of him—do you hear yourself, Pamela? What sort of a life is that?"

"It's the best one I can make for myself and the children now, Jamie. There won't be another man that I love outside of yourself and Casey. This is an arrangement, not a love match. He offered it as such and I accepted it in kind."

"You're a damn fool if you think he isn't hoping for more from you."

"I'll not short shrift him, he will have the things he wants—companionship, a woman to keep his home and his bed for him."

"So, you'll go to his bed?" Jamie's tone was level, but the fire in the green eyes was anything but.

"Yes. It wouldn't be fair nor right to do otherwise."

"Pamela, you're not a woman built for a relationship like that—without love, without dreams, without passion and desire."

She sighed; she was tired and knew this conversation was very dangerous ground for the both of them. She knew she should pull her hand out of his, and yet she couldn't quite make herself do it.

"I can't afford anything else, Jamie, you know that as well as I do. Seen in that light, it's the only sort of match that makes sense for my life."

"Can you at least consider what Casey would think of this? Would he want his children raised in a house with that bastard?"

"No, he wouldn't, but as he's gone, I can't make all my decisions based around what he would want. There are circumstances that he couldn't foresee."

"What circumstances?" Jamie asked, concern edging the tight anger in his tone.

For a moment, she wanted to tell him, she wanted him to take charge and fix things for her as he had done so often in the past. But many times, she knew, it had been at great cost to himself, and she couldn't do that to him again. Her life was moving in another sphere now and she owed it to Jamie and to Noah to remember that. As if to underscore her thoughts, a voice spoke behind her. "Pamela."

She whirled around like she had been prodded with a hot poker. Noah stood in the doorway; his stance was casual and the look on his face as cool as a fresh frost. A rush of sick adrenaline went through her as she wondered how much he had heard. When he spoke again, his words were directed at Jamie, though his gaze was fixed upon her and the hand which was still held in Jamie's.

"My fiancée is tired," he said, "an' I'm goin' to take her home." There was an unmistakable emphasis on the word 'home' as if to make it clear *he* was the man who would soon share one with her.

Jamie's eyes elongated and she could see he was about to make an angry retort. It was up to her to halt this before it went any further. She did not think she could manage a scene between the two men.

"Jamie, please," she pleaded, her voice little more than a whisper.

He looked at her for a long moment and then nodded and stepped back, letting her hand go. The sapphire felt twice as heavy as it had before he had touched her, as though it had gone through some physical change in those minutes.

The few steps it took to reach Noah, seemed like a journey across some other distance, one that could never be crossed again nor taken back. He reached his hand out to her, and she took it, though she could still feel the imprint of Jamie's fingers along her own. She followed Noah out of the room, and did not look back to where Jamie stood. It was one of the hardest things she had ever done.

Noah helped her into her coat and then she gathered the children together—Isabelle much appeased by the return of her crown and Conor darkly silent while she helped him with the buttons on his coat. She despaired of him ever truly thawing out enough with Noah to form some sort of relationship. Conor was a Riordan through and through and she had never known a more stubborn lot of men. 'Stubborn as the rocks in the field and twice as hard-headed,' Casey's grandmother had once said, and Pamela knew it for no small exaggeration.

They bid farewell to Patrick and Kate. She was grateful that Pat, who usually knew when something was awry, was too absorbed in Kate to notice the tension in their little group. The ride home was short in distance but very long on silence. Noah was not an easy read even at the best of times, but in moments like this one, fraught with things unsaid, he was about as decipherable as a pillar of stone.

The sun was setting as they drove down the lane to the house. Noah helped her with Isabelle, and Conor begged the key from her so that he could go ahead into the house. He would, she knew, disappear upstairs before Noah entered the house. Noah hesitated on the doorstep after opening the door for her so that she could carry the slumbering Isabelle in.

"Will you please come in?" she asked him, and he nodded, but still didn't speak.

The house was quiet around them, Rusty coming to curl about her legs immediately. Noah took Finbar outside. The dog was still a bit wary with him, but he no longer growled at him, which was an improvement.

She could feel Noah's presence even after he went outside. He didn't seem angry, nor did he seem particularly lighthearted. He might not mention what he had seen in the store room, but she was going to have to. The man would be her husband in a little more than two months and she didn't want things to start out on a shaky foothold. He had said he valued her honesty and so it was the one thing she could give him without stint.

She put Isabelle to bed, managing to remove her dress and shoes and socks, and even the much abused 'cwown' from her sticky fingers. She put her to bed in just her underwear; the night was warm and she would be more comfortable this way. She was aware of Conor's gaze following her as she tucked Isabelle in and smoothed her wild hair off her face before kissing her cheek and turning to her son, where he sat in his bed on the other side of the room, his damp hair and the strong smell of mint advising her that he had brushed both hair and teeth.

She sat on the edge of his bed. "Do you want me to read to you tonight?" Normally, she would worry that if she lay down with him to read, she would fall asleep. Tonight, it was likely that the anxiety of having to talk to Noah might well keep her awake if nothing else would.

"No, I can read to myself," he said.

"Are you sure?" He seemed unsettled, and she thought perhaps if she read to him it might help.

"Are ye okay, Mama?" he asked, small face concerned.

"I'm fine, Conor, just tired."

"You should go to sleep soon. Tell Mr. Noah to go home."

"I will, sweetheart." She smiled down at him, though she knew it was a tremulous smile at best. Conor looked at her with the dubiousness of expression that his father used to give her when he knew she wasn't being entirely truthful.

"Jamie looked sad today," he said. "He smiled every time Uncle Pat or Auntie Kate looked at him, but all the rest of the time, he was sad. I asked him why an' he said he wasn't sad at all, only had a headache, but I don't think that was true. Jamie doesn't lie, but I think he did today, Mama."

Which explained, she thought grimly, a tête-à-tête she'd observed her son having with Jamie.

"Sometimes big people do get sad, but then a few days later they are happy again."

"Ye've been sad for more than three days, Mama." Conor had worked out what 'few' meant some time ago, and was a stickler for accuracy.

"What do you mean?" she asked, wishing her son wasn't always such a perspicacious child.

"Ye've been sad for a long time—all the time since Daddy's gone."

Sometimes her son seemed to see her more clearly than even she saw herself. She *had* been sad for a long time but she had hoped, vainly it now seemed, that she wasn't quite so transparent to her son.

"I miss your daddy, Conor, just as you do. I will miss him all my life but that doesn't mean I'm not happy most of the time." The last bit was a lie, but she was happy in parts these days, oddly enough.

She smoothed his hair back from his face and kissed his forehead.

"Mama, you can come sleep with me, if you want to."

"Thank you, sweetheart, I might just do that." The thought of curling up next to his warmth, restless as he was at times, sounded infinitely wonderful. She held him and he gave her one of his big hugs which was entirely comforting.

She left Conor reading to himself and trod down the stairs slowly, feeling a little like a child about to confess to something which it knows will get it in a heap of trouble.

Noah had taken off his suit jacket and rolled up the sleeves of his shirt. His cufflinks glinted on the table where he had placed them, and hot, freshly-made tea scented the air. He sat relaxed, reading from a volume of Neruda. More specifically, a volume of his love poems, ones replete in sensuality and unfulfilled longing. Many were very erotic, leaving as they did much of the interpretation and imagining up to the reader. It had been on the shelf by the hearth.

He looked up as she came off the last stair, his expression impassive, blue eyes like rain-dark slate.

"Do you like him—his poems, I mean?" She asked, knowing the onus was on her to speak first.

"Aye," he said, "I know my Neruda, too. I know the poem Mr. Kirk-patrick referred to an' God knows I understand the infinite ache." He didn't look down at the book but merely spoke the words like they had been long housed in his memory. His voice was soft, but it had intent and she could feel each word as he spoke it, as though every vowel touched her skin.

...My thirst, my boundless desire, my shifting road!
Dark river-beds where the eternal thirst flows...

"Some say the poem is about his country, Chile, and not an actual woman," she said nervously, wanting nothing more than to avoid the gaze of those relentless blue eyes on the heels of the poet's charged words.

"That might well be, but I am not talkin' about a country, Pamela. I am talkin' about *you*."

"Noah—" she began but he cut her off.

"I understand that all too well, maybe most men do who have wanted a woman it seemed they could not have—the eternal thirst, the in-finite ache. Mr. Kirkpatrick was right. I do want more than what ye might think."

That answered her question of just how much he'd heard—a great deal apparently. She swallowed, wishing he was angry and primed for an argument, rather than this sad, vulnerable man who had just handed her his heart.

"I'm sorry that you overheard what you did, Noah, but you offered me marriage as an arrangement. We agreed it wasn't a love match, but that we could build it on our own terms. I don't see how that has changed."

"I didn't say it had, only that it's not quite as cold-blooded on my side as ye might wish."

"It's not cold-blooded on my side, either," she said defensively.

"I never said it was, Pamela. In fact, I believe it's likely to be anythin' but. Only that I do have feelins' that ye're clearly not comfortable with."

"I know that, Noah."

He was silent for a long moment and when he spoke again, his voice was quiet but carried an edge of steel in it.

"Pamela, I know ye had some sort of relationship with Jamie all durin' yer marriage with Casey, but I am a different kind of man, an' I can't countenance that sort of thing."

"He is the father of one of my children."

"And he can see ye in that capacity, but I can't abide anything beyond that."

"I don't think you need worry about that," she said. The truth was, beyond being parents of this child together, she did not think she could see Jamie anymore. Her heart had told her as much today in no uncertain terms.

He stood and crossed the room to where she was and she quelled the desire to step back from him. He put his hands on her shoulders—strong hands that could hurt her badly should he ever so choose.

"I'm a jealous man; ye might as well know that goin' in." He said the words lightly, but they sent a shiver through her body nevertheless. It was both admission of fact and she thought, a warning. "I take the notion of marriage very seriously. I hope that you will too."

"I do," she said, because it was true. She knew once she left this house, once she made her vows to Noah, her life would change irrevocably and there would be no going back down the road, no returning to the world she had known. She might well become someone different herself over time, but if it kept her children safe, she felt it was a small price to pay. With the loss of Casey she had changed forever anyway and there was a small hollow in the center of her soul that would never again be filled. What mattered now was raising her children in a home where she did not have to worry about leaving them orphaned every single day. And she was fond of this man; he was her friend and he had proven true in that regard. It was not his fault that he wanted more from her than she might ever be able to give. With luck, she might one day make him believe he had what he desired.

His hand moved to her neck, the touch soft but the desire clear even there in the brush of his skin against her own. She felt tired suddenly, and put her own hand up to his, wanting to halt him before he took it further. She wanted to go upstairs and drift off to sleep alone. She understood that they were at a very fragile juncture right now, as if they stood on a fault line and one wrong step would plunge them both into dark waters.

She reached up and kissed him, softly. His response was tentative, slow and with a restraint so tangible that it told her just what it was he was holding back and that if he ever truly unleashed it, it might well drown them both. He broke the kiss first, leaning his forehead against her own, his breath slightly unsteady.

She leaned back and looked at him. "Noah, we'll manage. It's only our business in the end. It's not for anyone else to say what we are to one another."

He nodded, the blue eyes dark with an emotion that made her put her head to his shoulder so that she wouldn't have to see it anymore. And then she let him hold her for a while because he needed to and because she had been tired and sad for such a long time, and needed to be held by a man who loved her.

Chapter Eighty

Loose Ends

ELSPETH HURRIED HOME from the post office through a sleeting rain, breathless anticipation causing her blood to run swiftly through her veins. Once home, she put the kettle on to boil and set out her good china pot and one good teacup. Every time she got a report from the private detective she went through the same ritual. Good china and good tea—the latter a Darjeeling she'd purchased from one of the fancy stores on Royal Avenue. She would sit down when the tea was ready and open the envelope carefully and peruse its contents down to the smallest detail. It was like delaying before opening the cover of a long awaited book, or a letter from a lover—something to be relished slowly.

She set the tea to steep and then slit the flap of the envelope. She would let the contents sit until her tea was ready.

It was probably time for one of her letters to the woman. She knew just the right bible verse—there were such a wonderful number of them pertaining to loose women—and a message, along with a lovely red scrap of silk she found which would look a great deal like blood. She wasn't above cutting her fingers and actually writing in real blood, either. She had done that the first time and also the last. She wished just once she could be there in the woman's house and see her face as she read one of Elspeth's letters. It gave her a delicious little shiver even thinking about it. She still had a bit of the woman's hair left, enough to maybe make another doll.

She wanted one for her own collection. She had taken the first one and put it in the woman's pocket to give her a fright. She took the hair and red silk out of the barrack box and placed them on the table along with expensive stationary and an envelope while she waited for the tea to finish steeping.

A few minutes later the timer went off with a dainty chime and she poured the tea into the beautiful translucent cup. Mr. Subha, who ran the teashop, had talked her into buying it, stating that a real lady should only drink tea from beautiful china. He swore it enhanced the taste. She had thought it was just heathen nonsense designed to part her from her money, but he had been right, the tea really did taste better when drunk from a pretty cup.

She sniffed appreciatively at the hot liquid, warming the tip of her cold nose in the steam. Mr. Subha had told her his people believed that Shiva, whose home was high in the mountains, blew a cool wind through the plants each morning and night to give Darjeeling its special flavor. That was heathen nonsense too, no doubt, but Elspeth liked the idea of a god's breath giving flavor to her tea here in rainy Belfast. She sat down and took a small sip of the tea, letting the taste warm the length of her tongue. Then she took out the contents of the envelope. Hiring the detective had been her birthday present to herself. Her mother had left behind a tidy sum when she died, enough so that Elspeth could afford to splurge occasionally on small gifts for herself. This was by far her most expensive indulgence and it had been worth every penny.

There was a small clutch of pictures along with his bi-weekly report. She read the report first, which was the usual reiteration of the woman's daily schedule. His summation was that he did not think Elspeth's fears about her husband were well founded as he had never seen the man whom she'd shown him the picture of with this woman. She then looked through the pictures. Two of the woman's house, an idyllic looking farmhouse tucked away at the end of a country lane. One of her driving past him, as the picture was blurred and she was little more than a ghostly-white face looking out the car window. Another of her with her children hopping along rocks near a stream, and then one with her looking almost directly into the camera. He must have used a telephoto lens for that one. She felt a twinge of annoyance, frankly the private detective seemed a little too enamored of taking pictures of this woman. She had only wanted to have a few photos of her so that she could use them to make another doll. She'd told the detective that she thought her husband was cheating on her with this woman. She was pretty but what of it? Why did a nicely arranged set of features count for so much in this world? Even Lucien (she had taken to using his Christian name in her head, even if she'd never dared to use it to his face) was weak in this regard. He had made it clear to her that he was helpless to resist the woman's all too obvious allurements. Men seemed ridiculously susceptible to a pretty woman.

"She is God's way of testing me and I am failing miserably, Elspeth." Lucien had said those words to her two weeks ago. It was the night on which he'd kissed her for the first time. Chastely and on the forehead only, but she had understood the deeper message. He felt clean with her and able to resist temptation. She was not some gaudy peacock of a woman with all her assets on display. He could be strong with her because she made him strong.

She picked up the last picture. This one showed the woman full length, standing beside her car, a frown on her face as she looked in the general direction of the camera as if she felt someone watching her.

Lucien had not exaggerated, he had failed spectacularly. She was pregnant. That whore of Babylon was pregnant with the Reverend's child. Elspeth felt a wave of fury so big it lifted her up out of her chair and before she even realized what she was doing she had taken her sewing scissors and was hacking at the pretty blood-colored silk, until it lay in tiny shreds around her feet, blazing scarlet in the last light of the evening. Glittering strands of the woman's hair lay scattered amongst all the shreds. It reminded her of a beautiful Japanese doll she'd been given as a gift long ago. It had been one of the nicest things she'd ever owned. The doll had been made from porcelain and had a white face with the palest pink blush to her cheeks. Delicate little slippered feet had peeked out from under a scarlet kimono which had been embroidered with tiny silver dragonflies. A matching parasol had sat just so upon the doll's fragile porcelain shoulder and a sash of silver and lavender had been wrapped around her porcelain waist. A small scroll that had come in the box with the doll said her name was Chiyoko and that it meant 'a thousand generations'. Elspeth had loved the doll and taken exquisite care of her. Her mother had smashed Chiyoko the night she caught Elspeth looking at her newly-budding breasts in the mirror. Vanity was a sin, her mother had said, and so she must be punished. The whore made her think of Chiyoko in some of her pictures, porcelain skin with that shell-like flush to it and the dark hair and perfect oval of forehead and cheeks and chin. Yes, men were weak to be pulled in by such simple things.

She took her bible down from the shelf above the table where she kept it. There was a verse that applied to this situation. It was in Genesis. She turned to the chapter and verse, for she had it memorized.

'And it came to pass about three months after, that it was told Judah, saying, Tamar thy daughter-in-law hath played the harlot; and also, behold, she is with child by whoredom. And Judah said, 'Bring her forth, and let her be burnt.'

This time she would send no letter. She did not want the whore to have any warning of her coming. Her path was clear now. She knew what she had to do.

Had anyone chanced to run into the Reverend Lucien Broughton that evening it wasn't likely they would have recognized him. His own mother would have trouble recognizing him just now, he thought, slipping a key into the side door of a garage he kept under an assumed name in the town of Newry. He went inside under the cover of thick darkness, just as he always did. He never visited this place in the light. It was too dangerous.

Inside there was a car and a sink and a hose. The car was covered with a heavy tarpaulin so that it wouldn't get dusty. He pulled on a pair of black gloves and then slowly folded back the tarp so that the car stood gleaming under the lone light bulb. He ran a hand along the hood. The car was in flawless condition. He'd stolen it a long time ago. It had been parked on a farm which he'd been acquainted with and he had taken it one night knowing he had a need for it. This car might be the truest love he'd ever known in his life. It had been utterly faithful to him and his purpose. It had kept his secrets. In return he had taken it on some of his grandest adventures. What few sexual experiences he'd had in his life had taken place in this car.

He was tying off loose ends, the car was one, Elspeth would be the next. Elspeth was slightly more unhinged than he'd bargained for. To use the Belfast street parlance, she was a right nutter. She was becoming dangerous, in a way he no longer cared for. He had known for a long time that she would have to go. She had seen the pictures he'd kept in the envelope in his bureau. He had never known exactly how much she'd understood of what she'd seen and, secretive wee bitch that she was, she'd never mentioned it. No doubt she thought it was further proof of her devotion and loyalty to him. He needed a loyalty that was completely blind and he feared Elspeth's no longer was.

He pulled a watch cap down over his pale hair and flipped up the collar of his dark coat. He hadn't taken the taxi out in a very long time. It was time to part ways. There was another garage waiting for it under the name of a different man, a man who could not be hurt by the discovery of this car. And it wasn't like the man had been entirely innocent. No, he'd had plenty of blood on his hands. A little more wouldn't hurt his memory. He wondered if Pamela Riordan had really put the wheels in motion to end the constable's life. If so, it made her more interesting to him. She was a more formidable player in this little game of his than he'd previously believed. He'd understood that when she joined forces with Noah Murray. She seemed to have little fear; he found that quality intriguing.

He drove the car out of the garage and parked it some way down the lane. Then he returned to the garage and doused the inside of it with petrol. He lit a match and watched it burn blue and gold until it touched his gloved fingers and then he threw it. The garage went up with a *whoosh* and there was that void in the center of the world that was fire, as it drew in a long breath before exploding outward in fury.

He would have liked to stay and watch, he was so rarely warm these days it seemed and the fire was throwing out a lovely heat. But he could not afford to linger. He walked swiftly to the taxi and got in, driving away into the dark slowly, for he wouldn't turn on the head lights until he was well away from here.

Once he moved the car and then tipped off the police on where to find it, this chapter of his life would come to a close. He would miss it, but it was time to move on. He was settling all his personal business because things had become slightly unraveled of late and a policeman, one who clearly didn't understand the Reverend's power, had come sniffing around recently asking some very inconvenient questions. This car was one loose end, and using it to make it appear that Constable Blackwood had been the man the police unofficially called 'The Butcher', was a tidy way to tie it off and relinquish it to his past. Then he needed to deal with Elspeth.

Chapter Eighty-one

Bittersweet Peace

SEPTEMBER HAD BEEN a long and beautiful month of fine days of sun and nights filled with soft winds. It had been a season of depth and sweet fire and she had inhaled it each day, savoring this final season in her own home—both the bitter and sweet of it. This season of mist and madness and mellow fruitfulness. Her garden had been plentiful, the lone apple tree bent with the weight of fruit. A certain peace had come to her this autumn, which had been entirely elusive in the years before, but it was a bittersweet peace, for it was, she knew, a reconciliation with loss.

Conor had begun school a few weeks before and had adjusted to it well as he did to most things, though he was annoyed by how much his attendance at school circumscribed his time out-of-doors. Today was Saturday, so he was free to play outside all day. It had been a fine day, if chilly, for they'd had their first frost that morning. Isabelle had played outside with her brother for several hours, and was now upstairs having a much-needed nap.

September had also been a month of pleasant surprise. She had gotten her first royalty check from her US publisher and while it had been miniscule it gave her a feeling of accomplishment. Another check had arrived too, from a publishing house in London, for royalties on the book of fairy tales Jamie had written and she had illustrated. This one was not so miniscule, and had gone some way to relieving her financial worry. The check had been large enough to make her think Jamie may have arranged to have all profits on the book diverted to her.

All the plans were in place for the wedding. It only remained for the paperwork to come through. Tomas thought it would be done and in her hands before October's end. She only wished it felt like a new beginning, rather than an ending. Nevertheless, she began her preparations for moving house. She had spent the afternoon packing up some of her special china and dishes, things that she didn't use on a daily basis. She thought she might leave the beautiful set of Belleek dishes here with Vanya, because the china had been a housewarming gift from Jamie and she couldn't see herself using those dishes with Noah.

Conor came into the kitchen, in his usual fashion, fast enough that he slid across half the floor. She sighed, she had just darned all his wee socks three days ago. He was wont to dash outside without his shoes or boots, though she always made certain his footwear was handy by the door through which he most often exited.

"What are you doing, Mama?" he asked, one small and thoroughly grubby hand digging in the cookie jar for the two cookies she had promised he might have for his mid-afternoon snack. She took a moment to answer him, for it wasn't a topic of which Conor was fond.

"Packing up the stuff we don't need every day," she said, and then went a bit further, because she suspected that he really didn't understand they truly were leaving this house in the next month or so. "We will have to start packing up your room soon too, Conor." She hated saying it, because she knew it upset him, and it put a sliver in her own heart but they did need to get on with the task of getting the house sorted properly.

"I like my room," he said, calmly. "I don't want a room in Noah's house."

She gritted her teeth. She understood Conor's feelings, but her patience was wearing a little thin in regards to his stubbornness.

"Conor, I know you don't like the idea of it. I understand that, sweetie, but I am marrying Noah and so we have to move."

"Ye're already married to my daddy," he said. His words struck her to the core, because he couldn't possibly understand just how true his statement was. She was, indeed, married to his daddy, in a way that neither death nor disappearance could lessen the hold of those vows on her heart. There was no way to explain a marriage of convenience and protection to a child. "What if Daddy comes home an' we're not here?" he asked, his dark eyes filled with worry.

She knew she had to answer him, for it was a real worry to him, this child who had clear memories of the father who had loved him and shown him the world around him in its beauty and detail. Who had made him feel safe in a way she could not. It was long past time, she knew, for her to be brutally honest with this wee son of hers. It made her feel sick. She hadn't said the words for his sake, but also for her own, because she did not want to say it and see the heartbreak in Conor's face, nor feel it in her own chest.

She went to where he stood and stroked her hand over his soft curls which were not the curls of his babyhood anymore. He was growing up, faster than she would have wished. She remembered the day he had been born, the terrible storm that had raged around the house, and she with only Casey to help her bring their child into the world. He had been afraid and worried, but he had been a rock for her. She needed to be so for this child they had created one night in a field, with the scent of grass and buttercups all around.

"Conor," she began, feeling the air heavy as stone in her lungs, as she sought for the words to tell him this thing, "Daddy has been gone a very long time. He loved us very much and if he was able to come home to us, he would have long ago. Conor, Daddy isn't ever coming home."

The dark eyes turned a deep grey. "My da' *is* goin' to come home," he said, a defiant note in his voice that was a direct echo of his father.

"Conor," she began, knowing it was important he didn't live any longer with the illusion that Casey was returning to them.

"He can't come home right now," he insisted, cutting off the words she was formulating to say to him.

She felt the sting of tears as she looked at her son, so like his father, right down to the stubborn set of his chin. She felt the helpless love and anguish of a mother who can no longer protect her child from the harsh realities of the world.

"Conor, if Daddy could come home he would, it's that simple."

"He can't right now," Conor repeated and she could feel the frustration in him building. He was slow to anger like his Uncle Pat, but once he exploded he did it with no small force. If he wasn't ready to acknowledge that his father was no longer in this world, then perhaps it was best for her to let it lie until he could more readily understand. His certainty made her want to believe, too.

"What makes you say that?" she asked, a small frisson of unease coiling its way around the base of her spine at his vehemence. Conor rarely got agitated and so she took it seriously when he did.

"Daddy told me so, that's how." There was no small defiance in her son's face and she gave him the dignity of not denying what he believed. He was a Riordan, so odds were she couldn't shift his mind anyway.

"Daddy told you what?" she asked, keeping her tone even.

"He told me he can't come home right now, but that he will some day."

"He told you? What do you mean? He talks to you?" She thought he might well have been dreaming about his father and that the veil between day and night being far thinner in childhood, he might believe he really had talked with Casey.

"No," Conor said looking up at her. His eyes were like smoke now, meaning he was nearing the end of his patience with his apparently obtuse mother. "He leaves me things in the fairy's home."

"What do you mean?"

"He leaves me things. I'll show you."

He ran off up the stairs to fetch his proof and she stood in the kitchen feeling cold all over. She couldn't fathom what Conor meant, but he was not a child given to fancy for the most part, if he said someone was leaving him gifts, then someone was. It wasn't his father, though, so just who in the hell was it?

Conor came back down the stairs at his usual break-neck speed, jumping off the last three stairs. He held a little bag made of rough canvas, contents bulging out here and there. It was only a small bag, brown and rather grubby, but Pamela felt a breathless fear that its appearance was entirely deceptive and that this bag was actually a Pandora's Box which should not be opened.

He sat down on the floor at her feet and opened the bag, small head bent over and the tender stem of his neck visible. Around them the kitchen glowed warm in the afternoon sunlight, but she felt a chill spreading out from her core which no amount of sunlight could penetrate.

Conor extracted the contents one by one, as he always did with treasured objects, and arrayed them carefully in an order, no doubt, known only to him. There was an agate, beautiful really, large and golden like a small sun sitting there on the pine floor. A feather that she thought had probably belonged to a barn owl and a length of bark which had the face of an old man in its rumpled folds. Last, there was a carving, and it was this item which made her vision go fuzzy for a moment, her breath caught high up in her chest so that it felt like she was choking. It was a small horse. It was beautifully carved with a proudly-curved neck and hooves caught in the act of prancing. It was made from silver driftwood. It looked like Phouka. It was the lines of the carving itself that made it so she had to sit down and clutch at the arm of the chair. Casey had always had a rare hand with wood, something he had told her he'd inherited from his own grandfather. He had carved Conor any number of toys those first few years of his life: animals both exotic and domestic, cars, fanciful figures from his own imagination, boggarts and sprites and a particularly wicked looking leprechaun which still gave her the wamblies when she came upon it unexpectedly. This horse had the touch of him in it. She would swear it had been carved by his hands, if she didn't know it was impossible.

"Conor, why do you think it was Daddy who left all these things?" Her voice was shaking and Conor looked up at her, a small frown wrinkling his brow.

"Because I found them in the fairy house. The aggie was in the kitchen sink, an' the feather under the bed. The bark was on the stairs."

She took a breath. All those items, while certainly things Casey might have given to his son, could be explained away easily enough. But the horse, the horse was another matter entirely. She picked it up and turned it over in her hands. The wood felt like satin to the touch, it had been sanded to a fine and flawless finish.

"What about the horse? Where was it?"

"It was on my window seat one morning," he said, head already bent back down to his treasures, unaware that what he'd just said had tilted his mother's world on its axis.

"In your bedroom?" She couldn't feel her lips and was surprised her words weren't slurred together with panic.

"Aye," he said, as if she were thick indeed, for what other window seat could he possibly mean?

"Conor, how long ago was this?"

"A while ago," he said and she took a breath, so that she wouldn't howl with frustration.

"Do you mean a week or in the spring time—last spring or winter maybe?"

Conor shrugged, his sense of time was somewhat malleable at this age. She did remember that he'd had the wee horse in the car that day they had gone to Noah's to see Khamsin. That had been two months ago.

She realized she was clutching the little horse like it could tell her exactly how it had found its way into her son's bedroom if only she squeezed it hard enough. She put it down and stood up, smoothing down the front of her sweater as if she could order her world by such a small gesture.

"Conor, let's go out to the fairy house. I want you to show me where you found each of these things."

He put his coat on, the beautiful brown shearling one Jamie had given him last Christmas. It was too warm for it really, but he loved it so much she didn't have the heart to make him change it for something lighter. Isabelle ought to sleep for at least another half hour which was more than ample time to go out to the fairy house and back.

They walked out into the brisk autumn afternoon; the wind had an edge to it and the scent of peat smoke was held in its threads. It had been cold enough to keep the fires lit today, the first day she had needed to this season. By the time the cold winter rains were falling, making fires necessary every day, she and her children would be living in Noah's house.

Here in the woods, the frost hadn't melted away with the morning's sun and the ground seemed to exhale cold air, thick with the scent of rotted leaves and chilled earth. She shivered, and pulled her sweater more snugly around her body. She hadn't been out to the fairy house in some time. It was one of those innumerable things that made her heart feel like it was filled with lead, merely by its existence. Casey had taken time and care with it and it had been such a beautiful surprise the evening he had presented it to them, that she couldn't bear the sight of it.

It rose out of the woods surrounding it, silvered with rain and wind, and the outside thick with moss and lichen. Skiffs of veined silver touched it here and there, where the morning's frost remained.

"Show me where you found all the things."

Conor glanced up at her, worry printed on his small face. She made an effort to change her tone to one that was soothing.

"Mama is just curious; just point out where you found each gift."

He pointed out the tiny shell sink and said, "That's where I found the aggie." Then he put a finger to the crooked stairs. "An' that's where I found the bark—it's special from the big cedar tree. An' there," he pointed under a delicate bed canopied with leaf skeletons, "is where the feather was."

"There's nothing new at all?" she asked, not certain whether she hoped there would or wouldn't be.

"No," he said quickly, too quickly she thought.

"Conor, are you sure? It's important that you tell me the truth."

"There could be something behind the trap door," he said reluctantly.

"The what?"

"The trap door," he repeated. "Daddy showed it to me, he said it was a secret an' that if I had anything special that I needed to hide, I could put it behind the trap door."

It was something Casey would do, so that Conor might feel they had a special thing only they knew about and that he was trusted by his father like no other person.

"Can you show me the trap door?"

He looked up at her, small face troubled. "I don't know, Daddy said it was only for him an' I to know."

"Damn you, Casey Riordan," she muttered under her breath, though Conor, who had ears like a bat, looked up at her in disapproval.

"You swore, Mama."

"Yes, I did, I'm sorry. Conor, your daddy wouldn't want you to keep secrets if they were maybe going to hurt someone."

He took a breath and seemed to weigh her words and then he stepped forward reaching his small hand into the room in the fairy house which was designated as the library. She leaned down so that she could see more clearly, watching as her son pulled lightly on one of the bookcases which Casey had constructed from twisted bits of driftwood, the shelves aslant but cunningly fashioned so that they looked as if they had grown rather than been built. It swung away from the rough bark-lined walls with ease and she realized that the shelf was mounted on a well-hidden hinge. There was a small cubbyhole behind the shelf, rendered invisible by the fact that the very structure of the house made it impossible to tell where spaces and hollows might exist. She wondered if Casey had only built it as something for Conor, or if he had other reasons for making sure he had a safe drop.

"There's somethin' in here, Mama," Conor said, wiggling his hand in further, the tip of his tongue stuck out between his teeth, in the same manner that Casey had when he was focused on something. He removed it and then held it out to her. She hesitated to take it, suddenly frightened at what it might contain.

"I think it's for you, Mama."

"Why would you say that, sweetie?" she asked.

He gave an expressive shrug of his shoulders. "I don't know, it just feels like it is."

It was a piece of paper, neatly folded in four. She took it and though she was afraid, she unfolded it. It was a drawing, simple in its lines yet beautifully detailed and very accurate. It was a cottage, if such a humble dwelling could be called so—shepherd's hut was probably the more accurate term. A simple one room dwelling, but graceful in its lines. She stood looking at the drawing trying to understand why it would have been left in the fairy house for Conor to find.

"Mama?"

She looked down at Conor, and realized several moments had gone by while she held the paper, taking in every detail of the drawing. She stood there in the chilly afternoon and heard the wind lamenting through the trees as if it had lost something long ago, but could not stop searching despite the hopelessness of it. She wondered how long the drawing had been tucked away inside this fairy house. The paper was damp, but it would be, sitting inside a hole in the tree. There was no telling how old it was, and if it had been placed there a week ago or three years ago. There was no telling anything, except what logic dictated.

She tucked the paper into her pocket and took her son's hand. And then, hand in hand, they walked back toward the house.

"My letters are gone," he said, and sounded pleased.

"What letters?"

"The letters I wrote for Daddy. I would put them in there, just like he said, if I had something special to tell him. So that's what I did. Mostly I just drew him pictures, but sometimes I put words, too."

"And they're all gone?" She glanced behind her, and shivered. The woods seemed suddenly alive, boughs whispering to and fro in the wind, the trees holding their secrets tight and watching, ever watching.

"Aye," he said, "all of them. That's why I think he's coming home soon, because he finally got all my letters an' I asked him to come home."

Patrick came over the next afternoon. In a complete act of bribery, she brought out a set of building blocks that she had been saving to give to Conor when they moved. She needed the privacy to speak with Pat without Conor present.

Pat looked at her, worry clearly written over his features. The poor man was probably wondering what she could spring on him at this point, between her pregnancy and impending marriage, she was sure he'd had enough shocks from her to last a few more years.

She came directly to the point. "Have you been leaving wee gifts in the fairy house for Conor?" she asked.

He frowned, clearly startled by her question. "Have I what?"

Her heart beat a little faster. "Gifts for Conor—someone has been leaving him small items in the fairy house that Casey built. I thought it might be you."

"No, 'tisn't me. What sort of gifts?" he asked.

"I'll show you," she said, wanting another adult with whom to share this knowledge and this worry. Only Pat would understand properly.

She fetched the small bag from where Conor had left it on the couch and then spread the items out on the table. She set the horse down last, and Pat drew in a sharp breath at the sight of it.

He picked it up in his big hands and turned it over, his touch as ginger as if he were handling blown glass. She watched his face, though in this way he was like his brother; he could shut his expressions down so that he was as readable as a stone wall. His hands trembled just the slightest bit and so she knew he saw what she had—that no hand, other than Casey's, could have carved that little grey horse.

"He might have carved it before—" Pat halted like his words had come up against a brick wall, neither he nor she could say the words still, "before he disappeared."

"He might have," she admitted, "but that still begs the question of just who left it in Conor's bedroom."

"Aye," Pat sighed and set the horse back upon the table as if it was an incendiary device. "That's the question, isn't it? I don't like the idea of someone bein' in the house that you don't know about."

"Also, Conor left a bunch of letters and pictures in the cubbyhole for Casey, and they are all gone. He said they were there for a long time and now, suddenly, they're gone."

Pat's eyebrows shot up at this. "Who else knew about the wee door in the house?"

She shook her head and sat down, her knees wobbly.

"As far as I know, just Conor and Casey. Casey didn't even tell me, it was a secret he had with Conor, something special for the two of them."

He gave her an assessing look, one similar to the ones his brother had given her just before he delivered a bit of bad news. She wondered if they had both inherited it from their father.

"Just spit it out and save your spleen, Patrick," she said tartly.

He raised an eyebrow. "Ye're truly a Riordan when ye're using my daddy's sayins'."

She returned his raised eyebrow with a green look of her own. "Patrick."

"I don't know what to say, Pamela." He put his big hands up in bewilderment. "I can't fathom where these things have come from. As ye said, it would be no stretch to explain the wee bits an' bobs in the fairy house, but this," he touched a finger to the arched neck of the horse, "this was carved by my brother's hand, I'd swear to that. But I...I have to believe that he carved it before he disappeared an' he found a way—found someone—to make these deliveries to give Conor a bit of magic, in case he was ever gone."

"Well, I would think that the obvious person for that would be you."

Pat shook his head slowly, his face troubled. "No, I got mad with the man every time he mentioned somethin' happenin' to him, or him not bein' here to look after you all one day. I regret that now; I regret it a great deal. "

She reached out a hand and put it over one of Pat's.

"I have the same regrets. It is only because neither of us could bear the thought of a world without him."

"Aye, I know he understood that. It's only that I sometimes feel he knew an' he was tryin' to prepare the both of us for what was comin'. An' frankly that pisses me off too, because if he knew then why didn't he stop it an' take you an' the children an' leave, move to the south. He might have just kept all of yez down in Kerry that last summer."

"He might have, Patrick but you and I both know him well enough to understand that was never a possibility. He had built a life here for us—the business, the house and his roots were here in the North. He couldn't change that about himself any more than he could have changed the color of his eyes. It was part of what I loved about him—his stubbornness and how he knew exactly who he was. He made me feel the same, as if I knew exactly who I was."

"An' who is that?" Pat asked, softly.

"The woman who loves him and is loved by him. The mother of his children, the woman he was meant to grow old with. The knowledge of that was what centered me and gave me a foundation from which to start each day and to end it as well."

"Ye were that for him as well. If ye could have seen him before he met ye, ye would hardly countenance he could settle down with the one woman an' be so happy that ye knew it was his destiny to be so. He was, as my daddy used to say, the one to give a man the grey hairs."

"It feels unfair to me, sometimes, as selfish as that sounds. To find him, for the two of us to find a way through all the hurt and trouble, and to really have a life together, with all the things we had dreamed about—our own wee house, two happy healthy children and each other at the end of the day—only to lose it and never to understand why."

"That doesn't sound selfish to me," Pat said and squeezed her hand softly.

"But it does in this country, Pat. I mean look at the Widow Coston down the road—she's lost her husband and both her sons to this messy little war we're all involved in."

"Aye, but the fact of that doesn't make less of yer own sorrow, Pamela."

"There's one other thing," she said, and took the paper from her pocket where she had carried it since Conor had handed it to her.

Pat unfolded the paper slowly and she could hear the quick thumping of her heart in her ears. Pat looked down at the sheet of paper in his hands, an odd expression on his face. She felt her vision blur slightly and blinked, fighting to catch her breath.

"Pat, do…do you recognize it?" she asked, wishing her voice wouldn't shake so, but knowing it didn't matter in front of Patrick.

"Aye, I do," he said slowly, eyes still on the paper.

"Where is it?" she asked, irritated anxiety making her words sharp.

Pat looked up. "It's a hut the men in my family used to go to sometimes in the summers. My daddy an' my granddad. Casey an' me one summer. It's high up in the Wicklow Mountains."

"Why would he leave a picture of that hut?" she asked.

Pat shook his head, his face truly troubled now. "Damned if I know. I will say this—my brother drew it, but I haven't a notion in hell of why. Do ye know when it showed up there in the wee hole? The paper doesn't look new, though it doesn't really seem as if it sat in a damp hole for three years either."

"You're certain he drew it?"

"Aye, aren't you, Pamela?"

"Yes, I am. But it's likely he did it years ago, and left it there for Conor to find one day. It probably got shoved to the bottom of the cubbyhole, under all of Conor's letters to him."

"Aye, well there's the thing—where the hell did Conor's letters go?"

"I know," she said, and found she was suddenly fighting tears.

"I'm goin' to make a wee trip down to Wicklow. I think it's worth havin' a look at the hut. I'll call ye as soon as I know when I can manage to make the trip. I'd ask ye to come, but it's a good hike in, an' I don't know that I remember exactly where it is."

"Be careful, Pat. We don't know who put this picture in there, it could be some sort of a trap."

Pat nodded. "Aye, though I don't see how anyone could know about the hut. And this picture was drawn by him, ye know his hand for such things as well as I do, Pamela."

Yes, she knew, but it frightened her all the same. It was that such a small thing could set her back months, could spark hope in her heart again just when she had managed to snuff it out. And she couldn't afford it anymore, because logic dictated that Casey had been dead for a very long time now and she was committed to marrying another man in a few short weeks.

"Pamela?" he said, and because she knew he understood all the emotions that were warring within her, she knew just what it was he was asking.

"Yes, go," she said.

Chapter Eighty-two

…And Did But Half Remember Human Words

WHAT WITH ONE THING and another, it was mid-October when Pat made the promised trip to Wicklow. He found himself oddly nervous on the ride down, though he couldn't have said why. He drove into the foothills of the Wicklow Mountains and then took a small byroad he knew, hoping to God that he could still find his way up to the hut. It had been many years since he'd been here, for neither he nor Casey had any desire to visit the place after their daddy died. From here, if he remembered correctly, it ought be about a two-hour walk. He wondered if it was madness, making this trip, the pure madness which was the distillation of hope. Heaven knew he had enough to do at present, and he would have loved to spend a day at home, painting the nursery for their impending child. But Kate, after he had told her about the picture and everything that Pamela had related to him, had said, "Ye have to go see for yerself, Patrick."

She was right, as she so often was; he wouldn't rest until he went and looked for himself and that had brought him here on this chilly October day. It was sunny at least, so hopefully he wouldn't encounter snow. It wasn't unheard of to get a sudden squall of foul weather up in these mountains at this time of the year.

It was a pleasant walk, with the landscape changing around him as the altitude rose. It was beautiful through the oak lands, with their understory of holly and hazel, the hollies growing to the height of a large house here. Ivy grew thickly up trunks and over shrubs, always grasping and climbing its way toward the light, lending the woodland a slightly exotic jungle air. Autumn had strewn its bountiful hand thickly along the forest floor with a vast array of mushrooms and toadstools, pricking the dun and smoke of the ground with lively spots of red and yellow, and the softer palettes of rust and grey. He spotted several he knew: tall shaggy ink caps, spongy yellow boletus, the aptly named Beechwood Sickeners and the cheery clusters of the flower-like chanterelles. Small whiffs of smoke arose each time he glanced a puffball with his shoes. Occasionally amongst the plants and fallen leaves and nuts he would spot the flash of a red squirrel, brisk about its business, gathering up winter stores. The woods smelled smoky, the way they often did in autumn, with the rich loam of decay an earthy base note. He breathed it in deeply, filling up his lungs, and removing his jacket as his body warmed from the exercise.

A bit of poetry from Synge came to his mind, something quoted to them by his daddy during one of their summers here.

'I knew the stars, the flowers and the birds,
The grey and wintry sides of many glens,
And did but half remember human words,
In converse with the mountain, moors and fens.'

That was what their daddy had tried to teach them, to converse with the mountains and the trees and moors and streams. It had been pure magic and the residue of that magic was still stored in his very cell and marrow, and he felt it sparking along the pathways of his blood as he walked, an understanding that was older than time and went as deep as the bones of the earth.

Higher up the mountainside there were patches of scree, where only lichen and moss and bilberries were hardy enough to establish a foothold. Higher still were thick swathes of forestry planted pine and spruce and Douglas fir, great stands of it like a cathedral in parts, dark and deep, and home to gods far older than those of Christianity. Above the pine was moorland, bright with the lavender mist of heather, the brown and gold of sedge and ferns readied for winter. A small herd of deer, seven in number, grazed contentedly on the heather and moorland grass, his presence only occasioning a flickering of ears and a casual glance in his direction. Ahead of him he glimpsed the feathered tops of a small pine wood, and knew he'd found his destination. He came up over the rise of a hill and then down into the lee of a small valley, tucked into the mountain's shoulder and sheltered from the worst of the winds and mists and swift sweeping rains that came across these mountains with great frequency.

It looked the same, a plain shepherd's croft with the thick pine wood at its back and a narrow path that ran straight to a crooked front door. It was empty, he could see that much even from a distance, but even so his heart was pounding with a sudden onset of anxiety. He could also see that it wasn't as rundown as he had thought it likely to be after years of neglect. He walked up to the door. The area around was still in the late autumn sunlight, and a fine mist hovered below the summit of the mountain so that the rest of the country disappeared from view. He hesitated a moment, his hand on the ancient latch, which he noted had newish looking screws fastening it to the door. He felt suddenly nervous, as if he was about to enter Bluebeard's chamber, and didn't know which would be worse—to find nothing changed or to find it all changed and still not know if that signified anything more than a tramp holing up here for a season. He lifted the latch and went in.

It was as he remembered, one room, simple in its lines, just a hut for a long ago shepherd, repaired and made sturdy by his grandfather's skill with wood and hammer and saw. The hearth, made of stone scavenged from the mountain, still stood, clean, with a box filled with dry, split pine to one side. The floor had once been hard-packed dirt, now it was tightly fitted with level pine planks. It looked almost identical to the floor in Pamela's kitchen. There was a bed covered in canvas to keep it from the damp, and a chair, a table and an array of tin dishes stacked neatly in a small hutch. Army utensils lay neatly beside the two plates, slotted together and shining a dull pewter in the afternoon light. The table had a light glaze of dust on it, maybe enough to indicate an absence of a few months. The table was new and handmade by someone who had great skill and an eye for the grain and flow of the wood. The chair matched the table and was sturdy and built to last. There was a bookshelf tucked in beside the hearth, cleverly made from stones and well-weathered boards, the stones slotted together at each end as supports and fitted so well that the shelves sat level. There were a handful of books on the shelves and he perused the spines—*The History of Ireland by* John Mitchel and *The Life and Times of Daniel O'Connell*. There was a worn copy of *The Tain* as well as Cecil Woodham Smith's *The Great Hunger*. There were a few paperbacks, dime store novels, and a copy of Ray Bradbury's *Something Wicked This Way Comes*. On the shelf below were two books of poetry—Seamus Heaney and Yeats. The array told him little, the books refusing to confess as to whether they were the property of one person, or the leavings of years' worth of tramps and vagabonds.

The windows had been changed, the glass still single-paned, but new with proper weather stripping around them. Someone had gone to a fair bit of work to make this place livable for the winter. Just what sort of mad soul might want to winter over here was the question. A man would have to be desperate to seek out this sort of solitude, considering the weather could sock him in for weeks. A man on the run might seek such a place. The Wicklow Mountains had long been a place of refuge for such men for the mountains were wild and isolated enough in parts for a person to hide for a long time.

He took a breath and put his hand to the back of the chair to steady himself. He realized now he had expected the hut to be unchanged, other than the weathering of the years. But it was clear someone had been living here recently, someone who had no small skill with carpentry. It could be anyone, though, it did not mean it was his brother, because he couldn't make sense of that in any way. Why would Casey be living here a few hours away from his family? No, it made no damn sense whatsoever. Yet, with the carving of the horse and the drawing in the fairy house and now clear proof that someone had been living here, what was he to make of it?

He ran his hand along the edge of the chair. The wood was sanded to a fine finish, and then oiled to bring up the honeyed beauty of the grain. It had been made with great care and the work of it must have taken weeks. He found it strange that someone had just left it here to the elements. Unless the person intended to come back and trusted that no stranger would come along to steal from the place.

He checked the cupboards then and found only tins of beans, peas and sardines. Only the non-perishables which wouldn't attract wild animals had been left behind.

It was then he noticed that there was a book sitting on the small three-legged table beside the bed. There was no cover on it and it looked well worn. He picked it up and it fell open to the final two pages, the paper yellowed, the book smelling like one found in the musty depths of a used bookstore. He read a couple of lines and recognized the words immediately.

'...and as I sat there brooding on the old, unknown world, I thought of Gatsby's wonder when he first picked out the green light at the end of Daisy's dock. He had come a long way to this blue lawn, and his dream must have seemed so close that he could hardly fail to grasp it.'

He sat down on the canvas-covered mattress, the book clutched fast in his hands. *The Great Gatsby* was Pamela's favorite novel. It was a popular enough book that anyone might have had it on their person, and lay here at night reading Fitzgerald's timeless words by the light of the lantern, the fire and the words providing an alchemy to keep the dark at bay. But that it, of all the books in the world, should be here in this hut...he closed his eyes and sighed. He didn't know what to think. He didn't know what he was meant to do. He was going to have to stew on it for a bit. It wasn't fair to give Pamela false hope when he didn't know a damn thing; it wasn't as though his brother was the only man who had skill with a saw and hammer and nails.

"Goddamn it, brother," he said in frustration, "what the hell happened to ye?"

It hit him with a terrible blow just how badly he missed Casey. It had happened before, and would again in the future. It seemed as if these moments ripped off the scab which had managed to form over the wound, in those in-between times, when a man felt like he was coming to a place of acceptance. Maybe you never could truly accept something when you didn't know what had happened, he thought. The missing were the ghosts that haunted a man forever.

He opened up his bag. He needed a bite to eat and some hot tea before he made the trip back down the mountainside. In the bottom of the bag was his camera. He'd brought it to take pictures of the hut, so that Pamela might see it was, indeed, the hut in the drawing. He wondered if he might do more damage by showing her such proof. For so long now she had hung on to hope, as frayed as the cloth of it was, and now she was moving on with her life, albeit in a way that he didn't like. He would be the first to admit though, it was better than her waiting for a man who wasn't returning. He understood what that kind of hope and longing did; it put your heart in stasis, and made you numb, and the worry for him was she would grow old and eventually when the children were grown, be alone, still waiting, like an old woman in a fairy tale. Except this was not a fairy tale and a young hero wasn't going to ride in from the west one day to return her to youth and love. He laughed a little at the image, being that Casey would have rather shot himself in the foot than ridden a horse.

He took the pictures anyway; he could decide later whether or not to show them to Pamela. He wouldn't mind having some himself, in case one day the hut was gone, and he wanted to show at least photographic evidence of it to his children. He took pictures of the interior and the furniture in close up, then the exterior too, as well as the surrounding area.

Inside the hut again, he took out his thermos of tea and the lunch Kate had made for him—sandwiches and fruit, and a slice of chocolate cake, as well as a wee note tucked away in the bottom that said 'I love you.' He smiled, a feeling of warmth blooming inside at the sight of the note. He was a happy man when it came to his marriage; he had found a passion and a contentment with Kate which he would never have believed possible even a few years ago. He still thought of his first wife, Sylvie, every day, but the pain of that was not as sharp as it had once been.

High on the shelf above the stove, he spotted a bottle of Connemara Mist, glowing a warm and inviting amber in the cool autumn light. He took down the bottle, uncorked it and added a slug to his tea. He sat for a time, eating his sandwiches and drinking the whiskey-fortified tea, his thoughts roaming backward in time, to when he had stayed here with his brother, and further back when their daddy had brought them more than one summer to stay. Those had been happy times, days of roaming and fishing and eating their catch for dinner and of learning all about the plants and trees and animals. At night their daddy had told ghost stories that made them shiver in their pajamas and at times lie wide-eyed at every noise that carried across the mountain. Casey had taken up the tradition of telling spooky tales on their summer alone here, but it had backfired badly and they had stayed up all night more than once, shivering and huddled up together on the bed.

The wind had picked up while he sat eating and was whistling now around the corners of the hut, carrying winter's tune in its notes. It was cold up here and the dark would set in early as it did this time of year. He needed to be back down the mountain and in his car before it came.

Nevertheless, he paused, wanting to absorb the memories of this place so that he might carry them home and feel them close for a time. If he closed his eyes he could conjure the men of his family here into being—the grandfather he had never known, his father, his brother and him. Gathered round about a fire, talking of times gone by and those still to come, the smell of trout cooking in a pan and the blue smoke of an autumn twilight gathering thick outside the windows. He felt a bolt of anger that it should never be so again and that he was alone, the last man standing in his family.

He stood, sighing, feeling a slump in his spirits. It was spooky up here today and if he didn't relish the thought of staying overnight, he needed to be off. The thin cry of a curlew cut through his nostalgia. The lonely sound seemed a part of the low violet light that edged the horizon and the deep solitude that came up out of the timeless mountain. He went outside, shutting the door firmly behind him, the copy of *Gatsby* tucked in his bag. He scanned the edges of the forest and then pulled the collar of his coat up, for the air had grown colder during his brief time in the hut.

In the periphery of his vision, a shadow slipped across the tall dark pines behind the hut, a being free of the fetters of the earth, who yet lingered amongst the rock and root and soil. Pat had the sudden sense of eyes upon him. He shook his head; it was probably no more than an inquisitive mouse, or a shrew eyeing him from the doorway of a snug burrow. Still the hair on the nape of his neck prickled, as if spectral fingers had reached out through time and brushed his skin. A liquid dusk had begun to flow in and around the tree roots, soft as a snake shedding its skin and he shivered, every nerve ending in his body alert.

"It was a bloody cloud, ye fool," he said out loud, the sound of his voice setting off a crow high in the branches of one of the pines. He was grateful for the noise, for it dispelled some of the eerie atmosphere. He set off down the trail, pine needles muffling his footsteps, and yet they emitted a damp hiss as well, like someone walked closely behind him, using the furled smoke of his breath to mask their own. He remembered a story from long ago that his daddy had told them, of a man who had a ghost that walked behind him everywhere, and the man had never been able to rid himself of said ghost despite the assistance of priests and shamans and wise women. He looked behind sharply, cursing himself for a damned fool with an inconvenient memory. There was, of course, no one behind him, neither man nor will-o-the-wisp ghost.

Just before he went over the rise where the land fell away to a steep pitch, he turned back to look at the hut one last time. The low violet of the gloaming had begun to creep up from the mountainside and he could see them for a moment, a trick of the light and longing—three men, big and strong, dark-haired and long of limb, standing together in the deep shadows of the hut and the mountainside.

"*Slán go fóill,*" he said, voice low but carrying across the landscape of greys and greens and rising dark between him and the men. And then they were no more, the trick of light and longing going to wherever it was such things went. He felt vaguely comforted by the vision, because he knew that some ghosts walked with a man forever, and sometimes, just sometimes that was a blessing.

Chapter Eighty-three

Great Hatred, Little Room

FOR THE REST OF HER LIFE she would wish she had not turned back that day and that she had not seen what she did. Because a moment could ripple out to the very ends of your life, it could change who you were forever. One minute could become a point of no return, and you crossed a river over which you could never journey back. She knew all this and had known it for some time now. And yet, she turned back.

Pamela was in Belfast delivering one last set of pictures before shutting down her photography business, such as it was. In her advanced state of pregnancy she wasn't up for roaming around at weddings or christenings taking photos. She had dropped the pictures off and was walking back to her car. She was only half a block away from the car when she noticed a crowd of people down the road from her. In their midst was a young soldier and even from the distance she was at, she could see he was lost. There was no way a soldier should be alone in the Lower Falls; he must have somehow gotten separated from his foot patrol. She turned and walked toward him.

The crowd circled him slowly, as if they were participants in an intricate dance. Time slowed so that it nearly stopped. She could hear the voices of the women. There were two protesting that he ought to be escorted to an army base. He was disarmed and he was crying, terrified out of his mind. He had committed the cardinal sin of getting lost in Belfast— one block down too far, one street over from the one you'd meant to go down, and you were a walking dead man. He couldn't be more than nineteen years old, probably fresh off the boat and just arrived on his first tour of the world's worst killing ground for a British soldier.

She knew she should walk the other way; there wasn't anything she could do to help him without putting herself and her unborn child in terrible danger. She made her mistake then by meeting his eyes. Two strangers in a strange land, locked together here in a place where time no longer mattered and space consisted of a narrow, dark city where the reaper had an inexhaustible appetite. She would look at him, for it was all she could do—hold his gaze and by so doing, give him some small sliver of humanity in this last moment of his life. Green eyes held to blue, spirit to spirit, because flesh was not lasting, and even when it was young and lovely, it was still far too fragile.

Once upon a time, a man she loved dearly had told her it was terror that wrote with the sharpest pen, delineating moments so clearly that you could not ever forget them. And so it was for she knew she would always see this moment as though it had been outlined with the darkest of ink and would always remember the silver tracking of his spent tears, tracing a line from eye to jaw, where a faint furze of whiskers darkened his chin. Always she would remember the exact color of his eyes, like bluebells opening in a spring wood—a blue that rolled on forever and lasted but a breath. And though he never moved a muscle, nor so much as blinked his eyes, she sensed a nod from him, as if he understood how fate and chance wove their terrible dark patterns and would go now into that merciless tapestry with what dignity he had left.

At last he blinked, or she did, she never knew which, and time started up with a lurch, the sound of a carbine releasing it to run again, releasing her, releasing him, the blue eyes rolling up even as he fell.

She felt strangely distant, as if she was watching a film, an old one, where the reel was disintegrating and she was only catching flickers of the pictures as they flowed past her. She thought it was shock, or it was living here so long and seeing too much blood and too much violence.

She backed away slowly, so that she was standing behind a parked car. Blood lust and fury did strange things to people. She could not crawl over to him, she couldn't risk it at all, the shooters might still be around and helping a British soldier, even one losing his life blood, was considered the act of a traitor. It would not matter that she was pregnant either; they would kill her. She waited for several minutes, knowing she needed to go, but was unable to move, as if the shooting had been one act of violence too many and had frozen her here. Like an object long petrified in a bog, someone might find her a thousand years from now, staring at a dead soldier in a bloody street.

Finally she moved out from behind the shelter of the car, scant as it was, and peered through the twilight which was fast closing in. She could make out the soldier's outlines, and saw that he was moving a little. She crouched as low as she could manage, and duck-walked her way over to him. She pushed two fingers into his wrist and then waited to see if she could feel a pulse. She thought she did—just a weak one, a small thread by which he held to life, but she couldn't be certain because her own blood was buzzing with adrenaline and thudding rapidly against her skin.

She pushed herself up off the street. Her hands were wet and sticky with blood; the copper and salt stink of it rising from her skin like a vapor. There was a pub with which she was familiar just up the street. It was a pub where Catholics drank but it had never been sectarian in nature. She thought she might be able to persuade the owner to call an ambulance.

Inside the lights were low and at first she thought the place was empty but then she saw the men sitting in the corner, eyes to the door, checking her out, looking for weapons. She didn't make eye contact, she didn't want to know if any of them had been out there circling that poor boy like wolves might circle a wounded deer.

She leaned across the bar, her belly rigid, baby kicking up a fury, sensing her mother's upset.

"There's a young man out in the street, he's been shot and he needs medical attention. Can you call an ambulance please?" She kept her voice low, not wanting to get the publican in any sort of trouble. She kept her hands tucked inside her sweater and tried not to look desperate.

The publican leaned over and smiled, as though she had asked him simple directions and he hadn't quite heard her. "I think ye mean the wee soldier. I'm goin' to get ye a glass of water, an' ye're goin' to hop up on the stool there an' drink it like it's the best drink of water ye've had in yer life. I can't call until the lads in the corner—don't look—have left, but once they're gone, I will. Sit ye tight until then, lass."

He came back with the water and a map, which he laid out carefully on the bar and began pointing out directions to her, and she nodded, asking the odd question so that it looked like she was genuinely lost. Should the men in the corner ask, her American accent would help to lend credence to the story that she had gotten herself hopelessly turned around in Belfast and was trying to make her way to visit relatives in Ballymena. She sat, looking earnestly at the map, even though it was just a blur of snaking lines and blobs of color, and sipped at her water. There was little else she could do; there was nowhere else to go to plead for help and the street was too risky.

With every minute that ticked by, the likelihood of the young soldier dying out there increased. And there was nothing she could do but sit here and drink her water, unless she wanted to die in a much less peaceful fashion than he had. The men continued to sit at their table in the corner, chatting in low tones, occasionally laughing as if a dying boy wasn't lying out there in the street.

Once they left, the publican went out immediately and then came back in a minute later. He shook his head. "He's gone, Army must have come an' collected him. There's a lot of blood on the street." He shrugged, a gesture of great eloquence that summed up the night. "It's not likely he survived losin' that much blood."

She nodded. There was nothing to say and it was far past time to be gone from here. She slid down from the stool, so tired that her blood felt like it had turned to wet sand while she sat.

"If ye give me a few minutes, I'll lock up an' walk ye to yer car," he said.

"No thank you," she said. "The car is only a block down, I'll be fine. Thank you for the water and for being decent."

"I'm only sorry it wasn't quick enough for the lad. Poor bugger," he said and shook his head.

She *would* be fine, for in the strange ways of Belfast, the streets had emptied entirely following the violence. Everyone had withdrawn to their various tribal enclaves and closed their curtains if they were fortunate enough to have them. Nevertheless, the publican stepped out into the evening and watched her walk down the block.

A cold wind carrying sleet, blew through her hair, depositing icy rain on her skin. The street was empty but hate still pulsed in the air, soaked into the very stones beneath her feet and the decaying façades of the buildings. Sometimes it felt as if all the hate and pain had maimed this city in its very heart, twisting it into something deformed which now bred violence and hate from that very deformity. It was a vicious cycle and one that looked to be unending in this wee city by the Lagan.

The poet had said it best, long ago, because so much in this country was part of the blood cycle, so that all things true became true once again on the sacrificial wheel. As she unlocked her car, she looked down at her hands and saw that the rain was washing away the blood which she had clenched her fists around only a short hour ago. But no amount of water would ever truly wash it away, for even the ceaseless and sweeping rains of this city were tinged with red.

Out of Ireland, have we come,
... great hatred, little room, maimed us from the start.

Chapter Eighty-four

There Will Always Be Blood

THERE WERE ONLY TWO weeks left until the wedding. Father Jim, after much convincing on her part, had agreed to marry them, though Pamela knew that he wasn't happy with the idea of her joining in matrimony with Noah. It would be a simple ceremony, or as simple as the special circumstances allowed. It would be just the two of them along with Patrick, Kate and Vanya. Gert and Owen had begged off saying they had commitments that day which could not be avoided. The truth, as Gert later told Pamela was that they could not bear to watch her marry 'that man'. Tomas had said much the same, only nowhere near as politely.

All that remained was to finish packing up the house. For the most part it would stay as it was, for Vanya was going to continue living in it. She was glad it would not be empty, and that he had agreed to keep Paudeen and Rusty here, as she didn't think they would be happy at Noah's, what with the several hundred cattle, barn cats, shepherd dogs and the flock of sheep. She wasn't certain what Finbar was going to make of it either, but she knew the children would not be able to leave him behind, not even in Vanya's loving care. As it was, Conor had suggested that he stay and live with Vanya. She had explained patiently that it was not possible, that he could not live away from her or Isabelle. To which he had said, looking as much like his father in a temper as was possible, that he liked living with them just fine in his own house, not Noah's, and stormed off to the byre. Isabelle, on the other hand, was happily rolling things up in blankets to bring 'wif me to Noba's homes'. Pamela feared that she thought it was just an adventure and that they would return to this house and to all their own familiar things, much as they had once done with Jamie. Only the children loved Jamie, and she feared that might never be the case with Noah. He was kind to them, talked to them, brought them wee gifts that he thought they might like and yet she knew there was a great reticence in their hearts, particularly in Conor's case. She couldn't blame them; life had been confusing for them since their father's disappearance. They had accepted Jamie into their hearts and lives, only to have him, for all intents and purposes, disappear like their father had.

She had packed three boxes that day with things she was taking to Noah's house. She supposed she would have to quit referring to it as 'Noah's house' and come to the realization that, from here on out, it would be her home, too. Today had been an especially hard day, because she had packed away some of Casey's things, put lavender in with his clothes and asked Vanya to put the boxes up in the small attic of the house. She had spent an hour sitting in the midst of the clothes first, smelling each garment of his, imagining that she could detect his particular scent in the weft and warp of every sweater and jersey. She knew it wasn't true, knew that the clothes were just wool and cotton, and that they didn't hold him anymore and that there was no essence there for her to take into herself and hold against the days to come.

Early that morning she had stood quietly in her kitchen and looked around her. The house was the same as it had always been from the day Casey had finished it until now. The only changes were those of life and the soft wear of a home which was well loved. It was strange to her that the house hadn't changed; that it could still have the same mellow patina to the floorboards, the same broad capability of counter and windowsill, that the same plants spilled greenery, the same mugs glowed warmly from the sideboard, that the level in the whiskey bottle was right where Casey had left it oh so long ago. As if even the inanimate objects were held in some thick amber, and waited upon his return. She knew for her it was true, that some part of her, particularly when she was here in their home, still strained for the sound of his step in the yard, his presence in the doorway, the comfort of his arms after a long day. The expectancy was not as sharp as it had once been, but it was still there, and she knew that it always would be to some degree. Perhaps it would lessen when she left this house and would become something other, something more like yearning and less like believing. She would live within walls that Casey had never seen, floors upon which he had not walked, a bed in which he had never slept, and she would roam fields which he had not tilled. But she was not naïve, and knew that wherever she went, however she lived, whomever she loved, some part of her, a ghost of a living woman, would still be standing here in this house, with this floor beneath her feet, waiting and hoping.

She'd been quiet through the evening after that, causing Vanya to ask her if all was well. She'd nodded, feeling weary and achy in all her bones. She'd been out of sorts ever since she had witnessed the killing of the young soldier.

"I'm fine, just need a warm soak in the tub," she said.

Which was exactly what she was doing, now that Isabelle was asleep and Vanya and Conor were reading together. She lay back in the lavender-scented water, feeling the ache ease out of her slowly as the warmth penetrated to her marrow. Her tub was one of the things that she was going to miss. It was an old Victorian, claw-footed monstrosity which Casey had recovered from some building before it was demolished. It was one of the few tubs in which the man could comfortably lie. She herself could wallow in decadent comfort with plenty of room to spare. She remembered when Casey had installed it and told her with a grin, that it 'was of a size for the both of them.' They had tested the idea out more than once and found that he was right, even if the floor was often soaked by the end of the bath. She sighed and closed her eyes, breathing deeply of the spicy lavender oil; it wasn't likely she would be frolicking in tubs in her new marriage.

She smoothed her oiled hands over the round of her belly and thought about the baby that floated inside, safe in her watery world, her whole universe warm and fluid, with the echoing assurance of a strongly beating heart. She wondered if she would look like Jamie. Considering the resemblance between him and Julian, she thought it was likely that the baby would bear his genetic stamp strongly. She would like that, a child who looked like Jamie, only she did not want anything that would make Noah resent the baby in any way, shape or form. Then there was the issue of Jamie and custody. She did not take his words lightly, and knew he was very serious about not wanting Noah around his child. Tomas had already cautioned her about the advice he was likely to provide Jamie as the baby's birth approached. She suspected his motive had been to scare her off marrying Noah, whom he referred to as 'that murderin' bastard.'

The baby, as if sensing her future was being fretted over, poked a tiny fist just under her mother's ribs. She lay her own hand over it, cupping it slightly and rubbing in reassurance.

She was half-drowsing, still stroking the tiny moving form, when Vanya's voice, sharp with anxiety, pierced her fog.

"Pamela, Noah is in the yard, something is not right with him. He is wanting you, but I do not like you to go to him."

"Why won't he come in?" she asked, getting up out of the water and wrapping a towel around herself. "Vanya, come in, and tell me what's going on. Why can't Noah come into the house?"

"He is all blood," Vanya said, poking his head around the door. His normally snowy skin sported a slightly green cast. While Vanya took most things in stride, blood was not one of them.

"Is he hurt?" she asked, frightened suddenly.

"I am thinking no; I am thinking it is someone else's blood he is wearing."

She dressed hastily as Vanya ran back down the stairs. The clothes clung to her bath-damp skin and her hair was still dripping as she followed Vanya down the stairs.

She was surprised at how calm she felt. If this country had given her one thing, it was this—a somewhat impervious attitude toward blood and injury.

"Pamela," Vanya was behind her as she opened the door, worry making him sharp. "I do not wish for you to go out there, he is not himself. Let me go, I will ask what he wishes to say and tell it to you."

"No, please just stay here with the children. Isabelle is asleep but I don't want Conor following me out. If it's me Noah wants, there's reason for it. Vanya, I'm not afraid of him. He would never hurt me."

"He might not mean to, but..." Vanya shrugged. She shook her head at him, to indicate that she was going. Vanya had never liked Noah, and he wasn't about to start now. It was just one more part of her life she would have to partition. Her life was starting to resemble Belfast's own tribal map, what with all the people she couldn't afford to have intersecting.

The moon was sharp tonight, but it shed enough light that she didn't need to wait for her eyes to adjust. She saw Noah at once, sitting on a stump, strangely still, his hand over his chest as if something pained him terribly.

"Noah?" she said, her voice low so as not to startle him. He looked up but his face was a pale blank, like someone moving through water, seeing the world through a clouded scrim. She recognized the signs of shock all too well.

She crossed the yard, a dreadful foreboding building low in her belly. Shadows rippled across him as clouds drifted over the face of the moon. She couldn't see the blood on him, but she could smell it.

"I couldn't think where else to go," he said, voice little more than a whisper. She touched his shoulder, gently, her heart hammering at the thought of what it would take to put him in this state.

He put his arms around her hips, startling her, his face to the round of her belly; he was shaking like a leaf in a gale. To her horror she felt something cold and slick soaking through the thin material of the shirt she had thrown on.

"Are you bleeding?" she asked, wondering if Vanya had been wrong in his assessment of Noah's physical state.

"No, it's not my blood," he said.

"Noah, whose blood is it?" She wanted to push him off of her but knew he had to be handled carefully. He felt like a tamped powder keg.

"There was...there was a little girl..." he sounded like he was choking on the words, as well he might. She understood now, for even though he was a man of blood and violence himself, children fell outside what he deemed acceptable.

"Noah, what little girl? Where were you?"

"I was at the church, I had a few details to discuss with the priest, before the weddin'..." he trailed off. "But the priest wasn't there."

"No, he's away just now," she said, "gone to visit family in the States."

"I was walkin' out the path an' there was a wee girl an' her da' gettin' in a car," he paused and pulled his head away from her. He swallowed and she could see his face stark in the moonlight, the bones taut to the skin, the blood black against it. "Some bastards came along in a car, an' they sprayed the car with the little girl an' her da' in it. The car looked just like mine, I am sure it was meant for me. I ran to the car, the father was already dead, the wee girl was still breathin', but she was drownin' in her own blood. It was everywhere. Everywhere, Pamela. She was gaspin' for air an' the look in her eyes..." he swallowed and she could feel the tremor that ran through his body, shaking him to his core. "She died right there in my arms. The ambulance came but it was too late."

Noah had seen more than his share of blood, but that it was a child was what appeared to have put him in this state of shock. It made sense, in the way that all the terrible things in this country made a terrible sort of sense.

"Just give me a minute," she said gently, "and I'll take you home."

He took her hand and put his face to her palm, as if seeking grace through her touch. She could feel the terrible tension in his jaw and the rasp of his whiskers pressing into her skin.

"I need ye," he said plainly.

"I know," she replied, and wondered that two simple words could be built from such sorrow.

Inside, the house was surreally cozy, as if such shelter and sanctuary could not be real but only an illusion—which it had proved to be; a lovely illusion for a time, but that time, for her, was now over. Vanya stood waiting, face pensive, arms crossed over his blue-shirted chest. She was relieved to see that Conor had not made his way downstairs.

"Vanya, will you please watch the children for me? I don't think I will be back tonight."

The amethyst eyes looked at her without blinking. "What are you doing, Pamela?" he asked in his usual forthright manner.

"I'm going to take him home," she said, grabbing a sweater that was hanging over the back of the sofa.

He nodded, though he looked suddenly sad. "Be certain, *moy podrooga*, of what you are doing and of what you want."

"Want doesn't have any bearing in this," she said and went back out into the night, where a man who needed redemption waited.

Noah got in the car with her and she drove the narrow, dark laneways to his home. It was silent and the night was held still and silver within the universe's hand. She did not speak, because there were no words to give him.

The farmhouse was dark and silent and there seemed to be no one about. She could hear the cows lowing far off in the pasture as she got out of the car. She stood for a moment in the moonlight, letting it touch her, wishing it could wash her clean, wishing it was like the hand of a priest filled with absolution. But there was no absolution, there was only life, and step after step on a road that led somewhere completely unfamiliar. She went around the car and opened the passenger door for Noah. He half-stumbled getting out and she grabbed him, then put his arm around her, the blood on his clothes filling her nose with copper-salt and something far darker; it was, she thought, the smell of butchery and the touch of it was a cold wind across her soul.

The house was quiet too, not even the sound of a fire to break the strange stillness that lay over the night, a stillness that waited for something, just as she had for so long now but as she no longer would.

She led Noah to a chair, and sat him down. His face was still that strange and desperate blank. She lit a fire; the house wasn't cold but if he was in shock, he would need the extra heat.

She checked the peat hod and saw that it was low. She picked it up and carried it outside. The peat pile was in a neat lean-to near the house. She filled the hod, the odor of peat like dark water in her nostrils; it was comforting after the thick and heavy stench of cold blood.

For a moment she stood in the yard, arms filled with the peat, the moon stark as a blade in the sky, and felt a chill breeze riffle through her hair as if winter had sent a breath back from where it sat hunkered and waiting for the turning of the earth. There was what a woman wanted and what a woman hoped for and then there was the truth. Her own truth was as hard as that blade in the sky, and as likely to run her heart along its deadly edge. Her husband was never coming home and Jamie was not going to swoop down from his hill to take her to safety and warmth and love. There was only herself, her children and this man, this bloody man of violence and shattered dreams. Sometimes it was hard to remember the road which had brought her here to stand in this stark light—this world that showed little mercy to its inhabitants.

Inside the house, she banked the fire so that it would burn long and hot and then she drew Noah a bath, running the water as hot as she thought he could stand. He followed her into the bathroom, and began to take his clothes off, though it was soon clear that his hands were shaking too hard to so much as unbutton his shirt.

"Let me," she said and so she undressed him there by the tub, a bag spread on the floor to catch the bloody clothes. He still seemed removed, though his eyes followed her every action. It was oddly intimate and yet not sexual, like she was simply tending to him as she would have one of her own children.

He stood naked for a moment, the smears of blood dark on his skin. Then he took a long shaking breath and got in the tub, the water rippling out from his body as he sank into it—little wavelets flowing out to the old porcelain edges. He picked up the cloth she had laid over the edge of the tub and fumbled it into the water, his hands still trembling.

"No, let me," she said again, and took it from him, knowing he needed something tonight for which he could not ask.

The water around him swirled crimson as she wiped down his body and then lathered her own hands to wash him as clean as was possible, considering the stains he bore. Her stomach pressed against the rim of the tub and the baby kicked in protest. She sat back on her heels and rubbed her hand down the side of her belly, and the baby rolled softly in response.

She looked up to find Noah watching her and she saw some spark of life there in his eyes, despite the dim of the old bathroom. She understood what he needed, even if she felt as hollow as a milkweed pod in the autumn, merely at the idea.

She took his hand and placed it on the top of her belly. The baby rolled again, poking out a wee foot. Noah startled slightly, his eyes hidden under his lashes.

"Life, asserting itself," she said, harking back to one of their first conversations and giving him a touchstone from their shared history.

"Aye," he smiled, his hand still touching her belly, though the baby had stopped her movement in the sudden way that babies did. She put her own hand over top of his, and saw the response in his face. He looked up, eyes dark with emotion and merely gazed at her for what seemed a very long time, while the ancient tap dripped clean water into bloody. At last she drew back and stood, the tension between them growing with every second that ticked past on the old clock in the kitchen, echoing into every other room in the house.

He got up, water spilling down his body and stepped from the tub and took the towel she held out to him. The room was dim, but not so dim that she couldn't see his outlines and feel the desire that emanated from him so strongly it was like a third party there with them, waiting.

She had been wrong when she spoke to Vanya earlier, for want did have bearing, and so did need, only love was absent, though not entirely, even if it wasn't in the form she would have wished. This man clearly wanted her, needed her tonight as he had not before, and he loved her, even if it was a love dark in its outlines.

"Pamela." It was all he said, just her name but he said it in such a way that she understood.

"It's all right, Noah," she said and led him, blind with shock, blind with need to his own bed.

The room was dark, the moon spilling its cold silver light on the other side of the house. For this she was grateful. He sat on the bed, with only a towel swathed around his hips, and she could feel his eyes on her in the dark. She took her clothes off, goosebumps rippling her skin as the chill air in the bedroom touched her.

He took her hand and pulled her toward him, still silent, the air between them bruised with the words neither could say because for her they would be lies; for him, because he would never be easy with words that left him vulnerable.

His hands trembled as he touched her, soft, with hesitancy in his fingers.

"Ye're cold," he said, even the low whisper loud in the stillness of the bedroom and the house and land beyond. "Come into the bed."

She lay down beside him, feeling like a ghost, as if part of her was still outside, and here only her body was present, her spirit waiting, waiting under the moonlight for a man who had long been a ghost himself. Here there was space for neither phantom nor memory. There was only what she could give to this man's need.

After, she lay in his arms, quiet, mind shut to that ghost-girl who walked the hills in the wind that soughed its way through the boughs of the trees and plucked with restless fingers at the eaves and the hearts of humans.

They did not speak, for Noah was, even now in the extremis of emotion, a wise man. They lay in the silence for a long time, touching, her giving him what tenderness time allowed, as none had done for him since he was a child. Finally, he slept, her hand stroking his head, softly, so softly, his breath warm and deep against her skin.

She lay awake listening to the wind fret around the house and the sound of leaves brushing against the bedroom window. It was a sound that she had loved as a girl, the whisper of leaves at the glass, as though they had lovely mysteries of which to tell. But she was not a girl any longer, and so she closed her ears to the secrets of the leaves. And then, she too, slept.

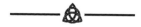

A cold, red dawn came up over the hills, spilling blood over the landscape off an edge so early that it was as narrow as that of a knife blade.

She sat at the kitchen table, feeling the warmth of the old kitchen lap around her. She was tired, and so distanced from her body that she felt as if she hovered above herself, looking down on the pregnant woman at the table, a cold, untouched cup of tea in front of her. Beside the cup, shimmering in the morning light, was a sapphire ring. She had been surprised by how much it hurt to take it off. Because she was going to miss him, a great deal more than she could possibly have understood even a few months ago.

Noah came out in worn denim pants, pulling a shirt on over his head. He would have work to do, farms waited only for first light, no matter the cost of the night before. The crimson wash of the morning caught him in movement—his tired face, the dark curling hair on his chest and stomach, the depth of the gentian eyes. He was, as she had thought all those weeks ago, a well-made man and he had been right, he would have kept her happy in the marriage bed. He had shown her that last night. He paused in the middle of the kitchen, barefoot and appearing far more vulnerable than was his norm. There was a question in his face, and she felt her heart crack a little inside her chest; it was only another fracture in a vessel which had become exceedingly fragile over these last few years.

"I can't marry you," she said, her voice sounding to her own ears like something hollow, that rattling seed pod emptied by the wind.

"I know," he said. His voice was as quiet as the red light that poured through the windows and wrapped about them, like blood, translucent and thinned. "If ye could tell me why, I'd as soon know."

"With you, Noah, there will always be blood. It was so with Casey, too, but…"

"But ye loved him, an' that made all the difference."

He had never been afraid to say the difficult things, this man.

"I've been making bargains with myself for so long now, Noah, exchanging one thing for another, telling myself that it was worth any price. But I just can't anymore. I can't marry any man, not even one who has convinced himself he would never need more than I could give. I'm sorry."

"Ye never loved me, I knew that; ye needn't apologize for it."

"I think, given time, I would have grown to, but I just can't now, Noah."

"Last night, why then? If ye planned to end things, why?"

"Because you needed me, and I needed something too. I didn't know until this morning that I couldn't go through with it, but I don't regret last night."

He came to her then and knelt down in front of her, taking her hands in his own, turning them over so that the palms were painted red with the dawn's light.

"A man could never accuse ye of dishonesty. It's one of the things I've liked since the day we met, ye know—yer honesty, an' yer courage."

She put a hand to his face, wishing she could smooth away the weariness she saw there.

"I wish," he said, "that ye had known the boy I was, I think you an' him might have got on quite well."

"We did get on," she said, and saw that it was true. For the last three years, his company had been the easiest for her to bear.

He touched the side of her face, gently. "I am goin' to miss ye, Pamela Riordan."

"I'm going to miss you too," she said.

She leaned into him and kissed him on the cheek and he held her for just a moment, there in the old kitchen bathed with light the color of blood.

"Noah, maybe one day—" she began, wanting to leave on words of comfort but he was not that sort of man, and did not need soft words which were not those of truth.

He shook his head. "Don't say things neither of us believe. You an' I have always been honest with each other, let's keep it so. These months with ye were my allotment of love; there will be no more. Ye gave me a glimpse of somethin' special an' rare for a bit, but it wasn't mine to have an' I think I always knew it."

There were things that hung unsaid, as they should, in the old kitchen that had seen far too many harsh words and unhappy moments. There were things she knew that she wished she did not—that for a man such as Noah there was no ultimate redemption, there was only what he could live with in his marrow, what he could live with alone. And that one day he was likely to die in a lonely blood-soaked hut, at the hands of a man just like himself. It would come, he knew it as did she, it was only a matter of which week, which day, which moment.

And so she left, because for the two of them, there was nothing more to do.

Chapter Eighty-five

Partners at Law

THE BRASS PLAQUE GLEAMED in the one liquid ray of sunshine which graced the building front that morning. Pat read it and then read it again, it said 'Egan and Riordan, Partners at Law.' He could feel his throat grow a little tight as he ducked in out of the rain. Their waiting room, if such a grand term could be applied to such a threadbare room, was warm and filled with the scent of tea brewing. A young man sat in one of the chairs and he glanced up at Pat with a nervous smile. A new client, and no doubt one who hadn't a penny to his name, but a problem that could not be ignored. He smiled back and nodded. "One of us will be with ye in a moment."

Tomas was in his office, and there was actually a small cleared space on his battered old oak desk.

"Tomas—the plaque outside?" Pat asked, wiping rain from his face.

Tomas looked up over the top of his ancient spectacles. "Aye, what of it?"

"Well, my name is on it. I'm just wonderin' when that happened?"

"It happened last night. I ordered the plaque a week back."

"Did I miss ye askin' me to be yer partner?"

"No, ye didn't," Tomas said briskly, "but I will tell ye this, lad. I haven't wanted to take on a partner in thirty years, so take that for the compliment it's meant to be. It's likely to be the only one ye'll ever get from me, so savor it. If ye don't wish to partner up, well no fault to ye, lad, we've a tough row to hoe in this country, an' I don't intend to take on only the easy cases."

"Thank ye, Tomas," he said, feeling rather stunned. It would take a bit, he knew, to fully realize the news.

"Don't thank me just yet, Patrick. That young man out in the lobby is goin' to be our next case, an' it's goin' to be just as interestin' as the last."

"By which ye mean," Pat said drily, "that he's got Republican connections an' not a single penny to his name."

"Aye," Tomas rubbed his hands together with what could only be construed as glee, "that's exactly what I mean. Are ye ready for another fight?"

Pat grinned, "Aye, I'm ready."

Chapter Eighty-six

Two Weeks from Yesterday

THE NIGHT WOULD BE a clear and cold one. The dusk was already gathering like translucent liquid poured from ancient cups, filling the hollows and furrows and the spaces between the roots of trees. It would be a night for the old ones to be abroad. Pamela shivered slightly.

It was near to the anniversary of Casey's disappearance. Two weeks from yesterday it would be three years. She had stopped counting the days at some point, though she didn't know exactly when. Only that now she counted in months, in years, in single moments like the day before when she'd caught Isabelle being naughty and told her she didn't want to see her doing that ever again and Isabelle had promptly responded with 'Just close your eyes then, Mama." It had taken everything she had not to melt into laughter right then and there. After, when she did have a good laugh about it, she had so badly wanted to share it with someone, with Casey or Jamie, as it would only mean as much to them. With Casey, because Isabelle was his flesh and blood, and Jamie, because he had been her surrogate father and loved her as a father would.

Things were either strained or ridiculously formal between her and Jamie now. She knew she should tell him her engagement to Noah was off so that he could stop any custody proceedings he might have initiated through Tomas. She knew things were not happy in his household. Violet seemed determined to hold him to a marriage which had been formed under strange circumstances—circumstances which no longer existed but still, she supposed if she were in Violet's shoes, she might try to hold on to Jamie by any means necessary, too. And she thought that Jamie did love Violet in a way, just clearly not in the manner Violet wished.

She stood for a long time in the yard and watched the ancient cups pour the dusk in its entirety, until the world was filled and the stars pricked out upon the smoke of a November sky. She was well chilled, and knew she should go inside and warm herself. But something kept her rooted there beneath the stars of a winter sky. It seemed if she waited long enough, something would step out of the bath of all that dark and would take her hand and lead her away to a fairyland which wasn't quite as forlorn as the one she had entered three years ago.

She thought that Casey would be proud of her. She had survived and the children were growing healthy, happy and strong. He wouldn't be best pleased about her having a baby out of wedlock but there wasn't much she could do about that particular situation. In truth, even had things been different with Jamie, she knew she wasn't ready for marriage or a commitment that required her whole heart. But she was making progress, or so she felt some days for she could touch the memory of Casey without pain now, or at least without the same sharp feeling in her chest which used to cause her to stop breathing. Often she felt like she was in a country where she had no map, and little familiarity with the terrain, and so she didn't always know where she was headed, or if it would be a good place should she ever arrive there. But at least she was moving forward, even if it was a slow journey.

Pat had told her what he'd found in the hut high up in the Wicklow Mountains. She'd understood why he'd feared telling her, and had taken the information in accordingly. It could have been anyone in that hut, and no reason to believe it was Casey. Life had moved on, and so must she.

She could hear the murmur of the children playing in the yard behind her—Isabelle's rapid paced chatter and Conor's measured answers. She turned to look at them. They were beautiful and happy and just now she could ask for no more. Conor's hair needed a cut and Isabelle's spilled over her shoulders in a rampant mess of curls from which Pamela was forever picking grass and leaves. Her wee face was flushed pink from the cold, dark eyes lit up with joy as Conor threw a handful of crimson and gold leaves around her, which shimmered in the light spilling from the windows of the house. Her son; her steady wee boy, who would never know until he was grown what an anchor he had been for her these last three years.

She took a breath of the cold air and walked toward her children, relishing the thought of the lamb stew she had left warming in the Aga and the fresh baked bread she had pulled from the oven before coming outside with the children. The fire was going and the smell of smoke was rich and inviting on the night. Something caught the corner of her eye—a flash of blue and not of the sort which naturally belonged to the landscape. She moved toward the edge of the wood and peered into the dark. She couldn't see anything. She would have to go find the torch and come back and have a better look. She would ask Vanya to come with her.

"Mama?" Conor, on his way into the house, turned back and looked at her. "Are you comin'?"

There it was again—the flash—only higher this time, as if it was rising in the air. What on earth could it be?

"I'll be in in a minute," she said, "Go on in and wash your hands and help Isabelle wash hers."

She stepped inside the tree line and the scent of pine resin rose around her. Pine trees had always smelled like Christmas to her. That was another thing she needed to think about—preparing for Christmas before this baby arrived. She was due in another week and so there was little time left as it was, particularly with her penchant for delivering babies early.

There it was again—a flash of blue, low to the ground like something running. She walked a little way further into the wood, and the fairy house, which Casey had made and presented to her and the children this very time of year, hove into her peripheral vision.

Behind her she could hear the children laughing with Vanya, and Conor calling to her once more. She turned to go back to the house and suddenly there was a blinding pain in her head and a sharp stab of something very cold in her shoulder. She grabbed her shoulder in shock and looked up. There was a woman standing in front of her with the strangest look on her face. Then the woman smiled and the world faded from view.

She woke to confusion and pain. At first she thought she was dreaming because she recognized her surroundings after the first few dazed moments. She was in the workhouse. The one Noah had taken her to that long ago autumn day. She sat up and then clutched her head. There was an enormous goose bump on the back of it. Someone had hit her very hard. She looked around; the room was empty and she was sitting on a dirty mattress which looked like it had been chewed on by a league of rats. She was groggy and her mouth was so dry it felt like it was filled with cotton. She tried to move, drawing her legs up and hoping she could get them under her sufficiently so they would bear her across the room and down the stairs. One leg pulled up, the other did not. Confused, she looked down the length of it; her vision was blurred as if she was looking through a stereoscope, enlarging things in the center of her field of view and miniaturizing them on the edges. And so it was that the manacle around her ankle looked small, like a delicate bracelet in shimmering silver worn for decoration and not restraint. The chain was narrow and attached to something solid which was currently beyond the edges of her vision.

She took three slow and careful breaths in an attempt to clear her head a little. It seemed to work for she felt a bit more stable. She had been drugged and hit—that much was clear. If she could remember what had happened then maybe she could figure out why she was here. There had been the smell of pine and the children laughing in the house. Oh God, what must the children be feeling? It had terrified them when the police carted her off, never mind her disappearing when she had been right behind them. Thank God Vanya had been in the house. *Please God, let them all be safe.* She put her hands to her belly then. What if the baby had been killed by the drugs? A reassuring thump of a small foot to her hand answered the pressure of her touch. She took another breath, this one of relief.

The room she was in was the dormitory room—long, narrow and open. She was at the end near the big hearth. There was no fire in it, however, and the air was damp and cold. The light outside was that of morning she thought, though it was hard to tell from where she sat. She must have been unconscious for several hours.

"Ye're awake, are ye?"

The woman had come into the room so quietly she hadn't heard her. She was small and had hair the color of dishwater and eyes that were near to colorless too—a pale, watery blue. There was something wrong with them too for they bulged unnaturally and looked raw and sore.

"Why am I here?"

"For yer sins. That's why ye're here. Because ye took a good man an' pried away at his weaknesses an' then led him down the path to sinnin'."

"You wrote the letters, didn't you?" she asked. She felt numb and cold but panic was spreading its dark wings in her chest.

"Aye, I did. Did they frighten ye, whore?"

"Yes, they did," she said. There wasn't much point in lying to the woman. "I don't understand why you sent them, though."

"It's because of what ye did to the father of that bastard ye carry in yer belly."

"I...I don't know what you're talking about," Pamela said.

"Are there so many men that ye don't know who it is I mean?"

"No, I don't.

"The most beloved man of God I know. The Reverend Lucien Broughton. I know that's his baby in yer belly, whore. And I plan to take it from ye. I'll raise it myself to be a child Lucien can be proud of. We'll be a family—just the three of us."

"What?" she asked, so confused that she felt like she had tumbled down a rabbit hole into some strange universe where nothing made sense.

The woman came across the floor and struck her across the face so hard that tears sprang immediately to her eyes.

"Don't lie to me, whore—he told me all about his weakness with ye. He told me how ye lured him with yer pretty hair an' yer fine skin. He told me how ye brought him to yer bed with all the allurements of a serpent an' its soft words. The child should not suffer for the sins of the mother though. I'll care for it well." She reached out a hand to touch the round of Pamela's belly.

Pamela shrunk back against the wall. She could not bear the thought of this woman touching her belly. This small mousy woman with the bulging watery eyes, seemed to believe, for reasons Pamela could not fathom, that the baby she carried belonged to the Reverend. She had encountered people who were unstable before, people who were on a fine edge or had toppled over it because of hatred or the blood-opiate of violence, but she knew she had never looked into the face of pure madness until today.

The woman smiled at her and Pamela swallowed down an icy surge of nausea. The woman stood then and walked over to the other side of the room. That was when Pamela realized there were three men as well. One was young, maybe in his early twenties with dark hair and a lean face. The other two were middle-aged and looked like the stereotypical hard man. Balding heads, beer bellies and mean red faces. Watching them as they huddled together and talked, it was clear to her that the woman was the one giving the orders.

The woman ignored her after that. Pamela took stock of her situation. She was shackled to the wall, firmly as it turned out for she couldn't get the bolt to move and only succeeded in badly bruising her ankle in her efforts. The men must have helped to bring her here unconscious and carry her up the stairs. The thought that they had touched her made her cold all over. She wondered what story the woman had told the men and if they thought her a harlot worth punishing too. There were some fanatical fringe elements in the Protestant faith in Northern Ireland that made it possible the men too, would see her as just a Catholic whore, not worthy to live. If the woman wanted her baby, she would have to look after her for now. That bought her a little time, though there was no way of knowing how much. The Reverend was evil and cunning but she didn't think he was crazy, at least not in the way this woman was. She didn't see him accepting her baby as being his. Why he'd led this woman to believe they'd been lovers she could not fathom. He loved to play games; she knew that fact from past experience. Perhaps this was all part of some elaborate game which he felt he was playing with Jamie, even if Jamie was an unwilling participant. Overall taking stock left her feeling doubly bleak. The drug's effects had passed and the baby was kicking furiously now, no doubt feeling the adrenaline flooding her mother's body. She was going to need to calm herself. Not that she had a clue on where to begin.

Later in the day the young dark-haired man gave her a cup of water and some bread and cheese. She drank the water too quickly and it spilled up the sides of her face and into her ears and hair. She slowed down after that, knowing she couldn't afford to waste one precious drop. She didn't know how often she would get fluids and needed to make certain to drink every bit that was given to her. She was allowed to relieve herself in a bucket a little while later. The young man had placed the bucket behind a screen of ivy which reached to the floor. It provided a bit of privacy, if not dignity.

"Why is this happening? I don't understand," she said when she returned to her mattress. She looked him in the eyes as she asked, hoping he would find it in him to answer her.

"It's not you, ye've been taken as a lure," he said.

"For what?" she asked, fearing that they wanted Jamie. If the Reverend was involved then it was likely. She did not want Jamie at that man's mercy and with the threat of her life and his unborn child's, he most certainly would be.

"Ye'll find out soon enough," he said and turned away from her.

She sat, having little choice in the matter, and watched the light fade outside. She had been gone close to twenty-four hours now. She closed her eyes and imagined she was home. Supper started and cooking in the oven, the children playing around her, Vanya telling her about his day and all the village gossip, who was marrying who, who *had* to get married, who was ill, who was estranged from their sister since the last village social, and who was having an affair with the neighbor. She went through it in detail in her head, hoping it would stem the rising tide of panic in her body. She needed to think rationally and calmly to see if there was any way out of this. Any way at all.

Her eye was caught by a remnant of newspaper on the windowsill, stuck there by some strange whim of fate, fluttering about its edges as if it, too, wished to flee this place. The word 'passage' was blazoned across it in big black letters. Passage on a steam ship to America, escape from this land of suffering and death. For the occupants of this workhouse it would have been too late, there wouldn't have been money for a passage over the sea. Escape, if it was to be made, had to happen before walking through the gates of this place. This piece of paper would have been a mockery, or perhaps a ghostly reminder of those already gone, who were as good as dead, for most families would never see their emigrant sons and daughters again. Just as, she thought, feeling utterly bleak, her loved ones were unlikely to ever see her again. At least not alive. Hopefully there would be a body for them to bury. Her children shouldn't have to wonder where their mother had disappeared to as well as their father. *Casey, if you're looking down on me from somewhere, help me, please help me.* It was a small plea, a flickering flame thrown out into a darkness as vast as the universe, but somehow talking to him in her head steadied her a little and made the panic recede just enough so that she could breathe.

There was noise on the stairs. Two of the men had gone out some time earlier. She shrank back into the corner as if the shadows could swallow her and render her invisible to whoever it was coming up those stairs. If the man had told the truth and she was here as a lure, then please God, let it not be Jamie whom her capture had been meant to draw in.

Three men came into the long dormitory room, and there was, indeed, one man she did recognize. At first she felt an uprush of hope in her chest, and then she saw the expression on his face as his eyes met hers, and the flare of hope died as swiftly as it had been born.

It was Noah.

They brought him to her after the first beating. She had learned courage long ago and so she stifled her desire to look away and not see the damage they had inflicted on him.

"What do they want?" she whispered to him when she thought he might be able to speak.

"Vengeance. They say they want information about the IRA in Armagh, but it's not true. The bald one with the blue eyes says I killed his brother five years back. It may be true. Either way, I can't give him what he wants other than my death. If there's something larger going on here, I don't understand what it is. The woman is the one that frightens me the most. The men are here because of me, but she is here because of you."

"I know," she said. They didn't speak any more of it because there was nothing to say. One couldn't really make sense of an upside down world of shadows and blood, and one could certainly not make it better by talking about it when it was far too late.

Some little while later she asked the dark-haired man for a cloth and some water. "You can give me at least that much," she said. "Please."

He walked away and she thought he was going to ignore her. But twenty minutes later he returned with a bowl of hot water and two cloths. He also brought a mug of beef broth.

"Thank you," she said. She was determined to stay on civil terms with this man as he was her only chance of humane treatment. The other two didn't care if she lived or died, she understood that just in the way they looked at her. The one mercy of being pregnant was that they weren't as likely to rape her. It wasn't entirely out of the realm of the possible, but it brought the odds down far enough that she could put the fear of it to one side. It was still there, but it was not a primary fear.

She used the water to wash away the worst of the blood. She was as gentle as she could manage but she could see it hurt Noah. There was no way not to hurt him. She bathed his face and neck and smoothed the dark hair back with a damp hand. It wouldn't heal him but she would give him kindness to combat the violence their captors had unleashed upon him. It was a small gift between them. She took stock of his injuries like she was making a list of things she needed to fix—first the ribs and then the eye, and then bind the ankle and straighten the fingers and somehow do all of it without medical expertise and painkillers. It was like making a Christmas list for Santa and then burning it in the fire and thinking the ashes would wind up in the North Pole where Santa could magically put it back together and deliver on impossible wishes.

"I'm so sorry," she said. She dabbed at a cut over his eye and he looked up at her. The gentian eyes were glazed with pain, but there was still an echo of his strength in them.

"I am used to pain," he said. "I can bear my own. If they hurt you then I'll break."

"I don't think they'll hurt me," she said. "The woman wants my baby, so until the baby is born, I'm safe."

"And after that?"

"I can't think that far or I'll go mad," she said, her tone matter-of-fact.

She tried to get him to drink some of the beef broth but he refused.

"Pamela, I don't need food anymore. I'll be dead in a few days at most. You drink it. Keep your strength up as much as you can."

She knew what she needed her strength for, and the thought of it terrified her. To give birth here in this haunted place without access to sterile tools and without medical help of any sort set loose the sort of panic in her body which she was doing everything to avoid.

He slept after that. She lay on the filthy mattress, shackled like a phoenix in a fairy tale, one who would not rise from the ashes but would instead die in her own blood.

She took stock of her physical self every other hour. They were feeding her well enough. The woman was worried about her nutritional needs but that would end once the baby was born. She found she was obsessing over every twinge of pain in her back or pelvic region. Being that she couldn't move around properly there was plenty of discomfort. Thus far, however, none of it felt like real labor pain. She found herself uttering a short prayer over and over like a rosary which held only three words— *Please be late, please be late, please be late.*

Vanya would have alerted Jamie and Patrick immediately. If it was at all possible to find her, Jamie would do it. The problem of course was that no one knew about this workhouse and it wasn't on any maps or lists either. It was so well hidden that it would be a challenge to find even if it had been marked on a map.

The man had dumped the bloody water out and brought her fresh water along with another rag and a bit of soap with which to wash herself. He'd given her toothpaste and a toothbrush as well. She brushed her teeth first, spitting into the cup in which the beef broth had been. Then she had an abbreviated bath not daring to remove her shirt or bare any of her skin in order to be more thorough. After, she lay down beside Noah. She was so exhausted that she fell asleep almost immediately. She awoke what seemed only minutes later to shouts and lights and the woman shrieking at her. It was an assault on her sleep-drenched senses and it took her a few minutes to understand what the woman was screaming about. Noah was gone. He was missing and they were searching the entire building for him.

The woman grabbed her hair and pulled her head back and then shone her torch directly in Pamela's eyes. "Where is he, bitch? Where is yer little lover-boy?"

"I don't know," she said, blinking away the light the woman kept shining in her eyes. "I didn't feel him leave."

He had to be in the building. She was certain his ankle was either broken, or at the very least, very badly sprained. He couldn't get far even if he managed to get outside. And while it might be naïve of her, she had a bone-deep belief that he would not leave her here knowing that he couldn't reach help in time. He would not leave her to the mercy of this madwoman who was clutching her hair so hard that Pamela felt as if a piece of her scalp was pulling away from her skull.

The dark-haired man came in just then. "We found him on the stairs. Let go of her. Ye're not goin' to treat a pregnant woman like this while I'm here."

He poked the woman with his rifle and she snarled at him like a rabid dog, but she let go of Pamela's hair. "Leave her be, or ye'll damage the baby," he said. This statement seemed to give the woman pause. "It's true, my sister's husband died when she was pregnant with their baby an' the baby was deformed when it was born. The doctor said it was from stress. So if ye want a whole baby for the Reverend, ye need to take care of her and not hurt her."

Pamela gave him a look of gratitude and he turned away. They both knew he could only keep her safe until the baby was born. She thought he hadn't fully understood what he was getting into with this kidnapping and torture, but now it was too late for him to back out.

They brought Noah back a little while after that. She was more pre-pared this time for how he looked and for the damage which had been done. Blood was their common element and she refused to shy away from it. She did what she could and even managed to get a tiny bit of water into him before he collapsed back into the mattress. He lapsed once again into restless unconsciousness.

Outside the light was growing. It was a pale November dawn, grey and then pink and then gold and she watched as the colors rose and built; even here in this dingy room there was a place for beauty. She rubbed her belly with long slow strokes, willing the tiny occupant to stay put for a bit longer and she would have faith that somehow, in some way, Jamie would manage to find them.

Sometime around mid-day everyone left the dormitory to gather in the smaller room next to it. The two rooms shared a chimney and because the mattress was near to the hearth a small bit of warmth leaked through. She could hear them arguing but couldn't make out what it was they were arguing about. Division in the ranks could be a good thing for her, if only she knew where the fault line was and how to exploit it.

She turned and found that Noah had awoken. She wished he hadn't. She wished she could grant him oblivion or even the peace of death.

"Listen," he said, his voice hoarse and so quiet that she had to lie down very close to him, in order to hear him. "I need to tell ye somethin'. If ye should get away there's somethin' I need ye to know. There's a crate of guns in the basement of this place. If ye could get that far, ye'd have a chance. It's where I was headed when they caught me. They don't know. They thought I was just tryin' to escape."

"Okay," she said. She didn't see how she could possibly hope to escape.

"I'm goin' to draw the directions on yer arm, Pamela," he said faintly. His breathing frightened her. It sounded wet and she wondered if his lungs had been damaged. She knew one of his ribs was broken and a jagged edge of bone could easily puncture a lung.

She put her arm gingerly on his stomach and he traced the directions on her skin with his broken nails and she spoke them in her mind. Right down the long hall off the dormitory, then right again, and a small set of choppy motions with his fingertip which indicated stairs, and then a gap, and another set of stairs. A long hall maybe and then a rectangle to the left indicating a room. He tapped her arm twice. This was the room where the guns were. She tapped her fingers twice on his chest to let him know she understood and she would remember. They both knew she wasn't likely to get the chance but it was hope, even if it was of the sort which was little more than a wraith on the air.

He passed out again after that. It wasn't sleep but it was mercy of a sort. She curled up next to him. She no longer cared about the smells of pain or blood or the reek of fear. None of it mattered. They needed the small comfort of human flesh next to their own. Or at least she did. Noah likely wouldn't know the difference unless he regained consciousness and she hoped he did not.

The day crawled past—lunch—tea, toast and an orange. Washing up with lukewarm water, rising to relieve herself in the bucket, lying back down on the mattress, each time praying that Noah would have stopped breathing and praying that he would still be there. He rose in and out of consciousness and she felt both a dull resignation and a sharp and blazing fury toward the men. She wanted to kill them all. Every last one. It was as she had told Noah—there will always be blood and now the fury of it, the want of it on her own hands had seized her.

They came and took Noah away again in the late afternoon.

They didn't take him as far away this time and the building with its old tall walls was the perfect forum for echoes. She made herself listen, though she didn't truly understand why. It was as if she was bearing the pain with him and by doing so, she could lessen it somehow for him. It made no sense and it was, she knew, in no way true, but she did it anyway. She supposed it was the same instinct that drove parents to find out the details of their child's suffering when they'd died by violence or depravity—as if the listening and the pain of doing so was owed somewhere in the universal balance.

At the very last there was one long scream, something inhuman, something beyond pain. And that was when she covered her ears and cried.

It was dark when they returned him to her mattress and she was cowardly enough to be grateful for that small mercy. She waited until the captors were in their little alcove, where they huddled near to heat and light, before she spoke to him.

"Noah?"

He didn't answer at once and she was afraid they had killed him and brought her his corpse.

He drew in a breath and it sounded like the gasp of a drowning man. Only this man was drowning in blood not water. "I'm alive," he said at last, though she could tell the words were difficult for him. She moved as close to him as she could manage without hurting him. They both desperately needed the warmth. She took her sweater off and placed it over him and then pulled the blanket the dark-haired man had given her over the both of them. She put her hand very carefully on his arm, in a spot where she could feel his pulse. Her belly pushed into his side and the baby rolled in response to the pressure. She went to move and Noah spoke.

"No, stay there...it's nice."

His pulse echoed against her own until it seemed as if they shared a strange place where time was suspended and this old building around them hardly seemed to exist. The world was just this—his pulse and their small warmth like a candle flame fighting against the wind.

She drifted then and dreamed. She was lying on the sofa in Jamie's study and there was a huge fire in the hearth, and she was warm. She could hear Jamie working away at his desk and then she could hear Conor and felt him snuggle in beside her. She must be in Conor's room now. She could smell his scent and she sighed, relaxing as her little boy's natural heat warmed her own flesh. Isabelle stirred across the room, clicking her tongue a little and then cooing just as she had done when she was a newborn. It felt real and yet she understood it was a dream, but it no longer mattered as long as she wasn't asked to wake up. A hand, strong and familiar, touched her shoulder. It was Casey. He hadn't visited her dreams in such a long time. He smoothed the hair back from her face, his thumb softly running the line of her jaw.

"I'm so glad you're here," she said.

"Aye, so am I," he replied. She could almost see him, but her vision was that of dreams—more impression than sight.

"Ye have to wake up, darlin'."

"I don't want to," she said. "I'm warm here. I just want to lie here beside you for a little while. You haven't come around for such a long time now."

"I know. I'm sorry for that."

"I thought you were mad at me and that's why you didn't come to me anymore."

"No, darlin', it wasn't that."

She felt one big hand cup the side of her face and she leaned into it. She was so tired. She wanted to just stay asleep forever here beside Casey because she knew outside of the dream he would be gone. He leaned down and kissed her forehead.

"Pamela, ye need to wake up."

"Why, why do I need to wake up?"

"So that ye can say goodbye."

"I don't want to say goodbye to you."

"Not to me, Jewel. To him. Ye need to say goodbye to him."

"Pamela. Are ye awake?"

She blinked. Casey was gone and so was the warmth she'd felt. Noah was terribly cold.

"Yes, I'm awake," she said.

"There is something I have to tell ye," Noah said, his voice little more than a reedy whisper.

"What is it?"

"That night in the byre. The Special Branch man. What he told ye."

"About Casey being an informant?" she asked, fighting to clear her head. She could still feel the touch of Casey's hand on her face.

"Aye," he shifted and lost his breath for a moment. "I'm referrin' to the bit where he told ye that Casey might have been sacrificed for someone in even deeper."

"Yes?"

"He was right, an' I believe he even suspected that it was me. If yer husband was killed, Pamela—an' I don't know what else could have happened to him—then the blood of it is on my hands an' no other."

"It was you?" She drew in a long shaky breath. All she could smell was the odor of pain and blood and exhaustion. "Noah, I don't understand." She didn't. How he could have gotten away with some of the things he'd done—if he'd worked for British Intelligence... She knew it was a dirty war the country was engaged upon but this—surely, but then no. There were likely no depths to which either side would not sink.

"I played both ends against the middle. They looked the other way when it came to the smugglin' an' gun runnin' for what information I could give them. They looked the other way for a lot of things."

"Did you kill Casey?" she asked. That much she did need to know.

"No, I didn't. I did think someone had discovered my secret, though, an' I talked to my handler about it. I didn't know it was him. In truth, I think he must have stumbled across somethin' accidentally. He was what he told ye, he simply passed names through the British spy who was yer friend."

"How long have you known?" she asked. There was no room left in her for shock and so she did not feel it.

"Once I started pokin' into it an' askin' questions—well, it wasn't too long after that I understood the road I was on didn't have any answers I was goin' to like."

"Most of the time you've known me then?" she asked. He didn't need to answer because she knew.

"Aye. It seemed too much of a risk to tell you. Both for you an' for me as well. An' then I liked ye an' valued yer friendship, an' I was too much of a coward to risk that. Then I loved ye an' it became impossible."

She couldn't absorb it and in truth, she wasn't sure it mattered anymore. They would both be dead in a matter of days. Hours in Noah's case. Why Casey had died no longer required an answer for her because answers wouldn't bring him back. And even if he could come back she would no longer be here waiting for him.

"Davison—did you kill him?"

"There was no other choice. He knew it an' that's why he tried to goad you into killin' him. As I said to ye that night, he thought a woman would give him a more merciful death."

"Was his death without mercy?" she asked.

"No," Noah said quietly. "I'm tired of blood too, Pamela. I see it in my dreams; I smell it on my hands even when they've been washed a hundred times since last there was real blood on them. I shot him. It was quick. I'm done with killing. It no longer matters for they will be done with me soon."

This was only too true. She couldn't quite wrap her mind around it. Death had happened around her nearly every week for some time. She had lived in terror of it and thought at times she had felt it coming. Once Noah was gone she would be alone here with these people until her child was born. She didn't think she could bear this much longer though. She couldn't countenance them hurting him anymore.

"Noah?"

"Yes," he said. He said it in such a way that she understood he was answering the larger question she had been about to ask and not merely the summons of his name. He knew. How to do it was the question. She was effectively shackled to the wall and well out of reach of a viable weapon.

"There's a tourniquet on my right leg," he said as if she had spoken her question out loud. "If ye release it, it will be done soon enough, an' it will be peaceful here with you. It's more than I deserve but it's how I would have it, if I've any choice."

She nodded and they were close enough that she knew he felt and understood her reply.

"We have a little time," he said. "Just speak to me. Whisper me one of yer pretty tales. They will wait the night. Even torturers get tired."

She whispered stories to him, ones Jamie had told to her and the children what now seemed a lifetime ago. And at the last, an old one which she thought her father had told her long ago—a story of a maid from the sea who had found comfort for a time with a man of blood and earth.

Before she finished, his hand rose and touched her face softly. He had maybe one unbroken finger and she knew the movement must be causing him agony, but she didn't move to stop him.

"It's time," he said. She thought it likely he wouldn't make the day any way, he was weak and he'd already lost a lot of blood and even a man as strong as he was could only bear so much. This would spare him a final day of pain.

She inched her way down, her fingers feeling lightly for the tourniquet. One did not ask oneself, at such a time, what was right and what was wrong; there was neither room nor leisure for such thoughts. She grasped it and then stopped for a second.

Noah's hand closed on hers and he pressed down. "Do it," he said, his voice no more than a hoarse whisper. She felt that she might well choke on the words she couldn't say. His hand was cool and sticky with dried blood.

"I'm sorry," she whispered and pulled. The bandage was wet and didn't come away easily, and she was afraid at first that she had tightened it, rather than loosening it. She tugged again, not wanting to hurt him, only wanting to give him an end with some kindness and love in it. The cloth gave in her hand. She pressed her lips to his forehead, and felt the first warm spill of blood against her thighs and felt a wave of terror that it was her water breaking, rather than his blood. It was his blood, though. And for a moment she felt a panic so intense that she considered trying to tie the tourniquet back into place. She was terrified of being alone. He might already be gone. His hand was so cold.

"Noah?" The space of a heartbeat and then another and then one more passed. She thought it was done and that he'd gone away from her and felt both relief and sorrow.

"I'm…just counting…the stars," he said.

She held him there even as his flesh grew cold, and the small beat of life which had been in him slowed and slowed and then ceased altogether, and she merely held the body, the spirit gone. The story she told to its end, knowing that the comfort of it was now for her, for the man in her arms could no longer hear, nor had he need of human stories to chase away the darkness.

He would know now if there was heaven or hell and what he had earned.

And still she held him, because here and now in this old building that had seen so much pain and blood, he was all she had left.

Chapter Eighty-seven

Devil's Bargain

Jamie waited for the Reverend at the appointed spot. Here in the Tollymore Forest Park there was a little stone shelter called the Hermitage which had been built long ago as a place for ladies to shelter while their husbands hunted. It was fretted with ferns and moss and it shone wetly in the dank November afternoon.

The park was wet and grey, the spaces between the trees filled with clinging mist. There wasn't another soul about, which was likely why the Reverend had chosen it as a meeting place. There was no danger of anyone stumbling upon them. There would be no witnesses regardless of what the man chose to do. He had the whip hand here and Jamie was certain he knew it.

It had been almost forty-eight hours since Pamela had been taken. The forty-eight longest and most terrifying hours of his life. Forty-eight hours during which he had pulled in every favor, listened to every whisper and rumor and turned up exactly nothing.

Kate had come to him immediately and told him Noah also appeared to be missing. It would have been nice to imagine they'd just gone off—as much as that idea might have galled him even a few days before. But the children and Vanya had been clear that she'd been outside with them and then the children had gone into the house and their mother had not followed. Then Kate told him Pamela had broken the engagement to Noah two weeks before and that the two had not seen each other since. Still, both of them disappearing at the same time was a bit too coincidental to his mind. And it was clear Noah hadn't planned to leave as he had left no instructions with his men and none of them—and he'd questioned them all—had any idea where their boss had gone.

Pamela was only a few days away from her due date. Her two births had been early and extremely precipitate with both children—Isabelle to the extent that Pamela had given birth in the middle of a forest.

Nothing made sense. The police had been pulled in and didn't seem to have any leads worth running down. To give them credit, those who knew Pamela from working with her over the years were concerned and doing their best to trace any clue as to her whereabouts.

It had to be the author of the terrible letters she'd received over the last few years. It made the most sense to him. He'd had a friend who specialized in forensics look over the one letter in his possession when he'd taken it from Pamela. There were no fingerprints on it, and the friend had said he thought it likely that the author of the letter had worn gloves while writing it. The tone of it made him think that if it wasn't the Reverend writing and delivering the letters it was someone within his sphere of influence. And so he had followed that lead and found out about the woman called Elspeth. He'd gone to her home and finding it empty, had quite calmly broken the lock and gone in. He'd spent thirty minutes going through her things and then he'd known for certain she was the author of the letters. He'd found pictures of Pamela and what appeared to be a series of reports from a private detective detailing her movements. That was when he'd asked the man for a meeting. The Reverend had chosen the place and time, and so here he stood awaiting him.

The Reverend appeared, walking toward him briskly, clad in normal street clothes—dark pants and a pale blue sweater. He looked, Jamie thought, rather normal and not like his usual water-pale and rather ominous self.

"How can I help you, Mr. Kirkpatrick?"

"I want to know where Pamela is, and don't even bother telling me you don't know."

The man made a good show of surprise. "What has happened to her?"

"She disappeared two days ago."

"What makes you think I know where she is?"

"Your little girlfriend knows, if you don't. Ask her."

"If you know that much then you know she also hasn't been home in several days. I don't know where she's gone."

"I don't believe that for a minute, Reverend. I think you know exactly what she's been up to and where she has gone."

Lucien looked up, eyes cold, but with a faint puckering in his brow which told Jamie it was possible the man hadn't anticipated this move in his game. "I don't know. If she had plans, she didn't see fit to inform me." His mouth was in a tight line that looked, Jamie thought, rather like fury. "She has gone out of bounds without permission."

It was an odd comment. Jamie took the letter from his pocket and handed it to the man. "Are you saying you don't know anything about this letter? And all the ones that followed?"

Lucien looked it over, his face smooth and placid. "This? No, what a horrible little screed. You're saying someone has been sending Pamela letters such as these for some time? Well, you know it is a rather moralistic country, except when it comes to murder. She has never truly seemed to understand that."

He was lying; Jamie was certain of it. He knew about the letters but he hadn't realized how far the game had gone without his permission.

"I believe Elspeth has taken her under some misguided idea that the baby Pamela is carrying is yours. Where do you suppose the woman got such a notion?" There were no good options as to what had happened to Pamela, but this one—being taken by this madwoman, was one of the worst. *Just be alive, sweetheart, just be alive. I will do the rest.*

"What are you willing to barter for this information?" Lucien asked coolly enough, but Jamie could see the pulse thumping in his neck. He was excited.

"I think, Reverend, we both know you're holding most of the cards in this game. So what is it you want to barter?"

"The things our kind usually trade in—information, blackmail, blood."

"Information?"

"Well, we could begin with the rather elaborate hopscotch you've indulged in since your return from Russia, all under the rather clever disguise of business trips—linen, whiskey, wheat, vodka and forests. And yet, there was always a double purpose to those trips. Meetings with others of your kind, traders in black secrets. All of you pieces on the board of intelligence and people dying horrible deaths for knowing too much or having seen the wrong thing at the wrong moment. And what was it that you sought, James? Once you found it, were you satisfied with the bargain you'd struck? To sell your soul for a woman you don't love and then have nothing left to give to the woman you do? That's a fool's bargain."

"Information has a variety of values—all scaled and weighted, one thing against another. So here's a question for you, Reverend. What about the kill squads? The off-duty policemen and the members of the UVF and UDA who have made it their part-time occupation to murder innocent

Catholics in their homes and on the streets these last few years. What is it you know about that, Reverend?"

"Why would you think I know anything about that?" The Reverend's voice was calm but there was a slight flush of color on either cheekbone.

"Because you're the root of that particularly poisonous tree, aren't you?"

"I'm a man of God, Mr. Kirkpatrick. I don't sully my hands with the acts of fanatics."

"No, you stir them up and give them names and then let slip their leashes as one does with dogs of war. Is that how you justify what you do? Because you believe you're involved in some kind of crusade? Blood always flows back to the hand which let it in the first place."

"Does it? I supposed you might know, Mr. Kirkpatrick, sins of the father and all that, not to mention your own sins."

"I'm not here to discuss my family history. I need to know where Pamela is. So which is it to be, Reverend? Information, blackmail or blood?"

"Information I have and blackmail," he shrugged, "it doesn't excite me these days."

"So blood then?" Jamie asked. He felt coldly resolved. He had known going into this it was possible the man might demand the ultimate sacrifice. And yet, because this man did not understand love, he could not know it was, in the end, not the ultimate sacrifice.

"You would hand me the means to your own destruction?"

"If that's the price you require for their location."

"What if I require your life—no tricks, no double cross?"

"No tricks, no double cross, you have my word." Jamie said, "I have to know Pamela is free and safe first. That's my one condition."

Lucien eyed him speculatively. "I find it interesting just how self-sacrificial love is. You would sacrifice yourself and she would mourn you for the rest of her life. It's madness of a sort, isn't it?"

"It's the only kind of madness that makes life worth living," Jamie said. "Now, tell me, do you know where she is?"

Lucien nodded. "Yes, I believe I do."

Chapter Eighty-eight

The Shooter

FINN HAD FELT the questioning of his cousin had merited an actual trip to Belfast. He had packed a small bag and told Casey he would be gone two days and no more. He left him in charge of the pub, which at least Casey thought gave him something to do with the time which seemed to hang heavier than a millstone around his neck. He had asked Finn to be discreet and not to tell this Tomas anything which might raise his suspicions. Until he understood his own history, he didn't want to spring any traps on himself.

Finn was gone three days and Casey thought he might well lose his mind at that point. He had refused to get his hopes up because he didn't feel that he could manage the crash which would come if there was no news on who he was, or worse yet, that no one was looking for him.

When Finn did finally return, Casey was certain the news was bad. The normally ebullient man looked like he had just come back from a funeral. He came in, shooed out the two customers Casey had been serving, flipped over the sign in the window to read 'Closed' and then turned to him.

"Take down the Angel's Ether, lad, an' pour us both a generous slug of it. I've a bit to say an' I suspect bein' a little drunk isn't goin' to hurt either of us by the end of it."

Casey did as he was told and then brought the drinks to the table where Finn now sat polishing his glasses.

"For the love of God, man, did yer cousin know anythin' or not?"

Finn took a swallow of the drink and then let out a long breath. Casey thought he might throttle him as a way of ending the suspense.

"Aye, he had information all right. Only he didn't need to give it to me. I found it for myself."

He thought he might actually pass out from the sudden lurch his heart took but he settled for a good-sized swallow of Finn's wicked brew. Finn reached into his coat pocket and pulled out a small pile of Polaroid photographs. He slid one off the top and pushed it across the table toward Casey.

"This man," he tapped the glossy surface of the top picture, "is yer brother. He works for my cousin, Tomas. I tell ye, lad, the day ye walked into this pub was fate, pure an' simple. I knew the minute I saw him, the two of ye had to be related. He's that much like ye. He's nearly as tall as ye, too; ye must come from a race of giants. He's a lawyer. He's got Tomas' respect which means he must be smart an' tough as nails. His name is Patrick."

Casey cupped the picture in his hand and stared at the man in the photo. He was tall, indeed, with a thatch of dark curls and a smile that would have melted the ice off a winter pond. His brother. His heart seized within him and for a second he felt dizzy and like he might pass out.

"Take a breath, lad, an' then take a drink. I had a chat with him, an' I asked the odd question, did he have siblins' an' the like. He said, aye, he'd a brother but the man had been missin' for three years. An' that brother left behind a wife an' two little ones. A boy named Conor an' a wee girl named Isabelle." He pushed another picture across the table. "Those two are your children."

He tried to pick up the picture but his hand was shaking too hard. Finn reached over and handed it to him, placing it gently in his palm. "Yer brother had them with him; they had dinner with us."

"They're beautiful," he said, though in truth he couldn't see them through the tears which stood in his eyes.

"Aye, they are that, an' both spirited as well. Yer lad is right smart, let me tell ye. He knows all sorts about plants an' animals, an' Tomas said he can ride a horse real well an' sail, too. The wee girl is a fiery one. She's a temper on her. Yer brother said, 'She takes after her daddy, that one.'"

"And my wife?" his voice shook even as he said it. She was real, the woman he'd longed for and dreamed about was real.

"Ah," Finn said, "well that's where things get a wee bit more complicated. She didn't come to dinner that night as she wasn't feelin' just the thing. So I thought to myself, 'Finn, ye can't go back to the man without seein' his wife,'—the question was how to do that. I'm not proud to say that I stole a book off my cousin's shelves an' took it to her house. I told her Tomas had asked me to drop it by for him as he remembered her wantin' to borrow it. She seemed puzzled, as well she might, bein' that she'd not asked to borrow it in the first place. She's lovely, an' I don't just mean the way she looks, but a lovely person all together. She had me in for tea. I felt terrible, I tell ye. I'm sure she thinks I'm a right strange one because I asked to take pictures of the house tellin' her I was lookin' to renovate an old farm house of my own. Then I insisted she get into the frame as well. She obliged me, though she was startin' to give me looks which didn't bode well."

Finn handed him the last picture. She was three-quarters to the camera and she was smiling, though she also looked a touch suspicious. He knew that look, he knew that face. There was relief knowing she hadn't just been a dream, she was real and she was his—or she had been for a time.

"God, she's beautiful," he said, feeling the tightness in his chest again.

"Aye, she is."

There was a long silence but Casey knew the difference between silence because there was nothing to be said, and silence because there was an enormous elephant walking about the room.

"What is it ye're not sayin', Finn?"

"She's pregnant."

Jamie Bloody Kirkpatrick had been the answer when he'd asked, with great calm, just who the father of this pending baby was. Well, Finn had just said James Kirkpatrick, Casey had added the bloody in himself. The damn woman had to make things as complicated as possible. And that, he thought, he *did* remember—just how bloody difficult and stubborn she was.

He had some thinking to do. It was a lot to digest—all the things that Finn had told him.

He wasn't surprised to find out that the wee farm with the fairy house was his home, or had been at least. He went there one evening and the house was lit up and he could see people moving about inside. He knew he couldn't just walk up to the door and knock on it. She was pregnant and the shock of it could hurt her or the baby. Besides, until he knew what he was doing, he couldn't just walk into their lives in such a manner.

So he'd done what he'd done for the last few years every time he was troubled. He walked. He walked and he walked, past seashore and farm, past city and field, he walked by day and sometimes well into the night. Since he had been told about his children, and now that he knew their names and the name of his wife, he felt like a man who had something to lose. Which was ironic, he thought, considering he'd already lost them. He kept walking until he had found himself back on the wee bit of land, standing beside the fairy house as a three-quarter moon rose over the thatched roof of the farmhouse. The house had been dark but it was late, and he thought it likely everyone had gone to sleep for the night.

He had brought a milk-white stone with him, and it glittered like a bit of the moon had fallen into his hand. He put it in the library of the fairy house and then checked the hole behind the shelves. There was a paper there. His heart thumped against his ribs and he felt both scared and excited. The letter was written in a child's hand, one who was just learning his letters. Conor. Each letter was big and clearly had been put to paper with painstaking effort.

Deer Daddy, it began. *I hop u got my uthr letrs. Pleez come home. Mama iz not goin to merry Noah enny mor. I miss u. Luv, Conor*

Not going to marry Noah? Who in bleeding hell was Noah? And why had Pamela been about to marry him when she was having a baby with James Bloody Kirkpatrick? He snorted, feeling a rush of anger. He'd been gone *three* years, not thirteen. The woman hadn't wasted a lot of time, had she?

And then he traced his fingers over those words again, crooked and misspelled and maybe, he thought, the finest words ever written. *I miss u. Luv, Conor.*

He read the letter through three times more and then Casey Riordan, who had for so long thought he was a man without a home, without love or connections, put his head in his hands and cried for the man he had been in another life.

Now here he stood, looking up at the old workhouse and still not certain about the best thing to do for the sake of his family. He had a longing to talk it all through with his brother, even if he didn't really know the man anymore. Still just having his name—Patrick—made Casey miss him.

He'd decided to spend the night here. Light a fire, have something to eat and get some sleep. He had nowhere else to go, truth be told, even if Finn had made it clear he was welcome to his spare room for as long as he liked. Now that he knew where home was, nowhere else felt right. And yet he couldn't go home. It was ridiculous.

He moved forward through the trees, wishing he hadn't left McCool behind with Claudia. He missed the damn cat. At least a man could talk to him and not feel like he was completely mad. He watched the ground as he walked, there were too many loose stones buried in the vegetation and he didn't want to risk a fall. Suddenly he realized that there was light falling on the tree branches above his head. He stopped and looked up. There was someone in the building. He froze to the spot, the branches above dripping sleet onto his head. He counted three windows with visible light. He knew immediately which room it was. The long one—the sleeping dormitory. It had a sound floor, though to his way of thinking, the room was a bit exposed. He felt slightly annoyed, like this was his house and someone had entered it uninvited. He turned to go, thinking he would walk back to his truck. Something compelled him to turn back—curiosity, he thought, a thing which always got a man into trouble.

There was a set of stairs at the far left of the building. They were in terrible shape and not the least bit safe, but he didn't want to walk into something he had no business witnessing. That was a quick way to get killed in this country. He knew there was an alternate route to the room though. There was a long narrow corridor which ran the length of the building right up to the dormitory section. He'd discovered that there was a secret hidey-hole in one of the rooms next to the dormitory as well, while rambling through the building one day. He'd thought at the time that someone had once used the hidey-hole, which was little more than a concealed cupboard, to spy upon the inmates of the workhouse. Inmates had been separated by sex and he thought it likely an overseer had put the spyhole in to watch the women in their sleeping quarters.

The stairs were even trickier than he had remembered and he held his breath several times as he clung to one edge and then the other until he made it to the second floor. From here it was the long hall that ran the length of the building. Once he traversed it, he would be really close and would need to access the area behind the fireplace. He would have to be quieter than the proverbial mouse if he wanted to get near enough to hear the people.

He removed his boots at the top of the stairs. He hunkered down low, his boots in his hand and moved slowly along the hall, careful to avoid any of the fallen pieces of roof and branches littering the floor. He asked himself what the hell he thought he was doing and why it mattered to him who was here in this building. It was not his and therefore no trespass had occurred, and yet he kept moving, compelled by he knew not what.

He made it to the room unseen. Inside it he moved carefully; there was only one wall between him and the main room now. In the corner was the cupboard and at the back of that was a small space which backed to one of the two hearths in the sleeping dormitory. He wedged himself in and shut the door behind him slowly and carefully so that it didn't make any noise and give him away.

The room was lit by two lanterns and a fire. There were three men, clustered together at present, arguing. Arguing over who was going to kill the woman curled up on a mattress in the corner. The pregnant woman on the mattress. He looked at her and understood why he'd been compelled to come and see who was in this building because the pregnant woman on the mattress was his wife. The fact of it slammed into him like a riptide had grabbed him about the knees and was about to pull him out to sea.

"I didn't sign up to kill a pregnant woman," the one man said heatedly. "Killin' that murderin' son-of-a-bitch Murray was one thing, but this is somethin' else an' I want no part of it."

Casey swallowed and pressed his head into the wall. He needed to keep his control. He needed to look in a calm fashion so that he could assess and understand the situation. Why and how she had ended up here didn't matter, only that they were going to kill her. He did not intend to allow that to happen.

She was clearly exhausted and terrified. Her hands were clasped protectively around the mound of her stomach. The pregnancy was well advanced, dangerously so. She was terribly quiet, almost as if she thought she might disappear from their view if she stayed silent. There was a bruise on the right side of her jaw, a stark black and blue blossom against her pale skin. Her hands were scraped on the backs, the knuckles slightly swollen. There was a glint of silver on her left hand and he remembered his long ago wish that his ring held the magic to lead him back to its match. In the future, he thought, he was going to have to be far more specific when he wished for things.

"Please, you can just go," she was saying. "Just go, I swear I won't tell anyone. I'll say you wore masks the entire time and that I can't identify you. Please."

"Shut up, whore!" A woman, whom he hadn't noticed up to this point, darted out and slapped Pamela hard across the face. She cried out, just a small cry but it broke his heart to hear it. She backed into the corner, cowering into the filthy mattress. He realized she was chained by one ankle to the wall. His hands fisted instinctively. He would kill the small mad-looking woman first. Just cut her throat, swift as that.

"If neither of yez is man enough to kill the woman, I will do it myself. So shut yer mouths an' quit yer bleatin' about it. We have to wait until the baby is born." She flicked a glance at Pamela. "It can't be much longer, she looks like she's about to burst with it."

He put his forehead to the crumbling stone, wishing he could just break through it and save her. Three men and one woman, which meant he had to count on at least four weapons. He couldn't take them head on, it was going to have to be an attack of a totally different sort, which would hold its own risks. He stood there a moment longer, hands fisted at his sides, the small cry she'd uttered when the woman slapped her echoing in his head. He had to go so he could come back and save her. The very idea made him sick to his stomach, but he couldn't take on three men and a crazed woman alone. He wanted to make sure the odds were in his favor as much as he could possibly stack them. And that meant he needed a gun. He pulled back from the wall and that was when a bit of stone, loosened by his touch, fell to the floor. It made a racket like a bag of marbles falling on glass, or at least it felt so to him. He stood there paralyzed, not even breathing, and furious with himself for his carelessness. It was the proximity to Pamela, he knew. That one simple fact had completely unmoored him.

"Did ye hear that?"

"Probably rats or birds, livin' in the walls," said one of the men. He could hear the crunch of boots on the floor, as the one who had spoken walked toward the fireplace.

"Go check the other rooms in the corridor," said the bald man with the extremely red face.

Casey thought wildly about the bag and the boots he had left in the room behind him. Please, dear God, let the fool overlook them, let the shadows be deep enough to hide them. If they caught him, he had no doubt they would kill him. The thought of it almost made him laugh—to come this far, to regain a little of who he had been and then to be killed in front of his own long-lost wife, would be beyond a tragic irony. It would be, he thought, with a bubble of panic building in his chest, really quite Irish in scope.

He could hear the man coming down the hall, stopping at each doorway to look. He knew the layout like the back of his own hand, and he counted the rooms off as the man halted and walked, halted and walked. The room with part of the floor missing but with all the window panes curiously intact. The room with the blue door hanging off its hinges, its brass door knocker long turned black. The room where the vines had crawled in through the window and overwhelmed everything inside, so that it seemed a secret garden held within crumbling stone walls. And then at last the room in which he now stood, with only a flimsy door between him and the man. He stayed perfectly still, certain that his heart must be echoing through the tiny space, it was beating so hard. Those goddamn boots. He couldn't believe he'd done something so stupid.

The man came in the room. To Casey, standing in the ridiculously small cupboard, sweating, it seemed that he looked around for several minutes. In reality it was probably only a few seconds before he went back out. It was dark in the room and clearly he'd missed the boots. Or he was standing out there in the dark corridor. Casey barely dared to breathe. He forced himself to count to one hundred before he eased open the door to his cupboard. He couldn't see anyone in the room; he stepped out slowly, aware that the man could be waiting in the shadows for Casey to pop his head out so he could blow it off.

He grabbed his bag and his boots and crept to the doorway. He hesitated for a second; he would have to risk it. He went right along the corridor, even though it went against every instinct he had to walk away from Pamela. He was halfway down the long dark stretch when he heard someone coming along right behind him. He went a few more feet and then ducked to the right down a set of stairs. Had the person seen his outlines moving ahead of him in the corridor? He didn't think so, or surely the man would have yelled out to warn the others before giving chase. He went down another set of stairs, thinking it was likely the safest option. The man was probably going outside and not into the bowels of the building, which is where he now appeared to be. He waited for a few minutes, breathing in the cold air and letting his heart resume a steadier pace. Above him a door creaked and a rush of cold air swept over him. The man *had* gone outside. He breathed out with relief and then reached into his bag, took out his torch and clicked it on.

He was in a cellar of sorts with a long tunnel running under the length of the building. He paused to put his boots back on and then walked along the tunnel. There were small rooms off to one side and he flashed the light around each one of them. With luck he might find some sort of weapon. One man had left. He thought it possible he could take two with something like a length of pipe. It was clear no one had been here in a very long time. Cobwebs fluttered in the dank air and he could hear water dripping further into the tunnel. He shivered. The atmosphere wasn't of the sort to bolster a man's courage. Some of the rooms held old half-rotted chairs, stacks of chamber pots and disturbingly, a bed with a heap of chain attached to its frame. Halfway down the tunnel, just when he was thinking he ought to turn back, he saw the crates. Two of them, covered in heavy canvas. He went in the room and pulled back the canvas, excitement running through his veins. It couldn't possibly be guns, and if there were guns there might not be ammunition to go with them. He pried the lid off of one crate, disbelieving his luck. Guns tightly packed in straw and in good shape. Clean, dry and in prime firing condition.

"Please God," he said and pried the lid off the other container to find his short prayer had been answered. Ammunition and lots of it. Enough to start a small scale war. It was odd that someone had chosen to keep guns here, but thank Christ and all the saints that someone had.

He chose two weapons and two boxes of shot. If he got in a fire fight he wanted to make certain he had ammunition enough to kill every last man in that room, before they killed him. He was a good shot and the months in the mountains had sharpened his skill. At close range he would have chosen a pistol, but at the distance he was going to shoot from he needed the long barrel of a rifle with a sight. The one he had picked was a short-action Mauser. It was top-notch for accuracy, and come hell or high water or damp it always worked. He wouldn't have to worry about it malfunctioning on him; he couldn't afford the slightest complication. He was going to have to take out two men before even one of them could get near Pamela. He put the pistol in the waistband of his pants. He might need it if any of the men managed to escape the building. He took a deep breath. He was as ready as he could possibly be.

Outside, he crept low and fast over the ground. There was an oak not too far from the building and not too close either. He knew it would give him the best vantage point. He slung the rifle over his back and began the climb into the tree. His knee hurt but he ignored the pain, focused only on getting level with that one window. The wind was blowing hard and the branches were slick with freezing rain. It made the climb difficult and it was going to make getting a decent shot hard, too. There wasn't time to wait for better weather and so he kept climbing, a strange calm settling over him now that he had begun on a course of action.

He found a branch he thought would bear his weight that was a tiny bit higher than the window. He took the rifle from his back and held it in his right hand, using his left to wipe the cold rain from his eyes.

Casey settled himself as firmly as he could, his mind buzzing slightly with panic. He looked through the sight and felt his heart drop as he did. The third man was back and was right next to Pamela. With the wind and the rain, he risked hitting her and missing the man entirely. He needed the man to move and wished he could will the bastard to step away from her and yet stay within sight of the window, giving him a clear shot.

"Make him move," he muttered between his teeth, uncertain if a higher power was likely to assist him in killing a man, but feeling a plea was worth a try. It seemed the universe was listening, for the man turned his head as if he sensed something. It widened the gap between him and Pamela to a scant few more inches, but it was going to have to be enough. God forgive him, it was going to have to be enough.

He couldn't think about the risk; he had a job to do and it had never been more important that he do it right. He felt a thin line of sweat break out on his forehead. He realized he wasn't breathing and that his chest was tight with the lack of oxygen. He stretched his neck a little and then settled his eye to the sight once more. He could feel the press of his rosary beads in his pocket. He would pray when this was done, or he would collapse entirely.

A man's voice, his father's voice, he realized, echoed through his head, as if the man stood now over his shoulder, his words there to shore up his son's courage.

"*Never seen anyone with a shot like you, son, ye could take the eyeball out of a gnat from a half mile away. Ye've a good steady hand on ye, and an eye like an eagle.*"

He took a long breath. "Daddy, if ye can hear me, keep my hand steady and steel my nerve."

For a second, he thought he felt the touch, light as air, of a big hand on his shoulder.

He let out his breath and took the shot.

Chapter Eighty-nine

I Rest in the Grace of the World

FOR A MOMENT she wondered if she was dead, and then she opened her eyes and realized she was, indeed, alive. Around her all was silent, except for a scrabbling in one corner. Rats, maybe, smelling the blood. All the men were dead. She couldn't see Elspeth. As far as she could tell, huddled here on her filthy mattress, all the men had been shot in the chest—shot dead center.

Her ears were ringing and she rubbed them a little, daring to sit up a bit more so she could better see. She thought there had been five shots all together. She hoped Elspeth had been hit by one of them.

The scrabbling in the corner coalesced like a spider emerging from a hole. Elspeth was still alive, but judging by her movements, badly injured. She was dragging herself along the floor, a gruesome noise which was both wet and scratchy at the same time. She'd been shot in her left leg. She was dragging herself with purpose and Pamela looked along her sight line to see that one of the men's guns had fallen away from him and was just a few feet beyond her mattress.

If she stretched out on her side as far as possible, she just might be able to reach it first. It was awkward getting over on her side but she used the mattress for a bit of traction, bracing her feet into it to push herself forward. She wiggled out across the floor, as Elspeth continued to make her slow way toward the gun, her left leg dragging behind her.

Pamela's fingers were at least an inch shy of the gun and her ankle felt like it was going to break if she applied any more strain on it. She stretched once again and felt something give a little in her back but it was enough to let her reach the gun. She wrapped her fingers around it and pulled it toward her just as Elspeth slapped her hand, wet with blood, on the muzzle. She pulled the trigger and Elspeth howled in pain, and then there was the sound of feet running up the stairs. Was it the shooter, come to finish the job, and more importantly, was he friend or foe?

Two men came through the door—one friend, one foe—Jamie and with him, the Reverend Lucien Broughton. The latter had a gun. She had thought her heart couldn't squeeze any tighter than it already had, but it did, as she realized the gun was trained on Jamie and that his hands were bound.

"Oh, Elspeth," the Reverend sighed, looking down at the woman now scrabbling to get up off the floor despite her leg and bloodied hand. "What a naughty girl you have been. You've made a terrible mess of things, haven't you? And now I'm going to have to clean it up. Pamela, slide that gun across the floor or I'm going to shoot your lover in the head."

She did as she was told so that the gun was well clear of Elspeth who, clutching her wounded hand, had managed to drag herself up into a sitting position. It became obvious why she'd been dragging her leg, for her kneecap was shattered and the flesh over top of it was torn wide, exposing the pearly gristle of tendon and bone. She had a knife clutched in her good hand though, and Pamela feared the woman was mad enough that she wasn't aware of the pain right now and so would not have its limitations.

She looked at Jamie then. Their situation was untenable and about, she knew, to become tragic but it was such a relief to see a loved face that she thought she might break down in tears just at the sight of him. He gave her a look, a question in his face and she answered in kind. What these last days had meant to him, she could only imagine. By that look alone she understood that Conor and Isabelle were fine, and that there was nothing beyond these walls she need fear.

"Here she is, just as I promised. And now brought face-to-face with it, will you keep your word?"

"I made a bargain," Jamie said. "I will keep my word and you must keep yours. She has to be clear of here first."

"Jamie—what bargain?" she asked. Her voice was barely above a whisper.

The Reverend looked at her, a chill little smile playing about his mouth. She had not seen this man since a night long ago, when he had killed someone who'd been intent on doing the same to her.

"He offered his life in exchange for yours and that of his child."

Pamela breathed out, horrified. "Jamie, no."

"Kneel down," the Reverend said and Pamela felt the world sway around her. She shook her head and realized tears were running down her face. He would do it, and Lucien would not understand the depth of the sacrifice nor the willingness with which it was given. Because love was not restrained by fear, and did not shape itself to such forms. Like water trapped amidst rock, love wound around, rose above or wore down all obstacles in its pathway. Love, not hatred. And so Jamie Kirkpatrick looked into the eyes of his own love, and kneeled down.

The Reverend smiled. "I had wondered if you meant it."

"Yes, I meant it," Jamie said. He did not look at Lucien but at her as he said it. "Now unshackle her."

"Do as he says, Elspeth. Take the chain off her leg."

"Are ye going to just let her go?" Elspeth said, a wild disbelief in her voice. "Ye have no right. I took her, I want the baby."

"No, Elspeth. Take the chain off her leg or I will shoot you." He pointed the gun at her, briefly, to show that he meant it. "The baby is not for you. The baby is theirs."

"The baby is his?" she asked, a dawning horror in her face.

"Yes, the baby is his. I've never touched the woman," he said and smiled.

"But you...you made me think..."

"I didn't make you think or do anything, Elspeth," he said smoothly. "You did all of this of your own free will. Only now you've taken it too far. Only I remove players from the board. Not you. You did not have my permission to do any of this."

"Permission? I saved you from this harlot," she said, spitting with rage.

"How?" he asked. "You made a fantasy in your head and allowed it to bloom into something dark and terrible. Now, remove the chain as I told you to."

Elspeth unlocked the chain around her ankle, though she did it so roughly that Pamela's ankle was bleeding by the time the manacle slid free. She needed to get to her feet and yet she was afraid to, for fear that if she stood, Elspeth would see that the back of her clothes were soaked. She understood what the pulling in her back had been. Her water had broken.

"Elspeth, get away from her. She is to go free. I am a man of my word and I promised she would go free."

"No, I won't do it. I want the baby." Elspeth had managed to drag herself to her feet. Pamela had been right—the woman was no longer feeling pain.

Pamela got to her feet, legs trembling, afraid that so small an effort was going to push her into full-fledged labor. Both Conor and Isabelle's births had been sudden and intense. She could not afford to have that happen here. The woman was right behind her and Pamela felt the cold prickle of the knife, right at the base of her spine. She froze in place.

"No," Elspeth said, her voice defiant. "I am not letting her go. I want the baby."

"Elspeth, shut up," the Reverend said, his patience clearly fraying. "I will deal with you after this is over. Take the knife from her or I will do it for you."

Elspeth slid the knife up a little to where, if she stabbed her, it would likely be fatal. Pamela could feel it poking into her back, just above her kidneys. One wrong move and she would be dead. She pulled a little to the right, where the window yawned open behind them. If the shooter was still there, and if he was indeed a friend, then maybe, just maybe, she could tilt the balance a little in their favor. Elspeth was so focused on the Reverend she might not realize where she was in the room in relation to the window.

Pamela felt strangely removed, like she had risen slightly above the woman who held her at knife point. It was many things—fear, dehydration, these last horrible few days. But mostly it was the man kneeling on the filthy floor, calmly trading his life for hers and that of their child. He looked at her, as though the other two people in the room, including the man who held a gun to his head, did not exist. There was for him only the two of them.

She did not know if she spoke aloud or if he did, or if they spoke as one mind, silent and together in this terrible moment.

I love you.

And I you, always.

Hanging there in the air between them was the vision of all that might have been. He smiled, a look to carry with her, along with all the gifts he had given her throughout the years of friendship and love. And heard the words inside her as if he spoke them out loud.

> *And I have fitted up some chambers there*
> *Looking towards the golden Eastern air,*
> *And level with the living winds, which flow*
> *Like waves above the living waves below.*

Soul within my soul. She could live within that which he would leave behind, and teach it to their child. His eyes were warm, the beautiful light-spilling eyes that had looked at her long ago and found within her gaze the missing parts of himself. This look was for her alone and there was nothing of fear or regret in it. Only love. *I rest in the grace of the world, and am free.*

Had she not been looking so fixedly at him, she would have missed the small flicker of his eyes. And then he did speak out loud. "Pamela, *move*."

Understanding was immediate. She dropped her weight away from Elspeth, having no other choice. She felt the shots before she heard them—two, almost simultaneous and she would have sworn too close together to come from one gun.

The air around her vibrated and she could feel the sway of the long ropes of ivy disturbed from their long slumber. She was afraid to open her eyes. But what was love if not courage and courage required one to look and to know, and so she opened her eyes.

Jamie looked back, his face fine drawn and ashen. The Reverend had toppled to his knees, and there was red flowering like a chrysanthemum across the white of his shirt. Then he fell all the way down, his eyes open. The woman lay still, the knife fallen from her hand, the blade gleaming dully in the lantern light.

Jamie came to her, and turned so that she might untie his hands. She did it swiftly, despite her fingers shaking with the shock of the last few moments. He kneeled down and shut the wide staring eyes of Elspeth, and then checked Lucien.

"He's dead," he said shortly. And then he came to her and took her in his arms. She was still afraid she was dreaming even though he was warm and smelled exactly as he should, despite the sharp-hot note of fear and fury that rose from his skin.

"The baby?" he asked, and she could hear the ragged note in his voice.

"She's fine, Jamie," she said just as the baby kicked hard as if to back up her mother's assertion. Jamie laughed and held them both tighter. Death lay all around, but here between them was life, moving and kicking.

"We need to go, Pamela, now."

He gave her his arm to lean upon for her legs were shaking and she felt distinctly faint. They crossed the room and she avoided looking at Elspeth or the four men who had been killed with such proficiency.

"Do you think he's gone?" She looked toward the window.

"Yes, he did what he came to do," Jamie said, a strange note in his voice.

Jamie was right, they must go now while there was the chance of it. But just before it was lost to her sight she looked back one more time through the window where a dark oak was framed in spectral bits of firelight, and said a silent *thank you*.

They went out of the building together, not speaking yet. The car, skewed sideways, sat waiting. Pamela felt more than a little surreal, like she was a tattered ghost who might rise out of her own skin and float away and rejoin all the spirits caught in that building.

Jamie got her into the car and then went around to the driver's side. He pulled away from the building and they were well on to the road when she finally took a long shuddering breath. She looked back as they drove out into the main road, the workhouse no longer visible. She half expected to see a figure in the narrow gap between the trees, standing and watching them leave. But behind her there was only the movement of the wind through the trees and the empty road where ghosts might walk, but no man did.

"Jamie," she said, gasping as the first real pain of labor struck through her lower back like a twist of lightning. "We need to get to the hospital."

Chapter Ninety

On a Deep November Night

KATHLEEN YEVGENA KIRKPATRICK was born late the next afternoon, when the frost lay thick upon the fields and folds of the countryside around. In comparison to her siblings and to the days which had preceded it, her birth was calm and easy. To both of her parents' great relief she was born healthy and sound, with a head of red hair which was startlingly bright.

Jamie felt like he couldn't breathe until the doctor was done checking her over. The doctor handed him the tiny bundle and smiled. "They're strong, these women of yours. Take good care of them."

"I intend to," Jamie said.

He took the first look at his daughter which was not blurred by terror, and found that she was, in all details, perfect. Skin fresh as a pearl drawn from the water and hair the color of fire in the dark—astoundingly red. So very tiny and delicate that it was frightening. And yet here and breathing and with no reason, the doctor had said, to believe her heart was anything but whole and strong. There would be, he knew, further tests, many of them likely, but for now he could breathe and just fall in love.

She opened her eyes and he fell into them. They were a deep jeweled green, and seemed wise far beyond her exceptionally new state.

Pamela smiled wearily, watching him and the baby. "She's perfect, isn't she?"

"Of course she is," he said, as if there had never been any doubt that she would be so.

Patrick and Kate arrived shortly after the birth with Conor and Isabelle in tow. Isabelle, uncharacteristically subdued, came into the room on the heels of her brother. The children had only seen her once since her escape from the workhouse and Isabelle could not be reassured that her mother was not going to disappear again for a long stretch of time.

"Mama?" she said uncertainly and when Pamela held out a hand to her, Isabelle ran to the bed, burying her face in the covers.

"Would you like to see your new sister?" Jamie asked, gently touching Isabelle's madly-curling head. She turned slowly and Jamie kneeled down with the baby in his arms, so that Isabelle might see her. Isabelle peered down at the small bundle.

"Sisser?" she asked tentatively.

"What's her name?" Conor asked from his perch beside his mother. Conor, always one to want the details sorted, was getting down to what he saw as the salient point.

Pamela looked at Jamie over the bundle in his arms, which was beginning to squirm. "I thought, if you'd like, we could name her Kathleen," she said. Kathleen had been Jamie's mother's name.

"Kaflee," Isabelle echoed, small face turned up to Jamie's.

"I would like that," he said, eyes meeting Pamela's. Her eyes shimmered with tears.

Jamie placed his daughter with great care into Conor's arms. He did not fear Conor would hurt her, for even at the tender age of five, Conor took a grave care for things and people. Pamela stroked her son's bent head, looking down at the baby with him. There was a hazy glow about her that made her even more beautiful to him than she had been before.

Isabelle crawled up into his lap and kissed his cheek. She'd had jam with her lunch. He could smell strawberries on her and the scent of sausage smoke in her dark curls. He kissed the top of her frowsy wee head.

"You goin' a stay here? Mama, Jamezie stay here a' night?"

"Of course, darling, Jamie can stay here. But you must ask him if he would like to." She looked up and met his eyes, a question in her own. He felt a constriction in his throat.

"Jamezie stay," Isabelle said with satisfaction and clambered off his knee and back to the baby as if all were settled in her mind.

"Well, would Jamie like to stay?" Pamela asked, her voice low, the murmuring of the children a flowing note between them.

A heartbeat and then another, and then one more. "Yes, he would."

Patrick, Kate and the children visited for another hour, Isabelle finally falling asleep beside her mother. Patrick came to Pamela's side and bent over, kissing her cheek.

"Congratulations again, she's beautiful. Ye're not to worry about Conor an' Isabelle. We'll look after them as long as ye need us to."

"How is Kate?" she asked, quietly.

"She's managin'. I think she'll want to talk to you eventually about what happened."

Pamela nodded, throat tight and prickling with tears. She could hardly bear to think about Noah, never mind find words to explain the nightmare from which she had barely escaped and which he had not. For Kate's sake she *would* find the words but she knew she would never tell her all that had happened.

Pat gave her a tight squeeze. "I'm so bloody relieved that ye're all right, Pamela. Don't hesitate if ye need anythin'. An' if the police come back, don't talk to them until Tomas or I are here with ye."

"I won't," she said. "I've been well instructed by Tomas." The police had been to see her and had questioned her, though they had been under very strict orders from her doctor to in no way upset her. Jamie had sat in on the interview which had the effect of keeping the questioning brief.

"I don't know who yer avengin' angel was," Pat said, "but I'm goin' to say a few prayers on his behalf tonight."

"Me too," she said, feeling vaguely troubled. She could have sworn she'd felt someone watching just before the shootings, just a presence that was different than the men who'd held her hostage.

"We're goin' to go while Isabelle is asleep here, or we might never get her away from ye."

Kate gave her a quick hug before they left.

"I'm sorry, Kate. About Noah," she said.

"I'm sorry, too, Pamela. You were there because of him. We might have lost you an' the babby too. Please don't fret yerself about it right now. We'll talk when ye're stronger."

It was only the three of them then as Pat and Kate left with the children, Conor having given a solemn kiss to his new sister and then hugging his mother so tightly that she couldn't breathe for a moment. The sun had set and there was a low flicker of light on the horizon outside the windows. Pamela realized suddenly how tired she was.

"You can sleep," Jamie said, "I'm happy to just hold her."

He looked down, silent, the dim light spangling his lashes. The baby was asleep in the crook of his arm, the delicate corona of her hair sparking red-gold as the light from the hall touched her and her father.

"Pamela. You know anything you need, or anything the children might need, I am more than happy to provide."

"Except you," she said, and then regretted the words immediately. "I'm sorry, Jamie, I shouldn't have said that, it wasn't fair."

"What did you say except the truth?" he replied softly. "I will do my best to be there for all of you. You, Conor, Isabelle and this little one."

"I know you will. I have complete faith in you." It was true, he would do everything he possibly could for all of them. She could not ask for more than that. "We can figure it out as we go," she finished softly.

When the hour grew late and it was clear Jamie was not leaving, a cot was moved into the room for him. A nurse closed the door so that they might have some privacy and the three of them settled in for the night.

Jamie stroked one finger over Kathleen's head. Now that her hair was dry it was springing into delicate curls, gossamer-fine around her face.

"She reminds me of Stuart," he said quietly. "She has the red hair and green eyes just as he did."

She smiled. "I'm glad that she has red hair. Mostly, I'm incredibly grateful she's healthy."

Jamie nodded but did not speak. He looked up, eyes dark with emotion.

"I have no right to say it, Pamela, but I find tonight I cannot help it. I love you, and I promise you I'm going to make this right."

"I love you too, Jamie."

His gaze held hers for a long moment, their daughter between them. She thought of all the things which had brought them here to this moment and found within her the echo of Jamie's own words to her, many months before. Within her, for this moment, there was no room for regret.

A little later, she fed Kathleen and then watched afterwards as Jamie changed her diaper and gently burped her. "Do you mind if I hold her a bit longer?" he asked, tucking the pink flannel blanket Kate had made for the baby more securely around her.

"Of course not," she said, smiling, "I believe she'll sleep soundest in your arms."

Jamie lay down on the cot with Kathleen tucked in beside him and a pillow propped under his elbow. The baby settled with a small coo, closed her eyes and was asleep within seconds. Jamie leaned over and kissed her forehead, one hand cradling her small fiery head. Pamela's throat grew tight looking at the two of them. She had never thought to see Jamie with a child of his blood in his arms. A healthy child, whole and sound and beautiful.

And so they slept father and daughter, the golden head and the downy red one glimmering in the low light from the bedside. Through the night, between spells of sleep, she watched them in their peace and wept a little for the family they would never be, and also for the family that they were.

Chapter Ninety-one

Cosan na Marbh

FATHER JIM ROSE FROM his prayers, and stood quiet for a moment at the wooden altar rail. The church was silent around him, though it had been as busy as a hive of bees earlier that day with the Ladies' Aid Society meeting, and a bible class study group, which had become rather contentious concerning a passage about loose women. It had taken him a good half hour to calm the class down and wrap it up so that he might have his tea before it was fully night.

He took a breath and looked out the window beyond the nave. Much good it did him for it was as dark as forty black cats outside with the wind moaning and cackling to itself like a demented being.

It was a night for ghosts, or so his gran would have said. Raining cats and dogs with a heavy dose of sleet. He realized suddenly that there was someone in the church with him, for he felt a presence strongly, enough to send a ripple up his backbone and raise the fine hairs on his neck. He didn't often get evening penitents coming in for confession in such miserable weather but occasionally a sinner would wander in from the streets looking to unburden his soul. Someone was in the confessional. There was the scent of the outdoors in the small church as if the person had brought the elements inside with him—pine and water and the twilight blue scent of fresh snow. There was no snow outside, just rain pissing down in proverbial buckets. The only place where there was snow in Ireland right now was high in the mountain passes.

He sighed. It was his job to listen to whatever this person needed to say but he had just taken a phone call from Patrick Riordan to say that Pamela was safely delivered of a wee girl. He had come into the chapel to light a candle and pray for the baby's health. He knew the fears of both parents were well-founded though he had a sense that the baby would be just fine. He couldn't really countenance any other thoughts for both Jamie and Pamela had suffered enough loss to last more than one lifetime. This child must be healthy and whole.

He adjusted his collar and touched his hand to the cross he wore around his neck before entering his half of the confessional.

The man on the other side of the screen was invisible, for the church was dark, lit only by the candles at the altar—lit in prayers for those departed, those lost, those mourned, those disappeared and never returned to the ones who waited for them.

"What can I do for you this evening?"

"Bless me, Father, for I have sinned."

"Do you wish to confess your sins, my son?"

"Aye, I do."

Father Jim frowned slightly as he took his rosary out, wanting the security of its worn beads clasped in his palm. He could have sworn for a second that the voice on the other side of the screen was familiar for it had set off a small bell deep in his consciousness.

"Any time you're ready," he said. The booth felt tight, and he had a shortness of breath that was akin to the anxiety he had been host to ever since one terrible weekend in a cottage in the mountains where he'd been brought to hear the confession of a doomed man. "Begin where it's easiest for you."

There was a short, sharp laugh from the other side of the screen. "Easiest—I think it might be easiest to list the sins I *haven't* committed. The list is long. Have ye time for this, Father?"

"Yes, of course I do."

There was a deep breath from the other side of the screen and then a long sigh. The words just came after that, a sober recitation of fact that made the blood plunge toward his toes a little.

"I've committed murder. I've carried rage so long now it's like breathin' for me. I've been involved in crime an' other things that would likely make yer blood run cold. I don't know that there's redemption for such as me, or if I should just resign myself to everlasting hellfire right now." The tone didn't match the words and the laugh he uttered at the end of this was without humor. Father Jim felt a strange sensation building in his stomach and small jets of adrenaline were going off throughout his body. He did know the voice, though he still couldn't place it. The man was admitting to murder. This wasn't entirely new in his experience for a man could not be a priest in this country and not have murder confessed to him at some point. Even if it was in a wee hillside hut with a blindfold over your head. The recitation of his sins after that was long, and Father Jim felt an exhaustion in the man's words which was at odds with the youth of his voice.

"Do you have a family?" He wasn't certain why he asked, only that he needed to say something.

"Aye. I have a wife an' children."

"Does your wife know about these things you've told me?"

"No, she doesn't," he said, "but I'm not certain that matters so much."

"It would likely matter to her," Father Jim observed. The tight feeling in his chest had increased and he feared anxiety was about to take over.

"I don't know that it would at this point, Father."

"What is it you really want to speak of?" he asked, feeling there was a reason beyond confession that this man had chosen his lonely little church this dark and rainy night.

There was a long silence from the other side of the screen, as if the man were carefully weighing what he said next.

"What I would speak to ye of is this—can a man ever really return to the world of the living, once he's walked years in the world of the dead?"

The spurts of adrenaline had turned to a waterfall flooding through Father Jim's body. He put his hand to his chest and stood slowly, wondering if he were actually asleep and having some strange dream which seemed more real than life. Either that or he was talking to a ghost.

"Casey," his throat almost choked on the name for it wasn't possible and if it was possible, it was so damnably late—too damnably late.

He stepped from the confessional into the steeped dark of the church, with only the candles for light, glowing softly with memory and prayer.

A man stepped into the shadows from the other side, a big man, bigger than most.

"Aye, Father, it's me."

And it was then that the words of the Irish poet came to him.

We can write but one line that is certain, 'Here are ghosts.'

35934110R00446

Made in the USA
Middletown, DE
19 October 2016